The Commander

Leslie Peppers

Book Two of
The Lyons Saga

This is dedicated to Hope

CONTENTS

ACKNOWLEDGEMENTS

I want to thank:

My daughter Nicole for
her encouragement to write this

JD Peppers for being at his studio with Haze
(his rare solid black German Shepherd)

Sam Blackwell, a US Navy Veteran,
for sharing more of his knowledge

An US Navy Veteran who wished to be anonymous
for sharing his deployment knowledge

&

Actor extraordinaire, Henry Cavill, for inspiring me
to give Commander Lyons a British ancestry
and so much more

FROM THE AUTHOR

When I began writing my first novel I decided to change a few things that bothered me as a reader. For example, in life during a conversation you know who is talking immediately, but in a book you don't know who is saying what until the middle or end of the sentence. I want to know who is speaking before they speak. I do not want to dangle in suspense. Therefore, I tell my reader who is speaking first and then what they say. Also, instead of writing he said, she said, they said one thousand times I mixed it up with he replies, she comments and they say.

During the editing process of *The Captain's Wife* I found out the things I changed were against the rules for writing that have been strictly enforced for decades. And only famous writers are allowed to break them. So, because I'm not famous yet, I have to change my style of writing? Here's a story that sums up how I felt about that.

For years every fall I have gone to New Orleans and walked around Jackson Square watching the people who work there. One year out of curiosity I decided to have a tarot card reading. After carefully observing them all I choose a friendly looking young man who introduced himself as Jerrick and motioned to the chair across from him. When I was comfortable I shuffled the deck, cut it and slid the cards across the table to him as requested. Next he laid out the cards, studied them briefly and began telling me what was revealed. Then he sat back in his chair smiling at me as he placed his finger on a card of a fair haired maiden with a floral crown, standing on grass holding a sword with the tip in the grass and said, "This is Defiance, she revolts against authority figures. The interesting thing is she appears twice." And he places his finger on the other one. "In all my years I have never seen her twice in a reading. You definitely do not like being told what to do. The sword means you will fight for your beliefs, no matter the costs, until you have won the battle." We talked about a few more things and then we were done I thanked him for the insight and went on my way.

A sister company for one of the Big Four in publishing was interested in publishing my saga, but because I was not willing to change my style of writing or edit out parts of *The Captain's Wife* relevant to the saga in order to get it under the recommended 400 pages or less for a first time author, as you can see, I went elsewhere. In my opinion it is past time to ease up on the rules in order to cease stifling a writer's creativity and give them freedom to express themselves.

My next subject addresses the aircraft carrier featured in *The Lyons Saga*. I did not clarify in *The Captain's Wife* USS Louisiana, aka Louise, is a fictional character. I created her to avoid tampering with the events of an actual aircraft carrier that participated in the Pacific Theater during the war. I feel artistic licenses should only go so far, after all it is history and in this book you will learn things not in any history book I know of, about what happened to the West Coast during the war. While researching the subject I was astonished at what has been left out. I carefully chose what to include and hope you enjoy reading about the events as they happen to my characters.

CHAPTER ONE

The day has finally arrived; Trevor is being reunited with his mother after being apart three long years. When I step out of my room I see all the bedroom doors are closed, so I knock on Théo's and quietly say his name. He opens it still wearing his pajamas. "Good morning, Gené. You look very pretty."

"Thank you. I need some reassuring words and a hug from my big brother." He immediately puts his arms around me. "Théo, his heart is going to ache when he sees his mother and I won't be there for him."

"I know, but Trevor is going to be strong for her. His emotions will eventually catch up with him, but when you get home you will make it all go away."

"I knew you would say the right thing. Thank you, Théo."

"This is what big brothers are for."

"We are cooking breakfast together at the apartment, so I need to go. Will you tell Mother and Father for me?"

"Certainly." He kisses my forehead and I go downstairs.

I want to be alone at lunch on my bench; therefore I need to make something for it fast. For some reason a peanut butter and boysenberry jam sandwich comes to mind. Pouring milk into my thermos I feel like I am getting ready to go to elementary school instead of work and before leaving, our mugs from the diner catch my eye and I grab them.

To save time I drive over to the apartment and while I go up the steps Trevor opens the door smiling. "Good morning, Baby."

"Good morning, Trevor."

"You look lovely today, more than ever."

"What a nice thing to say. Thank you."

"You're welcome. — What are you hiding behind your back?" I hold the mugs out. "Our mugs from Sam's. Let's fill those shall we? The kettle whistled before you got here." I give him a kiss and we go inside.

Trevor makes our coffee and before he ties the apron on me he gives me a proper kiss, which is British for a slightly passionate one, then we decide on Swiss cheese omelets. He grates the cheese and slices mushrooms as I scramble the eggs and put bread in the toaster. We cut up the entire time.

After we finish our coffee Trevor puts his dress shirt on over his undershirt and happily places each hand on my abdomen for me to roll up his sleeves. While he stands there smiling he asks, "What are you doing for lunch?"

"I am going to sit on my bench, eat a PB&J and wash it down with milk." He laughs heartily. "It was all I could think of. I was in a hurry."

"You are priceless. I do love you."

"And I love you."

He looks at his watch. "I'll walk you to your car."

On the way down I tell him, "I will park in front of the house when I get home, so you will know I am here."

"Thank you."

"You're welcome." The contraction gets a smile.

"All right, I will see you after school."

"I will be expecting milk and cookies." And in a blink I am dipped and kissed.

Of course traffic is unusually heavy and I am almost late for work. I enter The C's Room and when Emily sees my lunch she gives me a sweet, but slightly sad smile, because now she knows I intend to eat alone on the bench. When lunch time rolls around Emily and William try to talk me into going with them to The O Club, but when I tell them I have a PB&J they know to throw in the towel. While eating I'm so lost in thought I don't even care I forgot my book. I wouldn't have been able to focus on reading anyway. When lunch time is finally over I see Emily standing by the door alone waiting to walk back in with me.

Not long after returning to my desk I get a startle. I hear Trevor say my name and when I look up I thoroughly expect to see him standing at the door and he is not. I freeze. *What was that about?* Something must be wrong. I need to leave. How is the best way to do that without having to answer too many questions? The solution comes to me and I get up abruptly and go to the Ladies Room for a minute then I return, pull the cardigan that stays on the back of my chair and tie it around my waist with the sleeves as if I am covering a blood stain. Emily is watching me along with the others who quickly look away. I close down my desk and give Emily a nod as she gives me a sympathetic look and waves goodbye.

The moment I go into Mrs. Sloan's office her assistant Becky sees my cardigan then simply holds out her hand to take my files and tells me to return tomorrow. I make myself walk out at a steady pace when all I want to do is run to my car.

On the way home I remember the chapter in *Jane Eyre* when she is walking in a field and hears Mr. Rochester, the man she loves, calling her name on the wind. She gets in her carriage to go to him and finds his house has burned to the ground and he is blind. He does regain his sight, but nevertheless it was highly dramatic, sort of like this moment I'm having. And I drive a little faster.

The wall around our property is in sight and I drive through the gates straight to Trevor's apartment then jump out and sprint up the steps. I knock once and open the door. He is sitting at the dining table and when he sees me it startles him to the point his chair almost falls over when he stands up.

"Geneviève, are you all right?"

"I'm fine." Now he's in front of me. "I didn't mean to startle you. I got — spooked at work and I had to see you." Looking at him I notice there are dried tear stains on his shirt, undoubtedly left by his mother and his eyes are red. "Trevor, why are you here and where is your mother?"

"She's in the guest house getting ready to go to Micheletto's for a late lunch. I came here to change shirts. Mum is going to ring me when she's ready."

He starts shaking his head. "Geneviève, I was ill-prepared. My mum has aged beyond her years. And the circles under her eyes, they are so dark." Trevor swallows hard and it is taking everything I have to keep my wits about me. "The room was about to start to spinning when you showed up."

Trevor abruptly stops shaking his head and looks deep into my eyes. "What spooked you?"

I sigh heavily and reply, "While typing, I heard you say my name — so clearly that when I looked up, I expected to see you."

Without flinching he asks, "What time was it?"

"1:17."

"I looked to see what time it was when I left the guest house. It was 1:12. After being here a few minutes I called out your name, wishing you were here."

"And here I am." Suddenly his arms are around me and he melts into my embrace. When he steps back I notice there is a glass of water on the table and motion to it. "May I?"

"There's no need to ask."

Holding his hand I go to the table and reaching for the glass I notice small drops of water are in front of it. My heart sinks when I realize they are his tears. Trevor pulls a chair out for me as I pretend I didn't see them, drink some water and set it down between us.

Trevor looks at his watch then at me. "So — exactly how many laws did you break on your way?"

I chuckle and think. "Three."

"Just three huh?" His eyes are bright again and then the look on his face changes. "What did you tell Mrs. Sloan?"

Oh perfect, I was afraid he would ask me that. "Nothing, I didn't have to see her. I decided the quickest way to leave was to grab the cardigan on the back of my chair and tie it around my waist. When Becky saw it she simply held her hand out to take my files and told me to come back tomorrow. The only I thing I had to say was thank you and left."

"Aren't you quick on your feet? — Geneviève, that was pure genius. You would make an excellent field agent." I burst into laughter. "And you could use *your* passport."

"Commander Lyons, may I speak to Trevor please."

He laughs and says, "I'm here."

"Before the phone rings perhaps you should change shirts."

"Perhaps I should."

He gets a shirt out of the closet and goes into the bathroom. When he comes out Trevor is smiling showing me unbuttoned cuffs and I get tickled. We smile the entire time I roll up his sleeves and when I'm done Trevor asks, "I haven't kissed you since you got here have I?" I pout and shake my head.

Of course the phone rings while we kiss and he groans as he crosses the room. I get tickled again and have to cover my mouth as he answers it. The second Trevor tells his mother I'm here her voice gets loud enough for me to hear. He hangs up and looks at me for a few seconds. "I hope you're hungry."

My face goes straight at the thought of meeting his mother in — oh, two minutes, so I plainly say, "I need a mirror. Excuse me please."

He laughs and follows me. "Are you nervous?"

"Not at all, I'm excited to finally meet her. Now stop staring at me and get another handkerchief." His eyebrows rise. "Trevor, I did see your other shirt."

"It wouldn't be the first time you read my mind."

"Point made. I'm ready."

At my car Trevor opens the door and gives me my handbag. As he rolls up the window he gestures to my lunch sack on the floor board. "That is a telltale sign of hard breaking. Are you certain you only broke three laws?"

"Yes. Speeding, failure to stop at a stop sign, although I did slow down and the lights were yellow then they changed to red as I went under them. Before you throw a stone, remember you live in a glass house."

"Yes I do, a big one."

When we get to the doors of the guest house he knocks twice and pushes both of them wide open in order for us to enter side by side. The doors are still moving when his mother appears and her eyes are on me as she walks over with her hands out to hold mine. "At last, the woman my son is going to marry. I will try not to overwhelm you."

"Please do not give it a second thought, Mrs. Lyons."

"Evelyn, please call me Evelyn."

"I would be delighted to and please call me Geneviève."

"The moment Trevor told me your name, I knew you were lovely. Oh Son, I am so happy for you."

"Thank you, Mum."

"Let me see the ring." She lifts up my hand and gasps. "Did you say yes before or after you saw this?"

"Before." I laugh as I answer her.

"Had you hesitated that would have gotten him the answer he wanted."

While we laugh Trevor says, "That was the plan."

I smile at him and tell her, "I am fond of you already."

"And I you."

I take a step to her, "Welcome to Maison de la Mer." and kiss her cheeks.

"Thank you for the invitation. It is beautiful here."

Trevor steps over to the sofa table and picks up an apple from the bowl of fruit. "Excuse me. My stomach has given up and is no longer growling."

"Oh Son, we can talk in the car." This is when she lets go off my hands.

Going down to the car I can hear the poor thing eating. He suggests we walk to the arbor in order for him to finish his apple and for me to tell his mother about it. We toss our handbags in his car then she and I walk together as he follows. When we're close to the arbor I see an apple core go flying over my head.

We stroll along the cobblestone path and I tell her about the history of the property and the arbor, ending with my parents were married under it. I glance at Trevor and he says, "Mum, this is where we're getting married." She hugs her son then turns to me and gets still.

"Evelyn, I will not be overwhelmed if you hug me." The look on her face is touching as she puts her arms around me and even though we have just met, I hold her and when she gently begins rocking me I know what is in her heart. The love she has for her son and gratitude for all I have done for him and his family. When she lets me go Trevor is looking away blinking his eyes. I keep her attention by suggesting we leave for Micheletto's and we walk to the car while he follows us and regroups.

The moment we are inside the restaurant Trevor begins speaking Italian. He orders house salads, a bottle of Pellegrino and Italian Rosato along with a white pizza then waits patiently as our waiter pours olive oil in the saucer of crushed herbs to dip the warm Italian bread in. When the waiter leaves I pick up the bread basket, fold back the cloth and offer it to Trevor. This gets me a kiss.

After the waiter returns with the beverages he orders our entrée's then his mother sits back and says, "Now — I would like to hear how you two met and anything of significance after that." Trevor and I immediately look at each other and she begins to laugh. That is a lot of ground to cover, so while he eats more bread I tell her how we met and then he joins in. By dessert we have her up to date and she only makes a few comments here and there. But when Trevor told her he was getting out of the Navy she was quiet and we lost her for a moment as she absorbed the fact her son was finally going to be out of harm's way. On the way home she becomes quiet again and I hold her hand as we listen to the radio.

At the guest house I excuse myself to call Mother, because I know my car has been seen and my family needs to know what's going on. In the background I can hear Trevor handling ice and an ice bucket. When I end the call I see he is chilling a bottle of Italian Rosato and his mother is opening cabinet doors.

"Mum, what are you looking for?"

A few seconds pass before she answers. "I have forgotten." Evelyn closes the doors and stares at them as Trevor locks his eyes on me. We know what made her forget, month upon month on war rations and empty cabinets.

The mood needs to be lightened immediately if not sooner and I think to say, "I know you weren't looking for something to eat."

"That is for certain! It does narrow it down a bit. — Wine glasses. I was looking for wine glasses." And Trevor shows her where they are. "Thank you, Son. You know your way around here too?"

"All the kitchens are basically set up the same. Would you like to see the apartment I'm staying in?"

"Of course I would and when we return the wine will be chilled."

The first things in the apartment his mother notices are the photographs and she picks up the double frame with the ones from our first Summer Banquet. Trevor tells her, "Those were taken on the day we met."

"How fortunate you are to have these. The two of you looked like a couple already. And I see Joanna has not changed one bit. Who are the others?" Trevor points everyone out for her then the phone rings. Trevor glances at me, answers it and proceeds to have a significantly one sided conversation with Joanna. Then he explains to his mother we have lunch together three days a week and tomorrow is one of those days. Joanna would like for them to arrive early. With that the tour is over and we return to the guest house to drink wine until time to meet my family.

Evelyn and I sit on the balcony sofa with Trevor between us. He holds his mother's hand then puts his arm around my shoulders and we quietly enjoy the view. When I catch a glimpse of my grandparents going to our house the back way I excuse myself to go home and freshen up. Théo and Rachel arrive just as I reach the last step and he drives over to me, rolls down his window and asks, "Need a lift?" I laugh and reply, "Why not?" I wave to Trevor and his mother then get in.

Thank goodness I'm alone, because it is a little hectic when I enter the kitchen. Rachel stays close to Théo as I greet everyone and happily go upstairs, but when I wind up alone the image of Trevor's tears on the table and everything else catches up with me. Mother's voice calling me gets my attention and I step into the foyer less than a minute before Trevor knocks and comes in with Evelyn.

The moment I have been looking forward to for quite some time is finally upon us, my father welcoming my fiancé's mother to our home. Trevor makes the introductions and the evening begins. We are all so at ease it is as if she has been here for weeks, not hours.

Evelyn crossed several time zones that took her back six hours when she left London and today took her back four more. Due to that fact we move things along for the evening to end before she becomes too tired. Dessert and coffee is served in the drawing room instead of an after dinner drink. Soon after we finish our coffee his mother informs us she needs to go before an uncontrollable yawn overtakes her. That she has a delightful sense of humor comes as no surprise.

Trevor gets up to escort her and she asks me to join them. So we say our good nights and go to the guest house. On the way Evelyn tells us she simply wants to see her son and me together a little bit longer. A few minutes later she does yawn and Trevor insists she retires for the evening and instructs her to call around the property for him when she wakes up.

When Trevor and I are going up the steps to the house the lights in the drawing room go out and he asks if we can sit outside. The difficult day is almost over and he wants to spend some quiet time with me. He puts his arm around me and keeps looking at the guest house. I rest my head on his shoulder, because I too need this time with him.

Théo and Rachel eventually drive by then Trevor sighs and says, "Geneviève — you helped me through this day more than you realize. I don't know what I would've done without you." Not knowing how to respond I remain still. After the lights in the guest house finally go out he asks, "I can't remember the last time I went for a run in the evening. I'm familiar with the grounds now. Do you mind?"

"Of course not. In that case I am going to shower for an hour."

He laughs until it hits him, "You have long showers to unwind at the end of a day and now you jump in and out as if you're in the Navy."

"I prefer spending time with you."

"I miss being in the house with you already. Tonight I am tucking you in."

"I feel the same way. Now go run and take your time, then come to my room."

Trevor is happy as he opens the front door and gives me a nice kiss. Then he gently pushes me inside and is off. I want to watch him walk to the apartment, so I dash to a window. After he goes inside I decide to wait for him to come back out and in a blink he does. Trevor stands on the balcony wearing an undershirt and shorts, does some warm up exercises then runs down the steps and out of sight. I have a good image of him in my mind as I shower.

While untying the sash of my robe, Trevor enters the house. Since he likes to untie it I quickly tie it back as I turn around. He pushes the door open and my hands are still on it. He beams and says, "Allow me." Trevor's hair is wet and when he has the sash in his hands I notice his scent is strong and breathe him in. There is something about the way he takes my robe off of me that makes my heart flutter. And when he lifts my legs and pulls the covers over me I feel so close to him, because he loves taking care of me as I do him.

Trevor sits on the bedside chair and tells me, "The most incredible thing occurred to me as I ran." He has a slight smile as he thinks about it.

"What was it?"

"This is where I will be taking my runs from now on, because I am going to live here, with you."

"This would be a good time to kiss me."

"I agree." He puts arms around me, lifts me up and *he does*.

Instead of lying back down I begin placing pillows behind my back. He helps me and I sit up. "Geneviève, I would like to have breakfast here in the morning with you and your family. Is that all right?"

"Of course it is."

"Then I'll drive you to work. When I get back I doubt Mum will be up. She is so tired. I'm glad she came alone. I think Mum needed to get away by herself and regain her equilibrium."

"Mother mentioned she plans on taking her shopping and to a lady's lunch at the club Friday."

"Mum will like that."

All of a sudden I cover my face and he asks, "What is it?"

"I just remembered how I got out of work today."

"The real issue is why. That is something else altogether."

"There is no denying that. Trevor — it was surreal."

"You are connected to me in a manner that is most unusual. But as strange as it is, it gives me comfort in a way I can't explain."

"I feel as if it is proof we are meant to be together. Keep in mind I did not need confirmation. I know with every fiber of my being that ..."

"That we are soul mates."

"Yes."

Trevor sits beside me on the edge of my bed and places his hand on my face. He tenderly kisses my lips and says "I love you, Geneviève."

"I love you too."

"Will you lie back down so I can tuck you in before it gets any more difficult for me leave?" I nod and we move the pillows. He is still over me and I run my fingers through his hair that is not quite dry yet and pull him down by the back of his neck for my goodnight kiss. "Good night, Baby."

"Good night, Trevor."

Right after I turn off my lamp, instead of lying in bed wide awake I fall fast asleep and wake up feeling rested and ready for the day. Breakfast has returned to normal. It was just Trevor and I with my parents and Théo. Before we leave, Mother invites Trevor back to the house for another cup of coffee and a scone while he waits on his mother to call. Also he can watch her make coconut macaroons for tonight. Suddenly I am looking forward to dinner.

Driving into the parking lot at work we see William and Emily are standing by the Willys and she looks as if she is going to burst. We say good morning then Trevor tells her, "By the look on your face we're going to have to wait until lunch when we're all together to find out the date you two are getting married on."

Emily goes, "Yep." and sighs.

William gets tickled and tells her, "You've had to wait long enough. I think your health is genuinely at risk, so go ahead and tell them." She hugs him and exclaims, "We are getting married on Saturday the 18th of October. The two of you will be back from your honeymoon and then we can go on ours. Emily beams as she holds my hands. "Geneviève, will you stand with me as my maid of honor?"

"I course I will." Then it occurs to me I will be married.

"Why do you look funny all of a sudden?"

"Because I just realized I will be married and can't be a maid." William and Trevor burst into laughter as Emily's covers her mouth. William manages to say, "You're going to be a matron like Joanna." Emily gives me a hug. "As long as you are by my side I don't care what your title is. Thank you, Geneviève." She looks at William and tells him, "Focus please."

He looks at Trevor. "Since you're my best friend will you be my best man?"

"It will be my honor."

They shake hands as Emily looks around, then at her watch and gasps. "Gentlemen, we literally must run." Emily grabs my hand. I blow Trevor a kiss and we run to the building. We stop at the doors, take off our shoes and run down the hall. I don't ever want to do this again.

Noon at last and Trevor and William are here in the car. After Emily and I are in we get a kiss and William tells us, "We were thoroughly entertained watching you two disappear. Did you make it?" Emily responds, "Yes and that is all you are going to get out of me." I add, "I'm with her." Trevor tells William, "I really enjoy myself when these two are together." William replies, "So do I."

At the Mitchell's Evelyn is radiant, giving a new meaning to the words beauty sleep, which she obviously got plenty of. She is happy to see everyone again and to meet Emily. Best of all, Trevor looks like himself again, relaxed with eyes bright.

During lunch Emily and William announce the wedding date. When everyone quiets down William looks at Trevor and I. "Emily and I want to a have a small informal engagement dinner at The O Club. Since my parents will be here for your engagement party and it would be our two month anniversary would you two mind if the dinner was the day after yours?" Trevor dryly says, "Will you stop asking questions you know the answer to?" I recall his words earlier and tell Emily, "I really enjoy myself when these two are together." She bursts into laughter and Trevor bows as he tells me, "Touché."

After work Trevor and William are waiting on us engrossed in a conversation. William stays in the Willys and waves to me as Emily happily gets in. Trevor informs me on the way to the car Mother and Grand-mamma took Evelyn to the market today. She and my mother will be cooking dinner for us tonight.

We are the first ones home and when we enter the kitchen it is quite the little scene. My grandmother and Claudette are seated at the kitchen table drinking a glass of wine. Evelyn and Mother are also drinking wine as they cook and have the empty wine bottle on the counter close by. Trevor kisses the cooks on the cheek, looks at the label on the bottle and emerges from the wine cellar with two more. Soon my grandfather and father arrive. Minutes later Théo and Rachel join us and we all drink wine, talk and watch them cook. When dinner is ready we eat under the stars in the solarium and Trevor is on Cloud 9.

At the end of the evening Trevor and I walk his mother to her door and on to the apartment we go. He is not in the frame of mind for a run. Nothing has been said, but we are all aware his grandparents should be on their way to Canada via the transport flight then arrive in Georgetown tomorrow. Even though his parents safely made the trip, concern is still looming.

Trevor turns on a lamp. "Cognac?"

"Please." He hands me the glass and I give him a kiss. Trevor is being quiet, therefore I am. It is so quiet when the phone rings both of us flinch. We chuckle and I tell him, "That is your mother calling with good news."

Straight to the phone he goes and when he picks up the handset his mother begins talking. The man doesn't even say hello as he sits on the bed. He looks at me, nods and I sit next to him. A minute goes by and he says, "Yes it is." Another minute later he says, "I'll ask her. Would you like to have breakfast in the morning with Mum?" I nod. "What time do want us to be there?" Seconds later he says, "I will. Good night, Mum." and hangs up. "My grandparents made the flight. Father's going to ring Mum in the morning after they get to the house. They're out — and that is the end of that." Trevor stands, offers me his hand and asks, "Do you mind if I just sit on the sofa with you in my arms."

"Not in the least."

"After we finish these I'll walk you home." Trevor settles in the corner of the sofa and we curl up together.

At home Trevor tells me he will be back at 6:40 to escort me to breakfast. I give him a goodnight kiss and watch him leave. When I go upstairs Théo has his door open for me, so I go in and he has a few questions about my darkroom. I tell him it needs to be exactly the same, because I'm used to it as is then we visit for a bit. I fill him in on the status of Trevor's grandparents and ask him to tell our parents, because I will be having breakfast at the guest house with Trevor and his mum. He catches me up on how things are going with Rachel, gives me my kiss then I go to shower and get sleep I was not expecting.

In the morning Trevor walks into the kitchen where I am with my family. He only has time to say good morning and we go to the guest house where Evelyn greets us then surprisingly she hugs me first. "Son, your father rang a few minutes ago to let us know your grandparents are with him at the house." Trevor exhales slowly from relief with his eyes closed.

Evelyn sees this and instantly goes into Mother Mode by asking me, "How do you take your coffee?" And Trevor begins his deep laugh. She glances at him then motions for us to follow her into the kitchen. Trevor watches his mother while waiting for me to answer her. When I do Evelyn's pace slows almost to a standstill. "I have a nice French Roast your mother suggested." Then Trevor tells her, "Mum, she's not worried if your coffee's good. That's the way she takes it." She looks at me and gushes, "I love sugar too."

While eating the first breakfast Evelyn has made for her son in years she mentions being leery of going anywhere in the car we have provided. I ask her why and she informs me she is worried about finding her way back. That we left an area map on the front seat for her with an X over where the house is evidently doesn't matter. Trevor tells her to be ready at 1:30 to go on a tour of the city.

All too soon we have to leave and when we are close to the car I stop and tell Trevor, "Occasionally I drove to work with the radio off with the window down and just listened to the wind. Today would be one of those days."

"Why have you not told me this sooner?"

"Because it didn't matter until now."

"I'll walk you to your car."

"Oh — Trevor, I don't want to be alone. I just want to sit on the passenger side next to the window without the radio on." He smiles and opens the passenger door for me. We go down the driveway rolling down the windows. I kick off my shoes and pull my feet up onto the seat then Trevor puts his hand on my ankles.

In the parking lot at work Trevor breaks the silence in a big way. "I need to go to my quarters and check on things. Then I have to turn in my paperwork that covers my move off base and the date my marital status will change. Next I'll go see Mitch about the meeting tomorrow. What do you want to do for lunch?"

"That was a lot to absorb." He chuckles. "Umm ... eat a pizza on the bench."

"You read my mind — I bet literally."

"Moving on. Trevor, I need a favor. Will you get the film from this weekend out of my camera bag and take it to Mr. Blackwell while you're on tour with your mother?"

"I would be more than happy to. Mum can see the photograph of you and hear the story of how you became a photographer. And there goes Emily." We quickly exit the car, he waves at her and motions to William. "See you soon."

"See you soon."

William passes me with a wink and Emily and I go inside normally.

At lunch time Trevor is standing in front of the bench hiding something behind his back. I call out, "Don't make me wait."

He holds out a paper bag. "There are zeppole filled with ricotta and pieces of dark chocolate in here."

"Do I have to eat the pizza?"

"That's my girl."

We have such a nice quiet lunch together that when it came time for me to go back in, had he not made plans with his mother I think I would have walked into Mrs. Sloan's office and quit my job just to stay with him.

When Trevor picked me up from work he told me how much his mother enjoyed meeting Mr. Blackwell and she insisted they go back to his apartment so she could see the photo essay of his arrival. While having the apéritif before dinner she told me they were the most expressive photographs she had ever seen. At the end of the evening we did our new little routine, he ran, I showered and he tucked me in then read to me from his book. We are taking advantage of a peaceful moment before the hectic day tomorrow is going to be.

CHAPTER TWO

Trevor is going to the meeting with Mitch and their superiors about securing the base, so he comes through the front door in his Tropical White's. He smiles when he sees me coming down the stairs. "There she is." I pull the man into the study without saying a word. It has been a while since I saw him wear the uniform I met him in and his freshly shaven face is my weakness. I kiss him passionately and let him go as quickly as I grabbed him then casually walk away. We join my family for breakfast while his head is still spinning.

During lunch with the crew at The O Club nothing could be said about the meeting, but we could talk about coming back here tonight to watch the Swing Dancing. I may not know how to dance to the fast music, but I do know how to dance to the slow music and am looking forward to that. Emily can hardly wait, because all she has ever done is eat here.

After work Trevor is talking to William who is sitting in the Willys when Emily and I walk out. Trevor walks straight to the car, opens the door and says, "I have a surprise for you." He drives down the road we go parking on in broad daylight, but I just hold his hand wondering what he's up to. At the end of the road he turns off the car and says, "Indulge me." as he opens the door and we get out. He opens the back door and reaches into the seat. "Look what I found."

In his hand is *The Halyard* with my photographs on the front page. I glance at Trevor then look at it again. Without him the photographs would still be in a box unseen by the public. I wrap my arms around him and whisper, "Thank you for this." then I kiss him. A boat horn sounds causing us to realize we're out in the open and he is wearing a uniform. So, we get back in the car and I begin reading aloud. "Part One, that explains why the editor wanted so many photographs."

"Yep, didn't see that one coming."

"Trevor ..." then I begin to laugh. "I was about to say I cannot believe I forgot about this, but I can. You remembered though."

"Nope, I forgot too. After the meeting, the second I spotted the paper stand I knew what was in it. Mitch was right behind me. He looked at me and the paper then shook his head. He told me there was way too much going on around here."

"Tis true." I gasp. "Joanna knows."

"Yes she does and more than likely she's standing at the window sipping a martini as we speak. Perhaps we should head that way before runs out of olives."

I laugh as he starts the car then look in the back seat where I see a sizeable stack. "Trevor?"

"I admit it, I took half.

"And Mitch?"

"Half of what was left."

As suspected Joanna is looking out the window when we pull up. The second I enter the house she exclaims, "The photo journalist is here at last." She hugs me then asks, "Can you believe it? Part One?" She hugs Trevor and tells him, "We are so proud of her. This gives Happy Hour a new meaning." Mitch nods at us as he pours two more martinis.

The stack Mitch took is on the dining table next to his martini, so that is where we sit and toast to our success. In the distance we hear a Willys gearing up and when it gets close we hear it gear down. William and Emily are pulling up. The first person through the door is Emily holding *The Halyard*. "Look what my mom found at the commissary this afternoon."

I respond, "It was intended to be a surprise. My family is going to get one too as soon as I can get them all together."

"And what a surprise it is. Congratulations, Geneviève." And I get a hug.

William asks Trevor, "Joanna had something to do with this didn't she?"

"Of course she did. She met with the editor while Geneviève was at work."

"And she charmed his socks off."

"That was the plan."

Joanna interjects, "It's Happy Hour. Have a martini and join us." Mitch makes another batch and Joanna starts making plans. "I think we should finish these, get ready to have dinner at the club, meet back here for hors d'œuvres and more of these then close the place down and go to Sam's." Emily tells William, "Ooo ... I've never stayed out all night." I glance at Trevor, another night without sleep.

After work Trevor and I go see Evelyn to fill her in. My grandparents and parents are there, because are they are dining at our club. We are about to leave when Evelyn asks me to go with her and Trevor to the airport in the morning to pick up Trevor's father. I accept her invitation and we make a hasty exit.

Trevor walks me to the door and I ask, "Will you come up? I need your assistance in selecting a dress."

"This day just keeps getting better."

We enter my closet and I stand watching him go through my dresses. He looks at the hem of one and pulls it from the rack. "I fancy the peacock color and best of all; it's lined, so you don't need to wear a slip." I raise my eyebrows. "There is no doubt in my mind I am going to twirl you tonight." He gives me the dress and a kiss. "Shoes ... they should strap on. Do you have a pair like Flamenco Dancers wear?" I point to a sliding door as my mind goes all over the place. Then I hear him say, "We have a winner." He turns me around and puts his hand on my back to nudge me out. Trevor sets down the shoes and asks, "Anything else?"

"No. Thank you."

"Anytime." He dips me of course then it is his turn to catch me off guard with a passionate kiss. He stands me up and says, "See you soon." While my head is spinning he vanishes. All I need to do is put on evening makeup and jewelry then his selections. There is a chance I could be ready when he returns.

Making one last check in the mirror I hear the front door open and get out to the balcony toute de suite. "There she is." I descend the stairs and he extends his hand. "Hello, Beautiful."

"Hello to you too." He chuckles as I caress his freshly shaven face.

"Are you ready to dance the night away?

"Yes I am."

"After you." Trevor opens the door and so it begins.

We begin the evening eating hors d'œuvres and drinking martini's as planned. Everything tastes so good I finish my martini a bit too soon. Mitch offers to refill my glass, but when I decline Trevor points at it and Mitch happily drops another olive pick in it then fills my glass. I ask Trevor, "Are you trying to get me tipsy."

"I'm not trying; I am getting you tipsy, so you will let me twirl you tonight." While the others laugh Emily's eyes get wide and William points at her glass. Trevor and William are always on the same page.

The platters are almost empty and we decide to migrate to The O Club. We are going in Mitch's car. He's going to sip on vodka on the rocks, so he can drive us around the city in the wee hours.

Emily and William go in the club first and I hear Harry greet them. When I walk through the door Harry says, "Miss France. What a pleasant surprise. Welcome to the Night Club." I wave to him. "Thank you, Harry." Then he says, "Commander — Mrs. Mitchell, Captain," I glance at Joanna and she steps beside me. "Did you think we sit at home on the sofa for the weekends?" Quietly I reply, "Frankly Joanna, I try not to think how you two spend your weekends." She laughs with her mouth closed and Trevor makes a sound as if someone punched him in his stomach. Mitch sharply exhales with eyes forward while we walk to our booth.

As we take our seats Trevor motions for me to sit by Joanna and tells me, "Men on the ends." I see women sit next to each other here and notice they walk around alone, not in pairs. It really turns into a night club unlike any I have ever been in. It has its own set of social rules that are very relaxed, as it should be considering the highly controlled lives these men have.

Near the end of dinner the lights get dim. I look at Trevor and he has a glint. Two couples go straight to the jukebox while Harry turns up the volume. Trevor presses his cheek to mine and whispers, "It's Swing Time." I draw in a deep breath as Trevor winks at me. The first record drops and the drum beat begins.

"Trevor, I have heard these songs on the radio several times, but here it's different. I can feel it in my bones."

"I know. — It changes everything."

"It truly does. We are going to have such a good time."

"Yes we are. All right, what do you want to drink?"

"Something that will quench a thirst — a Vodka Collins."

"That should do the trick. I'll have the same. Switching from vodka could be detrimental to my health at this point."

"That was my thought."

William asks him, "What's the switch?"

"Vodka Collins." William looks at Emily and she gives us the thumbs up. Trevor motions for our waiter and orders for the table as I watch the couples dancing in complete disbelief.

The men hold the girls by the waist and sling them upside down into the air over their heads. The girls kick their feet then the men bring them down and sling the girls to their right side, then out and over to their left side. It looks as if the girls are swinging. And that's why it's called Swing Dancing. Who on earth started this?

Trevor turns to me. "It's a lot to take in at first sight."

"Yes it is."

Emily looks at me and drops her jaw. "There is no way I am ever doing that! Even though it looks like fun ... nope, not a chance. Where are the drinks?"

Joanna tells us, "We just watch and enjoy the show as we wait on a slow song. One always plays after two or three of these, because everyone needs to catch their breath." Mitch nods and sips his vodka.

The second I start watching the dance floor again I see a man do a leap frog over his girlfriends' back. He lands and dances what looks like a jig in a circle with her in the center. I have to consciously keep my mouth closed otherwise I would be as Trevor says, catching flies.

Time passes by quickly and I have finished my drink while engrossed in the world around me when a slow song finally plays. We are all on the dance floor in under a minute. William has to take a moment to get Emily in his arms; because this is all new to her while Joanna and I settle against our men. My head is resting on Trevor as he barely sways me in his arms. As usual we are not dancing, he is holding me as music plays and I love it.

The song ends and when we get close to the table I notice my glass has more than ice in it. I look at Trevor and he says, "As a time saver I told the waiter to replace empty glasses."

"And as a way to get us all tipsy."

He gets close to my ear, drops his voice and says, "I'm just aiming for you."

"And you never miss."

"No, I do not." I pick up my Collins and lift it to him. He smiles, touches my glass with his and we drink.

After two more slow dances and watching more fast ones he looks at me with a glint and I am no longer close to tipsy. "I think you've watched long enough. Are you ready to go for a spin?" He means literally.

I go, "Mmm mm." and shake my head.

"I know you like this one. I see your little foot move when it plays on the radio in the car."

"Trevor, what are you going to do?"

"Geneviève, I'm British." I have a small burst of laughter. That is his way of reminding me he is conservative. So, I hold out my hand and tell him, "You lead and I will follow." I glance at Joanna as I get up. She says, "Bon chance." I reply, "Merci." as he leads me to the dance floor.

"Did she just say good luck?"

"Yes she did."

"That's funny." Standing close to the edge of the dance floor he asks, "You have seen the tango?"

"Yes, guests from other countries at the club dance it."

"I'm going to use steps from the tango to spin you and then go where the music takes us."

"You are brilliant."

"We'll find out soon enough." He stands beside me with his chest against my shoulder blade, gets my hands and we take the stance that is right before a spin in the tango. "Are you ready?"

"As I will ever be."

He waits for the one count and immediately spins me out then back to him so fast my head almost goes back and we are off. Trevor keeps us near the edge of the floor and out of harm's way. We do a waltz with a little tango thrown in at an accelerated pace that keeps up with the beat and he spins me several times. This song is longer than I remember and when it ends we are out of breath.

Trevor says, "We pulled that one off."

I laugh and say, "We did."

"Did you have fun?"

"Yes — once I overcame my first case of stage fright. Did you have fun?"

"Oh yeah."

We applaud with the others and wait for the next record to drop. It's a slow one, but not our song. I look at him and he says, "I know. Come on."

He holds my hand, leads me to the jukebox and gives me a nickel. I drop it in and we scan the list. Trevor says, "Found it." He points to it then looks at me, "Press the buttons." I beam and carefully press each one. "We have two more to choose. Let's play another slow one and something else for the crowd." He makes the selections and we are done.

"Trevor, I am so thirsty."

"That makes two of us. Let's get a glass of ice water."

As we approach the bar Harry is filling a glass of ice with water. He hands it to Trevor, who hands it to me. As I drink almost half of it Harry fills one for Trevor and says, "That was some good moves for a pair of first timers."

"Were we that obvious?"

"No ma'am. I saw you get wide eyed when the dancing began and you *are* Miss France." Harry looks at Trevor, "I like her. She's got guts."

"Yes she does. She's a sailor."

"What? You found one from The Yacht Club?"

"I found her at The Yacht Club."

"Well all right then. How soon are you marring her?"

"Very soon; September 14th to be exact." Harry nods at me and refills our glasses. We thank him and join the others.

Everyone is so excited when we return. Mitch says, "That was exhilarating." Emily is nodding and Joanna says, "I taught these fellas how to tango." William says, "And we never danced it with anyone else until now." Emily raises her eyebrows at William and he tells her, "If he can do it I can." Trevor tells him, "You're going to have to wait, we played two slow songs."

Joanna lights up and drinks the last of her martini. Seconds later the fast song stops and we all get up to go to the dance floor before the first slow one begins. Trevor drifts us away from the others slowly for a little privacy so to speak in this crowd and then our song begins to play. Since I am a bit tipsy I sing to him as we dance. Near the end of it Trevor slides his cheek along mine and carefully grazes the corner of my mouth with his lips. Now that is romantic.

It is time for a fast one again and Emily and William are going to dance to it. Trevor asks, "What do you want to do?"

"Watch them."

"So do I." and we leave the dance floor.

There are fresh drinks on the table and we watch William sling and spin Emily around the dance floor. He *can* do what Trevor does and it is so much fun to watch them. When the song ends Trevor asks, "Are you ready to go again?" I offer him my hand and we dance the night away.

When the crowd begins to thin the men all leave a tip under their glass for the waiter and we go to the bar for them to sign their tabs and say good night to Harry. Being the gentlemen they are they tip him too. When we get outside Mitch asks,

"Are you ready for the next evolution?" William and Trevor say in unison, "Sir, yes, sir." Laughter erupts and we pile in the car headed for Sam's.

Carla is our waitress again and when Trevor goes to pass me a menu I hold up my hand and he gives it back to her. William says, "Hold it. Geneviève isn't looking at a menu." All eyes are on me as usual. "What are you getting?"

"A hamburger steak, medium well and two sides of scattered hash browns with a cola. I'm hungry."

Emily says, "So am I, make that two, please."

Trevor looks at everyone as they nod and he tells her, "Make that all around, please."

The diner is so busy Sam simply waves from the grill. We talk about the events at The O Club until the food arrives that we inhale and barely say another word until we are all done. While Carla clears away our empty plates Trevor orders a waffle and asks for two forks. Mitch and Joanna decide to share a piece of cherry pie. William and Emily share a piece of apple. Our plates are clean and we all order bottles of colas to go for the caffeine and pile back into the car. Before our minds can catch up with our bodies we are at the Mitchell's saying our goodbyes.

Trevor closes the car door and asks, "Where to next, Baby?"

"Willow." I pull the gate key from my evening bag and dangle it in the air.

Trevor gives me a kiss and whispers, "I love you."

"I know. I thought we could go below and make out. Then we can put a bunch of pillows and cushions on the deck, curl up under a blank and watch the sun come up."

"Geneviève, you are the one that is brilliant."

We stop at the gate to the marina and I slide over to pull the car in. This time after he closes it Trevor gets back in. We say hello to Willow and go aboard. I hand him a rope that is tied to the side with a mesh drawstring bag on the end and he puts the sodas in it then lowers it into the water to keep them cold. Below he turns on a few lights and I ask him, "Will you please pour us a glass of water while I change out of this dress?"

"Of course."

"Make yourself comfortable. I will be a few minutes."

I give him a kiss and go into my stateroom to change clothes. There I find a pair of my pajamas that are a few years old. As I put them on I discover the pajama top is tight across my bust and cannot button it up. After digging a little more I find a white camisole. The foundations were sewn into the dress so it is just me. Oh well. I take the hair pins out of my chignon, leave it in a ponytail and go out to Trevor. His jaw drops a little.

"I wore these before I blossomed into a woman."

"I see that."

While I was in my stateroom he took off his shirt and belt and is standing there wearing an undershirt. I turn off the main light, walk up to him and begin pulling on it. "I tire of stretching these out to feel your skin." The moment I finish the sentence he takes it off and tosses it next to his shirt. I pick up the water and reach for his hand then lead him to my parents' stateroom. There is just enough light shining through the draperies that we can see without having to turn on a lamp.

I set the water down, we take off our rings and watches then I pull on my collar. "I am wearing a silk camisole under this."

He looks into my eyes and begins to take off my pajama top. His hands do not brush along my body. This time he gently presses them against it. As he slides the pajama top off of me I begin thinking about his hands. "I love your hands, especially when our fingers are entwined. It feels ..."

"Intimate."

"Yes it does. It's why my heart began pounding when you were lying across me the other night and you held my hand like that. You were so passionate." I close my eyes and begin reliving the moment.

"Geneviève, open your eyes." I do and he looks deep into them. "Let me take you there again."

He holds my face and begins kissing me. When he gets me in his embrace so much of our skin is touching we get chill bumps. He dips me, but instead of being suspended in air he lies me down staying against me. The silk of my camisole is so thin from age it almost feels as if there is nothing between us.

Trevor whispers, "I can feel you. You feel — so — soft."

"And you feel so warm." I sigh and draw in a deep breath. "Trevor."

"I know, Baby." And we are lost.

Time passes and I whisper, "Trevor, roll over and pull me on top of you."

The dog tags on his chain fall off him onto the bed and I wind up lying between his legs as he holds me close. While he kisses my neck I whisper, "Let me go." Trevor knows what I want, so without hesitation he does and lies his arms down with his hands over his head. I reach for them and we are entwined. I have him completely beneath me and our bodies become so warm we begin to perspire. The wet silk of my camisole clings to my breast and seems to vanish. At one point he places his cheek against mine and whispers, "Geneviève, I can feel every subtle nuance of your body."

"And I yours."

Trevor slides his hand underneath my camisole at the small of my back that I arch the moment I feel his hand on my skin. There is going to be a passion mark on his shoulder where my mouth was when he did that.

More time spent in a state of euphoria passes then he asks, "May I roll us back over?"

"Please."

When his weight is on me my mouth comes open and I begin to draw in deep breaths as he kisses my neck. At last I can run my fingers through his hair and when I do he stops kissing my neck abruptly. I get still and he whispers, "I can't leave a mark on you." I nod and he kisses my mouth.

Soon his mouth is close to my breast and he is holding my hands. We are completely immersed into each other when his perspiration drips onto my body and I feel it run down my shoulder until it reaches my back and goes onto the sheet beneath me. There is almost too much to feel. I eventually close my mouth and swallow hard.

"Trevor." He sits on the edge of the bed, lifts me up and places pillows behind my back then hands me the glass of water. As I drink he brushes my hair from my face then slides his hand along my arm as he looks at my body. I set the glass down and he rests his hand on my waist. "I can't help seeing you and you are more beautiful than I ever could have imagined."

Trevor's hair is wet and has fallen onto his forehead. I lightly run my fingers under it and wipe the perspiration from his brow and slide my hand down his chest. "I love you."

"I love you too, Baby."

After he drinks some water and sets it down I pat my chest. He gives me a kiss and lies across me with his head on my chest and I feel him melt into me.

Lying with him in my arms I notice light filtering through my eyelids. "Trevor, I think we missed the sunrise." He sits up, looks at me and he reaches for his watch. "It can't be that late. Or has it switched to early now?" We laugh as he picks it up and looks to see what time it is. "We're good. It's 6:41." And we are up.

"Geneviève, we need those sodas."

"While you get them I'm going to peel off this camisole and put my dress back on." He laughs for a moment then gets quiet as he looks at me once more.

After getting dressed I open the door. Trevor says, "There she is." then walks in, gives me a soda and watches me as I put in my last hair pin. I hand him my comb and move back from the mirror. He combs his hair, turns around and kisses me. "Where to next, Baby?"

"The house and the airport?"

"That sounds about right." He looks at his watch. "Father is going to be there in a little over two hours."

"I cannot believe I am going to meet your father after staying out all night. I wish there was enough time for me to shower and wash my hair."

"You look beautiful." He kisses my neck and inhales. "And you still taste and smell sweet." Then he kisses the other side of my neck.

"Trevor, please focus."

He sighs and steps back. "I'm focused. Geneviève, trust me, all you need to do is put on a different dress and change shoes. May I help you choose?"

"That is a rhetorical question."

He lights up, "Are you ready to go?"

"Yes."

"After you."

The second we are on deck we squint. Trevor goes, "Whoa — if you want to close your eyes I'll guide you to the car and hand you your sunglasses." Laughing I pick up my shoes and reply, "Tempting, but I'll manage." We make it to the car without stumbling and we are finally on our way to Maison.

Trevor parks at the service entrance and inside we find my parents are in the kitchen. The coffee pot is still going, so they have not been up long. Mother says, "Our night owls have returned to the nest. Good morning." We say, "Good morning." in unison and she gets her cheeks kissed.

My father stands up. "Sweetheart, you look lovely."

Trevor glances at me with an I told so you look as I kiss my father and say, "Thank you."

"Dancing the night away ... ah, youth. When do you need to leave?"

"As soon as possible; we will be back ... later." Trevor nods as I grab his hand and drag him away.

We hear Théo stirring in his room as I touch up my makeup and Trevor is selecting my dress and shoes. I give him a kiss and he leaves to shave and change clothes. I hear his car start and get tickled. No running to the apartment this morning.

I dash into the kitchen to see Théo before I leave. Mother is wrapping two scones and he asks, "Did you Swing Dance, Gené?"

"Yes, to a degree. My feet did not get off the floor at the same time."

He chuckles and says, "We will want details."

I nod, open my handbag and Mother drops the scones in. "I love you all. I am off to meet my future Father-in-Law."

I hear Trevor pull up as I am walking through the foyer and when I open the front door he is walking in front of his car. "I feel ridiculous riding around here in my car."

Laughing I ask, "Are we riding to the guest house to pick up your mother?"

"Of course we are."

On the short ride over I open my handbag and show him the scones. "I love your mother. I'll get a soda from Mum's fridge for us to split on the drive."

Evelyn is dashing around when we get inside and she sings, "Good morning."

"Good morning, Mum. You look lovely."

"Really? Do you think your father will like my new outfit?"

"Without question. May I help?"

"No, thank you. I am almost ready." He goes to the refrigerator and she asks me, "Did you two have fun?"

"Yes we did. It was our first time to stay out all night." He comes back to me and we wait by the door. She joins us and kisses our cheeks. "Geneviève, I must say, you do not look like you stayed out all night. You look fresh as a daisy."

"Thank you."

"You are most welcome. Oh — my sign." And she walks away.

"Did Mum say sign?"

"Yes she did."

"Your mother gave me a piece of your typing paper to make this." She appears holding the paper up. It reads, LYONS. Trevor and I laugh and she says, "I hope that is what my husband does when he sees this."

On the freeway I get the scones out and Evelyn asks, "Trevor, is that breakfast?

"I'm not sure what this is. Our eating schedule is way off."

"I told your father I almost starved you when I arrived, so he decided to eat breakfast according to this time zone. Now we can have lunch on your time." I ask, "May I make a suggestion?" Trevor replies, "Please do."

"We could have a light brunch at the club then sit on the deck and listen to the Pacific until time for lunch by the pool. Or stay inside, whichever your parent's would prefer."

Evelyn gasps and asks, "Are you referring to the club your mother took me to lunch yesterday?"

"Yes, ma'am."

"That would be perfect."

Trevor tells me, "Were I not driving I would give you a kiss." He points at his cheek and lowers it to me. I kiss him, take the soda and replace it with a scone.

Evelyn tells Trevor, "She takes good care of you, Son."

"Yes, Mum, she does."

"He takes good care of me too." I pause for a moment. "Evelyn, your son is a good man. He is all I could have ever hoped for and so much more. Plus, I will never tire of listening to him talk. I love his accent."

Evelyn burst into laughter and says, "That is the first thing that attracted me to his father, that accent. It turns a girls head."

"How did you meet him?"

"I was sitting on a bench eating lunch with my father and sister on campus. He is a retired Sterling Professor from Yale Law. A gust of wind blew one of my father's papers around the courtyard and we watched Rowland chase it down. He was one of my father's students. Anyway, he walked up and said, "Excuse me, Professor Hutton; I believe this belongs to you." Our eyes met and I fell into them." I nod to her and turn to Trevor.

Admiring him I say, "When I looked into his eyes I could see so deep into them I could see his soul and time stood still."

Trevor locks his eyes on me for a brief moment as I realize I said what I was thinking aloud. He glances at his mother and pulls in a parking lot. Evelyn says, "Excuse me. I need to stretch my legs." and gets out of the car.

Gazing into my eyes he touches my face. "That is exactly what happened to me. I didn't know how to describe it, what I felt ... and time did stand still." Ours eyes are open as we kiss ever so tenderly. He lingers close to my face briefly then sighs. "I have to go get, Mum."

Her back is turned and she is genuinely taking in the sights. I see Trevor speak and she turns around then holds out her arms that he walks into. She gingerly rubs his back and he offers her his arm for the short distance back to the car. When she is settled in I am at a loss for words. Evelyn pets my face, begins to puddle and quickly says, "Shall we listen to music while the two of you eat?" Trevor smiles at us, turns the radio on then gets his scone off the dash and takes a big bite. He puts the car in drive and we are on our way yet again.

Luckily we are still a little early even after our delay and Evelyn is walking ahead of us and Trevor tells me, "When I was here Tuesday I began watching the people as I strolled to the gate. The things I saw were just as you described. One can tell so much about these people and their lives. Occasionally it felt as if I was invading their privacy, but some of the moments were so captivating I could not stop watching them." He begins smiling and slowing us down. "I can kiss you here." And he does.

We catch up to his mother who did not notice we had fallen behind. She is trying to find a good spot at the gate for us to wait on her husband. The aircraft is taxiing up to the terminal and I am anxious to see his father.

Doors open and we hear the aircraft engines shutting down. People begin to slowly flow inside and Evelyn holds up her sign as we wait. Soon a handsome gentleman is in sight that begins to laugh. Obviously he is her husband and that was what Evelyn hoped for. She is beaming as she glances over her shoulder at us. His mother has made sure the reunion with his son would not be emotional due to her humorous sign.

Rowland is all smiles shaking his head and pointing at the piece of paper as he steps up to his wife. He gives her a little kiss on the lips and with an arm around each other they face us. His father nods to Trevor then gives me a little bow. Evelyn quietly says, "There she is." He says, "The woman our son going to marry." After they said that I felt like a ton of bricks landed on me and acted like nothing happened.

Rowland goes to Trevor and grasps his forearms. "Good to see you, Son."

"Good to see you too, Father." When he holds Trevor I fight emotions again. Then they face me and I smile at Trevor. "Father, allow me to introduce you to my fiancée, Miss Geneviève Delcroix. Geneviève this is my father and I am certain he wants you to call him Rowland."

"Yes I do. It is a pleasure to finally meet you."

"Likewise and please call me Geneviève." I offer him my hand and he gently holds it with both off his then kisses it ever so politely.

"My wife told me a mere description of you falls short and I would have to see you to understand how lovely you were. She was spot-on, words cannot describe you. Son, I cannot believe you waited a month to propose."

"I asked for permission to marry her when I asked for permission to court her just in case." Rowland looks at Evelyn. "You did not tell me that." She exclaims, "I just found out!" They both are laughing when Trevor says, "Shall we get your luggage and go to the club?" Rowland asks, "The O Club?" He replies, "The one by the beach." Without another word Rowland offers his arm to Evelyn and we are on our way.

Trevor and I eat a light brunch and his parent's drink Mimosa's. We have coffee to get us through the next few hours. When they silently touch their glasses together Trevor holds up his coffee cup and we quietly toast to caffeine. While we sit on the deck listening to waves waiting to have lunch, his parent's look perfectly content. Then after a lunch that Chef out did himself on we make our way home.

The bags are inside the guest house and we are out on the balcony as his father stands and looks around our property for a few minutes. "My word, this place is beautiful." Evelyn tells him, "I woke up in the middle of the night and could not go back to sleep. About to get frustrated I remembered where I was. I slipped on my robe, made a cup of hot cocoa and sat on this balcony. There was a light breeze blowing as I soaked up ... everything."

Rowland sits next to his wife with his arm around her. Eventually he loosens his tie and Trevor tells them, "We have an errand to run. So take your time to settle in and then get ready for dinner with Geneviève's family. An apéritif will be served at 6:30 in the house on your right. We will meet here and go together." His mother responds, "All right, Son. We will see you shortly." Trevor kisses her cheek, shakes his fathers' hand and off we go.

Going down the steps I sense he is upset and when we are out of their hearing range I ask, "Where are we going?"

"To Blackwell's; I have had a stiff upper lip long enough."

He opens the car door, I get in and clasp my hands in my lap then he just drives off. He rolls down his window and props his elbow on the door with his hand on his forehead. I want to touch him, but I know from my own experience not to, for it could trigger the emotions he is trying to control.

We have barely gone a mile when he says, "I have never seen my father sit with his arm around my mum." He pauses for a while. "I wondered why there was such a drastic change between them and in front of you. Then I had a visual of them constantly sitting in the dark with his arm around my mum to comfort her as they listened to air defense sirens and explosions in the distance."

My eyes close and my head is down as I try to deal with my sympathy for him and his parent's. Seconds later Trevor's hand is over mine and I hear the cars' turn signal as he brakes. I look up to see he is parking at an overlook. My eyes are forward as Trevor opens the door and gets out then he helps me out and doesn't let go of my hand. We are alone, so he walks us to the front of the car, leans on the hood and gathers me into his arms.

When we have our equilibrium he says, "Geneviève, I don't want to put you through this."

"I don't want you to go through this without me."

"You do know it's not over."

"Yes — it's not even close to being over and we will get through it together." I push back to see his face and the smile he gives me I cannot describe. Without even looking around Trevor kisses me and then asks, "Are you ready to go?"

I shake my head for no, but reply, "Yes." And there goes the deep laugh. He's fine and we are on our way to one of my favorite places.

Mr. Blackwell is so happy to see us, because he is finally getting to tell me how much he enjoyed meeting Trevor's mother and he understands why I keep sending my film to him. We stay and chat a bit, but we really have to go. As we walk to the door I say to Trevor, "The wedding." He responds, "A photographer." and turns us around.

"Mr. Blackwell, do you still photograph weddings?"

"It will be my honor. Simply tell me when and where."

"The wedding ceremony will be at Maison on Sunday, September 14th. We will bring you an invitation." He marks his calendar and we thank him then actually make it out the door. I stop by the trunk of the car and tell Trevor, "I have been so focused on things concerning the engagement party I have neglected the wedding. I need to think."

"I'll drive, you think." And we get in the car.

Trevor pours us a Pellegrino at the apartment and we sit at the table. "What did you decide?"

"That the next several days are going to be hectic." We laugh nervously and I continue. "The gowns are a priority. I'm going to schedule an appointment next week after speaking with Joanna and Emily at the dinner tomorrow night. The invitations need to be ordered. I will have to get off early."

"Who does that?"

"The mother of the bride and the bride, which has never made sense to me; I have always thought the bride and groom should. — Since Mother chose the invitations for the engagement party, would you like to accompany me to the Fine Stationer and choose our wedding invitations?"

"Yes I would, very much. What else can I do?"

"Chose your groom's cake. My guess is you want the orange cake served on the first night you were here for our wedding cake, which is what I want."

"Your guess is spot-on and I know the groom's cake I want. It's supposed to be chocolate correct?"

"Yes it is."

"I want the raspberry one we had on Willow, with the dark chocolate ganache."

"Ooo, excellent choice."

"Thank you. All right, what else, Geneviève? We're on roll."

"Indeed. Hmm. The dinner menu can wait. My next concern is reserving a cottage for our honeymoon. That needs to be taken care of as soon as possible. It should have been taken care of the week we were engaged."

"Then let's go tomorrow after brunch. I'd like to see the place up close."

"Your view from Louise is a bit limited. What about your parent's?"

"Mum will be giddy when I tell where we're going."

"Point made. That's it for now. Shall we?" I motion to the sack of photographs. He gets them out and I see he had them boxed. "There is an extra one."

"I hope you don't mind. That one is for my parent's. I wanted them to see how happy we all are."

"Having a second childhood?" He nods and we begin going through them.

When the last one is turned over Trevor looks into my eyes, grabs my chair and turns me to face him. In an instant me and the chair are between his legs. He puts his hands on the chair back and his face close to mine. Softly he speaks, "Not too long ago I was lying beneath you." His cheek is against mine as he whispers, "Your scent is still on me."

"And I can smell the scent of you on me. What I really want is your mouth on me."

"Where?"

"Your choice."

Trevor puts his hands on my thighs and slides me forward on my chair as he pushes his backwards. He unzips the back of my dress and makes it fall off my shoulders. "Geneviève, are the dresses you're wearing this weekend going to cover you above your bust line?"

"If need be."

"I might leave a mark this time."

"Oooh I hope so."

My back arches as he puts his hands on my waist to pull me to him and his mouth is where I wanted it, on me. My head goes back and I become oblivious to everything but him.

When he is no longer kissing my body I lift my head and our eyes meet. He says, "I was going to kiss your lips, but I couldn't stop looking at you."

"You make me so weak — so easily."

"I see that. I would have taken you to the bed, but you have to go home and you might encounter a family member disheveled and wrinkled." That statement makes me wonder how much time has gone by. When I look at my watch I try to stand up, but my legs are pinned. Trevor pulls my dress over my shoulders then helps me up. "That late huh?"

I turn around for him to zip my dress. "I need to run, literally. Again."

"Would you like me to run you to your door?"

I laugh and spin around. "Just give me a kiss." He does and I sigh as I take off my shoes. He opens the door, steps aside and says, "I love you." I tell him, "I love you too." walking out the door. Trevor steps outside of course to watch the show. On the portico I wave and vanish before he gets his hand out of his pocket.

Mother is on the balcony by the phone. As I dash up the stairs she tells me, "I was trying to decide if I should call."

"Thank you, Mother." And I keep going.

After the shortest shower in my life I check my chest for a passion mark and there it is, at the top of my left breast. I pull the dress I planned to wear, hold it up and happily discover the lace overlay will cover it. I put on my makeup and get my hair done to perfection and step into my dress. There is a hook and eye closer on the back of it above the zipper that I cannot manage for fear of damaging the lace, so I slip on my shoes and open my door to go find mother. To my delight Trevor is reaching the top of the stairs in his Service Dress White's. "Good evening, Commander Lyons."

"Good evening, Miss Delcroix." He kisses my hand when he reaches me. "I must say you are beautiful and so is that dress."

"Thank you. I was going to find Mother." I turn around for him to see my dress is undone. He makes a little sound as the back of his fingers touch my shoulder blades and then slide to middle of my back. He hooks my dress and does not miss the opportunity to put his hands on my waist and gently kiss each side of my neck. He turns me around by my waist and softly says, "You leave me no choice when you wear lipstick, I have to kiss you elsewhere. And your mother's in the drawing room." I get tickled and he escorts me downstairs.

Trevor walks me to the entrance standing tall. All the handsome men of my family stand and everyone showers us with compliments. We thank them and I beam while telling them we will return shortly with his parent's.

The second I see Evelyn and her dress it is apparent she went to The Bridal Salon. The woman is stunning as she stands holding on to the arm of her distinguished husband looking quite dapper in his fine suit and tie.

After a brief greeting we go to the house where my family forms a receiving line and Evelyn makes the introductions. Things are run of the mill until she introduces Rachel as Théo's intended. Her eyes sparkle for I am certain this is the first time she has been called that. Even though it is not official it is accurate, Théo does intend to marry her.

While sitting at the dinner table I take many mental photographs. That his parent's are seated across from us is a little hard to believe, because it was no small task to get them here. And with each passing minute I grow fonder of his father that I think has become more like his son over the past few years. Then after dinner, conversation winds down sooner than usual, because once again we have a jet lagged guest. Which is fine by me, I have not slept in two days. When the goodbyes end Trevor and I walk with them to the guest house.

When we are the balcony an unusually loud car horn goes off that is down the street and Evelyn immediately looks up and begins scanning the sky. We freeze and when she lowers her head I quietly tell Trevor, "A shoe just dropped." He responds, "I'll get the doors."

I let go of his arm and he passes them then opens both doors wide. His father escorts Evelyn inside and I glace at Trevor as I follow them in. He closes them and offers me his arm while his parent's remain with their backs to us.

Then all of a sudden Evelyn turns to Rowland and the silence is shattered. She exclaims, "I do not want to live in Georgetown ever again. I want to go home. Rowland — I missed my parent's and I missed Meredith." Trevor places his hand over mine and I realize I am squeezing his arm. Then she begins to cry and motions to Trevor as Rowland tries to give her his handkerchief. "And I never want to be separated from my son that long again — ever." Tears begin to stream down my face as she motions to me. "And I want to get to know this lovely woman he is going to marry." Next she looks at me and gasps. Trevor whips his head around to me and I look up at the ceiling. I feel him place his handkerchief on top of my hand that is holding tightly to his arm. I let go of him to take it.

When I lower my head to wipe my tears I see Evelyn's hand is over her mouth and Trevor is beginning to unbutton his jacket. I decide to just cover my face with my hands. Seconds later Trevor's arms are around me and I bury my face in his chest and cry.

"Son, I do apologize. I did not mean to make her cry."

"Mum, there is no need to apologize. You have been through so much and Geneviève has been upset since she found out where my family was. She should have done this ages ago."

Rowland says, "Evelyn — please come here." She sighs and I hear muffled crying as Trevor begins to rock me in his arms. His father quietly tells his mother, "I promised I would make all this up to you. I will exchange our tickets for ones to New Haven. When we get there I will buy you any house you want."

His mother begins to slowly calm down then she says, "Oh no, Rowland, your shirt is ruined."

"Do we care?"

"No, we do not, but I think we care about the tie."

"Oh. I am certain there is a laundry service around here that can perform miracles on those Sailors white uniforms, therefore my dark tie should not be a problem." Evelyn sighs in relief.

All I can think is thank goodness things have settled down and the subject has changed. His father asks, "Son, what can we do?"

"Pour her a glass of cool water." They leave the room and Trevor whispers, "Geneviève, we're alone — so let's just be still." I turn my head and lay it against his chest. Soon I find myself listening to his heart beating and it all begins to fade away.

"Trevor, you may let me go now."

"I'm not going to ask you any stupid questions."

"Thank you, nor I you. — I am going to get your mum and go to the Powder Room." He kisses my cheek and I go to the kitchen.

Evelyn sees me and offers the glass of water. "Thank you." After drinking the cool water I ask her, "Will you assist me in the Powder Room please."

"Of course I will."

I give the water to his father and ask, "Will you please take this to Trevor?"

"Certainly."

I hold Evelyn's arm as we walk through the bedroom to the bathroom and tell her, "We are going to put this behind us as soon as you let me use some of your makeup remover." She immediately laughs loud enough for them to hear her and that will ease their worried minds.

Evelyn slows our pace. "I need a moment to summon the courage to look in that huge mirror in the next room."

"It is not going to be as bad as you think. Most of your makeup is on your husband's shirt."

"At least Trevor was able to protect that uniform."

"He was not protecting his uniform, he was protecting me. One day he hugged me and something stuck me. It never happened again."

"That is so thoughtful." She opens the door and turns on the light. "Time for the moment of truth."

We step up to the vanity still looking at each. No longer able to stand the suspense I look first into the mirror and get a pleasant surprise. Then she looks at herself and giggles. "It really is all on Rowland's shirt. How my lipstick got on it I will never figure out. I was amazed how quickly yours was off. You dried you tears, immediately unfolded his handkerchief and got most of it in one swipe."

"I am not fond of makeup and put on as little as possible. A surprising amount of it serves no purpose, what so ever. Ancient Egyptian's lined their eyes with kohl to keep the sun from blinding them."

"I did not know that. So, who are we mad at for starting all this, Nefertiti?" We have a good laugh and Evelyn hands me the remover.

After we cleanse our faces she touches my cheek. "I understand why my son fell so hard and so fast for you. — You are an exceptional woman." Evelyn hugs me then we join our men whom have been patiently waiting.

They stand and Rowland tells Trevor, "Look at those lovely faces. And they are so clean." Evelyn responds, "She does not care for makeup." Trevor laughs and says, "That is an understatement." He holds out his hand for mine. "I wish we could stay a little longer, but we have been awake over 45 hours and I am certain our I.Q.'s are dropping. We will see you at brunch and please do not wait on us."

His parents assure us they will go when they are ready and I pick up Trevor's jacket as he kisses his mum on her cheek. He shakes his father's hand; we say good night and close the doors. As he takes his jacket from me Trevor gives me a reassuring look and we begin walking to the apartment. Had he not been holding my hand I would have bolted to it.

"I'm going to ask a stupid question now." I have a small burst of nervous laughter. "Are you all right?"

"Not yet."

"That's what I thought, just checking."

"When I heard the car horn I thought, that's unusual."

"Then Mum looked up and you held your breath like I did as you waited for the other shoe to drop?" I touch the end of my nose and we shake our heads. "I can't decide what upset me more, my mum's breakdown or the reason it came to an abrupt end. When she looked at you and gasped I knew tears were streaming down your face and there was nowhere for you to go."

"So you gave me a place." I smile ever so slightly at him and he nods.

"I think it's safe to say the worst is over. My grandparents are going to be a walk in the park."

"I hope so."

"When you two went into the bedroom my father asked, 'Did she just make your mum laugh?' I said, 'You have a gift.' He responded, 'We're keeping her.' and I told him that has been my plan all along."

"Yes it has."

When we get inside I step in front of him and turn my back. "Help me out of this dress please." He unhooks it and partially unzips it. I turn around and hold out my hand. "May I have your undershirt?" He takes it off and puts it in my hand. I give him a kiss and go to the bathroom.

With the shirt on as I take off my stockings I realize I did not get anything to wear with it. It is long enough to cover my derrière and I am beyond caring about anything except for getting to him. So, I open the door and see Trevor has put on a tank shirt and is standing at the kitchen counter opening sodas. I slide my hands around him and hold him.

"Hey, Baby."

I place my head on his back and my muscles relax. He feels so good I go, "Mmmm." and do not move.

He exhales and puts his arms over mine. "You *are* soft."

I have no idea how long we stood there, but it was long enough for him to ask, "Geneviève, may I turn around now?" I quietly reply, "Yes." and he gathers me into his arms.

A few minutes later he says, "I am so tired."

"That makes two of us."

"Here, drink this. We're not going to make it without these. I thought about making a pot of coffee, but this was quicker. Sofa?"

"Please."

Trevor finally sees my legs and the look on his face is indescribable. "And once again you catch me off guard."

"It was out of necessity."

He gives me a kiss and when we sit down we find ourselves staring at a stack of *The Halyard*. I just slide them back and set my soda down. Trevor sighs and says, "I completely ..." and he falls silent.

"Forgot about those? So did I. Thank goodness I didn't tell my family before we left I had a surprise for them and we would be back soon."

"Geneviève ..." I place my finger tips on his lips and kiss him then we sit back and I curl my legs up on the sofa. Trevor pulls the blanket from the back of the sofa, covers my legs and puts his arm around my shoulder. "I'm staying at the house tonight. I come and go from there so often my parent's won't figure it out. After we sit here and cuddle for a little bit I'm going to pack for overnight and shower there, then I will tuck you in like I usually do."

"Then after Sunday brunch we will go decide exactly where we are going to spend our honeymoon."

"That we will." He gets quiet then asks, "Geneviève, do you want to go to the house now? It will give me more time to tuck you in." I fling off the blanket and get up. Trevor reaches for my wrist and says, "Indulge me."

I turn and stand between his legs then he slowly runs his hands down the entire length of my legs. This gives me chill bumps; he feels them and looks up at me with eyes gleaming. Then he puts his arms around my waist to hold me and I run my fingers through his hair. It is his turn to have chill bumps.

We finally pull ourselves apart and he goes to the chest of drawers. Trevor hands me a pair of his pajama bottoms. "It goes against every fiber of my being to give you these."

Laughing I have him hold them as I roll up the length, then in front of him I pull them on. While holding on to the waistband I lift up the undershirt. "Will you tie the drawstring for me?"

"Of course I will. I enjoy dressing you."

"I have known that since the night we shared our first kiss and you buttoned my sweater."

"I can't believe I did that."

"I was cold and you were taking care of me."

"Yes I was."

"It is a little different now though. You allow your fingers to get against me."

"That I do." He gives me a kiss then he begins to kiss me. Suddenly things are in reverse as Trevor runs his hands under the shirt and the skin of his arms are on my back. We are about to get lost again.

Time passes and when Trevor loosens his hold on me I have difficulty focusing. "Baby, I know we needed to go, but there are times when I cannot stop myself from touching you."

That statement gets me fully focused. "I recall having a conversation with you about constantly wanting to kiss you and I could not stop myself anymore. You asked me why I was trying."

"Point made." We gather our things and leave.

I cannot remember the last time I was so happy to shower. Wait a minute, yes I can, when we got out of the Grand Canyon. Anyway, clean at last and while braiding my hair Trevor walks in and says, "I'm guessing you enjoyed your shower as much as I did mine."

"Let me put it this way, for the first time ever I did not mind washing your scent off." He burst into laughter.

Trevor covers me up, sits on the edge of the bed and puts his hand on it to be over me. With eyes closed my entire body feels like it sinks into the bed. I sigh and open my eyes, look into his and hold my arms out to him. He hugs and kisses me then says, "Would you like me to begin telling you the story of the Sailor that fell in love with a princess?" I light up the room and respond, "Yes I would." He pulls the chair close to my bed and has a seat as I roll over on my side to hold his hand.

"A long time ago there was a princess that gave her parent's, the King and Queen of the kingdom absolute fits. She would constantly sneak off in disguise with her Lady-in-waiting. They took the horse drawn carriage the cook rode to market on and got into all kinds of mischief. During one such outing they went to watch a ship come in returning from The New World."

The next morning I awake with a smile on my face and in my heart because I drifted into a deep slumber listening to the story and the sound of his voice. I take a drink of water, grab my robe, open the door and see his door is pushed to. I walk across the balcony putting on my robe and open it to find him asleep in his bed. I have never seen him sleeping. I step in, push the door to and just stand there looking at him. I want to touch him, but he will wake up the second I do.

The need to touch him finally overtakes me and I gently place my hand on his face. "Trevor." He draws in a deep breath and places his hand over mine then kisses my palm. I sit next to him and softly say, "Good morning."

He opens his eyes and tells me. "Good morning, Baby." then puts his other hand on my waist and slides it along my side down to my thigh. "What time is it?"

"9:41. Where is your clock?"

"I did not want to know what time it was when I went to bed, so I didn't even get it out. I knew you wouldn't let me oversleep. In fact I fell asleep wondering how you would wake me up and how pleasant it was going to be. This was better than I imagined."

"It was a pleasant surprise for me. I have never seen you sleeping. Were it not for my desire to touch you I would still be watching you sleep. I wish I could lie down next to you."

"I wish you could too."

"Since that is out, I am going down to get a cup of coffee to drink while I get dressed. Would you like you me to bring you one up."

"I'll go with."

I get his robe and hand it to him while he slowly rises. When we enter the kitchen I am holding his hand and tell my family, "Good morning. Look who's here."

They all say good morning and Mother adds, "It is nice to see you in your robe, Trevor."

"Thank you. I was home sick." And he begins pouring our coffee as I walk over to Théo, whom I was not expecting to see. "Where is Rachel?"

"On her way. She told me I could pick her up for the dinner." Trevor hands me my coffee and I immediately take a sip.

"I have never seen her car. If I were to meet her on the street she would have to blow her — her horn to get my attention. Oooo, I really need this." I take another sip of my coffee and say in an upbeat tone, "If you all will excuse me, I need to dress for brunch." Théo reaches for me and kisses my forehead. I smile at everyone, place my hand briefly on Trevor's back and go up the stairs. Thank goodness they know I am sleep deprived, so I got away with that stammer.

I leave the door to my room open for Trevor and go in my closet to select the dress to wear for brunch, but more importantly, at the hotel.

"Geneviève?"

"I'm in the closet." When he steps in I ask, "Do you have time to choose my dress?"

"I'll make time. Which ones are the coolest?"

"The sundresses." And there is the glint. "Please pick one you have never seen me in." He sighs heavily.

In an instant he pulls a white one that has a hand embroidered bodice. "I like this one."

"Good choice. Thank you."

"You're welcome. I'm going to shave."

"Then I will give you a thank you kiss when you return."

"I shan't be long." I laugh as he leaves.

Dressed and almost ready to go I open my door. Within about a minute he is at my doorway. "I'm ready for my kiss." Then he focuses on me. "Geneviève, you look lovely.

"Thank you. So do you." He chuckles as I step right up to him. "Indulge me." Trevor gets still and I tilt my head. "Glide your face along my neck then I will kiss you." He does more than I asked, therefore I give him an extremely passionate kiss then I let him go and nonchalantly slip on my shoes. Trevor just stands there with his mouth open and his arm extended for me to hold on to. We go to my grandparent's and as expected we are the last ones to arrive.

During brunch we have the best time. Rachel and Théo are so happy together. And the good news is his mum looks fully recovered from her little ordeal. Before we go, Trevor tells his father they should take the car the family left for them in the garage and go to the Botanical Building at Balboa Park then have a late lunch at Mandarin Garden's. He assures us they will and we are off.

The ride on the ferry to Coronado Island is a welcome break from the activities of the weekend. We stand by the car with our arms around each other and soak up the warm rays of the sun while breathing the salty sea air. Then there she is, Louise, and I wave to her.

"What are you doing?"

"I haven't seen her in a long time and she did bring you to me." And we kiss.

The ferry lands and he drives us to the hotel. When we get close Trevor is rolling along, because there is more on the island than he was expecting. He parks and I suggest walking along the beach to view the hotel and cottages. I take off my shoes and we stroll along hand in hand as he takes it all in. The dome of the main building is impressive and the terrace is the length of the hotel. The landscaping is breathtaking and it unusually quiet to have so many guests milling about.

Finally we reach the cottages. We walk until we are at the last one and look at each other. He says, "That's the one."

"Yes it is. Let's go make our reservation."

We talk about our plans for the honeymoon on the way. I suggest we explore the grounds then and he agrees. In the lobby I go to the concierge desk, tell him my name and ask to speak with the hotel's general manager.

While we wait Trevor is beaming. "I have never heard you drop your name."

"It *is* late in the season and I want it."

"And you shall have it."

The manager welcomes us to the Del and introduces himself to me. I introduce Trevor as my fiancé Commander Lyons and tell him we would like to spend our honeymoon in the Sunset Cottage September 14th thru October 4th. He tells us he will handle it personally and apologizes we cannot visit the cottage, because it is occupied at the moment. I assure him it is not necessary. It has two fireplaces, one in the Master Suite upstairs and one in the living room and a fully modernized Master Bath. That is all we need to know.

We decide to have a late lunch on the terrace and talk about little details of the wedding and reception. When the waiter asks if we would like to see a dessert menu Trevor has to stifle his laughter as he responds with a yes. I just look out at the waves coming in, so I do not get tickled and a man catches my eye.

"Geneviève. What's wrong?"

"Oh — nothing. I thought I recognized someone."

"By the look on your face it would've been someone you do not particularly care for."

"I thought it was the man who took the photograph of Emily and me."

"The German?"

"That's the one. Here comes the waiter." He gives Trevor the menu and leaves us to decide. Then I begin to laugh in a high pitch.

"Why did my blood just run cold?"

"Keep looking at me and smile, because it is him. The camera like mine is hanging around his neck and he is sitting down behind you — about eight tables away."

"This is not good."

"I could not agree with you more."

"He has been on a very long vacation staying in a fine hotel across the bay from the largest Navy facility on the West Coast."

"Trevor, tell me this is my imagination running away with me."

"I can't. Geneviève, this situation goes beyond the Navy into Agency territory."

After I take a deep breath I tell him, "Trevor, you know how I am always catching you off guard?"

"Yes, ma'am."

"I am about to do that very thing. As fate would have it there is a card a man with The Agency gave me in my wallet. He told me I could call him anytime, day or night." To his credit Trevor does not visibly react. "I wish there was time for you to process what I just said, but I am going to the car to get it and call him. If we are wrong, I can live with that, but if we are correct." Trevor stands, pulls out my chair and gives me the car keys. "I am going to call from the lobby and be back as soon as possible. Order me something good."

"You know I will."

On the way to the car I begin to think what needs to be said. While I sit in the phone booth holding the card it all seems so unreal. I close my eyes, clear my mind then drop the nickel in and dial the number. It rings twice and a woman answers. "This is an operator. Extension number please."

"278."

"Connecting."

More ringing and a woman says, "You have reached the office of Mr. Collins. Who's calling?"

"Miss Geneviève Delcroix with an urgent matter."

"One moment please."

"Miss Delcroix this is Mr. Collins. My secretary said this is urgent."

"Yes, sir. There is a very good chance I have encountered a German man that is a spy."

"What is your location?"

"I am in San Diego at the Hotel Del Coronado on Coronado Island."

"Are you alone?"

"No, sir. I am with my fiancé, a commander in the United States Navy."

"I will meet you in the hotel lobby in approximately one hour and ten minutes. Just sit tight." Before I can respond I hear a buzz. He hung up. I look at my watch then get out my lipstick, put in on, smooth my hair and stroll to the terrace.

Trevor stands up and pulls out my chair as I give him the car keys. "Look at you, lipstick on and perfect hair. If anyone was watching you they will think you went to the Powder Room instead of a phone booth to call The Agency."

"That was my objective."

"The way your mind works is impressive. What next?"

"Mr. Collins will meet me in the lobby in approximately one hour and ten minutes." He glances at his watch. "What did you order me for dessert?"

"Cinnamon bread pudding with the scoop of vanilla ice cream on the side and a ginger ale."

"That sounds delicious. What did you order?"

"A shot of whiskey." I burst into laughter. "Chocolate layer cake and a cola."

"After dessert arrives I will tell you the story I thought I was going to take to my grave and answer all your questions. We have an hour."

"I'm not sure that's going to be sufficient."

"Here comes the waiter."

When he leaves Trevor says, "For the record, I think it is terribly rude of this man to show up while we are planning our honeymoon and enjoying a late lunch."

"It is in the worst of taste. I hope they lock him up and throw away the key, spy or not." There is the deep laugh I do adore.

While we eat I notice the waiter bringing the man a plate and say, "Oh good, he is having a late lunch, so we do not have to be concerned about him leaving any time soon."

"That's a relief." I smile and nod.

The waiter clears our dessert dishes and Trevor scoots his chair over then puts his arm across the back of mine. "I'm listening."

"In October Becky met me in the corridor after lunch to tell me Mrs. Sloan wanted to speak with me. When I went into her office there was a letter on her desk and two plain envelopes with our names on them. She gave me mine then handed me the letter. It was to her and read my services were required elsewhere the next day and if inquiries were made as to my whereabouts our response should be my services were required elsewhere. And nothing else, not even a signature."

Trevor comments, "That reeked of secrecy."

"Yes it did. I gave it back to her and she stood up, told me she was going to speak with Becky and to take all the time I needed. I opened mine and it read at 8 a.m. for me to be in the reception room for the office of the base commander.

"The next morning I went there and the commander's aide led me to a room, opened the door and two men in dark suits stood up. The aide motioned for me to go in and closed the door without saying a word. That little gesture made me even more uncomfortable."

"I bet it did."

"The man in charge, Mr. Collins, introduced himself and his assistant Agent Tidwell then he told me they were with The Agency. Mr. Collins seated me and Agent Tidwell poured me a cup of coffee without asking how I took it and glanced over his shoulder at Mr. Collins when he put in the fifth spoon of sugar." Trevor chuckles. "That was the only light moment during the entire meeting, subtly letting me know they knew everything about me before the meeting even began.

"Mr. Collins opened a folder and started telling me about my life. They knew about my childhood spent living next door to my grandparents and I spoke French flawlessly. That was their main interest in me and they liked the fact I was not married and had never dated anyone."

Trevor's raises an eyebrow. "I cannot begin to tell you how I feel about these people knowing so much about you."

"I had to stop thinking about it." I sigh and take a moment.

"They explained I would be trained in espionage at a camp before going out into the field. I had a most unpleasant visual of that place." Trevor smiles and shakes his head. "When they finished their speech they asked me to leave the base and think about their offer then return at the end of the day with my answer."

"Where did you go?"

"I drove around in disbelief for a while. I thought I was going to take dictation in a meeting of some sort." We laugh on that one. "When my stomach finally growled I went to Mandarin Garden's, because it's quiet there and they leave you alone. Then I went to places I don't normally go, hoping I wouldn't run into anyone I knew, especially Mother or Grand-mamma."

"That was smart."

"When I returned and politely declined their offer Mr. Collins gave me his card and told me if I ever changed my mind to call the number on it. I was rattled for days and had to act as if nothing had happened."

"That was a lot for you to handle by yourself."

"Mmm hm."

"Now that you are engaged they will more than likely lose interest."

"Yes, I am engaged, to a commander in the United States Navy."

"That blew up in my face. Do I have any eyebrows left?"

Once again I have to suppress my laughter. "They are a little singed, but you still look good. — Oh, how perfect. His waiter just brought him a piece of pie which means you can go to the lobby with me." Trevor looks relieved as he kisses my hand. "Do you have any questions?"

"Not at the moment."

"Then I'm going to change the subject. I've been meaning to ask what you learned at the meeting."

"Unfortunately the phone system is going to remain the same due to lack of funding. The estimate for the changeover is close to three million dollars."

"That's more than I was expecting."

"That makes two of us. The good news is they're going to begin a traffic count on the streets you listed to decide which ones to close or put sentry boxes on."

"I know those streets. That is going to be a boring task for a few Sailors."

"It requires three shifts for 24 hours a day over a weeks' time. And yes I am glad I am an officer." He begins looking at other tables and says, "Geneviève, we are going to have to order something if want to sit here and not draw attention."

"Lemonade?"

"That genuinely sounds good." He orders, pays our check and we sit quietly drinking our lemonade looking at the Pacific.

I break the silence and softly tell him, "Trevor, this is the calm before a storm."

"I know, Baby."

"He could really be a bad man."

"And if he is, they are going to take him away." He moves his arm up from the back of my chair and places his hand on my shoulder. Then in what seems like a blink of an eye Trevor looks at his watch and tells me, "It's time to go inside."

When we get settled in the lobby I tell him in an animated manor, "*I read* about these things. I am not supposed to live them." I hold my lemonade up and say, "Çest la vie." Trevor taps my glass with his. As we drink I see Mr. Collins enter the lobby. "He's here."

"Are you ready for the next evolution?"

"Sir, yes, sir."

"That's my girl."

Trevor stands and Mr. Collins says, "Miss Delcroix." He shakes Trevor's hand, "Commander Lyons." Then they sit down with me between them. "Miss Delcroix, time is everything."

"I'll be brief. On June 15th I went for a ride with my girlfriend in her new car. We stopped at a nearby overlook to take a few snapshots. She saw the man in question had the same camera I have and asked him to take a photograph of us. He asked her, 'Are you on vacation too, Fräulein?' then took the snapshot. We left a few minutes later. I noticed there was an Oregon plate among all the California ones as we drove off."

"Why do you know the exact date?"

"I met the commander on the 14th."

"The 15th it is. So, our man has been on at least a seven week vacation. Commander, I need you to show me exactly where he is. Miss Delcroix, please wait here. The commander will return momentarily."

Trevor squeezes my hand and walks out of sight. I look at my watch and cannot believe my eyes. That took place in just under a minute. They will not involve Trevor beyond identification, so if the man is still on the terrace he should be right back. I stare at my lemonade and all I can think is I am not supposed to be sitting here alone on this day.

"Geneviève." I look up as Trevor sits down and gently lifts one of my hands off the glass. "Your hand is cold. Where were you, Baby?"

"Adrift." He takes the glass from me and holds my other hand.

Trevor warms my hands and tells me, "We are to wait here for someone who is going to take us somewhere."

"That's vague. They move so fast I'm certain the someone will be here any minute."

"While we do have a minute I want to tell you I'm impressed with how calm you've been. Your synopsis of the encounter, under extreme pressure I might add, was brief and covered what he needed to know. That you noticed the Oregon plate was as nice touch."

"I owe that to my photographers' eye. It notices every detail."

"If this man is what we think, my guess is he has been working his way down the coast and this is his last stop. — It was a good decision to keep Emily's name out of this."

"They know so much about me and the people around me I knew he would key in on the daughter of an admiral. And just so you know, I didn't tell him your name, I told him your rank."

His face goes straight then he dryly tells me, "When the dust settles, his mouth is going to be watering for you." Trevor's hand goes up instantaneously, "Oh, Geneviève, please pardon the expression."

"The only problem I have with it is the fact it's accurate. My personnel record is going to get thicker and have drops of saliva on it." Trevor almost loses his composer.

Shaking his head at me ever so slightly he says, "That is one of the funniest things I've ever heard and most unexpected." Then he glances to my right. "Here we go. The someone is headed our way."

"It's Agent Tidwell. Could he be more obvious? Let's show him how it's done shall we?"

"Yes, let's."

Trevor stands and greets him as if he is an old acquaintance. I beam watching him and then join in. Agent Tidwell has us follow him and as we walk I ask, "Where are we going?"

"To meet Mr. Collins in the room of the man in question."

Trevor asks, "Where is the man in question and what is his name?"

"Richter, Karl Richter and he is off the premises in our custody."

Agent Tidwell opens the door and it is quite a scene. Agents are looking at pieces of furniture from every angle. One agent is on the floor looking under the desk. As Mr. Collins crosses the room to us I motion to a large Teddy Bear and tell Trevor, "That should not be here." Mr. Collins hears me. "It kind of jumps right out at you doesn't it?" He looks at his watch and asks the agents, "Where is our photographer? We can't make a move without him. How long does it take for that ferry to make a round trip?"

I respond, "40 minutes or so. It takes longer than you think due to loading and unloading. My camera and bag is in the car. I could get you started, but we cannot stay the duration."

"The job is yours."

Trevor says, "I'll get it." and leaves.

"Sir, our formal engagement dinner for family and close friends is this evening. The commander's parents managed to get out of London last week and his father arrived here yesterday, therefore we cannot be late."

"Yes, ma'am."

"I need to familiarize myself with the room. Will you excuse me please?"

Trevor returns and I tell him, "He is aware we are on a tight schedule. Will you please keep your eye on the time and tell me when we need to leave?"

"I most certainly will. I was wondering about that."

With camera in hand I say, "Gentlemen, I am not familiar with the procedure The Agency has for this. To save time we are going to proceed as follows: I am going to start with a 360 of the room at the front door and you will stay at my back as I turn. Then I will do the same for the bathroom. When you need me to take a photograph, call out the word shot. Any questions?" No one makes a sound and I step up to Trevor. "Please stay close." He nods and I move to the door then say loud and clear, "Gentlemen, shall we begin?" They follow my instructions to the letter, so things move at a rapid pace and it is time to begin tossing the room.

The first thing they do is pull the bedspread off. I take a shot of the bed and underneath it. Then they pull knives from their pockets and feathers fly. Trevor whispers, "I feel like I'm on the set of a movie and you're in it." Before I could respond Agent Tidwell calls shot. He has opened the closet door. Then Mr. Collins calls shot standing by an open desk drawer. I go over, take the snapshot and hear shot called again. They are moving fast. This time an agent has opened the bottom drawer of a tall chest of drawers. We are going to be a few minutes.

When the agent opens the third drawer I glance over my shoulder at Trevor and he steps up beside me. "Why do those boxes look familiar?"

"Because you've seen them in my darkroom."

Mr. Collins joins us. "What are we looking at?"

"Two boxes a case of film canisters come in."

"How many are in a case?"

"30."

He takes a deep breath, slowly exhales and opens a box. There are four canisters in it. I take a snapshot and move over. The next one he opens is filled almost to the top with canisters that have just been dropped in it. He lingers a moment then steps aside. Instead of taking a snapshot I stare at it.

"Miss Delcroix, would you mind thinking aloud?"

"My guess is these are all rolls of undeveloped film and if so, this is very good. It's possible these are the photographs he's taken here. He probably intended to mail them wherever in that Teddy Bear. I can go in the closet and open a canister to find out."

"Be my guest. Tidwell, clear out the bottom of the closet."

I hand Trevor my camera, pick up a canister and go to the closet. All eyes are on me as I close the door. When I open the canister and let the roll of film slide out on to my hand I hold my breath. I feel of it and breath. "I am ready to come out." Mr. Tidwell opens the door and I rattle the roll in the canister. "This is undeveloped."

Just about everyone in the rooms says, "Outstanding." including Trevor. An agent counting the canisters tells us we have 24 rolls of film. Mr. Collins says, "32 canisters are unaccounted for. Almost half of Richter's film has been used here. He had the layout of the land within a week. What is Richter so interested in?"

Trevor responds, "USS Louisiana, she's an aircraft carrier the Navy has been refitting since the 11th of June." The room gets so quiet one could hear a pin drop and I visibly react to the point that Trevor sees me out of the corner of his eye and looks at me. Mr. Collins asks me, "Do you have something to add?" Without taking my eyes off Trevor I reply, "No, sir." Still looking at me Trevor tells him, "I'm assigned to the carrier." Mr. Collins excuses himself and the noise resumes.

A few seconds pass and an agent says, "I have a receipt with June 5 on it from a curio shop in Long Beach for a Regina and in parenthesis it reads, 11 inch disc. Whatever it is cost almost 200 bucks." I announce, "I know what that is." Mr. Collins says, "We are all ears."

"It's a large square music box, approximately 15 inches wide and 9 inches tall with elaborately carved wood. Instead of cylinders it plays 11 inch metal discs."

"You are a wealth of information, Miss Delcroix. Obviously it's not in here. Who checked the car?" An agent replies, "I did and saw nothing like that."

My heart sinks as I tell them, "I think Richter put several rolls of film inside the mechanism and mailed it before he left for San Diego. I don't think he's married, so it went to his mother or a sister more than likely. It was smart to put them in a gift intended for a woman and US Customs agents would be reluctant to risk damaging it. As for the bear, that is intended for a niece and a parent was going to remove the film before giving it to her."

Trevor interjects, "You do realize she is spot-on."

"Yes I do." He turns around and announces, "Gentlemen, it is my firm belief Miss Delcroix just handed us a spy on a silver platter."

Every man in the room, including Trevor, go to a piece of furniture and begin knocking on the wood. They are honoring me. I look at each one of them and before I get misty-eyed I hold up my hands for them to stop. "Gentlemen, I am truly honored and I thank you all so very much." They bow slightly and begin searching the room again.

Trevor says, "We need to leave in 15 minutes."

"Help me get this film into a canister please."

While I get one out of my camera bag he quietly tells me, "I'm going to hit my head on something in that closet."

"Not if you put your back against the door like I did. Gentlemen, please do not open this door." There is a chorus of, "Yes, ma'am." as Trevor closes it. With his help we're out in under a minute and I hand the canister to Mr. Collins. "It's time for us to leave. Gentlemen, good luck with your investigation."

Trevor gathers my things and Mr. Collins sees us to the door. "The two of you will hear from me later in the week." He shakes Trevor's hand and then looks at me. "If you were a man I would shake your hand." I reply, "Don't let a little thing like me being a woman stop you."

He chuckles and shakes my hand. "Miss Delcroix, you are exceptional and seeking you out is the best thing I have ever done. I am in your debt. On behalf of the United States of America I thank you." He releases my hand and slightly bows. "Now, before I risk my reputation." He opens the room door; we go into the corridor and do not look back.

The first thing that leaps to my mind I say aloud. "I've never seen inside a mattress." Trevor laughs without restraint. "Do you still want a shot of whiskey?"

"More than before."

We go to the lounge, step up to the bar and Trevor tells the bartender, "Two shots of your finest whiskey, please."

"Right away, sir." He returns with our shots, tells Trevor, "That will be six even, sir." and walks off. We pick up the glasses, tap them together and drink the shot then set them down. Whatever it was it was smooth. Trevor puts a 10 dollar bill under his glass and we happily leave the building.

Standing by the car as Trevor unlocks it he says, "While I'm thinking about it, I've been trying to tell you this all day; I told Théo about Mum's little episode."

"When did you have the opportunity?"

"Last night he got home while I was still in your room. He stepped in because the door was wide open. When he saw me I stood and he motioned to you with raised eyebrows, which was big brother for is my sister all right. I nodded and he walked to your side. I moved the chair back then Théo knelt down and looked at your face." I place my hand on my heart and he nods. "Next Théo got up and shook my hand. I followed him out. He deserved to know what happened, so we went to the kitchen and had a nice talk."

"That explains the lingering kiss on my forehead this morning."

"I thought you wondered about that *and* I wanted you to know about the tender moment that took place as you slept."

"That's probably not the first time he has done that."

"I'm inclined to agree." He hugs me and we get in the car.

My arms are around Trevor's waist and we are propped against my car feeling just fine on the ferry ride back until we see Louise and all the other ships docked in the bay. I feel him tense up and lay my head on his chest. "Trevor, what were they going to do?"

"Don't go there, Baby. Come on, let's get in the car." While he opens the passenger door my breathing becomes erratic and I get in. Trevor walks around to the driver's side and in an instant he slides across the seat and hems me in. "I've got 15 minutes and I am going to take full advantage of them." And he does. When the ferry begins to dock he looks at me with eyes gleaming and says, "I like making out on a ferry. We should do this more often." At last, laughter.

Driving along our wall Trevor looks ahead. "Is that torches at the gates?"

I gasp, "Yes, it is."

"What do I not know?"

"On Christmas Eve we light the exterior with lanterns and torches. The interior of our homes are lit with candles. It's like going back to a time before electricity and my family is going to do that for us. You will not believe how beautiful this is going to be."

"Something else to look forward to besides seeing what you're going to wear."

"Not one hint will you get."

Trevor exaggerates a look of disappointment and walks me to the door. I give him a little kiss and turn to go inside. "I was expecting a tad more than that." I stop on a dime, go back to him and put my hands in his hair then kiss him as if we are on his bed. I actually rattle myself and have to gather my thoughts to tell him, "Now I really must go." He doesn't move an inch as I look at him while closing the door. Next I run up the staircase. My grandmother is putting my hair up and I have to get ready to go over.

Grand-mamma is waiting for me in her dressing room and while sitting at her vanity I remember the last time I was here. We were getting me ready for the Summer Banquet on the day I met Trevor. Fortunately this time I can step into my evening gown, because the bodice is surplice with narrow straps that widen as the go up to my shoulders and a zipper that goes from the top to below my waist. As she fastens the bracelet of the pink sapphire suite we selected I take several mental photographs of her in the glow of the candle light. My grandmother looks beautiful in her dressing gown. It's made of embroidered lapis blue bridal satin and has a short train, because it is from the turn of the century.

At the house I leave the matching wrap in the foyer then stand in front of the mirror in my room daydreaming after I have finished getting ready. When I hear Trevor enter the house I call out to him, "Stay in the foyer please. I want you to get the full effect." He chuckles as I blow out the candles in my room.

I place my hand on the banister of the balcony and step into his view. I slide my hand along it, because I am looking at him instead of where I'm going to watch his reaction when he is no longer seeing a side view of me. Not to mention he is so handsome standing there in his Dinner Dress White's at parade rest I do not want to take my eyes off of him. When I turn and face Trevor his mouth slightly opens, so I slowly descend the staircase. On the last stair he reaches for my hand and kisses it as I step directly in front of him.

"Geneviève, you take my breath away. In that beautiful evening gown it looked as if you were floating on air. — For you." He brings his other hand from behind his back and in it is a small bouquet of white tea roses.

"They're lovely. Thank you, Trevor." I immediately hold it up and smell them.

"You are entirely welcome. I must say your gown is a lovely shade of — pink." There is the glint and he kneels down. "Let me see your foot." I laugh as I place my hand on his shoulder and slip my shoe off then lift the full skirting of my gown. "There it is, Strawberry Fluff. How did you pull this off?"

"I painted one side of a quarter with the polish then put a top coat over the entire coin so it wouldn't chip off. The next day I took it to the seamstress and told her to find me a bolt of bridal satin to match it."

"Where's the quarter?"

I smile, reach into my pocket and hold it out to him. "This is for you." He takes the coin, kisses it as he looks at me then drops it in his pocket and tells me, "I am lost in my love with you." I am wearing lipstick, but I have to kiss him. With my hand on his chest I whisper, "Be very still." then ever so lightly kiss his lips.

Even though the sun has not set the glow from the torches can be seen as we walk by them. I like having them out in the summer. They would be lovely along the path to the arbor on our wedding day. We can discuss it when we are planning the details. For now I should focus on the present.

Looking ahead Trevor asks, "Who arrived in the two cars next to Joseph's I don't recognize?"

"The chef and the server named Eric is here to assist Joseph. We have grown in number to 14 people."

"14 and none of my grandparents are here. Aunt Meredith and William's parents will have us at 21. How many people can your grandparent's dining table extend to accommodate?"

"24. Beyond that we have to migrate to a private dining room in the club."

"I think we should migrate there at 21. And Claudette seems territorial."

"Because she is, but her motive for rushing people out of the kitchen is to spend time alone with Joseph. They are attracted to each other."

"Their actions are quite subtle, but I did pick up on that as well. Cupid has been very busy lately."

"Yes he has, but his work is done here. She was the last one."

"And we were the first.

"I love you, Trevor."

"I love you too, Baby."

He stops at the doors and asks, "Are you ready to be the center of attention?" I just look at him. As his deep laugh begins he opens the doors and we go into my grandparent's house. Claudette is waiting for us in the foyer and when she closes the doors we can see the glow from all the candles and the flames from the fireplaces illuminating the entire home.

After complimenting Claudette, who is wearing a lovely pale blue lace and satin gown, we enter the drawing room where I am taken aback by the scene. Every woman looks beautiful in their evening gowns and the men in their tuxedos are so handsome. Then there are the handsome Sailors looking impressive in their uniforms, which include my fiancé.

During the apéritif we discretely inform our friends my family doesn't know about *The Halyard* yet to avoid an awkward situation. Next I tell Emily and Joanna we can have an after hour's appointment Wednesday at The Bridal Salon to select gowns for the wedding. Joanna suggests the fellas should wait for us at The O Club and we can join them for dinner there. Emily is thrilled at the thought of sipping champagne and trying on gowns with the shop to ourselves.

Next Trevor and I join Théo and Rachel. I think Trevor hovering over me as I slept triggered something in Théo, because he suggests going on a double date soon. When he asks if that would be odd Rachel exclaims, "For crying out loud Théo, you took her to her Senior Prom." Trevor and I get tickled as Théo replies, "Touché." and taps her glass. I love her. She is so perfect for him.

Before we go join the conversation our parent's are having I pull Trevor aside. "I just had an idea."

"You have my undivided attention."

"Since you enjoy dressing me and choosing my clothing I thought you might like to select the gown I will wear to our engagement party."

"I *would* like that. Very much. When?"

"How does Thursday sound?"

"Not soon enough."

"You are going to enjoy this more than you think."

"Am I?"

"Mmm hm. Men do not go there often and when they do the staff treats them very well." Trevor's eyes are gleaming. "Consider this an engagement gift." He kisses my cheek and says, "You spoil me so."

Rowland stops in mid-sentence when he sees Trevor and as we get closer he says, "Son, you look as if she just promised you the moon."

"Because she did; I'm choosing her gown for the engagement party."

"It is the little things in life."

"Yes, sir. It is indeed."

Soon Joseph announces dinner is served and Mother chooses the first topic of our conversation. "Do tell us how your day at the Del went." Trevor and I look at each other while having a bout of nervous laughter. Due to the fact he is a highly trained officer in the Navy he was able to get his act together before I did, so he answers the question.

"It was a day filled with memorable events. The first was on the ferry ride over. We could see Louise from the water. Geneviève had not seen her in a while and was so happy to see her she waved." That information made them laugh and was a good cover for why we laughed. Then on a serious note he adds, "I'm used to seeing her while on land. She is quite magnificent from a distance in the water."

William looks at Mitch and I tell them in an animated voice, "I see a ferry ride in both your futures." William tells me, "You sound like a gypsy fortune teller." Emily chimes in. "I know you're joking, but she really does know things. I asked her if she had a crystal ball on the trip." Joanna sits quietly beaming as Grand-papa adds, "Women's Intuition, we are accustomed to it in this family." Simultaneously Théo, Trevor and my father begin nodding repeatedly then we finish telling them about our day. I let Trevor do most of the talking, because I do love his accent. Having his father here and listening to them talk to each other has been a treat.

During desert Evelyn comments on the wine and gets a surprise. Evidently Trevor has discretely left it to us to disclose the details of Château Delcroix. Tomorrow she will probably get another one, because the main reason we're having dinner at the club is the board meeting and I'm certain she doesn't know Mother is the chairwoman.

When we move to the drawing room Grand-mamma tells Joseph we will be fine on our own from this point. My grandfather pours Louis XIII, serves and then makes a toast to us, the future and the growing family. Next Trevor gives out the photographs of the weekend we celebrated our engagement here. His parent's are delighted by all the things we did. It was fun.

After we finish our cognac it's time for the women to put on their wraps and to stroll along the grounds lit by the torches. Before we go I tell Trevor I'm taking Claudette her box of photographs and let Joseph know we are going outside.

Upon entering the kitchen I see Claudette and Joseph are alone. The chef left after the cooking was done, but I did expect Eric to still be here. Joseph must have sent him on his way. He is washing dishes and she is drying. I set the box down and tell them what's in it then announce it's time to walk the torches. It comes as no surprise when Claudette declines to stay and help Joseph as she glances at him. On a whim I tell Joseph she enjoys walking along the torches and ask if he would mind keeping her company on the walk when they're finished. I simply cannot stop myself from giving cupid a little help and of course Joseph agrees to.

The second Trevor sees me he shakes his head and I just smile as I go to him. While he places my wrap on my shoulders he whispers, "I could see the twinkle in your eyes the second I saw you. What did you do?"

"Helped cupid a little."

"I knew it." I bat my eyelashes and it gets me a kiss.

My grandfather opens the doors and Trevor offers me his arm. The moment you step out onto the portico is when the magic begins. The place is transformed into something ethereal and our guests are speechless. As we stroll through the garden on the cobblestones I hear couples whispering to each other. It truly is perfection tonight; the moon is shining bright and its light dances on the water. The sky is filled with stars and tiny little clouds float among them made bright by the light of the moon.

The satin of the tuxedos and gowns shimmer and jewels sparkle. The medals on the Dinner Dress White's look like gold coins and the fabric of the uniform seems to shine. Trevor tells me, "We look like we're in a fairy-tale."

"We are, Mon Amour." I nuzzle him and we wonder aimlessly.

A damp chill in the air arrives and we go back in. Each couple takes turns pouring the cordial of their choice and settle in. How I do not want this to end, but the overwhelming desire to be alone with Trevor eases my melancholy. His parent's are the first to leave. Before they go Trevor tells them we are having lunch at The O Club tomorrow and invites them to join us. Without hesitation they accept and then gradually our remaining dinner guest's take their leave. Only family remains, which include Rachel and Trevor and we talk about how well the evening went.

A little later Claudette and Joseph appear. They are like the staff at Mandarin Garden's, quite as mice. Joseph says, "Please pardon the interruption. Monsieur Delcroix, the kitchen is in order and I would like permission to accompany Miss Bechard on her walk along the torches."

"Of course. Thank you for asking.

"Also, Miss Bechard informed me about the snuffing of the candles. May I add that to my duties for this evening in order for the family to retire early?"

"Yes. How kind of you to offer."

"It would be my pleasure, sir."

My grandmother asks Claudette, "Where is your wrap, Dear?"

"In my apartment."

"My white mink stole is in the foyer. Joseph, will you get it for her please?"

"Certainly, Madame Delcroix."

Claudette is positively glowing as she says, "Thank you, Constance."

"Think nothing of it. Now run along while the torches are still bright." They both say good night and take their leave. When we hear the door close Théo tells us he is going to take Rachel home and our parent's go home as well. Then I get an idea, grab my camera and go to a window. Trevor is on my heels. "What are you up to?" I reply, "Taking one photo of Claudette and Joseph. I'm going to give it to them on their wedding day." Without blinking at that little prediction he holds the draperies back for me; I snap the shutter and he lets them go.

With that taken care of we stay to have a moment alone with my grandparent's. Knowing they are tired we do not stay long and soon we thank them for the lovely evening and leave.

When we are crossing the portico I suddenly stop. "Trevor, I don't think we should walk in front of the guest house." He looks up and even though the house is dim inside he can see his father has his mum in an embrace. "If we take the back way we could encounter Claudette and Joseph."

"Change of plans, to the apartment we go."

Trevor cups my elbow as I carefully lift my gown with both hands to ascend the stairs. With his other hand he is unbuttoning his jacket and when we are inside without saying a word he takes it off, tosses it on the sofa then gives me his handkerchief. The second my lipstick is on it he places his hand on my stomach and moves me backward until I am against the door.

To stay off my gown he places his hands on the door and leans forward. He gazes into my eyes and begins kissing me with passion. I hold him by his neck and in the heat of the moment my hands are in his hair. Things escalate quickly from there. When he begins kissing my neck I tell him, "I want more than just your mouth on me." He instantly pushes off the door and stands up straight. Looking around I tell him, "This place needs a dressing screen. I can't take this off in the bathroom. Unzip me and stand against the door with your eyes closed."

"Yes ma'am. — It has been like being tortured seeing you all day and not being able to feel you. And I love seeing you in firelight." Then he gets quiet and rests his head on the door. While I run around he takes his watch and ring off and tosses them on the sofa as if his eyes are open.

Wearing only an undershirt and with my hair braided halfway I rush at him while his eyes are still closed. All the emotion we have suppressed over the course of this entire day is released the second he gets his arms around me. When we reach his bed and lie down he finds out my legs are bare by placing his hand on one to pull it over him. This is unexpected and makes him inhale sharply.

Near exhaustion we stop kissing and I lay my head on his chest and my leg across his. Then Trevor slides his hand down my thigh to my ankle and then back up to my thigh. The way he touches me makes me feel as if he has cast a spell on me; one that takes all my strength away.

Lying there suspended in time I begin experiencing fantasies for lack of a better word. One minute I was drifting away wishing I could feel the skin of his legs like when we were out on Willow and then the thought of breaking the chain of his dog tags to get them out of my way crosses my mind. Before I have another fantasy I hear a car start and we both slightly flinch. Trevor says, "That would be Joseph leaving. I know he walked Claudette to her door. I didn't even hear them come up the steps." He sighs heavily. "I am so tired of being concerned with the time."

"It's upsetting me too. Just lie here while I put my gown back on." When I have it on I tell him, "You may open your eyes now. Will you zip me back up please?" And he leaps off the bed.

The weekend has ended and normally I do not look forward to Mondays, but breakfast for just the five of us appeals to me and I practically bound down the stairs pulling on Trevor. During a lull in the family's conversation I ask him, "Do you think Joseph will be over this weekend to ask my grandfather for permission to date Claudette?"

"I think he has it set up to do that very thing."

Théo nods in agreement then Mother says, "I thought I was wishful thinking." Her eyes get misty and Father puts his hand over hers. "Are they truly attracted to each other?"

Trevor cautiously answers, "It seems that way."

Théo and I look at each other and he asks, "Mother, what do we not know?"

"The personal information on his employment application." She takes a deep breath and continues. "Joseph grew up at the orphanage."

My heart sinks. "Grew up? You mean he didn't get adopted?"

"That is correct. His application had a work permit attached, because he was only 15 years old. His one reference was a woman at the orphanage; therefore Mr. Murphy gave it to the board for review. There was an unofficial vote among the other board members for me to make the phone call. When I did the woman was so desperate for us to hire him she broke protocol and told me Joseph's mother was an unwed French Canadian sent here to stay with relatives and give him up for adoption before returning home.

"Joseph was very shy around strangers as a toddler. The fact that whenever strangers showed up one of his playmates would leave and never return made him even more so. Eventually he became like a turtle that goes into its shell. They tried to coax him out, but time passed and he just got older. Since the orphanage is state funded, at 18 they go out into the world or work there. The orphans get jobs when they turn 16 to save money for when the day comes. The woman knew he could have a good career at the club as a server; the problem was he had never eaten at a restaurant with servers. To get him a jump start she obtained the work permit.

"I reassured her the club would hire him and I personally would oversee his advancement. No one questioned me when I announced he was to begin training for our Silver Staff on day one. By the time he turned 18, Joseph had saved enough for a room in a nice boarding house. Now he lives in his own apartment."

Our mood lightens and I say, "That is why he dotes on you so; he has been under your wing for — over 12 years. What is his surname?"

"Côté, the ladies gave him a French Canadian one."

Trevor says, "Joseph Côté. He too was carefully named. Joseph and his coat of many colors; sold to into slavery by jealous brothers and one day he finds himself seated next to the Pharaoh as Governor of Egypt."

We all begin smiling then Mother asks, "What did you mean by 'he too'?"

"My middle name is Christopher."

Father says, "Indeed you were carefully named; by your mother no doubt."

"Yes, sir."

Théo says, "This has been an illuminating morning. I am going to fill my thermos with coffee and process all this on my way to the bank to see Rachel for a minute or two, maybe three." I tell him, "We will walk out with."

Mother gets a hug from each of us before we leave. Driving away we see Trevor's parent's drinking coffee wearing robes on the balcony enjoying the view. All of us wave as we pass by.

The morning declines when I get to my desk and find a plain envelope with my name on it. This time Mr. Collins wants me and Trevor to be in the reception room for the base commander at 8 a.m. tomorrow. I'll tell him at the apartment after dinner while he has a glass of something in his hand.

Since I wore a dinner dress to work Trevor and I go straight to the club. Joseph has the private dining room set up beautifully for us. My father is already here and soon Joanna, Mitch, Emily and William arrive followed by Rachel and Théo. It really is no surprise when my grandparent's walk in with Claudette who evidently went shopping today, because I have not seen the dress she is wearing. Joseph, who has always seated her because she is unescorted, compliments her. I quietly tell Trevor, "I wish Mother was here already." He kisses my hand.

Joseph opens another bottle of wine and maybe 10 minutes later Mother walks in carrying the red briefcase my grandmother had made when she became chairwoman. She refused to carry one that looked as if she borrowed it from my grandfather. It makes Mother look quite impressive and Evelyn has a look on her face that says, "What do we not know?" as she glances at Rowland.

Mother walks to the table with Joseph following two steps back as she says, "Good evening all. Thank you for waiting." Joseph takes her briefcase and Father seats her. Joanna of course finds a tactful way for Trevor's parent's to get the answer to their burning question by asking, "Madame Chair, is there something from the board meeting you can share with us?"

"The Pâtissier has planned wonderful seasonal desserts for next month." I light up and Trevor let's a chuckle slip. "Oh and the price of seafood has gone up, but the board voted not to pass the increase on to our members." I glace at Evelyn whose eyebrows are raised just a bit.

Since this is sort of a Bon Voyage gathering for Trevor's parent's we linger over after dinner drinks and discuss the engagement party that will have them on a return flight in nine days. Only nine days and I do not have an evening gown. I hope Trevor chooses something that does not require significant alterations.

I must have reacted visibly because Trevor quietly asks, "Is something wrong?"

"Our engagement party is in 11 days."

"I'm sorry I asked."

Before we leave the dining room Joseph and my grandfather step aside as Claudette clings to my grandmother's arm. Those of us who know what he is asking glance at each other. Outside we learn he'll be there Sunday morning.

At Maison Evelyn and Rowland wait in front of the guest house for Trevor to park the car to tell us good night and we go to the apartment. While he is turning on a lamp I go to the liqueur cabinet, pour myself a cognac and him a glass of whiskey. "Do I want to know why you poured me this instead of what you're having?"

"Probably not." He motions to the sofa and after I tell him about our meeting in the morning he is quiet for over a minute. "Perhaps I should have made that a double."

This gets him to laugh and he gives me a kiss. "The day is going to begin with seeing him and end with taking my parent's to the airport." I have a burst of nervous laughter. "Geneviève, are you all right?"

"Yes. It just occurred to me that we are having lunch with your parent's at Mandarin Garden's tomorrow and that is where I went the day I met Mr. Collins. More than likely I will have the rest of the day off again. I see sake in our future."

"I see my father as our chauffeur." While I laugh he jumps up and looks out the window. "Oh good, they're still up. I need to tell them I have to report for duty in the morning. You did tell Emily not to look for us?"

"Yes and she told me she has received requests for services required elsewhere for officers with secretaries out sick. I wish mine were due to a secretary with a cold instead of secret meetings with men in the CIA."

He gives me a noisy kiss and makes the call they are obviously used to getting. We relax for a bit as we finish our drinks and go to the house. When he tucks me in he continues with the bedtime story of The Sailor and the Princess. It is getting to a good part.

In the morning I hit the floor running and am ready when he is. At the breakfast table we barely join in the conversation that happens to be about the latest development with Claudette and Joseph, because we are focused on eating and leaving. Finally we realize they have stopped talking and are watching us. Trevor tells them, "I found out late last night I have to report for duty." Théo asks, "Is there anything we can do to expedite your departure?" Trevor replies, "Thank you for asking. Just make way when we get up to leave." I choke on my orange juice and he has to pat my back.

The humor continues when Trevor offers me his arm as we walk to the base commander's building. I get tickled and ask, "You're reporting for duty. Can I hold your arm here?"

"That's a question I don't know the answer to. I've never reported to duty with a woman." We slow down as he thinks. "I'm guessing no and I need to keep my hands to myself. I'm going to have to concentrate."

"Commander Lyons, once you get inside your training will kick in."

"Thank you for that reminder, Miss Delcroix."

"Think nothing of it."

He removes his cover and tucks it under his arm when we are inside. Each step we take Trevor changes more and more before my very eyes. So far he is the highest ranking officer walking through the building. Each Sailor we see says, "Good morning, Commander." Trevor acknowledges them with a nod and no one breaks their stride. When we enter the reception room for the base commander I see the lieutenant who is his aide; he properly greets Trevor and we follow him to the same room. This time he opens the door and only Mr. Collins is sitting at the table with folders and felt tipped markers in front of him.

He stands and says, "Good morning." Trevor tells him, "Good morning, sir." as I nod and think not really, because you're probably going to tell me something or show me something that will upset me. Anyway, we sit down and he pours coffee. He hands me a cup and then no surprise here, he begins making Trevor's without asking how he takes it.

Mr. Collins hands Trevor his coffee and sits down. "Let's get straight to it shall we? Richter's employer thinks his grandmother is on her deathbed in Austria and he's taking the risk to see her before she passes. The woman died eight years ago. Your call he has a sister with a daughter to send things to was on the mark. We have her and the rest of his relative's under surveillance."

Next he slides a folder over to us and I open it. "These are transcripts from pages in a travel journal Richter kept from day one of his trip. They are a wealth of information." I slide it in front of Trevor and he scans over the first page.

"Richter lived in Portland. His first paragraph is when he leaves for Astoria, Oregon which is at the mouth of the Columbia River that flows to six states and Canada. It was the best place to begin his journey. The man did his research. The river's water is deep. The boys in D.C. already had a plan in place to put a sub net there and watch towers. They're picking up the pace on that.

"Richter made his way south taking photographs from tourist boats, charters and ferry's that went along the coast. There are groups of entries that start with 1 and end with 24."

I say, "24 photographs per roll."

"Exactly. The good news, this is the key to all his photographs and thanks to you the enemy will never get it. The not so good news, there are 32 numbered groups beginning in Astoria and ending in Long Beach, the exact number of missing film canisters. We are going under the assumption the enemy did receive the film, because the Regina made it through Customs and out of the States, but they won't do them much good without his journal."

Next he slides two stacks of folders over, one to me and the other to Trevor. "These are the photographs from the film we intercepted and the main reason I'm here. You two can save us a ton of leg work by identifying the location of as many as you possibly can. Commander, yours are of the entire base. Miss Delcroix, you have everything else. What you can't identify put in a stack for you both to go through. Don't be concerned with keeping them in order; they are numbered on the back. Use these markers to write on the space provide on the front. Any questions?" Trevor replies, "I believe we're set."

Mr. Collins picks up his coffee cup and refills it. "I'm going to step out. If you need me or anything else the lieutenant is standing in the corridor by the door."

Trevor looks at my stack that is twice as high as his. "These will not take me long to go through. Thanks to our trip to Santa Barbara I can help with yours."

"I'm so glad you said that. I was a bit overwhelmed at the thought of doing most of these alone."

He chuckles and says in a voice like Mr. Collins, "Let's get straight to it shall we?" I laugh as I open my first folder.

Trevor lays a few photos in a stack between us and we are both moving along until I gasp. In front of me is a photo of the club taken from a boat. Trevor responds, "That is a little disconcerting. It's time for a break."

"I don't want any more coffee."

"What do you want?"

"A ginger ale will suffice."

He tells the lieutenant what we need as I fill out the label on it then he sits with his arm around my shoulders. "You should stop here, look at the ones I put in the middle and wait on me to finish mine. Then we'll finish yours together."

"I was dealing with all the others but this one ..."

"Was a bit much. I am ill at ease myself. The photos of Louise were expected, but I didn't expect to see that."

We sit together a few minutes until the lieutenant brings our sodas and get back to work. The second I pick up his stack I say, "This is of one of the streets on my list of one's to be dealt with."

"I think they all are."

Mr. Collins knocks twice and walks in. He sees what I am holding and asks, "Do those streets go onto the base?"

Trevor replies, "Yes they do and steps are being taken as we speak to decide whether to button them up with a barricade or put a sentry box on them."

"Excellent, now I won't have to bring that up in the meeting this afternoon." I glance at Trevor. "You both will leave the base after you finish up here." And he begins looking through the folders we have put on his side of the table.

Trevor closes his last folder and pulls mine over between us. It gets a little tricky, but we keep a steady pace even after seeing the park we went to the concert at. After looking at 576 photographs we announce the task has been completed. Trevor gives him a folder and says, "There are 43 photograph's in that. They are the ones we couldn't identify."

"That is well below the number expected. Thank you."

Trevor and I give him a nod and sit back to relax a minute, but we do not get to, because Mr. Collins begins talking to Trevor. "You speak Italian fluently and rudimentary Japanese."

"The last is an overstatement. I know a few phrases that allowed me to get around and be polite to locals when I was on shore leave in Japan."

"You can resign your commission next year. Would you consider becoming a member of The Agency?" My eyes are going back and forth between them. "You and Miss Delcroix would make a good team in the field and I am certain she can teach you how to speak French if she has not begun already."

I am trying to figure out a way to politely tell him what happens between us is none of his business when Trevor replies, "I'm going to take that as a compliment and thank you for asking, but I am certain she has not changed her mind concerning this issue and I am a Sailor."

"I would have been remiss in my duties had I not asked." Now he is looking at me. "Miss Delcroix, you shook things up that day at the hotel. When Banks finally arrived a rebellion took place. My agents wanted to continue with the way you were working the room. It was faster and far more efficient. When he was going to shoot a scene, before tossing it he would have us leave. We usually wound up in a corridor or somewhere drawing unnecessary attention to ourselves.

"On the return flight you were the topic of conversation instead of our spy. Not one of us had a clue what a Regina was and the other agents decided that efforts should be ramped up to get women involved. They know things we don't. I have already spoken with the director and changes will be implemented."

"This is flattering to say the least."

"I'm not done. The Agency wants you to consider becoming a field agent as a photographer for us and work scenes on the side. You would be able to keep your job here and they would only be ones close by that might require a short flight and there will never be a body on the scene. You would be issued identification's, work with my team and be well compensated for your time."

"Mr. Collins, time is something I need more of. We are getting married and our plans for the future have already been decided."

He nods and tells me, "Know this; there is not a time limit here. We would be happy to have you with us, even if it's a year from now." My hands have been clasped and resting on the table the entire time he spoke to us. On this note Trevor ignores the keep his hands to himself rule and places his hand over them.

"All right, let's wind this up. Miss Delcroix, due to the fact you are a civilian, the records on this case to protect you from anything further, especially his trial, read that I received an anonymous tip and acted on it. The only agents who know of your involvement are the ones you encountered and they have already signed a sworn statement confirming the report."

Finding myself at a complete loss for words I just sit at the table looking at Mr. Collins. When Trevor realizes it, he speaks for me. "We can't thank you enough."

"It's the least we could do for her after what she did for this country." He looks at me. "Which reminds me, now would be a good time to tell you this, President Roosevelt extends his deepest gratitude. When I speak with him it's full disclosure and he can be trusted to keep a secret."

As Trevor and I sit quietly processing what we just heard, Mr. Collins stands, takes a card out of his wallet and gives it to Trevor. "Our business here is concluded." We stand and he shakes Trevor's hand. Next he extends his hand to me as a gentleman. I place mine on it and he says, "Bonne chance, Mademoiselle Delcroix." then kisses my hand and bows.

At last I speak. "Thank you for making this as easy as you possibly could for me. I will not forget this favor, nor you. Bonne chance, Monsieur Collins." He nods and opens the door for us. As Trevor and I walk down the corridor I look over my shoulder and the man finally smiles at me.

We begin encountering Sailors again and after Trevor has nodded several times he says, "Why aren't these Sailors in an office? I'm beginning to feel like a bobblehead doll." In order not to laugh I sing, "Please do not get me tickled in this building." And he doesn't say another word until we are outside.

"I motion we go to our spot down the road."

"I second that motion."

Trevor parks the car and asks, "Geneviève, are you all right?"

"The jury is still out on that one. I've never said that. Why did I ... never mind. A trial? Those things are always in the news. Traitors and spies go to trial where they are found guilty and executed, immediately."

"Yes they are and it is to send a message to anyone considering becoming a traitor or a spy. Richter knew the consequences if he was caught and he still proceeded with his mission."

"Which was to gather intel for the enemy to plan an attack on the entire West Coast. Then Mr. Collins took a flight with that intel to the headquarters in Langley and then drove down to the White House to brief the President who asked him to tell me thank you."

"That's sums it up nicely."

"It sounds like fiction. — I could see the photo's you were looking at. There were so many of Louise it was upsetting and the one of the marina that showed Willows' masts was the cherry on top."

"That *was* an unpleasant surprise."

"It was an effort to keep my equilibrium the entire time we were in there. I was prepared for him to attempt to recruit you, but when he made the reference to our private life ... I'm glad I held my tongue long enough for you to step in."

"When your chin went up I had to. He was only doing do his job."

"While you were talking I realized that. You handled it very well, but I wasn't expecting the job offer he made us."

"Neither was I. He hit us in our blind side."

"He hit me twice. Once with the offer, then when he said there would never be a body on a scene I worked." Trevor burst into laughter. "Was he expecting me to say, in that case sign me up?" Trevor shakes his head and laughs even harder.

"Geneviève, you have got to let me catch my breath."

I stop talking and when his breathing is normal to a degree I add, "In the end though, he did show us the man he is when not on the job and he is a nice one."

"That he is."

"Oh my gosh. Trevor — I don't want to talk about this anymore. Will you please change the subject?"

He looks at his watch. "We are in our parking spot. Do you want to take advantage of it?" I hook him around his neck. "I will take that as yes."

When we hear the steam whistle for the construction workers lunch at 11:30 Trevor drives us to the apartment. While he is changing into civvies the phone rings and I answer it. Evelyn was surprised to hear my voice. I inform her when I have special assignments I leave when the job is done. Trevor takes the handset and tells her he wants his father to drive. When he hangs up we both say, "Sake."

Soon his parent's are waiting outside the apartment in their car. "I knew Father would be a good chauffeur." And he is. Rowland goes to the restaurant without missing a turn and then we proceed to have a very long lunch.

The nice thing about sake is that it makes you forget all your troubles and while we are walking to the car I have an idea. "Would you two like to go on an adventure?" Evelyn replies, "Indeed we would." When we get in Rowland looks at me in the rearview mirror and asks, "Where to Miss?"

"To the park please."

"Yes, ma'am."

He starts the car and I sadly tell Trevor, "I wish I had my camera." Evelyn says, "Rowland." He responds, "We *do* need a new camera. From here how do I get to Blackwell's?"

Trevor gives him directions and when we walk through the door Mr. Blackwell perks up. Rowland tells him they want the camera I have and everything to go with it. He teaches them how to use it; we thank him and continue our adventure by going to the Japanese Garden.

Once we begin strolling around soaking up the beauty Evelyn turns into a shutterbug. Soon we are posing for her everywhere. Then she gives the camera to Rowland and has him take several snapshots. Next she gets the camera back and starts walking toward a man. Rowland says, "There she goes. I hope he knows how to work that thing."

Trevor says, "I hope he's an American." His eyes get a tad wide as he looks at me and I get tickled. Poor Trevor's face gets red from laughing with his mouth closed. His father begins to laugh just from watching us desperately trying to get our composer. Perhaps we drank a little more sake than we should have.

Evelyn shows the man how to the work the camera while we fall apart. Then she joins us and the nice man that is an American takes three photographs to make sure we have a good one. Rowland thanks him and he bids us good day.

We are alone now and his father is looking at us. I feel Trevor should take this one, after all they are his parent's and he started it. Rowland looks at Evelyn then back at us. "May I ask what that was all about?"

"Long story short, Emily asked a foreigner to take a photograph of her and Geneviève the day after she got a new car. It eventually turned into a comedy of errors." I add, "Yes it did." Looking at Evelyn I ask, "When is the last time you rode a carousel?" She replies, "When Trevor was a boy. I hear the organ playing in the distance. Lead the way." And our adventure continues.

When the carousel is in sight she takes a snapshot then Charlie sees me in the distance and waves. Trevor goes to the ticket booth as I introduce them to Charlie and he comes back waving a short streamer of tickets through the air. Trevor gives them to me and when I offer them to Charlie he says, "Miss Delcroix, it's obvious this was a spur of the moment idea and you need to know that ladies riding side saddle are required to be on the horse's to the inside."

Suddenly Evelyn exclaims, "The brass ring game!" and we chose our horses then our men help us saddle up. They are in front of us so we can watch them and when Rowland grabs an iron ring Evelyn shouts, "Well done." after she takes a snapshot. Trevor gets one too of course. Eventually a little boy gets the brass ring.

After the ride Trevor is first at the toss box. Evelyn takes a snapshot as he hits the target hard as usual then exclaims, "Good arm, Son." Charlie walks over to Trevor. "We have choices today. There's a shooter, a top and a roll of shiny new pennies for Penny Candy. I light up and he says, "The pennies, please." I blow Trevor a kiss as Rowland steps up to the toss box and does exactly what his son did as Evelyn takes another snapshot. He tells Charlie, "I will take the pennies as well." Evelyn sings, "Thank you." Next I say, "Chaaarlie." He turns around raising his eyebrows. "If I promise to hold on with one hand at all times and he holds on to me and the pole may I ride on the outside to grab a ring?"

"Only because I know he will not let anything happen to you I am going to agree to this." I happily tell him, "You are the best." We get back on and I hold my arms out to Trevor who is shaking his head as he puts me on my horse.

Evelyn says, "Rowland." as she takes the camera from around her neck. She puts it on him and soon two unhappy men are holding on to their women when the carousel starts. We enjoy the ride a little while, then Evelyn and I get an iron ring. The next time around the brass ring is in sight and Trevor yells, "Mum, grab it!" And she does. Watching her waving it in the air was the highlight of the day.

When I hit the target with my iron ring Trevor says, "Good shot, Baby." I point at my cheek and he kisses it. Charlie gives me pennies without bothering to ask and goes to Evelyn who inquires, "What do I get?" He replies, "Your choice of what is on the shelves in the ticket booth." She smiles at Rowland and takes off. He is chuckling as I point at the camera. He hands it to me and catches up as we slowly follow him. Evelyn gives the brass ring to Beatrice then stands there giving serious thought to what she is going to choose. Eventually she says, "I want the light brown Teddy Bear wearing the brown plaid bow tie on the top shelf, please."

His mum proudly shows it to us and he is cute. I took several snapshots during the selection process that will make her very happy. Next we ask Charlie to take a photograph of us, we thank him profusely for everything and then walk to The Confectionery where the Penny Candy is.

What kind of candy I want requires no thought; I get two butterscotch discs and keep one of my pennies for a souvenir. Trevor does the same thing. Rowland gets the starlight mints because they are two for a penny and he can keep two pennies for them.

While we get candy Evelyn wanders over to the marble ice cream counter holding her bear. Rowland asks, "Who wants an ice cream cone? My treat." I raise my hand like a child at the same time she does. Our men and strangers laugh as we join her. Evelyn and Rowland order strawberry cones right away as I stand there thinking. Trevor says, "Let me guess, vanilla or that chocolate." I sigh heavily. "I'll get the chocolate and share." So, I order the vanilla and he gets a kiss on the cheek.

We choose a nice bench under a tree to sit down and eat our cones. Then after we finish our ice cream I take a really good photograph of Evelyn holding her Teddy Bear sitting between her husband and son. Next we slowly walk to the car talking about the fun we have had and go home so they can pack before dinner at my parent's house.

We are all so happy and the dinner conversation was lively. Just the stories from the park were enough to fill the entire evening. When it comes time to leave for the airport, even though his parent's will be back before we know it, there is a sense of melancholy as they say their goodbyes and thank my family for making them feel so welcome.

Waiting at the gate for their flight to be called Evelyn names the bear Diego and informs us he will be back. When their flight is announced over the speaker we all get quiet and Rowland picks up Evelyn's train case. She tells me she loves me and will miss me. I tell her the same. To lighten things up she tells us she will miss me more than Trevor and will give us a ring when they reach New Haven.

We stay and watch their takeoff and during the walk to the car I get a lump in my throat. I became attached to his parent's as quickly as I did him. Moments before my heart aches I remember the funniest thing said all day and begin laughing. "I hope he's an American huh?"

Trevor completely loses it. "I can't believe that came out of my mouth. I blame the sake."

"That's what I did the moment you said it!" Our laughter draws attention to us and we could care less.

On the drive home he tells me he will never forget the sight of his parent's on the carousel playing the brass ring game and his mum walking around the park *and* the airport with a Teddy Bear tucked under her arm.

When we get inside the apartment he asks, "Do you want to have a long shower tonight?"

"It doesn't matter to me. Do you want to go for a run?"

"No. I'm tired. I just want to lie down with you in my arms and rest." So that is what we do.

Trevor yawns and that is our signal to get up before we fall asleep. We never turned on a light, so we simply walk out the door to the house. The shower does feel good and I want to linger, but I know he is waiting to watch me braid my hair and tuck me in.

It is late when he pulls the covers over me and kneels beside my bed. He rubs my back and says, "I love you, Geneviève."

"Oh Trevor — I love you too." Soon after he leaves I fall asleep with a vision of him still by my bed.

In the middle of the night I wake up panting and trying to catch my breath. It is dark and I am confused until I realize I had a very bad dream. I want to cry and fight tears while pouring a glass of water. As I drink, it occurs to me Trevor is here. I open my door and go straight to his. He left it slightly open, so I go in and the second I close it he is wide awake. I am visibly trembling as he flings the covers back and gets up. I throw my arms around his neck and tears stream down my face. He softly says, "I've got you, Baby."

Trying to calm down I tell him, "I had the worst dream I have ever had in my life. I was in a court room on the witness stand and that horrid man was sitting at a table across from me. My family and our friends were there and I was looking at you. You were sitting between Mitch and William. A man behind you began standing up and everything started happening in slow motion. He had a gun in his hand and pointing it at me as he said, 'For the Fatherland.'

"I dropped to the floor keeping my eyes on him and suddenly I saw your back as you lunged toward him. Then I heard a gunshot and you went flying backwards. I was crawling on the floor to get to you and heard another gunshot. Someone shot him in the head. I stood up and started running to you. William and Mitch were carrying you to the aisle and laid you down. Your shirt was covered in blood.

"When I reached you I fell to my knees beside you and put my hand over the bullet wound to try and stop the bleeding. You looked at me and asked, 'Is he dead?' I said, 'Yes.' You smiled and said, 'You're safe.' Then you closed your eyes and breathed a sigh of relief. And you didn't draw in another breath." I begin to sob.

After a minute or so I feel Trevor is slightly shaking his head. What have I done? Why did I tell him I watched him die? I almost panic which calms me down some. "I should not have told you my dream."

"I'm grateful you did. I would've never asked you to tell me and I needed to know where your mind is in order to help you. And it's far worse than I thought." Tears flow again as he holds me. "Geneviève, you know this will never happen. You will not be at his trial. It really was just a very bad dream."

"It seemed so real."

"I know. I've had dreams like that."

"It will haunt me the rest of my days."

Trevor goes, "Shhhh." and rocks me in his arms.

When I sniffle he tries to wipe away my tears and asks, "Can you walk to the bathroom with me?" I nod and he holds my hand to lead me there. He gives me a tissue and says, "Blow your little nose and I'm going to wet a washcloth with cool water for your face." When he turns around I see his shoulder is shiny from my tears and his tank shirt is wet. No more crying.

While wringing out the washcloth he tells me, "I was hoping you wouldn't have a bad dream. When he said the word trial I thought things might go badly. It had been buried in your subconscious since the day you spotted him again and I hoped it would stay buried." He hands me the washcloth, fills a glass with water and drinks it as I wipe my face and neck. Next I wipe off his shoulder.

Trevor gives me the water and I drink some as he leads me to the bed. He gets in, moves over and lifts the covers. "Lie down next to me." I sit the water on his nightstand; he covers me up and strokes my hair. "Are you comfortable?"

"Mmm hm." I whimper because the vision of watching him die in that stupid dream is still all too real.

"Is there anything else I can do?"

"Just hold me, please." As I rest in his arms the dream fades away.

Eventually his bedroom has light coming in and we know it is time to start the day. Therefore we do. When Trevor enters my room I am standing barefooted in my closet at a loss wearing a slip. "More silk. If I let you feel my freshly shaved face will you let me feel you through that slip?" I place my hands on his face and he puts his on my back. "I love it when you tell me yes without a word." I am not sure what I enjoy more, feeling his face or his hands on me.

Things do not go any further. I need to get ready for work, so he asks, "May I chose what you are going to wear?"

"Yes and you may dress me."

"This day is shaping up nicely."

After he dresses me we decide to cook breakfast for the family, because it is very early. Trevor starts the coffee and I announce I'm going to make pancakes while pouring us a glass of orange juice, caffeine is something neither of us need. Things are going just fine until we hear footsteps on the staircase. "Oops, I think we woke up Théo." And there he is, fully dressed.

"Actually Gené, you woke me up. You were talking in your sleep during what I believe was a very bad dream. I was getting up to wake you when you woke up on your own. You were breathing so heavily I decided to let you get your wits about you before I tapped on your door. Then I heard it open and realized he was here. Gené — I'm concerned about you. Should I be?"

"No, Théo." I sigh. "It had to do with work."

"I knew the moment the war started your job was going to take a nasty turn."

"Théo, I will be all right now."

The next thing I know he whips his head around to look at Trevor and says emphatically, "You have a high security clearance level; there is not a doubt in my mind. She is not going be alone in this anymore. She has you." After he shakes Trevor's hand I ask him, "Would you like a glass of orange juice?"

"That would be perfect. Thank you. What are we having?"

"The usual with the exception I am making the best pancakes in the whole wide world." I give him the juice and he kisses my forehead.

We are all busy preparing breakfast, so busy no one hears our parent's until they enter the kitchen. Everyone says good morning and they make their cups of coffee. Théo brought the newspaper in and put it on Father's end of the table. After seating Mother he pushes the newspaper away as he has a seat. I fill plates as Trevor holds them then Théo serves. We begin eating and after maybe two minutes my father asks, "Théo, how much longer are you going to make your mother wait?"

At his moment I am thrilled he is the eldest. Théo thinks for a few seconds. "Gené woke us up because she had a bad dream that was triggered by something to do with work." Mother dryly says, "I knew the moment the war started your job was going to take a nasty turn." Trevor says, "That is exactly what Théo said."

Father asks, "Since you all seem to be fine, a solution to the problem must have been found. What is it?" Trevor replies, "I am going to be here for her, because I am in a position to do so." My parents look at each other and my father tells him, "We understand. It is good to have you back in your room, Trevor." He responds, "Thank you, sir. I'm glad to be back." Mother tells him, "It is us that should be thanking you." She gives him a warm smile then asks me, "Sweetheart, do I smell your wonderful pancakes warming in the oven?"

We recover nicely from the brief yet intense conversation and have a lovely breakfast. Mother got a break from cooking and Trevor and I thoroughly enjoyed the time with we had with Théo.

In the parking lot at work Emily is so happy to see me one would have thought I had been gone for days. Then she tells me looking at my empty chair was a drag. A drag? No doubt that is current lingo among the teens she picks up from her sister and the slang term is surprisingly accurate. When she brings up our appointment to select gowns for the wedding I pretend I have not forgotten.

When we separate for a private moment with our fiancé's I tell Trevor, "It's Wednesday and I cannot deal with lunch at The O Club."

"That makes two of us. I'll tell Joanna I'm craving something she cooks. William and I will pick you and Emily up. " He kisses my hand and I happily go inside with my friend.

By lunch the morning was a distant memory and we all decide to meet back here after work. We are going to The Bridal Salon in Joanna's convertible and the fellas are riding in the Willys to The O Club. Joanna tells them they will see us when they see us.

When it's finally five o'clock Emily literally pulls me by my arm to the Powder Room where we freshen up then she proceeds to pull me to her car. She is excited about where we are going and why. When we get to the Mitchell's Trevor is waiting outside propped against the back passenger side door of Mitch's car, so Emily waves and goes in.

He gives me a mischievous look as I approach him. After I kiss his cheeks I ask, "Is that whiskey on your breath?"

"Yes, ma'am. I waited for you out here for two reasons. One was to tell you it's Happy Hour in there. A bottle of champagne has been chilled for the ladies." He opens the car door. "The other reason was so you could taste the whiskey on my lips." I laugh as I get in. This time I corner him and oh how he does let me taste the whiskey, to the point we stay outside a bit longer than we should.

The second we go inside Joanna stops me at the door, hands me a glass of champagne and kisses my cheeks. Then she looks at me with eyes dancing. I say, "Do tell." She replies, "Darling, I smell whiskey on your breath." With a twinkle in my eyes I tell her, "There was some in the back seat of your husband's car." She draws in a deep breath and slowly exhales to keep from laughing. "Do you simply adore the woman in you that was just waiting to come out?" I quietly reply, "Yes I do and the man who brought her out." She taps my glass. "To the men we love to kiss." I echo her sentiment and take a drink of my champagne then swish it in my mouth as if I am at a wine tasting. Joanna finally gets tickled and I simply say, "William, Mitch." as I pass them to stand by Trevor.

He raises one eyebrow looking at me then gives me a kiss. "My ears were burning."

"I stopped talking about you before they caught fire." That statement gets me the reaction I wanted, his deep laugh.

After Happy Hour, which was only 40 minutes, Trevor walks me to Joanna's car. The top is down and as we drive away I feel compelled to turn around and look at him, so I turn around and kneel on the seat. They are in the Willys still parked watching us leave. Trevor is sitting on the edge of the passenger seat and we are close enough to make eye contact. We do not wave or anything. We just watch each other and I do not take my eyes off him until he is out of sight.

Inside The Bridal Salon the occasion turns into a celebration of the wedding. We drink champagne and I sit on the settee watching them going through gowns. I told them the color I wanted them to wear and to chose whatever style that made them feel beautiful. Joanna found exactly what she wanted in mere minutes. Emily found hers quickly too. After the fitting, barely an hour had passed and we found ourselves leaving before the sun set.

Since we finished much earlier than anticipated we decide to go back to the house before going to The O Club. When we are inside she tells us, "Let's get Bohemian." and starts throwing cushions from the chairs on the floor. When she motions to the sofa; Emily and I begin throwing the ones from it on the floor into a nice pile around the coffee table then we push the furniture in. Next Joanna has us kick off our shoes and sit on the cushions. She lights candles, turns off the lamps and pours glasses of Louis XIII for us and we get comfortable.

Emily wants to know all about her wedding and where they went for their honeymoon. Joanna tells us the highlights of the wedding and when she tells us they went to Versailles for their honeymoon we watch her drift away in thought.

When she returns Joanna looks at us and asks, "Are you two nervous about the honeymoon?" Emily is stunned silent by the question while I'm trying to think of how to answer it. Then Joanna laughs softly and says, "Oh, I know, you've spent years dreaming of falling in love, having a beautiful wedding and going someplace special for your honeymoon. Next you come back to a home and begin your life with the man you married.

"Then when you are well into your teens you begin having your cycle and all of a sudden you want a stiff drink before you go for your yearly physical." Emily I both get tickled because it is too true. "Next you find out what happens on a honeymoon. That information shakes you to your very core."

Emily is nodding and I say, "We are so venerable."

"Yes we are. We are naked and at risk of feeling pain instead of pleasure like the men do. Some men rush through the process and the experience is bad for the woman and they do not want to go through it again until they have recovered mentally from the disappointment and physically from the discomfort they have been left with.

"A good man and a smart man will learn everything he needs to know about the anatomy of a woman and what part of her body causes her to climax. Then he will slowly ease the woman into a life that includes physical love and her first experience will be pleasurable. Then she will look forward to it happening again."

I respond, "And we have good men."

"Yes we do; all three of us." She swirls her cognac and takes a sip. "I had many advantages growing up in Paris, one of them was the house was fully staffed and there was an upstairs maid. Her name was Oriana. She became my friend and as I matured she became my confidant.

"She was in her 30's and one day I asked why she was not married and she said, 'Members of a household staff rarely marry because it would require a place to live. I like where I live. I enjoy my work and do not need to marry to have the pleasures of marriage. I take lovers into my bed and fortunately my first one knew how to make wonderful love. He gave me such pleasure.

'This is what I have learned; foreplay is the most important part of making love. This is when the man creates desire in the woman for him, the longer the foreplay the stronger her desire and the pleasure of making love are intensified and you will want him again.

'Also, if a man has you positioned in a way your breast cannot be against his chest it is not possible for you to reach a climactic moment and only he will have the pleasure. Bring this to a halt and have a brief conversation. If he does not know this, continue in a way that will please you both. If he knows only he will be satisfied, then he is merely using you for his own pleasure, which makes him a selfish man. And, we do not need selfish men in our lives.'

Joanna sips her cognac to give us a moment to absorb and process what she has just told us. Emily and I are silent as we drink ours and I think how lucky we are to benefit from Oriana's words of wisdom.

Soon Joanna begins talking again. "Another advantage was going to the finishing school. Mitch was the first man to touch me, but I already knew what it was like to be touched by a man." My eyebrows rise just a bit and Emily's face is simply blank. "I have never told this to a living soul. Keep in mind my classmates are all young European women who have had their debut at a Debutant Ball and have never been allowed to be alone with a suitor.

"It is only naturally to wonder what it would feel like to be kissed and touched by a man. We had all seen foreign films that show more of what occurs naturally between men and women. We were assembled in small groups at the school that became tightly knit and we admitted we were nervous about what would happen when we finally had contact with a man. In order to quell these trepidations some of the girls decided to pair off privately to touch each other in the manor that a man would. To my amazement my best friend, who was also my roommate, asked me to help her get passed her fears and because she was dear to me I agreed.

"After I did as she asked she hugged me and said she could not wait for the day to be alone with a man because she knew it would be wonderful. I was happy for her and when she said it was my turn I almost choked on my own saliva. Not knowing what to do and to avoid hurting her feelings or making her uncomfortable I allowed her to reciprocate.

"It was one of the best decisions I have ever made, because when Mitch began courting me and we were finally alone I was not nervous in the least. I wanted him to touch me. I wanted him to kiss me, and he did, constantly."

Emily looks at Joanna and says, "I want to ask you a question, but it may be considered indiscreet."

"My Dear this entire conversation has been anything but discreet. Ask me your question and I will give you an answer."

"Did you feel that way on your honeymoon?"

"For the most part — yes. On the first night I was just so happy to finally fall asleep in his arms, then in the morning I woke up and he was still holding me in his arms. It really was a dream that came true. As things progressed of course I got a little nervous, even though I looked forward to what was going to happen next and the pleasure we would feel. Each day something wonderful happened and then one day we became lovers."

Emily made a sound and looked as if she wanted to ask another question. I knew what she wanted to ask, but could not bring herself to say the words and since I wasn't certain I understood her correctly myself I decide to speak up. "Joanna, you kept your virginity well after you were married?"

"Yes I did, because he wanted me to give myself freely to him."

As I look at her she nods and we share this moment that bonds us in a way I cannot describe. Then we notice Emily appears to be on the verge of tears, so Joanna quickly tells us, "The most unexpected thing about the honeymoon was I found out I was shy. I did not want him to see me nude and I turned into a turtle that wanted to stay in its shell. As you know one cannot coax a turtle out of its shell, you have to wait patiently for it to come out all on its own and my Mitch did."

She sighs and shakes her head as she begins to smile. "At one point, I thought if I could just put a blindfold on him I would be fine." As we begin to laugh I think for a second and tell her, "You know, Joanna — that was a good idea." She says, "I know. The only thing that stopped me was I didn't want him to think he'd married a woman who was insane. And that was the end of that."

We carry on for a few more minutes and then Joanna looks at her watch. Her mouth comes open and Emily says, "I think that means we need to go." Joanna gasps. "Oh my gosh, I hope they don't know what time it is. We can straighten up when we get back. Just help me blow out the candles."

With all the candles out, we straighten each other's dresses and make a hasty exit not slowing down until we are going up the steps to the club. Joanna gets the door and we casually stroll to the fellas who are standing at the bar cutting up with Harry and friends of theirs. When William sees us he exclaims, "Emily, I missed you." Clearly poor William has passed his limit and when we join them Mitch says, "Gentlemen, pardon us for not making introductions, but I have a Sailor who needs food. We thank you for the impromptu engagement celebration." A commander replies, "It was our pleasure, sir." And we walk away.

Going to our table Emily asks, "It's Wednesday, where did they all come from?" William replies, "An alert was sent out and it traveled like wildfire." Trevor adds, "Then they started buying us doubles. I had to tell Harry to make them singles on the rocks and no one caught on. Whew — still it was a tad much." Mitch dryly says, "I'm collateral damage." Joanna gasps and covers her mouth.

The waiter shows up with glasses, a pitcher of water and sets a basket of rolls down then Mitch takes charge. "The ladies will have the special of grilled chicken with vegetables. We will have the steak, medium well and baked potatoes, butter only. Bring a pot of black coffee and three Pellegrino's with lime, please." And after a hearty meal and plenty of coffee the fellas have somewhat recovered from their ordeal and we leave.

We are standing together in the driveway at the Mitchell's when Trevor pulls the car keys from his pocket and asks me, "Would you mind terribly if we went home?" I beam and tell him, "Not at all." This gets me a kiss. Then William asks Emily, "I'm still not right. Do you mind driving me to the BOQ?" She tells him, "I wouldn't mind one bit. In fact I think you should sleep in for a change." Trevor tells him, "I'll pick you up and take you to breakfast." William shakes his hand and waves to the rest of us then Trevor and I take our leave as well.

At Maison Trevor goes through the gates and starts to drive to the apartment. I tug on his sleeve. "You are you staying at the house now."

He steps on the brake and sighs. "What is wrong with me?"

"Aside from the fact we have been awake since four o'clock and you consumed large amounts of alcohol, nothing."

Trevor gets pale on the staircase and I tell him, "I am tucking you in tonight."

"That's fine by me." I turn him toward his room and he chuckles.

Even though I shower in record time Trevor is dozing off as I sit on the edge of the bed next to him. "Baby, I can barely keep my eyes open."

"Trevor, I'm exhausted too. Did you set your alarm?"

"Mm hmm."

"Then tell me you love me and I'll kiss you good night."

"I do love you."

"And I love you." I kiss him good night and stay until he is in a deep sleep and a few minutes more.

When I wake up a tidal wave of thoughts rush through my mind. When I get to the one where I am concerned if Trevor is awake and if so does he have a headache I grab my robe and go to his room. I knock lightly and he says, "I'm awake." He's still in bed with a glass of water in his hand. "They recommend hydrating after drinking large amounts of alcoholic beverages to avoid a hangover, something I never had and hope to avoid; especially since I'm going to choose your evening gown today."

He moves over and pats the bed. I sit next to him and kiss his cheek. "You hydrate and I am going to get ready as quickly as possible, so I can go say hello to Mr. Coffee Pot and tell him I've missed him." Trevor chuckles and says, "Tell him I'll be there in a minute." I nod and quietly exit the room.

Trevor enters the kitchen shortly after I do. He says good morning to my family and I finish making his cup of coffee. As we put food on our plates I notice he doesn't put as much on his as usual. Théo asks, "What happened to you?" He replies, "While they were at The Bridal Salon we went to The O Club to have a drink and wait on them to meet us for dinner. Since it was just us, a few friends decided to celebrate our engagements. Mitch was an innocent bystander." Everyone winces and he adds, "After I drop her off I'm going to check on William. He got hit the hardest." Mother tells him, "I think this would be a good time to inform you we have added you to our family's club membership. Now you can make reservations in your name and whatever else you need do."

Trevor is at a loss, so my father speaks. "You can show up for breakfast and brunch during the week. Perhaps you and William would like to go there this morning. I guarantee it will be as quiet as a library." I tell Trevor, "That is a very good idea. Joseph will take good care of you both and there will hardly be anyone else there."

With his thoughts gathered he says, "Thank you so much. I want to say more, but words elude me." Mother chimes in. "You are entirely welcome. Now we are waiting to add Rachel." Théo's face is priceless and we all begin to laugh. "Son, her parent's will be here in 10 days and you are going to ask for her hand in marriage."

Théo finally responds. "Should I be doing something?"

Trevor replies, "Getting a ring is a good place to start."

"I do not even know what size ring she wears and I refuse to call the mother I do not know.

I calmly say, "Théo, ask her friend Darlene, she should know."

"Why did I not think of that? What is going on with me?"

Mother gets tickled followed by the rest of us and Father tells him, "You are in love, Son." Trevor adds, "You're going to be scattered for at least a year." Our parent's nod and Théo shakes his head.

Around 11 o'clock as I sit typing at my desk it gets cloudy then it eventually begins to rain and I lose my place because there is a chance Trevor is going to show up under an umbrella.

At noon, because it is still raining, Emily informs me she is thrilled she drove to work in her car and is off to pick up William in it. I wait maybe a minute and I see Trevor, looking exactly the way he did that rainy day; a Sailor walking in heavy rain I can see only from the shoulders down, holding a black umbrella wearing his Service Khaki's. Trevor steps inside, closes his umbrella and says, "This brings back memories."

"I have been smiling since the first drop of rain fell." This time on the way to car he hides us under the umbrella and kisses me. Oh how things have changed.

Harry grins from ear to ear when we walk in as he sets two club sandwiches and cherry cola's on the bar. There are a few people here, so he waits for us to get close. "I knew you two would be in here. I remember that day because you were falling for each other and I decided to give it a little nudge with a nickel." Trevor says, "Best money you ever spent, Harry."

There are moments in life that you wish time would stand still, this is one of them. We eat and reminisce about that day, saying things aloud we did not dare and then we dance, drifting away and falling in love all over again. When we get in the car I think Trevor is going to give me a kiss, but he winds up kissing me passionately. Just as it was then, I am almost late for work.

At five o'clock it's misting, so we are able to sit in the parking lot and kiss unseen. For some reason we cannot stop kissing each other. Maybe it is the silence in the mist and the dim light of the gray sky that makes us feel alone in the world. Maybe it is love and the pleasure that it brings. Maybe it is all these things and so much more.

Time flew and soon we are standing at the door of The Bridal Salon. Trevor rings the buzzer and Mrs. Garner appears to unlock it. I introduce them and she tells me to ring the bell when we need her and goes through the door behind the counter. We enter the second section and there are beverage carts on each end of the blue satin settee in the middle of the room, one for ladies with champagne, sparkling and still waters all on ice with assorted glasses and one for gentlemen that has liquor decanters, an ice bucket and old fashioned glasses.

Trevor is soaking it all in and he looks in awe at everything around him. He strolls along the walls of gowns running his hand across them and makes his way back to me. He gazes at me then before I know it he has me in his embrace. "Geneviève, thank you for this, I am going to enjoy myself immensely."

"It is my pleasure. I wanted to share this with you."

"There are so many. How do I begin?"

"I focus on color first then choose the style." He nods. "Here's the good part; behind the door Mrs. Garner went through is a seamstress shop with a woman that works miracles. Any dress you see can be sized to fit me."

"That changes things."

Stepping in front of the liquor decanters I ask, "What's your poison, Sailor?"

"I do not find that remotely humorous."

"I'm having a glass of ice water."

"I'll have the same, thank you."

I hand him the water and he still looks a little overwhelmed. "Trevor, what are your top two requirements for the gown?"

"I want it to be in a color I haven't seen you in and it has to feel — sumptuous." He taps my glass, we drink, set them down and he holds my hand to lead me to where he wants to start. "All right, stay close." I nod and he begins.

Trevor sees a lavender one then he closes his eyes as he runs his hand down the gown. I knew this would be unusual, but I underestimated it. After he repeats his little ritual a few times he pulls a lavender one off the rack and holds it up to me. His eyebrows rise. "Oh, sorry, Baby. Now I see why you don't wear that color. It reminds me of an Easter egg." I touch my nose and he chuckles as he hangs it back up. "And we are moving on."

He holds my hand again and scans the wall. He sees one in the blue of my sundress he met me in then shakes his head. I watch him stand a little taller as we leave the size 2's and go to the 4's. He pulls a gown out that is a lovely shade of orange that is slightly pale. He holds it to me and lights up. "This is the color, but not the style. Do you like it?"

"Very much."

Trevor smiles and we move on. He spots the color again and then touches the satin with eyes closed. Suddenly he pushes the gowns back on the rack to look at the front. It is sleeveless with a jewel neckline and a wide waistband that looks like it could be for a sash and the skirt is fitted instead of being full. He pulls it out to see the back and it's backless. And that was a band for a sash that drapes down to about nine inches from the hem and it ties in a square knot. Then he discovers there is a rather high slit on the side.

"This is the one. It will show the shape of your body like the white gown you wore the day we met *and* your leg. It's time to try something on."

I set our water on my cart, begin pulling it alongside and tell him, "Follow me." We go into the bridal section; I let go of the cart by the settee as he stands in amazement. I open a dressing room door and ask him to hang the gown in it then ask him to choose a pair of shoes. He chooses a white satin D'Orsay pump in the proper heel height for a dramatic side slit. I take them and tell him, "Have a seat. I will be right out."

Once I have it on, I loosely tie the sash and look at myself in it. His taste is impeccable. It is beautiful and to be perfectly honest I would have never chosen a gown like this. It looks like something foreign actresses wear I see in fashion magazines. The slit alone is an eye opener. I take a deep breath and step out. Trevor stands to his feet as his jaw drops. I slowly walk across the room and step onto the pedestal facing him. "Geneviève — you are stunning."

"Thank you. Will you tie the sash please?"

"It would be my pleasure." As I turn around I watch his face in the mirrors. He slightly gasps and softly says, "Look at that."

"I know. I can hardly wait to see what it looks like with the sash tied properly." Trevor is a Sailor and he can tie any kind of knot to perfection, even one in satin.

He steps onto the pedestal then takes his time to tie it as his hands brush against the skin of my back. This is turning sensual. As I watch him my body flushes. When he finishes he runs his hands up my back and to my shoulders. I stand motionless as I see him lower his head and feel his lips on the back of my shoulder. My eyes close and I sigh as he slides his hands down to my waist and along my hips. Somehow I manage to get my hands in his hair and his passion heightens. Eventually I force my eyes open and raise my head to see him. He stops kissing my body and gets still as our eyes meet in the reflection of the mirror in front of us.

"Trevor." He begins turning me around by my waist.

"Geneviève ... I have to kiss you."

"Yes you do."

While we are kissing he pauses. "It is killing me I can't hold you tight. — I can dip you." And I find myself dipped to point I am close to feeling like I am lying in his arms. In the throes of passion he breathlessly says, "I'm going to stand you up before I leave a mark or do something to this gown."

After gathering our wits he steps off the pedestal and offers me his hand to step down then leads me to the cart saying, "This gown deserves champagne." And I raise my eyebrows. "It's just wine. I'll be just fine." He pops the cork and pours then without a word we make our glasses sing.

Halfway through the glass of champagne I ask, "Are you ready to watch the fitting?"

He gives me that deep laugh and replies, "By the sparkle in your eyes I would have to say no, I'm not."

I am laughing as I ring the bell and he helps me back onto the pedestal. "Trevor — have a seat." I sip my champagne as we wait. Then here they come. Mrs. Garner's eyes get wide and the seamstress, Mrs. Parker beams. Let the show begin.

A fitting is choreographed like a dance I know well. I stand with my arms bent at the elbow and raised to a height that I can still drink as pins are carefully put in the sides. Then Mrs. Garner holds my glass as I drop my arms for pins to go in the back. Next I slowly stretch my arms out then raise them like a ballerina until my hands are in the air over my head to see if it is too tight. Mrs. Garner hands me my champagne as Mrs. Parker checks the hem length.

Next is the elegant part of the dance, Mrs. Parker holds my wrist and elbow as she slowly walks me around the circumference of the pedestal in order for me to see every angle of the gown in the mirrors. I glace at Trevor several times during the process and he could not be happier. I stand and imagine how it will look when finished as Mrs. Garner fills my glass then Trevor's. I face him to let him get a good look at what he chose.

When I announce I am ready to change the ladies hold my wrists as I step down. Mrs. Parker escorts me into the dressing room in order to extract me from the gown without bloodshed and to keep the pins in place. Successful in her endeavor she leaves with the gown and I dress.

Trevor has set up an account by the time I join him at the counter. He tells Mrs. Garner he would like the shoes I wore dyed to match my skin tone and asks if there is silk chiffon to match the gown he would like a wrap made eight feet long and the width of the fabric. Then he holds my hand and goes to the evening bags.

He picks up a gold brushed metal one that looks like tufted fabric. I smile and we return to the counter. She wraps it in tissue paper, puts it in a box and bag then gives it to Trevor who has now selected everything. He signs the bill, we thank her and she sees us to the door.

When she pulls the shade down it gets dark and Trevor keeps us under the awning. "That was like watching a woman of royalty being dressed by her handmaidens. You were so graceful and looked completely at ease. I will remember this day always. This far exceeded my expectations." He gently kisses me.

"I will be reluctant to shop for another gown without you."

"I will be disappointed when you do since I'll know what I'm missing."

"Trevor, will you do something for me?"

"I will do anything you want."

"Take me to Micheletto's, I want to listen to you speak Italian."

He chuckles. "Of course."

"I am positively starving."

"That makes two of us. I can taste the white pizza already. Let's go."

We have a nice meal at a booth in the corner and head home with a box of zeppole. We drive through the gates and when I see Théo's car I gasp. Trevor says, "I'll get the stack of *The Halyard*. You run along." He gets a big kiss and I dash inside. My parents are in the living room; I say a quick hello and ask where Théo is. Father informs me he is upstairs working on the blueprints for our house, so off I go.

His door is open and I sing, "Théo, what are you doing home so early?"

"Rachel is doing something to her hair to make it shiny for the banquet and I was politely told to go home. Which was fine with me, I need to finish turning the guest house into your house. What is that smell?"

"Zeppole, I forgot to leave these in the kitchen."

"I am going get to eat two desserts tonight." I beam and he shows me the places I haven't seen on the blueprints. Soon I hear Trevor coming up the stairs. He steps in the doorway. "How's our nest shaping up, Zelda?"

"Hello, Fred. Nicely, due to our genius architect."

He shakes Théo's hand and put's his arm around me while my brother sits with a strange look on his face. Trevor sees the pastry box. "I see you were in such a rush those came up with."

"I was excited he's here."

"I know. I'm toying with you." He scans the room and says, "Théo, I have never seen any of your designs. That model is unlike anything I've seen. I quite like it."

"Thank you." He stands and moves back from his drafting table. "Would you like to see your house?"

"Yes I would." We stand at the table together and Trevor says, "This reads, 3 Levels Above Ground Storey."

"I decided to go out and up. Gené likes the overlook, so I thought I would improve the view by making it higher. The day the last guest leaves after the engagement party the crew is going to start working. They have a lot to accomplish in a short time. I am going to enjoy this."

"It's impressive. The place is going to look completely different."

"That was my goal."

"You have succeeded. Thank you for doing this for us."

"It really is my pleasure and I love my job."

Then Trevor looks at the pastry box again. "Zelda, in your haste you didn't call your grandparent's did you."

"Nope, excuse me." I step onto the balcony and make the call, then go back and tell them, "They are walking over." I look at Théo. "I have a surprise for the family. Shall we?" Théo picks up the pastry box and asks, "Better than this?" As we laugh Trevor and I nod.

Théo goes to the kitchen and we stop at the table in the foyer. Trevor cleverly put the papers in a drawer. I ask, "What do you think about laying them face down on the dining room table? That way they will see them simultaneously."

"That's a really good idea." And he follows me to the table. Trevor lays them at each seat while I stand at the end with my hands on the back of a chair getting a case of nerves, which he senses. "Geneviève, your family will be so proud of you." And he gives me a reassuring kiss.

Everyone is gathered in the living room waiting and all eyes are on me when we go in. I tell my grandparents, "Thank you for coming. The surprise is set up in the dining room."

Father motions Théo to the head of the table, so he can sit next to Mother and Trevor sits to my left. "I have waited a week for the best time to share this with you all. You may pick those up now and turn them over."

Théo's eyes are dancing. "Your photographs are in *The Halyard.*" Mother says, "This reads, Part One." I reply, "Part Two is being printed as we speak. I will have it tomorrow." Father says, "Sweetheart, these look good on the front page." Grand-papa adds, "Indeed they do."

"Thank you."

There is a moment of silence and Grand-mamma speaks to me, "Care to join?" She motions to the chair I have a grip on and Trevor immediately stands. "Allow me." I let it go and he seats me. She continues, "The dream is finally coming true, how happy you must be." I simply smile and nod. Mother says, "Your father and I were under the impression this was a hobby, because you never approached us to arrange a meeting with Mr. Cooper at *The Times.*"

Théo asks me, "May I?" I gesture to him. "Gené wanted to get this with her photographs, not her name, otherwise she would always wonder if she truly had talent."

"We all, over the years have told her how talented she was."

"Yes we have, Mother, but it is different when an editor tells you. It was the same for me, Gené. When my professor told me I had talent, it gave me confidence and I needed that."

"Exactement, Mon Frère."

My father says, "Very proud of you we are. Well done." The rest of my family echo's his sentiment and I am overwhelmed.

Trevor says, "Excuse me please. There is a bottle of Cristal with her name on it chilling in the kitchen." Théo adds, "There is also a box of zeppole with her name on it." My grandmother perks up; Trevor lifts her hand and tells her, "I have always had the suspicion she got her sweet tooth from you." He kisses her hand, "Thank you for confirming my suspicion." She replies, "Think nothing of it and it is my suspicion you had a hand in this." Trevor replies, "I will confirm your suspicion when I return. Théo says, "I'll go with."

Trevor pops the cork on another bottle of champagne. He makes a toast to me then we drink and eat our second dessert while Trevor and I tell the story of how this came to fruition. The evening has worked out very well.

Trevor and I insist on doing the dishes and after everyone is gone we are happily doing our chore when he gasps. "I have been trying to remember to tell you about breakfast at the club this morning. It had an unexpected twist."

"You have my undivided attention."

"The funny part first; William was drinking vodka on the rocks last night, so he asked Joseph if it was true having hair of the dog that bit you helps with a hangover. It was his first and I do believe his last. Anyway, Joseph told him some say yes, others say no. William tossed a coin and had Joseph put a splash of vodka in his orange juice."

Laughing I ask, "Did it help?"

"He looked better. Now here's the twist, he asked Joseph to bring him an application for membership to the club."

I gasp. "Emily is going to ..."

"Give my mate hearing damage when he shows her the membership card?"

"That really is going to happen."

"I know. Let's keep our fingers crossed he has the sense not to do it in a small enclosed space." I cross my fingers and he gives me a kiss.

Lights are out and on the way upstairs he asks, "Are you going to have a long shower?"

"Do you want to go for a run?"

"Not in the least. If you were I was going to tell you to wake me up when you got out."

"I will see you shortly. Are you tucking me in tonight?"

"Definitely. Geneviève, what are we doing tomorrow?"

"Crossing each bridge when we get to it."

"I love the way you think." I get a kiss and we go to our rooms.

After a quick shower I am crossing the room and taking off my robe when Trevor comes in. I toss it on my bench, sit on the edge of my bed and fall backwards on it. "Just kiss me good night and leave me here." He sits next to me and lies down. I turn my head to face him and say, "My arms are even tired."

"That is from holding them up during that fitting I enjoyed watching more than I can say."

"My gown." I sigh, turn my head, look up at the ceiling then close my eyes and picture it. "My beautiful gown; I have never even tried on anything like it. It makes me look like ..." I stop in mid-sentence to think and he says, "The woman you are becoming." My eyes open immediately. I look at him, prop up on my elbow and softly say, "It's very strange you said that." His raises one eyebrow as he says, "I'm listening."

"Yesterday, when we walked in to Happy Hour, Joanna told me she could smell whiskey on my breath." His eyes light up as he asks, "What did you say?"

"There was some in the back seat of her husband's car." By the look on his face I could tell he was astonished, but he remains silent. "She struggled not to laugh and asked, 'Do you simply adore the woman in you that was just waiting to come out?' I quietly said, 'Yes I do and the man who brought her out.' She tapped my glass and said, 'To the men we love to kiss.' then I repeated the toast."

Trevor pulls me to him and kisses me. "I watched you take that drink of your champagne and swish it in your mouth as if you were at a wine tasting. You did it to get the whiskey off your breath. No wonder Joanna got tickled. Then you just breezed by William and Mitch. When I told you my ears were burning your response was so provocative I knew you were being the woman I have been watching you become. I wished I could ask later what was said, but I know the rules. I am so glad it came up and you told me. It was better than I thought."

"I surprise myself constantly. I'm not sure what is going to come out of my mouth anymore."

"Neither am I. I find myself looking forward to what you're going to say or do next."

After holding me for a few precious minutes he gets up and slides me up and over to my pillow. Then he tucks me in and kisses me good night.

CHAPTER THREE

Conversation over breakfast is a sharing of information and updates on recent events. Trevor and I remind the family I have a half day at work because we are going to choose our wedding invitations. Théo found out Rachel's ring size from Darlene and has decided to begin looking for one from the Deco era they are both so fond of. Mother has invited Rachel to stay in what is going to become her apartment here the night of the banquet. And last but not least my parents ask us to give thought to the Joseph, Claudette development. Someone has to give him permission to court her.

On the way to the car Trevor tells me, "More and more breakfast reminds me of the morning briefings on Louise."

"Should I bring a steno pad to take notes?" We laugh as he opens the car door and make jokes the entire way to the base.

At noon we tell Emily and William we will see them at the banquet tomorrow and I get in the car with Trevor. When he pulls out of the parking lot and begins to drive to our road I'm so accustomed to this I just sit beside him without asking why. He parks at the end and says, "I drove to the base early in hopes *The Halyard* was already out." He reaches across me, turns the knob on the glove box and lets the lid drop. "And it was."

I am laughing as I get them out and say, "I glanced in the back seat for those."

"I knew you would and I wanted to surprise you."

"You did." And he looks so pleased with himself.

While we read the article Trevor's stomach growls, "Obviously it's past time for lunch. Where do you want to go, Baby?"

"I think we should have a toast to my latest achievement with a chocolate milkshake."

"Sam's it is."

On the way it occurs to me we haven't had the chance to speak with Sam since the morning we went to Santa Barbara and he found out exactly who I was. Trevor turns down the radio and places his hand over mine and I realize I am wringing them as they rest on my lap. "Geneviève, nothing has changed. Sam just needed a minute to absorb the information. The man found out for years he had been serving members of one of the most respected and influential families in San Diego. He had no clue because there isn't an arrogant bone in your body. You did give him your pancake recipe."

"Yes I did." Feeling much better I turn the radio up and carefully put my head on his shoulder.

While we order, Sam walks up to the table and acts like he always has then Annie runs him off. When she brings our milkshake's Trevor makes a toast to me and then I make a toast to the man that invented ice cream as I recall the first day Emily and I ate here. Trevor senses there is a story behind what I just did and I tell him.

Next stop, the Fine Stationer. And we are too happy there until we are looking in a second book at samples of invitations. Trevor quietly tells me, "This is taking an unexpected spiral downward. These are all such cliché's. How many have had overlapping wedding bands?" I reply, "I have no clue. I didn't know I should keep count. And these are ruining hearts for me." He sighs and asks, "Can we have an embosser custom made?"

"I think we are short on time. That book looks old. Let's look in it."

Trevor swaps the books and the first page is not bad at all, which gives us encouragement. And on the fourth page the clouds part and the angels sing; before us are two swans facing each other embossed in the top center of the invitation. Trevor says, "That's the one."

"They are perfect. Swans choose a mate for life." And he motions for the printing press operator.

The second he gets in the car I pull Trevor to me and kiss him like we are in his apartment because that was so romantic. I let him go as quickly as I grabbed him and he draws in a deep breath then goes, "Umm ... where to next?"

"The guest house please. I need to sunbathe. It has been a while and I am wearing a backless dress in a few days." With a glint in his eyes he says, "Yes you are." I shake my head smiling at him and ask, "I read when I sunbathe. Would you like to read to me and keep me company?" He begins to laugh. "I'll take that as a yes." We get home in record time. I think he was so lost in thought he didn't mean to speed. Trevor goes to my room and gets the book he has been reading to me. He was quick about it and I am trying to not get tickled as we go in the guest house.

I get a sheet and he follows me up to the lookout then I show him where the cushions are. "I'll set up while you change into your swimming suit."

"I won't be gone long." I give him a kiss and leave.

As I am changing into what I call my sunbathing suit it occurs to me Trevor is going to get a surprise when he sees me. I gather my things, put them in my straw bag, glance in the mirror, get two glasses of ice water and go back up. Trevor is standing looking at the view; when he hears me set the glasses down he turns around and becomes perfectly still.

"This is my sunbathing suit. As you can tell I had it made."

"That would explain why I've never seen anything like it. Your lower abdomen is exposed." I turn my back to him to and set my bag down. "You have dimples below the small of your back."

"Is that unusual?"

"I have no idea, but I find them quite alluring."

"Would you mind putting tanning lotion on me?"

"It would be my ... my pleasure." I made him stutter, how delightful.

"I am going to settle in then. Look at your watch please and let me know when 30 minutes are up." I hand him the lotion, lie on my stomach facing him with my arms up and let my hands dangle off the end of the lounge chair.

"Where would you like me to start?"

"At my neck then work your way to my feet. You should undo my straps first."

Trevor kneels, undoes the straps and lays them on the sheet covered cushion. When he begins to rub the lotion on my arms I realize I did not think this through properly. I thought it would be like having a massage by a professional masseuse. The man touching me happens to be one that stirs my emotions and this is like nothing I have ever felt. I love his hands on me through my clothing. This is going to be problematic. I may not be able to keep quiet.

Just I am about to get upset it occurs to me I should just go where this takes me and focus on his touch like always. Due to the warmth of the sun on my skin and hearing him breathing a bit heavy it doesn't take long for me to make sounds.

Trevor lingers at the small of my back giving me a massage I enjoy immensely. When he moves down to my left thigh and smoothes the lotion over every inch of exposed skin, my body becomes covered in chill bumps and I am not cold. Trevor works his way down to my ankle which means he is about to move to my right thigh and the thought makes my breath catch before he touches me. Trevor finishes and kisses my cheek. I softly tell him, "I will never sunbathe without you."

He whispers, "Is that a promise?"

"Yes."

Lying there with my eyes closed basking in the sun I could still feel his hands. I come out of my trance when I hear him turn pages in his book. Then there was a long silence, so I open my eyes. He closes the book and tells me, "I don't want to read."

"What do you want to do?"

"Sit here and look at you. Your body is so beautiful. Your skin is shimmering."

"Trevor, put down your book." I watch him looking at me for a moment then eventually close my eyes.

Time passes and Trevor quietly says, "You spoil me so." I keep my eyes closed as I smile.

More time passes in silence and I realize I am thirsty, but my water is not in front of me on the deck. "Trevor." He focuses on my eyes. "I wish I didn't have to pull you from your thoughts, but I'm thirsty."

"Geneviève, how long have you been thirsty?"

"Just a minute or two."

He immediately gives me my water and because he is standing, I sit up a little and take a drink. Trevor apparently looks at his watch because he says, "Has it really been 30 minutes already?" I sigh and lie back down. "I'll fasten your top."

With that done I sit on the edge of my lounge chair and he arranges it to recline. When I am comfortable I notice he is looking at me at bit puzzled. I realize he is thinking should he turn his chair around or leave so I can sunbathe without my top on. "Trevor, I just wanted to get sun on my back. We can go in if you are getting hot."

"I'm not hot, it's a nice day."

"I cannot believe I have not brought you up here before now to see the view." He raises an eyebrow. "On second thought, yes I can." He moves his chair by mine and we are just still. So much has happened in the past few days. Some things I wish I could forget and others have been wonderful; meeting his parent's and going to the park, the night we spent on Willow, Trevor choosing my evening gown, selecting the gowns with Joanna and Emily, then going back to her house and getting Bohemian as she tells us her secrets.

With that thought I put my hand over mouth. What have I done? I simply wanted to get some sun and have been lying here practically nude in his presence. Trevor will wonder what has gotten into me on our honeymoon, because I know I am going to be just like her and want to stay in my shell.

Trevor sits up, "Geneviève, where did you just go?"

I take my hand off my mouth and tell him "I'm here. Something occurred to me recently and I just remembered. — Trevor, because I do not want there to be any confusion on our honeymoon, I need you to know there is not a doubt in my mind I will become so very shy." I almost put my hand over my mouth again and sigh out of exasperation.

"I knew that." He reaches for my hand and holds it. "It seems the time to have the conversation about your virginity and the loss of it has presented itself."

Calm washes over me. I smile at him and say, "Yes it has."

"Can you shower off here?"

"Yes."

"While you shower I will gather my thoughts and open us a bottle of wine. What would you like?"

"Château Delcroix."

We go inside and as I shower I try to give him enough time to gather his thoughts, but not so much that he winds up becoming apprehensive. When I enter the living room he is standing in front of the French doors to the balcony looking out at the ocean and he turns around. Trevor gives me a tender kiss, motions to the sofa and after we are seated he hands me a glass of wine. He touches my glass with his and we savor its taste then he begins the conversation.

"After you mentioned the fact we will need to discuss this topic before we are married I realized we really should. I had a visual of you sitting next to me on the way to our cottage with your hands clasped resting on your lap getting nervous."

"That is exactly what I would have been doing."

"Instead you are going to be kissing your new husband because of what I am going to tell you." He gives me the sweetest smile and continues. "We have taken our time getting to know each other and after we are married we are going to take our time getting to know each other physically. On the first morning of our honeymoon you will still be a virgin and remain so until you no longer want to be. There are so many things that have to happen before we can even think about becoming lovers and I am certain you know that."

I drink my wine as I absorb those important words. Trevor drinks his a bit longer then tells me, "I will never forget the jolt to my nervous system I got when I found out exactly where the clitoris was and how small the area of a woman's body is that brings her to a climax." I quietly laugh and he adds, "I shot the doctor a look, then the first thing I thought was the scale is definitely tipped in the man's favor and how unfair it was. Then I realized the amount of pressure on the man and it was a tad much."

I respond instantaneously. "Imagine being a woman and finding that out. When the nurse showed me the *very* small area on the model of the female reproductive system I lost my composure. I was in complete disbelief. I asked her, 'Is that really it?' Then I motioned to the model of the males and said, 'A man has ... all that and we have that. It is almost nonexistent.' The nurse told me perhaps I should sit down, which I did for about a second before I stood right back up."

I shake my head; take a drink of wine and Trevor begins to laugh. "Geneviève, I am so sorry. It's not funny, but you are. I have a visual of you bouncing around the room and the poor nurse watching you."

"Oh ... she told me I wasn't the first woman to react that way. While I'm pacing she proceeds to tell me it is best for a woman to have her first climax before having intercourse. I stop pacing and sit back down as I learn about masturbation." I sigh heavily. "Then she tells me a man can do the same thing for a woman with his touch or by a word I had never heard and asked her to repeat, which was cunnilingus and she proceeded to tell me it was simply the oral stimulation of the female's clitoris by the male. My mind reeled at the thought. I told her I would reschedule my physical and left."

Trevor's face is turning red as he tries to control his laughter. "Trevor, you are going to have an aneurism. Go ahead, have a good laugh. I'll join you." And that was it for us. Eventually I tell him, "Fortunately the house was empty when I got home and I went down to the wine cellar with a glass and stayed for a little while. When it occurred to me I would probably never marry anyway I went to my darkroom with the wine.

"Since I was a girl I have been drinking small amounts, so I was barely tipsy when I finally emerged. Mother was cooking and I sat at the table with what was left in the bottle. I told her my appointment had to be rescheduled; she just walked over and kissed the top of my head."

"I knew this would be memorable, but I didn't expect it to be humorous."

"Neither did I."

We are quiet for a minute as we drink our wine then he says, "I have more to tell you. It may seem as if I'm changing the subject, so I need you to bear with me." I slightly nod and give him a reassuring smile.

"It was Plebe Summer before my final year at Annapolis. I am finally a Firstie and the long awaited privilege of full weekend town liberty is mine. It was 12 hours on Saturday's and Sunday's. William was expected to follow in the family footsteps and break in plebes. The decision was mine to make and I went with having some control of my life every weekend. It meant being able to eat when and what I wanted and go where I wanted for two whole days.

"Then there was the solitude. Since I was six years old I lived in dormitories with hundreds of boys and it had increased to over 4,000 young men, so I would just walk around town until I got hungry. There was a pub I ate lunch at often. I would sit at the bar and have a pint with a corned beef sandwich. It was the best.

"I also had a favorite place to eat dinner. It was called The Overboard, because there were tables outside."

I chuckle and interject, "That's clever."

"I thought so too. William and Don, a mutual friend of ours, would meet me there every now and then. One night when I was alone a woman I had seen in various places, usually alone as well, walked up to my table and introduced herself. The second she said her name I knew exactly who she was; Mrs. Sarah Wilcox, the widow who owned the service station in town.

"Her husband was a mechanic and he met with a terrible accident there that eventually took his life, but to everyone's surprise she kept it going. She asked me if I was expecting my friends. When I told her I wasn't she asked if I would like to join her. I said yes without hesitation. During dinner one of the things she told me was she married at the age of 23 and when she was 27 she became a widow. I meet her two years after that.

"The next thing I know William and I are sitting in her kitchen while she cooks dinner for us. She was a different woman by then. Sarah had purpose after work and our mission was to make her laugh as much as possible.

"On one of the nights I went alone we were sitting out back after dinner enjoying the cool of autumn and during our conversation Sarah got quiet. She went somewhere in her mind. I knew she was thinking about her husband and when she got back she said, 'I am so grateful for the time you have spent with me. You have eased the ache in my heart. I want to do something for you and the woman you marry.'

"While I was wondering what that could possibly be she said, 'Our honeymoon was disastrous. I blame the prude who was my doctor's nurse and his doctor. Neither of us had the slightest clue that making love was actually complicated and we suffered the consequences. One of them being we wasted precious time. I can tell you things no one told us that you need to know.'

"She paused, but not for long as I sat there speechless. Next she made a request. 'Before you turn down my offer I want you to meet with the doctor and ask to see the model of the female reproductive system. Then ask him to show you where the clitoris is and the purpose it serves. And if that doesn't convince you, I will tell you this, if you do not have a full grasp of the situation, chances are you will hurt her." That got my attention. And as you know I did as she asked."

Trevor begins to move on the sofa as if he is uncomfortable physically. "I am going to stretch my legs a minute and let you process what I've told you thus far." I just nod, because I have already been trying to process all this as he spoke.

As I place my back on the sofa and look at him standing on the other side of the coffee table anxiously watching me he asks, "Geneviève – have I upset you?"

"Not in the least. You have caught me by surprise, but it was impossible not to." He looks so relieved and I continue talking to him. "I think you are about to tell me that you are not going to be the blind leading the blind and I am not going to follow you off a cliff." He sighs heavily and says, "That is exactly what I am about to tell you."

I get up and go around the table to him. "It took courage for you to even begin this conversation and I am so glad you did. I love you, Trevor." I put my arms around him and he replies, "I love you too."

When I am certain he feels secure I step back. "Whenever you're ready, just pick up where you left off."

"Where was I?"

"You had been to the doctor."

Trevor groans and motions to the sofa. We get comfortable and he begins telling me the rest of the story. "When I went back the following Saturday to accept her kind offer, Sarah asked me to give her my word I would not use anything I learn from her with anyone I am not in love with. The reason was this; she had dated a man before meeting her husband and fell in love with him, but he did not fall in love with her and she was left with a broken heart. After she lost her husband, one day she realized she was experiencing emotions she had after her heart had been broken. Therefore when you lose someone you loved, it doesn't matter how, you mourn the loss." He exhales heavily. "I felt so sorry for her my heart actually ached and I gave her my word immediately. Then she told me we would begin the next day after lunch and we had dinner as usual.

"I remember the walk there, thinking with each step I was about to get in over my head, but it be worth it when I find the woman I want to marry. I went in and sat down at the kitchen table and she didn't wait until after lunch. She began talking as if we were having a casual conversation by saying, 'I am guessing you already know how to crawl, so I am going to teach you how to walk and then how to run.'

"I sat there silent wondering what she meant by crawling and decided to ask. She laughed a little and said 'I am referring to kissing, Silly.' I was 21 years old and didn't really know how to kiss. I made the mistake of sighing and she dragged it out of me. I reminded her I did attend an all boy's boarding school and had a kiss stolen from me occasionally during the summers when I was in my teens, then I went straight to The Academy. Her response was, 'Oh – I'm sorry. I can't really help you with that, but that will happen over time.'

Desperately I try to keep a straight face as I think things are different at schools for girls. They do things, and I wish I didn't know that bit of information right now. Apparently my eyes gave me away. Fortunately Trevor has no clue as to why my eyes are dancing, so he sighs and dryly says, "The way I learned how to kiss is actually amusing. Would you like me to tell you?"

"Amusing? Yes I would."

"It began the first time I was deployed and we were arriving at a port of call in Spain. A commander was talking to us in the Officer's Mess. It was more like warning us that for century's women have waited on piers for ships to come in to welcome sailors who have not seen a woman in who knows how long. So out of kindness, the moment you set foot on land you are given a welcome kiss. It took some getting used to and some of the women were more than generous. Over time I did learn how to kiss — with women I had never laid eyes on."

I am close to laughter as I tell him, "The first thing that comes to mind is I really appreciate those women. They taught you well." I hold up my glass and say, "A toast, to the women around the world." He strikes my glass and says, "To the women." After we drink I place my hand on his face, pull him to me, draw his bottom lip between mine for just a few seconds and release him. When I sit back to finish listening to his story he says, "I keep losing my place." I bat my eyelashes and he lights up.

"Ah, learning to walk. That begins with foreplay and it is the one of the most important thing to master, because it's 90% of making love when it's done the way it should be. She told me, 'Once a man penetrates a woman's body time folds and it is over all too soon.' There is a lot to foreplay and the end result should be the woman is totally aroused." I hold my hand up and say, "Elaborate please."

Trevor looks away from me because he has to think; after all it has been almost a decade since these events took place. He gathers his thoughts and tells me, "A woman's body will secrete a fluid when she is aroused by contact with a man that lubricates her vaginal wall and when so much has been produced that it makes its way outside her body it means she is totally aroused. Then and only then is when one should advance beyond foreplay."

My hand goes up again, this time to let him know I need a moment to think. With my thoughts clear I tell him, "Trevor, that has happened to me."

"The first time was the night you were wishing for a bottle of chloroform and you told me your body was wide awake."

"I didn't understand what happened to me until now." I look deep into his eyes. "I haven't been the same since." He sighs and tells me, "We can just hold back from now on." I shake my head. "Thank you for offering, but that is not what I want. I want things to keep moving forward. If you can stand it, so can I. — You were saying?"

"Your nurse was correct when she said it was best for a woman to have her first climax before having intercourse. It should be by touch and I am 99% sure I know how to do that, because Sarah was very clever. She figured out ways to demonstrate things and explain details to me in a way I could fully comprehend.

"For this she drew a small oval on the palm of my hand then told me to imagine it was a woman's clitoris and that all I need to do is touch the oval with the pad of my middle finger. Once I start this I am not to stray from the area because if a woman is close to climaxing and I do stray, she would have difficulties reaching that point again. Then Sarah showed me what to do by gently rubbing the oval on my palm with the pad of her finger. I asked her how I will know if I am doing this correctly and she told by the sounds the woman would make. Then she said, 'That reminds me and this is important. Do not be timid about making sounds or suppress them in any way for two reasons. One is it how you both can tell when you are doing something that feels good or not. The second is it will heighten the pleasure more than one could ever imagine.'

"While I processed this flood of information she adds, 'Oh — and bringing a woman to a climax orally is basically the same except it is done with your tongue instead of your finger and I highly recommend it.' My jaw dropped and she was so nonchalant about all this, that with her next sentence she stood and asked me if I wanted something else to drink with lunch. I almost told her something 80 proof or higher would be fine." I get tickled and he pours the last of the wine.

We sit quietly regrouping and while he looks into my eyes I slowly hold out my hand with my palm up. He cups it underneath with his left hand and sets down his glass. Trevor dips the pad of his finger into the wine and tells me, "I think you should close your eyes." I look at him, draw in a breath and close them as I slowly exhale.

The second Trevor's wet finger touches my palm my entire body tingles. I become so focused on what he is doing his touch is the only thing I am aware of. Strange that something so simple feels so good. My imagination can take me just so far, but it is far enough. As the wine dissipates Trevor slows to a stop and places his warm hand over mine. When I open my eyes they meet Trevor's. He was watching me. We do not utter a single word. One thing is certain, he is not blind and I am beginning to see light.

Still holding my hand Trevor begins to recline onto the pillows in the corner of the sofa pulling me over until I am lying on him. And there we stay for quite a while as we rest in each other's arms.

Eventually he asks, "Geneviève, do you want to pretend we're teenagers and go on a date tonight?"

While laughing I ask, "What do you have in mind?"

"Going to dinner and a movie, then to Sam's where I'll order us one milkshake with two straws. And after that we'll go parking at one of the overlooks."

"The perfect teenage date I never had."

"Neither did I."

Taken aback I blurt out, "What?"

"I was too busy academically and when I could date I was no longer a teen. Do movies still start at 8:00 on Friday night?"

"More than likely, we can check the paper at the house."

"Do you know which restaurant is popular among teenagers for dinner?" I begin to smile and nod. "That smile can mean only one place, Micheletto's for a pizza." I touch my nose then look at my watch, "I need to get ready."

He chuckles as we get up and go to the house. My parents are in the living room reading the evening paper, so we say hello and ask for the section with the movie times. My father hands it to Trevor and we are pleased to discover the show time is still eight o'clock and an encore of *Rebecca* is playing. Trevor gives the paper back to my father, thanks him and we go upstairs to get ready.

As usual I am in my closet trying to decide what to wear when he walks in grinning and picks out a dress in two seconds. "While you put that on I'm going to get the car. Then I want you to wait for me to knock on the front door with your parent's." He gives me a kiss and leaves.

When I go into the living room and sit with my parents Mother asks, "Sweetheart — what are you doing?"

"Waiting on my date to pick me up." They both begin to laugh. "This is all his idea."

"What fun. He has a good imagination."

"I should tell you, we are pretending to be teenagers tonight, because I am not sure how far he is going to take this."

Father says, "Thank you for clueing us in."

"You are entirely welcome."

Trevor knocks and when I open the door his face is lit up and I know why when I see notice the bouquet of flowers he is holding is wrapped in one of my grandmothers' linen napkins. I get tickled and tell him, "Good evening, Trevor. Do come in."

"Good evening, Geneviève. These are for you." He hands them to me and gives me a peck on my lips. Here we go.

He follows me into the living room and says, "Mr. and Mrs. Delcroix, nice to see you again." My father says, "Always a pleasure, Trevor." Then he tells them, "We are enjoying fine weather this evening." Mother is beaming as she says, "Yes we are." I walk to her trying to keep my composure and ask, "Will you put these in water for me please." She gets tickled when she sees the napkin and says, "Of course, Sweetheart. — Gérard, you are supposed to tell him what time to have her home." He thinks and responds, "Have her home by midnight, please." Trevor replies, "Yes, sir." And then I exclaim, "Dad! Midnight?"

There is a brief suspension of disbelief then Mother bursts into laughter followed by Trevor and Father. Even I get tickled and Trevor manages to say, "We are going to leave on that note." My parent's just wave and continue to laugh as we go into the foyer. He stops walking and gives me a kiss. "I can't believe you called your father Dad. That was hilarious."

"Neither can I. It just seemed like what a teenager would have said."

"That was sheer perfection. We are going to have such a good time tonight."

"Because this is such good idea." And off we go on our date.

At Micheletto's he orders a pizza and sodas. "Why didn't you order wine?"

"Because we're not old enough to drink, Geneviève." Once again I have to struggle to keep my laughter from getting loud.

Trevor is still on a roll inside the theater. He orders a large popcorn and cola with a box of jelly beans. We move to the end of the counter and Trevor begins laying napkins down for me to pour the jelly beans on, so I can pick out the licorice ones. "I told you about this a long time ago."

"And I have waited a long time to watch you perform this little ritual."

He happily watches then offers me his arm to go up the staircase to the balcony where there are only two couples on the front row. As we go up higher Trevor gets a glint and tells me, "I have waited years to do this."

After a brief hesitation I ask, "To do what?"

"Make out in the back row of a movie theater."

"We're going to be a make out couple?"

He chuckles. "I can see you are going to need a minute to catch up, so I'll get things situated." Trevor lowers a seat and sets the popcorn and cola on it as I cling to my jelly beans. He lowers one next to it for me, steps out of the row and says, "After you."

Actually I was looking forward to watching the movie. When the lights go down I relinquish my jelly beans and forget all about the movie while we make out. Then the sound of a throat being cleared gets our attention. Trevor whispers, "That is an usher. I am going to enjoy this." He turns and in a deep raspy voice asks, "Is there a problem young man?" And all of a sudden the usher standing in the aisle gets flustered. He replies, "Nnno sir. No ... excuse me ... please."

I cannot laugh. Oh my gosh, I cannot laugh, that poor boy will hear me. Trevor tilts his head and says, "I am too old to be reprimanded by a freckle faced usher." I am beaming as I shake my head. He winks at me and asks, "Where were we before we were so rudely interrupted?" And we pick up where we left off.

An actress in the movie begins laughing as if she is truly insane and of course we stop kissing and look at the screen. Trevor says, "Now would be a good time to eat our concessions. The smell of popcorn is starting to get to me."

"Trevor — I have been able to smell the jelly beans since I got them." As he quietly chuckles I hand him the popcorn and soda then immediately eat a jelly bean."

"What flavor did you get?"

"Orange."

"Ooo, give me a kiss." I do and then we whisper our thoughts on what we missed, eat and watch the end of the movie. I bet it was good.

Next stop Sam's, where we get a cozy little booth for two and he orders us a strawberry milkshake with two straws. Sam is too busy to come out, so he just waves because the diner is packed with teenagers.

Looking around I tell Trevor, "We're not the only couple sharing a milkshake tonight."

"No we aren't, but we certainly are the oldest."

Fortunately the teenaged crowd is loud, so when we burst into laughter no one pays any attention. When we strike bottom I give Trevor a come hither look, because the part of our date I have been looking forward to is upon us, parking on the cliff.

Trevor has his arm around me as we drive along the road looking for a good parking spot and I almost choke when we pass Théo's car. Trevor says, "That was unexpected. When he leaves, which way will he go?"

"I have no idea."

"I'm going to turn left and get us off this road. I'm concerned we may see Emily's car and I just can't." I gasp and get tickled. "The base it is."

When we get to our spot I tell him, "I like listening to the boat horns and the bells on the channel markers here anyway." He nods and we lower the windows a little then in a deep voice he says, "Come here, Baby."

The next morning after being awake all of two seconds I am smiling as I recall all the events of yesterday. When I smell the coffee I decide perhaps I should get up and find Trevor. I open my door and he is standing in his doorway tying his robe. We tell each other good morning and the moment we are close to each other I am twirled and kissed. Then he says, "Today is the last Summer Banquet. It's a big day. Are you ready to go down for the morning briefing?"

"As I will ever be." Théo's door is still closed, so I knock on it as we pass by. He says, "Down in a minute."

The usual things are being gone over until Théo tells us Rachel is coming over to help wash cars. While I'm thinking that is going to be fun, Mother mentions she needs to leave a message for Joseph concerning our table. My mind wonders and eventually I sit straight up. Father asks, "Is there something you wish to add?"

"I know what should be done for Joseph and Claudette."

Mother says, "Thank goodness. You have the floor."

"Joseph will be here tomorrow and we know Claudette calls her family every Sunday morning. More than likely she has told them about him and while Claudette waits with Grand-mamma in another room, Grand-papa can call her father with Joseph on another phone, properly introduced them and hang up. Then Joseph can ask her father for permission to court his daughter. Next Claudette can get on the phone and talk with her parent's as if they're here. Since Joseph speaks French fluently it should go off without a hitch."

Mother stands in an instant and as the men scramble to their feet she kisses my cheeks three times and says, "Excuse me." As she goes into the hallway to call Grand-mamma Father tells us, "There goes my wife." Théo says, "Gené, I think you should pick up the pace if you want to finish your breakfast."

While I do what my brother suggested Trevor says, "I had no idea Joseph spoke French." Théo replies, "We found out one day when he was serving us. Joseph greeted us with, 'Bonsoir.' and went from there. We realized had been working with a kitchen staff for years that the majority of are French and he just picked it up." Trevor smiles as he says, "Claudette found her match." I add, "A long time ago. It took our engagement to get them alone so they could finally talk."

Mother begins to speak before she's in the kitchen. "They are waiting on us to finish breakfast then we are to go over there."

"What did you tell Grand-mamma?"

"That you have the solution."

"They are going to be on pins and needles until we arrive."

Théo goes, "Mmm hm."

Mother and I sort of finish eating then get dressed. Father gives Mother a kiss as I ask Trevor to keep a scone warm for me. I quickly get a kiss from him and we leave with what is left of our first cup of coffee.

Through the glass of the solarium door I see Claudette is sitting with my grandparent's looking quite anxious. We join them and I begin to explain the solution. By the time the conversation concludes Claudette is misty-eyed, because Grand-papa is going to tell Joseph my idea tonight during his break. Claudette kisses my cheeks and asks to be excused. I leave shortly after she does and find Théo and Father doing the dishes and Trevor is missing.

"Where is Trevor?" Théo replies, "Talking on the phone in the hallway with his mother. She called a few minutes ago." My thought is this has to be good news as I set down my cold cup of coffee.

Trevor lights up when he sees me and motions for me to join him. He slides the note pad over to me and on it is an address that reads, Morris Cove Road. Evidently his parent's have bought a house on the beach with a view of the Atlantic. I give him a kiss and go back to the kitchen because I am determined to sit in the solarium with a fresh cup of coffee and eat my nice warm scone.

Just as I get settled Trevor sits next to me and I enjoy the last of my breakfast while he tells me all about his conversation with his mum. After a few minutes of peace Rachel arrives, which means it will soon be time to start washing cars.

When we step outside the antics have already begun. Théo's shirt is wet on the back and Rachel, with hair that is dripping wet, is holding the hose pointed at him. Just before she is about to soak him we hear Mother call out, "Cease fire." We are all laughing as she rounds the corner, sees me and says, "Oh good. Sweetheart, have you worn the evening gown you had for the first banquet?"

"No, dare I ask why?"

"Claudette wants to go to the banquet and she needs a gown." Théo and I whip our heads to look at each other. "Where is it?"

"In my armoire."

"Can you believe this? We are going to have to pull strings to get her an appointment at the hair salon this afternoon."

"If you show up with Claudette they won't turn her away. It is better sometimes to ask for forgiveness than permission."

"And this is one of those times. Your grandmother and Claudette will be so relieved." She kisses my cheeks and holds on to my arm. "Shall we go up? Excuse us please." Trevor waves and she pulls me away.

Mother is thrilled after I get a white organza gown out, because any accessory Claudette has will match it. When I ask her if she called the club to have another guest added to our table she makes a sound, which means no. More kisses on my cheeks and she is gone in an instant.

Back out to the driveway I find Théo, Rachel and Trevor standing together having a conversation. Rachel tells me, "Théo has filled us in. Claudette must be head over heels for Joseph."

"No doubt. None of us thought she would ever go to another one. She was quite clear that she felt like a fish out of water after she went to her first." Rachel sighs and says, "Love does shake things up a bit." Seconds after the words come out of her mouth we all look at each other and chuckle. Théo says, "That has to be one of the biggest understatements ever made in history." then gives her a kiss.

Théo informs us Rachel pays to have her car washed in the parking deck under the apartment building, so we talk her into letting us wash it. Even after adding an extra car the time ended too soon and Rachel goes to get ready. Watching her ascend the steps I ask them, "When everyone sees Claudette they are going to be taken by surprise. Should I call Joanna and Emily to tell them Claudette is going to be there and why?" Trevor replies, "Imagine being in their shoes." I give Trevor a kiss and add, "All right fellas, it is time for me to go make a couple of phone calls and get ready." Théo asks, "When did you start saying fellas?" I reply, "I have no idea. Joanna calls them that." He smiles and tells me, "I have never been called a fella. I rather like it." I shake my head and go up.

Ready for the evening to begin we follow my parent's onto the portico and they stop so suddenly we almost run into them. It doesn't take long to figure out why. Claudette's car is behind The Chariot. I tell my parents, "My guess is she doesn't want to leave early with Grand-mama and Grand-papa." Father adds, "This one is going to stand out in our memories." Mother goes, "Mmm hm."

Before we take another step I see Théo and Rachel round the corner of the house. Down the steps we go and when we are passing by the car's he sees Claudette's and comments, "That was unexpected." Trevor adds, "I think things are just getting warmed up." Everyone agrees and we go inside my grandparent's house where we have our apéritif then make our exodus for the club.

The arrival of the Delcroix family and friends is becoming a spectacle due to the number of cars alone, because William and Mitch waited on us at the entrance and fell in at the back of the caravan. My grandfather decides we should gather inside because we will crowd the valet's, so inside we go.

Since there are so many of us, Joseph and his assistants will serve our table only and keep an eye on it from a short distance. With this knowledge I have Trevor keep us near Claudette, because I want to see the look on Joseph's face when he sees her. When we enter The Banquet Hall his face does not change, but his eyes give him away and he goes to her post haste. His tone is different when he tells her, "It is a pleasure indeed to see you, Miss Bechard." She replies, "The pleasure, Joseph, is mine." and he slowly seats her. Those of us who hear this exchange are glancing at each other with slight smiles as the staff begins to serve.

The dining is done, so it will soon be time for Joseph to take his break and for my grandfather to speak with him briefly. Claudette suddenly looks pale. I decide to ask her to step outside with me for a bit of fresh air hoping that when we return my grandfather will be there with the results of the conversation.

Sitting by the pool it does not take long for me to reassure her Joseph will seize the opportunity being offered to him and he will be picking her up for their first date before she can blink. When we go back inside our timing could not have been better had we tried. Grand-papa is walking down the opposite end of the corridor straight toward us and when he sees us he nods to ease the suspense we are in and we exhale a sigh of relief.

When my grandfather reaches us he holds Claudette's hand. "Joseph thought it is a wonderful plan and asked what time you would like for him to arrive." She is silent and begins to tremble, so my grandfather takes out his pen and tiny pad of paper he keeps in the inside chest pocket of his jacket and asks, "Shall I write 8:00 a.m.?" She nods and he writes it down. "Geneviève, may I suggest taking a turn down the corridor and back before returning to our table." I reply, "We will be in shortly." He excuses himself and I find myself alone with a woman who is a bit shaken.

Without a word I hold her arm and gently start moving her forward then suddenly she begins to talk. "I feel as if I am in the fairy-tale with you as my Fairy Godmother who loaned me this magnificent gown. Thank you is not enough." I reply, "Yes it is and you are entirely welcome. As for the gown, it is a gift. I thought you knew." She gets misty-eyed and I firmly tell her, "Claudette, you will regret shedding one tear. It will ruin the makeup you are wearing." Her eyes get wide and my attempt to verbally shake her gently by the shoulders works. She exclaims, "All this on my face I am not used to. Thank you for reminding me."

"You are entirely welcome. Are you ready to go back in? I'm sure Joseph is watching for you." In true female fashion she regroups instantly and we go back inside where the first thing we see is my grandfather giving Joseph the note. Joseph glances at it then notices we are walking toward the table and he goes to stand by Claudette's chair. Trevor stands to pull mine out and as he slides it under me he says, "Look at you two. Cool as little cucumbers." Without taking my eyes off him I pick up my cognac and hear Joseph ask Claudette, "Miss Bechard, is there anything else you want?" She replies, "Not at the moment, Joseph. Thank you for asking." That was his way to let her know he will be there in the morning.

Soon after everything has been taken care of my parent's and grandparent's leave and Claudette stays without them for the first time and Théo asks her to dance. The dimmed lights in The Hall cause the ones on the stage to wash across the orchestra down to the dance floor he is gliding her around. It is more of the fairy-tale and over time Claudette has happily danced with each gentleman seated at our table, turning her head occasionally to look at Joseph who is making an effort not to watch her incessantly.

Our glasses are almost empty and while Mitch sits next to Joanna I recognize the look on her face. I softly say, "Trevor, Joanna is plotting something in that brain of hers." He glances at William, then to her which gets him to look her way. William discreetly looks at his watch then at us, holds Emily's hand and we wait.

"Mitch, do you know what I would like?" He replies, "No, but whatever it is I will get it for you." She nuzzles him and says, "A vanilla milkshake from Sam's." The plot is revealed; a way for Joseph and Claudette to spend time together this evening. I smile and say, "A vanilla milkshakes good to me." Emily quickly adds, "Chocolate." Rachel exclaims, "I want both." Théo tells her, "I'll get the vanilla." Then he asks Claudette, "What flavor do you want?" She looks at me and I give her a little nod. She lights up and replies, "Strawberry!" Joseph was able to hear her and steps up. "Miss Bechard, would you like a dish of strawberries and cream?" He took her by surprise which cause her to blush. "Thank you, but no. We are deciding what flavor of milkshake to have at Sam's Diner tonight." He responds, "Excuse me, please."

Before he even takes a step back Théo speaks up. "Joseph, since we are your only table, when we leave you may leave, correct?"

"Yes, sir."

"Would you like to meet us there and grab a bite to eat? You must be hungry."

"As a matter of fact I am."

"Then we will save you a seat." Théo stands up and shakes his hand. "Thank you for everything this evening, Joseph."

"It is always my pleasure, Mr. Delcroix." Théo slides Rachel's chair back and Joseph reaches for Claudette's chair. If only he could see her face.

While we wait on the cars Claudette thanks Joanna for making it possible for her to spend time with Joseph. If women were ambassadors for this country she would be one of the best in history.

Trevor leads the way to Sam's and parks The Chariot. When everyone has passed by he turns to me. "I wish Joanna had known about this place the day we met. I would have given anything for more time with you that night. But I have you now." He caresses my face and asks, "Do you want to wear that lipstick inside?" I hold my hand out and he gives me his handkerchief. The moment I am done Trevor begins to kiss me passionately, because we have not had the chance to kiss since we left the movie theater last night. And dancing in each others' arms all night long has pushed us beyond our capacity. In the middle of the July Banquet we slipped away for some privacy, but this one I left with Claudette and our opportunity never presented itself. He is taking it now.

The beams from car headlights go across our faces and I flinch. Trevor asks, "What is it?"

"I thought that was Joseph. He serves, he does not bus."

"We have to go." All of a sudden he places his hands on my thigh and slides me over to the passenger side which gets me tickled. "It will be easier to get you and that gown out from that side." And he gets out.

While we were in The Chariot three tables were pushed together and Carla has just begun serving water, so we were not in the car as long as we thought. She was about to start taking our order when Joseph arrives. Sam was walking toward us and changed his direction to Joseph. They shake hands and Sam motions to the counter then Joseph motions to our table. They speak briefly and Sam goes to visit customers at a booth. Now we know he comes here often when he leaves the club.

Claudette has not taken her eyes off him since he walked in. He is looking at her as he crosses the diner and pulls out the chair she saved for him. Joseph tells her, "Miss Bechard, it is a pleasure to see you again so soon." She softly says, "Likewise." Next he nods to Carla who has been standing by the table patiently waiting and she says, "*So* — Joe, would you like your usual?" He replies, "Yes I would. Thank you, Carla." She goes, "Mmm hm." Then he tells her, "The lady will have a strawberry milkshake." Then he asks Claudette, "Would you like anything else?" She beams and tells him, "Thank you, I do not want *anything* else." I glance at Joanna as she takes the rest of our orders.

When she leaves Sam walks over. "This is a drastic change from the last time I saw this crew. You all look pretty fancy. I haven't seen this many stars since my Navy days. When the captain walked in I almost said, 'Attention on deck.' to my kitchen staff." That gets a laugh. Mitch tells him, "Old habits die hard." Sam replies, "You got that right. Well, I'm going to make this young man his burger and reminisce about my Navy days." And he is off to man the grill.

After Joseph thanks Théo for inviting him by calling him Mr. Delcroix we spend the next few minutes asking him to call us by our names in nonprofessional circumstances. Then Carla brings our orders and Joseph begins asking questions. He wanted to know how long Mitch and Joanna had been married and where the other's were born and grew up; simple things that he couldn't figure out. This is turning out to be an excellent idea.

A few minutes after we finish our milkshakes Joanna says they have stayed out way past their curfew and soon we all are getting up to leave. Théo asks Joseph if he would mind seeing Claudette to her door, because it is quite late. She could not be happier.

On the way to our cars Rachel says, "I had a good time, but it was touch and go at first." Emily responds, "Wasn't it? Carla's slight hostility directed at 'Joe' came out of the blue." I say, "Obviously she has had her eye on him and he made it clear his eye has been on Claudette." Joanna adds, "He handled it beautifully. Thank goodness Claudette had her head in the clouds and didn't pick up on it." The fellas nod and Trevor says, "Never a dull moment." Mitch is quite droll when he responds, "It seems as if we have been running around this city since we arrived." William says, "Be careful what you want, Captain." He promptly replies, "Because I surely got it — in one fell swoop."

Through our laughter Joanna tells him, "Take me home, Mitch." He just smiles at her and we say our goodbyes. Before Trevor and I get in the car we see Joseph and Claudette have moved to a small booth by a wall for privacy. By the time Trevor tucks me in I expect to see light peak through my draperies.

In the morning when I wake up I do not move a muscle until I look at my clock and it reads 9:24. Then it hits me, Joseph has already left for the club and I can get the details of the event at brunch. I rinse my mouth and without putting on my robe I open my door to see Trevor's is slightly open which means he is still sleeping and the other bedroom doors are open. We are alone, so I dash into his room, pounce on him and start kissing his face. Laughing with his eyes still closed he says, "Geneviève — my alarm hasn't even gone off."

"Joseph is off on Tuesday's and I bet they are going to have their first date in two days." He lifts his head, opens those blue eyes and smiles that smile as I hand him his glass of water. He swishes some in his mouth, swallows then takes a drink and sets it down. Next he grabs me and throws me onto the bed.

His tone drops. "Where are the others?"

"Scattered elsewhere."

"Are you in a hurry?"

"Not anymore."

"Are you willing to risk injury to your face from my stubble?"

"Definitely." Several minutes pass before I go to re-braid my hair and that's all I need to do, because we have this brunch in our robes.

On our way we hear Théo and Rachel walking. We slow down and they catch up. After we say our good morning's Rachel says, "I feel so odd parading around in my robe outside." Trevor tells her, "Once it sinks in the total privacy one has behind these walls it changes things. I go for runs and for the first time in my life I do not have to keep my head up for vehicles or other people. My mind gets so clear. I just breathe in the salt air and the scents from the gardens and run."

We walk in silence to my grandparent's portico and then Rachel responds, "Thank you for sharing that with me."

"Think nothing of it."

Seconds pass as her eyes get a little wide. "Suddenly so many things are clear to me, especially how carefree these two are. They have had a place to escape prying eyes their entire lives. I want to be more like them, and you." Her eyes get wider as she sees me. "Please forgive me for speaking as if neither of you are here." I say, "There is nothing to forgive." I chuckle, look at Théo and add, "I felt as if we were eaves dropping." He responds, "I almost reached for you, so we could give them privacy."

Rachel gets tickled then exclaims, "Joseph was here. I wonder what happened." Théo tells her, "Rachel, if you will let me get to the door I will open it and we can find out before Gené makes a break for it." Trevor burst into laughter because he knows I am itching to go inside. Rachel asks, "What is going on with me?" Théo and I get tickled as he manages to tell her, "I am going to treat that as rhetorical." Rachel holds up her hand and just shakes her head while Trevor continues to laugh. That is how we enter my grandparent's house.

With one look at Claudette, questions are answered. She has a suitor and his name is Joseph. Also, they are going on their first date Tuesday. What we did not know was that while she waited with my grandmother they did not sit idle by, they cooked a simple breakfast and ate with him before he left. That explains why my parents are the only one's eating brunch as my grandparents drink coffee. Claudette is sipping on an espresso for the extra caffeine, which is something the rest of us need and have instead of a second cup of coffee.

Another thing we found out was that due to his unusual schedule he has permission to call on her late at night. This was decided after the phone call, because Claudette's father gave my grandfather carte blanche with the little things for the new couple. All is right in their world and they deserve it.

After brunch everyone decides to go their separate ways. My plan is to work for a little while in my darkroom which makes Trevor happy. We change into clothes, get cola's and go there. He gives me a kiss and asks, "What are you going to do?" I reply, "Something I have wanted to do since the week you arrived, develop an 11 x 14 of the Sailor's manning the rail, now with a slight change. I am hoping to crop it to where you and William are center."

Successful in my endeavor we stand looking at it as it hangs to dry then Trevor starts guiding me backwards to the counter as he whispers, "I have been waiting for quite some time to come down here with you." He picks me up, sets me down on it and places his hands on my thighs instead of by them. Then I begin to remember; this is where I wound up the first day he was down here after I threw myself on him when we were in total darkness.

A slight smile appears on my face as I look into his eyes and he asks, "Are you remembering the last time I put you on this counter."

"Yes I am."

"Several things happened that day. The woman you are becoming made her first appearance and I told you I was in love with you."

He kisses me tenderly and I whisper, "Yes you did."

Tender kisses become passionate and as I put my arms around him I slide forward until my knees are pressing on him in a somewhat sensitive area. I decide to separate them a little and in an instant our bodies collide. His hands stay on my thighs and he begins to tighten his hold on them. Soon he lets go of one and puts his arm around me. When his mouth is on the slope of my neck I moan to the point it gets our attention. Trevor relaxes his hold on my thigh and slides me back just a bit. I rest my hands on his shoulders as we look at each other and calm down. He exhales slowly and asks, "Geneviève — how did I wind up with your legs around me?" I reply, "I put my arms around you and slid forward. My knees were pressed ..." He quickly interjects, "I know what happened. It's fine."

We are silent a moment then I tell him, "And another aspect of foreplay has been discovered." And there goes the deep laugh I simply adore. He hugs me then says, "Yes it has. Let me know when you're no longer weak at the knees and I'll get you down. What is it about this darkroom?"

"I have no idea, but I am thrilled there is going to be one in our house." The look we give each other says it all and Trevor gets me down.

Things return to our normal routine after that. We enjoy a light lunch in the solarium and he massages my aching feet until it's time to get ready for Sunday dinner. Trevor remembers to bring *The Halyard* with Part Two of the article and my photographs before we go and of course everything is perfect. Claudette even joins us when we have our cognac. She is still in disbelief she is going to be dating Joseph in two days and is filled with anticipation.

Trevor tucks me in and stays for only a few minutes. We were up into the wee hours and the only way we can recover is to sleep. When the alarm goes off in the morning I'm disoriented until I hear Trevor calling in for any messages and this time he has one. I drag myself from my nice cozy bed, slip on my robe and open my door. He hangs up and gives me a good morning kiss then says, "I have to report for duty at 1:30. I'm going to the West Annex?"

"That is where the intelligence division is." He is none too happy and I add, "At least you aren't going to the base commander's building."

"I am cheered. I love you."

"I love you too."

At the morning briefing Father tells us my grandfather has hired a chauffeur to drive us to our dinner party in The Chariot. Next Mother gives Trevor two Letters of Recommendation and tells him when he gives them to William inform him he should get the one from Joanna and take them to the club this morning. With luck he could have the cards by Thursday and present it to Emily on the day of their engagement dinner. This reminds me to ask Mother for an invitation to ours for Harry. He should be there and Trevor agrees wholeheartedly. Last but not least, Théo tells us he has the permits for his building and the Ground Breaking Ceremony can finally be scheduled.

Everything falls into place from that point on. Trevor tells me on the way in The O Club for lunch with the crew he and William did go to the club. Next Harry is taken aback by the invitation to our party and graciously accepts. Joanna announces it is Happy Hour again today, then Emily and I go back to work and Trevor is going to find the Annex.

Typing away I am when the most unexpected happens; Becky steps in front of my desk with a little grin and hands me a note. Filled with dread I cover my typewriter, get my files and glance at Emily. When I enter Becky's reception area I see Trevor and he stands up with eyes forward, so I walk passed him and go into Mrs. Sloan's office. She is holding a letter for me again. It reads the usual with the exception I am to go with the driver sent for me. Mrs. Sloan escorts me out and Trevor stands back up. She says, "Commander Lyons, this is Miss Delcroix." He nods. "Miss Delcroix, this is your driver, Commander Lyons." and I nod to him not knowing what to say. The entire time Becky is looking back and forth among us. Obviously she knows who he is. Trevor motions to the door and says, "After you, ma'am."

When we are halfway to the front doors he speaks quietly. "We are going to see Emily's father." I'm relieved it isn't Mr. Collins, but I'm unhappy about being summoned to the Annex, even if it is to meet with Robert.

Trevor opens the back passenger door and I get tickled. He says, "I had to report for duty to be your driver, so we are going to take this the whole nine yards." I get in; he walks around, starts the car and I ask, "What is going on?" He replies, "This is sort of your doing. It is in regard to the page you typed on the security issues the base has. Robert told me he would make everything clear when I returned with you."

"I knew Emily's father was in the intelligence division."

"Dare I ask?"

"I used my powers of deduction." This gets a chuckle. "Emily never said what division he is in and the intelligence division is the only one never mentioned."

"You are spot-on. No one is ever in intelligence."

"I work in the secretarial pool." Trevor laughs and shakes his head.

While we are going toward the building he tells me, "There is a passage to the left after we go through the security check. We will enter it through a door that looks as if it's to the janitor's closet. I was escorted to his office through the center of the building. He walked me out through a door in the back of his office, down the passage and told me to bring you in that way. Allow me to do the talking until we are in his office."

Trevor opens the outer door that goes into an empty space. Then he opens another door and I find myself in a darkened vestibule that resembles a court room with two Sailors wearing a sidearm on opposite sides of the building. We go to a tall desk with a lieutenant standing behind it and Trevor says, "Commander Lyons, Plus One reporting." and a Sailor standing by the desk swings open a gate and we go through.

As we go down the passage that is narrow with just doors and name plaques on them I quietly tell Trevor, "Now I understand why he sent you."

"Mmm hm."

"Plus One is a term used for someone they do not want on the records."

"Yes it is and you are my first Plus One, which I find is normal for things concerning us as of late." He begins looking at the plaques. "Here it is."

Trevor taps on the door twice with his knuckle. It opens within seconds and there is Robert. He motions us in and closes the door. "Geneviève, it is nice to see you again. Thank you for coming. I apologize for the cloak and dagger. Please have a seat." Trevor holds my chair and seats me then sits next to me.

"Long story short, my wife is cooking dinner and casually tells me, 'I do not understand why the traffic is being monitored on the streets now. When school starts the numbers are going to change drastically. Why are they not waiting until after Labor Day?' All I do is shrug my shoulders. I can't tell her time has become an issue, but she had a valid point. The next day I made an unofficial inquiry and Captain Mitchell was mentioned along with your fiancé. Next I wound up with a piece of paper without a typist line. I added 2 and 2 and got you. Knowing you could expedite matters I requested to take this on and I really didn't want to hand you over to strangers."

"I appreciate that, Robert."

"Think nothing of it. All right — we are going to step over to that table where there is a map of the base. I'm going to call in my secretary to take notes as you tell me which ones to barricade."

Within minutes we are done and his secretary is gone. He says, "Problem solved and in under five minutes. The man hours and headaches you just saved us. Thank you, Geneviève."

"You are most welcome."

"Have a seat please. There are some things I would like to say to you both. In order to do so I am going to bring up a subject neither of you can discuss with me, so I fully expect to hear crickets when I pause between sentences."

Trevor says, "You have our undivided attention, sir."

"One fine Saturday I was sitting in my favorite chair reading the paper when the phone rang. Next thing I know I'm in uniform sitting behind this desk. I was coordinating a flight coming in from L.A. with transportation to The Coronado. As I watch several agents leave the hangar it occurs to me Emily told us you two were going there that day and I hoped you would not encounter those gentlemen.

"When they finally came back I added a Plus One to their return flight and cargo. For some reason as the aircraft taxied out of the hangar I remembered Emily joking about a German spy you both happed upon and a chill went up my spine. Instead of going home I returned here and pulled your file. There is more to you than meets the eye, Miss Delcroix." He pauses and we hear crickets.

"A flood of information came through here over the next few days concerning a compromise of the entire West Coast. I figured out it was you who spotted the man responsible and without hesitation you took immediate action.

"In the midst of something that caught you completely by surprise I trusted you didn't give them Emily's name to protect her and you did. I know this because my daughter never came home slightly unhinged needing to talk with me in private. I chose to bring this up to tell you I admire your courage and to thank you for protecting my daughter. I will be eternally grateful."

It pains me not to respond. He touched my heart and I have to sit and be silent. Just before things get sticky Robert looks at Trevor and says, "Don't think you're off the hook." I had to literally bite my tongue not to laugh.

"The Navy doesn't train us on what to do in the face of adversity with the women we love by our side. I cannot imagine what you must have been going through. I did read you were the best in your weight class at Annapolis. I bet it crossed your mind if you could just have one minute alone with that man, because it was all you needed. I admire your restraint. If you ever decide you want to stay on land, let me know. We could put an officer of your caliber to good use here." He raises his eyebrows and gives Trevor a nod. Robert meant that.

"All right then, I'm really looking forward to seeing the two of you at your engagement party Saturday and our little celebration Sunday for Emily and William's engagement. I've got a lot on my plate this week."

Trevor chuckles and tells him, "Yes you do; entertaining William's father, the grandson of a full blown historical figure of the Navy." I look at Trevor then Robert who asks me, "What do you know about William's great-grandfather?" I reply, "He was an admiral of some importance." He tells Trevor, "She should be in the same boat with the rest of us. Fill her in."

Trevor looks at me and draws in a breath. "The admiral was in the first graduating class of The Academy and had a stellar career aboard ships and in our Office of Naval Intelligence. There is a bust of him in the museum on campus."

As I sit speechless Robert adds, "I can still see that thing in my mind and the plaque on the pedestal that reads, Admiral William Snowden, and my daughter is marrying the forth one. I never even thought she would marry a Sailor. Life is filled with the unexpected." He chuckles and as he looks at us.

Trevor and I control our laughter as I say, "For instance being here and listening to you talk about things that never happened."

Robert slaps his desk and laughs. "We should end on that note." He stands up, motions to the door and thanks us for meeting with him. Trevor and I do not utter a word until we get close to the car and I tell him, "Your boxing things are in your quarters. Would you like to go get them?"

"Geneviève, what is going through that mind of yours?"

"When we met I realized you knew how to box and I have wanted to watch you do that very thing since. I can put those pads on my hands."

"I do not know where to begin on the list of problems I have with that."

With those words from him my heart sinks. Is he actually going to deny me this? My mind becomes a whirlwind of thoughts as we continue to the car and I relive the disappointment of being at home listening to the Louis and Schmeling fight on the radio. I've wanted to watch a boxing match for ages and years will pass before the men of the boxing world will let a woman in. The skill and the strength they have, he has, and the dream I had of seeing him was gone in an instant.

Trevor opens the car door for me and instead of getting in I take off my sunglasses and face him. "Trevor ... what is the worse that could happen to me? You will make my hands sting?"

"That was one thing."

"I can cast off an 85 foot ketch and raise her sails. Do you think those lines have never stung my hands?" He is silent. "Trevor, trust your skills and please do not deny me this because I'm a woman and you're concerned I will get hurt." He closes his eyes and sighs then looks at me.

"I forgot I was talking to a woman who tried to go to a boxing match dressed like a man." In an instant I begin to beam and almost kiss him.

Trevor goes to his quarters and walks out with his things. I put my head on his shoulder and we listen to the radio all the way home. When he gets his bag out of the car I pull him by his hand up the steps to the apartment. He is laughing the entire time. I open the door myself and pull him inside. He closes the door and sets his bag on the coffee table and motions for me to sit, which I happily do.

He unzips the bag and takes out a pair of black leather gloves with a thin pad on top with the fingers cut in half. "These are my practice gloves. I wear them when I'm using the speed bag or these." He pulls out the pads I referred to. "These are called punch mitts." I smile and nod. "This is all we're going to need."

Trevor takes off his shoes and socks then gets up. He takes off his shirts and picks up the mitts. "I can't believe I'm doing this." He holds my hand and leads me to the middle of the room then slides the mitts on my hands. Trevor pushes the coffee table back and puts on the gloves. I get lost for a moment as I watch him standing in front of me bare footed and only wearing his khaki pants. When he turns to the side and starts swinging his arm through the air my jaw drops as I watch his muscles flex. He stops, faces me and chuckles as he steps in front of me, so I close my mouth.

"Geneviève, when I swing I'm going to punch your right with my right and your left with my left. When I make contact with a mitt use resistance, but if I hit it with enough force your arm goes back just quickly move it forward to where it was. I am going to begin slowly and go through the motions without making an impact. When you have a grasp of the way it works I will gradually increase my speed and make impact."

He positions my hands and takes a big step back then he begins to swing and moves forward making light contact with his left then his right. After a few slow hits on the mitts he speeds up a bit and makes my left arm go back a little. I bring it back into position and he smiles at me. "I got it, more resistance."

Trevor takes a stance, swings, hits the mitt and my arm doesn't go back. He starts a breathing pattern as he boxes and I am soaking up every second. Even though I am enjoying this immensely I know he is holding back because neither of my hands has felt the slightest sting. His control is impressive, but I want to see more. Finally I say, "Time out." and he gets still. Before he can say anything I ask, "This is all you're going to give me?" His eyebrows go up. "If my arms get tired or my hands begin to burn I do have the sense to throw in the towel." I lower my voice. "Come on, Trevor — show me what you've got."

Trevor has a glint in his eyes as he draws in a deep breath and steps away from me. Suddenly he looks like a boxer waiting in his corner shifting his weight from foot to foot and shaking his arms. Then he starts swinging through the air as he works his way to me as if I am an opponent. Here we go. He makes a wide sweeping motion with his left using his entire upper body twisting at his waist as he moves forward, then he hits the mitt and I feel a sting. Now he is boxing.

Trevor moves fast and I keep up. My heart is racing and soon he begins to perspire. I watch him duck as he moves away then he closes in on me and swings, shifting his weigh from each foot. His entire upper body is where the strength behind the punch comes from and his legs are involved as well. I am learning so much about this incredible sport. One minute he is completely focused and the next he is smiling at me.

He is magnificent. Trevor is fluid and powerful with every move he makes. I am pulled in to where he is mentally and become mesmerized with him. The phrase poetry in motion comes to mind as I watch this beautiful man before me. He surpasses all my expectations.

I barely notice my hands are stinging, but when my arms tire I know it's time for this to end. I let him take a few more swings and when he moves back I breathlessly tell him, "I am throwing in the towel." He nods and we begin to catch our breath.

While taking the punch mitts off me he says, "I'm impressed."

"And I'm so attracted to you right now. Trevor — do something."

He looks straight into my eyes as he dries off. "Geneviève, please tell me there is something under this dress I can see you in."

"I'm wearing a silk camisole and half slip."

"That is music to my ears."

Trevor takes off his gloves and belt, then kneels on one knee. As he begins to unbutton my dress I place my hands on his shoulders. While he works his way up the buttons slowly rising to his feet I can feel the heat radiating from his body. The moment he reaches the last button he slides the dress off of me and I find myself in his arms being kissed with such passion I can barely keep up. My arms glide across his back due to the light perspiration on his skin after he dried off and he feels incredible because his muscles are defined. In this moment there is not a doubt in my mind that if we were already lovers we would make love now.

He guides us to the end of his bed until his legs are against it and I am standing between them. Somehow he manages to get us on the bed and up to the pillow while lying beneath me. What follows is a blur of pleasure and moans we both make. He slides his hands under my camisole and I feel the skin of his arms on my bare back again. What is it about our bare skin touching that feels so good?

I push myself up to look at his face and notice there is a passion mark on his shoulder so dark it looks like the result of an injury. The sight of it makes me wince. Trevor's eyes twinkle. "I'm guessing you've spotted the passion mark on my shoulder."

"Yes I have. Trevor, that is going to be sore."

He laughs deep and says, "It already is." I gasp and he touches my face. "Don't get upset, Baby. I'm glad I can feel it, so I will not forget it's there, nor why."

Relieved I lay my head on his chest. Then all of a sudden he chuckles and tells me, "I will never be able to box again without thinking of you."

"That should make things interesting."

"The next time William asks me to spar a few rounds he might get a point or two he wouldn't otherwise." I get tickled then he flinches. "William — Happy Hour. What time is it?"

"I'm afraid to look. You do it."

Trevor turns his head. "Time is barely on our side. We've got 27 minutes."

We get up and Trevor happily puts my dress back on me. He loves the one's that button up the front and so do I, but for a different reason now. I try to stand still, but I keep touching him and cannot stop myself. I cause him to miss a button and Trevor playfully chastises me as he redoes them.

The fun continues at Happy Hour. We all are determined to enjoy our last moment as just the crew before the world ascends on us Wednesday for the parties and invade every aspect of our lives. Trevor, William and Mitch make jokes about the night they all came close to getting drunk for the first times in their lives, because William is drinking beer. Mitch tells them it will not be the last time they will be rescued by their women and we, the women, agree.

While going over the schedule for Wednesday I notice Emily is staring at me and I finally ask, "What's on your mind?" She replies, "I know I can't ask where you went, but I can ask how you got there. I've always wanted to receive a request for my services elsewhere and find a driver waiting for me then sit in the back seat like my dad does sometimes. They know so much about our movements on the base I'm certain they knew you didn't have your car. Did they send a driver?"

"As a matter a fact they did. They sent him." I motion to Trevor and all jaws drop. Emily dryly says, "They know a little more than I thought." Joanna looks at her husband as she finishes her martini and hands him the glass to refill it. Emily adds, "There has to be humor in this story. We are all ears."

"After Becky handed me the note I got my files and went to see Mrs. Sloan. When I walked into Becky's reception area I saw Trevor sitting with eyes forward. As he stands up he looks right through me, so I decide to ignore him and go into Mrs. Sloan's office. A minute later she escorts me out and introduces me to my driver. We continue to act as if we don't know each other and the entire time Becky looks like she watching a tennis match. Obviously *she* knew who he was."

The look of disbelief on their faces is too funny as they began to chuckle and Emily blurts out, "I can't believe Mrs. Sloan has never seen you two together. Where has she been, under a rock?" Then Joanna asks, "What is she, a truffle?" In an instant we all burst into laughter. Emily is laughing so hard William begins to fan the back of her neck.

We are enjoying our selves so much Joanna invites us to stay for dinner. After she tells us they spent half the day at the commissary buying food to stock the cupboard in order to feed the masses we all accept the invitation. The masses are parents; hers, Mitch's and last but not least, William's. Trevor calls Mother to let her know we will not be home for dinner and soon we are seated at the table feasting on the fruits of our labor and laughing well into the night.

The next day we all pair off for lunch as usual, but this one is significant. It will be almost a week before we will have the chance to be alone for lunch again. Therefore Trevor and I sit peacefully on the bench eating our lunch he brought from the club.

He picks me up after work and we go to The Bridal Salon for my gown and shoes. He is excited until I inform he can only enter the first section and I am not coming out of the dressing room, because I do not want him to see the gown in its full glory. Luckily there was orange silk chiffon available and I have a lovely wrap to match. This I show him and he is elated.

When everything is safely in the car we get in and Trevor says, "You do know we have to take every opportunity to be alone today. The arrivals begin tomorrow morning and we are going to be spread thin among them all. Therefore I made reservations at Mandarin Garden's for us." I sit quietly absorbing and he asks, "Where's my kiss?" I touch my lips and reply, "Right here. If you want it, come and get it." And he does. We were almost late for our reservation.

After a nice dinner with warm sake we go back to the house and all the outside lights are off and there are no torches lit. Plus there are no interior lights visible because draperies are closed. Since Joseph picked up Claudette for their first date tonight, something is definitely up.

There is a half moon shining, so we are able to see as we make our way to the service entrance and inside we find my parents sitting in the dark drinking cola's in the solarium. Trevor apologizes to them for turning on a light in the kitchen and I finally ask, "How long are you going to leave me dangling in suspense?" He hugs me and says, "There is going to be a spectacular meteor shower tonight." I gasp. "We are going to watch it from the lookout of the guest house."

As I hug him around his neck Trevor picks me up and puts me on the kitchen counter. "What are you doing?" He replies, "Giving you another reason to marry me." I laugh as he gets out a sauce pot along with milk and sugar. Next he vanishes into the cupboard, appears with cocoa and steps in front of me. "I make the best hot cocoa you will ever taste." I laugh and ask, "Why did you not tell me this before we started dating?" He chuckles and replies, "I would have had I known you had such a serious sweet tooth." He gives me a kiss, pulls something from his pocket and begins making the cocoa.

While the milk warms he gets my thermos. "Your Mother told me blankets and anything else we may need is in the guest house. We have to stay up past midnight and it will get chilly." His back is to me as he stirs the aromatic mixture.

"Evidently I am the last member of my family you told about this."

"I also told Joseph yesterday when I went to the club with William."

"Their first date will be watching a meteor shower on a blanket somewhere?" He looks over his shoulder beaming. "I do love you."

"I love you too." He sets the pot on a trivet to let it cool. "Now let's get you down from there, so you can change clothes and I am to going to get my jacket."

Trevor follows me into my closet and closes the door. "Do you want me to kiss you now or after I get you out of that dress one more time today?" I reply, "After." He kneels and here we go again.

When he finally goes to get his jacket I put on trousers and a sweater then we go back to the kitchen. He fills the thermos with the hot cocoa and we tell my parent's good night.

The moment we're settled on the lookout under a warm blanket we see the first meteor. "This is called the Perseid Meteor Shower. It occurs when Earth passes through the debris trail of Comet Swift-Tuttle. It slowly builds from the end of July and peaks late at night usually on August 12 and since we have a clear, dark sky we might see as many as 60 meteors an hour tonight." That revelation causes me to inhale deeply. "You haven't heard the best part yet. The first recorded observation of the Perseids was in 36 A.D. by Chinese astronomers, which means this meteor shower has been occurring for 1,975 years we know of."

"I've never heard about this and I go to the planetarium often."

"I didn't know about it until I attended Annapolis. Several Sailors had seen it from the deck of a ship in the middle of an ocean. They told us it was something to see and they were correct. Of course I watched it on land, but I will never forget watching it from Louise's deck."

"We'd be on Willow's deck right now was it not for the arrivals of our guests wouldn't we?"

"Yes we would, but I promise you this; come what may, next year we will be out on Willow. Now — are you ready to taste the best hot cocoa you've ever had in your life?"

I sit up and eagerly wait as Trevor pours and hands me the cup. The second I taste it I realize he wasn't overstating. "This *is* the best I have ever tasted. I detect a hint of something unusual in this. What is it?"

"I harassed a cook on the ship years to tell me what it was and just before he retired he told me with one condition, that the only person I could tell was my wife. I gave him my word I would honor his request."

"And I am not your wife yet, therefore I must wait." He nods with a glint in his eyes as I drink a little more, then hand the cup to him.

We lie back down and watch the beauty unfold. I have never seen anything like this. It seems like a dream state instead of reality. Knowing him is beyond what words can convey. I treasure him above all things.

When the meteors become less frequent we decide to go to the house. Joseph has not returned with Claudette and Théo is still with Rachel probably on the roof of our building downtown. My parents have already retired for the evening, so after showering Trevor reads to me from his book then he kisses me goodnight. And what a night it was.

CHAPTER FOUR

Breakfast was beyond a briefing, it more like a warning of things to come; catering vans, florists, linen trucks and a house staff that will arrive daily after breakfast or brunch to maintain the apartments. And last but not least, I will meet Trevor's maternal and fraternal grandparents, and his Aunt Meredith.

When we finish eating there is a hasty exit made by all to get out of the way. Trevor's kisses me and we are a little down as he puts me in my car, because he cannot take me to work. He has to move back into the apartment this morning and stay there until next week when the last guest has left. Then Trevor is going to the airport and wait on flights to arrive in the concession's atrium that runs between the gates with William, Mitch and Joanna. It was decided that Emily with her family and I are to meet the families of our friends and William's in a private dining room at The O Club for lunch. And this evening I am going to meet the rest of Trevor's family at the guest house.

For a change Emily and I are going to The O Club in my car, because she has taken a half day off and as soon as we get in she tells me, "I'm a little nervous. Can you get over the story about William's parents?" I step on the brakes and pull over. "What story?"

"It's long. I can't believe you don't know it. Drive slowly and I'll talk fast."

She draws in a deep breath and begins. "William's father was married to the Navy until he was in his mid-forties. Umm ... William's mother, Judith, lived in Annapolis and lost her father who was in the Navy during World War I and her mother lost most of her mind shortly after. Judith refused to put her in a ... facility, hired a live-in nurse and stayed by her mother's side. Years later the nurse talked his mother, who was in her thirty's, into going to the Ring Dance they still received an invitation to for some unknown reason. She met Williams' father there that night and he is in his late seventy's now."

"All right then. Good synopsis under pressure"

"Thank you. Oh, when you see him you will understand why he caught her eye. I saw a recent photograph of them and the man is still handsome, surprisingly handsome."

"Like father, like son." Emily beams as she nods.

Inside we go and down the corridor that leads to the private dining room. Trevor and William are waiting for us with Emily's family at the entrance. Kelly is holding her little brothers arm so tight his sleeve is wrinkling. Meeting what she called 'Navy royalty' has her nervous. Emily's mother is calm and immediately greets me by saying it is so nice for them to finally see me again. I just go right along and pretend I didn't see Robert two days ago. Next William escorts Emily into the dining room with her family two steps back. Trevor and I walk in last and there they are, the parent's of my friends that I hold so dear.

There are so many officers it distracts me momentarily. I am looking at two four star admirals, a captain and two commanders. And they're all wearing Service Khaki uniforms, which are appropriate, yet it's funny to me because I know the uniform of the day was not discussed among these men.

William and Trevor introduce the Prescott's and me informally for times' sake and when we sit down I am in awe. Joanna's father Howard and his elegant wife Lorraine are seated by their daughter then seated by Mitch are his distinguished parent's, Albert and Sandra, the couple Trevor is grateful they moved to Savannah because of food. Next there is William's parent's; the admiral whom is indeed handsome with a dignified yet boyish charm which is endearing and I see why his lovely mother fell for him.

We had 50 minutes together and it seemed as if in the blink of an eye Trevor was walking me to my car. Trevor told me he was going back in, but will be leaving soon because he wants to visit with his family. He assures me they will be gathered at the guest house when I get home.

This is one of those days I drive with the windows down and listen to the wind as I go home. When I drive passed the guest house I look in my rearview mirror and see his family on the balcony waiting for me. I wonder where Trevor is then I see him standing at the bottom of the steps to the service entrance. He opens my door, tells me he missed me terribly and wraps his arms around me.

My entire family, including Rachel is in the kitchen. Mother hands me her Manhattan, I take a drink and we go to my bedroom for me to freshen up. Trevor goes straight into my closet and chooses a dinner dress for me. This one has a side zipper with hook, so he gets to help dress me. I kiss him, which is something I have wanted to do for hours then put on lipstick and we go out the front door.

Evelyn showed me photographs of her family; therefore I recognize her father who is standing next to Rowland at the railing of the balcony. Rowland waves and so does Spencer which triggers activity on the balcony. When we reach the top of the steps Evelyn is there to give me a hug, followed by Rowland. Next flurries of introductions begin and I find out Trevor calls his maternal grandparents Poppy and Pops. That had to be adorable when he was small.

His Aunt Meredith is just as I expected, outgoing and loaded with personality. I knew that Hildegard was shortened to Hilda, but was mistaken as to why. This woman has a sultry side to her and it is most unexpected. Tobias looks like the quintessential British gentleman, but I know those looks are completely deceiving because he encouraged Trevor to be a card shark as a teen. I am going to have a soft spot for him, because no doubt he is who Trevor takes after. He calls them Granddad and Grandmum.

We walk to the house with his family and at long last our families are together. Introductions are made with first names only. Trevor and I could not be happier. While the apéritif is being served at my parent's house I finally hear the bell Meredith wears. Trevor looks at me with eyes dancing. When she is talking to Théo and Rachel he smiles ever so slightly as he tilts his head. He doesn't miss a thing, even though there are 15 people milling around our drawing room along with Joseph and Eric. Claudette is staying in the kitchen on Cloud 9 no doubt.

It wasn't long after dessert that our guests dispersed to collapse in their private quarters. Red eye flights from coast to coast will get you every time even if you do sleep most of it. There are too many family members in too many places for us to see them to their doors, so we say our good evenings in the foyer then Trevor and I go to the kitchen to thank the staff before going to his apartment. Obviously there is strength in number because the counters were cleared and only Claudette and Joseph were sitting at the table drinking a glass of water.

Joseph stands immediately and I say, "We were going to thank the staff." He tells us, "Claudette runs this kitchen like, Chef. They finished up toute de suite and left." She is glowing either from the high praise or that he calls her by her first name at long last.

Next Joseph holds his hand out to shake Trevor's. "I want to thank you for telling me about the meteor shower, it was the highlight of the evening."

"You are entirely welcome. I knew you both would enjoy it."

Claudette adds, "It was like being under a canopy of falling stars to wish upon."

"Yes it was. Trevor and I watched it from the guest house lookout."

"He took me to one of his secret places."

Joseph explains, "Over time I have explored every nook and cranny of our coastal area and have discovered a few secluded places."

Trevor says, "We shan't keep you a minute longer. On behalf of my family I thank you for everything." Claudette says, "It was our pleasure, Commander." She kisses my cheeks and we bid them good evening. Walking to his apartment we bask in the glory of the knowledge their first date went so well.

When we are inside the first thing is I see is a pastry box on the table. "Is that what I think it is?"

"If you think it's two dozen pecan sandies from Sandra, yes, it is. She cared for three boxes during the flight."

"That was a nice surprise."

"Mmm hm. — There is something I have been itching to tell you all day." As I kick off my shoes and pull my feet up on the sofa I ask, "That good huh?"

"Yep. Mum is traveling with the bear." I laugh and say, "Diego." He nods and continues. "I'm standing at the gate watching for them and I see a little girl close to my mum as they enter the terminal. They have something in common; they're both holding Teddy Bear's. — I have no idea what has gotten into my Mum.

"Geneviève, here's the thing. At the airport a reunion took place as each flight arrived. Since it was the first time we've all been together in almost a decade we delayed leaving the atrium pulling tables together and Diego became a topic of conversation. By the time we were leaving it had been decided a trip to the park should be on their itinerary. It came back up at The O Club after you left."

"Let me guess, everyone wants to go." He nods. "The only time we can all go is after Sunday brunch. Trevor, there are 31 people involved. It would be a convoy from where, the base? We could fill a bus." I watch Trevor think for a few seconds. "Our personnel buses carry 36 passengers." My mouth opens, because I know what he's thinking. "I could get one from the motor pool legitimately. There would be two admirals, a captain and two commanders on it." I ask, "Who would drive it?" He replies, "Yours truly."

Suddenly a glint is in his eyes. "Trevor, I know exactly what you're thinking and I cannot begin to express how much I do not want to stand in the front of a bus holding on to a pole pretending to be a tour guide."

"I'll be driving."

"Only if someone asks." He gives me a kiss and with dread in my voice I add, "Someone *will* ask."

"My guess is Joanna. Do you want a glass of cognac?"

"Please. Then I want you to kiss me until my heart is content."

On the walk home we see Evelyn and Meredith sitting on the balcony. Sisters staying up late talking; how delightful. They hold up mugs and Trevor slows us down. "I have to take a mental picture of that." I take one as well as we wave and Trevor sighs heavily. "I am not going to get to tuck you in." I ask, "Why did everyone show up so early? The party is not until Saturday. Helen is waiting until Friday." He chuckles and says, "When we get inside I'm going to pin you against the door before I leave." He does what he said he would and I am cheered.

The next morning, just before breakfast I hear a light knock on my bedroom door and Trevor quietly says, "Geneviève, it's me." I start laughing and tell him, "What are you doing up here? Give me a minute." Then I hear, "Good morning, Théo." I put my hand over my mouth so I can hear. "Good morning, Trevor." And Théo keeps going without another word.

"You may come in." Trevor rushes me and says, "I'm here because I met you two months ago today and if I don't steal a kiss now who knows how long I will have to wait." He has the presence of mind to hold my face and not wrinkle my clothing as he kisses me tenderly then we go downstairs.

What followed were two days and nights of meals and stolen moments between me and Trevor. Breakfast is served at my parent's house; lunches are in the private dining room at The O Club in order to include Emily and me; also to accommodate 30 people. The apéritif for our guests are served at my parent's house then dinner's are in one of the private dining rooms at our club, because not even my grandparents' house can seat everyone.

Hilda and Tobias asked us to spend time with them at their apartment Thursday night. They have a wonderful sense of humor and I see their traits are evident in Trevor. Helen arrived Friday in time to get settled in our guest room, aka Trevor's room, and meet his family before we went to the club for dinner and we stayed quite late. The one thing I am not happy about is Trevor was successful in getting a bus from the motor pool. My fate is sealed.

It is Saturday at last, so we all sleep late and are going to have brunch at my grandparents. Once again before I'm ready Trevor knocks on my door and I open it wearing only a slip. He immediately gathers me into his arms and holds me. "I miss you, Geneviève. I miss our time alone."

"I miss it too."

"After brunch we're going to disappear and no one will see us until we're at the club." He gives me a kiss and leads me into my closet. "What would you like to wear when we choose our wedding bands?" I get emotional as I throw my arms around him and oh such wonderful kisses follow.

It is supposed to get quite warm today so I tug on the sundress I wore the day we met and he lights up. "This is going to exceed your expectations. My hair is done and that goes over my head, so I will need you to help me dress." I place my hand on his chest and move him slowly out of my closet. "I have to change my lingerie. Give me a minute please." He nods and closes the door.

When I open it Trevor is taken aback by what he sees for I am wearing a foundation garment on my upper body that goes to my waist and a half slip. I walk toward him and he manages to ask, "What are you wearing?"

"A strapless longline bra." I slowly turn a full circle to let him see it is backless.

"I've never seen anything like that."

"One has to go *inside* a lingerie boutique to see these things."

Trevor nods just a bit. "This is what you've been wearing under that dress?"

"Mmm hm."

"When I see you in it I will never look at you the same again."

I laugh lightly as I go back in my closet, get the dress and hand it to him. My fiancé is mesmerized. "Trevor." He looks in my eyes. "I need you to focus, so you do not destroy my hair. We need to go."

"You're going to have to talk me through this."

"I know. It will be easier than you think."

"I hope so."

Trevor carefully follows my instructions and in an instant he is successful. After he pulls up the zipper I let him put the belt on for me and he says, "That is the closest to heaven I have ever been." We kiss and go next door.

Poppy is the first to compliment my dress and once again the story of the day we met is told. Thankfully is not a boring one I will never tire of hearing or telling. After we eat Trevor announces we have errands that should take the majority of the day and we will more than likely see them at the club.

We get to my car and I notice a beautifully wrapped gift in the front passenger seat. Trevor tells me, "Please do not let that slide around as I drive."

"What is it?"

"A little something for you on this special day."

"I have something for you in the trunk."

"Do I need to be concerned with it?"

"Not in the least. I've been hiding it in there for days. Normally I would have hid it in my closet." He chuckles and we leave.

Even as Trevor holds the door for me to enter the jewelry store I am still in disbelief over why we're here. It doesn't take long for us to make our decision; we both want a plain yellow gold band. Mine was easy; I wanted one the same width of the shank of my engagement ring. Trevor wanted a ring wide enough it would not look small compared to his Academy ring, but had no idea what size ring he needed. After finding out we tried on white gold bands, because we didn't want to wear ours until we are married.

Leaving there he informs me our next stop is to buy the first furniture for our house. To be specific, a bedroom suite due to a time constraint; it has to be refinished, because Trevor likes the black furnishing of my bedroom. Choosing it takes a while, but we find perfection then we look for pieces to go in front of the sitting area by the fireplace. I tell them to deliver everything to the shop that refinished mine then Trevor asks me what he needs to do. I suggest going there Monday morning before the delivery, introduce himself to the owner and throw money at him. Then we leave for our next destination, the music store.

At this point I feel as if I am just along for the ride, because he is a man on a mission today. When we walk in Trevor tells me we are there to make a wish of his come true. He only has a radio, because not much can fit in his bags and he has wanted a record player since he had to leave his behind when he went to Annapolis. My heart twinges and I tell him to get whatever he wants.

Trevor proceeds to select one that is more like a piece of furniture due to its size, then we happily walk to the record department. He goes left, I go right and we meet in the middle. The stack on the counter is so high during check-out we get tickled and he decides everything should be delivered to his apartment.

It is passed time to eat and he asks me to decide where to go. I choose Micheletto's, because I'm in the mood for dark chocolate zeppole and listening to him talk with the waiters. The best thing about late lunches is one misses the crowd and it's quieter. When he tells me we are going to spend the rest of our free time aboard Willow my eyes dance. That is going to work out in my favor.

The first thing at the marina I do when out of the car is hold out my arms and exclaim, "Willow." She really is a beauty, her hull is a bright, shiny white and when a wave gently rocks her you can see the royal blue of her keel.

While Trevor tells her hello I take my keys from him and find the one to my trunk. I hand the key to him and say, "It's time to open your present." He lights up I and follow him to the trunk. As he opens it he begins to see something he thinks belongs to me until it's wide open and he realizes what his present is, a new leather satchel that has Willow Wisp embossed in the leather. Trevor glances at me then lifts the brass tag. On it are his initials. "Geneviève — I'm at a loss."

"Now there are seven of these. This makes it official; you are a crew member of Willow Wisp."

"This means more to me than I can put into words." He holds me and softly tells me, "Thank you." I respond with a kiss.

With one last look at it he closes the trunk, gets my gift and we go up the gangway. He leads me to the galley and opens a bottle of Château Delcroix then we go into the lounge where he serves and as we drink it I try to be patient waiting for him to give me my gift.

Trevor finally bursts into laughter. "I can't make it another minute. You have the patience of a Saint." He takes my glass and hands me the gift cautioning me it is heavy. When I get the wrapping paper off I find I am holding another box from France that is larger and always has frosted crystal in it. I lift the lid and reveal a crystal ball. I gasp and lift out the beautiful sphere to hold it up into the sunlight.

After we admire it he sets the frosted crystal base for it on the table. "I do not want to take my hands off this." I look at him and set it in the stand then let it go for maybe 10 seconds before putting my hands right back on it. We get tickled and he tells me, "Perhaps I should've given this to you when we were on land."

"The timing is perfect. I love it. Thank you."

"I simply could not resist getting this for the gypsy in you."

After I give him a lingering kiss he helps me get it nestled safely back in the box then we sit quietly and sip our wine as I try to think of a way I can throw myself on him without getting disheveled and crushing this dress. Then it occurs to me and I look into Trevor's eyes. He says, "And there she is, the gypsy."

I motion to a bar stool. We walk over to the bar and I step back. Trevor smiles and takes a seat. With a lilt in my voice I say, "Your sweater please." He pulls it off and hands it to me then I step between his legs and place my hands on the bar with him between my arms. We don't have long and make every minute count.

Trevor parks my car at the service entrance and I ask him to take my gift to his apartment along with our wedding bands, give him a kiss then dash up the steps without turning to watch him walk away. Of course we are running a bit late. When I enter the kitchen Théo is there and I exclaim his name. "Gené, you are way too happy to see me. What are you going to have me do?"

"I need to change the color of my pedicure and I do not want to risk damaging my manicure."

"Gené, that whole I will do anything for you thing — you're pushin it."

"I know. You can finish protesting upstairs." He sighs as I grab his hand and drag him up the stairs.

The house is empty and I am in my room dressed and slipping on the shoes Trevor chose for me. I hear the front door open and as he ascends the staircase he says, "The Chariot is out front and there's a stranger standing by it." I burst into laughter and try to get my composer before he sees me.

He enters my room and says, "There she is."

"Trevor, will you finish that sentence out loud for me this once?"

"The woman I am going to marry."

He closes the space between us by putting his hands on my waist and we kiss a kiss that is the perfect expression of love. Next he moves a bit and says, "I knew you would be beautiful tonight, but Geneviève, you have far exceeded my expectations." I place my hand on his face and he gives me that smile then runs his hands down my arms to hold my hands and looks up and down my body. "Trevor, my sash needs to be tied" He grins and says, "I wonder why I forgot that." He places his hands lightly on my waist and I slowly turn around. As he gathers the sash I feel his warm hands brush against the skin of my back. When he finishes I stand perfectly still as he slides his hands along my back to my shoulders and this time I feel his lips on my neck. Trevor sighs as he turns me back around. He did not want the moment to end and neither did I.

To lighten things up I say, "I have to tell you this; when I walked by my mirror out here I caught a glimpse of my leg and stopped cold in my tracks. He laughs that deep laugh and says, "I knew you didn't see that view at The Salon." I shake my head adding, "I am going to have to resist the urge to tell everyone you picked this out." Then I gasp. "I was barefooted. I bet the slit in this gown looks even higher with my shoes on."

While Trevor is trying to keep it together a sudden calm washes over me. "There is something I want to show you. Slip off my shoe."

He looks at me inquisitively as he kneels. I lift my foot and Trevor takes off my shoe. "I can't believe it, Orange Taffy. I chose a dress the exact color of that polish. It must have been in my subconscious after seeing it when I purchased the Strawberry Fluff." He puts my shoe back on and stands. "I actually picked it up and when I read what the color was I remembered you had that one. And you put the two together."

"Not until last night. I am going to share something with you, but I want you to give me your word you will not repeat it."

"This is going to be good. You have my word."

"Since then I've been trying to figure out a way to change the color of my pedicure without damaging my manicure and when we got home I discovered Théo in the kitchen."

Trevor begins to laugh immediately. "How much did he protest?"

"A good bit. He actually told me I was pushing the whole he would do anything for me thing. I didn't mind though. I knew he was being playful, but you on the other hand would not even playfully protest."

"Frankly, I would've offered to paint them for you." And he caresses my face.

"We need to focus on the matter at hand."

"Yes we do, for instance kissing you one more time before we leave." And I am kissed.

Trevor watches me put on my lipstick and drop it into the handbag he chose for me. I drape the wrap over my arm and he says, "Shall we?" As we go down the stairs I tell him, "By the way, I had the dessert tonight changed to orange sorbet."

"No unsatisfied craving for me tonight. I adore you."

"I adore you. Also, the chauffeur is not a stranger. His name is Elliot. Grandpapa hires him for special occasions." Trevor opens the door and when we step outside Elliot tips his hat and says, "Good evening, Miss ... Miss Delcroix."

"Good evening, Elliot. It is nice to see you."

"Thank you, ma'am."

Trevor tells him, "I have this." Elliot nods and goes around.

I whisper, "Trevor — my dress made him stammer."

"I know. — I'm going to enjoy this evening more than I thought."

In the car we find a bottle of Cristal chilling. "I need to open that before we're on the street. Elliot, pull over please." Trevor opens the car door, steps out and uncorks it without an incident.

We arrive at 6:24 and at the curb we are able to see there are still several people milling about the lobby who did not receive invitations. They know how these things work here. A cocktail hour is held in one of the private dining halls adjacent to The Banquet Hall for guests. This begins at six o'clock and family members arrive at 6:15. Therefore they have already seen a parade that included two admirals, a captain, three commanders, three lieutenant commanders and two lieutenants.

The couple arrives shortly after family and friends who will be members of the wedding party and joins them in order to have a few minutes in private and for photographs to be taken. Next a receiving line is formed and the guest's enter The Banquet Hall.

Walking through the lobby Trevor tells me, "They are still here hoping to get a glimpse of you."

"I beg to differ; they are hoping to get a glimpse of me *and* you. Even though the females have seen that uniform they want to see you in it again." With a lilt in my voice I tell him, "And I speak from experience."

"How I do love it when you talk to me like that."

When we are almost to The Banquet Hall Trevor walks by the doors then stops and moves us beside a potted tree in the hallway. We can't kiss so what is he up to? He softly asks, "Will you give me an Eskimo Kiss?" I slightly gasp and reply, "With pleasure."

I give him my handbag; he tucks it under his arm and places his hands on my waist. I hold his neck, look into his eyes and begin to move the tip of my nose slowly along one side of his then the other. We close our eyes as I continue to move and when I feel his warm breath enter my mouth I remember the first time I breathed him in. Then I hear Trevor whisper, "I love you." And I whisper, "I love you too." I nuzzle him once more, step back slightly and open my eyes to find Trevor is already looking at me.

We stand there and savor the moment then Trevor gives me my handbag and says, "After you." And we step inside. There are a few gasps as we walk to our family and friends. I see Théo, whose eyes are sparkling as Father and Mother kiss my cheeks.

Joanna begins to laugh with pure delight. "I have been waiting anxiously to see the gown he chose. I knew it would be unlike anything I have seen you wear. Darling, you are stunning. Well done, Trevor." He is beaming as Mitch asks him, "What did you think about your first trip to a dress salon?" Trevor replies, "The ladies know how to make a man feel welcome." Mitch says, "They certainly do."

William asks Emily, "What have I been missing?" She replies, "I have no clue." Théo tells William, "I think we should find out." He responds, "I could not agree with you more." Théo looks at Rachel and she tells him, "I was planning on going there Tuesday. I will make a call first thing Monday morning." And he kisses her hand as William sighs heavily. Emily tells him, "There is not a doubt in my mind I'll need something from that place before this month ends and you will be most welcome."

William lights up and I see one of Josephs' servers emerging with our bottle of Cristal from The Chariot in a champagne bucket. He is on Joseph's heels as they go to our table. In no time Joseph is standing by me and Trevor with two glasses of the champagne on a tray. We tell him good evening and take our glasses. It is time for a toast and Théo makes it. "I have a toast inspired by Shakespeare for this occasion. The best of happiness, honor and fortunes, keep with you both." Everyone raises their glass and drinks to us.

At this point Trevor finally encounters Helen and he is astounded. Wearing an evening gown and makeup with her hair styled she is almost unrecognizable to those who do not know her well. Now he sees why she and Mother became friends. Helen did not look like she just rode up on a horse at college.

After posing for photographs Trevor asks the pianist to play Chopin's Nocturne No.8 and we are off. After we float around the dance floor and the music ends, because we are among friends and family this time when he dips me and I dramatically turn my head away from him he kisses the slope of my neck in a very sensual manner. Oh how he stirs my emotions.

While we are still lost in our world leaving the dance floor service doors open and the orchestra files in; they set up and begin to play. This means it's time to form the receiving line and have our guests who have been waiting in the next room enter The Banquet Hall. And the evening begins.

While meeting and greeting guests their reactions to my drastic change in appearance border on humorous. Club members are caught off guard. Most of them made it known by complimenting me and others by their facial expressions. When Harry introduces his companion I recognize her. She's is a co-manager of the jazz club downtown. She speaks to me and Théo when we go there, but she doesn't recognize me until I motion to him. Trevor was indeed entertained.

In the distance I see Reginald and his wife Norah. They step up, greet us in the usual manner then Norah says, "Geneviève, you are stunning." Looking at Trevor she tells him, "I love her evening gown. Commander, you have exquisite taste." Trevor swallows so hard I see his Adam's apple move just before he says, "Thank you, ma'am." She responds, "Think nothing of it." Norah turns, winks at me and they move down the line. That is going to be one of the highlights of the evening. It took everything I had not to get tickled; someone actually called him on it.

When after dinner drinks are served a flurry of activity begins. Mother secures Joseph for Claudette by asking him to check our table frequently in the presence of his servers; this way he can go to the table alone. Then we all are off to the dance floor with the exception of Claudette who is seizing the opportunity for stolen words with Joseph. Helen takes Meredith along as she circulates around The Hall introducing her to the people she calls the cream of the crop.

The first two dances are with Trevor and afterwards my dance card is instantly filled with family and friends and family members of my friends. Eventually when we are all seated taking a break Trevor announces he will be my every third dance. I was pleased to hear him say that because I was beginning to miss him.

All the men I have never had the pleasure of dancing with have enjoyable personalities on the dance floor. Rowland dances like my father I think because I am like a daughter to him already. Tobias dips me unexpectedly and due to his age he can get away with it. Spencer is light on his feet and likes to twirl his dance partners. Howard, due to years in the diplomatic services, glides a woman effortlessly across the floor. Albert is relaxed like Mitch but his head sways along with the music. I do believe living in Savannah has influenced the man.

After a nice break between dances spent sitting close to Trevor and sipping Louis XIII, William's father who likes to be called Bill, asks for the next dance. When we are on the dance floor I discover he is more interested in talking to me than dancing. He begins the conversation by saying, "I waited weeks to finally meet the woman my son speaks so highly of and I have waited four days to have a private moment with you."

I blush and he continues, "Like the gentle influence the moon has on the tides you influence the people around you. Not one person I know in this tightly knit group is the same. My son has his head up finally and is seeing the world. Then from what he has told me you have been helping him find his way with Emily, the breath of fresh air you brought into his life. And he is sailing again, the reason he fell in love with the sea, like all the Snowden men.

"For the first time I am seeing Joanna being herself, because you brought her back into the life she left behind, which has made Mitch a very happy man. And I do not have to tell you what you have done for Trevor." He pauses to twirl me.

"Then there is Théo who from what I have pieced together found his intended because of you. And last but not least the lovely wallflower is being courted by the dashing young man waiting on her hand and foot, also because of you.

"Geneviève — modesty has you in denial that all this change has been brought about through you. Keep this in mind; you had purpose the day Joanna met you. Fate had her wondering aimlessly and led her to you."

I look straight into his eyes and he slightly nods then says, "So, before you get overwhelmed, how about letting an old man take you for a spin around this dance floor?" I tell him in earnest, "Bill, you are anything but old. I was told age is in the heart and the mind. My guess is you are in your mid-forties. That *is* the age you were when you met your lovely wife?" He smiles and answers, "Yes it was." He tilts his head as he looks at me and chuckles then asks, "Shall we?" I reply, "Yes, please." And we are off. More than before, I do see why his Judith fell for him.

When the music stops I go from one admiral to another. Robert must have been watching us talk most of our dance because he steps lively and does not say a word until our dance is over. Then he gets a most unexpected glint in his eyes and dryly tells me, "Remember — if anyone asks, you never danced with me." He hands me over to Trevor and goes toward the table. Within seconds I get tickled and have to use everything in my power to keep my composure. Trevor says, "When you can manage to speak do tell. I saw that glint in his eyes."

While we dance I get myself together. "We should go outside. I need some fresh air and you should be where you can laugh out loud. I'm a bit light headed from suppressing mine." He responds, "It was that funny?" I nod and as we cross the dance floor he sees William and Emily. Trevor slows down and tells him in passing, "If we're not back in 15 minutes come outside and find us."

When we're sitting at our table by the pool I tell him what Robert said and Trevor bursts into laughter and finally so do I. After we catch our breath he says, "Geneviève, you've been on your feet all night, are you in pain?"

"My calves have been burning."

"That was not the answer I was expecting."

"Trevor, when women dance, most of the time our weight is on our toes. Théo and I learned how to dance barefooted and I was on my tippy-toes." Trevor chuckles. "My grandmother would say that to me as we took a stance. This served two purposes, it simulated the heels I would eventually be wearing that would put my weight on my toes and the other was to teach Théo to stay off a woman's feet. We had so much fun and it worked like a charm."

"That explains why you're so easy to lead and why you told me, 'You lead and I will follow.' with such confidence the first time we went to The O Club on that memorable rainy afternoon. Sometimes it feels as if you are floating on air."

I whisper, "Because I am."

While wishing I could kiss him Trevor looks to my right. "Eric is headed our way with two glasses of ice water."

"Pardon the intrusion. Joseph sent these." Eric sets them on the table and before Trevor can say thank you he vanishes.

"Joseph does take care of you and yours." Then he looks to my right again. "That time flew. It's Emily and William."

I motion to the chairs on the other side of the table. "Join us, please." Trevor glances at me. "At this point the only people who realize we're gone are the serving staff and the people at our table." Emily says, "She's right. Most of the guests have drank enough to be in a world all their own."

With that said they settle in and I tell William, "Your father, I am quite fond of him." He replies, "And he is of you. I don't know what you said to him during your dance, but he came back a changed man. The change is subtle, but he sort of reminds me of the father from my youth." Emily tells me, "You always know the right thing to say at the right time. It's remarkable." I respond, "That is sweet of you to say. Do you think everyone is enjoying the evening? The reason I ask is I have not been able to sit still long enough to make the assessment."

Trevor begins to laugh followed by them and says, "None of us have." William adds, "Why do you think we sat down without hesitating?" Emily is nodding as Trevor lights up and says, "It's Théo. He's alone and has his glass of cognac."

Théo begins to speak when close enough for us to hear him. "Mother sent me out of concern, not propriety. You *have* been on your feet all night, Gené."

"I'm fine; I simply wanted to be still a few minutes. The pace is dizzying."

Instead of reporting back Théo pulls a chair up next to mine and sits down. "Théo, are you all right?"

"I'm just exasperated. Introducing Rachel as my girlfriend 110 times was annoying. And the ring I want to give her has proved to be impossible to find." William tells him, "I know how you feel. When my father offered his grandmother's ring for me to propose to her with I felt like he pulled me out of an abyss." Théo says, "That settles it. Mr. Simmons told me they keep all their molds and sketches. I'm having a Deco ring made. I hope it doesn't take long." Trevor says, "I'll tell you what your sister told me this afternoon, throw money at him."

The weight of the world lifts from my brothers' shoulders and he smiles for just about 10 seconds because Trevor says, "Incoming. Gentlemen, on your feet." As they stand Théo asks, "Is it Mother and Helen?" He replies, "Nope — worse; it's

Rachel and Joanna." William says under his breath, "We're in for it." Emily and I smile at each other then wave at them.

Joanna says as they approach us, "Nice evening to be outside for almost 30 minutes." Jaws drop. "Mmm hm, time flies when one is avoiding guests. Ladies, we were going to powder our noses and thought perhaps you might like to join."

I respond, "Yes we would. Thank you for asking."

"Think nothing of it." Trevor and William help us from our seats as Rachel gives Théo a kiss on his cheek to let him know he's not in hot water. "Gentlemen, we will see you inside?"

They all say, "Yes, ma'am." in perfect unison. We are not able to make it inside holding our laughter.

Back in The Hall we find everyone is out on the dance floor with the exception of our men who have joined Mitch who has been kept company by Judith and Bill along with Claudette during our absence. After we are all seated Judith tells me, "This has been a lovely evening. I cannot remember the last time we enjoyed ourselves this much." I tell her, "Thank you. We are so pleased you accepted our invitation." Joanna says, "It has been memorable and it shows no signs of slowing down." Bill discretely looks at his watch. "It is 11:38. May I ask why?" Théo replies, "The club holds a banquet each month of the summer and they end when the last guests leaves. It appears it is causing some confusion." William interjects, "We need an exit strategy that will give the guests a subtle hint it's time to leave."

To our surprise Claudette is the first to speak looking at Théo. "May I suggest having Joseph and his staff begin clearing our table?" Everyone lights up and Trevor says, "I'll ask Eric to tell Elliot to bring The Chariot around. When this song ends Geneviève and I will go to the dance floor for our last dance. And while all eyes are on us when we return to the table we will say our goodbyes and leave." Judith tells Bill, "We should leave shortly after they do." Bill asks Trevor, "Would you ask Eric to have our driver be out front as well?" Trevor nods and William tells Emily, "After we watch them dance for a moment we'll join them for our last dance and when they leave we will thank their parents for the wonderful evening and make our exit." Théo adds, "Rachel and I will be on your heels."

Joanna looks at Mitch and tells him, "We should stay in the trenches with their parents." He nods in agreement and Claudette says, "I will stay as well." William says, "We have our exit strategy. Let's execute it."

It was just in time too. The music stops and here they come. When everyone is seated Théo tells Mother and Father, "We have a plan." As quickly as possible he fills them in and we watch it spread around the table. Eventually everyone is smiling and Father motions for Joseph.

Trevor stands and holds his hand out to me. "Ma ravissante fiancée, danse avec moi?" He takes my breath away and I reply, "Bien sûr, Mon Amour." Trevor kisses my hand and leads me to the dance floor. "I am going to waltz with you. I have wanted your body against mine all night and can wait no longer."

After a wonderful last dance for the evening we go to the table and say our goodbyes. Trevor drapes the wrap around my shoulders and we take our leave. The Chariot is waiting for us out front and we are on our way home.

The first thing I do is ask Trevor, "Who did you ask how to say ravishing?"

"Théo — and he told me he was stealing it."

"I find it difficult to believe he hasn't called Rachel that yet."

"Geneviève, it is a close relative of ravenous."

"And that means eager for the gratification of wants or desires. I see your point." I glace at Elliot whose eyes are on the dark road ahead and softly tell Trevor, "Your handkerchief please." As he gives it to me he whispers, "Once again, you catch me off guard." We hold each other and kiss the entire way.

Elliot drives through the gates and Trevor tells him to drive to his apartment. The Chariot is parked under these apartments, so while we go up the steps Elliot opens the garage door and puts it away.

Trevor turns on a lamp; I immediately slip off my shoes and collapse on the sofa. He takes off his jacket and opens bottles of ginger ale as he says, "Right now I'm really glad I've attended weddings of shipmates and know the bride and groom leave the reception early and it continues without them." I laugh and say, "That is the only thought keeping me sane." He gives me a kiss and hands me a bottle then sits down. Next he pulls my legs across his and begins to rub my calves.

After silently enjoying the massage a few minutes I tell Trevor, "I enjoyed meeting your shipmates tonight. They are all very nice."

"I'm glad you liked them. Do you know what an arch of swords ceremony is at the wedding of an officer?"

"It just so happens I do."

"The officers you met tonight are the swordsmen I have selected for ours."

"Oh Trevor, that's wonderful."

"I desperately wanted to surprise you, but since our wedding is going to be private I didn't want you walking up to the arbor wondering who those unexpected guests are and I'm not sure where to place them to form the arch."

Within seconds I know the solution. "I wasn't going to tell you this, because I wanted to surprise you as well. For formal outdoor weddings the bride walks on white runners to protect her bridal gown. They will begin on the portico and end where we stand under the arbor. After the wedding ceremony they can stand out from under it on opposite sides of the runner."

"That sounds perfect. — White runners. Those are going to be a nice touch. I'm sorry you had to spoil your surprise."

"Don't be. Due to the reason, I was more than happy to tell you."

We sit quietly looking at each other then I say, "The woman you are going to marry."

"I've been waiting a long time for you to ask me about that."

"I thought I knew the answer since the first time you said it was when you arrived to pick me up for our first date."

"What did you think I was saying?"

"The woman you were falling in love with. Then after you told me you loved me I thought it changed to the woman you are in love with."

"That makes sense. It wasn't the first time I said it though. You just didn't hear me." Wide-eyed I sit quietly.

"I started attending and being in weddings after I graduated from Annapolis. Eventually I began wondering how old I would be when I got married. My thoughts were when I was 25, maybe 27 at the latest. After turning 27 I began wondering, 'Where is she?' When I was about to turn 30 I started to get — concerned. Keep in mind I did know Bill."

"A man who married well into his forties."

"Mmm hm. On the day we met, when I saw you in the lobby I whispered to myself, there she is, because I knew you were the woman I was going to marry."

Trevor slides out from under my legs and stands up. He offers me his hand and asks, "Do you mind?" I reply, "Not in the least." When I get up he takes me in his arms like he does at The O Club. I rest my head on his shoulder and he begins to sway with me. Before long I sigh and so does he. Shortly after, he says "Geneviève, I think I'm rocking us to sleep." I open my eyes. "I think you are too." And he stops swaying. "It's time for me to walk you home. This has been a long day and tomorrow is going to be another one. Plus we have to get up early and go to the base for the bus before brunch." I groan then say, "I forgot about that." He gives me an incredible kiss and we walk to the house.

This time as he helps me out of my gown he merely unhooks it and lowers the zipper for me then leaves to get ready for bed. He wants me off my feet. When I am ready to get in bed I open my door and find Trevor waiting on the balcony. He happily tucks me in.

CHAPTER FIVE

In the morning I get up and put on my jeans and boots because last night while we were persuading Helen to stay and go to the park she told us all she had left in her bag was jeans and boots. Therefore she didn't want to go and as she put it 'stick out like a sore thumb'. In an act of solidarity those of us whom are young with Western attire agree to wear ours and she gave in. Of course I was ecstatic at the thought of a valid reason to wear my jeans around town.

Trevor comes in and I am already in the kitchen putting scones on plates. He is wearing his Service Khaki uniform and I look at him inquisitively. "I thought showing up at the motor pool dressed like a cowboy would be unwise."

"I see your point. Good morning, Trevor."

"Good morning, Baby. I'll get us a couple of sodas." He opens the refrigerator and chuckles. "You have to see this." I walk over and see a full sized glazed ham. "Now we know what Mother was doing yesterday while we were running errands."

"I bet there is one just like it in Joanna's." He closes the door, opens the sodas and we prop against the counter to eat our scones. When we finish eating I pick up my camera bag, he carries our drinks and we are gone.

Trevor drops me off at my bench and goes to get the bus. When I hear the bus I put the strap of my camera bag over my head and across my chest then run down into the street to photograph him as he drives up. He begins shaking his head and gives me a disapproving look for being in the middle of the street. I just smile and wave as he stops and opens the door. He says, "Geneviève, really?" I take another snapshot, get on, give him a kiss and we cut up the entire way home.

Trevor parks the bus in front of my grandparent's house and while he changes clothes I photograph it while I have the time. The odds of this being on our property again are slim to none. In no time I hear Trevor's boots on the steps and turn around. Forget the bus, new subject, my man looking so handsome walking toward me with his hat in hand. He says, "I do like the way you look in those jeans." I reply, "Likewise. How about a kiss Cowboy?" In a flash Trevor hooks me around my neck then I am dipped and definitely kissed.

When the kiss ends he fans me with his hat and my side hurts from laughing so hard. Then he asks with an American cowboy accent, "Are you all right little lady?" Still laughing I reply, "Yes. Let me up. I can't breathe." I look at him as he puts on his hat. "Just how many Westerns have you seen?"

"Every one when I'm on land. I've probably missed one this time, but that's all right because I was the leading male in one and at the end ..." In mid sentence he switches back to the American accent, "I rode my trusty steed into the sunset."

I finally pull my bandana out of my pocket and wave it in the air. "I give. Lead me to food." I tuck it in my back pocket and he puts his arm back around my neck. "Why are you wearing your hat anyway?"

"To get a reaction from Mum." I chuckle and give him a kiss.

Inside at last, I leave my camera in the foyer with a picnic basket I do not recognize and four camera bags. When we enter the dining room for brunch his mums' jaw drops and she says, "Son?" Everyone burst into laughter, including us.

After brunch Grand-mamma announces it's time to go the kitchen and we all get up carrying our dishes. There we find Claudette acting unusual. Trevor says, "Claudette is almost giddy. What have we missed?" I gasp and reply, "Joseph serves Sunday brunch and takes a half day. He returns to serve dinner. I bet he is meeting her at the park." Trevor nuzzles me as his mum breezes passed us. Then we notice three picnic baskets, mine included, are by the kitchen island as my father gets the ham Mother made out of the refrigerator. Then his mum returns with the basket that was in the foyer, takes a blanket out of it and goes to a chair where there is a stack of those.

Théo and Rachel are on the dishes, so Trevor and I bring in the chafing dishes and put away leftovers. While we did that an assembly line was formed to make sandwiches. Evelyn is slicing bread and Mother is buttering it with my father next to her at the ham with the carving knife. Meredith is by him with the wheel of cheddar. Poppy is wrapping and Hilda is packing while my grandmother and Claudette are cutting vegetables and Helen is boxing cookies.

Those of us not involved get out of the way and I get my camera. Our families are together and working as one. It looks as if they have done this before. I stop by Trevor, get a kiss then continue taking the occasional snapshot.

With everything almost packed Trevor tells everyone, "We need to go get something and will be back in a minute." He grabs my hand and heads to the solarium. "We need your blanket. Can you run in those boots?" I raise my eyebrows. "Forget I asked." And here we go.

At my car Trevor lets go of my hand and runs inside to get my keys. When he comes out I ask, "Why are we running?" He opens the trunk and replies, "So I can do this." Trevor reenacts our first kiss and as I stand there speechless he gets the blanket, tosses the keys on a car seat and we run back to find men are already carrying baskets out into the hallway and women have blankets. I grab my camera bag and we make our way to the front of the line. Trevor opens the front doors and we go out first as everyone gets the rest of their things. Trevor and I dash to the bus; he sits in the driver's seat and I begin taking snapshots as they get on.

Finally I sit behind Trevor and he closes the bus's door. When he starts the engine his mum asks, "Son, do you have a license to drive this?" Trevor chuckles. "Mum, the Navy wouldn't have let me reserve it without one." And a light bulb went on over her head. Next stop, the Mitchell's.

As Trevor drives by the house to turn the bus around I see draperies move. He parks so the door to the bus is lined up with the sidewalk and opens it. I get out taking snapshots of Joanna then Mitch, who is carrying a large picnic basket and their parents, who have more blankets.

Next we go around the corner to the Prescott's and only Emily and William are waiting on the patio. When they get close I take a snapshot and ask Emily where her family is. With so much going on she forgot to tell me Bobby's team is playing an important baseball game today and they went to watch.

Thankfully we have only one more stop to make which is to pick up Bill and Judith. William tells Trevor the way and he parks aligned with the sidewalk to the very nice house they're staying in. I get out there too and they don't seem to mind one bit being photographed as I greet them.

I get on the bus and take a final snapshot of all our passengers. While I do, Bill says, "I cannot remember the last time I was on a personnel carrier." Joanna says, "Bill, this isn't a personnel carrier, it's a touring bus." I glance at Bill as she turns around beaming. I look at Trevor and there goes that deep laugh. The ones who know what has happened are all smiles while the rest of our passengers look puzzled. I was prepared for this in one way and in another I was not. Théo is going to be beside himself.

As I put my camera away my mind is reeling. I am at a loss until I realize they are family and friends old and new who gathered here to celebrate our engagement and I'm going to give them something to remember as a token of my appreciation.

I take a deep breath and say, "Good morning everyone. First we would like to thank you for choosing San Diego Tour Lines. My name is Miss Jenna and I am going to be your tour guide today. This is our driver, Tex." Trevor tips his hat grinning. "Before we get under way I would like to take this opportunity to ask all passengers to please refrain from distracting the driver in any way for my safety and yours." After the laughter I resume my speech. "Our destination is Balboa Park. If you have boarded this bus by mistake please raise your hand."

After scanning our amused passengers who are steadily taking snapshots I tell Trevor, "Tex, we are ready to proceed." He takes off his hat and I hold on to the pole as he slowly pulls away from the curb. "Our tour is starting at the US Destroyer Base, San Diego established in 1922 and is homeport to the pride of the Navy's Pacific fleet, the aircraft carrier USS Louisiana." Immediately our passengers become enthusiastic, as well as Trevor.

On our way to the park I stop being a tour guide and point out places for our guests who have not been here and answer their questions. When we are close to the park I turn into the guide again and tell them how large the park is and about some of the main attractions, but the most important thing, I explain how to play the brass ring game and win prizes.

When we reach the field that has several shade trees close to the carousel where we are going to have our picnic Trevor pulls over to the curb and stops the bus. I announce, "We have safely reached our destination. Once again we thank you for choosing San Diego Tour Lines. We hope you ride with us again." They give me a standing ovation and I curtsy in jeans and boots.

We all unload the bus then Trevor asks me to go with as he finds the parking area for buses. The second we are out of sight he pulls me onto his lap and I ride there. I discover the steering wheel is larger than it looks sitting at it and realize it requires more skill to drive the bus than I thought. After he parks I tell him, "I am impressed with how well you handle this thing. I think you deserve a reward. Would you like a really good cookie?" Trevor laughs and goes, "Mmm tempting, but I would like a really good kiss instead." I reply, "Help yourself." And he does.

While we were gone everyone was busy putting down blankets overlapping them to form one large patchwork blanket for us to mill around on and arranging picnic baskets. Someone went to the concession stand and bought sodas, therefore we're ready to go. When Trevor and I are in front of the group he shouts, "To the carousel." and we lead the way holding hands.

Trevor and I walk up to the ticket booth and wave at Charlie. He tells Beatrice "27 tickets please." This is over half of the capacity of 52, so her mouth is open as she picks up a pencil to do the math and says, "That will be $7.00 please." Trevor pays her, she hands him a streamer of tickets then he gives them to me.

I wave the tickets in the air, we all go to gate and I say, "Hello, Charlie." He tips his hat and his eyes are wide. "Hello, Miss Delcroix. I see you've brought a few more people with you this time." I smile and say, "Our engagement party was last night and this is our close friends and family." Then I elevate my voice as I say, "Everyone this is Charlie, he owns and operates this fabulous carousel. Charlie, this is everyone." They wave and I give him the streamer of tickets.

Thankfully only a few other people are here, because suddenly things get serious for those who are going for the bass ring as they choose an animal to ride on the outside circle. Trevor rides a horse on the inside next to mine and tells me, "I think this is going to become competitive." Emily who is behind me says, "Yes it is. I want a Teddy Bear." I hear William clear his throat as I hand Trevor my camera. "Take only two snapshots please. I want to save my film for the toss box." I get a thumbs up.

Round and round we go and Trevor is holding two iron rings for me because I decide to take one every time I pass the dispensing arm to help get the brass ring down. Then finally from the other side I hear, "I have it." It was a man's voice, but I couldn't tell who's over the organ music. I look at Trevor and he shrugs his shoulders then William tells us, "That was my father. I bet Mother is ecstatic."

The prizes today are pennies and marbles. 26 people have to take their turn at the toss box and everyone watches each person toss their rings. I photograph them all and then Trevor photographs me while Judith waits patiently to choose the bear she wants. When the last ring is tossed our group goes to the ticket booth led by Bill and his happy wife who chooses a darling black one with a red bow.

By the time we're done it's time for lunch and as soon as we're all settled on the blankets Joseph appears. To top it off he is holding a white bear with a pink bow. Claudette jumps up and gives him a hug. He must have talked Beatrice into selling it to him. How thoughtful and sweet is that?

Trevor and I sit with his family and after savoring the picnic I ask Poppy, "How did Trevor wind up calling you Pops and Poppy?" Trevor lowers his head as Poppy squeezes my hand and replies, "I am so glad you asked. There is a soda pop shoppe near the university the student's frequent and they call the owner Pops. Being stereotypical grandparent's we started taking Trevor when he could walk and one day out of the blue he started calling Spencer Pops and me Poppy. Trevor must have thought it sounded similar to Penelope and that was that."

While Poppy waxes rhapsodic about her grandson several minutes Trevor finally says, "If I may, I would like to motion for a change in subject." Hilda tells him, "Motion denied." We all burst into laughter and even he chuckles. At this point I realize we are surrounded by legal minds. Hilda's husband Tobias is a barrister and her son Rowland is an attorney who is married to Evelyn that just so happens to be sitting next to her father, Spencer, the law professor who taught her husband. In the future when we need legal advice we can simply call a member of Trevor's family.

Hilda, after giving Trevor a look tells him, "Your lovely fiancée is enjoying this immensely. In fact I have a few stories of my own to tell her." Trevor, who was propped up on his side, groans, closes his eyes and rolls onto his back. I put my hand on his chest as he lies there in exasperation. His grandmother's are teaming up on him and I am so happy. He places his hand over mine as Poppy says, "I yield the floor the floor to Hilda." who replies, "Thank you." and looks at me.

"This is my favorite one." Trevor opens his eyes wide for about two seconds, closes them and sighs heavily. This is going to be good. "Tobias and I took Trevor to the zoo in D.C. when he was two years old and we discovered he had learned several animal sounds; for instance the sheep goes baah and the tiger goes grrrr. When we reach the lions he says, "The lion goes roar." Then he whirls around to face us holding his little hands up as if they are paws with claws extended and tells us, "I am a lion. ROAAAR." and he slashes his paws through the air at us. We pretend to be frightened and desperately try not to get tickled, because it was the most adorable thing we had ever seen."

My hand goes over my heart and I gush, "Oh my gosh, that is the cutest story I have ever heard." I sigh and everyone is nodding. Then Spencer tells us, "I have one." Trevor props up and exclaims, "Pops, you too?" His mum tells him in a very motherly tone, "Son, I find it is best to get these things over with in one fell swoop." And the stories continue.

Eventually William and Emily stand up and he announces, "I am on a mission. Would anyone care to join?" All the young adults get up and go ride the carousel as the Mitchell's and the Moore's join us. Trevor is handling this well, because the stories are rather embarrassing, but they do reveal how thoughtful he has been his entire life.

The rest of our group returns after what I believe was three rides on the carousel. Rachel is holding a cream colored bear and Théo is beaming. Obviously he grabbed the brass ring. William drops a handful of marbles on their blanket. "One more ride and we will enough for a game of marbles." Emily is being a good sport about not having the prize she wants and it's on the two month anniversary of meeting William.

Whispering to Trevor I ask, "Do you remember what's behind the candy counter?" Wheels begin to turn and he says, "Teddy Bears, nice ones with bags of candy tied to their wrists. I'm up." He helps me up and I go put my arm around Emily's waist. "I think you need an ice cream cone." She nods and seconds later everyone is on their feet and following us to The Confectioners. As 29 people file in two by two the teen aged boys wearing white shirts and aprons with red bow ties stand perfectly still. The ponytailed girls at the candy counter smile and welcome us. Next we hear a high pitched, "William!" Emily has spotted the bears.

After Emily introduces us to Benjamin Bear, who has brown fur, a plaid bow tie and a bag of chocolates we decide to stay inside and eat our ice cream. This works out perfectly, because the man who operates the taffy pull machine starts it up. Only my family knows when the taffy is ready he will wrap fresh warm pieces of it and throw them into the crowd. He is making the strawberry taffy; it is the sweetest, therefore I am thrilled.

Howard catches the first piece and gives it to Lorraine. When she announces it's warm things turn slightly aggressive. Luckily the taffy man recognizes me and I easily catch a piece. Trevor has never had fresh taffy and I give it to him. Théo was watching me and his jaw drops. I ignore him and when I look at Trevor he is pulling it apart then he gives me the big half, thus I give him a kiss on the cheek.

With pockets full of taffy and Penny Candy we walk back to the carousel. There are hardly any people in line, so we seize the opportunity to basically have it to ourselves and ride it twice in a row. Odds are now in our favor someone among us will get the brass ring each time.

My grandfather hands me the longest streamer of tickets I ever seen, because he bought them for both rides. There are 58 tickets in my hand and when I give them to Charlie he doesn't bother counting them and motions us all through as he unhooks the chain. I ask him if he would take a few snapshots of three generations on his carousel. He simply smiles and reaches for my camera. When the rides are over Sandra and Helen walk away with bears. Helen tells us hers is going to be in the seat next to her on the train to keep strangers away.

When Joseph announces he has to return to the club we all get quiet, because we know we should be leaving too. Trevor goes to get the bus as everyone scrambles to fold blankets and throw things into the picnic baskets. We are waiting by the curb when he pulls up with the doors open and then he holds his hand out to me. When I get on the bus there is a big black Teddy Bear wearing an orange satin bow sitting in my seat. I ask, "Is orange taffy in that bag?" He nods and I throw my arms around his neck. Everyone gets on the bus and pretends we're not there. On the way to the base I ride in the seat behind his with my hand on his shoulder holding the bear that is a testament to the fact he can run like the wind, he had to in order to get him for me.

After stopping at the Mitchell's we proceed to the Snowden's and discover several boys riding on the side walk. Trevor slows to a roll and Emily yells out the window, "Bobby, who won?" At the exact same time they all raise their fists into the air and shout, "We did." She tells them, "Congratulations." Bobby waves and calls out, "We're going for ice cream." And they pick up speed. I ask, "Why is everyone so excited?" Emily answers, "They just advanced to the World Championship game. There are so many boys on the base there are four teams. They have a play off and the two teams left go to the World Championship and it is called that because the boys are from all over the world."

"That is too clever." And it hits me, "I've heard about this, the game is played on the field at the community center." William says, "Yes it is and the game is Saturday. We hope to see you there." I look at Trevor and he tells them, "We wouldn't miss it." Emily is beaming as I step close to Trevor and tell him, "Now I know what we'll be doing on the afternoon before our wedding rehearsal." Trevor is catching flies until I wink at him and he continues to where the Snowden's are staying. William and Emily get out there.

At Maison we all unload the bus and tell Helen we will see her soon and my father takes her to the train station. With my bear in my arms I ask Trevor to meet me in my room after he gets ready, because I'm going to need him. He gives me a kiss and I dash upstairs.

The only thing I am wearing is my kimono robe over my tap pants when Trevor walks in my room. The silk is thin enough that the details of my breast are visible. He slows down and lays his jacket on the bench. "That you allow me here when you are in a robe or your slip, I see it as a privilege. I do love you." With those words I put my arms around him and we kiss.

When I loosen my hold he chuckles. "You taste like orange taffy."

"You gave me candy."

"And of course you ate it."

"I thought about it while showering, so I ate a piece while I dried off." His face goes straight. "What is it?" He shakes his head and replies, "In a split second I had an involuntary visual of you walking in here dripping wet with a towel wrapped around you and had to stop it before it went any further." I cover my mouth as he sighs and asks, "What am I supposed to be doing?" I take my hand down and tell him, "Looking for a dress Emily hasn't seen." Trevor smiles and goes into my closet as I get out a pair of stockings and sit on the bench.

It doesn't take him long for I have just started putting on the other stocking. I glance up as he stops in mid-step for a moment then comes a little closer. "I haven't seen you put on stockings." With that in mind I move slowly for him and finish putting it on. "I'm getting a glimpse into a woman's world and I've seen enough to know I am going to be fascinated after we're married." The look on his face is so sincere that I stand up and caress it then look at the dress on the hanger he is holding.

Trevor focuses. "I want to see you in this again because of the memories it brings to mind. You were wearing this when your father gave me permission to ask for your hand in marriage and I got you in a swing."

"Yes you did." He gives me a kiss as I take it and go into my closet. When I come out I let him zip the dress and look at me a moment then I turn around, pick up his jacket and hold it out. The ribbons on his chest make Trevor more handsome than when he walked in. I continue to admire him as we go to the driveway. When the families are gathered, everyone gets in cars together and we lead the way to The O Club even though they know how to get there.

The private dining room looks completely different; flowers and candelabra's are everywhere and covers of pastel floral cotton are on the chairs. Emily looks radiant and so poised with William by her side. I wished for my camera, but Kyle was doing a good job staying in corners taking photographs of the very happy couple and their guests.

The best thing about the entire evening is that instead of hiring musicians to play during dinner and for the dancing after it, Emily and William rented a jukebox. To top it off, the clever pair had little drawstring bags filled with nickels at each place setting. The evening was perfect and so much fun. Mitch played a couple of Big Band records so he and Joanna could join in this time and do our version of Swing Dancing. Rachel was thrilled that on the second one Théo jumped in. We would've danced the night away had it not been a Sunday evening.

While we are leaving Emily whispers to me she and William are going to stay after everyone is gone. I could see them slow dancing through the sheer draperies as we pass by. Romance, I adore romance.

Trevor stops at the guest house to drop off Meredith and his parents then goes to the apartment. He turns on the radio and pours us a cognac to share. Looking at the box with my gift in it I say, "Trevor, I would like to keep my crystal ball here because I spend more time here than in my room. Is that all right?"

"Of course. Geneviève, you don't have to ask me things like that." I kiss him and we carefully get it out and set in on the dining table. Next he lights two candles and sets them near the crystal ball then turns off all the lights and we dance. When another song begins to play Trevor softly says, "Geneviève — the smartest thing we've done is deciding to get married on a Sunday. We're going to be able to leave by nine o'clock to be considerate of our guests."

"Etiquette is on our side for once. I cannot tell you how happy that makes me." He goes, "Mmm hm." And we sway until it's time to walk me home.

Our wedding bands have been on the coffee table with the boxes open, so before we leave I close the box his is in and as I take it I tell him, "This is going on my nightstand." I clutch in my hand and we leave.

When Trevor is tucking me in he picks up my bear from the chair. "There are gifts you should receive during a courtship. Ours was cut short, but it's never too late. I bought him because I thought maybe you would cuddle with him in your bed until I can take his place." I caress his face then Trevor gives him to me and I hold my bear as he covers us up.

"You haven't asked his name yet."

"I wasn't sure he had one."

"I named him while hugging you after you gave him to me."

"That didn't take long."

"Because it required no thought; his name is Christopher."

Trevor looks at me with pure adoration and we kiss. Then he tells me good night and I fall asleep holding a Teddy Bear, something I have not done in years.

The morning briefing mainly concerns Théo and Rachel. After working maybe two hours he is taking the rest of the day off, because he is going to the jewelers to select the engagement ring, so they can get started on that. Rachel has taken the week off while her parents are here. She is picking them up this morning from the airport and cooking lunch at her place, which is where Théo will meet them. We're meeting them over dinner at the restaurant in the hotel they're staying in.

With that out of the way things become comical when Trevor asks, "Geneviève — would you mind if I took you to work on the bus?" When I ask, "What?" in a high pitch, they all begin to laugh and so do I after I recover from the shock. Then I reply, "Emily's going to wish she had her camera." Théo says, "What a photo op, you getting off a bus at work. Is Emily's number on the note pad by the phone?"

"You have been having several laughs at my expense."

"Which reminds me; I thoroughly enjoyed you being our tour guide."

"Oh — you did? I wasn't sure since you got off the bus without giving me a tip."

"Clearly an oversight on my part."

He gets his wallet out, hands me a five dollar bill that I happily take and says, "I am leaving while I still have money to buy flowers for my future wife and mother-in-law. Mother, thank you for breakfast, I will see you all at dinner." And out the door he goes. We are on his heels.

When Trevor and I get on the bus he tells me, "Miss — the bus fare." Laughing I ask, "How much is it?' He says, "For you, a kiss." And I give him the bus fare.

On the base Trevor makes the block and in the distance I see William and Emily near the curb and she has her camera. Trevor says, "That is a coincidence."

"Théo is not going to believe this. I don't and I'm seeing it." Next I stand up to get ready to be photographed arriving at work on a bus driven by my fiancé.

Emily and William wave as Trevor stops and opens the door. She takes a few snapshots as William tells me, "Emily called it. She told me you would let him bring you to work on this bus." Emily is beaming as she steps back. I give Trevor a kiss then step down out of the bus with Williams' assistance and we wave as he drives off. After that, the day returns to normal. He picks me up in his car for lunch with the crew and their families at The O Club.

Back at Maison while Trevor helps me dress for dinner to meet Rachel's parents he asks, "Where are we going?"

"Downtown to The Brava."

"That sounds posh."

I smile because he hasn't said that word yet and reply, "It is."

On the way to the hotel I cannot get past the fact we have abandoned our house guests for the evening, but they assured us it was fine and not to give it another thought.

The Janssen's, Elise and Hugo have an excellent sense of humor and are a nice looking couple. This is no surprise when one takes into consideration they do have a gorgeous daughter. And they are thrilled with her choice for a husband.

Fortunately the evening was short by our standards and we were all on our way back to Maison by 9:30. When Trevor and I get there, his mum and Meredith are on the balcony. I ask him, "Do you think they would mind if we joined them?" He replies, "Of course not, but to be polite I'll ask." He stops the car and steps out.

"Ladies, may we join you for a bit?" Meredith answers, "Only if you make us your hot cocoa?" I get tickled and he tells her, "Deal."

When I get out of the car Trevor goes to the trunk with me following him out of curiosity and after he opens I see four Teddy Bears. He tells me, "Three grown men ran an errand today." I laugh as he selects one for Meredith that matches the one his mum has, but it is a little darker. Evidently he too talked Beatrice into selling him one. Trevor hides it behind his back and when he is standing in front of her he holds him out. Meredith gasps, takes the bear and stands to hug Trevor as she gushes how thoughtful he is then he goes inside to make the hot cocoa.

After a bit of small talk about meeting the Janssen's, Trevor comes out with a tray of mugs filled with another reason I am marrying him. When he gets settled I tell Meredith, "I have to ask, what is the story regarding the bell?" Evelyn lights up and she replies, "I was the first born and Mother was a nervous new mom. Soon after I started walking, one day while Mother was washing dishes I decided to go upstairs. By the time Mother realized I wasn't in the kitchen and found me, I was halfway up the staircase.

"That afternoon we went to the jewelers. She had a pin made with a sterling silver bell and belled me like I was a cat." I laugh and say, "Oh how delightful — and intelligent." She nods and adds, "Mother told me when I got older she took it off and that did not go over well. Apparently I liked the sound of it and have been wearing it ever since. Evelyn was born three years later and since we were always together Mother didn't bell her."

The setting was perfect for telling that story. There they sat together holding Teddy Bears and drinking hot cocoa like little girls. Trevor was so happy I could see his eyes sparkling in the dim lighting. These women are wonderful and I'm glad I helped make it possible for them to be together for him.

A bit later Trevor tells us he needs to take care of something in the apartment and insists I stay and join him later which I happily do. We talk about him and I answer questions to fill in blank spots for Meredith about our courtship. Then I ask about the trousers they wore to the picnic. I find that San Diego shops are woefully behind the times. Evelyn promises to get my sizes and send me a few things from New York City. The train ride is two hours from New Haven.

Due to the combination of the hot cocoa and cozy robes they are wearing they begin to get sleepy, so I tell them good night. At the bottom step I sit down and take of my shoes and stockings to feel the cool cobblestones on my bare feet as I stroll to Trevor's and reminisce on the day's events.

The first thing I notice in his apartment is the record player has been delivered and he is on the sofa opening records drinking more hot cocoa he just made. How I do want to kiss him, so I push him back and lie across him. He taste like cocoa and it takes me back to the first time we went parking for so long we couldn't see out the car windows.

The time flew and I need to leave. As I get up Trevor says, "I was going to dance with you tonight, but this was better." I say, "Much." and pick up my shoes then tell him, "It is late; therefore I am going to walk home with you happily watching me, shower and curl up with Christopher." He gives me a goodnight kiss and off I go.

I wave to him before going in the house, go upstairs and am thrilled to see Théo's light is still on and the door is slightly open. I knock lightly and he opens it with his face lit up. I go in and sit on his chair as he sits on the ottoman and begins telling me how everything went with Rachel's parents, which was smooth as silk. Not to mention they went on and on about the family and Trevor.

He has selected her ring; the center stone is going to be a 2.5 carat Chatham cut, framed with brilliant cut diamonds set in platinum with scroll work under the center stone. Théo is beaming as he describes it in detail and I can see it in my mind. Last but not least he tells me he has put his name on the waitlist for the penthouse apartment where she lives, even though he has not seen it, there is no reason to. The rooftop is part of it.

As we sit and talk I am thrilled we are having a late night chat. I miss these moments. When all was said between us, Théo being the gentleman he is, escorts me to my door, hugs me and kisses my forehead. I was on Cloud 9 as I curled up with Christopher and fell asleep.

I wake up still holding Christopher which starts my day with a smile, but getting dressed I feel lonely, because Trevor isn't here. It's odd how quickly one can get used to something.

When I get on the balcony I see Trevor is in the foyer waiting on me holding a gray Teddy Bear with a pink bow and a bag of strawberry taffy. We tell each other good morning and kiss before going into the kitchen. After saying good morning to my family, without wasting a second he goes to Mother and holds out the bear. She is struck silent as she takes it from him and looks at it, so Trevor tells her, "My mum walked through the airport gate holding Diego near a little girl holding her bear. Later it occurred to me women have a part of them that will always be a girl just like men can be boys. Consequently I decided to give all the women who are dear to me a bear." I hand Trevor his cup of coffee and Mother who is holding the bear in her lap finally speaks, "Thank you, Trevor." He nods and we sit down for the morning briefing.

The work day is over and I am sitting at the club where our group has gathered for dinner before the migration back to the East Coast watching Trevor give a bear to Poppy and Hilda while Mitch gives one to his mother and Joanna's mother. During dessert Trevor quietly tells me, "The next time we're all together, you and I will be days from becoming husband and wife." I gasp quietly at the thought.

On the way to the airport in a caravan as usual, Trevor mentions he should have kept the bus, because there are three cars following us. While we all sit in the atrium waiting on flights to be called I become upset, because I do not have my camera. Before me are several dignified women sipping coffee, holding Teddy Bears and acting as if it's normal. Lorraine stands out the most for she is wearing a navy blue Parisian suit with matinee and opera length stands of pearls. Like mother, like daughter.

One by one their flights are called and the crew is all that remains. We unanimously vote to have lunch at Sam's tomorrow, because we are tired of The O Club then get up to leave. Joanna is downhearted as she walks next to me, so I ask her to describe her bear and she lights up like a candle. The thing bothering me is I have to follow Trevor in my father's car. I want to ride with him and for a brief moment I actually miss the bus.

Trevor pulls up behind me at the house and gets out with his car running. He walks to me and says, "I'm going to pack an overnight bag for now. I miss my big comfy bed." He gives me a kiss and gets back in his car. When he drives away I run up the steps into the house. Trevor is moving back in.

Wearing only my nightgown I sit at my vanity brushing my hair with the door open waiting for him. I hear his footsteps getting closer then the words I long for, "There she is." When Trevor is by my side he kneels and puts his arms around my waist then whispers, "I have missed you, Geneviève." I lay down my brush and tell him, "I have missed you too." and wrap my arms around his neck.

When Trevor stands he picks up my brush and begins brushing my hair. "I've been watching you braid your hair for quite some time. May I try?"

"Yes, you may."

Watching him in the mirror I see he is focused and determined to do this right. It takes him a while, but he finally reaches for the elastic band to secure the end and steps back. He begins to smile and runs his hand down my braid then gives me my mirror and turns me around in order for me to see it. I gush, "Trevor, you braided my hair."

"Yes I did. I have wanted to do that for a long time. It's a bit loose at the top, but with practice I will perfect it."

"I have no doubt."

"Did I earn a kiss?" I give him the kind of kiss he earned, a passionate one.

Afterward he slowly leads me to my bed. I sit on the edge and he gathers my gown as always and lifts my legs then he picks up Christopher and gives him to me. We are tucked in and Trevor sits in the chair. Quietly he says, "Tomorrow is a monumental day for us. The transition of the guest house into our house begins."

"I wish I could be here. Will you take a few photographs of Mother packing and the movers taking the furniture down to the garage for me?"

"I can't believe I didn't think of that."

"Oh, this is important; I would love ones of Théo working. Is there anything else I haven't thought of?"

"Geneviève, if I see anything good I will photograph it."

"Thank you."

Trevor tilts his head. "You look comfortable holding him."

"He's soft." I nuzzle Christopher and Trevor kneels beside my bed, lies across me and the bear and kisses me more than good night. And then he is gone.

The next morning I wake up holding my bear and say, "Good morning, Christopher." I sit him in the chair, then stop and ask myself, "Did I really just talk to him?" I shake it off and get dressed. When I open my door I see Trevor's is open. Luckily he's still in his room unpacking. When I go in he stops and spins me around as he says, "Good morning." Next he begins kissing my neck and I whisper, "If you persist I will reciprocate and skip breakfast." He stops and looks at me. "You would wouldn't you." I go, "Mmm hmm."

The next thing I know I am being led to the kitchen. When the subject of preparations for the remodel are being gone over Mother asks Théo if building materials should be part of the Janssen's first impression of our property. After all, they *are* coming here for dinner tonight. He announces he needs to make a few phone calls and excuses himself. While he does that we finish eating and Trevor takes me to work.

During lunch all Trevor tells me is that seeing is believing concerning what is going on at Maison. After I get off work and we drive through the gates it looks like nothing happened. Trevor parks by the house and tells me to wait by the car. He goes inside and returns with cola's then starts leading me around for the second time today.

The first place we go is inside the guest house to the kitchen. "This is where I found out where Claudette and Joseph went on their date yesterday as we packed; we being me, the heavy box lifter, your mother, your grandmother and Claudette. They went to the zoo, a place I have yet to visit."

"We can put a trip to the zoo on our honeymoon places to visit list. Saturday we need to choose a china pattern and other things for our Wedding Registry. Plus looking for more furniture to fill this place that is going to grow over the next three weeks would be good."

Trevor is catching flies as he would put it then he says, "Moving on." Out onto the balcony we go that has nothing on it, not even a plant and then down to the garage. He presses all the door buttons and we stand back. Soon I see it is filled with construction materials. "Where is the furniture?" He replies, "On the second floor of the Master Building Company." Now I'm catching flies. "It gets better. I believe your mother was standing in this very spot talking to your grandmother when a plan was hatched. Follow me please."

We start walking to the apartments by the house and he opens a door to the one on the right. Everything that was in Trevor's apartment by my grandparent's house is inside. "Your mother thought I should be here when I can't stay in my room and had the movers swing into action. I was about to tell her it wasn't necessary and she spoke first, telling me it's our place for privacy and should be closer to this house. She liked the record player by the way."

I collect my thoughts and tell him, "This is a pleasant surprise. The only problem I have is this one mirrors the other. I was used to it to say the least." He adds, "I know, the kitchen is on the right side and the bathroom is on the left. I hope I don't wake up in the middle of the night and ... never mind." I get tickled and when I realize he's embarrassed I quickly say, "When Mother gets an idea in her head there is no stopping her. He goes, "Mmm hm, just like another woman I know." He kisses me and asks, "What I am wearing to dinner?"

"Whatever you wish. I am wearing a simple dinner dress." And there goes the glint. "Yes, I am going to change clothes and you may choose what I wear, but I should dress myself tonight." He is genuinely disappointed as we go to the house.

Trevor is all smiles when he comes out of my closet. He hands me a dress with a zipper and hook in the back. "You did that on purpose." He responds, "Guilty as charged, but I do fancy it. I'm going to change into clean clothes and return momentarily to fasten your dress." And he is gone.

I don't even bother closing my door and slip on my dress. I go to my jewelry armoire and am looking at earrings when he returns. As I stand there he kisses my neck softly and zips the dress. "May I choose your jewelry? I've not had the opportunity to look through this." I step back and he goes through every section then chooses the pearls I wear most often. Next he pulls out my princess strand of pearls and puts them on me, followed by the matching bracelet and ring.

As he leads me to the mirror to admire his choices we hear Théo's car door close. Trevor has us half way down the staircase before we hear the other one close. We make it to the drawing room with seconds to spare and the evening begins.

Before dinner we walk the grounds with Rachel's parents drinking our apéritif. Théo even tells them about the changes he is making to the guest house and how little time he has to pull it off. I know workers will begin tearing the place apart tomorrow and it will be done with time to spare weather permitting.

Throughout the evening we discover Rachel and her parent's interact similar to us and the dinner went off without a hitch. When Théo is getting ready to leave and take our guests to their hotel he tells me not to wait up. This is not a disappointment for I am tired. Trevor senses this and leads me to my vanity bench and seats me. I feel like a woman with a hand maiden, because he carefully takes off my jewelry and puts it away then unzips my dress and leaves for me to shower.

After he tucks me in we realize we can have lunch alone tomorrow for the first time in over a week. We are going to sit on my bench eating food from Mandarin Garden's. With this thought lingering in my mind I fall into a deep sleep.

During work, all morning I find it difficult to focus and coffee is not helping. Five minutes before noon I start covering my typewriter and slowly shut down my desk. Emily noticed I was lethargic and tells me while we walk down the corridor she feels the same way, because we just went through a marathon. I remind her mine has not ended due to Rachel's parents. She hugs me outside and goes to the parking lot as I go straight to Trevor. I kiss his cheeks then we sit quietly and feed each other with chopsticks. After we eat our almond cookies Trevor puts his arm around my shoulder and we drink our ginger ale's listening to the leaves being blown by a breeze.

Suddenly I shatter the silence, "I know how to get the direct dial phone system for the base." Trevor laughs and says, "That is out of the clear blue. I'm listening."

"My father and *The San Diego Times* editor can meet with the CEO of the telephone company and explain this is a matter of national security that cannot wait. Also the country needs it companies to step up to the plate. Mr. Cooper will seal the deal by promising coverage of every move they make; announcing the donation to the base on the front page with a photograph of the men involved, the ground breaking and everything in between up to completion."

"Geneviève, you deserve a reward." Before anything else could be said we hear footsteps approaching and soon Emily and William are standing in front of us. Obviously lunch is over.

On the way home Trevor tells me he watched Théo work today and I am envious. He sat on the balcony at his apartment and watched him instruct the workers as they demolished the guest house and when I see it, demolished was accurate. The overlook is missing along with the entire roof. Trevor took snapshots the entire time the men worked. When this is finished I believe we are going to have an excellent photo essay.

There is no time to linger because Rachel is cooking dinner for us all at her apartment and I am excited to see it. While Théo was home from college one summer we went inside the building to look around the lobby. Théo dropped our name and told the doorman he was going to be an architect, so we were allowed to go up in the elevators and roam the corridors. We couldn't go to the penthouse floor; a key was required to access it. More than likely the elevator doors open to a foyer. I will find out one day.

My father drives us there and because Rachel gave us a parking pass we don't have to park on the street. I'm the only person who has been here; therefore everyone is going to be pleasantly surprised as we make our way to Rachel's apartment. Inside it is just as I had envisioned; the view from the balcony is spectacular and I want to stay. Following a delicious meal we have our after dinner drink on it and leave soon after. We all are still tired.

After Trevor tucks me in we make our plans for tomorrow that is thankfully Friday. Joanna is cooking lunch then having Happy Hour. Théo got us out of eating with Elise and Hugo, so after Happy Hour we are going to the market and buy things to cook dinner together for the first time. The thought of being alone all night has us filled with anticipation. I am certain I fell asleep smiling.

The morning briefing has wonderful news from Théo. He wound up alone on the balcony with Hugo while Rachel and her mother cleared the table. He seized the opportunity and asked for permission to marry his daughter. Of course the man gave it to him and now it just a matter of time before Théo can introduce Rachel as his fiancée.

I'm on Cloud 9 all day until it's time to leave work for Happy Hour. Trevor and William greet us with big smiles and as Trevor and I walk to the car I ask, "What on earth has happened?"

"How do you know something's up?"

"Your smiles may have fooled Emily, but your eyes gave you away. Please answer my question."

"There's an article in *The Halyard* that is going to upset Emily."

He opens the car door; I get in and pick it up. The caption reads, Hollywood Is Coming To The Luce! And it is so true. The list of movie stars is staggering. They are performing a charity show to benefit the San Diego Naval Aid Society at the Luce Auditorium. What makes this bad news is they are going to be here for two nights beginning on Saturday, October 18th; the night Emily and William are getting married.

While I absorb this news Trevor parks the car and we go inside. Joanna greets us at the door with a martini and a whiskey on the rocks. Mitch says, "Can you believe this?" Trevor and I shake our heads as Joanna sets drinks in front of two empty chairs. Then we sit silently waiting on the other shoe to drop.

There is only one olive remaining on my pick when the door opens. Emily sighs, sees the martini, sits down, removes the olives and proceeds to drink a third of it. William doesn't sip his sipping whiskey and asks, "Has anyone come up with any ideas yet?" We all look at other and Joanna dryly says, "Personally I would not even consider changing my wedding date simply because Hollywood is coming to town." Emily chuckles and so do we, which breaks the tension.

Joanna tops off Emily's martini and I say, "The curtain goes up at 8 p.m. and will drop in the wee hours. You and William will leave the reception around 10 o'clock, no one will leave before then and if people want to see the show they can still go." Emily replies, "That's true, but they will be keeping an eye on their watches." Mitch tells her, "They will only do it once if I see them." We all agree and Happy Hour begins.

As I look at Emily I know she needs a break from her routine and I give Trevor a look. He smiles and I tell Emily, "I think you should spend the night with me in one of our apartments. The fellas could get a couple of pizzas and bottles of wine. Then at midnight we can raid Mother's kitchen." Trevor adds, "And the guest house is a must see." I nod and finish with, "Then in the morning we can go to Sam's for pancakes."

William is nodding at Emily and she says, "I can't turn down an opportunity to raid your mothers' kitchen. I'll need to go home and pack an overnight bag." Trevor responds, "Then we should get this ball rolling."

We say our goodbyes and go outside where Emily stops cold in her tracks and tells us, "You all should stay here. If you come with, we'll get stuck there. My parents have read *The Halyard* by now. I'll assure them I'm fine and am spending the night with Geneviève. I won't be long." And she is off.

While we wait by Trevor's car William tells me, "Thank you for this. I wasn't sure what to do or say. After Emily read the article she told me there is going to be a dark cloud over our wedding day. When I told her nothing was set in stone and we could move the date up or down a week Emily was quiet. I could tell what I said upset her. I understand being upset; I am too, but not as much as she."

I glance at Trevor then tell William, "More goes into choosing a wedding date than you realize." He looks bewildered as Trevor shakes his head and bluntly asks, "William, are you daft?" I almost get tickled as he responds, "Obviously I am." I sigh heavily and say, "You shouldn't be alone with her again until you have a full grasp of the situation. Since she could return any minute I am going to hit you between the eyes.

"A woman does not want to be on her menstrual cycle during her honeymoon and that is taken into consideration while choosing the date. Discussing that would take some of the romance out of it, so it goes unsaid." Poor William looks up to the sky and closes his eyes. Trevor lowers his head and props on the car. I remain still, thinking I cannot believe I had to discuss that subject with William, but it was for a good cause.

William finally looks at me and says, "I am at a loss for words."

"Oh good, because the less said the happier I will be."

I hear Trevor's' deep laugh then William chuckles and gives me a hug. "Thank you, Geneviève."

"Don't mention it — ever — please." And they burst into laughter.

Just as we quiet down Emily returns and is herself again. She rolls down her window. "I'm ready to go." Trevor motions to William and says, "He's not." We all look at him inquisitively and he tells William, "You need to pack for overnight yourself. You're staying with me." Emily lights up and says, "Hop in." I tell them, "We'll see you at Maison." And they give me a thumbs up.

Seconds after we are in the car I start laughing and say, "Are you daft?"

"Awww ... I haven't been aggravated with him in a long time."

"I took everything I had not to laugh. I knew that wasn't the first time you've said that to him."

"Nope and I'm sure it won't be the last."

"I've realized we have something else in common."

"And what might that be?"

"When my emotions are high I speak in française and you speaking in ... British."

"This day *has* been memorable."

"And it isn't even close to being over." After I say that we ride in silence and enjoy our brief time alone.

At home I go inside to fill in my parent's then go right back out. While standing at the trunk of the car waiting I tell Trevor, "I'm getting married in a little over three weeks and am about to have my first sleep over." He gets tickled. "And there is only one bed in the apartment next to yours." Still laughing he tells me, "Say no more." Trevor steps in front of me and holds me, but not for long. He moves back and places his hands on my waist then says, "I was going to tell you this later tonight, but we might not be alone until who knows when. Théo told me there is a four star restaurant in The Posh. Since the Janssen's are going to be dinning with Darlene and Marshall at their place tomorrow I made reservations there. I'm hoping we won't know anyone, because it's in a hotel and we can have a romantic dinner for two." I throw my arms around him and we begin to kiss.

Only until Emily's headlights are on us do we stop and the antics begin. When they get out, Trevor motions to the guest house and their jaws drop. After a few minutes of discussing the demolition William gets Emily's bag and Trevor tells him, "Get yours too, my apartment is over here now." William dryly asks, "Josephine?" Trevor replies, "Yep, she said my name in the way that makes your blood run cold then handed me an empty box." And they begin laughing.

When William is inside he says, "Oooh ... it's reversed." Trevor goes "Mmm hm." William doesn't say another word and we go to the apartment next door.

Emily glances at the queen size bed and I tell her, "If you prefer your own bed we can go where Trevor was." She replies, "I don't mind sharing the bed. You're not going to kick me in your sleep are you?" The fellas chuckle as I tell her, "I ... I'm not sure. Are you going to kick me?" We have a small burst of laughter and Emily replies, "Gosh, I hope not." Trevor says, "All right then, that's settled. I'll go open a bottle of wine and we can drink it under the arbor."

At the arbor Emily asks me, "Do you mind if I take off my shoes and stockings? I've had these on all day." I reply, "Of course not. In fact I'll join you." After we sit down Emily waits a bit then says, "William, avert your eyes please." He stammers something as he turns around and Trevor glances at me with eyes gleaming then looks down to pour the wine.

It is a nice evening. There is a cool breeze and Emily seems to have forgotten her woes. She is occupied with tomorrow. They're using their club membership for the first time. William made lunch reservations poolside. They are going to swim and lounge by the pool then move to the beach and watch the sunset. Afterward they are going to dine with Joanna and Mitch at Mandarin Garden's.

When there is not much wine left in the bottle we decide it's a good time for the fellas to get the pizza's and a house salad. They're going to choose the dessert, because it is a Friday and the special for tonight could be something good. Emily and I agree to shower and change into comfortable clothing while they're gone and I need to pack a few things.

We are setting the table when they return. William has the pizzas and Trevor is carrying the salad with a pastry box on top from my favorite bakery. He lights up when I immediately take only it from him. Inside I find the glazed petit fours he bought me on our first date. I say, "Pardon me please, I am going to kiss him." William responds, "We'll fill bowls with salad while you do that." Trevor chuckles and I stop him with a passionate kiss for a good 30 seconds, because their backs are to us at the counter.

Once he regroups Trevor softly tells me, "Those were in the apartment. I bought them this afternoon to eat after the dinner we were going to cook tonight." I whisper by his ear, "I love you." He brushes my cheek with his lips. "I love you."

The stolen moment is over and we open a pizza box as William turns on the radio. We all sit down and have a very relaxed meal and just enjoy each other's company, drinking wine and talking about every little thing.

After the table is cleared and the dishes are done Emily drops a deck of cards on the table "We've never played a game of cards and I think tonight would be a good one for the first of many to come." Without a word Trevor and William remove the leaf from the table and I get a pencil and note pad. Emily begins shuffling the deck and tells us, "Let's have some fun." William asks her, "What do you consider to be a fun game of cards?" She beams and replies, "Go Fish." Trevor and I whip our heads to look at each other with eyes dancing.

William responds, "I haven't thought about that game since I was a small boy. Where did that come from?" She sits back and speaks slowly, "Years and years of babysitting." This makes us laugh *and* give her sympathy.

Just as Emily wanted, we did have fun to the point we decide to stay and eat more petit fours instead of raiding Mother's kitchen. During our midnight snack she tells us, "Drinking wine instead of soda pop while playing Go Fish is far more amusing. Not to mention I can actually play to win for a change."And when the game was over win she did after years of losing to countless children. William asks her, "You're a little shark aren't you?" While she pretends to be aghast at the accusation Trevor and I burst into laughter because we were actually playing cards with one and I'm engaged to him. Then she announces, "To the victor go the spoils." Trevor and I look at each other in disbelief. There are way too many coincidences happening. William asks her in earnest, "What would you like?" We watch her think and she replies, "My mind is a blank. I'll get back to you on that." He chuckles and tells her, "Gimme a kiss."

It has been a long event filled day and we wind down by listening to the late night songs play on the radio. When Emily yawns William tells her, "It's time for me to kiss you good night at the door." Trevor tells her, "Sleep well, Emily." She nods and says, "You too, Trevor."

The sound of the door closing can still be heard as he scoops me into his arms. Here we go. "Geneviève, you were supposed to be lying next to me over two hours ago. I'm about to make up for lost time." He is a man of his word. Somehow he manages to kiss me while holding me with one arm as he unbuttons the top part of my blouse enough to kiss my neck and shoulder. While my head is still swimming Trevor buttons my blouse then leads me to the door. Emily and William are on the balcony holding hands looking at the view. They stand and Emily trades places with Trevor then the fellas motion for us to go inside and we do.

Emily goes behind the dressing screen as we change into our pajama bottoms. When she walks around it her eyes go straight to my neck. Did he leave a mark? I must have made a face because Emily tells me, "I apologize for staring." I reply, "No need to apologize." and sigh. Then she says, "I couldn't help but notice your skin is a bit red from Trevor's five o'clock shadow." Relieved I tell her, "Oh is that all, I thought he left a passion mark."

The second I finish the sentence I want to take it back. Standing there trying to think of something to say Emily responds, "You've had a passion mark? Did it hurt?" While I am still speechless poor Emily exclaims, "That is none of my business. Geneviève, I do apologize. Please forget I asked." I can talk now and hold her hand. "Emily, it's fine and of course you have questions. Feel free to ask me anything." She freezes up, so I smile and answer her question. "As for a passion mark, it does not hurt when you get one. It is quite the opposite. Although the next day it might be a little tender, but you don't care because it reminds you of how it got there."

"Really? They look like a painful bruise."

"A bruise is caused by a blow hard enough to bring blood to the skins surface, therefore those do hurt. A passion mark is made with a kiss."

"Point very well made."

"I don't know how to describe it to you, but William will eventually give you one and then you will understand." Emily nods as I go to the refrigerator and pour us glasses of water. "Let's lie down and talk, so we can at least rest." Emily perks up, takes the water and says, "It'll be like when we were on Willow; that was nice." I go, "Mmm hm." and we turn out the lights then get in bed.

When we are cozy in bed the first thing Emily does is sigh heavily, so I ask, "What's troubling you?"

"William won't leave a passion mark on me until we're married."

"Why do you say that?"

"We're always standing or sitting next to each other in places it isn't possible. Vehicles are always passing by when we're on the patio and when we're parked at the cliffs just for some privacy he does kiss me, but my neck is not accessible."

"You said sitting. You don't turn around in the car seat and pull your legs up on it so you can lie across him in his arms?"

"No. I've seen it in movies, but I would have to initiate that and haven't the faintest idea how."

"One night when you're tired, ask him if you can rest in his arms and he will take it from there. Plus you should stop wearing collars on dates and switch to a u-neckline or a ballet."

"Oh my gosh — you want me to lie across William."

"More to the point, you don't?"

"Why can't I be more like you? Nonchalant about the possibility there could be a passion mark on you and you know things now I won't until my honeymoon and I'll be a bundle of nerves."

"Emily, let's get up and talk. Bring your water." She follows me to the sofa and I turn on a lamp. "Tomorrow at the club William will be shirtless and you will be in a swimming suit. When he puts his arm around your waist or something, notice his skin against yours and his muscles, how firm they are. And look at him, he is tanned and his hair will be dripping wet and beads of water will drop on his chest. Notice these things and you will find you want to touch him and for him to touch you. It is normal to be physically attracted to him beyond how good he looks in his uniform and I think you will not go there."

"You are correct, I won't."

We sit silently as I think and it occurs to me the only way to get her to move along is if she knows what it feels like for him to touch her, like Joanna told us. She will never that ask of me and I'm going to have to offer. Emily is my friend and she needs my help. I wish this water was vodka.

I get up my nerve and ask her, "Would you like me to give you an idea of what you are missing?" Emily swallows hard and replies, "I was afraid to ask, because that it is a lot to ask of you and yes I would." She is misty-eyed, so I know I have made the right decision.

As I stand up I cannot believe what I am about to do. Then Emily steps up behind me and gives me a hug. This time it was different. There are layers of clothing between us when she hugs me; bras, blouses and even cardigans, but this time we both are wearing only camisoles and I felt her breast on my back. The next thing I know I am remembering the night when Trevor was standing at the kitchen counter opening sodas for us. I put my arms around him then rested my head on his back and he said, 'I can feel you on my back. You *are* soft.' and now I know why. Trevor could feel my breast against him.

We are soft, our bodies and our skin. We feel fragile, but we have strength. This is why he constantly wants to hold me or run his hands along my body and kiss me with such passion. Calm washes of me like water and I turn off the lamp then take us to the middle of the living room area. I hold her hands and softly say, "Emily, I want you think of a moment you were in Williams' arms and he was kissing you passionately then imagine he slows down and loosens his hold on you."

She closes her eyes and I give her a moment then let go of her hands and slide mine up her arms then in an instant she is me and I am Trevor. When I get to her shoulders I caress them exactly like he does mine. I step close to her and run my hands along her neck then slowly down her back and gently hold her in my arms. I slide my cheek across her shoulder and nestle my head on her neck so she can feel my hair on her skin; then Emily sighs. That is what William will want to hear.

Next I slowly move my hands along her sides down to her waist then glide my cheek up her neck and my lips graze her skin. I place my cheek on hers with my mouth close to her ear and exhale as I relax. I feel chill bumps on her and realize she heard and felt my breath. Then the unexpected occurs, Emily softly makes a sound that is close to a moan.

Suddenly her entire body stiffens and I step back. She whispers, "Did you hear that?" I reply, "Yes I did. I think we should sit down." She nods as I turn on the lamp and we return to the sofa. We reach for our water and take a drink at the same time which makes us get tickled. Then we sit back and are quiet.

Emily begins to smile and says, "Well — that worked like a charm. I actually forgot for a moment you were not William, because everything felt so very nice. I came around when I made that unusual sound."

"Caught you of guard did it?"

"Yes it did. What was that?"

"Your reaction to pleasure and it is what he will be waiting to hear. It lets him know he is doing the right thing, so don't ever suppress those sounds. And when your breathing becomes erratic do not give it a second thought, just disappear into William and he will take care of you, I promise."

"Geneviève — I want to go next door and wake him up." I chuckle and tell her, "I understand that. Would you like to switch to cognac?" Without hesitation she replies, "Yes, please."

While we sip our cognac and Emily processes what she has discovered I remember to tell her, "This is important, try to remember what and how he does things you enjoy, so you can reciprocate."

"Oh my gosh ... he has never felt these things either."

"William has been true to Louise, just like Trevor."

"Now they are true to us. Geneviève, isn't that romantic?"

"Very."

Sipping our cognac Emily starts looking around. "I like this apartment. What's along the wall?"

"That is several closets of my mother's gowns she has worn over the years and is stored in. There are some matching accessories as well."

Emily lights up and asks, "Is her wedding gown in there?" I nod and she exclaims, "May I see it?"

"Absolutely. I need assistance though, it's cumbersome."

Emily bounds to her feet and we get the large boxes down then set them on the bed. I carefully begin getting the veil out and hand it to her. Then I get the gown out and lay it across the bed. Mother's wedding gown is Victorian and when I let it go Emily gasps. It is off the shoulder with yards and yards of silk ivory satin and lace, complete with a chapel length train and veil. The accessories are shoes, a fan and a little drawstring bag made of the same lace.

Emily asks, "Are you getting married in this?"

"Unfortunately no, it is far too fragile. Then there is the issue it will not fit through a car door. My parent's rode to their reception in a horse drawn carriage."

She sighs then says, "Your mother had a fairy-tale wedding."

"Yes she did — but you do not have to ride in a carriage to have one. We are going to have fairy-tale weddings and we are going to live happily ever after."

Emily eyes almost puddle. "It's true. We are, aren't we?"

"Without a doubt."

Next I answer several questions about my parent's wedding as we finish our cognac and go back to bed. This time we fall asleep.

Knocking on the door wakes us up and wide awake we are. It's almost nine o'clock and I go to the door, peek through the curtain and see Trevor then tell Emily it's him. She ducks behind the dressing screen, so I open the door wide. He smiles and says, "Good morning." then kisses my cheek. "William tossed a coin and I won."

"Won what?"

"The opportunity to witness the flurry of activity when I wake you two up. Good morning, Emily." We hear a faint, "Good morning, Trevor." from behind the dressing screen. He asks, "Should I tell William that you two will be ready shortly and will come next door? We're starving." Emily steps out wearing her robe and replies, "Tell him we'll be ready in two shakes of a lambs tale." Trevor grins and tells us, "There is way too much girl stuff going on in here. I'm leaving." He hooks me around the neck, dips me and I get a noisy kiss then out the door he goes. I whirl around and tell Emily, "I have to get ready in my bedroom. I will see you at their place." She nods; I fling on my robe and literally run out the door.

After getting ready and running down the staircase I stop in the mudroom to get my handbag and my composure. When I open the door they are standing outside by the cars. Emily has an odd look on her face, but the fellas are grinning from ear to ear. "Trevor, why does Emily look frayed?"

"William and I wanted to be waiting for you out here by the cars to toy with you by making you feel slow," I shake my head at him, but cannot stop smiling. She did ask to be included in future practical jokes.

They open the car doors and when Emily and I are about to get in I stop and ask, "Fellas, exactly what time did you wake up?" Their eyes get wide and William eventually responds, "I think we'll take the Fifth Amendment on that." Trevor is nodding as I say, "That's what I thought." Emily shakes her head at William as she gets in. I on the other hand get Trevor to confess they had been up maybe 15 minutes before waking us; which means the second they were ready William tossed the coin.

The diner is packed, so Sam visit's briefly, but the coffee is very good today, therefore we stay and have a second cup before going separate ways. Our first of many stops today is at Simmons & Co. to choose china, silver and crystal. As we walk by rows of china patterns we see one bordered with traditional Chinese design elements of butterflies and honeycombs in a cinnabar color and decide to get it in a service for 12. Trevor motions for the clerk and she makes the first entry for our Wedding Registry. While writing she tells us we have exquisite taste, because it is made by the company that makes china for presidents in the White House. We glance at each other and proceed to the section of sterling silver flatware where we choose a simple pattern.

Then we go to select stemware and we stop at a pair of Deco candlesticks in clear and black crystal. Trevor and I can see them sitting on the mantle in our bedroom. We have those boxed deciding anything for it will be purchased by us. For fun Trevor suggests we put an extravagant gift on our list to see what happens.

After well over an hour we have made decisions on everything required for a registry. Trevor and I walk out with our candlesticks in need of a quiet place to have lunch. We take a risk and go to the club where we eat in the lounge hoping Emily and William will not see us. It worked out perfectly.

Next we pop into Blackwell's to get the prints from the week spent with family and friends then proceed to shop for furniture. We pick out the must have's; sofas, settee's and upholstered chairs, with paisley or solid colored throw pillows for them. One of the many things we agree on is nothing navy blue or floral and to choose the rest over time after we are living in our home. The dining room furniture has to be refinished in black and will join our bedroom furniture.

As we stand under the awning of the third shop Trevor suggests we quit for the day. We stop at the bakery and he buys oatmeal cookies with pecans and we go to the apartment. We have cookies and milk while looking at all the incredible photographs then he settles into the corner of the sofa with his feet on a pillow placed on the coffee table and I get to stretch out on the sofa. There we stay until time to get ready for our dinner at The Posh. Best of all, Trevor packs his satchel to bring his things back to the house again.

My entire family is home getting ready to go out to dinner, so Trevor goes to into my closet first thing to choose what I'm wearing as I sit on the bench watching him. I enjoy this little routine, but not as much as he does though. This time he has found something I bought on a whim but never wore, a three quarter length sleeved dinner suit in powder pink silk shantung. He hangs it on the closet door, asks if he can choose my jewelry again, gives me a kiss and goes to shave and shower. A smooth face will be here soon.

The house empties as I get dressed, so I open my door and soon Trevor walks in wearing his black suit with a black tie looking incredibly handsome. I was expecting him to be in a uniform. "Trevor, you look too good."

He chuckles. "Thank you. We're going to where no one knows us hopefully and if they do this suit will throw them off. Geneviève, you look lovely."

"Thank you." I move closer to him and run my hands down his lapels and as I pull on them ask, "I want to feel your face on mine." Trevor smiles and holds my shoulders then places his cheek on my cheek and I take it from there.

After the interlude he says, "Time for pearls." and goes to get them. He hands me my earrings, I put them on then he puts my bracelet and ring on for me. Next Trevor motions for me to turn around and face the mirror. Then like a magician he begins pulling a long strand of pearls out of his jacket pocket and fastens them around my neck. They are a matinee length. As I stand there speechless admiring them I notice he begins to pull another strand from his other pocket. When he drapes them over me I gasp for these are opera length.

"I watched you admiring Lorraine at the airport. And I am aware that women of a certain age wear dinner suits and long strands of pearls, but I noticed this in your closet a few weeks ago and since I'm engaged to a revolutionist I got these for you, because I knew in your heart you wanted them and now you have them." No longer content to look at his reflection in the mirror I turn around to look in his eyes and am speechless, thus I gently kiss him and caress his ever so smooth face.

The evening is like a dream. We do not know a soul at the restaurant and are alone in the crowd. He did not tell me there would be a small orchestra there and we dance the way we want to dance without a care in the world. While sipping on Louis XIII we decide to return after we are married and stay for a weekend just to have breakfast in bed. Room service is one of my favorite little luxuries.

At the house we hear music coming from the drawing room and look down the hallway to see it is dimly lit. We slowly go to the entrance of the room and my parents are dancing a slow waltz. We try to slip away without being noticed and are unsuccessful in our endeavor. My father says, "Oh, please join us." We of course do and when I'm in full view Mother gasps. "Sweetheart, you are ..." Father adds, "A vision to behold." He looks at the pearls, then Trevor and says, "Well done." Trevor slightly bows his head to them and offers his hand to me for this dance.

While the record changes my father places his hand on Trevor's shoulder to cut in then he goes to Mother and holds out his hand. When we switch partners again we dance to a few more records then my parent's bid us good night. When Trevor is certain they are in their suite he says, "Alone at last." After several minuets spent in sheer bliss we shut down the house and go up as well.

Trevor kisses me as he takes off the strands of pearls then he slowly unbuttons my jacket looking into my eyes. When it's off he gathers me into a passionate embrace. I would have stayed in his arms longer instead of showering, but my hair needs washing. Hair lacquer doesn't brush out; it breaks your hair if you try and you wind up looking like you went to a barber shop instead of a salon.

As Trevor tucks me in I tell him, "This was a perfect day. I don't want it to end." He sits in the chair and says, "Then I will finish telling you my bedtime story." Trevor holds my hand and I listen to the sound of his voice as I watch him using his imagination in the most wonderful way. When he finally says, "and they lived happily ever after." my heart soars.

CHAPTER SIX

The next morning my sleep is shattered by the unknown. I sit straight up and inhale sharply. Something must be terribly wrong; it's not even eight o'clock. I get out of bed, fling my bedroom door open and see my parent's door is the only other one open. There is no smell of coffee yet, so I go down the back staircase in a rush. I reach the kitchen to find Mother dressed and sitting alone at the table drinking orange juice. "You get more like your grandmother each passing day." Then she looks toward the staircase and says, "Trevor, do come in." We glance at each other when he stands beside me; neither of us is wearing robes or slippers. Mother sighs and tells us, "A situation has developed in Aix. Gérard went outside to get the newspaper and saw Joseph's car then he came in and called his parent's. He is over there now." Mother sighs again. "Claudette made her Sunday morning call to her family and was told a brigade of German soldiers arrived in town Friday evening."

"How many officers are staying at the Château, Mother?"

"I will not ask how you know that. Two are there and one is staying in the maison for our vigneron."

"That explains why Joseph is here."

"I was trying to think of a way to wake you all up gently when you thankfully appeared. Will you wake your brother please? I am going next door." I nod then she kisses our cheeks and leaves. Trevor hugs me immediately and softly says, "Still reading what you type." He holds my hand and tells me, "Let's go up stairs. I will stand close by as you wake up, Théo."

On the way I decide what to do and as I knock on his door I sing, "Théo, it's time to wake up." We hear stumbling then he says, "Gené – I had 10 more minutes." He opens the door and stops smiling. "What has happened?" After I answer his question we all get dressed and walk next door together.

Everyone is in the kitchen. Joseph is standing with his arm around Claudette who is dabbing tears from her face. As we make our cups of coffee my grandfather continues to speak in French and I begin quietly translating to Trevor. "As a precautionary measure Monsieur Bechard is going to walk his wife and two daughters to the main house each morning where they will pose as members of the staff. Family members and the men and women working at the château have been instructed to stay in pairs at all times. A window of opportunity for anything unfortunate to happen will not be opened."

My grandfather stops talking and is looking at Trevor. He has realized I have been translating. Before he gets even more upset I say, "We should start breakfast. I'll scramble the eggs." Théo out of habit says, "I'm frying the sausages." Trevor chimes in, "That leaves me with the toast." and we swing into action. Normally Théo and I cut up when we are cooking, but I had to count the eggs twice, so he stood quietly beside me as I was lost in thought.

It is common knowledge that France, after surrendering to the enemy, was divided into occupied and unoccupied zones. The occupied zones were places where the enemy moved in and stayed, mostly in the best cities. The unoccupied zones were in rural areas that were farm lands or olive groves and vineyards. Provence thankfully was unoccupied.

What was not common knowledge, because it wasn't reported in the news is that brigades were constantly on the move going through the unoccupied zones. The soldiers arrive in towns and quickly take over. They fill the inns and high ranking officers are placed in the nicer homes living with the owners as guests that are most unwelcome. I know of this and more due to my job. When Joseph starts getting out plates and flatware I lose my train of thought which is fine by me.

We eat at the kitchen table and Théo, who ate very little looks at his watch and says, "I have to go meet the Janssen's for Sunday brunch. I will keep this to myself and call as soon as possible." I tell him, "We will go with." Trevor slides my chair out and we leave.

The second we go outside Théo tells me, "That was a graceful exit. I imagine the only thing holding you together is your skin. The only thing holding me together is you have him to talk to." We begin walking to the house and he says, "Gené, you know I want to call and cancel." I reply, "Of course I do." Théo shakes Trevor's hand as he tells him, "I am leaving my sister in your capable hands." Trevor nods and Théo looks at me. I say, "Théo, the only thing we can do is hope for the best and they will watch over each other day and night. So go upstairs and get ready to go be with Rachel and her parents." He kisses my forehead. "I love you, Gené." I respond, "I love you too." Théo glances at Trevor and goes inside. When Trevor lightly touches my hands I realize I began wringing them together the moment Théo's back was turned. He motions to the apartment and asks, "Do want to go for a walk or there?" I shrug my shoulders and he says, "After you."

Going to the apartment Trevor doesn't touch me until we are on the stairs and then he only cups my elbow in his hand to keep my steady. He remembers not to handle me when I'm emotional and I am truly grateful. Inside I begin pacing and Trevor says, "I don't care what time it is, I'm pouring you a glass of wine." I follow him to the counter and watch him open the bottle then pour it into the glass. He hands it to me then props on the counter. Since I just look at the wine he puts his hand on the bottom of the glass and raises it up a little. "Hint, hint." He manages to get me to smile and I take a sip. A few seconds later I begin wondering aimlessly around the apartment and he stays still watching me.

Eventually he sighs quietly. I know he is concerned and wondering what is upsetting me, so I tell him, "I'm afraid if I start talking I will not be able to stop."

"Geneviève, you don't have to talk. I'm just concerned about you. Obliviously what you know is bad."

"It is worse than you think."

"That's what concerns me. I do know about some of the things happening over there."

"Do you know they are conducting inquires that resemble witch hunts? These brigades are searching for more than people of the wrong religion or helping members of the French Resistance. They are looking for anyone they consider to be immoral or corrupt. Men are being put in front firing squads." As I take a deep breath and take a sip of wine he says, "Geneviève ..." I interject "There is a cross on top of the family mausoleum." He sighs in relief and I continue.

"Most of these soldiers are horrid men, using the war as an opportunity to commit crimes. They ransack homes taking what they want or what they think is valuable. And the soldiers have been attacking women, even married ones, they don't care. For years I have known the atrocities men are capable of; deceit, intimidation, veiled threats and lies to manipulate women merely to get what they want — but this?"

"I cannot begin to tell you how much I wish you did not know these things. I wish I didn't. Baby, please stop reading what you type."

"I did, weeks ago, when the brigade reached Dauphiné."

Trevor pours himself a glass of wine and sits down. "I just got my family out of that mess and now yours has been plunged into this ridiculous war. All your relatives are at risk and poor Claudette, her entire family is."

While he speaks I stand still on the other side of the coffee table in front of him and set down my glass. He is silent for a moment then looks very serious as he tilts his head and asks, "Veiled threats and lies; where did that come from?" I close my eyes and lower my head with my hand over my face. "Is this something I need to know?" I look up, sigh heavily and reply a simple, "Yes.", then sit down and ask, "May have a glass of water please?"

While Trevor pours glasses of water I begin talking. "It was summertime; I was 15 years old and sitting by the pool reading. Two girls who were best friends since childhood had just graduated from high school and were talking at the table next to mine. They thought I was so immersed in my book I wouldn't hear them, but one girl was so upset the tone in her voice caught my attention. She was pregnant and her intended she was in love with was not going to marry her. The cad told her he was testing her to see if she was virtuous." Trevor's jaw drops a little.

"The girl decided to go somewhere in Europe for the remainder of her pregnancy, give the baby up for adoption and then attend a European finishing school. Her friend accompanied her and they stayed. Eventually they married European men and rarely come back."

"My word ... you were at a tender age to hear that." I nod and continue.

"The next incident was maybe a year later. It was before noon and a married woman with three children was drinking a Bloody Mary telling her best friend last night her husband wanted to copulate. She told him she was ovulating and didn't want to risk having another child. They had been to a party earlier where he drank too much and he told her the refusal was grounds for divorce. It was a threat to intimidate her into submission. When she got passed her disbelief at what he said it made her angry. That night she realized she fell in love with and married the man he had been pretending to be all those years and the man he really was finally made an appearance. The woman told him there was no need for him to file for divorce, because *she* was going to, which she did." Trevor smiles and says, "Good for her." I go, "Mmm hm."

After drinking some water I sigh and tell him, "I need to warn you, this last one is a tragedy."

"Perhaps you shouldn't go there."

"I went there already. It changed me and I should tell you now. I will have to one day because it haunts me." I sip on my water a minute then begin.

"It was the beginning of my senior year and a woman I was very fond of and had known for years was drinking Mimosa's during brunch by the pool. She was with her close friend watching her little girl playing in the pool with her friend's children. Her husband wanted her to have another child and was telling her his father was pressuring him for a boy to carry on the family name and legacy. She almost died having the girl, but he reminded her second pregnancies are statistically easier. She was convinced her husband loved her, even though he was asking her to risk her life. Her friend pleaded with her not to give in.

"It took everything I had not to tell her he is not the man she fell in love with while he was courting her. She fell in love with the man he was pretending to be, not the man he really was, just like other men I knew about. To my dismay she gave in and my worst fear befell her. She died shortly after giving birth to a boy." Tears well up in my eyes and Trevor sits listening to me visibly shaken.

"Théo heard me crying the night I found out. He came into my room and sat next to me. I was crying for several reasons; a woman I knew had tragically passed away, an alarming percentage of men could not be trusted and more than likely I would never marry. When I told Théo what I knew and the reasons why I was crying he held me as I wept."

Trevor is silent and still as he tries to process all I have told him and watches me fight back tears. His voice is strained as he quietly asks, "What can I do to help?" I shakily tell him, "I am at my wits end and cannot be strong any longer. Just hold me." When he has me in his arms I begin to cry my heart out. The past and the news this morning is all too much.

Once again I find myself in a bathroom with Trevor helping me clean my face after crying. With that done we go back to the living area and he opens all the French doors to let the breeze blow in and we settle on the sofa.

Trevor's arm is around me and he starts thinking out loud in a sense by talking under his breath. "Théo took her to her Senior Prom, she didn't attend her Debutant Ball and then she focused on dual careers. No wonder she ran from me." He gets quiet and I remain quiet not wanting him to lose his train of thought or realize I heard him. It may cause him to feel uncomfortable, because I sure am.

Time passes and he finally says, "Geneviève, I can't believe you gave me the time of day."

"I knew you before I met you — through Joanna." Trevor carefully moves me so he can see my face and he has an inquisitive look. "Joanna only told me a few things. You and William attended The Academy together. You both were assigned to the aircraft carrier eight years ago and why you spoke with a British accent. The rest I pieced together. I knew Mitch was a good man because Joanna is so in love with him and he is your mentor. Therefore you would treat a woman like he treats her, because you observed them together for so many years."

He responds, "I knew you before I met you. I was aware you had a great deal in common with her and you were French by blood. Plus she was so fond of you in such a short time I knew you were a good woman. I was looking forward to meeting you, yet I was not sure surprising the two of you was the way to go about it and I was spot-on. The first thing she did was call him wicked, which is her way of discretely scolding him." I have a small burst of laughter and he says, "Do tell."

"I thought wicked was an odd term of endearment — and it wasn't."

"His main interest was meeting you and curiosity simply got the better of him. Looking the club over was a plausible excuse. You were just as I knew you would be with the exception of your age. I thought you were close to hers and so did Mitch. Then there was the fact she neglected to mention you were stunning with soulful brown eyes. I actually scolded her for not telling me you were beautiful or your age. Joanna told me she must have only mentioned what you looked like to Mitch, but she didn't know your age. When I told her anyone could tell you were in your mid-twenties Mitch nodded in agreement. Her response was, 'You did get a pleasant surprise.' and that I did."

"Trevor, I cannot believe I am going to tell you this. Joanna neglected to tell me you were handsome. When I met you it caught me off guard you were so handsome and after the two of you left I scolded her for not telling me. Her response was she was used to being around handsome men, so she didn't give it a second thought anymore."

"That woman is something else."

"Yes she is. — I knew you were a good man, but after spending time with you I found out you were an exceptional one. I'm glad you chased me."

"I'm glad you slowed down a minute. — If I didn't need to shave I would be kissing you right now."

"That has never stopped you before."

Trevor gets up immediately and closes most of the doors. He walks back to the sofa, picks up his glass of water and tells me, "We're going next door. I'm not worrying about one of us falling off a small bed."

Lying on the bed we kiss, but he holds me more than anything. He wants to comfort me and I need comforting. The only conversation between us is him asking if I am comfortable. I was indeed; to the point I get a little drowsy and for a change my stomach growls. Trevor chuckles and says, "We're in the right place for that. There's salad and leftover pizza in the fridge. Have you eaten cold pizza?"

"No, but I'll try it."

"If you don't like it I'll toss it on a pan and heat in the oven."

"That is how you reheat pizza?"

"How do you reheat it?"

"In a skillet with a lid, the crust becomes crispy again and the cheese melts nicely." I watch a light bulb turn on over his head.

"It's simulates a brick oven where the pizza cooks on the bricks. That's a neat trick. It's time to learn something else fun to do."

Trevor bounces off the bed, goes to the kitchen and starts getting everything out. Watching me reheat the pizza he asks, "How do you know about this?" I reply, "Mama Micheletto told us a long time ago." He dryly says, "I speak Italian and not one person has ever told me this." I try to contain my laughter and tell him, "Perhaps that's why no one has, we're French." Trevor grins and says, "You're probably spot-on."

While the first two pieces I reheated cools, he reheats two more. When all is done we sit at the table to eat our impromptu feast. After he eats his first bite of the pizza he exclaims, "This is delicious. I am both happy and mad." I push his glass of wine closer and get him to laugh.

After we eat petit fours I slide the box over and say, "These are staying here." He gets tickled and gives me a kiss then tells me, "I love you." We go sit on the sofa and enjoy each other's company until it's time to get ready for the Sunday dinner which includes the Janssen's.

On the way to the house we notice Joseph's car is still here. "The cooking. Why did they not call me?" Trevor looks at me with raised eyebrows. I go straight inside to the phone and call my grandparent's. Grand-papa answers and tells me what is going on. I hang up and tell Trevor, "Joseph took the day off to stay here with Claudette and has insisted on helping her cook and he's going to serve while she stays in the kitchen. They are cooking as we speak. He thinks she should stay busy to keep her mind occupied."

"Joseph is taking excellent care of Claudette and your family. He must feel so good about being here for you all." Going upstairs he asks, "Do you want me to choose a dress for you?" I reply, "Of course I do." He goes in my closet and takes a little longer than usual and comes out with a simple dinner dress. "I fancy this and it looks comfortable."

"It is actually. Thank you, Trevor."

"You know it's my pleasure. I'm going to shave now."

As he leaves I'm laughing then I abruptly stop when I realize he'll be back shortly. Into my closet I go and dress. I get out a pair of shoes and sit at my vanity, put on a little makeup and un-braid my hair. As I pick up my brush Trevor walks in and without a word takes it from me and brushes my hair out. For some reason it feels nice and it relaxes me. I watch his reflection in my mirror and Trevor looks content with eyes bright and a slight smile. After my hair is up Trevor kisses me as I caress his face then he hands me my lipstick. I'm ready, so I get his jacket and help him put it on. At this point it feels as if we're married.

Dinner goes flawlessly thanks to Joseph stepping in. When Rachel asks where Claudette is, my grandmother tells her she is not feeling well tonight. I glance at Théo, because now I know he has been carrying his burden alone all day. He just smiles like the rest of us and carries the conversation.

While we're in the foyer bidding our guests good night Théo quietly tells Trevor and me he is taking her parents straight to their hotel. Next he plans to take Rachel to her apartment in order to fill her in on the day's events before he loses his mind. He kisses my forehead and turns on a dime like Trevor. Théo is a blur as he escorts Rachel out. It is a comfort to know she will see to his needs and I can stop worrying about him.

No one says a word as we go back into the drawing room and collapse. It's not easy to keep your chin up and pretend you haven't a care in the world when it has crumbled at your feet. Joseph steps in and asks if we need him. Grand-papa thanks him for all he did for us and tells him to just stay with Claudette.

The next morning as Trevor is taking me to work we see Joseph's car is still here. I ask, "What do you think happened?"

"She probably fell asleep on the sofa while he was holding her. He didn't have the heart to wake her and eventually fell asleep himself. I know he was exhausted."

"That worked out. The moment she woke up I know she started crying again and he was there." Trevor slows down and stops in the middle of the driveway. "What is it?"

"It's too early to have a stiff upper lip. You're speaking from experience and I just had a vivid image of you waking up that next morning and Théo in the chair being ripped from his sleep having to comfort you. Yesterday it actually crossed my mind to go look for that man."

"I understand. Théo and I had to stay away from the club for a while. He — and I'm quoting, 'wanted to beat him to a pulp'. We told Mother I simply couldn't bear to see him, which was the truth. She would check the reservations and when he didn't have one, we would go to the club. Fortunately that didn't last long. He moved and since his wife asked her friend to be the children's Godmother she and her family moved too." I sigh heavily. "Trevor, I'm fine now. It was a long time ago."

"I know that, but I just found out yesterday and I'm upset."

"I see your point." He goes through the gates and I wait a mile or so then say, "This is going to come from out of the blue, but speaking of broken hearts." He glances at me. "I have wanted to ask you this; do you know what became of Sarah?" He slightly chuckles and replies, "As a matter of fact I do. I would've told you that day, but you held your hand out." We smile at each other then he begins telling me the rest of the story.

"We were all together in the spring having lunch at The Overboard when one of our professors stopped at our table and I introduced them. He was courting her before we left. Sarah married him the following November. William and I have stayed in touch with her through letters and we visit them when we see his parents. William saw her and the professor along with their two sons when he went home."

"I'm so glad I asked. She found happiness. Trevor — does she know you and William are getting married?"

He shakes his head emphatically. "I will take care of that today."

"Our invitations for the wedding and the reception go out tomorrow. You could add her to the wedding mailing list."

"She would like to receive an invitation. That's what I'll do." He is smiling again as we ride to the base with the windows down.

It has been a full day that included lunch with the crew and dinner in the restaurant at The Posh with the Janssen's before Théo and Rachel took them to the airport. Trevor and I are sitting on the portico looking at the progress on our future home and talking about the framework for the second floor when I change the subject.

"I have been trying to talk with Father for a week about my idea for the phone system on the base."

"May I make a suggestion?"

"Please do."

"It will take you maybe five minutes for that. I can go for a run and after you've talked with him you could have a nice long shower then I can tuck you in."

"I love you."

"I love you too. Let's go inside."

We coast through the next day together with no one to meet anywhere or entertain. We have a quiet lunch on my bench and when we get home we discover Théo has brought Rachel for dinner. My grandparents are next door having dinner with Claudette and Joseph. This is his day off and I hope Claudette is feeling better.

When Théo leaves to take Rachel home we sit on the portico again looking at our house. There's another load of lumber outside, because the first one has been assembled nicely on it. Next Trevor goes for a run and I have the pleasure of another long shower.

The following day was smooth sailing through our new routine until we're sitting on the portico enjoying the cool night breeze and Claudette appears at the bottom of the steps. Trevor stands up as she says, "Please pardon the intrusion, I will only use a minute." I tell her, "You are not intruding at all. Please, join us." Trevor goes to the steps and extends his hand. She slowly takes it and after he seats her she looks at me.

"May I speak with you when the time is good this week?"

"Trevor was about to go for his run, is now too soon?"

"Oh, not at all."

After Trevor excuses himself and goes inside Claudette carefully places her hands on her lap. "Geneviève — each night it hurts when I say good night to Joseph. I feel lonely terribly and told him this yesterday then he had an idea I like very much. I did not know this, when Joseph asked my father for permission to court me also asked for my hand in marriage." I cannot hold back a tiny burst of laughter and tell her, "Trevor did the exact same thing." She responds, "It is romance?" I reply, "Yes, it is romance." And she absolutely glows.

"Like your father, my father gave him both; hence Joseph has suggested we marry soon and we would not consummate the marriage until I am certain I want to remain so. If not, we could easily have it — dissolved and I would have my virtue still. I love him as he loves me and will not want our marriage dissolved."

I am nodding when we hear Trevor make a lot of noise to warn us he is about to open the front door. He emerges with two glasses of Pellegrino; we thank him and he runs away. Claudette and I pause to drink then she resumes. "Next is something I must ask. Joseph works day and night. Lost I would be somewhere else. Is it too much to ask for Joseph to live here?"

"It is not. Of this I am certain; the family will welcome Joseph to live here with you in your apartment." Claudette's eyes puddle then she lights up. "I did not tell you the most important part. He told me when the war ends he will take me home and it will be his home. I love him more for this and want to become his wife."

"Joseph is a good man and will be a good husband."

"Fortunate. I am fortunate. — My reason for telling you these things are I am in need of advice; how to have this private life conversation with Constance."

"Would you trust me to speak with her on your behalf?

"Indeed I would. You are most kind."

"Think nothing of it. I am happy to do this for you."

We are quite for a moment then I manage to think and ask, "Do you know when and where you want to have the ceremony." She replies timidly, "Saturday next and here, on the boardwalk along the beach." I put my hand over my heart and ask, "What time would you like it to take place?"

"When the sun is setting and I want to look like a ballerina in a Degas."

"So you shall."

Claudette holds my hands. "Will you be by my side as my honored maiden?"

"Yes, it would please me, more than you know." She throws her arms around me. "Thank you, so much."

"This will be taken care of when I get home from work tomorrow and Friday morning Grand-mamma and Mother will help you begin planning your wedding."

"Geneviève — I am marrying Joseph. I want to be there when he arrives, so I go now." When we stand she hugs me tightly, then kisses my cheeks and I watch her dance as if she is a ballerina as she goes to her apartment.

While I am sitting down trying to process what just happened Trevor shows up dripping with perspiration. Looking at him my mind goes blank for this is my first time to see him after he has made his run. He is smiling at me and gets closer as he uses the towel around his neck to dry his face. Next he gives me a kiss and sits by me. "Is everything all right?" This brings me out of my Trevor induced trance and I reply, "They are more than all right. Joseph and Claudette are getting married next week."

Trevor smiles at first, then looks at me with the strangest face and dryly says, "They are going to beat us all to the altar."

"Oh my gosh — they are. But they have known each other for years."

"Indeed they have. Is there anything else you can tell me?"

"I am going to be something I thought I would never be, especially since we are getting married soon; Claudette asked me to stand with her as maid of honor."

"I'm so happy for you, not to mention Claudette. Your grandmother is about to be busy, but with you and your mother assisting, Claudette and Joseph will have a beautiful ceremony wherever they decide."

"The decision has been made. They're getting married here, on the boardwalk as the sun sets."

"It's a shame your mother has probably gone upstairs. You are going to toss and turn until morning. Fancy a glass of cognac?" I get tickled and nod. "After we shower I will meet you in the drawing room." I grab the towel and he makes a sound of surprise as I pull him to me with it and kiss him most passionately.

The next morning Trevor enters my room as I am picking up my handbag. I sing, "Good morning." give him a kiss and drag him down the stairs. His deep laugh continues on the way. When we enter the kitchen I sing, "Bonjour tout le monde." My parents are looking at each other as Théo says, "She must have good news." Mother responds, "We are all listening." Trevor tells me, "I'll make your coffee." then pulls out my chair.

"I have an announcement. Joseph and our dear Claudette want to get married next week, on Saturday at sunset, here." Théo and my father get wide-eyed as I ask Mother, "Will you have Grand-mamma here when I get home please?" She replies, "Of course, Sweetheart." Father looks at Trevor. "It would be best to stay clear of the ladies. I will meet you in the study." Trevor asks, "Whiskey?" My father nods and while we eat I tell them what I can.

After work Trevor pins me against the car when we get to the house. He says, "I will miss you." I chuckle and we go inside to find my mother and grandmother sitting at the kitchen table with three Manhattan's next to pens and paper. Trevor greets them and goes to the study to wait on my father. A few minutes later he arrives, kisses Mother and keeps going. My grandfather walks in soon after and follows in his footsteps.

Our papers are covered in notes when the phone rings. Father steps in the doorways and tells us, "Pardon the interruption, we have been summoned next door." And we are up and off.

The first thing we notice, Joseph is here and then we hear Théo's car. Rachel rolls down the window and asks, "What's happening?" Father replies, "We have not a clue." She adds, "Can you believe this?" Mother responds, "Just barely." Théo parks and they walk in with us.

When we enter the drawing room we see two bottles of Roederer chilling. Joseph is holding Claudette's hand and begins to speak. "Thank you all for coming here. We want to announce it is official. I proposed to Claudette and she accepted this ring." She lifts her hand and we gather around them to see it. After we congratulate them Grand-mamma tells her, "The ring is beautiful, Claudette."

"Thank you."

Grand-papa says, "Well done, Joseph."

"It was not I who chose the ring, my fiancée did. I wanted her to have the engagement ring of her dreams; therefore I took her to Mr. Simmons and asked her to choose. Next we went to a special place for us and I proposed." I kiss Claudette's cheeks and quietly say, "Now that is romance." She lights up the room.

Joseph walks over to Théo. "I have known you since we were in our teens and Claudette knows you well. I would be honored if you stood by me as my best man." Théo extends his hand and tells him, "I will be most happy to. You honor me." A few of us get visibly emotional because Joseph was so sincere and we are the closest thing to family he has.

After a toast my Grandfather invites Joseph to live at Maison with Claudette after their honeymoon, he accepts and Claudette is elated. Then Joseph informs us he must go to the club, but hopefully since it's Thursday he will not be there long. My grandmother suggests we dine at Micheletto's and for Joseph to join us when possible. This is a good plan. No one need change their clothing, plus we can relax and enjoy the evening with someone else cooking. Claudette walks him to the door and we scatter to freshen up then reassemble at the cars.

Lingering over appetizers and wine pays off, because Joseph arrives in time to order his main course. Not one of his regular members showed. Fate smiled upon the happy couple and we celebrate. I remembered to get my camera and take only a few snapshots to capture the occasion. I have never seen Claudette or Joseph look so happy.

The next day is Friday. Emily and I are on our way to meet the crew for lunch and I can hardly wait to tell everyone about the newly engaged couple. Inside we notice Joanna apparently sent Mitch to The Flying Dragon, because there are several take out boxes setting in the middle of the dining table with plates that have chopsticks and napkins lying across them. The thing that catches my eye is the sake cups by the plates.

We get kisses from our men and sit down. Trevor touches the sake cup and looks at me with eyes gleaming then says first thing, "Geneviève needs the floor."

"I have an announcement, Claudette and Joseph are engaged." I give them a moment to react then add, "The private wedding ceremony will be held by the beach at Maison de la Mer on Saturday, September 6th." Jaws drop and Joanna says, "This can be handled easily. It's like an elopement." I respond, "Exactly." Mitch chimes in, "We should start eating and have a toast to them with the sake." Next Trevor and I ask Joanna and Mitch if they have plans tomorrow night and fortunately they do not, so we invite them to dinner at the apartment to see the progress on our house. When Mitch makes the toast Emily and I take two small sips of sake, we have responsibilities. And all too soon due to those responsibilities we are back at our desks.

After work Trevor and William are waiting together by the Willys and when they see us Trevor goes to meet me at his car. We wave to our friends and I place my head on his shoulder for I am weary. "Baby, do you still want to go to the market?"

"Yes, I want us to cook our dinner and do whatever it was we had planned last Friday."

"Can you believe a week has gone by?"

"Not really. I hope we can slow down and enjoy some of this weekend."

"Don't give it a second thought, because I am a man a mission to achieve that very thing." This gets him a kiss and off we go to the market together for the first time. I am making my smoked salmon and as we buy the ingredients Trevor keeps me completely entertained.

At the apartment we set out the greens for our salad and put the other things away. While Trevor opens a bottle of wine I tell him, "I am going to call Mandarin Gardens and pre-order a crispy duck for dinner tomorrow." Stammering he asks, "Did ... did you say crispy duck?" I chuckle and nod. "I haven't had one of those in months and months. Do you know how much I love you?" And I get a glint for a change. "You can show me after dinner." While he stands there with his mouth open I call the restaurant and then Mother to find out what I've missed. At the beginning of the call Trevor hands me a glass of wine and sits beside me then I hang up and fill him in. "Mother and Claudette went to the wardrobe department of the ballet company today where she talked them into loaning them a corset and tutu from 1887. After Claudette and I have lunch inside at the club in order for Joseph to serve us, we are taking the fragile items to The Bridal Salon to have it duplicated and that is all that involves me."

"I heard your end of the conversation and made a decision on how to spend my time apart from you. First I am going to the base and then I am having lunch at the club by the pool then go for a swim. Just pretend I'm not there if you see me."

"That won't be easy to do." After we laugh I tell him, "I have an idea you are going to love."

"You definitely have my attention."

"I'm going to throw my swimming suit and a few things in my straw tote before leaving. When we are done at The Salon I'll have Claudette drop me off at the club and join you."

"I can't believe it. I'm finally going to get you in the pool." Trevor takes my wine glass and sits it on the coffee table by his and pins me against the sofa. There we stay for quite some time, because he doesn't wait until after dinner to show me how much he loves me.

As we prepare our meal together I tell Trevor, "To have only cooked a few basics you certainly know your way around the kitchen."

"For years I've watched Joanna and Mitch cook. It's probably going to surprise us both how much I know." I give him a kiss and the asparagus.

With Trevor, cooking is almost completely different. He brushes up against me every chance he gets and I do likewise. We reach around each other and steal kisses with the occasional pause for a proper kiss. When it comes time to set the table and eat I'm a little disappointed because the time flew, but I can plainly see he isn't. Trevor has been waiting a long time for this meal.

Next he does something else he has been waiting on, to finally play music on our record player. I watch him carefully choose each record then turn it on and adjust the volume to a nice low. He lights the candles on the table and kisses me once more before seating me and whispers, "Now this is a romantic candlelit dinner; to the first of many." We hold up our glasses and make them sing.

Just before dessert, which is a mystery to me, our song begins to play. Trevor looks at me with a little smile as he stands and offers me his hand then we sway and nuzzle each other. How I do enjoy dancing with him when we are alone.

When the song ends he asks me with eyes gleaming "Are you ready for dessert?" I begin to laugh and he adds, "That was a rhetorical question." Still laughing I nod as he opens the freezer. Looking so pleased with himself he holds out a container I recognize. "In this is homemade vanilla ice cream from The Confectionery at the park. You can show me how much you love me afterwards if you wish." I reply, "Oh, I wish."

When we have savored the last bite of ice cream he stands and pulls me up from my chair then leads me to the bathroom. "I brought my shaving kit from the base, so we can make out and not chap your chin." I smile as I think just my chin is no longer accurate; he kisses far more than my lips.

Trevor shaves and holds out his hand for mine. "Geneviève, follow me please." I do as he asks and he opens a drawer. Next I see he is holding one of my camisoles and pajama bottoms. "These were on the bench at the foot of your bed." He offers them to me and I go back to the bathroom. When I come out I place my hands on his face and he whispers, "Do you have any idea what you do to me?"

"Tell me."

"You smell and taste so sweet. And you are *so* soft. Then there is the way you touch me and the sounds you make. I find myself reaching a point I want to devour you."

"And you hold back." He nods. "Trevor — devour me."

He looks deep into my eyes then holds on to my waist. Trevor slowly kneels before me and lifts my camisole to expose my abdomen then he begins to kiss my body there. When my breathing gets inconsistent to the point I get light headed and pull on his shirt, I decide I want it off of him. As I begin to take it off he lets go of me and holds his arms up. It is gone and so are we to the bed.

The strength in my arms has waned and I cannot manage my body anymore. I tell him breathlessly, "Trevor, look at me." He gets still and looks into my eyes. "My strength is at its end. You have devoured me." He smiles ever so slightly as we catch our breath. Trevor tenderly kisses my lips and lies down beside me.

Eventually I notice the flames of the candles flickering, which means they are about to go out. Those candles burn seven hours, which means it's around two o'clock in the morning. Then I realize something else. "Trevor, the flames of the candles are flickering and need to be blown out before the candlesticks crack. He sits up, "It must be later than we think." He crosses the room as I tell him, "They burn seven hours." He glances over his shoulder at me and after he blows them out he asks, "Geneviève, do you want to change?"

"Not really. I'm going to sleep in this and shower in the morning." I sit on the edge of the bed; drink some water and Trevor returns with my things then puts his rumpled shirt back on that has been lying on the floor and we walk to the house. Passing Théo's car I hope he is in bed sound asleep. Seeing him the way we are dressed would be awkward. Fortunately the house is dark and we go upstairs quietly not to disturb anyone.

Trevor tucks me in and kneels by my bed. "Geneviève, I'm not sure if this is an appropriate thing to say, but thank you for allowing me to devour you. I love you."

"Oh thank you — very much. And I love you too." We kiss goodnight and I fall asleep with the scent of him all around me.

The smell of coffee brewing wakes me and I am so happy it's Saturday I do not know what to do with myself. I jump into the shower, put on a nightgown and robe to have breakfast in the solarium and open my door. Trevor's is still closed and when I reach it I do not here a sound. After lightly knocking I hear a groan that gets me tickled. "Geneviève, I can hear you. Come on in."

He sees me and becomes wide awake. "You're showered and ready for breakfast."

"And all before you were even awake. Good morning, Trevor."

"Good morning, Baby." He moves over and I sit down.

"I will only stay a minute and bask in the glory of last night with you then I'm getting out of the way while you do some Navy things to get downstairs" He chuckles as I touch his face. "Still pretty smooth; you don't need to shave yet."

"Shaving after dinner was a first."

"I did appreciate it." He slides his hand along my thigh. "Trevor, I'm going downstairs before I change my mind." I go to the door and before pulling it open I turn to him and say, "By the way, there is a passion mark on my abdomen." The look on his face is priceless. I smile demurely and tell him, "You might want to get that yellow feather out of your mouth before you have breakfast with the family." I close the door and hear his deep laugh as I walk away.

We linger in the solarium after breakfast and Rachel arrives. No doubt she slept in. Entertaining her parents had to be exhausting. Trevor and I stay a little longer, but Claudette will be here shortly and we must excuse ourselves. I have a lot to do and Trevor is more than happy to help. We dress and he comes in to put everything I need in my straw bag while I finish getting ready for a ladies lunch at the club. Then we go out to the cars in time to see Claudette round the corner with a very large box and her handbag swinging on her arm.

Trevor runs to her and takes the box that is obviously from the ballet company and she hovers as he sets in the back seat. Trevor helps her in the car and after giving me a kiss with a little longing in it he helps me in. We will only be apart a short time, but I feel a twinge as we leave. Saturday is ours.

The moment we drive through the entrance to the club there is a change in Claudette's demeanor to the point she even takes out her compact and checks her lipstick, something I have never seen her do. Inside I insist for her to walk in front of me in order for Joseph to see her first. Claudette is petite and tends to hide behind whomever she is following. Reluctantly she does and is thrilled she did because Joseph, knowing we are punctual, was standing by our table waiting on her to arrive. He looks professional like always, but his eyes give him away.

After having one of the longest lunches in history we are on our way to The Salon. I am so proud of myself; for I resisted the urge to look for Trevor. He was there and I know how he looks when he is swimming. It was indeed a struggle.

The ladies at the salon are expecting us, but they are not prepared for what is in the box. They have to put on gloves to handle it. While Claudette and I look at bolts of fabric I catch a glimpse of my wedding gown. The majority of it is covered with cotton sheeting my name is on and I wish there was a way to look at it alone before we leave.

Claudette is going to wear a crown of flowers with ribbon streaming down the back of it just like the ballerina in the Degas and I am to wear pink. She wants my dress to be styled almost exactly like hers, in a tea length which I have not worn since I was a teen.

There are several shades of pink satin on the shelves. The bolts of fabric are grouped by color making the selection process simpler. Suddenly I am caught off guard by Claudette exclaiming, "Your name is on the tag hanging from this bolt." She has discovered my Strawberry Fluff. "This is the satin your gown was made of for your engagement dinner. That was the night Joseph and I strolled through the torches together and we expressed our love for one another."

"Claudette, it seems appropriate my dress for your wedding should be made from this."

"You would not mind wearing the color twice."

"In fact I am thrilled at the thought of an opportunity to wear it again."

She hugs me then chooses two accessories which takes almost no time at all. Like all brides-to-be she has a vision of her wedding and saw herself wearing slippers that resemble ballet shoes. Mine are going to have a heel and be dyed to match my dress. Her something blue is a white handkerchief with a hand embroidered edge in the perfect shade of blue to be tucked in her bodice as she walks to her groom then it will be placed into her bridal purse at the reception. When I return I am going to ask them to make her a small fan to match her ensemble that can fit into it. She is going to need one.

Not even an hour has passed and we're in the car. Trevor will not be expecting me so early. It will be a nice surprise. When I get my keys out Claudette reaches to hold the hand they are in. "Geneviève, I am in need of a favor."

"Simply tell me what it is."

"I do not know how to choose the nightgowns. Will you help me?" My eyes get wide as my jaw drops. "Geneviève, what is the matter?"

"Not one thing have I purchased for my Bridal Trousseau."

Claudette covers her mouth as I start the car and drive toward the lingerie boutique. Did something this important really slip my mind? I need new everything; undergarments, peignoir sets, slips, tap pants; oh the list is long. I will not be surprising Trevor early after all.

We swoop into the boutique and I tell the clerk why we are here and she goes away. "Claudette, I am guessing you want to be modestly dressed yet feminine and want at least one peignoir set in white."

"You guess correct."

She is a size two petite and as I look through the rack I tell her, "Stop me when you see something that catches your eye in any color, you need at least three." She nods and looks determined. We are about to reach the end of the section when she says, "That one." And it is an excellent choice, a white silk satin nightgown trimmed in lace with a matching lace peignoir. My brother could see her in it without flinching it is so modest. We pull it and soon she spots one in a lovely pale blue. Then there are no more left to look through and she is obviously sad.

"Claudette, you prefer pajamas. Perhaps we can find one's suitable for the occasion." I motion for the clerk and explain we want feminine pajamas and the woman perks up. "There is a new line from a designer in Hollywood I think will meet your needs." We follow her and Claudette is happy again. They even have matching bed jackets, thus we have struck gold. She is in her element, so after choosing a set for me I go shop for a few things on my list.

Fortune smiles on me *and* I find things for her. Soon we are in adjacent dressing rooms and we are two elated women when we are done. The poor clerk calls for an assistant and they begin pulling tags and putting thing in garment bags and boxes upon boxes carefully keeping our purchases separate. And once again I have to bring the car around in order to load it.

Claudette drops me off at the club entrance to the pool and happily goes home to admire her things. I open the gate and see Trevor immediately. He is swimming laps and I get close enough to where he can see me. Lucky me, I am able to watch him for quite a bit before he does. He lights up; here we go, I remember this sight very well, dripping wet with muscles toned from the laps looking too good.

"There she is." He climbs out, dries his face, kisses my cheek and I look the man up and down. Trevor is amused. I look into his eyes and say, "I am going to change into my swimming suit and gather my wits." and walk away listening to the deep laugh that doesn't help my situation at all. My desire to get my hands on him is going to be an issue, therefore I go to the bar, order a vodka Collins and begin drinking it as I change my outfit and put my hair in a tight French braid.

Marc opens the door for me and I make an entrance for I am in full on club poolside attire that includes tan kitten heeled slides, a wide brimmed straw hat and sunglasses. The best item is the turquoise colored open front cover up that blows in the wind showing my white strapless swimming suit. My bag is over my shoulder and my drink is in hand as I go to Trevor whose mouth is open as he stands to seat me. "Geneviève, I am not sure how to give you a compliment and not sound inappropriate."

"I will take that as your compliment and say thank you." He removes his sunglasses after sitting down to get a better look at me and tells me in a hushed tone, "You have caught me off guard once again." I must admit I am enjoying this immensely.

A few minutes later Marc comes over and I order a dozen boiled shrimp on ice to go with my drink. Trevor orders a vodka Collins and pushes his soda aside. I smile demurely and he shakes his head. Marc brings him the Collins and he eventually thinks to ask, "How did the outing go?"

"Very well, thank you. Both of us wound up shopping when we went to the lingerie boutique." Trevor's face goes straight and he dryly says, "Lingerie?" and puts his sunglasses back on. I finally get tickled and say, "That was not intentional, but I am enjoying this moment."

"That makes two of us. — Baby, I almost didn't recognize you. But I know those legs, every inch of them." I push my sunglasses down and look over them at him. "I'm going to be quiet now."

My voice drops as I ask him, "Why? I enjoy the way you talk to me now."

"The gypsy in you is going to get the best of me."

"Oh — I hope so."

Trevor's eyebrow goes up then he glances away. "Here comes Marc with the shrimp. I hope I don't get choked on one."

This just keeps getting better. He is so focused on me he doesn't realize how focused I am on him sitting there with one button done on his shirt in those swimming trucks. I rarely see his legs. This is only ... the third time. The other night when he was running, doesn't count. It was dark. I'm moving us to the lounge chairs after we eat, so I can get a better look at him.

Trevor does not choke on a shrimp even though we flirt shamelessly the entire time. In due course I stand, remove my cover up and drape it on the chair back then suggest we move to lounge chairs. He unbuttons his shirt and I stare at him while he hangs it on his chair. Sunglasses are so handy, one can stare a hole through someone without them knowing.

We are all settled in and I ask Marc to bring us two ice waters. When he leaves I get out my suntan lotion and begin with my legs. Trevor is obviously watching and eventually tells me, "That is my job."

"Not here, Mon Amour, but it is acceptable for you to put it on the back of my shoulders."

"I will take every inch I can get."

After the lotion is on my arms I offer the bottle to Trevor. I am positive his eyes are dancing as he stands; I can almost see them through his sunglasses. Before he begins, Trevor gets close to my ear and whispers, "At last I get my hands on you." I glance over my shoulder at him and he slowly proceeds.

When he is done I lie down, close my eyes, remove my sunglasses and sigh. The sun is warming my skin and it feels so good. A slight smile comes over my face when I realize I can feel his eyes on me. Then it occurs to me why are mine not on him. It's the reason I moved us. Casually I reach for my sunglasses and put them back on. When I turn to look at him he is of course looking down at my legs. I seize the opportunity to admire his entire body unbeknownst to him. This has quickly become the best day I ever spent at the pool. The phrase 'tall drink of water' runs through my mind while I feast my eyes on him.

Eventually I want a drink of water and I guess the sound of the ice in the glass brought him out of his trance. "Are you enjoying the day?" I sigh and go, "Mmm hm. And you?" He looks over his sunglasses and replies, "Quite." I laugh softly and ask, "Are you ready for another swim?" He nods and drinks some water as I pull the thin straps out of my suit and tie them around my neck. His eyebrows are raised as he stammers, "I ... I didn't know those were tucked away." Trevor sighs heavily then stands and helps me up.

He follows me to the deep end off the pool and asks, "Will you wait for me to reach the shallow end and swim to me?"

"Of course." I look at him smiling and add, "I have not been swimming since last summer. I just forgot how to dive." This gets a laugh.

"While I swim perhaps it will come back to you. I will see you at the other end." He kisses my cheek and dives in. I do not take my eyes off him as he swims under water and when he reaches the shallow end Trevor turns around smiling and holds his arms out. I dive in and swim under water toward him. When I reach him and come up out of the water we forget where we are and embrace.

"Geneviève, you dive gracefully and swim like ... you are beautiful."

"Trevor — thank you. I am taken aback."

"As am I. What do you want to do now?"

"This." I begin swimming on my back almost floating, slowly moving my arms and he follows alongside me swimming with his head above the water and we just watch each other. To the deep end and back we silently go, again and again.

Eventually I break the silence. "This is nice, I like swimming with you."

"Likewise. We need to make a day of this on our honeymoon."

"I could not agree with you more. I don't want to ask, but what time is it?"

"You're wearing a watch."

"Yes I am. This is my first time to wear it swimming." After looking at it I tell him, "Thank you for this. I do enjoy wearing it. I always think of you when I check the time and I don't have to take it off to shower." Trevor stops swimming and puts his feet on the bottom of the pool. "Geneviève, sometimes I do wish you would think before you speak. I have been in your bathroom and have seen you sunbathing on your stomach with very little on. Visuals enter my mind before I have the chance to stop them." I get so tickled that the serious look on his face goes away and he finally sees the humor of the situation.

We get out and as we dry off he tells me, "You have been toying with me mercilessly since you arrived."

"Only ... three percent was intentional."

"I know, but that other 97%. Don't hold me responsible for my actions when we get in the car." With that said we climb up the pool ladder and quietly gather our things.

As we walk to the table I hear, "Gené." We stop cold in our tracks and turn to see Théo and Rachel sitting close by. There is a partially eaten plate of fried calamari on their table and I ask, "How long have you two been here?" Théo replies, "Over half an hour. We chose not to disturb. If memory serves this is the first time you both have been in the pool, not by it. Can you two join us for a few minutes?" Trevor replies, "Of course we can." When we do Théo tells us, "Rachel and I were hatching a plan. *Rebecca* is still showing and she wants to see it again. Have you seen it?" Trevor and I smile, but the answer to his question eludes us. Saying we saw the end is inappropriate. Rachel steps in. "What he means to ask is would you like to meet us tomorrow for the matinee?"

Trevor gives me a nod and I answer looking at Rachel, "We would love to. Thank you for asking."

"Think nothing of it."

Marc steps up and asks, "May I bring you something?" Trevor replies, "The check, please." He bows and leaves then I tell Théo, "Joanna and Mitch are going to be our dinner guests tonight at the apartment and we are going to show them what you have done thus far on our house. It is shaping up nicely." He replies, "It is and I do not have to hover over the men, they are working hard for you."

Before I can respond Marc returns with the check. After Trevor signs it we stay just a bit longer then say our goodbyes. On the way to the car Trevor tells me, "I am pleased we ran into them, but it did change things."

"Nonetheless, I will not hold you responsible for your actions."

"That will be putting the key in the ignition, starting the car and leaving against my will."

"And mine." We sigh and get in the car.

Pushed for time we decide to split up to accomplish all that needs to be done. He parks out front, walks me to the door and gives me a kiss. While I get ready, he is going to get ready and pick up the take out. Men do have the advantage; they are ready in minutes. If I move at a fast pace I could have the table set by the time he returns.

In a rush I get the picnic basket and put our bottle of sake along with a sake set in it and go out the front door. The first thing I do is put on a pot of water to warm the sake in the Tokkuri then begin setting the table. Trevor arrives just in time to take over the sake. The last thing I do is place the duck on a platter and it smells delectable. Trevor turns on the record player, lights the candles and there is time to sneak in a passionate kiss which we stop when Mitch knocks on the door.

Joanna kisses our cheeks then begins a conversation that changes subjects with each sentence as she looks around. "Trevor, so this is where you live. Ah — a crispy duck, it has been ages and pineapple cakes. This record player is nice." She draws in a breath and I ask, "Would you like to have a seat?" and motion to the table. Mitch is shaking his head as he slides her chair forward and Trevor pours her sake. While eating we laugh more than anything enjoying excellent food and marvelous company. What more could one ask for?

The mirth continues as we walk to our house. The dry-wall is in and soon the painting will begin. Théo is going to paint patches of our color choices on a wall in each room first. He has not said anything, but I know his main concern is with our choice of burgundy for the walls of the master suite. Trevor and I can imagine how nice the black furniture and my black and white photographs are going to look.

On our way out Joanna puts her arm around my waist and I hers then she stops us standing under the frame work for the solarium. Mitch glances at her and she gives him a slight nod. We all are focused on Mitch as he moves to stand close to Trevor and begins to talk. "Geneviève, do you know our plans for when I retire?"

"No, I don't."

"We decided years ago to buy a beach cottage on the East Coast to be near our families. As always time and events have a way of changing things. Joanna and I have been discussing the events of late and have decided that when I retire we are going to stay here."

Mitch places his hand on Trevor's shoulder, "I am not sure when or how it happened, but for years Joanna and I have referred to you and William as the boys. Now we have two girls and neither of them wants to leave San Diego." He glances at me. "Emily has been vocal." He looks back at Trevor who is at a loss. "The way we see it, Louise will be here when I retire. Therefore I am going to make my wife very happy by giving her a house off a Navy base."

Joanna beams as she tells us, "We have already been looking at lots in the area. And as fate would have it we recently made the acquaintance of a local architect who is quite talented." Mitch adds, "He works for a highly recommended building company too. By the way, you both are the first to hear this." Trevor replies, "I am speechless." and looks at me.

Once, maybe twice it crossed my mind they would move away and the thought upset me so, mostly for Trevor, and I promptly cleared it from my mind. Hearing this news has me fighting tears of relief and joy, thus my silence. I expect Trevor is silent for similar reasons.

After giving us a minute to regroup Joanna asks, "Geneviève, will you join me for a stroll around the gardens?" I nod as she holds my hand and walks to them. Joanna gives Mitch a kiss and kisses Trevor cheek then steps back. Mitch kisses my hand and I look into Trevor's eyes for a moment and give him a kiss. Joanna adds, "We will see you fellas back at the apartment." and we go down the steps.

When we reach the cobblestones she quietly says, "I thought they needed privacy. You already knew we called them the boys; Trevor has a lot to process and you do as well. I will enjoy the gardens until you ..." I stop her in mid-sentence by giving her a hug. She tells me, "I feel the same way."

Quietly we stroll as she holds on to my arm all the way to the boardwalk. Then she tells me, "I have been wanting some time alone with you for a while."

We sit next to each other on a lounge chair and I respond, "Likewise."

"I will get to the point, is there anything else you want to know before you go on your honeymoon?"

"Thank you for asking, but there is not one thing I can think of. I am not nervous in the least. I trust Trevor and we did have an in depth conversation at my behest. I had questions only he could answer."

"Good for you, Geneviève. Women seldom speak up and they should. Silence is the enemy for so many reasons. A couple should discuss everything, covering from what seems to be insignificant to the glaringly obvious. Otherwise things can go very wrong that could have been avoided by a simple conversation." I nod in agreement then we sit in silence listening to the ocean.

Time passes and she asks me, "How long have we been here?"

"I have no clue, which means we should probably start back."

We walk to the apartment and find them sitting on the sofa and love seat drinking cognac. Mitch says, "There they are." Trevor adds, "We were about to form a search party." We sit next to our men and they hand us glasses of cognac on the coffee table they poured and we begin warming it. They were busy while we were gone, different records are even playing.

When the glasses are empty Joanna ask Mitch, "Are you ready to take me home?" He replies, "Yes I am." He turns to us and we walk with them onto the balcony where we say our good nights. As we watch them drive away I find myself in Trevor's arms being spun round and round as he makes his way inside with me. He puts me down and says, "Now I'm going to tell you the main reason I went ahead and bought the record player. I want to teach you how to tango."

"Are you going to start tonight?"

"If you want me to."

"I want."

"Kick off your shoes."

Trevor takes off his and while he changes the record he tells me, "If you trip, know I have you." and we take a stance. The record begins to play and he sweeps me off my feet figuratively and after the third time we dance he sweeps me off them literally to the sofa where he unbuttons my dress and gently bites the slope of my neck. Thankfully tomorrow is Sunday and we can sleep in.

CHAPTER SEVEN

We have a late brunch while the rest of my family and Claudette sip coffee after having breakfast with Joseph. Their wedding, being just days away is the main topic. My grandmother has the task of a mother of the bride to fulfill and my grandfather has those of a father of the bride. The tasks are not overwhelming for they do not want any musicians and want only a small dinner at the club for their wedding reception. My parents are acting as one's for the groom. The rehearsal dinner is going to be at Micheletto's, so that is a phone call for Mother. Father gets thrown in the mix, because the happy couple wants the ceremony to be spoken in French and he needs to call Reginald. It is short notice, but we are hoping he can officiate the wedding and if not, perhaps he knows someone who can.

After brunch we decide to walk around our house for a little while then go to the apartment and clean the kitchen. Once again the dishes sat overnight. There isn't any time to relax on the sofa today, because we're going on a double date. I've been looking forward to spending time with Rachel and Théo for days and seeing the rest of movie, the ending *was* good.

We enter the parking lot and I instantly say, "There is Théo's car. Oh — don't get close."

"I see them kissing. I'll drive around until they stop."

Trevor finally parks after making a few laps and we get out. They see us and walk our way. Rachel is aglow and I whisper, "Oh my gosh, Théo proposed." They close in fast and he cannot respond. We greet each other and Théo says, "You two are going to be the first to know; I proposed less than two hours ago. I exclaim, "Oh, Théo." and hug him then Rachel and tell her, "I am going to love having you for a sister." She replies, "Likewise. We are going to have so much fun teaming up on these two."

I nod repeatedly and am all smiles as Trevor shakes Théo's hand chuckling and tells him, "Allow me to be the first to congratulate you."

"Thank you, Trevor."

"She's a catch." And we all burst into laughter.

Rachel manages to say, "I am a catch, literally, in the bigger net he cast and it was suggested by you."

This gets me another hug as I desperately try to get a glimpse of the ring he gave her. Théo is watching me with eyes dancing. And that is enough of that. "Rachel, may I see the ring?" The woman becomes completely calm and holds her hand out. "It's more beautiful than I imagined."

Rachel gushes, "I can't get over the fact he had an Art Deco ring made for me."

"I know exactly you feel. Théo, you have always had impeccable taste."

"Excuse me, can we go back in the conversation just a bit? Geneviève, I sense your ring has a story. May I ask what it is?"

"Of course. Trevor showed up one morning in the parking lot before I went in to work with coffee and chocolate croissant. It was the only time he was going to be able see me that day. Trevor didn't know how I took my coffee yet, therefore he called the house when he was certain I was gone and asked Théo how I took it. What I did not know, was he asked Mother my ring size in the same call and was driving to Beverly Hills to get my ring at Cartier after he left."

Rachel gasps. "Cartier of France because you're French. How romantic."

Théo looks at his watch and tells Trevor, "Maybe they will follow us if we start walking." He replies, "Let's find out shall we?" Rachel shakes her head and I say, "We heard that." Théo replies, "Oh, good." Trevor motions to the theater and adds, "Ladies, after you — please." Rachel and I breeze passed them and continue to talk as Théo buys tickets.

At the concession stand when Rachel discovers what I am doing with my jelly beans she tells me, "You are brilliant. I never eat those here because I hate black licorice. It tastes medicinal." Théo takes the box of chocolate covered peanuts she is holding and exchanges them.

Rachel happily goes up the stairs to the balcony with her licorice free jelly beans as Théo says, "I hope the front row isn't crowded." I almost gasp as my eyes get wide. Luckily I am looking down at the stairs and no one saw my face. All I can think is I am in for it.

We are walking in pairs now and they are in the lead. Rachel is the first one to see the balcony and announces, "The front row is not crowded; in fact we are the only people up here." I briefly close my eyes and think here we go. Théo looks to the back row and says, "I can't believe there isn't a make out couple." Trevor burst into a contained laughter then says, "I *have* to know why you said that."

Théo chuckles and begins to answer him as we have a seat. "Gené and I always sit up here and when she was young I told her couples would be kissing in the back and it would be best for her not to turn around. When she was older Gené found out the term for what they were doing and she started calling them make out couples, and it stuck."

Trevor has to cover his mouth in order to muffle his laughter. I dryly tell him, "We are at a higher altitude where there is less oxygen. I hope you pass out." Théo and Rachel get tickled and Trevor has to take his hand off his mouth in order to breathe. Some people on the lower level finally turn around to see what is going on. I just shake my head and take the popcorn from his lap. Rachel says,

"Théo, you know she is going to get even with you for that." He replies, "I know, but it was worth it." They settle down when the lights dim.

I give Trevor the popcorn back and eat a jelly bean. He whispers, "What flavor did you get this time?" Without looking at him I coolly reply, "Lemon." Trevor softly chuckles and his response is, "That you taste sour does not deter me in the least." I can't help it; I smile and look at him. He lights up and says, "Give me a kiss. I know you want to." I sigh and of course I kiss him.

The movie is good, as I thought it would be and I am on Cloud 9 sitting between the man I love and my brother who I have been missing and is at last engaged. I know Théo has been missing me too, because he holds my hand a little while and kisses it before letting it go. This is a good day.

As we walk out of the theater Théo announces, "This is first time we've been together like this and I feel like celebrating. Are you with me?" Trevor and I nod. "Excellent. Rachel, where would you like to go?"

"To The Brava for a bottle of champagne and hors d'œuvres."

"The perfect choice." He gives her a kiss that makes her glow even more. Then Trevor lights up. "We're going to The Posh." Théo and Rachel give us a look and I inform them, "That is what he has been calling The Brava." Rachel laughs and Théo says, "Very British. I'm going to call Mother and tell her they should have the apéritif without us and we will join them for dinner."

Seated at The Posh things become humorous, because the first thing Théo tells us is, "I do not want to wait on a wine list and therefore I am about to utter words I thought would never come out of my mouth." So, when the server walks up and asks what we would like to start with Théo glances at me and replies, "A tray of the finest hors d'œuvres and a bottle of the best champagne, please." The server says, "Right away, sir." and gives him a nod. We have to wait a moment before the laughter could begin.

While waiting on the champagne to chill Trevor and I finally get to hear the story of the proposal. They were sitting outside on the balcony enjoying the morning view and when Théo went inside to warm their coffee he decide to go back and propose. He returned with the coffee and got down on one knee. Rachel tells us it was so early he completely caught her by surprise.

The champagne arrives and we are relieved when we find out their best is a Roederer. After it is poured Trevor holds up his glass for a toast. "Everyone, please raise their glass." This is not going to be for only Rachel and Théo. "To being incredibly happy and clichés." We laugh and make our glasses ring loud and true then drink to a well stated toast. Shortly after, Rachel glances at Théo and looks at me. "Geneviève, I want to ask you something. Will you please stand by side while I marry Théo?"

"Oh — I would love to. I am taken aback."

"You were expecting me to ask Darlene, but she did not bring us together and she will understand." Théo adds, "And it is appropriate, because Trevor, I want you to be my best man. Would you do me the honor?" Trevor responds, "It would be my pleasure. I am the one who is honored."

While they shake hand Rachel jumps in. "The ceremony is going to be on Saturday the 22nd of November." I gasp and Théo nods as he says, "Our rehearsal dinner will also be a celebration of our grandparents' 55th wedding anniversary." I respond, "How romantic — and a little sneaky." Trevor comments, "You two are as thick as thieves." We proudly nod and then he gets distracted. "Excuse me for a moment."

Trevor goes to the server who was hovering at a short distance and asks for the check. He gives it a quick look, hands him money and returns. "Pardon me, but that server was watching us like a hawk and I wanted to make sure we were not interrupted. I will fill everyone's glass. What did I miss?" I reply, "Just more plotting against our grandparents. While he laughs I ask Rachel, "Are there any details yet?"

"We are getting married under the arbor at 11:45, when it will be the warmest and having a private luncheon at Maison. Then we will go on our honeymoon to an undecided place and hopefully arrive in time for dinner. The only big event will be an engagement party at the club." Théo adds, "We have learned by the events planned by you two along with William and Emily. Collapsing from exhaustion after our wedding is not an option. We'll barely have to time to catch our breath between everything already scheduled." Rachel chimes in, "Today is the last day of August and there are two weddings in September and one in October. November has Josephine's birthday and Thanksgiving, which is on the day before the rehearsal, slash anniversary dinner and the next day is our wedding."

After Trevor and I process the information I tell Rachel, "I hope you like to shop." She replies, "I do, but not this much at once. We need six gowns to finish out the year and one of them is a bridal gown for me." My jaw drops and Trevor smiles as he pulls the champagne bucket over and fills our glasses. We thank him and I tell her, "Trevor chose my gown for the engagement party and by his smile I can tell he will be volunteering to help me shop."

Rachel looks puzzled and asks me, "At The Bridal Salon?"

"Yes. Those women really should make this known. After hours appointments can be made to include men."

"Instead of dwelling on the fact I wish I'd known this sooner I'm going to revel in the thought of Théo helping me."

Trevor adds, "This is all I am going to tell you both; the experience will surpass your expectations." He gives Théo a nod then glances at his watch. "I think the race to dinner should start." I respond, "You said race." Rachel tells Théo, "Don't look, let's just leave."

While waiting on the cars we plan a strategy. Théo is going to drop Rachel off at the door of her apartment building and wait by the curb like a chauffeur. We are to meet in the foyer of the house and go next door together. Luckily Rachel and I only need to put on a little more makeup and change dresses. The cars arrive and we are off to the races, literally.

At the house Trevor and I sprint upstairs and go to our rooms. Finding a dress that didn't have to go over my head was a time consumer, but Trevor helps me make the loss up by selecting my shoes and jewelry. I give him a kiss and put on lipstick as he puts on his jacket and down the stairs we go.

A minute passes maybe, then there is a commotion outside and my brother flings open the door for Rachel. As Théo takes two stairs at a time he says, "Give me two minutes." She has a strange look on her face as she emphatically tells us, "I don't ever want to do that again." She turns her back to me and asks, "Are my seams straight?" I go, "Oooo." She sighs heavily. "That's a no." Quickly I say, "Rachel, I will straighten them for you." Trevor clears his throat. "Ladies, do I need to be here for this?" We get tickled and I tell him, "We'll go down the hallway to the mirror." He replies, "Thank you." as we walk off.

With seams straightened we go back to the foyer in time to see Théo descending the stairs with tie flying and the French cuffs on his shirt down. We are cutting it close, so as we go next door Théo puts on his tie tack and cufflinks. At the doors Rachel straightens his tie as Trevor looks at his watch and proudly says, "17 seconds to spare." and opens a door. We get excited because we made it and enter the house beaming.

Everyone is standing in the drawing room near the fireplace instead of sitting and Mother says, "You all look so happy." Théo responds, "We are; I proposed to Rachel this morning." They are instantly surrounded.

When Claudette disappears and returns with a bottle of Cristal already chilled Théo shakes his head at Grand-mamma. "Easy this was to predict. Neither of you have ever missed the apéritif." She does have a point and when we all have glasses filled with champagne my father looks around the room with Mother holding on to his arm. It is a lot to take in. Not long ago his children were free as the birds that visit our gardens and in a fraction of time they are getting married.

In due course Father glances at Mother and says, "This moment is worthy of an eloquent toast, yet this is what keeps going through my mind." He holds up his glass and says, "Everyone please raise your glasses and drink with me ... to love." We all echo his words and glasses ring in notes that sound like a song being played.

During the candlelit dinner Théo and Rachel tell the plans for their wedding and one can see the wheels of my mother and grandmother turning. I nudge Trevor so he doesn't miss this. My guesses; Mother is thinking how to pull off a Thanksgiving Dinner to accommodate the wedding guests. Grand-mamma is focused on the fact Théo and I have indeed got what we wanted, a celebration of their 55th at the club. Watching them is entertaining; the looks on their faces keep subtly changing. Trevor smiles and winks at me.

Back in the drawing room a bottle of Louis XIII is opened for the momentous occasion. As we sip the cognac there is a knock on the front door as it opens. Claudette looks as if Santa's sleigh just landed on our lawn as she goes to the foyer to greet Joseph. He enters the room and immediately congratulates our newly engaged couple, then Father tells him and Claudette Reginald will be able to officiate their wedding. After a short celebration of the good news Joseph asks, "Has the destination for your honeymoon been decided." Théo replies, "Not yet, but the night is young." Claudette says, "We have. Do tell them, Joseph."

Joseph is reluctant, but he begins to talk. "We plan on taking turns going to places we want to visit and do something special there. Claudette and I will pack the car Sunday morning and drive to Hollywood first. I've been there and told myself if I were ever fortunate to find a woman who would marry me I would take her there and we would go to the Chinese theater, look at the footprint's of movie star's and stay at the elegant hotel across the street. Then that night we would go watch the movie showing there." Claudette lights up and adds, "After that I have chosen to go to Helen's ranch."

Josephs' face changes as he tells us, "She told me how beautiful it is; therefore I am looking forward to it, but I have never ridden a horse. Claudette assured me it is not difficult and I will be riding one named Whiskey." Trevor jumps in. "No worries, mate. I hadn't been horseback riding since I was quite young and recently rode Whiskey. He does all the work; you just sit tight in the saddle." Joseph is visibly relieved.

In the midst of all this Théo decides we should dance. Thus the men begin moving furniture and ladies select records; then the dancing begins. In the middle of the second song Trevor tells me, "You have not stopped smiling."

"I adore hearing you speak British and you seldom do."

"When I'm relaxed it tends to surface."

"Will you say something else please?"

"You *are* lovely and I do fancy that dress."

"I love you, Trevor."

"I love you too, Baby."

"Would you like to go make out?"

Trevor looks at me with eyes gleaming and when the record stops he says, "Please excuse us, there is something I want to give Geneviève at the apartment. Rachel, Théo, we are so happy for you. Constance, Théodore, thank you for the lovely evening. Good night everyone." We smile and nod at the others and leave.

The second we are outside I ask, "You want to give me something?"

"Yes I do; a passion mark on your body wherever you want."

"I need to change out of this dress."

We walk silently to the house and upstairs. Into my closet I go and close the doors. I hear Trevor hanging up his jacket as I change into the shorts and shirt I wear washing the cars adding a camisole underneath. When I emerge Trevor's jaw drops. "My favorite outfit. Once again, you catch me off guard." Without a word I glide my hand across his face as I pass by him to go wash off my makeup.

At the apartment he changes into pajama bottoms and a tank shirt. After I pour us a glass of water I tug on the tank and he takes it off making his dog tags rattle. My hands are on his broad shoulders as he unties the knot in my shirt and says, "I can't believe I am getting to do this." Trevor looks at me lovingly as he unbuttons the shirt. "When I dress you or help you undress, buttons are my favorite."

"I know and you started this on our second date. That we have reached this point is beyond me."

"It is because you indulge my obsession for the sweet taste of your skin I cannot get enough of." Trevor takes off my shirt then holds my face as he softly kisses me. "Let's go lie down and talk for a bit. I've been thinking."

We get comfortable, which includes Trevor pulling my bare leg across him so he can glide his hand over my skin and he begins telling me his thoughts. "When I went to get your ring I noticed couples walking along the street Cartier is on. They were shopping together and not by appointment. This is what I've been thinking. After we're married, which will be in exactly two weeks, and are settled into our home I thought we could go up for a weekend. I want to stay in a posh hotel, order room service and take you shopping for the things I already know about and all the things I am going to find out about."

"Care to be specific?"

"What comes to mind first is slips; they follow the shape of your body and feel so good. Oh — and when wearing one you are always barefooted. Dresses that button up the front or zip in the back and anything I can find that is strapless. I'm especially interested in a bustier."

"A bustier? I do not recall telling you when I was wearing one. How do you know about those?"

"I saw one in London. It was on a mannequin and — wait a minute. When did you wear one?"

"During the weekend we celebrated our engagement."

"Under the fragile black lace gown."

"Mmm hm and yes the bustier was black, as well as everything else I wore."

"I think we should find you another black gown on our shopping spree."

"For New Year's Eve I plan to wear one made of black velvet."

"Velvet — and you will be my wife."

"Mmm hm." He rolls me onto my back and hovers over me tossing his dog tags over his shoulder.

"Before we are lost in euphoria, where do you want the passion mark?"

"My abdomen; the dress I am wearing for the wedding has thin straps. Please be careful elsewhere."

"I will be."

As we lie on the bed together it eventually begins to rain. He is tenderly kissing my neck and whispers, "I like being in bed at night and listening to the rain."

"So do I. I hope it rains an entire day during our honeymoon."

"And we will lie in bed all day and all night."

"Yes we will." And then he gets my earlobe between his lips. "Ooooh — Trevor — that feels so good. I love your lips."

"Baby, I love the sounds you make. I'm moving to your abdomen."

Trevor slides his hand under my camisole and along my side to raise it. I put my hand on his back and slide it across. I love his skin too. Then he finally gives me what he has wanted to give me, a passion mark, which gives me chill bumps and my breasts react. All I can think is I want to feel his warm body against them. "Trevor — kiss me." When he lies across me his breath goes "Whoooh." and I moan, because it feels indescribable to be against each other. There is no doubt in my mind the moment there is nothing between our bodies, it will take our breath.

While in a state of euphoria headlights go across the wall and we get still. It was Joseph leaving, therefore it's late. Trevor sighs as we sit up and drink some water, then I rest my head on his shoulder. "Geneviève, what is about rain?"

"It's like music playing softly in the background of a scene in a movie that stirs your emotion."

"On the first rainy day we spent together, when I held you on the dance floor I knew I wanted to hold you the rest of my life. And your breath smelled like cherries. I wanted to kiss you so much and taste them."

"That explains why you kissed me with such passion after lunch on the next rainy day. You were finally getting to taste the cherries."

"Yes I was. Now you taste like ... you." Trevor caresses my face and softly kisses my lips. Then I ask, "If you begin kissing me again will you be able to stop?" He responds, "Not for a while. — We're going to get drenched on the steps and be chilled to the bone. My umbrella is at my quarters. Another reason for me to move my things off the base, which I intend to start tomorrow if it isn't raining. I'm going to get my books first. Baby, what's the plan?"

"Throwing a blanket over us and making a run for the carport."

"Good plan."

We are barefooted and the cobblestones feel like ice cubes. When we're inside not even a hug helps; a long hot shower is the only solution. Even by Trevor's standard he has a long shower as well. After tucking me in, the second he let's go of me I curl up with Christopher. Trevor looks at me with a very straight face and says, "I will be replacing him soon." and closes the door.

It's a Monday and we find out at the morning briefing my parents are dinning at the club and Théo is taking his new fiancée out to a candlelit dinner. Trevor and I have decided to dine with my grandparents who will be thrilled when he calls them later in the day. The rain stopped and the men who install the glass for the solarium arrived before we left for the base. Joanna made a large pot of a tasty stew for lunch we almost emptied as I announced Théo's engagement and told them the highlights. Trevor stayed to pack his books and William volunteered to be a 'lifter of heavy things' to help with the move. By the time five o'clock rolled around two tired men were in the parking lot. Books are heavy.

At the house we discover my parents are already gone and take advantage of it for a few minutes. Then I notice a note on the kitchen table from Mother and ask Trevor to read it aloud.

"To Trevor, A delivery truck from Simmons was here. The packages are in the study. A freight truck was also here with two large crates addressed to you in care of Geneviève from your mother. Those are in the garage of your house. Have fun you two." I am beaming as he asks, "How did she know I would read this?"

"I am going to treat that as rhetorical. Let's go see what's in the crate's first." He chuckles, opens two colas and holds my hand as we walk down the hallway. Trevor says, "Seeing the words in writing ... it really is our house. Even though we don't live in it yet, it is ours." I look at him and say, "I had the same epiphany after you read them." Outside he looks over to the apartment. "William and I lugged my footlocker up all those steps." He puts his hand on his back and groans to make me laugh.

Upon entering our garage we have a reaction to the size of the crates. "Your mother's note did read a freight truck delivered these." We chuckle and walk over to them. One reads, Open Me First printed in very large letters. We recognize the handwriting; it's his mum's. And there is a hammer and two pairs of leather gloves on it placed there by Father no doubt. He hands me a pair and I put them on while he pries the top off.

With the lid safely removed we see newspaper pages and strips of torn sheets with things wrapped in them and small boxes. Lying on top of these items is a letter with his name on it, also in his mum's handwriting. Trevor opens it and begins to read it aloud. "My dear Son, The embassy sent over a crate to each house and told us pack what we want to bring on the transport flight, it was all we would be allowed. Your grandparents and father agreed with me since you will have a home soon, to pack all your belongings in London into the crates. We love you, Mum."

Trevor is overwhelmed by the words she wrote and what is before him; the things from his childhood and beyond are in these crates. He looks into my eyes and gives me the sweetest smile then puts the letter back in the envelope and reaches for the first item.

As Trevor carefully unwraps the sheeting a gray elephant pull toy is revealed. "This is Bradley Bull and I have no recollection of where Bradley came from, but I learned a male elephant are called bulls at the London Zoo. He followed my everywhere for years. I would carry him to go down or up stairs. He's made of mohair that used to be fuzzy." I interject, "You wore the fuzz off." He lights up and nods. "Bradley, this is my fiancée, Geneviève. Geneviève, this is Bradley." Trevor hands him to me and I say, "It is so very nice to meet you, Bradley." He replies, "Bradley says likewise."

There are so many treasured things in the crate. Holding Bradley I watch him unwrap tiny suits with short pants and shoes, framed photographs of him as a baby to a little boy, rattles and even a toy drum. When we realize it's time to eat with my grandparents we leave reluctantly and I take Bradley. During dinner we tell them what is in the crates. They are thrilled for Trevor and understand why we ask to be excused early.

A dress in no longer necessary and we go back to the house for me to change into my jeans. On the way when I suggest taking milk and plate of oatmeal cookies for the children we are being to the garage he beams, but when I suggest for him to get the milk and cookies while I change clothing he pouts.

Time passes with more treasures revealed and Trevor finally reaches the bottom layer. As he begins pulling a blanket out he gasps. "My toy chest and my train set." He lifts out three wooden boxes with sliding lids that contain his train set and puts them on the lid of the crate. The muscles on his back flex as he begins to lift the toy chest and when it is visible I cannot believe my eyes. Before me is a circus wagon with red wheels and black bars painted on it with a lion behind them.

He kneels in front of it and I stand next to him as Trevor softly tells me, "There was a toy shop in town and everything in it was made of hand carved wood. There were no walls in order for the children to see the men working. I thought it was what Santa's toy shop would be like, except with elves. I was young and vaguely remember picking this out. Years later Mum told me the story of us walking around the shop while she held my hand letting me look at all the toy chests. When I saw this one I said, 'Look Mummy, there's a lion on it and that's what we are. I want that one.' I wish I could remember those details, but one of my first memories is of this toy chest."

Trevor reaches for my hand and gently pulls me down to kneel beside him. He lifts the lid and the first thing I notice is a flour sack made into a drawstring bag laying on top of his toys wrapped in newspaper pages for shipping such a long way.

The sack is what he picks up. "These are in my first memories." Out of it he pours wooden Alphabet Nursery Blocks on top of the things in the chest and after pausing to look at them he picks one up and hands it to me then picks up another for himself.

"Mum taught me the alphabet using these and The A.B.C. Song when I was a toddler. We sat on a large rug that was under this and she put them on the lid with the letters in sequence and sang the song slowly as she pointed at each letter. I eventually started singing it too and one day we sang it at the tempo it was supposed to be sung at. Mum scooped me up in her arms and rocked me as we hugged, telling me what a smart boy I was.

"After that we started playing the game. She put them in the sack and we would take turns pulling one out and rolling them like dice. Whatever was on top I would tell her what it was; a number or punctuation mark and which one. If it was a letter I even told her capital or small. For drawings I would tell her what it was and the letter it started with. I was not wrong once and one of my blocks never went back into the sack to try again."

"My favorite was the G block. I liked saying gorilla. Now I like saying Geneviève." He reaches to hold my hand and gives me a kiss. "We played with these for hours over months and months even though I knew everything on the sides of each block. After dinner sometimes my father played the game with us. It was fun. The nanny was more like a maid that would occasionally babysit. My mum raised me."

After he tells me the story I get misty-eyed. Trevor just told me his fondest childhood memory and I can see him in his mum's arms. I find myself holding the block tightly in my hand and over my heart when Trevor asks, "Geneviève, are you all right?"

"Yes, I could see you and your mum, then I thought maybe one day we might teach our children with these."

"That would be ... more than I could ever hope for."

For that I have no reply, just the need to hold him and I do. Within seconds he says, "Your arms are almost cold. I have an idea. Let's take my train to the house. I will get a fire going in the study, make my hot cocoa and then we can put the train together by the fire."

"I love you."

"You do have the most unusual ways of telling me your thoughts and answering my questions that I quite like. And I love you too." Trevor covers the toy chest with a blanket to keep the salt air off of it and we go to the house with his train.

We seem to be walking on air until we reach the study and see our wedding gifts. I gasp and then we burst into laughter. Trevor goes, "Mmm mm mm mm mm." My parents are in the next room therefore he whispers, "I think it would be best that we never, ever, tell a single soul we forgot we had wedding gifts waiting for us." I respond, "I think you are spot-on." Trevor chuckles and says, "You're British is coming along nicely." He gives me a kiss and starts a fire.

On the way to the kitchen we stop in the doorway of the living room and he asks my parent's, "I am going to make hot cocoa, would you two like some?" Father answers, "Thank you, but no, we were about to go upstairs. We glance at our watches and Mother tells us, "Time does fly when you are having fun. Enjoy the rest of your evening." We say our good nights and go to the kitchen.

The fire is roaring now and we take off our shoes and kneel. He slides the lid off one of the boxes and in it is an abundance of track pieces that include a trestle. Trevor places the box between us and we start laying the track. When we are done I find I am in the middle of an oval that is at least 12 feet in length and 5 feet across with a trestle that is two feet long. "Trevor, this is huge."

"My father got enough track for us to fit in the middle without crowding each other."

The next box has the cars and I sit and watch him make a train yard with them. The last box has buildings, trees and thing one sees along a train track such as a water tower and signs. I help with this part of setting it up asking where each piece goes and he remembers as if he set this up yesterday. The beauty of this train set is its simplicity, for the wood is not painted and time did not damage it. Paint would have chipped and faded.

With the train track and what surrounds it in place Trevor picks up the engine and begins adding a car to it with each lap. He pulls it around his half of the track and I pull it around my half until the caboose is on. The trick is not to allow the train to slow down during the hand off and I master this in no time.

We are playing in our little world when we hear Théo say, "Bonsoir." We look up and I exclaim, "Théo, did you have a nice evening with your fiancée?" He replies, "Yes I did. Thank you for asking. That's a nice train set." Trevor tells him, "Thank you." Théo scans the study and asks hesitantly, "Are those wedding gifts?" Instead of answering him we look at each other. "I am clearly intruding. Pardon the interruption." Trevor responds, "You're not intruding; we're embarrassed." I tell Trevor, "We can make him take an oath." He chuckles and says, "Pour a nightcap and join us." Théo laughs, walks over to the liqueur cabinet and asks himself, "What have I gotten myself into?"

No longer kneeling we remain in the middle of the train track; I am on my hip with my legs bent and Trevor is sitting tailor-style. Théo walks over with his cognac, kicks of his shoes and sits like Trevor across from us. "I have not sat like this in years. It is entirely possible I will require help to get up." Trevor looks down at his legs and I get tickled.

Trevor begins telling Théo about our evening. I pick up my cocoa that is still warm, because it was close to the fire and sip on it letting Trevor tell the whole story. When he's done Théo understands why the wedding gifts haven't been opened and assures us our secret is safe as he holds up his right hand at my request.

My brother is looking at the train and Trevor asks, "Are you ready to see it in motion?" He responds, "Yes I am. In fact I've been waiting on you to ask." Trevor looks at me with a smile as he slowly uncrosses his legs and we kneel again. It's stopped on his side and he gets it going then I pull the train around my side of the track and over the trestle back to Trevor flawlessly. Théo tells me, "Well done." I reply, "Thank you, I'm new at this." Trevor adds, "Your sister caught on fast. We've been playing for over an hour. Would you like to play?"

"I need to go upstairs and catch up on some work I brought home."

"Good luck getting up."

"I'm going to need it." Théo shakes Trevor's hand and moves slowly as he manages to get to his feet then he kisses my forehead and we are alone again.

"Geneviève, what are we going to about those gifts?"

"Open them. Sleep is for the weak. Now help me up."

Laughing we make our way to the desk and he asks, "Where should we start?"

"They say good things come in small packages, but I think it's the opposite in this case, so let's start with the big ones."

"Good thinking."

He finds the biggest one, picks it up and goes, "Ooo, this is heavy." He sets it in front of me then stands at my side. I pull the bow and together we tear the wrapping paper off the box. He lifts the lid and we are looking at an ebony flatware chest used for storing a silver service for 12 with the small card that has the name of whom it is from laying on it. I pick it up and tell him, "Mr. and Mrs. Tobias Lyons." Trevor looks at me. "Every piece available in the pattern we chose is in this — which would explain the weight."

After he manages to get it out of the box I immediately toss it on the floor, so he can put it back down. Trevor says, "You should lift the lid." When I do we see he is correct, the chest contains every single piece, down to the gravy ladle.

I motion to the sofa and tell him, "Those boxes are the size of one's that contain 5-piece place settings of china and there are 12. Care to hazard a guess?"

"Poppy and Pops."

We go to the sofa and he opens one then hands me the card. It reads, Mr. and Mrs. Spencer Hutton. "Trevor, that was not a lucky guess was it?"

"Mum loves stemware and that's what is in those stacks of boxes on the floor."

I open one and get the card out. He knows his mum. "Trevor, it will take us half a day to check all this for breakage."

"I can't say I'm looking forward to that. All right, let's open the rest of the random ones on the desk and call it a night."

The last box to open sits before us. We silently lift the lid together and look at the card. It reads, Captain and Mrs. Everett Mitchell. There are three pieces wrapped in tissue paper. I lift out the one from the middle and know exactly what it is, a crystal vase. Trevor unwraps the other two, which are matching candlesticks. This was not on our registry. "Trevor, they gave us a set for a romantic candlelit dinner for two." My eyes get misty as Trevor takes the vase and sets it down. He holds my face and the instant his lips touch mine I get chill bumps.

The next morning I wake up and know in a split second my legs ache and I am going to need coffee until it's time for lunch. Dressed and ready to go down stairs I notice Théo and Trevor's doors are closed. "Good morning, fellas. I will see you both down stairs." Théo says, "Down in a minute." Trevor opens his door and motions for me to wait on him. When he focuses on me getting closer he lights up and says, "Good morning indeed." then gives me a kiss. "Geneviève, your dress has buttons."

"I am sorry to burst your bubble, but I am wearing this to avoid destroying my hair at The Bridal Salon when I try on my maid of honor dress. We are going there straight from work to meet Claudette and Joseph."

"I remember now."

"Trevor, why was I ready before you?"

"I was moving slowly, my legs are a tad stiff."

"Mine too."

"What I don't get is I can run for miles and I'm good to go, but sit in the floor for an hour and I'm incapacitated."

"You weighed less when you were a child."

"Ah, I was crushing them."

"Mm hmm."

"I feel better ... mentally."

Théo catches up with us on the stairs and I ask, "Legs stiff?" He somberly replies, "Just a bit." Trevor's says, "Join the club." We go into the kitchen, say our good mornings and line up at the coffee pot.

There is a lot going on today besides going to The Salon. Trevor is wearing his khaki uniform, because he is packing things in his quarters. Joseph and Claudette are getting their marriage license, we are getting ours Friday. Théo and Rachel will be here for dinner and last but not least, my father along with Mr. Cooper is having the meeting with the VIP's of the phone company this afternoon.

After work we spend a minute with Emily and William before going to The Salon. Sitting in the car, we look their way to wave goodbye and they are locked in an embrace. Trevor asks, "You have noticed that since the night they spent at Maison those two have been behaving like us?"

I manage to keep my face from turning red and reply, "Of course I have."

"Why aren't we doing that?"

"You started talking."

"I have nothing else to say."

As I laugh Trevor lifts my right hand and kisses it then slowly works his way up to my upper arm stopping at the edge of the cap sleeve of my dress. He is about to kiss my neck and I sigh heavily. "Trevor, we can't get carried away."

"We're parked in the back corner of the lot."

"I need you to focus; Claudette is going to a bride in four days."

"It is disconcerting how easily distracted by you I am." He lets go of my arm and starts the car.

Traffic was in our favor and we make good time. As we pull over to park Joseph gets out of his car and walks around the front of it to open the passenger door for Claudette. "Trevor, she still sits on the passenger side. That's not good."

"I couldn't agree with you more."

"Let's show them how it's done shall we?"

"Yes — let's."

Trevor waits until they are looking at us to get out and I slide over as he helps me out of the car. Joseph was watching us and Claudette seemed oblivious as she stood by him beaming. We only get to say hello, because Claudette starts toward the doors. Trevor and Joseph open them for us and stay outside.

I am first to try on my dress. When I come out Claudette gasps even though it is loosely on me because of the back lacing. Mrs. Parker tightens the laces and it fits me perfectly. The tulle is pretty and Claudette fluffs it a little as Mrs. Garner places the matching pink shoes at my feet. I slip them on and Mrs. Parker hands me a faux nosegay made of pale pink flowers to hold. When I am standing as if I am about to walk down the path Claudette gets misty-eyed and takes a step back. "Geneviève, you are a vision of loveliness. Are you pleased?"

"Yes I am. Your taste is flawless."

"Thank you for this."

"Claudette, it is my pleasure." And the ladies help me down from the pedestal. "You are next."

Claudette is wide-eyed as she goes to her dressing room. Without thinking I go to the settee to sit down and thankfully Mrs. Garner stops me before I crush the tulle then she quietly asks, "Miss Delcroix, we need you to try on your bridal gown. Should we wait?"

"Please and thank you for your discretion." She nods and goes to the pedestal.

The dressing room door begins to open slowly and there is the bride. She barely takes her eyes off me as she is helped up onto the pedestal. The ladies lace her up, slip on her shoes and hand her a faux bouquet. When they place a faux floral crown on her head that looks similar to the real one she will wear I go, "Oh my goodness. Claudette — you're beautiful. Degas would have painted you." The dear girl begins to tremble. I drop the nosegay and go to her immediately.

Her eyes puddle and she says, "I wish my family could see me." Tears well up in my eyes and I dare not blink. The ladies gasp for they know her circumstance. Mrs. Garner gets two handkerchiefs and dashes to us, because tears cannot get on these dresses. We dab our eyes while Mrs. Parker flicks open a fan as she walks over and begins fanning us the moment she is close. The gentle breeze stirred by the fan has a calming effect. My tears subside, my mind clears and words come to me. "Claudette, we will have two photograph albums made and send one to your family. Then after Joseph takes you home, when you celebrate your wedding anniversary, wear this."

A smile appears on her face and she dries her tears then holds me tight. "Geneviève, you always know what to do. I chose wisely." I hear the ladies sniffle while we hug.

With that handled we turn to face the mirrors. "Joseph will have his breath taken by your beauty when he sees you walking down the garden path."

"I hope so. I do want to take his breath just once."

"Claudette, I have seen you take his breath on several occasions."

"You have?"

"Mm hmm. The first time was when you went to the New Year's Eve Ball and I watched the napkin draped over his arm slide down it when he saw you."

"I wish I had looked his way. We are shy."

"The two of you are making up for it."

We get tickled and she responds, "Indeed we are." Then she gasps. "He is waiting for me on the sidewalk."

"Ladies, we need to be unlaced." Mrs. Parker tosses the fan, which makes Claudette and I get tickled again. Laughter is a nice note to end on. When we go out to our men who have been patiently waiting we talk briefly then Claudette and

Joseph are on their way. I tell Trevor, "I need to go back in alone. Do you want to know why?"

"Since I can't come in, yes I do."

"I am going to try on my bridal gown for the first time." Trevor looks at me with adoring eyes and we kiss then I go inside.

Mrs. Garner pulled the shade down on the doors after Claudette and I went in and when I open a door to leave there he is, propped against the car with his ankles crossed; a scene I have come upon many times yet never tire of. He lights up when he sees me and I go to him, kissing him the second I reach him. Since we are in public we keep it simple.

Next Trevor tells me, "Wait right here." He reaches through the car window and pulls out a bouquet of flowers.

"Trevor, you went to the flower stand."

"It only took me three months."

"They are lovely. Thank you."

"You're welcome. Are you ready to go?" I nod, kiss him again and we are off.

Driving through the gates we see cars, including Joseph's, parked in front of the houses. Trevor says, "All right, tell me what's going on. I know you can."

"We're all going to Micheletto's for two reasons. The wedding planning has left no time for cooking and to quietly celebrate the news the phone company is going to donate the direct dial system."

"Your father and Mr. Cooper talked those VIP's into making a three million dollar donation. I'm going to feel better about the security being stepped up."

"That makes two of us. By the way, you are going to be asked to order for us again, so you might want to give it some thought on the way."

Inside everyone is waiting for us in the drawing room and they all say, "Bonsoir." Then Grand-mamma says, "The wedding planning is consuming all our time, thus the need to dine out. We have decided on Micheletto's and are ready to leave when the two of you are." Several heads nod as Trevor looks at me. I respond, "I'm good to go." He chuckles and we turn around. Walking through the foyer Father slowly passes us and says, "The base will be getting a new phone system." Trevor just looks at me, but I know what he's thinking.

The only people who ride together are my parents and grandparents, the rest of us pair off and we become a convoy again. After dinner Joseph and Claudette are going to his apartment to continue packing. Théo and Rachel are going to her apartment and we just wind up together.

At the restaurant they do ask Trevor to order for us. I am not the only the one who enjoys listening to him speak Italian. The highlight of the evening is when Théo announces our house will be finished Thursday as scheduled. And for the first time I watch Joseph being himself; at last completely relaxed around us. Claudette does make it easy by flirting with him. In fact we are all flirting with our men. Love is in the air.

At Maison Trevor parks at the apartment and as we ascend the steps I ask, "Did you unpack the other crate this afternoon?"

"While packing my things back in the other one I decide we would unpack it when we live there and can leave my things out in our house." And we go inside.

"Did you pack the train?"

"I was going to when I was there this afternoon moving our wedding gifts into closets, but your mother came in and asked me not to." My face lights up. "That is what your mother looked like when I told her I would leave it out. It's those eyes. No man can look into those brown eyes you two have and refuse what you want. And you both know it." I give him a kiss and go to the liqueur cabinet. "Would you like a glass of cognac?" He is shaking his head as he replies, "Yes I would. Thank you."

We sit on the sofa and he says "Baby, I have a little story to tell you."

"You have my full attention."

"After I packed my things I went to the quarters of Mr. Barnes, one the lieutenants' you met, to tell him something. He enjoys taking photographs and doesn't man the rails. I was looking at the new ones on the cork board above his desk and spotted this." Trevor reaches for a photograph face down by an envelope on the coffee table, turns it over and hands it to me. I look at it, gasp and am rendered speechless. In my hand is a photograph of me sitting on the roof of my car when Louise arrived. I turn to him and he says, "That is exactly what you looked like the first time I laid eyes on you."

"Trevor — this is unbelievable."

"I thought I was hallucinating and reached for it. Mr. Barnes said, 'You saw her too huh? She was a sight for sore eyes.' I responded, 'I'm marrying this woman next week.' He stood immediately and told me he meant no disrespect. I told him there was none taken and he took it down. The negative is in the envelope. Mr. Barnes told me it was between us exactly who you are. He could not believe the coincidence and neither could I. He did ask me how we met and when I told him, he couldn't get passed the fact you were already a friend of our captain's wife. I thanked him more than once and walked out of his quarters in a daze."

"Trevor, I can't believe we have this photograph."

"I've had time to absorb this and I still don't. By the way, I would like at least a 5 x 7 of this, soon." I burst into laughter, look back at the photograph then tell him, "This explains why you and everyone else saw me. I did not blend in with the scenery."

"No you didn't and you never will." He gives me a loving look and a proper kiss. "I think we should play some records, dance a little — then make out." Trevor takes the photograph from me and pulls me into his arms. We skip the dancing.

The next morning is two days before the wedding and things are getting a little hectic. The morning briefing made my head spin and I was happy to go to work. Lunch with the crew was going fine as usual until Joanna asks, "Geneviève, on the wedding invitation for Claudette and Joseph it reads, The Delcroix Family. I understand why her parents are not listed and but what about Joseph's?"

Trevor and I look at each other and I reply, "My parent's will be standing for Joseph. I should let everyone know this just in case. Joseph was a ward of the state at infancy and grew up in the county's orphanage." We could've heard a pin drop for several seconds as our friends process the answer and trying to tell them as little as possible I continue. "My family has known Joseph for over 12 years. The county issued him a work permit when he was 15. Mr. Murphy showed Mother his application and she gave her approval to hire him. She has kept an eye on him ever since. We just learned this from her recently. Mother could not discuss information on his application. It is an invasion of his privacy, but circumstance left her with no choice."

Mitch says, "We understand. Thank you for the insight. In all likelihood you just kept us from being blindsided on their wedding day." Joanna says, "I will have a handkerchief in the bodice of my dress." Emily is blinking her eyes as she says, "I wish I had one now." William hands her his as she sighs and adds, "He never got adopted? That is so sad. Couples usually want a boy." I respond, "Yes they do. He was painfully shy." My heart aches as I remember the tragic past. I clasp my hands and slowly place them on the table. Trevor, who has his arm on the back of my chair, doesn't move a muscle.

William slightly changes the subject. "Is there anything else we need to know?" I reply, "My family and all of you are the only people Claudette knows and Joseph did not invite anyone to the ceremony nor to the dinner at the club. From what I understand he is being diplomatic, not wanting to risk slighting anyone he works with. And our servers are going to be his associates; therefore there will be no one to meet."

Joanna responds, "Excellent, we can relax and be ourselves. New subject; is there any way to see Théo and Rachel before Saturday? Congratulating them on their engagement during someone else's wedding seems inappropriate." My response is immediate; "I was thinking the same thing yesterday. Perhaps lunch tomorrow at Sam's." At last, smiles. Trevor says, "All right then, Sam's it is. We will inform Théo tonight we have made plans with his life." We all laugh and lunch ends on a happy note.

The work day is done; my grandparents are home going over last minute wedding details with Claudette and we gather in the kitchen. Father selects a good wine for us to drink and while three ladies cook, our men set the table.

Before dinner Trevor tells Théo, "At lunch today the crew made plans with your life."

"Where am I going?"

"To Sam's tomorrow with your fiancée to celebrate your engagement."

"Those are good plans." Rachel spins around and looks at Théo. "Since we can't make a reservation we'll go early and get tables." Rachel gives Théo a kiss.

While drinking our wine Trevor tells me, "I rang Grandmum and Mum today to thank them for sending my things. Mum informed me we should open the other one tonight, because there is something on top we will be interested in." I go, "Oooo, a mystery that should be solved immediately." He gives me a kiss and asks Théo, "Would you and Rachel like to play with my train?" Rachel answers, "We would love too. Thank you." Théo glances at her and she tells him, "I can help you up." Laughter erupts. He told her why he was stiff the other day. Mother adds, "We will do the dishes, you children go play." We all reply, "Yes, ma'am." in unison and go our separate ways.

With the lid off the other crate we see laying on top what appears to be a photo album wrapped in a thick hand knitted baby blanket. "The blanket I mentioned going home in." He carefully lifts it out. "Geneviève, do you want to go look through this at the apartment? I'll start a fire." I reply, "I would love to." We put the lid back on and leave.

Settled in with a fire crackling Trevor unwraps the album and hands me the blanket I fold and place on my lap. "This is more like a scrap book my mum made over the years with things I enclosed in letters to my family during my Annapolis days. He opens it and I see photographs from monumental events, newspaper clippings and snapshots taken by his friend Don.

Eventually he turns to a page that causes me to gasp for I am looking at a newspaper clipping with a caption under a photograph that reads, Navy Beats Army! In the photograph I can see The Brigade in the stands waving their covers in the air to the team standing together on the field facing them holding their helmets in the air. "What a sight it must be to see that in person." He says, "I should take you to a game one day. I haven't been to one in years." I throw my arms around his neck.

Trevor is to the last pages and I gasp again when I see a photograph of him and William. "This was taken after the Color Parade at Worden Field. It's the last full dress parade for graduating class members. We received our commissions the next day and went on to serve as leaders in the Navy."

"Trevor, you look glorious. Your uniform is resplendent. All those buttons and you're wearing your sword. Where is that?"

"In my footlocker that I promise we will unpack when we move into our house and you can see all these things and more." On the last page is a portrait of him before he left The Academy. We take a good look at it and he closes the album.

We are quiet, he is thinking about the past and my mind goes elsewhere. "Geneviève, you look as if you're contemplating changing the subject to something a tad serious."

"Am I that transparent?"

"To me you are." He gives me a kiss then I pick up my glass and look at it. "Is there something in your drink?"

"No, I was just thinking you should have poured yourself a glass of whiskey instead of this."

"Cognac isn't adequate?" After a bit of nervous laughter as I think he says, "I'm sitting on a pin already; if you don't start talking I might feel a needle." After more nervous laughter I start talking.

"Trevor, are you aware after The Revolution French titles of nobility were abolished and continue as a necessity for passing heirlooms or the deed's of an estate to the next heir?"

"Yes I am. Would you allow me to ask a burning question now, then you can fill in the details?"

"Of course."

"What title does your grandfather hold?"

"Marquis; the title is a Noblesse d'épée, Nobles of the Sword. These were appointed by kings to men who served him in battle for two decades or more. One of our ancestors did that very thing. The title is given to the male children and grandchildren at birth. My grandmother is his Marchioness.

"This means you are a Marchioness?"

"Yes, but not like Grand-mamma through marriage. The title of Marchioness was given to his wife separately, a Noblesse Uterine, Nobility of the Female Line. It's held through the female bloodline and inherited by female heirs; therefore the true title is mine. I am the 10th Marchioness Delcroix. My French citizenship includes my title. Titles are still regulated by a bureau of the Ministry of Justice."

"You are nobility in your own right." He stops talking, sips his wine and softly says, "Dignified sitting in a swing." Then he sits quietly processing a tremendous amount of information. "Since I'm aware the signet rings you and the members of your family wear represent more than a coat of arms; why do your father and grandfather wear theirs for wedding bands?"

"French nobility wear them on the ring finger of their left hand outward when they are unmarried and turn them inward when married. Théo decided years ago to break tradition and wear his on his right. The only ring he would wear on that finger was a wedding band."

"Good decision. Does Rachel know this?"

"Not yet. I was waiting on the right time to present itself to tell you. Théo is motivated by fear."

Trevor chuckles and asks, "Fear?"

"Absolutely; if Rachel gives birth to a son there is the distinct possibility instead of attending university he may go to France and eventually take his place as heir of Château Delcroix d'Aix-en-Provence."

"Ah, fear is the correct word. Poor Théo."

"I feel sorry for him too. I was apprehensive about telling you and our children will be staying, but here is the best part. My grandfather has our ancestors' sword he wore into battle and the sashes for the star's that was presented to them by the king. He also has the Delcroix Tiara that was presented to his wife, all in safe keeping."

"The tiara has a name?"

"The king commissioned it and royal jewels are named. I inherited it along with my title. Grand-mamma wore it when she married Grand-papa, Mother wore it when she married Father and I am going to wear it when I marry you."

"Something else to look forward to seeing on our wedding day."

"I've been thinking about that and have a request. I want you to see the tiara before then. My request is for you to accompany me to the bank Friday to pick it up and take it to the ladies at The Salon. They need to attach my veil. And you can see the sword; it is centuries old."

"I am at your service."

"Thank you. Trevor, do you mind if we just sit together quietly?"

"I do not mind in the least." He puts an arm around me and pulls me to him.

Happily at ease we eventually hear Théo leave. Trevor says, "I know what that means. I place my hand on the photo album and ask, "May I take this to my bedroom?" His eyes gleam as he tells me, "By my guest." I pick it up and clutch it to my chest. Trevor shuts the apartment down, picks up the envelope, puts the photo of me in it and we go to the house where he tucks me and Christopher in then kisses me and kisses me.

Lying in the dark I begin to get restless and realize sleep is going to elude me for a while and it occurs to me; I have never written him a love letter. I throw off my covers, go to my desk and turn on the lamp. With pen in hand words begin to flow.

My dearest Trevor,

My mind is filled with thoughts of you; your gentle touch, the softness of your lips — the taste of you. Then there is the warmth of your body, the rhythm of your heart beating slowly and how soft your hair feels as it brushes against my skin.

As my thoughts pour from my pen onto this paper I can hear your voice and the things you say to me when we are alone. I can see the look on your face when you have been waiting for me and the waiting is over because at last you see me. You are such a beautiful man; so kind and sincere, but the way you love me is the most beautiful thing of all.

Words I have read again and again have new meaning; yearning, hunger, desire and surrender. I want to share everything with you. I want to tell you my inner most thoughts and to experience all that there can be between us. I am so in love with you and know we are grazing the surface of a passion that runs so very deep. Sleep will not come easy to me until I am able to drift away in your arms.

My heart is yours,
Geneviève

4 September 1941

With the letter carefully folded and tucked into the envelope I seal it with a kiss, write his name on the front and hide it in my desk drawer. Still wide awake I pick up the album and get in my bed. As I turn each page it is beyond my comprehension he is going to be my husband in a few days. Look at him, he is magnificent; noble and true, with the purest of hearts, like a young woman dreams about and hopes with every fiber of her being he exists.

Just as tears are about to stream down my face I hear a light knock on my door. He is standing on the other side. I cannot reach the door fast enough. Without thinking about the noise I'm going to make at such a late hour I fling the door open, throw my arms around him and hold him tight; almost as tight as he is holding me. He whispers, "I have never been so glad to see a light on in my life."

Trevor waits a moment and lifts me off my feet as he closes the door. I tell him, "Please don't let me go yet."

"I didn't intend to. I want to kiss you." And he kisses me tenderly.

"Geneviève, I need to talk to you." I hold his hand and go sit on the edge of my bed. He stands in front of the chair and pulls it toward me then sits with my legs between his and his knees touching my bed. Trevor holds my hands and tells me, "You gave me more to process than I realized. It caught up to me when I hit my rack. My mind went in several directions. Oddly the first thing was an understanding of Claudette and her asking for permission to do things and Théo expressing his frustration. She met you all at Château Delcroix and I am certain the staff formally addressed your family."

"I was still a child the second time we were there and it was all fanciful to me thank goodness. When she arrived here we had to insist on no titles and give her time to adjust." He nods and looks at me pensively.

"Then I was overwhelmed when it occurred to me our children will have Titles of Nobility before their names."

"Just like you."

"What?"

"Trevor, you are a Noble of the Sword as well. You took an oath to defend this country with your life and do each time you are deployed. And your title is Commander, one you earned."

"Thank you for telling me that."

"You are entirely welcome. Mine was inherited and it is of little significance."

"I beg to differ. You have earned yours by things you did before you met me. For instance the night in the Grand Canyon, you volunteered for watch duty to make certain no harm befell your parents as they slept and you watched Théo's back. I have also seen several instances with my own eyes. I will chose — two. On our way to Santa Barbara after the flare went up and we were separated, instead of sitting below deck wringing your hands you were devising an attack plan if things took a turn for the worse and I have no doubt you would've gone through with it.

"Immediately after that, without hesitation you went over to Mr. Harding. I saw his leg too. Geneviève, it made me whence. Do you have any idea how worried I was about you? And there was nothing I could do. You knelt by him and cupped his head in your hands to comfort him without flinching. Then you placed that strap his mouth. The man was in agony and you got him through the horrible ordeal. I watched you in awe. That is when I found out how brave you are."

"Trevor, anyone would've done the same."

"Geneviève, once again I beg to differ. I've seen trained men crack under less pressure."

"That's not good."

"No it isn't, especially when you're an officer and expected to lead men during a conflict. The second instance and I apologize for bringing this up, but it has bearing on the case I'm presenting. At The Coronado, you literally came face to face with the enemy, rallied the troops so to speak and led them to his capture. I just kept on eye on him. When it was over you drank a shot of whiskey and went on with the rest of your day. My point is, you have strength and courage; I am honored by your consent to marry me and have felt this way ever since."

I kiss him and ask, "Will you lie down with me until we get sleepy?"

"I was beginning to think you were never going to ask."

In the morning, we feel well rested and are cutting up before going down to what we hope will be breakfast instead of another briefing. We're looking forward to lunch and our house is supposed to be finished today, so Trevor and I are filled with anticipation. Then to our delight, we had breakfast.

Noon finally rolls around and out the doors Emily and I go. The rest of the crew is waiting for us and we are at Sam's in no time; Mitch has a heavy foot quite often. Upon our arrival we see Théo and Rachel have taken care of everything, tables are together and our orders have been placed.

The moment we are seated Annie brings everyone a chocolate milkshake. The first thing Trevor does is hold it up and tell us, "Raise your glasses please to join me in a toast." Milkshake's with straws are in the air as he says, "To the beyond happy couple and the person who invented ice cream." As we laugh Théo and Rachel get to raise their glasses because the toast was not just for them. Then Trevor confesses, "I can't take full credit for the toast. I got the last part from Emily." She beams as he gives her a wink.

Théo was so thorough he asked Annie to alert us when it was time to wind things up. He knew time would get away from us and it did for we were enjoying ourselves. Everyone felt better when Joanna reminded us we would be together again in two days for a wedding.

Trevor picks me up after work and when we get close to the house he says, "Geneviève, I see your brother." I gasp for I know why he is waiting outside on us. Trevor parks the car close to him and we get out. Théo looks so proud and his eyes dance as he tells us, "Gené, Trevor, I am pleased to announce your house is finished." I beam as he squeezes my hand. "You two go on and look around. I'm going to wait inside while you marvel at my genius. When you're done, call me and I'll join you." Trevor nods to him and reaches for my hand. As we walk slowly to our house Trevor asks, "Where do you want to start?" I reply, "The solarium."

Standing at the doors to it he gives me a kiss then opens them and we go in together, hand in hand. We walk in silence as we look at the details. Standing in the middle soaking up the view Trevor tells me, "This is perfection. The black metal will disappear at night."

"Théo has outdone himself."

Next Trevor opens a pair of the French doors and we go inside with our arms around each other's waist. "Baby, we have a house."

"Yes we do and it is beautiful."

After looking at the living room we go to the kitchen and stare at the far wall. "Geneviève, I don't remember that."

"With good reason; it wasn't there." We gasp when we figure out what is.

"Your brother put in a dumbwaiter. The child in me just came out." And like two exuberant children we go to it. Trevor slides the door up and there it is.

"I don't know how many times my grandfather sent Théo and me up in theirs."

"My family did that with me at the houses in London."

Suddenly it occurs to me why Théo did this. "Oh my goodness. Trevor — he put this in for our children."

"This is my favorite part of the house, hands down. Your brother thought of everything."

"Yes he did. I'm anxious to see how our bedroom turned out."

"We'll go there next."

Trevor quickly opens a door to it and our doubts are allayed. We go in and he tells me, "The bedroom is beautiful. I can see our black furniture in here. You did good, Baby." He gives me a kiss and as we walk to the windows I comment. "It's much longer in actuality than on the blue prints."

Trevor chuckles, "Yes it is. I'm glad we chose furniture for the sitting area when we chose the bedroom suite. It's going to be cozy by the fireplace. We need a nice rug and more throw pillows."

"And a trunk to store thick down comforters in." I sigh and Trevor looks deep into my eyes. "I'm having ... a daydream and I hope you make it come true."

"Oh I hope I do." Trevor wraps his arms around me. "We're down to a single digit; our wedding is in nine days."

"I can't believe the two months are almost over."

We relax in each other's arms for a bit and suddenly Trevor stiffens up. "Théo ... Geneviève, we should breeze though the rest of the house."

"Oh my gosh — he's already pacing."

Trevor holds my hand and says, "Lead the way."

It pains us when we begin quickly going through the rest of the house, but fortunately it became humorous as we sprint up the stairs to the second floor. When we reach the overlook we do take time to admire the new view. The second story did raise it substantially and it is better than ever. Trevor and I linger in a kiss then go back down and I call Théo.

We go out on the balcony and I call out, "Well done." when he is close. Théo stops and takes a bow, therefore we applaud and he comes up. The first thing I do is give him a hug and get my usual kiss. Trevor shakes his hand and we step inside commenting on the black metal of the solarium first. This time we are going at a slow steady pace.

In the kitchen Trevor and I thank him for the dumbwaiter and Théo tells us he learned they were the fashion for houses of the affluent in London while studying for his Masters and he was certain Trevor took many a ride in one too and would appreciate it. My brother is exceptional and we do marvel at his genius.

When we are on the overlook I see the back of Rachel through the window of my parent's house. Théo informs us our grandparents are there as well. I look at Trevor and he goes downstairs to call the house and invite everyone over. Claudette decides someone should keep watch over the food for dinner and stays.

This time the tour started at the top and went all the way down into the garage. We wanted to see what it looked like and as suspected Théo had done a few things. The laundry area cabinets had been remodeled and a new table sat in front of new appliances. There was even a fresh coat of paint on the walls, trim and ceiling. As we leave I think it has to be the nicest garage in the neighborhood.

During dinner Trevor expressed his gratitude to my family and Mother told him to think nothing of it. Their motives were not pure; they want us to stay and reminded him if ever we feel the need for a larger house to simply tell Théo. After the laughter ceases Trevor assures them we will.

My grandparents stand to take their leave after finishing their cognac and I tug on Trevor's sleeve and he stands to slide back my chair. He is intuitive to say the least and offers his arm to my grandmother as I step close to my grandfather, who offers me his. "Going to ask me for a key are you?" I reply, "Yes, Grand-papa."

We go to the study where the key is and have a seat. Grand-mamma says, "At the last minute you tell him as did your father. Théo is doing the same. Your grandfather was fortunate I knew before meeting him he was to be a marquis." My grandfather nods repeatedly as he stands and goes to one of the book shelves, pushes on a section and it swings out to reveal a safe behind it. Trevor glances at me and I know what he is thinking, first a hidden passage and now this.

My grandfather pulls out passports and then the small case the safety deposit box key is in. He takes it out, hands it to me and while closing the safe tells Trevor, "When you remove the sword from the scabbard do keep in mind it is still sharp." He replies, "Yes, sir." My grandmother tells him, "As if it were yesterday I remember seeing it for the first time. It is beautiful as is the Delcroix Tiara that graced my head when I married this man."

While my grandfather kisses her hand Trevor and I look at each other and he tells them, "We have much to discuss about the next day's events. Thank you for everything." My grandfather replies, "You are entirely welcome." And we leave to give them privacy.

Standing on the portico Trevor tells me, "I feel like I'm in a dream. Before I awake, kiss me." In his embrace I drop the key when I open my hand to have his hair around my fingers.

We kiss for a long time and when Trevor picks up the key he says, "One of my favorite things about Maison de la Mer is the stones and pebbles; they remind me of old cities in Europe. Concrete and asphalt have never appealed to me. I have grown to love this place and everyone here."

Strolling to his apartment he looks up at our house. "I thought Théo was joking when we were in the study and he told us the safe was behind that bookcase."

"I wondered why you smiled and shook your head."

"My family has absolutely no imagination. Their safes are behind paintings." And I get tickled. "I'm changing the subject. We need furniture for the solarium; why did we not pick some out the other day?"

"I have no idea, but we should try to fit that in tomorrow."

"What we should do is make a list tonight."

"After that, can we practice the tango?"

"Of course, Baby."

"When are you are going to pass me a rose while we dance?" And he gives me just what I wanted, his deep laugh. A rose truly is preposterous, they have thorns.

Sitting at the dining table I resemble a secretary waiting to take dictation from him. As we discuss the day the list gets long. When we finish our task Trevor takes it from me then offers me his hand with a glint and pulls me swiftly up from my chair right into his chest. We are definitely going to tango.

In the morning, just like a little girl, I wake up and hug my Teddy Bear then tell him I am going to the court house with Trevor this afternoon to get our marriage license. Next I get up and tuck him under the covers then dress for the long day ahead. Before opening my door I get the love letter I wrote Trevor and slip it into my handbag. My plan is to place it in the middle of the front seat of the car as I get out and let him find it when he is about to leave.

Sitting at my vanity I hear light footsteps toward my room then Trevor's deep laugh as he walks in and says, "You tucked the bear in." My response, "Christopher is still sleepy." He laughs again. "Good morning, Baby. I do love you." and kneels next to me. "I love you too." Then he whispers, "Geneviève, I am going to kiss you." My fiancé places his hands on my face and kisses me to the point that when he stops I am disoriented. "Trevor, I do not recall what I was going to do next." He looks me over. "You were going to put on your earrings." Thus I finish getting ready and just as we reach the door I call out, "Sleep well, Christopher." He gives me a look. "When exactly did you start talking to him?" I sing, "A few days ago." He shakes his head smiling and downstairs we go to step into the whirlwind.

In the parking lot at work as Trevor gets out of the car he is distracted by Emily and I put the letter on the seat unnoticed. Trevor helps me out and closes the car door without looking back. When it's time for Emily and me to go inside I give William a hug and tell him, "I will see you Saturday at Maison." He gives me a nod then I become French by kissing Trevor's cheeks and tell him, "See you soon." He has a glint and goes, "Mmm hm, see you soon." Halfway to the building I turn around and look back to see him talking to William. There's no telling how long it will be when he finally gets in the car.

The moment I begin typing it's clear I'm going to have to concentrate. This works out because time flies and Emily is standing at my desk waiting for the other ladies to leave for lunch. When we're alone she tells me, "I can't believe Claudette is getting married."

"Neither can I. Fortunately her wedding is going to give me a serious practice before I'm the bride."

"Oh my gosh — I'm so glad you're getting married before me, I get a practice." She gives me a hug. "William is waiting. See you later." And off she goes. With my desk in order I take my files to Becky and I am filled with anticipation going down the corridor to leave. What will his reaction to the love letter be?

Slowly I round the corner to get a glimpse of him before he sees me and there he is, propped on his hood and looking lost in thought. The second I step in sight he tilts his head and when I am two feet away he says, "There she is ... the woman *I am* going to marry." We're alone because I'm the last one out and he holds out his arms and uncrosses his ankles for me to step between his legs so he can hold me tight. "Geneviève, Willow is close, do you mind if we go to there?"

"There is no other place I would rather go."

Those were the only words spoken until we go below and into the lounging area of Willow where I see the letter on the coffee table. Trevor holds my face and softly tells me, "For some reason I felt compelled to come here and read your letter. After I read it all I wanted to do was bring you here and it felt like time was against me, but you're finally here and I can do what I have been longing to do."

Trevor kisses me so tenderly and so caught up in the moment was I that my knees give completely. In a blink he catches me in his arms then carries me to the sofa. I have my arms around his neck and when he puts me down I do not let him go and pull him down. He lies beside me placing his head on my shoulder and whispers, "Spoken words seemed inadequate, so I decided to *show you* how I felt about what you wrote to me in the letter." I whisper, "I understood each and every word." Instead of kissing we lie in each other's arms as Willow gently rocks us.

I think we would have fallen asleep had I not started feeling funny. "Trevor ... my body just; I'm not sure how to describe it."

"Does sank describe it?"

"Yes it does."

"It's way passed lunch time. You need to eat something. Eh-sap. I'm going to slowly sit you up, so you don't get dizzy and then I'm going to the galley."

Trevor disappears and just as I am feeling a little dizzy he returns with a wheel of cheddar and a knife on a cutting board in one hand and a glass of water in the other. Tucked under his arm is a box of water wafers. I drink some water and in no time he gives me a chunk of cheese and says, "Take a big bite of that please. We have a long day ahead of us, again. This changes things. You should have something substantial for lunch." I wash down the cheese and respond, "That means duck is out." He nods and I sigh then suggest, "Filet de bœuf from the club?" My fiancé lights up and asks, "That is French for mignon?" I nod and he adds, "I forget about those. Not even The O Club serves them." Trevor eats as well and soon we are at the club.

To our surprise we are told Joseph is here and when he walks up, instead of saying hello I exclaim, "What are you doing here?" He replies, "Working my last shift as an unmarried man." We're smiling as he asks, "Two house salads and Pellegrino's?" Trevor says, "Yes, please." Joseph motions to Eric and asks, "For lunch what will it be?" Not having the chance to tell Trevor what else I wanted I order for myself. "Filet de bœuf, mashed baby red potatoes and what do you suggest, Joseph?" He smiles and replies, "Asparagus tips are being served today, Miss Delcroix." I respond, "You know me too well." He nods and looks to Trevor who says, "I will have what the lady is having."

Oddly Joseph drifts away and I touch his forearm. "It occurs to me you are wise in your choice and I should have the same before leaving. Something tells me the rehearsal dinner could be a late supper." Our faces go straight while Eric serves the salads and Joseph leaves us with that thought.

After we eat Joseph tells us, "I have taken the liberty of ordering two espressos and the Pâtissier is baking coconut macaroons for this evening. The first ones are out of the oven."

I light up and Trevor chuckles. "We will be having those. Thank you, Joseph."

"It is my pleasure, Commander."

The second Joseph turns his back I begin eating a piece of my roll and Trevor's laugh is deep. As I look at him inquisitively he tells me, "One of the things I adore about you is your love of dessert. No matter what the circumstance, if it's possible you will clear your palate. The day you made my nest and we ate pizza before working, you pulled a piece of the crust then ate it before eating the cannoli. Watching you I thought everyone else is rather dull compared to you." I want to respond, but I can't because my mouth is full.

After we eat our dessert Trevor signs the check and Joseph walks with us to the lobby to be away from prying eyes. He tells us it was nice we were his last table, because it calmed him down and several details need to be covered before he leaves the club since he will not return until after their honeymoon. A minute later Joseph is off to continue his day as are we. Next stop, the court house.

The second Trevor and I enter the County Clerk's office we see a couple who is obviously getting married today. A young woman wearing a knee length bridal dress holding a bouquet is what tipped us off. I tell Trevor, "They're eloping, which makes them the smartest people in this room." He pulls me aside saying, "I know you're being serious. Geneviève, why did you say that?" I sigh heavily and reply, "I am beyond tired of telling you good night and watching you leave."

Trevor is at a loss for words then I have a bought of nervous laughter and say, "I speak to a stuffed animal when I wake up." He covers his mouth as he laughs. After settling down he tells me, "We do what we must to survive. — Now would be a good time to let you in on something. I'm not certain how long I've been doing this, but when I wake up, the first thing I do is look at the photograph I took of you and tell you good morning." Without a care in the world I kiss him while we are surrounded by people and he returns the kiss.

While doing that the couple left and we walk right up to the window and begin answering questions. When the woman asks about our citizenship and Trevor says he is American she slightly raises an eyebrow. I almost get tickled, but maintain my composure. We sign it, he pays the woman and we barely make into the corridor before bursting into laughter.

"That woman had *serious* doubts didn't she? I thought I was going to have to leave and get my passport." He offers me his arm and says, "Let's get out of here before she changes her mind." We cut up walking to the car then he asks, "Where are we going next?"

"You have the list."

"Yes I do." He pulls it out of his pocket. "Pick up tiara. I can't believe we forgot that. To the bank." All of a sudden Trevor stands as if he is holding a sword and says, "En garde." as he lunges toward me and pretends to slice through the air. I can't breathe.

We go to bank still acting up and when he parks the car I tell him, "Trevor, we cannot behave like this in the bank."

"Kill joy. Give me a kiss."

I give him a kiss and we get out. I check my handbag for the safety deposit box key and exhale slowly with my eyes closed. He asks softly, "Are you ready to go inside?" I smile reassuringly and tell him, "Yes, I am."

Several minutes later, after signing my name 15 times, we enter the vault and the assistant and I place our keys in the door of the safety deposit box to unlock it. The man pulls out the long box and takes us to a room with two chairs and a table on which he sets box. I thank him and he nods, leaves and locks the door. Then I tell Trevor to lift the lid. A beautiful old piece of French Blue velvet is draped over and underneath the contents. Trevor folds it back to reveal the sword, six antiqued white satin pouches, four French Blue Duchesse Satin sashes and two pairs of white gloves. I pick up the gloves and we put them put on.

I remove the pouches and tell Trevor, "You may pick up the sword now and yes it is as heavy as it looks if not more so." With self assurance, which impresses me, he moves steady and smooth with it and after admiring it Trevor removes the sword from the scabbard as if it weighs nothing and looks at the blade. I wait a bit then tell him, "My grandfather showed Théo and me this years ago and said, 'This sword and your ancestors' skill kept him alive through many a battle. It should be respected and honored in his stead.' Those words still have an effect on me."

With the sword put away we have a seat and I pull all the sterling silver jewel cases out of the pouches and open each one. "These diamond stars are worn on the sashes of the marquis and his marchioness by marriage. These are worn by the marchioness heiress and her husband. He nods as he thinks. "Wait a minute, that's for me?" And I have to think myself. "Did I not tell you after we marry you become a marquis?" He shakes his head. "Oh, I was nervous. This signet ring is for you too. It will be sized for you." And I move on to the small stars like his medals hanging from French Blue satin and the star brooches.

"Signet rings and stars were provided for two more generations. Father and Mother wear the set with diamonds and rubies. Théo wears the diamonds with sapphires and Rachel will wear the brooch and ring when she becomes his wife."

I move the case that holds the tiara between us and raise the lid. I tell Trevor to take off his gloves as I take off mine and lift the tiara carefully, because it has pearls that dangle from the top. I hand it to him and let him look at it a bit then say, "The pearls are older than the tiara, they were gifts to the king. The metal is 20kt yellow gold. This along with the star and sash was presented to me by my grandfather on my 18th birthday, which is a time honored tradition."

"What was that like?"

"There was a banquet held in my honor at my grandparents. Family members and close friends from Aix attended. It was similar to our engagement dinner, except it was white tie. My family wore their stars and I wore my first ball gown."

"I bet it was beautiful. Will you describe it to me?"

"It was white satin of course and had a train. The neckline was sweetheart with small puffed cap sleeves. After we return from our honeymoon, remind me and I will show you the portrait painted of me wearing it."

"Why have I not seen that? Where is it?"

"In storage. My grandmother had all the official portraits put away before your arrival, stating that dealing with the emotions of falling in love with me was enough for you to handle."

"Your family hid them from me."

"Mmm hm." And his deep laugh follows. "Claudette told Grand-mamma she was not telling Joseph until they moved to Aix."

"Talk about a well kept family secret."

"At least it wasn't a skeleton in the closet."

"Thank goodness for that."

"My grandparents left those at the Château." Trevor shakes his head at me and laughs while I put everything away except my tiara which I pick up and carry.

"I would offer to carry that for you, but I'm going to be looking over my shoulder." I chuckle, give him a kiss and then he opens the door.

Trevor parks in front of The Salon and says, "I kind of feel sorry for the ladies. I was uneasy holding it merely looking at it. They have to attach a veil to it."

"This will not be their first time to attach a veil to a headpiece. They do have lovely faux ones. Umm — Trevor, there is a chance the ladies have seen us."

"By that statement I gather your mother called to fill them in. I'm going to be quiet from this point on. I don't talk when I'm on guard duty." Of course he gets me tickled before we go inside.

The moment Mrs. Garner sees us she rings the bell and Mrs. Parker emerges from the back wearing white gloves and carrying a piece of white silk to wrap it in. When I pull the case out of the pouch the ladies gasp. It is pretty, our family crest is engraved on the lid. When I lift out the tiara they are silent and I hand it to Mrs. Parker who begins to slightly tremble. Thank goodness mother called and made it possible for us to leave shortly after that awkward moment.

Trevor walks straight to the car's trunk and says, "I'm so glad I decided to drive your car. We can wrap the case in the picnic blanket and safely tuck it away. Otherwise our next stop would be at your grandparent's house." All I can do is laugh and hand him the case.

Our next destination is to a department store, this allows us to relax again. Trevor and I choose the all important furniture that will go in the solarium and a trunk. Then we pick out the rugs for our bedroom. When we look for one that is thick to put in front of the fireplace I almost blush.

With all our errands taken care of we go to our house and wait on the overlook for the black lacquered furniture to be delivered, because it's the only place there are seats. We decided to have the teakwood chairs and lounge chairs brought back. They have memories of watching a meteor shower and him watching me.

There is a lot going on too and we are at a safe distance from it all. The delivery van from the florist is parked in the middle and people are carrying floral arrangements to both houses and a freight truck is parked in front of my parent's house. Then there is Joseph who is carrying boxes up to what will soon be his apartment as Claudette opens doors for him.

While we soak up our surroundings the sound of a big engine gearing down can be heard in the distance. Trevor looks at me and to my surprise there is a glint in his eye. "Last one down." and he immediately takes the lead. I do not mind at all because I know the quickest way down and I'm certain he doesn't. When we get to the kitchen he goes toward the front of the house and I take the door into the garage. When he's descending the steps I appear at the bottom beaming. "The second I heard that door slam I knew you had me again."

"I was motivated by the thought to the victor go the spoils."

"I am not going to mind losing am I?"

"Not in the least."

Where the furniture is to be placed has been decided already. All we do is show the men where each piece goes and they are gone in no time. The piece that got my attention was the bench at the foot of our bed, so I go to it first pulling Trevor along. Running my hand over the upholstery I tell him, "That they had black fabric was astounding, but this is sumptuous. It feels like the cashmere — your black suit is made of."

His eyes are gleaming when I look at him and he explains. "When you told me it was doubtful they would have black you were spot-on. They didn't and not willing to compromise I started thinking where I could find black fabric suitable to serve as upholstery. The word suitable triggered my train of thought that led me to Bertucci's. Arturo was taken aback my request, but as you can plainly see they sold me what I wanted."

"You are brilliant." Next I slowly slide my arms around him. "The way your mind works ... mmm."

"Geneviève," he whispers, "would you like for me to pin you against our sofa — in our house?"

Suddenly my heart sinks. "I cannot be disheveled or wrinkled, the rehearsal."

"Allow me to rephrase. Would you like to pin *me* against our sofa, in our house?"

"Yes, I would like. May I take the lead?"

"Please."

With my hand on his abdomen I start pushing him backward to the sofa. "I saw a movie at the Foreign Film Festival last year."

His eyes lock on mine. "The first time you said Foreign Film Festival you touched my lips with your fingertips."

"Mmm hm." With a lilt in my voice I say, "A woman's lover was sitting on the sofa. She walked over to him and sat on his lap in a way I had never seen. It was a way to get close to him ... and kiss him." Trevor's legs are now against the sofa and I use my foot to put his feet together then gently push him down until he is sitting.

I slip off my shoes and lift my dress just a bit as I place my right knee on the sofa next to his thigh and my hand on his shoulder. Then I do the same with my left thigh and let go of my dress, so I can place my hand on his other shoulder and sit across his lap. He exhales and softly asks, "Where do you want my hands?" I whisper, "On my back." I nuzzle him and say, "This is nice." He whispers, "Yes it is. I want to kiss you." I respond, "Take the lead." And he does.

In his embrace our passion goes somewhere without us and we have to catch up. Then Trevor does something he has never done, he unbuttons my dress and pulls it off both of my shoulders. I place my head against his and become acutely aware of his body beneath mine. He is warm, so warm and his mouth; what is happening? When I realize his hands are on my face I look at him. "Geneviève, I understand the effect the weight of my body has on you." I nod and his kiss is ... heated.

The room is getting a little dark; the sun is shifting and reality sets in. "Trevor." He looks at his watch. "Please tell me we do not have to stop this abruptly."

"We do not." I sigh in relief and he softly kisses my lips as he pulls my dress over my shoulders and slowly buttons it back up then puts his arms back around me. "I don't want to let you go."

"You know I don't want you to, but soon you won't have to."

"And I won't. I love you."

"I love you too. More than I can say."

We stay as we are a little longer then I carefully stand up. After he stands Trevor moves me backward a little to look in my eyes and softly says, "I can't believe you initiated that. Geneviève, you are spoiling me."

"You are spoiling me by giving me my way."

"And I will continue to do so."

I nuzzle his neck with a sigh and say, "I need to look in a mirror."

"You look like you did when we walked in."

I run my fingers through his tousled hair then ask, "Are you ready to go?"

"Yes. Umm ... where are we going?"

"To — my grandparent's."

We get our heads on straight and the tiara case out of the trunk. As we walk there Trevor says, "I'm famished."

"That makes two of us. Let's go in the back way and set the case on the desk in the study. And don't forget Reginald is in there. He flew in today."

"I did forget. Give me a kiss."

We slip through the back door; drop off the case and go to the drawing room. Trevor perks up at the entrance. "Salmon canapés and martinis. Let's join the party shall we?"

While the rehearsal is being discussed in detail things get a bit humorous when Reginald asks who is going to stand in for the bride and we all look at Rachel. She handles it well volunteering on the spot and we go outside.

While those who are not in the wedding party walk to the boardwalk I stand at the main garden path with Claudette, my grandfather and Rachel then I see chairs from my grandparent's kitchen on the boardwalk. Obviously nothing is being left to chance. When they reach it everyone takes their place, either sitting or standing and we begin walking to the garden path that leads to the arbor at the back of my parent's house.

At our destination we realize there is a slight problem, everyone will be to our right as we go to the arbor and the bride can be seen as my grandfather escorts her there. The first time Joseph sees her should not be a side view. My grandfather says, "Between the four of us we will come up with a plan." Claudette replies, "My brain is paralyzed." Rachel and I stare at each other trying to hold back nervous laughter as my grandfather rubs Claudette's back.

I focus and it doesn't long for me to solve the problem. "Claudette — if you walk on the left side of my grandfather to the arbor, he and I can shield you from being seen. When we are under it you get situated on his right." Claudette gives me kisses and leaves to watch us near the boardwalk to make sure it will work.

While we wait for Claudette to reach her spot my grandfather begins looking at Rachel who asks, "Why are you looking at me like that?" He replies, "Taller than her you are." She shakes her head. "And I'm wearing heels. My stockings are going to be ruined." I tell her, "Rachel, even barefooted she might see you and your blonde hair. You are going to have to crouch down." Grand-papa is nodding with eyes dancing. Let the fun begin.

Rachel asks me, "Exactly how much am I going to have to bend my knees and walk at the same time?" My grandfather offers her his left arm and I take a few steps back. Rachel crouches down and I motion for her to go lower, then I give her a thumbs up. She immediately tells us, "I need to practice this." While they walk around sympathy keeps me from laughing. She eventually nods and we go to the start of the path.

Things are fine as we walk toward the arbor and Rachel dryly says, "It is going to take Théo all of five seconds to figure out I am crouching down. His face will be beaming from the visual he will have." We are halfway there when she quietly exclaims, "Oh my gosh, my calves are burning. *I* am out of shape. I blame the elevator in my building. It calls to me." I get tickled as my grandfather coughs.

We are finally in the middle of the arbor and I stand in front of poor Rachel as she slowly straightens her legs. My grandfather tells her, "My dear, things will go smoother when you stand in for Geneviève next week." She breathes a sigh of relief. I become a bundle of nerves.

Next he says, "Ladies." and motions to a chair. In it are two nosegays, one of Stargazer lilies for Rachel and white tulips for me. He hands them to us and we are overwhelmed. Rachel gushes, "Théo knew I would stand in for her. We are going to marry such romantic men." I respond, "Yes we are." She hugs me and I go stand at the front of the arbor and Claudette gets my attention because she is ecstatic and giving us a little wave. We pulled it off.

Trevor is looking at me and I place my hand over my heart. He does the same and I begin to walk toward him. I love the flowers and the thoughtful man who gave them to me. Then it occurs to me, was I supposed to wait for a cue from Claudette? Nevertheless I set the pace as if I am a woman leisurely strolling through a garden looking at each and every flower she passes. The sound of the ocean is like music; Claudette and Joseph were wise not to have a musician play, it will complement the beautiful simplicity of their wedding.

When I finally take my eyes off of Trevor I notice my family is aglow looking at me. As I step onto the boardwalk I turn my head as I pass Trevor then face forward to see my brother wink at me. Joseph gives me a nod and I take my place. This is when Rachel and my grandfather step forward and we can see them at last. My thoughts go to how lovely a bride Rachel will be as they slowly draw near and how pleased my grandfather looks.

Reginald breaks the silence when Rachel and my grandfather are in place by calling Claudette over. He speaks in French to her and Joseph then Théo and me and the rehearsal is over. My brother leads me to Trevor then we all agree to meet out front in five minutes to leave for Micheletto's and scatter like leaves caught in the wind.

In the kitchen I immediately get two vases out then Rachel and I fill them with water for the flowers we received as Théo and Trevor stay back. Next we proceed to the foyer escorted by our gentlemen where my parent's and Reginald are waiting, then out the door we go. Our destination is the family dining room in Micheletto's they allow large dinner party's to reserve. Trevor and I are the last to leave because I thank him properly in the car for the lovely flowers.

Things move quickly at the restaurant; all the food was ordered in advance. We wait for the wine to be poured and a toast before filling our appetizer plates with fried ravioli and a red garlic sauce. A sort of silence falls in the room as we eat what is on our plates and breadsticks. We are a hungry little group. Reginald cleaned his plate first. The rest of us were not far behind.

Conversation gradually begins and the first subject is what went on while they waited on the four of us to appear during the rehearsal. This is when we find out Joseph finally asked Théo if it was too late for Claudette to get cold feet. Théo jokingly replied no and dryly told him on the day of the day of the wedding it's called being left at the altar. Trevor tells us the look on Joseph's face was priceless. After more than two hours fly by we are dropping sugar cubes into the Asti Spumante for the last toast of the evening.

When the motorcade is back at Maison, I call it a motorcade because we have a Justice among us, Claudette and Joseph go to her apartment and the rest of us go to my parent's house to visit with Reginald. Trevor and I go upstairs to freshen up and when we are on the balcony I see two large boxes on the bench in my room and practically drag Trevor to them as he chuckles. I read the shipping labels and gasp. "My trousers." Trevor closes my door in an instant, because I was a bit loud. "This one is from your mum and that one is from Meredith. I can't open them now. This is cruel and unusual punishment."

Trevor bursts into laughter as he pulls out his pocket knife. "We need to take time for a quick glimpse, otherwise you'll miss parts of conversation thinking about these." He knows me all too well. I give him a kiss and he opens the boxes. I tell him, "You get the one on the right." and we begin taking turns getting things out.

The boxes are filled with the most wonderful things; trousers with shirts and blouses to match. And the suits are beyond my expectations. They even picked out lady like trouser socks with shoes and handbags. When I get to the bottom of mine there is a letter and Trevor says, "Baby, you are going to have to read that later." I nod, put it down and kiss him again before he goes to his room.

I absolutely adore Reginald, but when he announces he has had a very long day and is going to retire for the evening I become giddy. When he leaves we all swing into action. My grandparents are the first to leave. Rachel gets her flowers and they do not linger then I tell my parent's Trevor and I are going to my room and why.

Trevor is sitting on the bench while I'm in the closet trying on another outfit and I hear my mother ask, "May we come in?" From the closet I call out, "Take a seat; I'll be out in a minute. Read the note." It was sweet; they thanked me for giving them an excuse to spend the day together shopping and have lunch at the Russian Tea Room. And they are looking forward to another trip. I hear mother go, "Ohhh." and ask "Are you all ready for me to come out?" Trevor replies, "We are waiting on you." which gets a laugh and I emerge. Mother takes one look at me and tells my father emphatically, "We are going to L.A. while they are on their honeymoon." He nods and gets a kiss.

They stay for one more outfit then retire for the evening. There are only two outfits remaining for me to try on and after that Trevor and I decide to stay at the house and have a glass of cognac in the solarium. It is nice to be still indeed and does not take long for exhaustion to set in. I barely have the strength to shower and get ready for bed, but Trevor helps by braiding my hair.

My back hurts from walking in heels on the cobblestones too much and he massages it as I lie on my bed. Trevor does take such good care of me and I love him for it. So relaxed am I, that when he pulls the covers up and kisses me good night I can barely keep my eyes open as he leaves.

CHAPTER EIGHT

The next morning I awaken and think I see Trevor sitting in the chair by my bed. "Trevor?"

"Good morning, Geneviève."

"Good morning. I thought I was dreaming." He sits up and touches my face with the back of his fingers.

"I had a dream. I was asleep and woke up with you in my arms. You felt so good against me through the silk nightgown you were wearing and it seemed so real that when I actually did wake up I expected to see you. Knowing full well I would not be able to fall back asleep I got up and came in here. There was enough light for me to see you lying there and I could hear you softly breathing. You are so beautiful."

My door is pulled to and I whisper, "Where is my family?"

"Your parents are in the kitchen and I think Théo is still sleeping."

"Then hold me."

He kneels down beside my bed and I untie the sash of his robe then slide my hands under it as he gathers me in to his arms. With his head resting on my shoulder he goes "Mmmm. This is where I've wanted to be all morning."

After several minutes of bliss we hear Théo stirring and I know the day is about to begin. Trevor lifts his head, smiles and then kisses my cheek. "I'll be back in here as soon as you open that door."

This day requires running around attire, so I put on old trousers with a blouse and loafers. When I open the door Trevor gives me a startle, because he is already standing at it. He did tell me he would be back in my room as soon as I open it. The next thing I know we are making out in my closet. He is in rare form today.

When we enter the kitchen instead of saying good morning my father tells us, "It is safe in the house; outside, not so." Trevor and I go into the solarium and see men are everywhere placing runners on the boardwalk while others are carrying chairs and our torches are being placed carefully along the path. Théo joins us for a minute then says, "This is nothing compared to next week." and goes into the kitchen. He was referring to our wedding. Trevor and I just look at each other.

After breakfast we all stay at the table sipping coffee as we each take a section of the newspaper and tell the others anything of note. Next we all pitch in and solve the crossword puzzle, which is highly entertaining because we make silly guesses that are quite funny. This of course causes time to pass quickly and Théo gets up to go find where Joseph's apartment is. He is taking him to lunch at The Posh where it will be quiet.

Théo steps into the hallway and there is a knock on the door. Mother tells him "That must be the florist." Théo goes to answer the door and we hear him say, "Yes she is. One moment please." and the door close. He comes back looking puzzled. "Gené, there are two men on the portico with a delivery for you. They are dressed like the guards in Simmons, but they are from somewhere else."

Trevor pulls out my chair and everyone follows me to the door. Théo opens it as Trevor stands by my side and I see two intimidating men; one is holding a clipboard and the other is carrying a satchel with a lock on it. No wonder Théo looked the way he did. A guard asks, "Are you Miss Geneviève Delcroix?"

"Yes I am."

"We have a delivery for you and it requires your signature."

They scan the property looking at all the vans and men everywhere then give me a calling card that reads Thomas J. Harding III and ask, "May we step inside please." Stepping back I bump into Trevor and reply, "Of course." They come in as I show the card to Trevor then give it to Théo and sign my name. The satchel is unlocked; one guard holds it open as the other begins taking out jewelry boxes and gift bags placing them on the center table with the floral arrangement.

They close the satchel, nod to me and go toward the door without a word. Trevor catches up to them, opens it and the men are gone. As I stand in front of the table Father asks, "What have we here?" I respond, "Gifts from Mr. Harding." and Mother begins to smile. Obviously she had a hand in this.

Cards are on top of each box slipped under cord with the formal names of everyone who went to Santa Barbara written in calligraphy. There are three brown leather boxes, one for each gentleman, and three boxes from Van Cleef & Arpels for the ladies. "One of the last things Mr. Harding told me was a remark about sending extravagant gifts." Théo responds, "And he did. I wish I could stay." He gives me my kiss and dashes down the hallway.

Looking at Trevor I ask, "Do you want to open yours?"

My parent's chuckle and he responds, "Geneviève, ladies first." and hands me the one with my name on it. I slowly raise the lid and find a delicate little fairy with wings of diamonds and she is holding a fairy wand that has more of them for sparkles around the end of it. I stare in disbelief and say, "A fairy." Trevor tells me "She's lovely." I add, "She's a clip. I want to pin her on ... something." We look at her a little longer then I hand her to my parents.

Trevor picks up the calling card and still looking at it says, "Mr. Harding is Thomas J. Harding, the owner of Harding Publications and one of the most influential men in the country." He is silent for a moment then adds, "One would expect him to have a longer yacht." I get tickled then respond, "He does. Morning Glory is his private one. Mr. Harding loves sailing."

Picking up the box for Trevor with eyes dancing I tell him, "Your turn." He says, "You open it. I'm positive it's a pocket watch." I glance at him then raise the lid and there it is, a gold pocket watch with his initials engraved on it. I show it to my parents and handing it to him I say, "Do tell." He chuckles and tells us, "Officers do not wear wrist watches to white tie events or with dress uniforms when attending an official ceremony."

"How does he know that and I don't?"

"The burning question is how he knew none of us own one. Joanna carries a watch in her handbag and we bother her all night."

As we laugh he hands the watch to Mother and I focus on her. She says, "Mrs. Harding called and asked if I knew their initials and I called Joanna." Trevor tells my father, "There should be more women in intel. They can find out anything with a phone call and the op is over while the men are busy preparing to go covert." Father replies, "It makes me proud to say I understood what you just said." Mother and I laugh; Trevor is learning French and teaching us Navy speak.

Mother hands me my fairy and I say, "I know those other boxes have fairies in them. I wish I could give them to Joanna and Emily today." Trevor tells me "Your wish is my command." and goes to the study where I can barely I hear him say, "Joanna." In a minute he returns with my handbag. "Emily and William are meeting them at their house then going to Sam's for lunch. They're going to wait on us." I give him a kiss and we pick up the gifts. "Do you need anything else?" I reply, "Just you." Trevor tells me, "I like your answer." and out the door we go.

On the way I tell him about showing Emily my mother's bridal gown and what was said and that is what the fairy represents to me, a fairy-tale wedding and living happily ever after. This gets me a nice kiss before we go in.

Trevor opens the door and announces, "We come bearing gifts." Faces light up and after we're seated he asks, "Has anyone figured out exactly who Mr. Harding is yet?" They all look at each other and Mitch says, "Here we go." All eyes are on me therefore I step in. "His full name is Thomas J. Harding III of Harding Publications." After a brief silence Emily stammers, "My ... my mom buys two of his ladies magazines every month." Mitch says, "One would expect him to have a longer yacht." We all get tickled then I respond, "That is exactly what he said." Trevor adds, "I did."

Things quiet down and I start getting out the gifts. While Joanna looks at the bags from Van Cleef & Arpels she says, "Now things are makings sense. The gifts are from Mr. & Mrs. Harding." I hand out them out and get out mine. Emily just looks at the box and William tells her, "I'm sure whatever's in that is inanimate." She giggles and tells him, "I'm apprehensive because I know there's something stunning in here." She slowly opens the box and her eyes get wide followed by William's. "Geneviève, it's a fairy — as in a fairy-tale wedding." I nod and show her mine. Joanna wastes no time in opening hers. We watch her heart melt as she says, "And they lived happily ever after." then kisses Mitch.

While the ladies look at each other's fairies Trevor says, "The brown boxes are worth opening." Joanna gives Mitch his and tells him, "*Open* it." He does then grins. "If I did not know better I would think we had been investigated, but the man is that sharp." Joanna looks at the watch and exclaims, "Thank goodness. I just retired as the official timekeeper for the fellas." William opens his and explains what she meant to Emily. Then Trevor says, "Josephine told us she and Joanna gave our initials to Mrs. Harding." William says, "Women are so efficient it's unnerving." Joanna beams and asks, "Who's hungry?" And the exodus begins.

We order our usual at Sam's then he comes over to tell us Joseph dropped by for breakfast and told the staff he would be back late at night and occasionally in the morning for pancakes. Sam informs us they are the only thing that keeps him from losing his bachelor customers after they marry. He thanks me and as Sam goes to man the grill it occurs to me Joseph will only be here for late nights, Claudette has known my secret ingredient for years.

Happily we all eat everything down to the last fry then leave to get ready for a wedding. I keep my head on Trevor's shoulder the entire way home. We are going to be apart for a long time. The gentlemen will visit with Théo and Joseph at my parent's house until it gets down to the wire and then join my family along with the wedding guests at my grandparent's. I will be with Claudette at her apartment; we are going to dress each other, due to the lacing. At the house Trevor and I steal a few moments together then go to our rooms.

Standing in my dressing gown at my jewelry armoire putting on my pearl earrings Trevor enters wearing his White Dinner Dress uniform. "You are so handsome." And I slide my hand down his chest. "Geneviève, you are a vision in that. I can't wait to see you in the dress." Trevor gently kisses my lips then goes to my neck. He does love to kiss me there.

When he begins to expose my shoulder I tell him, "Just a minute. I need to hold my dressing gown together. My upper body is bare."

Trevor takes a step back with his eyes locked on mine. "The things you say." I grasp the opening between my breasts then pull it up to loosen the fabric from the sash and it falls from my shoulders. "That is the most sensuous thing I have ever seen." Trevor places his hands on my waist and tells me, "Please keep leading."

Placing my hand on the back of his neck I pull him to me and place my cheek against his that has just been closely shaved and whisper, "Je t'adore." Then I move my lips close to his and hesitate, for there is longing in the anticipation for a kiss. He says, "Geneviève." as his hold on my waist tightens. He can wait no longer and neither can I.

Sounds from downstairs make their way to us and I tell him, "The gentlemen are waiting for you and Claudette for me." He nods as we still hold on to each other. "I'm going to slip out the back." He tells me, "See you soon." I reply, "See you soon." then slide my hand down his sleeve to his hand and he leaves. Gathering my things I have to concentrate, thinking of Trevor causes me to lose my train of thought. Descending the back staircase I can hear their voices. Joseph is talking to Théo and Trevor is laughing.

On the way to Claudette's I admire my surroundings. The torches are lit and golden chairs between two elegant floral arrangements in floor stands are on the corners of the carpeted boardwalk. There are white clouds scattered in the sky and the sun is getting low making things glisten. It is going to be a lovely ceremony.

Claudette hears me on the steps and peaks through the curtains of a pair of doors. When I reach the top I see her eyes are sparkling and soon both doors magically open for me to enter. Inside I am taken aback by the new dressing screen and the presence of Joseph's things. Claudette is overjoyed by all this and is aglow as she shows me a photograph of him taken when he was a child sitting on the floor playing with a toy fire truck.

We hang my dress with hers and she models the new dressing gown she is wearing. Next she shows me the flowers we will be carrying and her floral crown that is perfection. Now is a good time for me to give her the matching fan I had made. When I hand it to her she begins to puddle and I suggest using it. Laughter follows and we begin to get ready.

Suddenly the sound of a car gets our attention. I am elected to do the peaking and I see Kyle parking at the other apartment. He has arrived to get familiar with the grounds. Claudette tells me Joseph filled him in on the details at work. Well over half of the wedding involves the club and it has been very convenient.

I begin dressing first and put on the lining for the tulle that is so well tailored it looks like a satin pencil skirt and then the corset. While she loosely laces it we realize things are about to get complicated. There should be a sheet covering the rug to keep anything from getting on the layers of tulle that are going to wind up on the floor, because they cannot go over our heads this time. With the sheet in place we let the skirt float down onto it and land in a full circle then I lightly step onto the layers of tulle then into the middle of it holding her hand.

After a bit of effort I am ready and it is time to dress the bride. Claudette steps out from behind the dressing screen wearing the lining and the corset is hanging on her body by the straps. I loosely lace her up and next we have to get her in the tulle skirt. After it floats down we stand by it for a good minute. The thought of stepping on hers makes us nervous, so I suggest a glass of cognac we should have poured when I arrived; better late than never. After sipping on it our nerves are settled and I hold her hand as she steps ever so lightly on the tulle. When she is in the middle we breathe a sigh of relief and I tighten her lacing.

Next Claudette puts on her slippers and to the mirror we go to admire her and we tilt our heads at the same time. Claudette asks, "What is different?" I reply, "The skirt is not as full as it was. It has been hanging too long." Looking at her with no clue as to an easy solution to fluff all those layers I watch her eyes get very bright. "I twirl, like a ballerina." I move back as she gracefully raises her arms and twirls. The beauty of her movement takes my breath.

With her bridal gown taken care of beautifully she gets her crown of flowers and hands it to me. I make certain the ribbon streamers are straight and place it on her head as she watches in the mirror. I get misty-eyed admiring her and I think of a diversion, getting her bouquet and my nosegay. She has me stand beside her and tells me, "Thank you for this." I respond, "You are most welcome. I am happy to be by your side." Claudette opens her fan and once again we feel its calming effect. The moment is fleeting because we hear cars arriving and she exclaims, "I hear our guests." as she tosses her fan and gets my hand to lead me to the door for more peaking. It's Joanna and Mitch with William and Emily following. When they get out we see cocktail dresses and white uniforms. Claudette is giddy.

Next she sees the time and tells me, "We have over 10 minutes to spare. We should pick up the sheet."

"You will need it when you return. Joseph will hold your hand as you step out of the tulle. Then he can loosen the lacing for you." And she looks a little panic stricken. I hand her the cognac and she takes a nice sized sip. "Claudette, when you come home tonight Joseph will be your husband and he can assist you with things like that. After he loosens the lacing simply get undressed behind the screen and put on your peignoir set. More than likely he will change into his pajamas in the bathroom while you're doing that."

Claudette nods and reaches for my hand. "Speak with you I must about a personal matter." I pick up my cognac. "Joseph has told me he will sleep on the sofa until I am comfortable with his presence. I do not want to upset him, but ... Geneviève, that night he stayed, we were sitting on the sofa and I fell asleep while he was holding me. He did not mean to fall asleep. But when I woke up, it was such a comfort to still be in his arms. It was not romance. It was life and he was here when I need him most. Tonight I want romance."

"Claudette, it's your wedding night and it should be romantic. Since you want to sleep next to Joseph, tell him. He loves you and will happily do whatever you ask of him."

"Joseph said that very thing to me."

"He meant it."

"Yes, he did. I will not hesitate again."

We finish our cognac talking about how pretty the wedding is going to be and then I call the house to let them know we are ready to begin. Claudette draws in a deep breath as I dial my grandparent's number.

"Bonsoir, Gené."

"Bonsoir, Théo."

"His bride is ready?"

"Yes and she will take his breath away."

"Of that I have no doubt. I am looking forward to seeing you a well."

"Oh, Théo."

"I will send our grandfather up."

"Thank you. We will see you shortly."

When I hang up I notice Claudette looks light headed. "I am going to peak outside and after Joseph passes by you can join me." She is giddy again, mission accomplished. At the curtains I tell her what I see. "The doors are opening, it is my grandfather, followed by — Joseph and Théo; handsome men they are."

"I wish I could look."

"Just a few more seconds; Reginald is escorting Grand-mamma and oh, Joseph just looked up. He knows his bride is waiting in here."

"More romance."

"Indeed. There are my parents. Trevor is escorting Rachel. Théo and Joseph are about to round the corner and — you may look outside now."

She reaches the other doors and says, "Your grandfather is on the steps."

"Are you ready for him to come in?"

"I hope so."

"Shall I open the door?"

"Please."

"Grand-papa, you look debonair."

"Merci beaucoup." He carefully kisses my cheeks then sees Claudette. "Magnifique, vraiment magnifique." She blushes and replies, "Merci beaucoup." I stand beside her and he says, "You both are beautiful, a lucky man am I. Shall we?" Claudette responds, "One moment please, I need to speak with my family before I marry." My grandfather tells her, "We will wait for you outside. Do take your time." She nods as he offers me his arm. I pick up my nosegay and cannot get through the door fast enough.

Safely on the balcony I put my hand to my face. "I did not see that coming."

"Nor did I. Blindsided by a bride."

I have a small burst of nervous laughter and ask, "What does Rachel say?"

"For crying out loud. When she says it to Théo I do enjoy it so."

"It is hilarious. I adore her."

"As do we all. — Geneviève, do you have a handkerchief?"

"Yes. We hid one among our flowers. Joseph's wedding band is in here too. I slipped it on a slender leaf."

"Imaginative girls."

We get quiet and look at the sky. It is changing colors. The show has begun and as if on cue Claudette emerges with her hands full carrying her bouquet, bridal purse and my evening bag. I take it from her and start down the steps then wait for them at the bottom. When they reach me my grandfather offers me his other arm. We go to the front of his house where he dashes inside with our bags.

He returns toute de suite and while we stroll along Claudette says, "Recently, sad for my father I was and it occurred to me he has two more daughter's he can walk down the aisle. Théodore, I am pleased it will be you. I adore this family."

"We adore you as well. Thank you for sharing your thoughts."

"You are most welcome. Besides, how may brides have a marquis escort them to their groom and a marchioness stand by their side?" Claudette's eyes sparkle as she looks at us. We are speechless.

Soon we are at our destination and switch sides to shield the bride from view. In a huddle we proceed to the arbor and I get butterflies in my stomach. How odd. Hidden by the arbor Claudette and I check each other then I go to the front and stop while they get situated. Reginald is smiling as I hear her softly say, "We are ready." I nod to Reginald who motions to us and everyone turns in their seats.

Slowly I begin to walk toward them looking at Trevor. He almost stands when our eyes meet and he catches himself then sits very still. It is a habit for him and I am touched. When close, I glance at the others then focus on Joseph and Théo. They are beaming and it's only me.

When I am in my spot and facing the arbor my grandfather and Claudette finally appear. Everyone stands and I hear gasps then I take my eyes off her to look at Joseph in time to see his chest swell from a deep breath he takes at the sight of his bride and my heart leaps. Emotion overtakes me for a moment and I quickly look at Joanna; she will help me get my wits. Our eyes lock because she is watching me and I get a wink. That does the trick. I can always depend on her.

Claudette only has eyes for her groom as she steps up to him and my grandfather places her hand in Joseph's. He sits next to my grandmother and the ceremony begins. How beautiful the words are when spoken in française. It is lyrical and the sounds of the waves are the music, just as she had imagined.

As soon as Reginald says, "Vous pouvez embrasser la mariée." I see Trevor smile out of the corner of my eye; he does know the word for kiss. And such a kiss they make. She reaches for her bouquet I am holding and they take their first steps as husband and wife. The second they pass Trevor I get to look into his eyes and just before I fall into them Théo steps to the middle. I refocus and move toward him. He softly says, "I knew you would be a vision." I smile at my adoring brother and he escorts me away, passing my fiancé whom I cannot wait to steal a kiss from.

In the drawing room Théo and I are at last with the one's we are in love with. I squeeze Trevor arm and he whispers, "I missed you terribly." I whisper, "I missed you too." He adds, "By the way, I fancy that pink you're wearing." and takes the quarter with Strawberry Fluff on it out of his pocket.

After drinking a little champagne Kyle informs us before it gets dark he needs to take photographs, therefore we all go back outside. Going toward the boardwalk I exhale heavily and Trevor asks, "What was that about?"

"Something just caught up with me."

"Talk to me."

"My grandfather walked into the apartment, complimented us and made a few sweet comments then asked, 'Shall we?' and Claudette told him, 'One moment please.' The tone of my voice drops. "She needed to speak with her family before she married. Grand-papa told her we would wait outside and outside we went." Trevor's jaw drops. "Unbelievable; you were blindsided by a bride." I get tickled and tell him, "My grandfather said that while we were outside trying to regroup. The rest is a blur." Laughter *is* contagious and he gets tickled. Trevor places his hand over mine and we quiet down then I go to pose for photographs.

William makes his way over to Trevor with Emily on his arm; Mitch and Joanna are on their heels. Father along with Mother and Rachel step in close on my grandparents and they all appear to be talking nonchalantly, but I know Trevor and Grand-papa are telling them we were blindsided. Rachel will tell Théo the story and that will take of that.

Kyle finally announces he will see us at the club and Reginald begins telling everyone goodbye for he has a flight to catch tonight. After watching him round the corner to the apartment he stayed in we hastily return to the drawing room. Champagne is chilling in there.

We are all reveling in the moment; it is such a happy occasion. After Théo eloquently makes his toast Joseph raises his glass and toasts his bride. Then he turns toward my mother and says, "For years I have waited on an opportunity to properly thank you and your husband for watching over me. If anything ever happened to me I knew without a doubt I would be taken care of. That knowledge gave me peace of mind and sustained me throughout the years. And as if that were not enough, I now have a wife due to this family. Please join me as I raise my glass and drink to the Delcroix's."

This catches my family and our friend's off guard. We were expecting a toast, not a heartfelt speech. As he raises his glass to my parents I am clinging to Trevor and smiling while, "To the Delcroix's." resonates through the room. When Joseph nods to me I continue to smile, but inside my mind is going in every direction possible and I wonder what is going to happen next.

Thinking keeps my emotions in check and I'm fine for about a minute because next he says, "If you all would be so kind as to indulge us for a moment; Claudette's parents are waiting to speak with her and for the opportunity to properly welcome me to their family." Everyone in the room shifts ever so slightly and my grandfather tells them, "Please, call them on the phone in the study and take all the time you require."

When they turn around movement among us immediately begins. Some of us look up to the ceiling, others glance around the room. I turn to Trevor who is visibly shaken, as are we all. I am hanging on by a thread and the split second we hear the doors of the study close Mother cries out, "Gérard, I do not know why it did not occur to me — Joseph is no longer an orphan. He has a family now." Tears escape onto her face. My grandmother wilts as I hear gasps and murmurs. My jaw is trembling when my father sternly says, "Josephine, give me your hand. You cannot go there now. It will take too long for your return." She tries to take a deep breath as she nods. Trevor reaches for my glass and I see the champagne is about to spill out because my hand is shaking.

Earlier when I put down the nosegay I had the presence of mind to get my handkerchief out and tuck it into the corset; therefore I am able to catch the tears welling in my eyes before they land on my dress. Trevor turns his glass up and empties it before setting it down. Next I notice there is a handkerchief in a hand of most of the people here. Mitch is helping Joanna, my father is carefully attending to mother and Rachel is busy with herself and Théo. My grandfather takes care of Grand-mamma looking stoic then I hear Emily tell William, "My mirror." and see him holding her evening bag open as she takes out her compact. I look around for mine and Trevor says, "It's in the foyer. I'll get it." I am gripped with fear until I see the damage was minimal.

Next I hear Joanna clear her throat. "Excuse me; it would be best if we were doing something when they return." Théo responds, "Cognac, serving cognac." Grand-papa tells him, "Well done." and they swing into action. Trevor hands me the champagne I was drinking and I turn my glass up. Mitch scoffs, "This is white wine with bubbles." and empties his glass. That comment got a light chuckle and we are on the road to recovery. By the time Joseph and Claudette join us everyone is swirling a glass of cognac and two glasses are waiting on them.

When I focus on Claudette one more problem arises. Her eyes are red and her makeup is almost gone. It obviously did not survive the tears she shed. Grand-mamma says, "Geneviève, my dressing room." In no time, with our cognac and evening bags, Claudette and I are on our way. As we begin to repair her makeup she says, "If I tell, I will cry." My response is, "If I listen, I will cry." And that was our entire conversation.

Back in the drawing room things are back to normal. Joseph kisses his bride's hand and Trevor kisses mine twice upon our return. Fortunately there are no guests waiting at the club and we take our time to enjoy the reception. No more toasts were made thank goodness and the mood elevates steadily as we admire their wedding bands and mill around the room.

Soon the time for their dinner is upon us and yet another exodus begins with Joseph and Claudette in front. For some reason each couple is driving there separately, so we begin the walk to our cars after the bride and groom are in theirs. It has writing in white shoe polish on the back window that reads, Just Married. My grandparents get in Grand-mamma's car, because The Chariot seemed inappropriate. Father puts Mother in their car and Théo attends to Rachel.

Next we see a limousine with Reginald in the back going down the driveway and Trevor tells us, "He probably feels guiltily for leaving early. He has no clue how lucky he is. An explosive device went off in that room." William says, "I have permanent hearing damage." Mitch nods in agreement as Joanna dryly remarks, "I have internal bleeding." Emily whimpers, "So do I." Trevor says, "Geneviève took a lot of shrapnel. Baby, should we stop by the ER before we go to the club and have you checked?" I reply, "I can make it through dinner. We can swing by on our way home." He laughs along with the others, puts me in the car and kisses my hand before closing the door.

There is quite a disturbance when Joseph and Claudette pull up to the valets. Apparently the staff is as closed mouth as is expected of them, discretion is a motto here. What a fuss; poor Claudette is so close in proximity to Joseph it impedes him as they go inside to make their way to the corridor where the private dining room is to wait for us.

After gathering in the lobby we begin walking down the corridor and as expected her back is to us and when Joseph looks our way she turns around so fast her dress twirls out and mouths come open, including Joseph's. I'm so pleased everyone was able to see that. Next William and Mitch step forward and stand by the doors. Joseph looks at Claudette and she nods then they open the doors.

The first thing I notice is Trevor and I were not the only ones to drop their wedding gift off here, because there is a table stacked with several more. Some I believe are from members of the staff. Personally I am happy to see the dining table, so I can stop carrying this nosegay. Down it goes and Claudette does the same thing with her bouquet.

The only servers in the room are those who work with Joseph and we are all quite relaxed as the wedding dinner begins. The best of the best is being served starting with caviar and champagne. When it's time for the main course we get a surprise; Chef enters the dining room with the plates for the bride and groom. When he nods at Joanna I almost get tickled knowing he supplies her with white truffles.

When the Pâtissier carries in the wedding cake and the Sous Chef has the groom's cake we are not surprised. They wanted to wish them well and they acknowledge me with a nod, which delights Trevor. The Bride and Groom cut the cakes as Kyle takes several photographs of them then they feed each other and hook their arms together to drink the champagne as most newlyweds do. The cakes were delectable and after dessert my grandfather has a bottle of Louis XIII presented to them. Joseph insists on it being opened and served.

As we sip the nectar I ask Joanna to accompany me to the Ladies Lounge. We walk arm in arm complimenting each other and having small talk then she opens the door. This is when things take an unexpected turn for the worst. We hear a woman say, "Have you heard the Delcroix family is here in a private dining room?" I freeze as does Joanna. Another woman replies, "No, do you know why?"

"The little French maid they brought over married that waiter Joseph tonight; the help marrying the help."

"What is wrong with that?"

"It is so common. It could have been worse. Théo could have married her."

I look at Joanna then face forward. My chin goes up as I tell her, "I am going to verbally stab that woman in the chest with a dagger." Joanna gasps as I step further inside for the women to see me and they do in the mirror. They both face me and I know which one I am after. Staring her down I quickly close in on her. "It was impossible not to overhear your conversation. You are sadly misinformed. Miss Bechard, currently Mrs. Joseph Côté, is the daughter of the vigneron for Château Delcroix in Aix-en-Provence. She is a close friend of the family who came here to further her education and in the process became a refugee from the war. As for Joseph, he is a member of the elite Silver Staff of this club. It is an honorable profession made difficult by people full of their own self-importance making unreasonable request of them. Now you may consider yourself well informed." I glare at the woman and leave the lounge area into the powder room. Joanna follows me and closes the door instantly.

"Darling, I know this is wrong, but if I do not eavesdrop, I will never forgive myself." I laugh and tell her, "Joanna, you go right ahead." The woman lights up and presses her ear to the door. She whispers, "Can you hear me?" With my hand over my mouth I go, "Mmm hmm."

"Mean one: We are going to be blackballed. Nice lady: Not we, you. And Miss Delcroix is not vindictive, so that won't happen. She will keep this incident to herself and protect her family from the knowledge this vicious rumor is going around. Mean one: You think so? Nice lady: Do you have any idea who the Delcroix's are? Silence now, I think the mean one is paralyzed with fear. Nice lady: They are the most prominent member's here. This club was built on land they own." Joanna chuckles and listens, then says "The mean one gasped and told her let's get out of here. — And they are gone. I have never eavesdropped in my life and I thoroughly enjoyed it."

"I see that." Placing my hand on the doorknob of a water closet I add, "Joanna, I am the maid of honor." She responds, "Oh, we can walk and talk in a bit."

With noses powdered and lipstick reapplied we enter the corridor and Joanna excitedly says, "I cannot wait for the crew to hear this one."

"What? Wait a minute. Joanna — I don't even remember half of what I said to that woman."

"I do. Please let me tell them."

Shaking my head thinking, I finally say, "Joanna, I better not regret this."

"Oh, thank you. You won't." She squeezes my hand and opens the door. The gentlemen stand and Mitch is giving his wife a look, so she announces, "Geneviève had to stop and talk with some members. Eventually she told them to excuse us." Mother says, "How inconsiderate. They had to have known why you are here." I reply, "They did." Joanna's eyes are still dancing and she covers beautifully. "I am thrilled to be here. We did not miss anything I hope." Mitch tells her, "Not anything of note.", but his eyes say quite a bit more.

It's time for a distraction, therefore I announce, "It is not the custom to open gifts at a dinner, hence we ask you all to indulge us. Trevor, would you give them ours please." He places it on the table between them and Joseph pulls the ribbon then Claudette lifts the lid. As she folds back the tissue paper they inhale deeply and look at each other. Claudette picks up her fan as Joseph manages to say, "At a loss we truly are. This was taken shortly before I told my bride I was in love with her." Sighs fill the room.

Joseph takes the photograph out of the box and after they look at it he hands it to Théo. As it is passed around the table I tell them, "When I grabbed my camera Trevor raised his eyebrows at me. I told him I was only going to take one and we were going to give it to you both on your wedding day. He held the draperies back for me; I snapped the shutter and he let them go." When it gets back to Claudette she holds the frame in her arms and the look she gives me told me everything she wanted to say.

When our glasses are almost empty Claudette quietly speaks to Joseph. "The day is beginning to catch me and I so much want to enjoy the drive along the coast in the morning. Would you mind terribly if we left soon?" He replies, "I will take you to our home now if you wish." She tells him, "I wish."

Joseph motions for Eric and asks him to have the gifts put in their car. With the servers gone we have a moment together and they thank us profusely for everything then request for us to stay and finish our cognac instead of seeing them out. Claudette is ecstatic when Mother tells her she does not have to toss her bouquet because all the ladies are spoken for. Looking at the floral arrangement in front of me I suddenly pull several petals from an unsuspecting peony to toss on them as they leave. To my surprise everyone follows my lead and we shower the newlyweds with the petals as they go into the corridor. It was the perfect send off. Romance filled the room and each gentleman gave their lady a tender kiss.

My grandparents wait until they are certain Joseph and Claudette are gone to take their leave, as do my parents. Théo tells us keeping an anxious groom occupied most of the day has exhausted him, so he gives me my kiss then he and Rachel slowly exit the dining room.

When the doors close Joanna motions for Eric and ask for 15 minutes of privacy. This cannot be happening; she is going to tell everyone about the incident now. Mitch tells her, "I take it you are going to share with the rest of us what has had you quietly entertained since you and Geneviève returned." William looks at Trevor and says, "I knew something was up." Trevor replies "She is transparent to those who know her well. Joanna, you have the floor."

"First I want you all to raise your right hands and repeat after me." I have an outburst of nervous laughter and she adds, "I'm serious." Hands go up and she begins, "I give my word I will not repeat the story Joanna is about to tell." They take their oath and lower their hands grinning.

Here she goes. "It began when I opened the door to the Ladies Lounge and we heard a woman talking. I am going to be quoting verbatim and mimicking. She said to her friend, 'Have you heard the Delcroix family is here in a private dining room?' We froze in our tracks and the friend replied, 'No, do you know why?' The woman tells her, 'The little French maid they brought over married that waiter Joseph tonight; the help marrying the help.' The nice lady: 'What is wrong with that?' The mean one: 'It is so, common. It could have been worse, Théo could have married her.' At that point Geneviève looks at me then faces forward. Her little chin goes up in the air and she tells me, 'I am going to verbally stab that woman in the chest with a dagger.'"

There are multiple reactions; the main one is from my fiancé who looks at me laughing and says, "That is the best line I have ever heard." Mitch gives me a thumbs up. William exclaims, "I better get to steal that one day." Emily is wide eyed covering her mouth as I tell Trevor, "I have no idea where that came from." He responds, "I do, utter infuriation. First she insults Claudette beyond all comprehension and then she goes after Joseph. Her fatal mistake was bringing your brother into it." Everyone looks at him nodding.

Joanna says, "It gets better."

Trevor tells her, "You have my undivided attention."

"Well, I gasped as Geneviève stepped further inside for the women to see her and they do, in the mirror. They both spun around and she knew exactly which one to go after. Geneviève closed in on her so fast the woman flinched and she proceeds to verbally stab that woman in the chest."

As Joanna continues to tell the story it occurs to me I did. I told her exactly who Claudette was and I mentioned the Château. Oh, and Joseph, I insulted her over that comment about him. Never will I live this down.

When Joanna begins to confess she eavesdropped I calm down, because I didn't expect her to do that, but it is the best part. What was said after we went into the powder room was hilarious and the image of her with an ear pressed against that door will stay with me for the rest of my days. By the time she finishes telling the story Mitch's eyes are watering.

Finally a staff door opens and Eric cautiously steps in followed by the other servers. "Miss Delcroix, we were wondering if you and your guests would like something else." I glance at the crew; they all give me a slight shake of the head and I reply, "We require not another thing. Thank you all for making the evening memorable." He responds, "It was our pleasure. Good evening, Miss Delcroix." I tell them, "Good evening, gentlemen." And we will be alone from this point on.

Emily says, "Excuse me please." and goes over to the wedding cake. She cuts three tiny pieces from it and wraps them in cocktail napkins. Emily places one in front of Joanna and me then tells us, "For sweet dreams." It is a lovely sentiment, placing it under your pillow to have sweet dreams, but it never gave them to me and I stopped. This one will go under my pillow though, for it is special.

Instead of sitting back down Emily puts her hand on William's shoulder and asks, "Would you like to take me to the overlook?" As he stands William replies, "That's a rhetorical question if ever I heard one. My friends, we bid you good night." Mitch and Trevor begin to stand and Emily tells them, "Gentlemen, please keep your seats." William shakes Mitch's hand and kisses Joanna's then walks to us and does a repeat. We cannot help but chuckle, the man is not wasting time. Emily blows us kisses as he escorts her through the doors.

Mitch looks at me and says, "Geneviève, you have had a busy day. You were blindsided, hit by shrapnel and had to draw a weapon. I think Joanna and I should take our leave and give you two some privacy." Joanna gets tickled as we all stand for hugs and kisses, then Trevor and I are alone.

The first thing he says to me is, "I am going to verbally stab that woman in the chest with a dagger. I do love you." He throws his arms around me then adds, "It is ridiculous how much I love you."

"I love you too."

"What would you like to do, Baby?" I am silent as several things go through my mind. "Do you want to go home?"

"Not really."

"Let's sit on the deck and listen to the ocean. Then if you feel up to it we can go for a walk on the beach."

"That sounds good to me."

We gather my things and go to the deck. To our surprise we find ourselves alone and I finally get the kiss I have been longing for. Next we sit down and he puts his arm around my shoulders as we listen to the waves. The good things that occurred this evening slowly begin to overshadow the unexpected ones then I begin thinking about us and how close we are to having our dream, but it has seemed as if that day will never arrive.

After I exhale a deep breath Trevor says, "Let's go for that walk." and kneels at my feet. "Do you know how long I have wanted to do this?"

"Since you saw my dress and realized I had Strawberry Fluff on my toes."

"I would touch my nose, but I'm preoccupied at the moment." I laugh as he begins to takes off my shoes. "Ah, of course you are wearing stockings. This dress is not full length — and they are silk."

Looking at him I decide I am not about to go inside to take these off and since we are alone, without taking my eyes from his I pull my dress up along my right leg just enough to reach under it and get my hands on the garter. As I slowly pull it down my leg to take it off he sees it and says, "You're wearing garters to hold your stockings up." His eyes are gleaming as I slip it over my foot. When I hold it out and offer it to him Trevor takes it from me and slips it into his pocket keeping his eyes on mine the entire time.

Next I reach under my dress for the stocking and move it to a place where it can slide down my leg and take it off. As I lay my stocking on the seat looking at him I hear his thoughts clearly and say, "I wish you could take the other one off too." His eyes lock on mine. After it is off I straighten my dress and he rests his hands on my thighs as I place my hands on his shoulders.

"Trevor, we watched a couple begin a life together today."

"Mm hmm. And we're next." Trevor gives me a reassuring look as he gathers me into his arms and holds me close.

"Geneviève."

"I'm listening."

"Eskimo?" And I happily do as he asks.

Driving through the gates at Maison we notice the only sign left a wedding just took place is Josephs' car parked in front of his new home with Just Married still on the back window. Knowing those two, my guess is that will be removed before leaving for their honeymoon, because it is an invasion of their privacy.

As for us, Trevor parks at the house and we go in the front door. The only light on is the lamp by the phone upstairs. The second we set foot on the balcony he takes a stance from the tango with me and says, "I have wanted to do this since I watched Claudette's dress fan out." And he spins me out then he spins me right back against him. Next he gives me a sly grin and a kiss then loosens his hold on my hand as I tighten mine on his. "Trevor — I need you to help undress me." His eyes turn the most beautiful shade of blue and I lead him into my bedroom.

Instead of pushing the door to, he closes it. "I am at your service."

"Undo the tulle skirt and let it fall to the floor." When it lands I turn to him and extend my hand for him to hold as I step out of it.

"I thought this was pretty with the tulle. Baby, you are stunning. That underskirt fits you like a glove. Promise me you will wear this on a special occasion."

"I promise. — Are you ready for the best part?" I turn around, look over my shoulder, and point at the laces. He exhales heavily, kisses the slope of my neck and slowly begins to loosen them. When it is loose enough to separate he discovers I am not wearing anything under the corset and slides his hand under the laces along my spine. My eyes close as my head goes back and I do sigh. I am not sure how he did it, but Trevor moved in front of me and kept his hand in place and the next thing I know we are in the throes of passion.

He eventually whispers, "Again, I do not want to let go of you." But he does.

"I'm going to rinse off and wait for you." Trevor gives me a kiss with yearning in it and leaves.

For some unknown reason I decide to put on one of the peignoir sets I intended to wear during our honeymoon. The robe is white with lace over satin with satin covered buttons. The matching nightgown has satin ribbon that makes the straps and wraps around under my bust line like a Grecian gown. Instead of admiring it I sit looking at myself in the mirror feeling strange as I braid my hair waiting on Trevor. He comes in just when I finish.

I stand up with the small piece of wedding cake, give him a kiss and go place it under my pillow. I turn around and see Trevor is walking slowly toward me as he looks at me from head to toe. "I would remember this. It has buttons — and it's lovely."

"I'm glad you like it. I got it for you."

"How you do spoil me."

Trevor reaches for the buttons looking into my eyes as he unbuttons them. When he slides it from shoulders the nightgown is revealed and his jaw slightly drops. "Your nightgown is beautiful — *you* are beautiful." He sighs and caresses my face, then simply runs his fingertip along the ribbon.

After soaking in everything he sees he puts my robe on the bench as I sit on my bed. Trevor kneels at my feet and waits a moment before lifting my legs onto it then slowly covers me up. Sitting on the edge Trevor tenderly kisses me then with his hand on my neck he whispers, "I love you. Good night, Geneviève."

"I love you too. Good night, Trevor."

It doesn't take long for me to notice Trevor left without tucking me in with Christopher and when I turn my head to look at him the sweet aroma from the cake wafts from under my pillow. As I lie there alone it occurs to me at this very moment Claudette is blissfully sleeping in the arms of Joseph and without warning a tear rolls from the corner of my eye onto my pillow. Where did that come from — and why? *Am I envious?* That is not like me. A wave of emotion overcomes me and I sit straight up, then my mind becomes turbulent with thoughts I cannot grasp. Before I know it I am going down the staircase of the foyer headed to the liqueur cabinet.

Picking up a glass I wonder what I am doing. I don't want a drink. I want to cry. And that is it. Putting the glass down I turn and as quietly as possible run down the hallway then outside through the service entrance. While running barefooted across the cobblestones to the closest apartment my nightgown flutters in the cool night breeze and it reminds I am supposed to be wearing this in bed with him. Why did I wear this? Inside at last I stand in the dark trying to catch my breath. Then I see Trevor's shadow at the door and he steps inside.

"Geneviève, what are you doing?"

"Running away from myself." He looks very concerned as he walks over to me and stands silently keeping a little distance between us. "Trevor — I was becoming someone I am not. When I smelled the wedding cake underneath my pillow it occurred to me that Claudette was sleeping in the arms of Joseph and a single tear rolled from the corner of my eye. Trevor, I am not a person prone to envy, but something came over me."

"Baby, the same thought crossed my mind. It wasn't envy, I wanted to be them. I wanted to fall asleep with you in my arms. Instead I wound up chasing you."

"You chased me?"

"Yep. I heard you downstairs and was at the top of the stairs about to come down when you came running out of the drawing room and dashed down the hallway. I couldn't call out your name to stop you, so I took the back stairs hoping to cut you off at the pass, but you were gone. I chased you the entire way here and was not too far back. You are fast. The nightgown didn't slow you down one bit." I cannot help but laugh, then I put my arms around him and he holds me tight.

"Thank goodness you heard me. I was in an emotional free fall. This is all my doing. I chose to have the proper ... everything. I just wanted our families to be here."

"Geneviève, we made this decision together and I still say it was the correct one. Their wedding ... just turned on us."

"It did. The smell of the cake under my pillow sent me over the edge."

"I think we should remove it when we get back to the house. For now I am going to pour you a glass of water, you must be thirsty after that run." He makes me laugh and goes to the refrigerator. When I start drinking it I realize I am thirsty.

After I hand the water to him he asks, "Do you want to lie down and at least rest together for a bit?"

My face goes a little straight and I hesitate before answering him. "Under one condition."

"You have a condition? — What is it?"

"When the inevitable happens and we become passionate, I do not want to worry in the back of mind I might find myself lying completely beneath you. It is distracting and taking away from these moments we share."

"I think it's time to move a boundary." He reaches for my hand. "Shall we?"

"Please."

Trevor leads me to the bed, places his ring and watch by the glass of water then pulls the covers back and over to the other side. He looks deep into my eyes, sweeps me off my feet and puts a knee on the bed in order to lie me down in the center of it. As he stands looking at me Trevor takes off his tank shirt and tosses it on the covers. I do not take my eyes off of his torso while he gets on the bed. When he is on his side against my body he caresses my face and kisses me tenderly then he gathers me into his arms. And so it begins.

In the midst of a passionate kiss he rolls me over until I am lying on him. My arms are beside his shoulders and his legs are between mine. I prop up and place my cheek against his and kiss his earlobe because I discovered he likes it. Then I work my way down to his shoulder with every intention of leaving a passion mark on it. While his skin is in my mouth he rolls us over. I instinctively hold on to him with my arms and legs. When we get still I find myself lying completely beneath him. I am so taken aback my mouth opens and I lie my head down on the pillow.

The weight of him does not prevent me from drawing in a deep breath and when I exhale I notice his breathing is shallow. I open my eyes knowing his will fall into them the moment I do.

We remain perfectly still in order to feel ... everything: warm bare skin touching, each others breath on our faces, the weight of his body on mine and my body beneath his.

"Trevor, — mmmm."

"Geneviève, I know. Believe me, I know. I can feel how soft you are ... everywhere. I'm afraid to move."

"Don't be. Whatever happens ... happens. You may kiss me now."

Trevor presses his forehead to mine then he unleashes his passion. After I run my fingernails along his spine there is a blur until without thinking I drop my arms onto the pillow. The moment I do he stops kissing me and I open my eyes. His begin to gleam as he caresses both of my arms slowly working his way to my hands that are waiting to be entwined with his. When the wait is over I find myself beneath him with the full weight of his body at long last on mine.

We look at each other and wait a moment to catch our breath then begin to kiss. And next he proceeds to kiss every inch of the exposed skin of my upper body. Even though my heart is pounding he ignores it.

Finally it is me who has to interrupt this moment of pure bliss. "Trevor, I have to get a drink of water." He nods and begins to move off of me then he gets strangely still.

"Umm, Geneviève. I seem to be tangled in your nightgown." I begin to laugh until I realize our legs are wrapped tightly together in it. When I move my legs a little to try and loosen it nothing happens. "Baby, wait a minute. I think you're going to cause further damage to it."

"What do you mean by *further* damage?"

"Oh, I do not want to tell you this, but somehow my foot went through the lace. I can it feel around my ankle. It must have happened during all the rolling around we did." I burst into laughter.

"Trevor, what are you going to do? I'm thirsty."

He starts laughing then says, "Give me a second to think."

"Take your time. I do have the ability to speak." He chuckles and nods.

"The way I see it rolling around got us into this predicament and rolling can get us out of it. Hold on to me, Baby."

Halfway to the side of the bed we start laughing and I wind up underneath him when we stop. When I reach up and turn on the lamp he rolls us on our sides. "All right, you take it from here."

I give him a kiss, drink some water and survey the situation which causes me to get tickled. "We look like we're in a cocoon."

He lifts his head and chuckles. "Yes we do, now will you please get us out off it. — Geneviève, you have a glint in your eyes."

"You enjoy helping me undress. All you have to do is pull down the zipper, close your eyes and I can slip out of this." Trevor shakes his head at me.

On that note I get to work and after an effort that takes a few minutes because we keep getting tickled, I get us untangled then hand him the water as he sits up. I

"I seriously need to rethink my trousseau. Nightgowns are lovely, but not practical in the least. I am so glad this didn't happen on the first night of our honeymoon."

Smiling he says, "It definitely would have changed the mood."

Nodding the solution leaps to mind. "I'll wear my new undergarments instead. I have lovely satin tap pants with matching bralettes."

"Your legs will be bare?"

"Mmm hm. What are you going to wear?"

Trevor's eyes dart around the room then he looks at me. "All I have are Navy issues. I need to go to Bertucci's Monday morning for some civvie skivvies and the same day laundry near the base."

"Since our wedding is next week that's a good idea."

"Geneviève, you're still going to bring the nightgowns on our honeymoon?"

"Yes, I will wear them while eating dinner in our cottage and I'll change before we go to bed. — Eventually you will take them off of me before we get in bed."

Trevor sets down the water, pulls the strap off my shoulder and gently kisses it. "Bring this one please." I nod and move a little closer to him then his stomach growls. "Baby, please ignore that this time."

"I cannot refuse you, but when it happens again."

"We'll go to the house and I'll pour the orange juice."

He carefully lowers me back down onto the bed and I honestly think he willed his body to stay silent, because we were lost in each other before it made another sound.

It is way after four o'clock, so we decide to make the bed later in the day and turn off the light then go outside. The first thing we notice, Théo is not home. Trevor says, "I hope we don't run into him."

"It would be the most awkward moment in history. I think we should leave the same way we arrived, running."

"I think you're spot-on." He grabs my hand and we do not stop running until we are in the mudroom, then we sneak upstairs and go to our rooms. I change into pajamas and a robe I wore when I was in my late teens and open my door to find him waiting. He just had to put on a robe and slippers. We go downstairs and breathe a sigh a relief because we did not encounter Théo.

We decide to skip coffee and go to bed after we eat then sleep until lunch time. There are going to be long days ahead of us when his family returns Thursday for the wedding. While Trevor keeps his word by pouring orange juice he tells me, "I think Théo and Rachel have stayed up all night making plans for their wedding or should I say rearranging them?"

"The latter, the wedding had an effect on them too."

Trevor starts making noise chopping ham for our omelets and comments, "Your parents having their suite built on the other side of the house was pure genius. They can't hear a thing coming from this side."

"It made mine and Théo's life simpler, because we started raiding the kitchen when we were very young."

While cooking we hear Théo walking down the hallway, who obviously parked in front, so he wouldn't disturb our parents at five o'clock in the morning. He enters the kitchen with his tuxedo jacket over his shoulder. "I'm not surprised to see you two. That wedding backfired." We nod as he sighs heavily. "When we got to Rachel's she told me to get comfortable because we needed to have a discussion then she changed into her big girl PJ's, which I see you are wearing."

While whisking the eggs I tell him, "We're making ham and cheese omelets then going to bed after we eat and sleep until lunch. Do you want one?"

"Rachel made us breakfast. I left after we finished eating. We decided to do the same thing. I'm going back for lunch. Can I help?"

"You can set the table and heat scones."

"A scone, that sounds good."

When we sit down I tell Théo, "You have our undivided attention."

"Long story short, Rachael and I are not having an engagement party at the club. We changed our wedding date to Saturday, November 8th and will return from our honeymoon the day of our grandparents' anniversary. And we have you two to thank."

"What did we do?"

"You both decided to follow etiquette by having a formal engagement party and wedding reception, thus giving our family the joy of an elaborate celebration of a marriage." Trevor and I look at each other thinking the same thing. We made the correct decision, without a doubt.

"The other thing we discussed was after we are married she will be given the title of Marchioness, because I will be the 14th Marquis des Château Delcroix d'Aix-en-Provence. And she will be wearing the Delcroix Tiara that belongs to you during the ceremony."

I put down my fork. "How did she react?"

"Rachel told me she was almost positive my grandfather had a title, because he wore a signet ring instead of a wedding band. Then when she met Father she was positive and has been waiting on me to fill in the blanks. Rachel learned a lot reading French literature."

Trevor dryly says, "The French literature I read didn't mention any of this, so your sister blindsided me."

Théo refrains from laughter and tells him, "Apparently you rebounded quickly. I didn't even know she told you. Rachel and I need to spend more time here." I nod repeatedly then we start eating our scones.

After the dishes are done we notice it's daybreak and Trevor says, "Since we are all still up I think we should sit on the portico and watch the sunrise."

Théo replies, "I haven't seen one of those in a while. It will be a nice way to end this extremely long day."

"Mon Frère, I could not agree with you more."

Théo leaves Mother a note to let her know how late we all stayed up and we will be sleeping until it's time for lunch. Next we turn off all the lights and Théo puts his jacket back on as we sneak outside where we manage to squeeze in together on the settee with me in the middle. Trevor's arm is around my shoulders and Théo is holding my hand. We are on Cloud 9 until we hear a noise then look to our right and see Joseph; he has suitcases in his hands. Of course they're going to start their honeymoon by riding on the interstate watching the sun come up. Théo quietly says, "You two are in the clear. I'm still in my tuxedo."

"Gentlemen, worst of all, we are going to be invading their privacy."

Trevor tells us, "We'll get spotted going in the front door, it will take too long. We need an exit strategy."

"That is clearly your department." Trevor glances at me, then while he thinks Théo slips off his shoes. "I have it. When Joseph goes back in we are going to jump off the side of the portico." I give him a thumbs up and so does Théo. I have to cover my mouth.

All eyes are on Joseph watching him go up the steps and when he goes in we all jump to our feet. Trevor leads us to the side and he puts his left hand down then does a move like he is dismounting a pummel horse. I'm wearing a robe, so I decide to sit down. The second I do Trevor grabs me by my waist and gets me down, then to my surprise, Théo does the same thing Trevor did. Next we run to the service entrance like thieves in the night trying not to get caught.

Safe inside the mudroom the laughter begins. When we calm down Trevor says, "That was not how I saw that playing out in my mind." I bury my face in his chest. Théo says in exasperation, "This day needs to end." I tell him, "It will when we get in our beds." Trevor motions me to the doorway.

Upstairs not a word is spoken as Théo shakes Trevor's hand, gives me my kiss and goes into his room. Trevor follows me into mine and closes the door. We sit on the edge of my bed and I pour a glass of water from the pitcher on my nightstand and drink it immediately. I hand it to Trevor who is shaking his head, but there is a gleam in his eyes. "I am a commander in the United States Navy and just ran around this house like a mischievous boy hiding from grownups." I have to put my hand over my mouth again. "Let's get you tucked in, and please, stay in your bed this time." All I can do is nod and he pulls the covers over me then reaches under my pillow. He gets the piece of wedding cake out from under it, puts in his robe pocket and then sits beside me.

"You're not sleepy are you, Baby?"

"I was until we saw Joseph."

"Same here. I'll stay and we can wind down together." I sigh in relief.

"Trevor — thank you."

"For what?"

"Moving the boundary."

"It was my pleasure."

"It was mine as well." Trevor caresses my face. "Geneviève, do you want to get comfortable and let me rub your back?" Without saying a word I roll over onto my side and he puts Christopher under my arm. I snuggle him to my chest and Trevor starts rubbing my back.

"Will you set my alarm for noon before you go? I want to wake you up."

"Of course I will. I like for you to wake me up, especially when I know there's no one upstairs."

"I love you, Trevor."

"I love you too." He kisses my cheek and continues to rub my back.

That afternoon as I walk across the balcony to Trevor's room I notice Théo's door is open, which means he left already, and draperies are still drawn. When I open Trevor's door he is out like a light. I decide to get on the bed and lie down next to him, so I go to the other side. When I am on the bed getting under the covers he wakes up smiling and holds his arm out for me to lay my head on his chest. Trevor puts his arm around me as I sigh heavily and close my eyes.

"I don't hear any noise coming from downstairs. Where are your parents?"

"I think my parents have gone sailing."

"We're alone?" I smile and nod. "What do you want to do?"

"I want to stay here."

"We'll fall asleep."

"I think it's time to move another boundary."

"We've already moved one today."

"Yes we did, but several hours have passed."

Trevor chuckles and rolls me over onto my back, gives me a kiss and then he throws the covers off of us. While I pout he gets up and I make him pull me to the edge of the bed. After I get up he gives me another kiss and I go to my room listening to him laugh.

When we go downstairs and enter the kitchen he says, "There's a note on the table. — Your parents *have* gone sailing. Your mother left lunch for us in the fridge and they will see us at dinner."

"Mother makes pasta salad when they go sailing."

Trevor's face lights up as he goes to the refrigerator. He opens it and hands me two plates and gets out two colas. We retreat to the darkness of the dining room to eat and linger to read the Funny Paper. Next we decide to go make up the bed in the apartment and when we go in I walk over to the bed and collapse. He smiles and lies down beside me.

"Your father has to be a happy man. I can picture his face as he casts off with your mother at Willows' wheel. — When William and I went to the club I picked up a brochure about the sailing lessons. I like it that your grandfather had the idea for the club based on making those available."

A few minutes pass in silence then Trevor sits straight up. "I know what I want to do." This causes me to sit up and look at him. "When I get out of the Navy I want to become a sailing instructor for the club."

"What a good idea. You would be in high demand."

"Why do you say that?"

"There would be so many people wanting to brag they were taught how to sail by a commander who attended the United States Naval Academy."

"And I no longer wonder if I would get enough students to make it worth my while." I get tickled and he asks, "Who would I talk to?"

"Mother." And there goes his deep laugh.

"I think we should make out." And he tackles me down onto the bed.

Back at the house to get ready for Sunday dinner Trevor is thrilled to learn he doesn't have to wear his uniform and I am wearing a pairs of trouser from his mum because when the family goes sailing we don't dress for dinner. Théo and Rachel drive up while we are walking to the house and she gets out of the car wearing trousers too. Théo remembered. We gather in the drawing room to wait on my parents and when they step through the doorway my father, who got some well needed sun, looks years younger and Mother is windblown and radiant.

The evening begins with Théo announcing their wedding plans have changed and Rachel has finally been told the family has titles of nobility. Then Trevor makes his plans to be an instructor at the club known. Mother can hardly contain herself at the thought. The evening ends with Théo drinking coffee with his dessert instead of wine, so he won't get drowsy on the drive back from downtown. Trevor and I retreat to the solarium to enjoy the last moment of tranquility we will have until the day after our wedding.

The next day the flurry of activities begins. After taking me to work Trevor goes to Bertucci's for some last minute shopping and he moves our wedding gifts into our house. Tuesday we go The Bridal Salon and he waits outside while I try on my bridal gown with the tiara and veil. Perfection has been accomplished and he assists me in putting them in the car and then into my room. Wednesday is a monumental day for Trevor, because he goes to his quarters for the last time then turns in his room key and it's official, he no longer lives on government owned property he has lived on for over 12 years. Instead of having lunch with the crew we meet at the bench for a quiet lunch and some time for him to process the drastic changes taking place in his life.

Trevor picks me up from work and since he is going to spend his last night in the house with me, because his family arrives tomorrow, we decide to pick up dinner from Mandarin Garden's. When we get to the house it's empty. Théo stayed downtown with Rachel and my parents dined at my grandparents' to give us privacy. Trevor and I decide to eat in the dining room then shower and change into our sleeping attire to sip cognac in the solarium. Even though we will be living together as husband and wife in three days we are taken aback a little that life as we have come to know it will end and it has been wonderful.

Trevor and I finally go upstairs and into his room. It will be the last time I tuck him in here. I untie the sash of his robe and place it on the bench then pull the covers back. Suddenly he gathers me into his arms. "Geneviève, I have so many incredible memories made in this room. I will miss it. Is that strange?"

"Not in the least. I feel the same way. This is the nest I made for you."

"And I needed it so. The happiest days of my life have been spent here, living under the same roof with you." He gives me a tender kiss and gets in bed, then I cover him up and sit next to him. "Baby, I'm not going to like being so far away from you in the apartment."

"I'm not going to like it either."

"There are going to be a few restless nights ahead."

Caressing his face I softly tell him, "Close your eyes and drift into the embrace of night and rest in its arms." Then I whisper by his ear, "Remember, soon you will be resting in mine." I give him a kiss and pour all the love I have for him into it I possibly can. And once again I find myself in his arms.

CHAPTER NINE

Trevor and I decided last night I should wake him for several reasons, so when my alarm goes off I swing into action and take off like a shot to his room as I put on my robe. After carefully turning the doorknob trying not to make a sound I see him. He is still sleeping and lying there looking as if I just tucked him in, because he didn't move. After watching him sleep a moment I lightly kiss his lips. He draws in a deep breath as he opens his eyes and pulls me down onto him. "You certainly made the last time I wake up in this room memorable."

"Plus I gave us a few extra minutes."

"I do love you." And he runs his hand down my braid. "In three days I will be waking up with you."

"It will be the best Monday morning of my life."

"I'll make sure of that."

Rising up I look into his eyes. "Before my imagination runs away with me I'm going back to my room." I give him a kiss and leave to the sound of his heavy sigh.

In the parking lot at work, since we're cutting it close on time, Trevor lets me out and waves to Emily, who hands her car keys to William. He follows Trevor and watching them leave she asks me, "Why aren't we going to the airport?"

"To avoid the chaos at the luggage carousels."

"Good point. Let's go inside."

For lunch it the usual gathering of everyone at The O Club. Walking passed Emily's car we see Judith's Teddy Bear on the front seat and Hilda's on the back seat. Unable to resist the urge to go look in Trevor's car we see three in his then go inside to get hugged for five minutes before we eat.

After work the four of us are standing in the parking lot talking, because I chose tomorrow to begin my time off for our honeymoon. Then suddenly Emily wraps her arms around me. "Oh my gosh, you won't be here for three whole weeks. What am I going to do?"

William points at himself, "What am I, chopped liver?"

She lets me go and hugs him. "We'll see you at the game Saturday. I'm going to go make him feel wanted." Williams' eyes begin to gleam and we go our separate ways.

When Trevor and I reach Maison we notice there is not a soul outside. Since the guest house is our house now, no one is on the balcony. Most of his family members are staying in guest rooms at my grandparents'. Hilda and Tobias are in the apartment next to Claudette and Joseph's. Reginald and Norah will stay in the one next to Trevor's when they arrive tomorrow and Helen will be staying in what is once again our guest room.

Instead of going inside Trevor wants to go parking under the carport and it sounds good to me. We are interrupted by the arrival of Rachel and Théo, then the hunt for family members begin. We decide to begin in our drawing room, but alas is it empty, so Théo takes the opportunity to pour whiskeys for the men and make martinis for us, then we steal a few minutes to savor our drinks and get mentally prepared to go next door. This proved to be a wise decision because an unexpected fuss was made by Trevor's family over the engagement of Rachel and Théo and her custom made ring.

After dinner I tell Trevor I want him to push me in a swing and he suggests inviting Rachel and my brother. They of course want to join us and minutes later we are quietly enjoying ourselves. Lights start going out at my grandparents' house and my parent's wave to us as they walk by with their arms around each other's waist. Shortly after, we hear a car in the driveway and realize the newlyweds are home. Minutes later they appear at the garden path and freeze.

Théo motions to them and when they join us he says, "Welcome home, Mr. and Mrs. Côté." They immediately smile and relax. While Joseph tells us they just wanted to stretch their legs after the drive I motion Claudette to a swing and within seconds she sits in one. Joseph begins pushing her and we learn he surprised her with a trip to Napa Valley before they went to the ranch. Claudette told us it felt like home and gushed over how thoughtful he was. When Joseph tried to control a little stretch from being sore after driving 220 miles from Santa Barbara she had him stop the swing and they were gone.

Watching them leave I have an idea and turn to Théo, who is already looking at me. "Théo, Joseph is perfect and Claudette would be elated."

"Everyone will be."

"You know she had to have been her fathers' little shadow."

"And learned everything there was to learn. She could pass it on to him easily. Gené, we can start him on an apprentice salary next week and he could work fewer shifts at the club. I'll get the ball rolling Monday."

"Then when her father retires Joseph will become the next vigneron for Château Delcroix."

Trevor goes, "Ah, I thought that was where you two were headed with this. — Joseph is going to work with the family too."

For a split second Rachel gets a faraway look in her eyes only I see and say, "Théo, speaking of."

"The time *has* presented itself." And he gives me a go ahead look.

"Rachel, be prepared to be caught off guard. The first thing I should tell you is I have already spoken with the family about this." Her eyes get a little wide and she stops the swing. "In about 15 years Mother is going to step down as chair of the board and we would like you to take her place. The pattern that has been set *is* the wife of a Delcroix chairs the board."

Rachel looks at me in disbelief for several seconds before she looks over her shoulder at my brother. "Théo, will that lovely red briefcase be passed down to me?" He laughs while nodding. "Then my answer is yes."

Trevor and I get tickled then she stands up and so do I because I know she is going to kiss my cheeks. "This means the world to me. I love your family and am overjoyed at the thought of being a part of it."

"I'm thrilled my brother chose you."

"Thank you for ... everything. Théo, it's time to take me home."

As soon as they're gone Trevor says, "Now that all those family matters are taken care of I think we should go to the apartment where there is a pair of pajama bottoms waiting on you." I leap out of the swing and Trevor tucks me in very late. Before leaving he puts the phone in my room and tells me to ring him when I wake up.

After stretching and reveling in the thought I don't have to wake up to an alarm for the next three weeks I pick up the phone and he speaks first. "Good morning, Baby."

"It is a good morning."

"How are you feeling this fine day?"

"I feel divine, simply divine."

"I was getting dressed when you called and I know everyone is next door. I hope you will still be in your bed when I get there."

"I won't move a muscle." The phone begins to buzz. I realize I should at least rinse my mouth and rush to my bathroom. Pulling my covers back up I hear him on the stairs.

"There she is." And I find myself in a passionate embrace. When Trevor sits up he asks, "After breakfast what would you like to do today?"

"The laundry service made a delivery to our house yesterday. Would you like to go to hang monogrammed towels and put the bed linens on our bed?"

He stands up and flings my covers back. "I will be waiting out here to button your blouse." After I stop laughing I give him a kiss and go into my closet.

We eat a late breakfast with our families while members of his sip espressos and the rest of us drink coffee; time zone changes *are* brutal. When we finish our second cup we announce we're going to begin getting our house in order and go on our merry way.

We stand in our living room holding hands where there are richly colored rugs and furniture and that's about it. The end tables only have lamps on them and our mantle is bare. Each room in the house is the same. Trevor finally asks me, "Where to begin?"

"I think hanging the draperies is a priority."

"Yes it is. I'll get the step ladder." I am dipped and kissed before he leaves.

We only hang the ones for downstairs and while we admire them the phone rings. It's time for lunch and we're starving.

Upon returning to our house we decide to hang the towels then unpack some wedding gifts next. And after a lot of walking here and there deciding where to place what, the house looks like a home with crystal sparkling and silver shining in all the rooms except our bedroom that we saved for last.

The box with our pair of Deco candlesticks is already in it, so we carefully unwrap them and place them on the mantle. Next we go to the bench at the foot of the bed our bed linens are on and I get the bed skirt. Trevor pushes the bench away from the bed with just his foot then lifts the mattress as if it weights nothing. As we put the skirting over the box springs I'm looking forward to watching his display of strength when he puts the mattress back.

When we begin putting on the fitted sheet things take an unusual turn. The laughter and talking we have been doing while we work stops as we run our hands across it to smooth out the creases looking into each other's eyes. Next we unfold the flat sheet and lift it up then let it float down onto our bed. Our hands touch in the middle and Trevor gives me a kiss.

By the time our marital bed is made and the throw pillows and bolsters are in place he softly tells me, "Geneviève, it is taking everything I have not to place you among all those pillows."

"Will you settle for the sofa?"

"I wouldn't call that settling if you do what you did last time."

"Then you will not be settling."

Trevor holds my hand and turns off the lights as we go to the sofa. He stands in front of it perfectly still smiling at me. "You do like me to lead."

"I love you to lead." I gently push him down onto the sofa and take my spot.

Before we know it the phone rings again and I reluctantly get up to answer it. "Hello, Mother."

"Hello, Sweetheart. I thought you two might like to know Reginald and Norah are on their way and Helen is here."

"We'll be there in a minute. Thank you, Mother."

"Think nothing of it." I put the handset down, fill Trevor in and we are off.

Trevor goes inside with me to say hello to Helen and while we are standing on the portico just before he leaves, Reginald and Norah's limousine drives up. We wave and Trevor tells me he will greet them and for me to go get ready. I give him a good kiss and dash back inside.

Everyone gathers in our drawing room for an apéritif and to coordinate who rides with whom to the club, including Claudette and Joseph. She talked him into joining us, probably bringing up the fact we will be in a private dining room and he has to start dining with us there sometime.

It's decided Trevor and I will lead the way. When we turn onto the street he looks in the rearview mirror and jokingly remarks, "The transport bus sure would have come in handy this weekend, especially for tomorrow. I can't believe every single person wants to go watch the baseball game."

"Neither can I." We shake our heads and he turns on the radio.

After we return to my grandparents' house for a night cap and couples begin to take their leave Trevor and I wind up alone with Tobias and Hilda. Trevor pours a little more Louis XIII into our glasses and while we describe our house to them we realize no one in his family has seen it, therefore off we quietly go.

The timing is perfect because we discover our house shines inside at night like a Rose Moon with the crystal and silver scattered throughout it. For some reason I am pleased we found this out with them. I think is due to the fact they give me an idea of how Trevor and I will be when we're their age, still having our arms around each other and resting my head on his shoulder just like they are as we sit in the solarium watching the ocean sparkle and barely saying a word.

After Tobias yawns we tell them good night and eventually we kiss under the stars in our solarium for the first time. There will be many nights like this for us, but it is the first and we are reluctant to leave. Knowing tomorrow is going to be a long, long day gives us the motivation to go to the house.

Instead of leaving while I shower and get ready for bed Trevor stays and sits in the chair by my bed. I come out with wet hair wearing only my robe. I walk over to him and give him a kiss then he follows me to my vanity. When I pick up my comb he takes it from me and combs my hair. Braiding it he begins talking to me.

"I could hear the water splashing on the tile and I knew what you were doing as you showered. I heard you rinse your body off then you started bathing and soon you rinsed off the soap. You wash your hair last and then linger under the water after the shampoo is rinsed from your hair. Knowing your every move was ... indescribable."

"Trevor — kiss me. Kiss me."

I love the way he holds me and kisses my skin he keeps inhaling the scent of. And his mouth is so soft. When my robe falls off my shoulder to the point my breast is almost exposed he holds me close to keep it from falling further and we slow down. He eventually walks me to my closet for me to put on a nightgown. I didn't expect him to stay by the door and sweep me off my feet then carry me to my bed where he does not let me go.

He touches his forehead to mine. "I do not — want — to leave. The only thing keeping me sane is the knowledge that after tomorrow night I will not have to. Marry me, Baby."

"I will. I promise. You have my heart and soon you will have my body."

"And you will have mine."

"I must admit, I want it so."

After looking deep into my eyes he hands me Christopher, covers us up and kisses me good night. I watch him close the door and drift into sleep.

In the morning I hear Trevor taking two stairs at a time. I'm already dressed; therefore my door is wide open. He stops cold in his tracks when he sees me. "I was afraid I was going to miss helping you dress."

"You are so spoiled."

"Yes I am." With eyes gleaming he gives me a kiss.

"I did hope you would be wearing your Tropical White's."

"Every officer who can be there will be in the same."

"There will be more stars and anchors gathered in one place than I have ever seen."

"Yes, ma'am." I grab my sunhat and get another kiss.

While we walk down the hallway of my grandparents' house I ask, "Why is it so quiet?" He stops smiling and when we enter the dining room faces light up. Everyone looks *too* happy and Trevor asks, "What do we not know?" Mother responds, "The Harding's arrived in the marina last night aboard Stargazer and it made the front page. Somehow the reporter knows they are here to attend your wedding reception." I reach for the paper. "Worry not. Your father is going to call the police chief and request police officers to be at our gates and the entrance to the club."

After looking over the article I am stunned into silence, but Trevor isn't. "There is no need to have ones here. I'll call Mitch to tell him we need two more swordsmen and why." Father says, "Well done, Trevor." and we eat in peace.

Théo leads the five car motorcade to the baseball park and upon arrival we hear the sound of baseballs being hit and the voices of teenage boys. After listening to the sounds around us we all get our camera bags then move in an orderly fashion to the gate. When we reach the bleachers it's not a problem finding the others because blankets are on three rows going up behind them to save our seats. Joanna is wearing the sunhat she wore the day Mitch returned to her. Emily, Faye and Kelly however are wearing baseball caps with the number 17 on them. This family is serious.

Trevor and I are in front of our group of 20 people and when Emily spots us she shrieks and jumps to her feet. After we all make the climb, everyone just waves at each other because there are 13 people in their group making us a crowd, which will be cheering for Bobby and his team the Silver Stars. Admirals wear one or more of them according to rank. They're playing the Eagles, captains wear those.

The others have already been to the concession stand, so while Emily asks Claudette where they went on their honeymoon several of us go there before the game starts. Trevor's eyes gleam the entire way. When we step up to the counter he asks, "What would the lady like?"

"I would like a bag of caramels and popcorn with an ice cold cola."

"I will have what he lady is having. — I've been curious about what you wanted here, because you had only one scone."

"The caramels taste like my coffee, except a tad sweeter."

"When I drank your coffee it reminded me of something, but I couldn't put my finger on it. Your coffee is liquid caramel." I smile, kiss his cheek and grab my bags of treats. He chuckles as he picks up my cola.

The stands are filled with people from the base. There are more silver stars on shoulder boards of all the admirals than players on the field and civilians are in awe of how many Sailors are present, including me.

When the practice ends Bobby runs by waving. All 33 of us stand up and call out his name drowning out the others cheering for their boys. His chest puffs up with pride. Soon the game begins and so does the fun. We begin clapping, cheering and raising our voices to talk to each other over the crowd. Clearly not civilized behavior and I enjoy breaking the rules. We even switch seats, especially at the end of an inning when someone returns with treats from the concession stand. Emily and I sat next to each to share a fluff of pink cotton candy William came back with when he went to get a bag of roasted peanuts to eat with Trevor.

Poppy went there alone and came back with a large bag filled with butterscotch discs then went through the rows giving them out. Apparently everyone knows Trevor keeps them in his pocket, but they don't know why. The things I make him crave and how he gives in to whatever it may be is amusing. Trevor gets his disc unwrapped first and offers it to me with a glint. Since all eyes are on the game once again I touch his finger tips with my lips. He of course licks his fingers.

It's the bottom of the ninth inning; the Stars have one out remaining, players on first and second base and are trailing by two home runs. Bobby is next up to bat and he gets a strike on the first pitch. At this moment the fun comes to a screeching halt and we are all on the edge of our seats. Bobby is swinging the bat in circles while he waits on the pitcher to throw the next pitch. He sets up and within a split second the ball is headed his way and I am holding my breath like the rest of us. He swings, hits the ball and sends it to the fence of right field. Now the bases are loaded and a player steps up to bat. The crowd starts chanting his nickname, Hack, after a famous big league player named Hack Wilson. The man hit 54 home runs in one season, so we have high hopes.

Hack's first hit goes foul, then the next pitch is called ball one. The boy twists the toes of his left foot into the dirt just before the next pitch and I take a snapshot because I have a feeling this is it. Hack swings and there it is, a home run. The crowd gets loud and we chant, "Bobby, Bobby, Bobby." as he steps on home plate.

We stay to watch the base commander giving out trophies and the team posing with them for *The Times* photographer. The entire time we have been here I have been taking photographs and am almost out of film. I saved enough for after the game and take a few of Bobby holding his trophy standing with his family. Before leaving Trevor's parents make sure everyone knows they're invited to the rehearsal dinner, but Robert, Faye, Kelly, and Bobby are going to a celebratory dinner.

On the way to Maison I tell Trevor, "That was so much fun. I'm a little tired from all the excitement. Perhaps I'll fall asleep at a decent hour tonight."

"I was just thinking the same thing. I do not want to be playing solitaire into the wee hours the night before we get married."

"We haven't been apart before midnight on a weekend in ages."

"'Tis true."

"Trevor, what are you wearing tonight?"

"What you want me to wear."

"I would like you to wear one of your new suits."

"Thank you."

"You're welcome, but why?"

"Even though I have to wear a tie, the suits are more comfortable because of their light weight. I'll ring Mitch and William to tell them my plans."

"I'm glad your parent's decided to have the rehearsal dinner at The Posh since several of our wedding guests are staying there. Joseph will be at ease seated next to his new wife there too." Trevor nods as we roll down the widows and ride in silence the rest of the way. Our ears are ringing from the noise level at the game.

Driving through the gates we see deliveries were made while we were at the game. The trellises are up, golden chairs are under the arbor and a white stage for the baby grand piano is behind it a few yards away to the right. Tomorrow it will look completely different with floral arrangements on white pedestals and white fabric draped and wrapped around just about everything, including the swing set, which is my little secret. We take a brief glance at the grounds and go inside.

Trevor walks me to my bedroom door and stops there, placing his hands on the door jamb. "I'm going to shave, again, and shower. I'll wait for you in the drawing room with the others. I suppose your mother will help you dress." He sighs heavily and kisses me. We stop when we hear the voices of Mother and Helen, then in no time they are on the balcony. I wave to them over Trevor and he turns around. "Josephine, Helen." They wave and vanish. "I'm going to speak with your father a minute then leave. I love you, Baby."

"I love you, Trevor." He kisses me once more and closes the door.

When I emerge from my room needing help with my side zipper I hear Mother and Helen in the guest room. I knock and tell them, "It's me." When I go inside Mother is hooking Helen's dress. "Next, please." Mother zips and hooks my dress and down the stairs we go to find our gentlemen waiting for us with Reginald and Norah all sipping on Roederer. My father is wise, start with champagne and stay with it throughout the evening.

We hear the front doors open while we take our first sip and see our wedding party being shown in by Théo and Rachel. Emily, who looked like a teenager earlier in the day with her ponytail and cap, looks older than she is. Joanna looks the same, gorgeous. Mother and Father serve them a glass of champagne and Mother calls next door then we go outside to begin the rehearsal.

Mitch and William take their place next to Trevor, who is by Reginald. The others take a seat and my father escorts me to the other side of the trellises followed by my maid and matron of honor and my lovely stand in, Rachel. We have a brief discussion and I go back to the arbor. They slowly make their way down and in no time the rehearsal is over. That is until Trevor looks at Reginald and says, "I need to speak with you and my fiancée."

Everyone walks to me and Trevor holds my hand. "Geneviève, when you join me, before the ceremony begins, I'm going to want to talk to you sort of privately. I know it probably breaks some kind of etiquette rule, but do you mind?"

"Not all. I love you for bringing up. Reginald is this acceptable?"

"I don't see why not. You two may take all the time you need."

William says, "We'll move back and give you privacy."

Trevor responds, "Thank you." and turns to Reginald. "The part when she vows to obey me, I would like that to be removed. It's antiquated. Geneviève, is there anything you would like to change?"

"Yes there is. I would like for us to be announced as husband and wife instead of man and wife."

"Perfect. Shall we go to The Posh?"

"Yes, please. I would like to eat some real food." This makes everyone laugh. The food from the concession stand cannot sustain us much longer.

When the motorcade arrives at the valet station the head valet blows a whistle for reinforcements. And in short order we are entering the private dining room where the rest of our dinner party is eating hors d'œuvres and drinking Roederer. Evelyn and Rowland obviously have thought of everything to make our rehearsal dinner perfect.

When we begin eating the first course, two servers enter the dining room pushing carts with champagne bowls on them filled with six clear bottles, which means they are Cristal. The head server says, "These are compliments of Mr. and Mrs. Thomas Harding." Looking at me he asks, "Are you the Bride-to-be?"

"Yes, I am."

"Mr. Harding would like you to save him a dance tomorrow night."

"Please tell him I will and my party sends our regards."

"Yes, ma'am."

When he leaves Joanna's mother asks, "Are those from the Harding's of Harding Publications?" Joanna nods and Mitch responds, "Lorraine, do you remember the story we told you about the rescue at sea on our way to Santa Barbara?" She nods. "He was the man we rescued, but we did not find out exactly who he was until recently." His mother Sandra dryly adds, "That helps explain the article on the front page of today's *San Diego Times*." Bill and Judith are shaking their heads as she shoots William a look. To them it's like letting an admiral sneak up on a Sailor. Trevor is the first one to laugh and the crew quickly appoints Mitch to tell the story. He begins with the flare, the others jump in and it ends with the fairies. By this time dessert is being served and the servers have trays of petit fours. I offer my hand to Trevor for him to kiss. This was his doing.

Due to lack of sleep for our guests from the East Coast, instead of having an after dinner drink Rowland makes a final toast with champagne and brings the dinner to a close.

On the way to Maison I get butterflies. "Trevor, suddenly I have no clue as to what to do when we get to the house."

"Earlier in the week, when my head was on straight, I gave tonight some thought. We're going to my apartment where there is a bottle of Louise XIII waiting for us and two crystal glasses I bought to drink it from. Then we are going to curl up together and talk and kiss until it's close to midnight." I kiss his cheek then place my head on his shoulder and we ride in silence.

Settled on the sofa warming our cognac he dives right into a subject. "Our first kiss as husband and wife, have you given it any thought?"

"As a matter of fact I have. A long time ago Grand-mamma mentioned before lipstick was invented women would stain their lips with the juice of raspberries. She showed me how that day and I am going to stain them tomorrow so I don't have to worry about getting lipstick on my veil and you."

Trevor gets tickled and glides his fingertips over my cheek. "Knowing your lips are going to be stained changes things. I personally do not want it to be one of those pecks we give each other constantly. And since we will be with close friends and family, I want it to be like our first kiss."

"Ooh, I would love that."

"I won't be able to hold you tight because of my medals, but I'll hold you as close as I possibly can."

"That sounds perfect. One thing though. To avoid pulling on my veil, you should slide your hands under it when you gather me into your arms — for as long as you want."

"For as long as I want?"

"Mmm hm."

"I know you are going to feel so good. I've become quite familiar with bridal satin, which is what you are wearing now. — Dance with me."

Trevor loosens his tie and then to no music we dance like never before, caressing each other and kissing until finally he has me pinned to a wall. And there we stay.

Eventually he looks at his watch and his demeanor changes in an instant. It must be time to walk me to the house. My heart sinks for I am nowhere close to being ready to part from him then Trevor says, "This will be the last time for the next three weeks I will let go of you before I am good and ready."

Lost in each other's arms we hear his clock click signaling we have 15 minutes, so I let him go. He puts his jacket over my shoulders and opens the door. The cool night air fills my lungs and my head is clear as we walk to the house.

We step inside and he lays his jacket on the table in the foyer. Holding my hands he tells me, "Tonight you are my fiancée. Tomorrow night you will be will my wife."

"And you will be my husband. I am going to miss you tonight more than ever."

"I'm going to feel the same way."

After a brief silence his eyes get bright. "Geneviève, take the phone into your room and call me the moment you wake up. We may not be able to see other, but we can talk."

"Yes we can. I feel so much better."

He scoops me up into his arms and kisses me. "I love you, Geneviève."

"I love you, Trevor."

He touches his fingertips to my lips and we do not utter another word. We kiss once more and he turns to leave. He stops with his hand on the doorknob and we look deep into each other's eyes, then he leaves. Before my emotions can get to me I run up the stairs and into my room where the thought of showering has no appeal to me. I want his scent on me.

While sitting at my vanity braiding my own hair, missing him becomes almost unbearable. And then I hear a light knock on my door. Théo is home early for me. He really is the best brother a sister could ever want.

"Gené."

"Théo, please, do come in."

He steps in with eyes gleaming and asks, "Do want to go raid the kitchen?"

I have a burst of laughter and reply, "There is nothing on earth I would rather do." The second I finish my braid I get up and hug the air out of his lungs. He draws in a breath and gets tickled, then holds my hand like when we children and leads me to the kitchen down the back stairs.

Happily eating our ice cream I ask, "What was Rachel's reaction when you told her you were leaving early to raid the kitchen with me?"

"She told me I was the best brother in the whole wide world and stood to show me to the door saying something about beauty sleep. Then the next thing I know I am kissed goodnight and standing in the corridor."

After we stop laughing we begin talking about fond memories of the kitchen raids of our youth and a few details of the wedding ceremony. Then I decide to take our conversation where he is apprehensive about going. "Théo, if you were my sister instead of my brother, you would ask me if I am nervous about the honeymoon. And I would tell you not in the least. Trevor made it abundantly clear I would be making every decision for it."

Théo smiles sweetly and says, "I am so glad I never threatened his life."

I laugh and tell him. "There was no need, Hank did."

"Whoa! From Hank that is not hyperbole. How did Trevor react?"

"He didn't even flinch and calmly said, 'Yes, sir.' Then Hank handed him his fathers' revolver to shoot targets with."

"Wait a minute ... did he get a nickname?"

After I stop laughing I reply, "Sort of. They call him Commander."

"Out of respect, as they should. But it doesn't make feel better about it."

Théo stays up with me until I wind down, which took close to two hours. We shut down the kitchen and go upstairs. I grab the phone in passing and he says, "Calling him when you wake up. That's a good idea."

"It was his."

Standing in my doorway Théo holds me for a bit then kisses my forehead and gives me a nudge into my room then closes my door. I have a smile in my heart and on my face as I get Christopher and tuck him in with me. The light coming in around the draperies allows me to be able to see and I look around my room I have lived in for over 25 years. It is so familiar to me. Then I see Trevor's jacket hanging on my closet door and I fall asleep thinking all this will become my past, for the future is upon me.

CHAPTER TEN

The sound of activity outside wakes me up. When I realize those sounds are being made by people setting up for our wedding my heart skips a beat, then I grab the phone and start dialing. It rings once and he answers, "Good morning, Geneviève."

"Good morning, Trevor."

"Did you and Théo have fun raiding the kitchen last night?"

"How on earth do you know that?"

"When I got to my apartment I stood on the balcony and looked at our house. Then I started looking around the property when I noticed his car and it was not in his usual parking place. So, I knew what he was up to, surprising you. I went inside, got ready for bed and fell asleep knowing you were happy."

"So, you slept well too."

"Yes I did. I was worried we would toss and turn all night after I left you and we'd be tired tonight, but thanks to Théo we'll be just fine."

"And when we finally do fall asleep tonight, it will be in each other's arms."

"Something I have imagined and looked forward to more than I can say."

"At long last my heart will be utterly content."

"I love you, Geneviève."

"I love you too. — How long have you been awake?"

"Not long. It's so quiet here and there was a noise outside, so of course it woke me up. I thought it might wake you too and it did."

"Yes it did and then my heart skipped a beat."

"Mine too. We're getting married today."

"It seems too good to be true."

"I know exactly how you feel. — What am I supposed to do after brunch at your grandparents' house?"

"Go to our house. I got you a little something and it's in the solarium. I'll be waiting for you to ring me."

He chuckles and says with a thick British accent. "All right Miss, I guess we better get this day going. Cheers." As I laugh uncontrollably he hangs up.

Sitting at the kitchen table after brunch with my parents and Théo, I sip on a glass of orange juice instead of coffee, knowing I will be running on adrenaline all day, waiting for Trevor to call and talking with my family. I imagine the scene next door is the opposite of here with all his grandparents, parents and aunt added to my grandparents and Helen along with Reginald and Norah. It must make for a lively conversation I visualize Trevor sitting quietly soaking it in.

The phone rings and I sprint into the study, pick up the handset and hear him laughing. "Hello, Trevor."

"You bought me a set of luggage in British Tan leather."

"When the salesman told me the color of the swatch I couldn't resist."

"No doubt. The set is beautifully crafted. You even had my monogram put on each piece. Thank you, Geneviève."

"You are entirely welcome, but my motive was not pure."

"I know. You had a visual of Elliot getting out your beautiful set of burgundy luggage, then setting my seabag next to them."

"I did and then I thought you are going to be traveling as my husband, not a Sailor."

"I like the sound of that."

"So do I. — Wait a minute, you said seabag. Let me guess, that is what I call a duffle. And you've even said it. Why?"

"I think it's adorable, so I didn't tell you."

"That's a really good answer. I'll keep calling it a duffle just for you, but around others I will use the correct term. New subject. Did you get a laugh when you went outside and realized the draperies were closed at both houses?"

"Yes I did. Your family is not taking any chance of us getting a glimpse of each other. Here's the best part, Claudette's are wide open. No peaking for her today." I burst into laughter. "Joanna and I caught a glimpse of slightly parted curtains on the doors when we came out to go to the arbor. She threatened me and I kept a straight face."

"I adore her *and* am a little embarrassed at being caught."

"It was priceless. Umm ... Geneviève, what am I supposed to next?"

"Take your luggage to the apartment and start packing. Oh, I put a case for albums in there. I'm taking my turntable."

"I'll pick out our favorites."

"All right, it's time for me to go outside and check on how things are going. I'll call when I'm back inside."

"Have fun."

"I will, talk to you soon."

The second I hang up I dash up the stairs to get dressed, then get my camera and go outside. The moment I walk through the vine covered trellises between the houses my jaw drops. Three men with ladders are at the swing set wrapping it in garlands with white flowers and white sheeting on the seats. The top of the arbor is draped in the garlands on all four sides and golden chairs are in rows. It's going to look exactly as I visualized when the runners and flower stands are in place.

Next I hear a freight truck backing up behind the house and go over. Three men get out and raise the door to reveal a baby grand piano covered with quilts. I show them where it goes and get out of the way, taking photographs as I watch the transformation of our property.

Soon Théo is in sight being followed by two men helping him carry torches. He is going to make sure the men put them where they always go and gives me a wink as he passes by. Next my parents emerge. Father kisses my cheeks and joins Théo. Mother holds my hand and stands quietly by my side until we hear another truck arrive and a man shouts, "Is there a Delcroix out here?" Mother announces,

"I have this one." and walks around the corner. She returns with two men carrying a large roll of the white runners.

While I am watching the runners being unrolled I hear Evelyn in the distance. "Geneviève, may I join you?" I smile and motion her over. "I was getting fidgety. Did you want this to be kept a surprise? If so, I can go back inside."

"You are most welcome here. What do you think?"

"I can't believe my eyes. This is going to be stunning when those torches are lit. The swing set is an unexpected touch I quite like. Your idea no doubt."

"Inspired by your son."

"I remember now, he got you in a swing his first time here. How romantic — you intend to get on one and have him gently push you. I am getting misty-eyed already." She hugs me and says, "I am going to take my emotions inside and hopefully leave the majority of them in there when I come back out for the wedding." I get tickled and she leaves, then I sprint into the house to call Trevor.

"Hello, Geneviève."

"Have you finished packing?"

"Yes I have. In fact I was about to pour myself something to drink."

"Oooh ... don't do that. You should go to my grandparents' house where I am sure the women in your family will be more than happy to dote on you."

"Tis true. I'll call when I get there to you let know you can go back outside."

"I will stay by the phone."

"Talk to you soon." And I hear the buzzing sound. Maybe two minutes go by and the phone rings. I pick up the handset and he says. "I got surrounded the second I walked through the door."

"I bet you did. Would you like to go ahead and call Mitch and William to have them here a little early?"

"Actually, I wish they were already here."

"Will you have Mitch tell Joanna to call me after they leave please?"

"Of course. I love you."

"I love you too."

Waiting by the phone I look at my watch. I need to start getting ready as do my father and Théo. This will soon become No Man's Land. So, after I talk to Joanna and Emily I call next door. This time my grandfather answers and I ask him to find them and send them over.

Théo steps in my doorway and sees I am holding a bottle of polish remover and cotton balls. He sighs heavily then smiles and asks, "Do you need my help?"

"It's sweet of you to offer, but today calls for a manicure and a pedicure."

"All right then, I'm off to the races. See you shortly."

I am fanning my feet with a magazine to dry my polish when he returns. I stop immediately, then carefully walk over to him and place my hand on his chest. "Théo, how handsome you are, even with your bow tie in your pocket."

"Thank you, Gené. How I have been looking forward to this day."

My father appears and asks, "Am I intruding?"

"Of course not." I motion him in and he kisses my cheeks then stands next to Théo. I admire them and just before tears well up in my eyes, I have a thought inspired by my fiancé. "Two dapper gents." And the wonderful sound of laughter fills my room.

Théo kisses my forehead and tells me, "We're going to get out of here before another female shows up." I walk out onto the balcony with them and suddenly the front doors fling open. Helen and Mother have returned together. When Mother sees them she dryly asks, "What have we here, two men in No Man's Land?" Father responds, "We are on our way out." They go down the stairs and he gives her a kiss as they pass by.

On their way up the stairs Helen asks, "Geneviève, did you know there are two intimidating officers from the Navy wearing swords guarding the closed gates? Also, I think there are at least four more walking the grounds and one on each end of the wall down at the beach. They act like FDR's in here." After Mother and I have a good laugh they go into the guest room.

Next I decide to call Trevor to find out if Mitch and William are here. He tells me they are and the swordsmen followed them here. That explains their early arrival. Then I ask him to tell Grand-mamma I am ready for her to put my hair up and I hear him chuckle as he hangs up. What is going on over there?

My grandmother finishes my hair in a perfect French Twist and leaves just in time to miss the rather hectic arrival of Joanna and Emily carrying train cases, shoes and their gowns. While they hang the gowns in my closet Emily says, "I must confess I feel silly. From the neck up I look like I'm going to a gala and from the neck down, a baseball game." I nod and chuckle because the description is accurate. Joanna adds, "I walked out the door with my head down hoping no one would see me."

We talk a little more then they take turns putting on their dark red gowns and after they are dressed to perfection all attention turns to me. When I open my armoire which was basically emptied to hold my bridal gown and veil Emily and Joanna are rendered speechless. Before them is a white bridal satin corset with thin straps that hang from the sides. When I am wearing it will look like they slipped of my shoulders. The best part is the satin covered buttons that fasten the front. The skirting is flat and fitted in the front, but on the back the satin is gathered and has tulle underneath to make it resemble a Victorian bustle that raises my train to keep it from dragging too much.

Emily steps up to the veil and almost touches my tiara. "Geneviève, this is the most beautiful thing I have ever seen. It's a family heirloom isn't it?" Joanna's looks at me and I answer, "Yes it is. The tiara has graced the head of many a Delcroix bride over the years." Joanna quickly asks, "What do we need to do."

"Go to the kitchen and bring up the tray of our flowers in the refrigerator. And take your time please; I am going to need about five minutes. Then you two can help me put the skirting of my bridal gown on." Joanna gives me a nod as she escorts Emily out and closes the door.

Seated on my bench slipping on my stockings and garters I think about Trevor and get butterflies again. He will be taking them off and my mind goes astray as I finish. Before I get more butterflies there is a knock on my door. "Sweetheart, may I come in?"

"Oh Mother, please do."

She opens the door looking beautiful in her rose colored lace gown holding two glasses and a champagne bucket is beside her. I stand and take the glasses. She brings in the Cristal and tells me, "I think it is time for the Bride-to-be to start celebrating." and closes the door. She pours, hands me a glass then without a word between us we make them ring.

"I am getting married, Mother." She nods smiling and we hold hands. Before our eyes puddle she opens the door and we see a large tray of flowers making its way toward us being carried by two very happy women. They set in down and Joanna brings in the tray of glasses sitting by the phone installed for the man I am about to marry.

Mother calls my grandmother to join us and when Helen is ready, she does. Soon we all have a glass that is half full and Mother takes mine. "It is time to get you into your bridal gown. Ladies." She helps me take off my dressing gown and it begins. I step into the corset Mrs. Parker laced to perfection for me then sit on my bench in order to get the skirting on. It took all of them to get me in it. They congratulate each other on a job well done while I happily slip on my white satin D'Orsay pumps.

My grandmother and mother pick up their corsages to smell the golden orchids. I pin those on them and kiss their cheeks then squeeze Emily and Joanna's hands as I give them their nosegays of dark red tea roses. I take Trevor's wedding band out of the box and hand it to Emily. She slides it over a tiny rose bud while I put on clear lipstick to make my lips moist, earrings and my engagement ring on my right hand. Next I get my bouquet of white orchids with the stems wrapped tightly in white satin ribbon and tuck my little fairy in it. Only Trevor knows I named her Primrose, after Evening Primrose, because she blooms and shines at night. I take a sip of champagne and stand close to the full length mirror that is no longer in my closet, for it is time to put on my veil.

Mother picks up the tiara and everyone gathers around. Grand-mamma gets the four inch hair pins of gold for it and stands close by. Mother places the tiara on my head, carefully secures it with the hair pins and moves to my side for me to see myself. To my amazement I surpass what I had envisioned. Trevor will be taken aback when he sees me at long last.

Once I am passed that revelation I am showered in compliments and then silence falls. Mother eventually hands me a handkerchief and says, "Sweetheart, this was tucked in my corset when I married your father, now it will be your something borrowed. I love you."

I gasp and tell her, "I love you, Mother." then tuck it into my corset.

"Are you ready for me to call your father?"

"Yes, Mother, I am."

She looks at my grandmother and Helen, then they step in front of me standing side by side. Simultaneously they curtsy to me like they did the first time I wore this tiara, then they slowly turn and leave my room.

Joanna is holding Emily's hand and her eyes are sparkling as she gives me a slight nod. I think she has figured out I have a title and is delighted. Emily is just beside herself, because it was like a fairy-tale. Joanna tells her, "It's time for us to go out onto the balcony and let her gather her thoughts as she waits on her father.

We will be waiting with the others." She picks up my bridal purse and fan then they leave and she closes the door.

Alone again I step up to the mirror and admire my bridal gown. Eventually I hold my foot out from under it to see my shoe. I smile thinking the first thing Trevor will do is kneel to slip it off my foot. Then it hits me how much I want to see him and wonder what he is doing at this very moment.

While lost in my imagination about the future a knock on my door brings me back to the present. It is my father. "May I enter?"

"Yes, you most definitely may."

The door opens and he immediately puddles. "Words fail me."

"I know."

Father kisses my cheeks and I set down my bouquet then get the orchid that is for him and place it into his lapel. He carefully holds me for a bit then opens the door. "Josephine, I need you to help me pull this veil over our daughters' beautiful face." Mother steps back in and soon my veil is in place. We join the others and my grandmother calls her house to tell them I am ready.

Mother is the first to walk down and to my joy and surprise she opens a drawer and lifts out a camera. Then one by one, all the lovely ladies descend the stairs and stand in the foyer looking up at Father and me. We stand at the top for Mother to take a photograph of us then she puts it down and when they open the door to leave I hear the pianist is playing Chopin's Nocturne No.8. Trevor and I chose that to play as our grandmothers and mothers are escorted to the arbor and for Emily and Joanna's walk there as well.

Father looks at his pocket watch, then we descend the stairs slowly and when I am safely on the floor he looks at it again and out the door we go. The second we are on the steps I am overwhelmed as the bell atop my grandparents' house begins to ring. When we reach the cobblestones I look up and see an officer is ringing it. Trevor — my thoughtful Trevor, this was his idea.

When I realize the officer is wearing navy blue I look for the guards at the gate and see they are wearing Service Dress Blue uniforms. This means I am going to see Trevor in dress Blue's for the first time and suddenly I am in a hurry to reach the trellises.

Now standing between them, Father and I can be seen and the pianist trails off the Nocturne. I immediately see Trevor and discover he is wearing his Dinner Dress Blue uniform and standing tall. He is resplendent. The waist jacket has three gold stripes and a star on the sleeves with a gold cummerbund underneath and I am certain that is the white tuxedo shirt I unbuttoned and the black bow tie I untied during an unforgettable evening.

While I am trying to get a better look at him through my veil the pianist starts playing again with a cellist accompanying him. This is my surprise for Trevor, I am walking to him while the Sonata plays that was playing during our first kiss. In an instant Trevor places his hand over his heart and we begin walking toward him.

Even though we're closer I can't see his face clearly and realize he can't see mine or my upper body at all. "Father, I need you to something for me. This veil is difficult to see through and I want to see Trevor's eyes. I'm going to stop and you are going to step in front of me and pull it back." I hear him swallow. "It's easier to pull back than to pull it over. Trevor was going to do this alone, without practicing, so you can do this."

I stop and he sighs while stepping in front of me. "Only my daughter would turn into a revolutionist on her way down the aisle." I get tickled and try to hold still as he slowly lifts my veil. He tilts his head to the side and I see Trevor's eyes at last and they are gleaming as his shoulders slightly move, which means he is trying not to get tickled.

When Father is at my side I hear gasps and focus on Trevor. I have never seen him look so proud and this handsome. This is his best surprise. Then I notice how handsome William and Mitch look in their Dinner Dress uniforms. Emily and Joanna are going to look incredible when they are escorted down the aisle by them after the ceremony. I'm going to glance over my shoulder. I didn't get to see them walk down. I was being hidden from view.

When we are almost to the arbor I slowly look around at my family and friends then at Théo. He bows and I get a rush of emotion, the first of many to come.

At last I am standing near Trevor and he holds out his hand. My father places mine on his then I step up and stand beside him. After he kisses my hand he whispers, "There she is, the woman I am going to marry."

"Yes you are."

"Geneviève, I missed you so much."

"I missed you too."

"You are the most beautiful bride I have ever seen and your bridal gown has me at a loss." He stops himself from touching a button. "You had this made for me. — You spoil me so."

"And you me. Trevor, you are unbelievably handsome in that uniform."

"I wanted to surprise you."

"You succeeded. I desperately wanted to see you clearly."

"No doubt. I tried to be still and for the first time in my life I simply couldn't."

"I saw your shoulders move."

"Thankfully everyone was looking your way. When your father moved and I could finally see you, I was mesmerized. — Baby, where's Primrose?"

"Where fairies hide." He looks in my bouquet and smiles.

"I love you, Geneviève."

"I love you, Trevor."

We glace at Reginald and our wedding ceremony begins. Trevor is all I can see, feel or hear. Reginald's voice seems like it is being carried on the wind and guiding us. With each I do and each I will, we become closer to being married. When he asks for the rings I remember we are not alone.

William hands Trevor mine before I turn to Emily and she already has his ring out. I smile at her and Joanna, then take his ring and hand her my bouquet. Trevor and I place them on the book Reginald is holding and he tells us they are the symbols of our love and offers the book out to Trevor. He picks up my ring and looks at me as I lift my hand. He slides the ring on my finger then looks deep into my eyes as he places his lips on my hand and the ring in a lingering kiss. He even closes his eyes for a moment and my heart takes flight.

It is such a beautiful expression of his love for me I need a minute to gather my thoughts. Then I reach for his ring while holding his hand. Facing Trevor I glance as his hand then fall into his eyes as I slide it onto his finger. I look down at the ring, then at him as I lift his hand and place it close to my heart holding it there for him to feel it beat as he has done many times. Trevor's chest swells from the deep breath he takes in and slowly exhales.

I move his hand away as he gets my other hand and holds it tight. Then I hear the words I have longed for. "I now pronounce you husband and wife. You may kiss your bride." Trevor caresses my face with both hands and mine rest on his shoulders as we are about to have our first kiss as husband and wife. It begins like our very first and changes into one that is somewhat passionate as he slides his hands around my back and has me in his embrace.

I am not sure how long we kiss and then hold each other, but when we stop he whispers, "I am holding my wife in my arms."

Close to his ear I whisper, "And I am holding my husband in mine."

He loosens his arms for us to look at each other and when I see his face his eyes are gleaming. "I can say this now. I love you, Mrs. Lyons."

He takes my breath away and I give him a kiss. "Oh, Trevor — I love you too."

We hug and he asks, "Are you ready, My Bride?"

"Yes, My Groom, I am."

I take my bouquet from Emily then he nods to Reginald and we turn to face everyone. "Ladies and Gentlemen, it is my honor to introduce you to Commander and Mrs. Trevor Lyons." They all stand and the swordsmen take their place. As we pass by smiling at our family and friends I notice the majority of them have red eyes, but no sign of tears and realize Emily looked the same way. They shed tears of joy and we took so long kissing and holding each other it gave them time to regroup and return our smiles. How lovely.

When we reach the swordsmen the arch of swords ceremony begins. An officer commands, "March, march, march. Detail ... HALT. Center ... FACE." They are standing toe to toe. "Open ranks ... MARCH." They take three steps back and are off the runner. "Officers ... DRAW ... SWORDS." And they point them up straight, close to their shoulders. "Officers ... PRESENT ... SWORDS. Blades away." And the arch is formed. We walk under it and the last two officers lower their swords and cross them in front of us then one of them says, "A kiss is required to pass." Suddenly I am dipped and kissed. When he stands me up I am not the only one laughing and I notice Mr. Blackwell, who just took what is going to be one of my favorite photographs of our wedding.

The bell starts ringing again as we walk to my parents' house. I gently tug his arm as a thank you for the bell and Trevor just smiles. Then we reach the bottom of the steps and stop at the same time. "Trevor, I've only gone down steps." He looks at me, takes my bouquet, cups my elbow and I lift my gown. Problem solved ... moving on.

Next my father says, "Allow me." as he goes around us to open the doors. Trevor walks me straight to the table in the foyer and puts down the bouquet. We turn around and without warning we become a two person receiving line. It begins with my mother and ends with Joseph. Everyone is in the drawing room and we stay by the table overwhelmed.

"Trevor, I need a drink of water."

"We also need to be alone for a bit."

"I am depending on you to make that happen ... Eh-sap." And there is the deep laugh I love.

He goes to the entrance of the drawing room and announces, "My Bride and I are thirsty, so we are going to the kitchen for a drink of water and a moment to ourselves. We will return shortly."

Father says, "Take as long as you need. We are going to start celebrating." And a champagne cork pops.

Trevor gives me a kiss and offers me his arm to escort me to the kitchen. When we are standing in the middle of it Trevor slowly moves in front of me looking serious. "Let me look at you." He caresses my face, touches my lips and then slides his fingertips down my neck to my corset.

"You want to touch my buttons."

"Mmm hm. I have been since you were finally close." And he begins touching the buttons one by one, making his way down to the last. Then he puts his hand on my waist and as he walks around me looking at my bridal gown he slides it along the satin. After going full circle he places his other hand on my waist. "Your bridal gown is more beautiful than I imagined and you are beautiful in it.

"When I heard the bell begin to ring I knew I would be seeing you any minute and then, there you were. What a vision you made. One of the first things I noticed was I could see your bare shoulders through the veil. I expected they would be. Then I realized I couldn't see your face and desperately wanted too. Just as I was about to get upset you did something I didn't expect. You became a revolutionist on your way down the aisle to me. I couldn't believe it, but on the other hand, I could. When your father moved back to your side I could see your shining face and the rest of your gown. I know my heart skipped a beat."

"Mine did too when I could finally see your face clearly and this uniform that was most unexpected." I place my hand on his chest. "I love this one and you are beyond handsome in it." I tug on the bow tie. "I thought you bought a bow tie to and shirt to wear with your tuxedo, but you were wearing these."

"Mmm hm." He caresses my shoulders and softly kisses each one then gathers me into arms and we kiss most passionately.

"Geneviève, you been on your feet since you put this on haven't you?"

"Indeed I have."

He goes to the table and pulls out my chair. Then he looks at my gown and pulls it out further. I get tickled as I walk over and try to manage the gown to sit down without crushing it.

"Can I help?"

"Just keep a good grip on the chair." He chuckles and I get situated.

"I'll get us that well needed glass of water." As he moves around the kitchen I cannot take my eyes off of him.

We sit in silence drinking the water and looking at each other. Eventually I see a glint in his eyes. "Trevor, what are you about to do?"

"Something you want me to do."

He offers me his hand and when I am on my feet he leads me to the mudroom and outside. When he heads to the swing set I get tickled again and he tells me, "The second I spotted it was covered I knew you wanted me to push you in a swing. I am guessing my job is to hold it perfectly still while you take a seat." I touch my nose and he kneels down. When I am seated he walks around the swing and pulls it up toward him until I am high enough for him to kiss. And after he does, he lets me go and I gasp. After taking a step back he stands there smiling, watching me swing.

"This time you look very elegant in a swing. I will always have this image of you in my mind. The tiara gracing your head suits you, Mrs. Lyons."

"Say my name again."

"Mrs. Lyons."

"Trevor, embrasse-moi." He stops the swing immediately, kneels beside me and kisses me tenderly, but passionately.

"Would you like me to push you now?"

"Yes I would." And he does.

All too soon out of the corner of my eye I see him pull out his pocket watch I completely forgot about. "Geneviève, since you are already in the swing, let's have our bridal party join us for photographs." I nod and he puts his fingers to his mouth and does that really loud whistle. While I sit there with my mouth open, William appears on the portico with his arms out. Trevor pretends to have a camera in his hands and William gives him a thumbs up then vanishes.

Next thing we know a very large group of people are headed our way. Trevor says, "And our privacy is over."

I laugh and watch Mr. Blackwell work his way to the front. "I knew I was going to get an unusual wedding photograph when I noticed this swing set all wrapped up. I'm glad I came out of retirement for this."

He picks his spot and photographs us then I ask Joanna and Emily, "Ladies, care to join?" Emily says, "I've been looking forward to this. William, hold my swing please." Joanna adds, "Darling, this will not be forgotten and I adore you for it." Mitch gives me a wink and kneels down to hold the swing for his elated wife. Mr. Blackwell takes a few shots then I say, "Rachel." And motion to a swing. She covers her mouth and Théo beams as he escorts her to the swing set.

Once she is settled Trevor calls out, "Gentlemen, on my mark, give them a little push. Three, two, one … MARK." And we are swinging.

Our men move around to see our faces and we swing until it comes to a stop on its own. Then they have to get us out. Joanna and I are up first and how I wish I could see William's face. I know it has to be amusing, because having his hands so close to Emily's hips have to make him uncomfortable. Emily is focused with a very straight face and Rachel is simply too happy to care.

Trevor motions to the swings and says, "Next." Before we, the wedding party go to pose under the arbor I see Hilda grab Tobias by his arm. They are followed by Poppy and Spencer. By the time we are at the arbor Evelyn, Rowland and Meredith have joined the fun. It's hard to pay attention to posing while we watch them and then to my utter delight I see Claudette has a camera in her hands photographing them. I wondered why Joseph rushed off.

After the outdoor photographs we go inside and my grandfather asks our guests, "Please excuse us while we go next door for formal family portraits." Helen chimes in, "I will be your hostess in their absence." Walking into the foyer I hear her lower her voice and she adds, "Let's raid their wine cellar." And the house fills with the sound of laughter.

When we enter the drawing room I lead Trevor to the draperies and we stand together as husband and wife for our wedding portrait. After Mr. Blackwell is happy with the photographs, he arranges our families by placing our parent's by our sides then grandparents and Meredith. With that done Trevor escorts me to Mr. Blackwell and I tell him, "We're going into the study briefly and when we return, what you see will need to be kept in complete confidence."

"I give you my word I will, but what am I about to see?"

"My family will be wearing sashes and medals given to our ancestors by a king of France in a ceremony where he and his wife were given titles of nobility."

"That explains the tiara." And Trevor chuckles.

My family and Rachel follow us to the study where Trevor spots our sashes and medals on the desk. I lead him to it and everyone gathers around. When I hand my sash to Trevor his face goes straight and I motion to my grandparents. He watches them drape their sashes over each other and nods to me. "Drape it over my veil and after it's in place you'll be able to easily slide it out." I give him a reassuring look and lower my head then he skillfully gets it passed my tiara onto my shoulder and gets my veil out. Trevor straightens the sash then takes two steps back and without warning he full on bows to me and says, "Marchioness." The man is beaming as I motion for him to rise.

"Trevor, I cannot believe you did that."

"I've always wanted to bow to someone with a title. I *am* British." And we all burst into laughter.

When everyone is ready we go back to the drawing room and jaws drop even though Trevor told his family weeks ago about our ancestral heritage. After the photographs are taken we remove our symbols and pose for a family portrait anyone can see.

Rachel returns to her spot next to Mr. Blackwell after taking Théo's medal and I look at her and say, "Next time you will be wearing this." as I motion to my tiara. She gets wide-eyed then smiles at Théo as he goes over to her. Mr. Blackwell asks, "When will I be back?" Théo replies, "November 8th, please and thank you."

We join our guests and have time for toast's which my father begins with the traditional one as he raises his glass, "To the Bride and Groom." After glasses are lowered he continues to speak. "Trevor, I have been thinking about what I want to say to you on this auspicious day and realized you know what is in our hearts, therefore I will simply tell you words I have waited to say, welcome to the family and to your house by the sea." He raises his glass and we drink to my husband.

"I want to thank you all for the many things that have been done for me. Welcoming me here and letting me get to know Geneviève at her home. Allowing me to find out what privacy is like, something I was not familiar with until I was within these walls. And I thank you for bringing my family together." Trevor smiles at me and continues. "More than any of those things, I want to thank you for this exceptional woman who at last stands beside me as my wife. I am indeed a fortunate man. My friends and family please raise your glasses and drink with me to the Delcroix family."

Rowland speaks next. "My son took over half my little speech I had planned. Therefore I will skip to last sentence." He raises his glass to me. "Geneviève, I would like to be the first to tell you, welcome to our family, who you reunited." His entire family nods in agreement and they drink to me. I manage to place my hand over my heart without tearing up.

Mitch being quick on feet pulls out his pocket watch and gets our attention. "I called the club just before we walked out the door and was informed we are going to have to drive through reporters outside the gate, so perhaps we should get the show they are waiting for on the road." Glasses are emptied and ladies grab handbags as we go through the foyer. Trevor gets my bouquet and out the doors we go.

The cars are lined up with The Chariot last. Elliot tips his cap and says, "Good evening all. Reporters are gathered at the gates of the club. Drivers, stay close to the bumper in front of you and try not to slow down. They'll get between the cars if you do." He opens the car door for me and Trevor helps put me and my bridal gown in, then he walks around and lets Elliot open his door. The first thing he sees is another bouquet and slides it over to get in as he looks at me. "I have no intention of tossing my bouquet to the single ladies. I am keeping it."

"Good thinking. I never understood tossing away something so sentimental."

With the door closed I tug on his sleeve and he moves over to me. "Trevor, raise the glass partition please." He does as I ask and I tell him, "Talk to me."

"When I heard the cellist play his first note I knew you were going to walk down the aisle to me as we listened to the Sonata that was playing during our first kiss. My emotions soared. I love you." And he stops talking as he carefully gets me in an embrace. Our kisses are beautiful and the little things we say to each other are beautiful as well.

We realize we are close to the club when poor Elliot has to tap on the glass. When we let go of each other and look ahead our jaws drop. Reporters with bright lights are everywhere. Trevor rolls down the partition and I spot a motion picture camera. "Trevor, do you see what I see?"

"Yes I do. I've only seen one of those in newsreels."

Elliot interjects, "Commander, Mrs. Lyons, may I suggest not looking ahead anymore. The lights for that will blind you temporarily."

Trevor tells him, "Thank you for the warning." and picks up my bridal purse. "Baby, this might be a good time for you to check your appearance" I get out my compact and it is alarming I do not need an interior light to be turned on. The glows from the ones ahead are sufficient.

Next he hands me my duplicate bouquet and tells Elliot, "Please secure the vehicle after you park and keep the keys. There is a diamond brooch in the bouquet Mrs. Lyons is leaving on the seat."

"Yes, sir. Would you like me to say with the vehicle, Commander?"

"Thank you for offering. It will stay out front and the valets will take care of it. We want you to dine with the other drivers. It's going to be a long night for you."

All the cars make it through the reporters without slowing down thanks to Elliot and his advice to the others, but we are still seeing spots as we go through the parking lot as Trevor asks, "Are you ready?"

"Yes, I am."

"Then we can sit here and watch the others get out for entertainment. It's nice being last sometimes." So, we watch a parade that consists of Helen, Meredith, Reginald, Norah, Claudette and Joseph go in. Joseph is going to alert the emcee we have arrived in order to get our guests seated. Soon after, the wedding party is walking through the lobby and down the corridor in the order we are to enter the reception then we reach the closed doors that two ushers are stationed at with a list of names that received invitations to keep the uninvited out. On Trevor's signal they open the doors for the grand entrance to begin.

Théo and Rachel are first into the doorway and just before they are announced he says something to Grand-mamma. She turns around and speaks to Hilda, this continues until it reaches William, who is in front of us. "Guess who's sitting next to Helen." Trevor's eyes are gleaming as I exclaim, "Hank!" William nods and my husband says, "She told us he would change his mind at the last minute and to make a place setting for him. And he did not disappoint."

By this time all the grandparents are inside. Next in line are his parents, followed by mine. Joanna and Mitch are getting close to the entrance when she glances over her shoulder at us and pretends to walk with a cane two steps while Mitch maintains his composure the entire way to the entrance where they announce her as Matron of Honor. Emily regains her composure by the time she and William are announced.

While we wait on them to be seated Trevor says, "I love you, Geneviève. You are perfection."

"I love you too, Trevor. And *you* are perfection."

We are finally in view and hear several gasp before the emcee announces, "Now for the Bride and Groom. It is my honor to introduce Commander and Mrs. Trevor Lyons to the public for their first time." Our guests begin to applaud and we walk though, stopping at our table for me to put down my bouquet and bridal purse. Leading us to the dance floor for our first dance as husband and wife he tells me, "I found out this orchestra, when it plays elsewhere, has a lady that sings with them during current songs they play."

I glace at him wondering what he has done now. He gives the conductor a nod and a lovely lady walks across the stage and stands in front of the microphone. We stop in the middle of the dance floor and he asks, "Mrs. Lyons, may I have the pleasure of this dance?"

"Yes, you most certainly may." And we take a stance.

The orchestra begins to play and I recognize the song on the first note. It is "Embraceable You". Just as I get misty-eyed he suddenly holds me against him. Our first dance as husband and wife and we are going to dance the way we should. As he sways with me in his arms memories of that rainy day wash over me. And we are alone in our world.

When the song ends he doesn't let me go and whispers, "That was just as I imagined, how we would dance to our song when we were finally married."

"I thought it would be at our beach cabin tonight, but you arranged for it to be our first dance. You are so romantic. I can't wait to find out what you do next."

"Suffice it to say I am looking forward to it."

He gives me a kiss and we hear applause and get tickled. "Hmm ... I do believe it's time to join our wedding party." I slightly sigh and we sit at our table that has champagne buckets with Roederer in them. Then the serving of the seven course meal begins. We chose things that are sentimental or a favorite of ours. The first course is a traditional Vichyssoise to honor Mother. After the third course there is a break for a speech by William. He introduces himself in case anyone has forgotten he is the best man and tells the guests he has been Trevor's shipmate for longer than he cares to remember. He goes on a bit then ends with a wish for us to fall in love with each other over and over again.

During his applause Emily tells everyone at the table, "He did that on his own. When I found out one of my duties was to make a speech I had a panic attack. William calmed me down by having me call Joanna." Mitch is shaking his head and Joanna is tickled as she says, "I invited them over and poured her a martini. She was able to focus after that." The servers bring out the fourth course of roasted duckling and Emily enjoys is to the point she forgets her speech is next.

When the servers remove the plates William gives Emily a little nudge on her elbow and she becomes poised and eloquent. She introduces herself and talks about the first time she met me, then Trevor and that she knew we would wind up here one day. Emily holds up her glass and quotes an actress who said, 'Love has nothing to do with what you are expecting to get, only with what you are expecting to give, which is everything.' Several people stand as they applaud, including William and her father.

Soon the last course of fruits and cheeses on cold marble cheese boards are on the tables. This means the dancing will begin. And when the emcee announces it is time for the father of the bride to dance with his daughter my father stands and offers me his hand.

The moment we set foot on the dance floor "La Fille aux Cheveux de Lin" by the French composer Achille-Claude Debussy begins to play. It translates to "The Girl with Flaxen Hair". This has been our song since before I can remember. He rocked me to sleep by this when I was an infant. It is slow and beautiful. When we begin to dance he says, "I knew you the first time I cradled you in my arms. I knew you were going to be intelligent, beautiful like your mother and with a mind of your own." He pauses to keep his emotions and mine in check. "Today is one of the best days of my life. I watched you marry a fine man whom I know will make you happy beyond your dreams and you love each other deeply. I witnessed that when the two of you exchanged rings. There was hardly a dry eye under the arbor afterward. *And* we found out Emily and Joanna had handkerchiefs hidden in their nosegays." Of course he gets me tickled to lighten the mood.

We are silent the remainder of our dance and when it ends he kisses my cheeks. "My Daughter, I love you so."

"I love you, My Father.

Walking to the table we notice Mother and Grand-mamma are trying not to puddle as Trevor escorts his Mum to the dance floor. Near the end of their dance, Evelyn was facing my way and I was able to read her lips as she told Trevor, "I am happy for you, Son and I love you." He said something then spun her around to make her laugh.

Our parents and grandparents decide to have their dances together to save time and the rest of us agree to join them after a minute has passed in order for our guest to be able to join us on the dance floor after being seated so long. Trevor kept us centered as we dance, so we can watch everyone.

When the music stops Théo and Rachel walk over. Without a word Trevor offers his hand to Rachel and Théo whirls me away. "I couldn't wait any longer for us to be alone and talk. Gené, you are stunning."

"Thank you, Théo."

"I forgot how beautiful the tiara is."

"It's the veil."

"Oh my goodness, you and that veil. My sister, the revolutionist on the aisle."

"Trevor and Father called me that too."

"Did you hear the muffled laughter?"

"No, I didn't."

"It was great and I didn't know Mr. Blackwell could still move so fast."

"He took a photograph?"

"Yep and one of us, that is why he had to shake a leg."

I get tickled. "I am not the only one Trevor has had an effect on."

"No you are not and we are enjoying it more than we admit. — Do you have anything you want to tell me before I make your head spin?"

"Not a thing." And he literally makes my head spin.

After eating a few pieces of an orange to quench my thirst along with some champagne my grandfather offers me his hand and while we are dancing he talks about the future and its possibilities, telling me Trevor and I can make the life we want and to always follow our hearts for that is where our love lives.

The music ends and he kisses my cheeks. Then Rowland steps up and whisks me away. Half way through the song he informs me Spencer will be out next. The men of Trevor's family are three. I'm not sure I can make it through four dances in a row without something to drink. Then Trevor dances by with Meredith and I realize he is going to dance with the women. We are in this together.

Spencer barely speaks, he wants to dance, which is sweet and then when he is twirling me around I see Tobias walking up. He taps Spencer on the shoulder and cuts in. After we start dancing he tells me this was planned, so I could clear my dance card and sit down with my husband. This gets him a kiss on his cheek.

Eventually the song ends and Trevor escorts Hilda to us and we switch partners. At last I am with my husband again. Tobias leads the way to the table and Trevor seats me next to Joanna who hands me a glass of water with a smile and tells me, "I remember this part of our reception with mixed emotions. I loved dancing with all the men of the newly united family, but even my toes began to hurt." I almost spew my water on her because mine are stinging. She pats my back and motions for the rest of the crew to join us. When Hank walks out onto the dance floor with Helen, Trevor happily tells everyone who he is and the story of how he literally threatened his life.

When the laughter quiets down Eric steps up to us and asks if we would like to have our cakes brought out. Trevor and I glance at each other and light up then Eric just vanishes. Two minutes later the Pâtissier and his sous chef appear rolling out our spectacular seven tiered wedding cake. It is solid white on a silver platter with a silver cake knife and two champagne glasses next to it. Our guests begin to applaud and they bow then step back from it. Trevor shakes their hands as I gush about how beautiful the cake is and thank them profusely. Next Eric rolls out the grooms' cake being followed by his assistant who has a pedestal champagne bucket with a bottle of Cristal in it.

Standing alone in front of our wedding cake Trevor picks up the cake knife and gives it to me. I hold it and he puts his hand over mine then lightly grips it. He whispers, "Baby, you take the lead." I get tickled for a moment and then we cut into our cake with me guiding us. We make the second cut and my groom holds the plate as I place the first slice from our cake on it.

Trevor sets it on the table and hands me a fork to cut the bites for us to feed each other. Then I get an idea and cut one long piece from the top and turn it on its side so he can see it looks like a petit fours. He has a gleam in his eyes as he looks into mine. I cut it in half and he picks up a piece and when Trevor feeds it to me his fingertips touch my lips. Still looking at me he licks them and gives me a kiss while I chew. Of course I repeat what he did and it almost gets him choked, for a lady never licks her fingers. After he finishes eating he tells me softly, "The gypsy makes an unexpected appearance in public. Mrs. Lyons, you catch me off guard yet again." With a lilt in my voice I tell him, "She will be back soon." And Trevor is speechless.

When we hear the Cristal shift in the ice we leave our world and come back to the club. Trevor turns to the champagne, picks it up and pops the cork. He pours it into our glasses and hands me one. Then he looks odd. "Geneviève, there is one thing we did not discuss."

"Yes there is."

"That being the case, do you want to entwine our arms when we drink?"

"Is that a rhetorical question?"

He laughs and says, "Which means you want me to decide. — We only get one shot at this, so, yes, let's." I smile, give him a slight nod and we make our glasses sing then entwine our arms and slowly put them to our lips and drink. After we cut the groom's cake Trevor tells Eric, "Place a piece of my cake on your tray and the cork, please."

"Yes, sir."

"Also, my wife's parents will take the top layer of our wedding cake home and please give our chauffeur the second layer of both cakes."

"Consider it done."

"Thank you, Eric."

"My pleasure, sir."

While Trevor and I cross the dance floor with our champagne I tell him, "I wondered why you asked the Pâtissier for an extra layer. I adore you."

"I adore your appetite for sweets."

"I owe you a kiss."

"And I'll be collecting that as soon as we're in The Chariot."

"When we finish our cake I'll be ready to leave." And there is the deep laugh.

After we are seated and served Eric sets things in motion. Ten servers with large trays appear that are soon covered with plates of our cakes. William looks at our plates and tells Emily, "I'll get the chocolate one I recognize from our trip." She says, "And I'll get the one that has orange filling between the vanilla layers that I know is going to be delicious." Mitch tells Joanna, "Sounds like a good plan to me." Joanna responds with several nods as she looks at our plates. Thankfully the wedding party is served first and they all deserve it.

After we share our desserts I tell Trevor, "Next, I would like to dance with Reginald."

"I'll ask Norah to dance." Then he shifts his attention away from me and I notice unusual smiles on the faces of the rest of the crew. Then I see why. Mr. Harding is walking over with a silver handled cane in his hand.

"Good evening all. Pardon the intrusion."

Father stands and shakes his hand. "Good evening, Thomas and you are not intruding. My guess is you would like to speak with my son-in-law."

"Your guess is correct. Excuse me please." And he steps up to Trevor. "Congratulations, Commander."

"Thank you, sir."

"May I dance with the bride?"

"If you give me permission to dance with your wife."

"You have it and she will be overjoyed."

"Excuse me please." And he is off to find her.

"Mrs. Lyons, may I have the honor?"

"You may." He hangs his cane on the side of the table and offers me his hand. I glance at the cane as he helps me up.

"I only use that to make Mrs. Harding happy. My leg is fine due to you and your crew." He gives them a nod and starts walking us to the dance floor.

"Mr. Harding, I am so pleased you and your wife are here."

"As are we." Then we begin to dance. "Mrs. Lyons, after what we have been through I believe it is passed time for you to call me Thomas."

"Thomas, please call me Geneviève."

"It will be my pleasure. You have a lovely name I rarely hear and ..." He lowers his voice, "I go to France more often than people know."

"That does not surprise me in the least."

"Something surprised me recently."

"Do tell."

"While looking at copies of *The Halyard* not too long ago I read a two part article about Sailors returning home and noticed the photographs were by a G. Delcroix. I was impressed with your photographic essay. For years I have watched you wonder around the harbor with a camera. Geneviève, I thought you were a shutterbug. You have a good eye and if you ever want to be a professional give me a call at home. Your mother has our number."

"Thomas — your reach is longer than I thought."

"By the way, I had it leaked to the press Mrs. Harding and I would only be attending the reception to keep reporters away from your home."

"That explains why there were no disturbances. Thank you, Thomas."

"It was nothing." He gets a glint in his eyes then says, "You are a lovely bride and this is the most beautiful bridal gown I have ever seen. It's time for me to show you off." Then he takes us to the edge of the dance floor.

After sitting at the table for several minutes Trevor asks me, "Would you mind borrowing your mothers' wrap and stepping outside with me for some fresh air?"

"Not in the least."

With Mothers' wrap carefully placed under my veil we are finally outside and alone on the deck. "Baby, you have been looking at me as if you have to tell me something since you danced with Mr. Harding."

"That is because I do. Long story short, somehow he gets his hands on *The Halyard* and has offered me job."

"What do you want to do?"

"Ask him if I can work part time."

"You're not going to turn in your notice on the base?"

"I planned on surprising you with this on your birthday. I'm going to turn in my notice the fifth month of your deployment. Now when you're giving sailing lessons I'll go places with my camera, otherwise I will spend my time with you. I want to spend as much time with you as I possibly can for the rest of my life."

"Geneviève — I love you." He sighs heavily and caresses my face. "There is something I was going to surprise *you* with when the time was right and it appears to be now. Twelve days before and after a deployment Sailors stand-down, which means we are off duty."

"Twelve days? If Mrs. Sloan will not give me the time off, I'll turn in my notice before you leave."

He kisses both of my hands and holds them tight. "I can't tell you how much I want you in my arms right now."

"What time is it?"

"8:32."

"After 28 minutes you can hold me as long as you want. Will an Eskimo Kiss suffice for now?"

"Yes. Yes it will." And he gets very still.

Back inside Trevor does not seat me and says, "Gentlemen, it is time." Théo, William and Mitch stand up and offer their hands to their ladies then begin leading us to the dance floor. I ask Trevor, "Time for what?"

"To tango."

Emily's voice is high pitched as she says, "What? William, I thought Mitch and Joanna were teaching us that so we could tango at The O Club. My father's here."

"What does your father being here have to do with anything?"

"I don't know. I'm panicking."

I quickly jump in. "Emily, remember there is strength in number." She begins to calm down as I look at my brother. "Théo, you tango now?"

"Rachel and Darlene took dance lessons for fun, so she taught me."

"Trevor, I thought we were going to dance this at The Posh."

He smiles with eyes gleaming and I look at Joanna. In an upbeat tone she says, "Welcome to the Navy."

"Thank you."

"Think nothing of it."

We are by the stage now and the music has stopped. Trevor motions to the conductor, then calls out, "Fellas, take your corners."

On the way to ours I notice the dance floor is clearing. "Trevor, how long have you been planning this?"

"A while."

"This isn't very British of you."

"Neither is drinking iced tea."

Glowing I tell him, "You lead and I will follow."

Now in our corner I look around and see we are all in the same stance then look in Trevor's gleaming eyes. The music begins and we are dancing the tango, at the club, and I am wearing a bridal gown. Not even a minute passes and we are joined by our swordsmen with their ladies. These men are worldly in every sense of the word and one of them is now truly mine.

Oblivious to my surroundings Trevor's unusual movement gets my attention. This is when I notice members of the club are out here with us. The place will never be the same and all because of my husband. On several occasions my grandfather mentioned the club needs to change with the times and it has.

We go all over the dance floor doing the dramatic walk of the tango I love so much and Trevor even makes his way to our table and spins me for our parents and grandparents then twirls me away to get close to Théo and Rachel. We are having the time of our life. William even manages to bump into us and call him a Brit. Trevor of course calls him a Yank. Next Mitch passes by so he can give Joanna a spin for us. When the music ends my hand is on the back of his neck to keep my body against his during a dramatic dip. And our dance is complete.

We all applaud and soon Trevor and I are surrounded by men in uniforms and no surprise here, Bill is among them. They are all so handsome in their uniforms. I adore Sailors. All those years watching them pass by on the base and I had no idea what was within these very controlled men.

Overtaken by thirst the crew sits silently drinking water. As I sit by my husband I begin looking at the faces of everyone at our table I notice Claudette is beaming. What a night it has been for her, dancing with all the men of the wedding party and then for the first time she has danced with Joseph here, which they did every chance they got. It must be a dream come true for them both because of all those New Year's Eve Balls they could not. It is so romantic I turn to Trevor and give him a kiss that he makes a little more of. I want to be alone with my groom.

"Trevor, instead of going to tables of guests, can we have our last dance and the tossing of my bouquet? I'm ready to leave."

"We can do that." He motions for Eric.

While Trevor tells Eric the change in plans, Théo, who is seated next to me now, reaches to hold my hand; he overheard. "Gené, I will miss you and I love you very much."

"Théo — I love you too." After I stand up he shakes Trevor's hand and gives me my kiss on my forehead. I have to fight tears as my groom leads me to the dance floor after the emcee announces it is time for our last dance of the evening and Trevor gets my mind elsewhere immediately. "Geneviève, since you knew you were going to walk down the aisle to me with our Sonata playing, when we decided our last dance would be to this, why didn't you suggest something else?"

"Walking to you and dancing with you are two entirely different things."

"Yes it is and it's slow, therefore we can dance like we do at The O Club."

Swaying in his arms my thoughts are of past memories and then the one we are making now. So much has happened since that day and it all led to this.

"Geneviève, once again, when the music stops I am not going to let you go, but this time I am going to kiss my bride." I can feel the twinkling of my eyes as I look at him and he doesn't wait.

When the music does end our kiss continues until the unusual silence brings us out of it. We look to our table and Emily is standing up with my bouquet in her hands to bring it to me. She is performing her last duty as my maid of honor. When she hands it to me I tell her, "Thank you for being by my side. It has meant the word to me" Her eyes puddle as she nods. I kiss her cheeks and then she turns around and walks back to William who is still standing.

The emcee announces it is time for the tossing of the bouquet and for all the available females to get out on the dance floor. Trevor says, "I do enjoy this part, watching the ones who happily get up and the ones who are reluctant, slowly getting up and slowly walking across the dance floor." Suddenly Trevor abruptly turns his head. "What are our mothers doing?"

"My guess is their first act together as family." He glances at me. "Just wait."

"Unbelievable. They are going to get Aunt Meredith and Helen. Look at the smile on Hanks' face. I wish I knew what they were saying."

"I know Helen and she just said, 'Josephine, I will never forgive you for this.'"

"Aunt Meredith is telling Mum, 'Evelyn, get away from me. I mean it.' Mum tells her, 'We are family now, Meredith, so get up.'" While we are entertaining ourselves Hank stands and tugs on both of their chairs. "This is getting better by the second." I am so tickled I can't speak. "Geneviève, you know they are going to stand in the back and you are going to have to give it all you've got when you toss that thing." I look at him and turn around.

"Oh my gosh. I should have practiced this with ... something." And there goes his deep laugh as he steps back so he can see my face.

"The second you turned around they moved over."

"Commander, you are going to have to give me some coordinates."

That statement gets him tickled. "Give me a second. — Umm ... they are at my two o'clock."

"Got it. Thank you."

"Mmm hm."

I lower my arm then toss it with everything I've got and the instant it leaves my hand I spin around and watch it arch then start falling and it is going straight to Helen whose eyes are opening wider the closer it gets. To keep it from hitting her in the face she has to catch it and the second she does Meredith laughs heartily.

"Well done, Baby."

Laughing I reply, "*Thank you.*" And Helen shoots us a look before she turns around. "I hope Kyle caught all that on film."

"As if that image will not be in our minds for the rest of our lives; it was like watching something in slow motion."

"It was."

"Let's join them, shall we?"

He offers me his arm and when we get close to our table everyone stands and applauds. Joanna tells us, "Good job you two." Mitch adds, "And that's why he's my navigator." Emily and William give us the thumbs up and my grandfather asks, "What exactly do we not know?" Trevor replies, "She asked me for coordinates and I told her Helen and Aunt Meredith were at my two o'clock." Laughter breaks out and Théo holds up his thumb.

Trevor and I give them a little nod and he says, "On that note we are going to take our leave. We love you all." Trevor hands me my bridal purse and since there are so many friends and family we decided earlier to just kiss our mothers on their cheek before we go.

With that done we walk toward the doors that now have tables on each side. White porcelain baskets with handles for the ladies and without for the gentlemen as mementos of our wedding are on them, filled with rose petals to throw at us.

We are showered with the petals down the corridor, into the lobby and out the doors. It was like walking through the Japanese Garden when the cherry trees are in blossom and a breeze catches them. Our fairy-tale wedding is ending beautifully as we get in The Chariot that has a white satin bow tied on the hood ornament and matching streamers on the door handles.

Waving while Elliot slowly drives away I take a mental photograph and Trevor raises the glass partition. At the same we see another bottle of Cristal and he asks, "Water?" I pick up two glasses and he pours it from the decanter. After we pass through the gates that still has a few photographers left Trevor asks, "Mrs. Lyons, would you like to begin kissing your husband now?"

"Yes I would." And he pins me in the corner. We stop kissing on the ferry to look at the base. It looks otherworldly because of the small lights everywhere and we sit quietly soaking it all in.

Elliot drives off the ferry and we can see The Del. "Geneviève, this place is glorious at night."

"We are going to be so happy here."

"I'm already happy." I give him a kiss and we ride holding hands.

Elliot pulls under the awning and swings into action. He gets out, goes inside, gets our key and drives to the cottage. We stay in the car and kiss while he takes in our luggage and even the pastry boxes our cakes are in. At last he opens Trevor's door and walks around to open mine. I stand beside Trevor and he extends his hand to Elliot. "Thank you for helping to make this a perfect evening."

"It was a privilege, Commander Lyons, Mrs. Lyons. I wish you both all that is best in this world. Good evening." I nod and he turns on dime and drives off as Trevor helps me up the steps.

At the doors he points at my feet, which means stay where I am and he opens them. "I am going to carry my bride through the threshold." Trevor slides his hand along my waist avoiding the veil and sweeps me off my feet. I put my bouquet on my lap and my arms around his neck then he carries me through the doors kissing me.

"I don't want to put you down."

"Then don't." He kicks the doors closed.

Eventually he whispers. "I am going to put you down, but please keep your arms around me." I toss the bouquet on a chair and the moment my feet touch the floor we are in a passionate embrace. While he is holding me he says, "I want to hold you closer. It's time to get this jacket off me and that veiled tiara off you. I can't kiss the shoulders you bared for me."

Trevor turns on a lamp and stands there admiring me as I do the same. "Geneviève, will you indulge me for a moment."

"I will."

"Please do not misunderstand this. I did want to see your lovely face through the veil and lift it to kiss you."

"I understand. I wanted that too, but I wanted to see you more. Turn around please." He does as I ask and I go to find a mirror. Fortunately there is one across the living room.

With my veil back in place and holding my bouquet I say, "I love you for this. You may turn around now." When he does his jaw drops a bit because I am close enough for him to see my face. I slowly walk to him as if I am on the aisle and stand in front of my husband. Moments later he takes the bouquet from me then carefully puts it down and holds my hands as we get lost in each other's eyes again. Then I say, "You may kiss your bride." He titles his head and smiles, then he lifts the veil. This kiss is not like the one after our ceremony.

When it is over he studies me. "We need to get this tiara off. It must be heavy by now."

"You have no idea."

"Tell me what to do."

"There are five gold hair pins holding this in place that are four inches long. I am going to look down and hold onto it and you pull out the pins."

After he has the second one out he says, "These added weight. You poor thing, I had no idea."

"I'll be fine once it's off. I speak from experience."

It doesn't take him long to announce, "I have them all. What's next?"

"After I lift it up take it from me and I will get one of those pillows on the sofa for you to place it on."

When it is on the pillow Trevor offers me his hand and we go stand in front of the sofa. He pushes the coffee table away and tells me, "You take the lead."

The first thing I do is take off his Academy ring and then run my hands down his lapels. Next I slide my hands down his sleeves to the gold stars and stripes to get a closer look at them. I untie his bow tie and toss it on the coffee table then undo the top two gold studs and rub his neck. This gets me a thank you kiss.

The unusual thing about his jacket is there are two gold buttons connected by a two inch gold chain buttoning it up that is even with the top of the cummerbund. I unbutton one and it dangles by the chain. I smile while carefully taking his jacket off and lay it out on the coffee table then ask, "Would you like to take my shoes and stockings off now?"

"Yes I would." He seats me and I hand him a pillow to put his knee on as he kneels down, because I know he is going to be kneeling for a while.

Trevor slides my shoes off and softly says, "Gum Drop." As he rubs my calves I sigh. "I've been looking forward to this since the day I had to watch you do this." And he begins to slowly move his hands up my leg under my gown until he reaches the garter. Trevor slides it down and over my foot. "Something blue." and puts in his pocket. Then back up my leg he goes running his hands along it for the stocking. When it's off he tells me, "I am keeping these." I just nod because the pleasure of his touch is exceeding my expectations. Then he begins to take off the other garter. When it's visible he whispers, "My button. I knew it was on you somewhere."

"Like I know there is a pink coin in your right pocket." He reaches in the pocket and there it is.

Trevor puts it back and proceeds to take off my other stocking. This time he takes much longer and by the time it is in his hands I have to pull him up and kiss my husband.

Time passes and he tells me, "I need to sit down and take off my shoes."

"Then you are going to begin taking off my gown after I get you out of that shirt." He looks at me the entire time he takes off his shoes and socks. Soon he is on his feet and so am I.

While he kisses my shoulders I slide my hands down his back, unbuckle his cummerbund and drop it. Then I push his suspenders off his shoulders. "Baby, when this really is foreplay ..."

"It will go a little differently. Right now I would like to remove those cufflinks." He holds out his wrist and those are gone. I undo the rest of the studs and just drop his shirt, because he has kissed his way down to the top of my breast.

"Trevor, my knees are getting weak."

"Where do I begin getting you out of your bridal gown?"

"The skirting has a hidden zipper on the right side. When you find it, unzip it. As you pull the skirting from under the corset let it fall to the floor and I will step out of it."

He is still my holding my hand as I stand in front of the skirting while he admires me. I am only wearing the corset and a pair of white satin tap pants. "Geneviève, you are stunning."

"Trevor, embrasse-moi." While we kiss he realizes he can finally hold me close and he holds me so tight I can barely draw in a deep breath. When I begin to untuck his undershirt he whispers, "Baby, just take it off." He steps back and before it lands on the floor he has me in his arms again.

While he is nibbling on my neck it occurs to me I could probably breathe if I didn't still have on the corset. "Trevor — there are some buttons waiting for you to unbutton."

He slowly stops and slides his hands down my arms then holds my hands as he takes a step back and looks into my eyes. Trevor runs his finger tip down the buttons then he begins with the bottom one working his way up them slowly while I watch him.

When he unbuttons the top one the straps slide down my arms and it falls onto the floor to reveal I am wearing a strapless bralette made of thin white silk. So thin it is close to transparent and he is able to see my breast. "Geneviève, will it make you uncomfortable if I just stand here a moment and look at you?"

"Not in the least."

He caresses my face then holds my hand. The man is mesmerized and when the moment has passed he says, "I want to feel you against me."

"And I you."

When I am firmly in his arms we draw in deep breaths. Warm, our bodies are so warm. We hold onto each other for a while because we have to catch our breath before we kiss.

Eventually I am pulled from pure bliss when I notice I am in pain and it is being caused by his dog tags. I manage to toss them over his shoulder and he lets me go. In an instant he takes them off, throws them onto the coffee table and has me back in his arms.

While kissing his neck Trevor loosens his hold on me and I know what he is about to do. "Trevor, it pains me to tell you this. You can't carry me to our bed yet."

"What? What else needs to be done?"

"My hair, I need to take it down and rinse the lacquer out. I don't want to separate from you, but ..."

His sweetly smiles as he nods and I am close to being distraught when his eyes begin to gleam. He grabs my hand and says, "We're going upstairs. I have an idea."

We go into our bedroom and he tells me, "Wait right here." He goes out onto the balcony and returns with a teak wood chair. He sits it down, reclines the back and tells me, "When I was a little boy I went to the beauty salon with my mum. Get two pillows and follow me."

Laughing I get my train case and the pillows then follow him into the bathroom. He sits the chair in front of one of the sinks, takes the pillows from me and puts them on the seat. Next he drapes a bath towel over the chair and gets a hand towel that he folds and places in front of the sink. "Mrs. Lyons, your chair is ready."

I give him a kiss and start pulling out hair pins. When I have the last one in hand I lay them on the counter and he looks at me with raised eyebrows. "Now I completely understand. You hair looks the same. I thought it might come down at least a little." Trevor turns on the hot water to let it get warm then seats me in what he has made a very comfortable chair.

"I am going to enjoy this."

"So am I. How I do love taking care of you. Now place your head in my hand please." He fills a glass with water and pours it over my hair. "Is that too warm?"

"It's perfect."

Somehow he turns a simple thing into something sensual and I begin to get chill bumps from how pleasurable it becomes with each pour of warm water over my hair. I can't describe the look on his face, but he too is getting pleasure from this.

When he turns off the water I am disappointed for this to end until he begins to use a towel on my hair. Even it feels good.

"Let's get you up and move you to the vanity bench. I need your comb and a band before you sit down."

I open my train case, hand the things to him and take a seat. He kisses my shoulder then gently begins to comb through my hair. I watch him in the mirror and he occasionally glances at me in it until he begins braiding. When he puts on the band I tell him, "Thank you, Trevor. That was wonderful. I owe you a tip. What would you like?"

"A dance." He turns off the light, helps me to my feet and takes a stance. Then I begin our count and he twirls us out into the bedroom and we kiss and dance to imaginary music around the room. Then suddenly he sweeps me off my feet and carries me to our bed. He places me on it then lies next to me, caresses my face and tenderly kisses me. After a good bit of time passes I realize he still has on his trousers, so I tug on the waist band. He chuckles and tells me, "I should have taken these off before I rinsed your hair." I get tickled as he gets up. When he is finally undressed and standing at the foot of our bed wearing a pair of dark blue cotton sateen undershorts I recall him telling me he needed to buy some civvie skivvies. And there they are. Don't get tickled now. Obviously there is a twinkle in my eyes he can see, even in this dim light, because he grins and asks, "Do you like my civvie skivvies?"

I allow myself to get tickled and go, "Mmm hm."

"So do I." And he begins to crawl up the bed until he is over me and gives me a kiss. "Can you believe all we had to do to get in this bed?"

"Not really. At least we didn't have to worry about the time."

"And we won't have to for three entire weeks."

"We are in a dream come true."

"Yes we are. — Geneviève, what do you want me to do next?"

"Let me feel the weight of your body on mine."

Trevor kisses me and gently places his knee between my thighs. I move them apart and his knees are together as he slowly lowers himself onto my body until his full weight is upon me. I hold him in my arms and then I notice I have my calves lying on the back of his. So much of our skin is touching and I feel our bodies get warmer. Our breathing alters and we just lie still. "Trevor."

"I know. Geneviève ..."

"I am your wife. Talk to me."

"You are softer than I could have ever imagined. Whooooh, you feel so good."
I hear him swallow hard.

"Trevor — no more holding back."

Suddenly he slides his arms under and around me, which lifts me up to a point he cannot get me closer. Every muscle in his body is taut. His scent is intoxicating and I find myself in the most passionate moment of my life. As he moves to my shoulders his soft hair brushes my neck that he has left passion marks on. I felt each one. They will be the first of many on us both. I can already see one on the slope of his.

He savors every inch of my skin as he works his way around my breast and down to my abdomen where he lingers with his head resting on it. His neck must be aching.

A few minutes pass while I stroke his hair as he rests. Then he tells me, "Now I am going to do something I have wanted to do since the day I watched you sunbathe." He rises up, unbuttons my tap pants and exposes my lower abdomen then he begins to kiss and taste my skin. The pleasure is indescribable and so intensely felt that I grab his forearms and hold on to them tightly. As he glides his tongue over my skin the sounds I make are like none before.

When he begins to move I manage to tell him, "Trevor, I'm not sure how much longer I can make it without a drink of water."

"I'll pour us a glass."

Sitting on the bed sharing the glass of water I try to gather my thoughts looking at him and he tells me, "This day is catching up with me."

"Why are you smiling?"

Speaking each word with emphasis he responds, "Because, I will finally be falling asleep with you in my arms." And I give him a lingering kiss. "Baby, are you still thirsty."

"No, but I need to go back into the bathroom."

"I'll go to the one downstairs; your things are in this one."

We scoot to the edge of the bed and he helps me up straight into his arms where I am passionately kissed, then we go on our way.

When he returns I have our bed straightened and the covers turned back. He gives me a kiss and chuckles. "I thought you might not use toothpaste either. I noticed you didn't that first time you woke me up, knowing you didn't want to overwhelm me with the taste and smell of mint."

"I can't believe you noticed that."

"I notice everything you do." And he gathers me into his arms for a nice kiss then carries me to our bed. After he lies me down he climbs over me and pulls the covers over us. "Now we have to figure out how to sleep together." My eyes get wide. "You get comfortable and then I will figure out how to lie beside you." I fluff my pillow and lie on my back. "Geneviève, that is not how you sleep. You lie on your left side, turn over a little and raise your right leg."

"My back will be to you."

"And I am going to put my chest against in it and my left leg over yours and my right arm around you. Then you are going to put your arm over it and entwine you fingers in mine. I'm not sure what to do with my left one."

"Try putting it under my pillow, but before I get on my side kiss me goodnight." And he gives me the best goodnight kiss he has ever given me.

When we are finally settled for sleep, it took so much effort I am not really sleepy anymore. "Trevor, are you sleepy?"

"Not after all that. It's time for pillow talk, but first I have to ask if my leg is getting heavy?"

"Not at all, I am quite comfortable and very happy. I hope I wake up and you are still holding me."

"I hope you do too."

"You said that with melancholy in your voice."

"I have slept on my back in one place since I was at The Academy. Racks are narrow and you did not want to fall onto the tile floor. Due to my sleep habit I might roll over."

"Then I will roll over and lay my head on your chest."

"I love you, Geneviève."

"I love you too."

"It feels so good to lie beside you and hold you like this."

"I love feeling your heart beat. It's soothing to me."

"I love being able to smell your hair."

"That you rinsed and braided. You spoil me."

"You are my wife."

"And you are my husband." I rub his wedding band thinking at long last I am going to fall asleep in his arms.

CHAPTER ELEVEN

A slight movement of his body wakes me up and I feel its warmth. I squeeze his hand and press his arm that is around me, against me. "Yes, Geneviève, I am still holding you." Unexpected emotion washes over me and I roll over to see his face and hold him in *my* arms. "Good morning, Baby."

"Good morning, Trevor."

"I am going to kiss you until our hearts are content." And he does.

With a content heart I ask him, "Do you want some of our wedding cake?" And there goes his deep laugh.

"I think we should order room service."

"We're on our honeymoon."

"Yes we are and we need to keep our strength up."

"You have a point. Kill joy. I'm going to find out what I look like and spruce up. Order me the salmon and asparagus please."

"If you let me take down your hair."

"I'll open the door."

With my hair re-braided we put on our robes to go downstairs and I get out my camera to take photographs while we wait on breakfast. When I'm finished he immediately goes over to my bridal gown. "My uniform is carefully laid out, but we leave this in a heap on the floor." He picks up the pieces and starts laying them on a chair.

"It's fine. My bridal gown will be cleaned and placed in a box for safe keeping."

"I feel better."

"I'd feel better if I was eating breakfast. Suddenly I am starving. I'm going to look outside and see if there is a person with a tray headed our way." I open the draperies. "Nope. Where's my car? I know Théo and Rachel didn't forget."

"I'm sure it's around here somewhere. After breakfast do you want to get dressed, look for your car and go for a walk on the beach or the gardens?"

"Yes I do. That sounds good."

Trevor puts on his Academy ring then picks up his dog tags. "I won't wear these while we're at the hotel." And he places them back on the table.

"Thank you. You deserve a reward. What would you like?"

Trevor closes the space between us, unties my robe and then there is a knock on the door. "Of course. I'll answer the door." He sighs tying my robe.

He opens the door and two waiters with trays are on the veranda. One has our food, the other has a pot of coffee and a carafe of orange juice. They set the trays down on the dining table, Trevor signs the check, thanks them and shows them to the door.

After we inhale our breakfast we go upstairs to dress. I point to the suitcase I want, he puts in on the bench at the end of the bed and then puts his next to it. Next I turn and ask, "Will you unhook my bralette please."

"It would be my pleasure." He kisses my shoulders and I place my hand on it to hold it in place and he unhooks it. I toss it and get a real one out, then put it on. Without having to ask he hooks it for me and I turn around. "Once again you catch me off guard." I give him a thank you kiss as he stands catching flies as I put on a pair of slim leg trousers, roll them up and get out my deck shoes. I put on my blouse and when he's dressed he buttons it for me.

"This is the first time we've dressed together. Does this wrinkle easily?"

"Yes it does." And he unbuttons it then lays it on my suitcase. With his hand on my abdomen he slowly moves me back until I feel a wall and I am pinned. After a passionate kiss he drops to his knees and unbuttons my trousers then makes me weak by kissing where he exposed my skin.

When I no longer care where my car is and am about to ask to be carried to our bed he begins to button my trousers then stands up. "I have a new weakness."

"That makes me weak."

"Then the next time I do that we will be on our bed." He holds me and begins to rock. Was it not for the secret plan I have been waiting to carry out today for weeks I would start undressing him.

We make it outside and hold hands as we walk around the parking lot looking for my car. "Oh my gosh. Trevor, the white Jaguar I told you about is here."

He leads me over to it, reaches in his pocket and pulls out a key dangling from a key ring. "Théo and Rachel did bring your car, just not the one you were looking for. This is my wedding gift to you." I look at the car then at him. Words elude me, so I hug him. "You're welcome, Baby." And I keep hugging him. "Do you want to take me for a ride?"

"Yes I do. You want to go to the marina?"

"I'll go wherever you want."

"My driver's license." He pulls it out of his back pocket and holds it up.

I take the key and my license from him and he opens the car door. I bounce into the car, start the engine and begin looking at the dashboard. After he gets in I ask, "Why is there under 50 miles on her? She was built three years ago."

"We can't make out in a convertible on the ferry, so I'll tell a story instead."

"A good one no doubt." I put my hand on the gear shift. "You should know this, I haven't driven a stick since I test drove her."

"By the time we reach the ferry you'll have your touch back." I grab him by the back of his neck and give him a passionate kiss before putting her in gear. And we are off. To my relief he was correct about getting my touch back, because I get us on the ferry with ease.

"You have my undivided attention."

"This began over a month ago and the first thing I found out was the dealership was in Los Angeles, therefore I told Mitch and Joanna what I wanted and he told me they were in. The next morning I met them at their house. They left and I stayed to accept collect calls. The first call was just before lunch. He told me a car collector in Hollywood had her. I knew this was going to make things a tad difficult because the man would be reluctant to sell her, so I told Mitch to make him an offer only an insane person would turn down." I burst into laughter.

"About two hours later he called again and it turned out the man was sane, but had a stipulation. She had to be brought down here on a flat bed truck."

"That explains the mileage. — Over a month ago. Where has she been all this time?"

"Under a tarp in the parking garage where Rachel lives."

"Every one of us can certainly keep a secret."

"Yes we can."

"Where do you want to get a lunch to take to the marina?"

"What are my choices?"

"Trevor, any place you want."

"The Flying Dragon."

When we get off the ferry I admit it, I speed. He glances at my speedometer and gives me a look. "Blanca likes to go fast."

"I see that. You've already named her. Blanc is French for white and you made it feminine by adding an 'a'. I quite like that." I smile and go a little faster.

Inspired by my new convertible we are at the marina in no time, but I do go the speed limit in the marina and slowly pull up to Willow as Trevor says, "Look at that. Willow has a striking new neighbor." I park the car and he gets out. As he walks around to open my door he says, "Hello, Willow. It's nice to see you." I hop out and sing, "Bonjour, Willow. We shall return after meeting your new friend."

Standing at her bow he tells me, "She reminds me of an ocean liner, all white above deck, a black hull, which will keep her warm in these waters, very clever, and a red keel. That takes me back." With eyes gleaming he asks, "Do you think I could make the owner an offer that only an insane person would turn down?"

I smile at him as I pull a key out of *my* pocket. "That won't be necessary. She's my wedding gift to you." His face goes straight. "Trevor, allow me to introduce you to Gypsy. She has been patiently waiting to meet you."

"Geneviève ..."

"While you think of what to say, I have a story to tell *you*. The day after you looked at the photographs of Azure I asked Father to sell her to me. I gave him a dollar and he signed her over. Then the fun began. I had her stripped inside and out, replaced everything that needed replacing and the galley and head remodeled. Father supervised the entire thing for me. She is renamed and signed over to you."

He looks deep into my eyes then kisses me as he gathers me into his arms. Then he holds my hand and walks to her stern. "You named her Gypsy."

"I knew you would have."

"I can't believe you did this for me. Thank you, Baby. I do love you."

"And I you. — I'm ready to go aboard when you are."

He goes to Blanca, gets our lunch and motions to the gangway, "After you."

After spending a long time on deck we go below and discover fresh flowers along with one of my cameras. He looks at me with raised eyebrows. "My parents offered to stock the galley with staples this morning. The flowers are Mother's touch."

"The fabrics for everything are your touch. How did you pull that off?"

"Mother hid swatches in my armoire."

"The one place you won't let me look in."

"Mmm hm. By the way, she told me our stateroom is a must see."

"You haven't seen it?"

"This is my first time below deck since the work was finished. I thought this is something we should see together, like walking through our house." He takes me by the hand, spins me around and to our stateroom we go.

"Geneviève, you've outdone yourself. This is unusual. It matches the exterior."

"I am so pleased you like it. I was uncomfortable making all these decisions without you. If there is anything you want to change, just tell me, it won't hurt my feelings. She is yours."

"I don't want to change a thing and she's ours."

I throw my arms around his neck and he lifts me off my feet. Going to put me on the bed he slows down. "What is it?"

"Aww ... there's a note taped to the closet door."

"Put me down please."

"I knew it."

"You *can* pick me back up."

He sighs and reads the note. "You two may need these."

Trevor slides the door open and reveals two black jackets hanging. I pull one out and we see Gypsy, San Diego, CA embroidered in white on the front and he just looks at it. "You were taking me to the bed because you think we can't take her out today. Trevor, I know about the re-naming ritual to appease Poseidon."

His eyes sparkle. "Of course you do."

"I had Father put my Peace silver dollar, some index cards with notes, a bottle of champagne and a tag with Azure written on it in the galley. And the tag with ..." I gasp. "Gypsy written on it is in the glove box of my other car." Neither of us can manage to hide our disappointment. "Wait a minute. Who else knew you were giving me Blanca?"

"Just your parents, I needed to ask them a few questions"

"My father never misses a beat."

Trevor grabs my hand and we go on deck. "Stay put, I'll go look." I nod and give him a kiss for luck.

Sitting on the passenger seat he looks at me then slowly opens the glove box. Two seconds later he raises his hand in the air holding the tag. I shout, "Thank you, Father." Trevor nods, lays it in the driver's seat and is back on deck in an instant. Then we go below to the galley and he asks, "There's a small refrigerator in here. When did those become available for pleasure crafts?"

"I have no idea, but when Father told me I was giddy."

"No more lugging an ice chest aboard for me." Nodding I open its door and we discover a bottle of Roederer. "Poseidon is going to appreciate that."

"And so will we." I open a drawer where the other things are.

"Baby, I've been on a sailboat during this, so I don't need the index cards." I chuckle and get the coin and tag.

Back on deck we go to the bow and the ritual begins. He asks Poseidon to remove the name of Azure from his ledger then drops the tag into the sea. He rings the ships bell and asks him to write Gypsy in his ledger then pours half the champagne into the sea walking from east to west. Then he pours more for the gods of the four winds as he faces North, East, South and West reciting words of the ritual. He rings the bell again and says, "On this day, 15 September 1941 I name you Gypsy." And we take a drink from the bottle and toast to her name, then I give him my silver dollar which serves as a talisman and he wedges it under her mast reciting more words. Next we toast each other and he goes ashore to get the tag. Back onboard with her name he rings the bell and puts the tag under the post for her wheel.

He hugs me, gives me a nice kiss then asks, "Are you ready to take her out?"

"I sure am."

"Take the wheel, I'll cast off." My husband is overjoyed.

Instead of sitting on the bow I take my spot between his arms and we go into the open sea. We both breathe in the salt air and he turns into the wind to start raising the sails. Now I begin taking photographs of him doing what he loves for the first time on his own sailboat.

When we get to where our house is he says, "In three weeks we will be living our lives together there." I place my head on his chest and we sigh at the thought.

Several minutes later I feel him stand tall. "What do you see?"

"The wind on the water up ahead is shifting. And this is one of the reasons The Academy taught me how to sail backwards."

I turn around to face him. "You know how to sail backwards?"

"Yes, ma'am."

"I'm impressed. Umm ... Trevor, you said one of the reasons. What is the reason you're going to sail backwards now?"

"To impress the gods who are watching me sail."

"I didn't know sailing backwards was part of the ritual."

"Because most people can't and it has been ignored and forgotten over time."

"You are a true Sailor." I give him a kiss and duck under his arm. "Where do I need to be and may I photograph this?"

He points to a line. "Hold on to that and yes you may."

Trevor's entire demeanor changes and he is totally focused on his task. I hardly take any photographs because I watch him in amazement. And somehow he has

Gypsy sailing backwards. I feel my blood rush through my veins. This unlike anything I have ever experienced and find myself attracted to him even more.

After his glory moment he begins to lower the sails for her to slow almost to a stop in order for him to change her course forward. He holds me at his side as we drift.

After over three hours of sailing along the coast we are back on land, wearing our new jackets and admiring Gypsy. He says, "65 feet of head turning beauty." Then he turns to me. "And a little over five more feet here. I am a lucky man."

While he gives me a hug I ask, "What do you want to do next?"

He slowly and softly replies, "Go to our cottage, order room service, shower, read to you in our bed and then hone our skills of foreplay."

"Put me in the car please."

At the cottage while Trevor reads the dinner menu aloud I notice my gown and the rest of his uniform should be taken upstairs and start gathering our things. Then he stops and asks, "Baby, where's our wedding cake."

"In the freezer. Having a craving?"

He gives me a smile and I go upstairs with my arms full then return with a small paper bag and sit it on the menu. "I believe this is what you really want."

"You bought me a bag of vanilla gumdrops. I adore you."

"And I adore you. I will have what you're having, but I'm craving the bread pudding. Now, I am going to shower." He stands up, dips me and kisses me.

When I return the food is not here. "What did you order?"

"Lobster. I forgot they take a while to cook. I'm going to shave and shower."

"May I watch you shave?" He gets my hand and leads me upstairs.

Trevor gets the ebony filled travel case I selected for him on that memorable day and pulls out the vanity bench for me then tosses his shirts on the floor. When he takes off his dog tags I light up and he looks at me. "Room service will get here before I get out. I'm not sure I want those men to see you in that kimono."

"Only you will see what's under it." He raises an eyebrow as he shakes his head. I just smile and he begins to shave.

Soon there is a knock on the door and I jump up. "I'm starving. I will see you downstairs. He tries to give me a kiss with shaving soap on his face. I shriek and successfully dodge him as I close the door. I can hear his deep laugh as I walk through the bedroom.

Of course he is downstairs in a silk robe and pajamas before I turn on the record player. He seats me and we savor every morsel as we talk about our wedding gifts for each other and how much we enjoyed the first day of our honeymoon. And it's not even over yet.

While I showered Trevor got a fire going in the fireplace of our bedroom. The glow and crackling from it fill the room with an aura of romance. He places his book on the nightstand and I step up to kiss him as I untie the sash of his robe. I lay it across the chair by the bed he is not going to sit in tonight and then proceed to do something I haven't had the privilege of, taking off his tank and pajamas.

I do not take my eyes from his as I feel my way along his sides and pull off his tank. It is going to take some time for me to get used to how beautiful his torso is without those distracting dog tags. I glide my hands along his chest down to his waist and to the string that holds the pajamas up. I have to look down to see how it's tied and find a slip knot. I pull the end that unties them and they fall to the floor. He steps out them and moves us forward by holding on to my waist. He is only wearing a pair of burgundy undershorts and without thinking I slide my hands from his waist over them down to his skin. The sateen is thin and I can feel how muscular he is.

Trevor softly kisses me as he unties the sash of my kimono then kisses my neck as he slowly slides it off of me, holding on to it. He lays it by his and focuses on me. I am wearing just a bralette and tap pants again. "Geneviève, these are pretty. I love you in petal pink." He runs his finger tips along the straps down to my breast. "May I slide my hand between your breasts to reach your waist?"

"Yes."

How many times has he placed his hands between my breast to dress or undress me, or to feel my heart beat? But this *is* different, this time he is feeling my breast and his touch is gentle. I can still feel the sensation as he picks me up and sits me on the edge of our bed. My husband starts piling pillows up on the head board and tells me, "Now, I am going to read to you."

He sits on the bed, settles among the pillows then he slides his left foot up toward his body and raises the knee of his leg. Then he moves the other one until they are far apart and holds my waist as he slides me between them until I am against his chest. It is like he has become a soft chair for me to put my back against and rest my head on. "Are you comfortable?" I go, "Mmm hm." Trevor picks up his book, opens it and lays the bookmark on the bed. Then he puts his arm across my body and begins reading to me.

Listening to his voice and feeling the steady beat of his heart is like he is casting a spell on me. I move my head over until it is by his neck and ever so slightly I begin to rub his chest with my shoulder blades. I realize he has stopped reading when he whispers, "Geneviève."

"I'm listening."

"I know, but you are listening to the sound of my voice, not what I'm reading. I think you're becoming aroused. Are you?"

"Yes, completely."

"I need to do something in order for you to make sense of everything you're feeling and have been feeling for far too long."

"Talk to me."

"I am going to slide my hand over your tap pants and down until it is over the place that stimulates you. Then I will press my hand against your body and keep it perfectly still. If or when you want me to stop just lift my hand."

"I understand." He puts the book on the bed and releases a breath as I close my eyes.

Trevor lowers his head to mine, places his hand on my hip and moves it to the middle of my lower abdomen then slowly down and stops. He presses his hand against my body which cause me to open my eyes and sharply inhale then exhale. I immediately put my hand over his and press it against me. Breathlessly I tell him, "That is what my body has been wanting, you to touch me there." I move my hand away and onto his thigh. "That feels so good."

"Baby, what do you want me to do?"

"Let me catch my breath."

He lifts his hand and holds me. I relax and my breathing is a little closer to normal. "You were right, it all makes sense now. — I want more."

"Do you want me to bring you to a climax with my touch?"

"Yes. Yes, Trevor. I do."

He picks up his book, places it on the nightstand and gives me a glass of water. I take a drink and then he turns off the lamp. Holding me he speaks softly. "I'm going to undo that button and then I am going to keep my left arm around you. If what I think is going to happen happens, you need to hold on to it to keep yourself still and perhaps you should put your hand back on my thigh."

I get situated and after I do he undoes the button and exposes my lower abdomen. When he lays his warm hand on my body my eyes close. I can feel his breath on my neck when he goes, "Whooooh." He's nervous. Rubbing the palm of my hand with his fingertip and what he is about to do are two entirely different things, but I know he has confidence in his abilities to adapt. I do.

Fortunately he moves slowly and it gives me time to wrap my mind around where his hand is about to be. When he is there and his fingertip touches the place I want him to touch my entire body shivers. He pauses for a moment, I think so we can both gather our wits, then he begins to slide the pad of his finger in a circular motion and I moan. How can such a tiny thing yield so much pleasure? Within seconds I find myself griping the wrist of his arm that is holding me and his thigh. What follows is a blur beyond description. Suddenly I feel as if I am falling and then I am overwhelmed with pleasure. My moans turn into other sounds, and just when I think I am going to hyperventilate Trevor stops moving his fingertip and leaves it in place as my body flinches. I feel his chest swell against my back as he draws in a deep, deep breath. My body no longer feels as if it is falling and my breathing is rapid.

Trevor carefully lifts his hand and places it on my lower abdomen then my body relaxes to the point I cannot move, even if I wanted to, which I do not.

When I can finally speak I tell him, "Trevor, hold me. I am so weak." And he wraps me in his arms, but soon I feel a bit of a chill. "Trevor my body is so warm I feel chilly." And he pulls the covers over us.

After being cozy under the covers a while I begin to talk to him. "I know why it is called a climax. I felt as if I was going higher, higher and higher, then suddenly I felt as if I was falling and I fell into ecstasy. Trevor, I'm not sure if these are the correct words, but thank you for giving me that."

"Believe me, it truly was my pleasure. The way your body feels is indescribable, and the sounds you made were like a beautiful song, the likes of which I have never heard before and I want to hear it over and over again. I am so lost in my love for you and I do not ever want to find my way back. — May I kiss you?"

"Why are you asking?"

"Because I need to move you. Are you ready to be moved?"

"Yes. I want to lie down with you."

Trevor sits up holding on to me and rearranges the pillows then he carefully lies me down and lies down beside me.

I'm not sure when, but we fell asleep and while it is still dark I become wide awake and make a little sound that wakes him up. "Baby, are you all right?"

I get tickled. "I'm fine, but I need to ... powder my nose."

He chuckles. "I'll meet you back here." And we fling the covers off.

Trevor returns and throws another log on the fire. "It was a little chilly down stairs, so I turned the heater on low."

"Good. I'm hungry."

"It's only five o'clock, but we have 24 hour room service. What do you want?"

"A mushroom and Swiss cheese omelet, croissant, orange juice and hot cocoa."

"Without coffee we'll get sleepy again."

"Mmm hm and then we'll go back to bed and sleep til noon."

He picks up the phone by the bed and places our order. Then we kiss until we hear a knock on the door and he answers it while I stay in bed. The waiter asks him if we want our breakfast served downstairs on a cart or on bed trays. This is how we find out there are bed trays in the kitchen. Obviously we haven't opened all the cabinet doors in there. I hear Trevor tell him on a cart.

When they leave I go downstairs and see the cart is by French doors we can watch the sunrise at. Trevor says, "The last time we tried to watch the sunrise it didn't work out." I laugh and give him a kiss remembering our run around the house to hide from Joseph.

After we finish eating we sit on the comfy sofa facing the doors and sip our hot cocoa as we watch a beautiful sunrise. When he yawns we take that as our cue to go back to bed.

The sunlight around the draperies wakes me up. This time I immediately recall having my first climax and I become hyper aware of his body I am beside. I wake him up by running my hand over the muscles of his back. Before I can say anything he rolls me over and slides my bralette straps off my shoulders. Next he proceeds to leave a passion mark on my neck then kisses his way down to my breast. Then he whispers, "Geneviève, are you aching for my touch yet?"

"Yes I am." And he takes me higher than before.

While resting by Trevor's side he tells me, "My stomach just sank. I'm going to get an apple."

"I'm going to lie here basking in the pleasure you gave me."

I listen to his footsteps as he goes down the stairs and across the living room. There is a moment of silence then the distinct sound of him taking a bite of an apple. Upon his return he gives me the apple and I take a big bite then we share it.

"We need food. I'm ordering us sandwiches."

"I want smoked turkey with Baby Swiss on a dry croissant with carrot sticks, Pellegrino with lime and a piece of cheese cake with caramel sauce."

"Hungry?"

"I'm famished ... and have the food served on bed trays please. I'm weak due to lack of food — and you." He gives me a sticky kiss and orders.

After we eat I lie down and have an idea. "Trevor, hand me the receiver please. I'm having our kitchen stocked." He hands me the receiver and I get a kiss. "This is Mrs. Lyons. We need our refrigerator and pantry stocked with a smoked ham and turkey, raw vegetables, an assorted basket of bread and one of scones, a wheel of cheddar, water wafers, a basket of apples, four plates of grilled smoked salmon and asparagus, six bottles of Pellegrino and a lime, a pitcher of orange juice and sweet tea without ice." I look at him and he gives me a thumbs up. "That will be all. Thank you."

"You took command of that situation like an officer in the Navy."

"I am married to one."

"Yes you are." And he kisses my wedding band. "Where is your engagement ring?"

"In the refrigerator with Primrose." He chuckles. "I'm going to go get them and after I watch you shave I'm showering and then turning this cottage into our home while the staff stocks the kitchen. See you soon."

Beaming he says, "See you soon."

I slip on a dress after I shower and then go downstairs where I hear the staff in the kitchen briefly, because they were gone in a blink. Minutes later he joins me wearing a polo and khakis looking around. Surprisingly I even had time to set up my record player. He smiles and looks at me. "Geneviève, you're not wearing a bralette."

"I decided we're going to stay inside. After we eat would you like to open the doors and enjoy the view?"

"Yes, I would." And we go to the kitchen.

Curled up on the sofa a breeze begins to blow the white sheers as we listen to the sounds of the ocean and soak up the view. After I feel his freshly shaved face against my cheek we wind up rolling around on the sofa. And when it gets dark we order dinner then go back to the sofa to watch the moonlight dance on the water. Eventually I wind up beneath him with my legs around him and he whispers, "Baby, put your arms around my neck and hold on." I do as he instructs and he gets us up then holds on to my thighs and walks to the bedroom kissing me. Carrying me has now become foreplay.

He reaches the bed, gently lies me down then he takes off his polo and khakis and lies down beside me. After passionate kisses he moves to my neck, inhales the scent of my skin and starts unbuttoning my dress. When his hand is between my bare breasts he hesitates and I manage to speak. "Don't — stop." Suddenly he puts his hands on the bed, pushes himself up and hovers over me. His face is so straight. "Trevor, what is it?"

"Just a minute. It's fine." He moves over and sits beside me.

When it occurs to me what I said I sit up. "Oh Trevor — I do apologize."

"Baby, there is no need to apologize." He puts his hand on his forehead. "Thank goodness that happened now. As it is ... I still think I'm going have gray hair." He sighs while I am shaking my head as he takes a moment to get his wits about him. "We need a code word for stop." I cannot help but laugh. "Did I really just that?"

"Yes, you did." He shakes his head and chuckles. "Between the two of us we have over 15 years of experience. One of us should be able to come up with something." Now he laughs.

We scoot back and sit up with the pillows on the headboard. Trevor puts his arm around me and I put my head on his shoulder. He says, "It has to be a word neither of us would say during times of passion." We sit in silence for a few minutes then I say, "Glue." Trevor lights up and says, "Glue. That's perfect."

"Thank you." I am beaming.

"That is completely random I might add. Now, where was I?"

"You were about to expose my breast and stopped."

"And you told me not to."

We lie down and without taking his eyes off mine he begins unbuttoning my dress again. When it's completely unbuttoned Trevor slides his hand along my body moving my dress until it falls onto the bed. I rise up and he pulls it out from under me. "Trevor, I want to feel my breast against your chest."

Laying beneath him he slowly lowers his chest until it is against my breasts and we both inhale deep breaths from the sensation it gives us. I hold him in my arms and wrap my legs around his. The skin on his legs is almost hot. There is something about the weight of him on me and my bare breast against the skin of his chest that causes me to become extremely passionate. I cannot hold him close enough and I cannot kiss him with enough passion.

As we kiss he slides his hand up my leg along my hips and side to my face. I put my hands in his hair and begin to kiss his neck. This causes my body to move under his and the unexpected pleasure from it makes me clinch my teeth. I inadvertently catch the skin of his shoulder and lightly bite him. Trevor inhales sharply and then he moans in a deep tone. I am so relieved I didn't hurt him I place my head on the pillow. He gazes at me then starts kissing his way down my body to my abdomen. I feel his hands on my waist and he unbuttons my tap pants then folds them back and begins to kiss my hip bones.

While lost in the pleasure he is giving me Trevor says, "Geneviève."

"I'm listening."

"Do you want to keep these on?" He keeps kissing my body.

"Are you ..." My eyes open. "Do you want to bring me to a climax?"

"Yes I do."

"Then take them off."

Trevor lies next to me and moves my leg until my thighs touch then he slowly slides my tap pants down and off. I am nude and he is seeing my body for the first time. Even though the bedroom is dark I have never felt so uncomfortable in all my life. Much to my relief he reaches for the sheet, covers me and lies down on his side next to me. He looks into my eyes as he puts his hand over my heart. It is pounding. He says, "Let's wait until you are calm again, all right?"

I whisper, "Yes ... please." He leaves his hand over my heart and begins to kiss my lips so gently my stomach sinks. "I want to lie beneath you as we were in the beginning." I lift the sheet and soon feel the weight of his body on mine again. I drop the sheet and it falls below his back that I put my arms around.

He whispers, "Let me know when you are ready for me to move again. Until then I will happily stay right here." And he kisses my earlobe.

Within seconds we are lost in a passionate embrace. My desire for him is more than I can stand and I say in a breath, "Move." Then Trevor slowly begins to move. He is finally going to taste my entire body.

Trevor kisses my shoulder and his hair is against my neck. My legs are still around him as he kisses along my arm until he is at its bend, then he pulls the sheet off of us. "Trevor, I am no longer apprehensive. I want to know what your tongue is going to feel like."

"I am going to move your body so you can find out." There is a blur that follows of his mouth and hands gliding over the skin of my legs and then I feel his hair against my thighs. Lost with this man I am when I feel his tongue glide over the area of my body that brings me to a climax. His tongue feels ... indescribable, and I experience so much pleasure. I draw in the deepest breath and gather the sheet beneath us in my hands to keep still. My neck and back arch as I try to focus and figure out where to put my hands on him. I realize his forearms are against me and hold on to them. His mouth is warm and it feels so soft. And then it is as if nothing else exist, only him, and the pleasure I am feeling.

When I reach the point I am going to climax I hold on to him tightly and then I feel and hear him moan. Not expecting to climax so many times mere seconds apart I can barely catch my breath.

After I can finally breathe somewhat normally all I can think is I want to feel the warmth of his body over mine and I tell him, "Hold me — please hold me." And he lies down with me beneath him. I love being completely under him for many reasons, but right now it is because I can wrap my arms and legs around him feeling more of the warmth and strength of his body.

Trevor whispers, "The sounds you just made were beautiful. I can't put it into words how they made me feel."

"I had no idea anything could feel that good. Your mouth was so ... so warm. Your tongue ... the way it felt, it is indescribable. Trevor, kiss me."

As we kiss passionately Trevor becomes aroused, so I begin to calm us down. His member has to cause him discomfort being pinned between us. And with that thought he tells me, "I am going to lie down on the bed for a moment, all right?"

Trevor lies down next to me. I drape the sheet over us then carefully lie on my side and across him. He puts his arms around me and I softly tell him, "I am so weak."

"Just rest, Baby."

After time passes I tell him, "I cannot stop thinking about how you felt and what you did."

"I love you, Geneviève."

"I love you too, Trevor, so very much." And we rest in each other's arms.

Eventually Trevor sighs, "I do not want to separate from you, but I am starting to become self-conscious. I'm going to shower off."

"Oh Trevor, I completely understand."

"I shan't be long. I promise."

He gives me a kiss and goes to shower. As I lie there I begin thinking I want to see his body. So I make a decision, get up and slip on my robe. The bathroom door is pulled to and I can hear the water splashing. "Trevor, may I come in?"

"Of course." I step in and he asks, "What's the matter?"

"Nothing. I didn't realize I would alarm you. I apologize. I have invaded your privacy." I turn and reach for the door knob.

"Geneviève, please don't go." I turn back around. "Tell me why you came in."

I walk closer to him. "I am so shy and you have been so sweet and patient as you try to help me overcome this. It is placing undue pressure on you and I want to try and take some of it off. While I was lying there listening to you shower I began thinking how beautiful your body must be and wished I could see you in the light. Then it occurred to me you have to feel the same way about me. The reason why I came in is — I want to join you."

Trevor steps back from the shower door and pushes it open. I turn off the light in the shower stall then slowly draw in a deep breath. I take off my robe, cross the room, step in and close the door. He turns the hot water up and smoothes his hair back. I am so taken by his nude body I forget for a moment I am nude. The muscles just below his waist are so defined and the amount of hair that runs down the middle of his lower abdomen was unexpected. I had only felt it. He is perfection and I want to touch him.

Trevor stands still as I go around him, get under the shower head and close my eyes. The warm water relaxes me as it flows over my body that is still sensitive. When I open my eyes he is looking straight into them. I step forward until the water is on my back and he says, "I need you to tell me what you want to do." I nod, pick up the bar of soap and lather my hands. "I want to bathe you." He tells me, "I am yours."

I place my hands on his shoulders, give him a kiss then slide my soap covered hands down the back of his arms to his wrist then I glide my hands over his chest and abdomen without taking my eyes off of where my hands go. I slowly walk around to his back never taking a hand off of him and begin bathing his sides. I stop and lather my hands again to bathe his back and without thinking I run my hands around his waist and press my body against his. Trevor sharply draws in a breath and every muscle in his body flexes. I tell him, "I was not prepared for that either. I just wanted to hold you. You feel so good."

"Oh — so do you." I slide my hands up to his shoulders and hold onto him. A moment passes and he says, "Geneviève." I let him go and tell him, "I am yours."

Trevor turns around, wraps me in his arms and we immediately begin to kiss. The soap makes ours body's slide about and he loosens his hold to get us stable. As I expect, he eventually becomes aroused again and we continue to kiss.

He moves back until the warm water flows over us. The soap rinses off our bodies and he begins kissing my neck and shoulders. My head goes back as he moves to my breasts and I become oblivious to my surroundings due to things caused by sheer pleasure.

We reach a point I have to tell him, "I need ... a moment." We are breathing heavily as he stops kissing my body and holds me with one arm while placing his hand on the wall to steady us. Maybe a minute passes when I say, "Trevor, I am about to catch you off guard." I pause briefly. "I want to bring you to a climax with my touch and I don't know what to do. Will you help me?" He takes his hand off the wall, puts his arm back around me and holds me as he says, "Yes — I will. I just need to gather my thoughts."

"Trevor, I do understand what you're going through. You are my husband now and you shouldn't need a bottle of chloroform." He begins a contained laugh and says, "I don't need it." I am instantly lost, then I realize he is no longer aroused. I cannot help but begin to laugh too as I loosen my hold to see his face and tell him, "I did warn you I was going to catch off you guard — unlike you."

"What?"

"Do you want to keep these on?"

"Point made. I'm going to rinse off and get towels." He steps under the shower head and closes his eyes. "There is also a risk of running out of hot water."

"In other words, shake a leg." He laughs as we trade places and he wraps a towel around his waist. I rinse off and he hands me one. I wrap it around me covering my breasts and when I focus on him my eyebrows go up. He turns off the water and says, "Let me guess, I have a few passion marks on me."

"Yes you do. Do I?"

"Mmm ... mmm hm."

His timid response alarms me just a bit, so I open the stall door and go to the mirror with Trevor on my heels. I expect the ones on my neck and shoulders, but the ones on my forearm and my thigh, not so much. This leads me to open my towel to see the rest of my body. They are located on almost every place his mouth was. My chest has one, there are several on my upper and lower abdomen and then I see one on the inside of my upper thigh. I smile and close my towel.

As I touch the ones on Trevor he says, "I didn't get the chance to say this earlier. Your body is beautiful."

"Your body is perfection. I knew it would be."

"I can't believe you came in here and the reason why. Thank you, Geneviève."

"For what?"

"Thinking of me and understanding."

"I love you and want to help, for lack of a better word."

"I know what you mean and I love *you*."

Trevor holds me close for a moment then we go sit on the edge of the bed. He asks, "What would you like to do tomorrow?"

"I was thinking about going for a swim, but since I look as if I was in a hail storm, that's off the table."

We both begin laughing as he says, "It really is."

"I'm hesitant to even go outside." Trevor falls back on the bed as he laughs. "We can stay inside or wait until the coast is clear and make a dash for my car to go for a drive." Trevor is still laughing.

"Geneviève, please. I'm going to hyperventilate." I stop talking and he sits up to take a drink of water. "When I imagined our honeymoon, going from the heights of passion to laughter never crossed my mind. And it keeps happening."

"The rapport between us has not changed a bit. Only what happens between us physically is changing and our wardrobe." I tug on my towel. "I'm going to change out of this."

I toss him a terry cloth bathrobe then come back wearing one. He has lain back down, so I sit next to him and he begins rubbing my back. I remain quiet because I know he is thinking. Eventually he says, "I have been trying to figure out how you can bring me to a climax. The main thing you need to know is I will guide your hand when need be." I nod. "We should be in the shower, because you will need soap and water. You might be able to stand behind me, against my back ... and reach around me in order to do this. If not, we will work it out. There really is not more to say ... we will just have to be in the moment."

"You are obviously uncomfortable." I exhale heavily. "Trevor, I asked to do this for you; you did not ask this of me. If I find I am uncomfortable in any way, I will tell you." He sighs in relief.

"Thank you. I feel much better." He pauses briefly then asks, "Do you want to play a game of cards?"

I laugh and reply, "And to the victor go the spoils?"

"Most definitely."

"You deal."

Never in my life have I wanted to win a game of Go Fish so much and to my relief, I do.

Trevor asks, "What do you want?"

"To get back in the shower."

Trevor eyebrows go up as I reach for his hand to lead him to the bathroom. Without hesitation I take his robe off, but I have to summon the courage to take mine off. We hold hands as we go to the shower stall and get in then I turn on the hot water and hold my hand under it until it's warm. I make the temperature nice and step under it pulling him to me. We kiss and we kiss, even after he is aroused, then I ask, "May I touch you without the soap?"

"Geneviève, do what you want until you need me."

With him in my arms I move around to his back and press my torso against it. Then I slide my hand down along the ripples of his muscular abdomen until I reach his member. I gently hold it in my hand and notice I am touching the softest skin, but underneath it he is solid. Reaching for the soap I move us over to get out from under the stream of water then I lather my hands, put my left arm around his body and slide my hand back down to his member. "Tell me what to do."

"Hold me in your hand, tighten your grip a bit and slide your hand up and down in a slow continuous rhythm. Eventually I will hold your hand in mine to change the rhythm and let it go."

The first time I slide my hand along him Trevor moans and his head goes back. For some reason I like the way he feels in my hand. Moments later he guides my hand to a different rhythm and he suddenly puts his hands on the wall of the shower stall and moans. I love the sounds he begins to make. Every muscle in his body flexes, his breathing is erratic and then I feel his member throbbing. Trevor reaches for my hand and holds it still. He climaxed.

"Baby, you can let go now. I'm going to stand here for a minute, but please hold me. When I'm able I will turn around and hold you."

"Take your time." And I hold him close.

When he turns around Trevor holds me as he buries his face into my neck. Eventually I notice the water is getting cool on my feet and there are no towels. "Trevor we are about to get cold. I'm going to get our bathrobes."

I barely open the door, grab our bathrobes and dash back in. He puts on his, then helps me put on mine. Back in his embrace he tenderly kisses me and whispers, "I love you. How you do spoil me."

"I love you too and you spoil me more."

"Geneviève, allowing me to spoil you, spoils me as well. Come on, Baby. Let's go lie down."

In the bedroom I tell him, "Your undershorts are in the top left drawer."

"You even unpacked?"

"I had time. You showered like a civilian."

"The water felt good."

I give him a kiss and turn on the lamp on the left nightstand while he gets ready for bed. The second I turn it on he says, "You brought a safe light. We're going to put that to use."

"Yes we are. Will you chose something for me to sleep in? My things are in the top right drawer." He opens it and looks at me smiling. "Why are you smiling?"

"I've never seen your panties. They are pretty."

"Pick out a pair and I'll sleep in them."

"This just keeps getting better. What else do you want?"

"A camisole. Those are loose and comfortable."

"I knew those bralettes weren't." He gets one out shaking his head.

Dressed for bed we get in it, he turns off the lamp and gives me a goodnight kiss. We are settled for a few seconds and I say, "Nope. Trevor, I need to sit up. He lies on his side and asks, "What's wrong?" Sitting up I look at him and begin taking off my camisole. "I can't feel your skin on my back. I've never slept without wearing a top and I'm going to find out if I can." I throw it on the chair and lie down on my back then ask, "May I have another goodnight kiss?"

"You may have anything you want." He puts his arm over me, pulls my body against his and gives me the kiss I want and a little more. Eventually Trevor lies on his back and I lie on my side next to him with my head on his chest and my leg and arm across him, then we drift into a deep sleep.

I am awaked by Trevor lightly caressing my shoulder and I sigh because we are still in the position we fell asleep in. Then my sense of touch has me wide awake. My bare breasts are against him and as I recall the events of last night my heart rate goes up. He says, "I can feel your heart beating. When I woke up, mine did the same thing. I thought the sound of it might wake you up."

"You muscles are so thick I didn't hear it." I lift up and get the glass of water on his nightstand. I swish some then drink some. He lifts his head and does the same thing. The second I set the glass down he rolls us over and I am beneath him once again close to nude. Whispering I tell him, "Trevor, it just occurred to me, we haven't been nude together in our bed."

"And you want us to be."

"Yes."

He moves to my side. "Raise your hips." And he takes off my panties then he takes off his undershorts. "Where do you want me?"

"Where you were."

He nods and the moment his body is lying on mine we gasp and fall into a trance filled with moans and pleasure. Magnificent time pass and eventually his stomach growls. We exhale simultaneously out of exasperation and get tickled. "Geneviève, I'm going to the bathroom downstairs and then throw some salmon and asparagus on a pan." He puts on his undershorts and reaches for our robes. "It's cloudy and will get chilly in here." I put on my robe while he turns on the heater and he looks at me with a gleam in his eyes. "Maybe it will rain today. I shan't be long."

When he returns I am sitting on the edge of the bed and my husband walks straight to me and unties my robe then he lowers me to the bed in his arms. Time flies and all too soon Trevor leaves to get our breakfast.

Eating in bed he says, "When we finish this I am going to build us a fire and then I am going to read to you. How does that sound?"

"Perfect. This time I will listen to your words." He chuckles and gives me a bite of his scone.

While he builds the fire I arrange the pillows and he is my soft chair again. Finally he gets to the chapter I had stopped reading at. Listening to him read it in English with his British accent makes me so content. Then we hear rain begin to landing on the roof. He kisses my check, snuggles me closer to him and continues to read.

When he pauses to rest the arm and hand that has been holding the book and get a drink of water he says, "This is a good book. The man is obsessed with her. I am getting curious how this will end. Is it wrong to hope the phantom gets his head on straight and the girl?"

"Not in my opinion."

"I don't know what I would have done had I not got the girl."

"Geneviève, talk to me."

"I love your skin against mine and your tongue feels like velvet."

He moves me until I am in his arms as if we are in the car and gives me a tender kiss. "And you taste sweet — just as I knew you would. It is the sweetest taste I have ever tasted. Now I crave you."

"That is the most sensual thing you have ever said to me." And I intentionally leave a passion mark on the slope of neck for remembrance of this moment. Next he buries his face into my neck and begins to slightly rock me. Just as I am getting a bit sleepy a see light through my eyelids and a second later there is a loud clap of thunder. He says, "That was close. Perhaps we should eat lunch in case the power goes out and we can't open the fridge. I can't make it on a piece of cheddar with water wafers and an apple."

We decide on pasta salads and to let a piece of his grooms' cake thaw while we eat. Listening to the storm we barely speak as we eat. After we finish the cake I look into his eyes and he asks, "You are slightly nodding. Why?"

"Because I have learned a lot these past few days and I know some things." His eyebrows go up just a bit. "First I learned that I have a part in reaching a climax."

"You do?"

"Yes. I do indeed. The second time you were touching me, I decided to relax a bit and the instant I did, I stopped going higher and almost lost some height. Then I realized I should not relax and needed to go where the intensity takes me. The next thing was while I was holding your member in my hand covered with soap lather I realized the size of it would not cause me any pain."

"You're certain of that?"

"Yes. Yes I am."

"That takes a weight of my shoulders."

"And I'm not done."

"You have my attention."

"I know what is going to be like when we are finally making love." I pause for a moment to allow him to stay with me. "It will be as if we are composing music together. We will begin ever so slowly and gradually the tempo will increase until it reaches a crescendo, then the tempo will slow down — drastically — until there is silence."

I watch him absorb the things I told him and he responds, "That is what it will be like."

"Yes it will. Soon, I think we will reach a point when everything will simply fall into place and we will be lovers."

"I love you, Geneviève."

"And you show me how much you do every day." He kisses me and once again he tastes like chocolate.

The lightening clouds are over the ocean now and we curl up on the sofa to watch the storm. Hours pass as we talk like the husband and wife we have become. Eventually he rubs my chin. "Would you like to watch me shave and have our first true shower together?" I nod smiling. "Then I will order us a four course meal and we will dress for dinner and dancing."

After he gets a fire started we go into the bathroom and take off our bathrobes and he puts towels in the shower. This time when he shaves I load the brush with shaving soap and hand him his razor. Then after he rinses his face I pour a few drops of shaving balm onto his hand to sooth his skin. After it soaks in he lets me have my way with his face and then he pulls off my camisole and I step out of my panties while he takes off his undershorts then I lead him to the shower. "You're leading, so what do you want to do, bathe each other or bathe ourselves?"

"Oh ... I want to watch you bathe." His eyebrows go up yet again.

"I didn't expect you to say that. I have to confess, since we've been here I've imagined you bathing and I want to see you with my own eyes."

When the water temperature is perfect I step underneath it and un-braid my hair. He hands me the soap and a wash cloth. I lather it up and begin to bathe. Trevor stands close and watches me with adoration. As I let the water flow over me rinsing off the soap his eyes gleam then he pours shampoo into my hand. He seems mesmerized as I wash it.

When we switch places and I watch him bathe there is something sensuous about watching the soap rinse off his body and I understand why he had a gleam in his eyes watching me.

With the shampoo rinsed from his hair he pulls me under the shower head and lets the water flow over us a few minutes then he turns off the water and begins to dry me off. As I had hoped, he makes it pleasurable.

After he finishes I wrap the towel around me and get one to dry him off. This is when I familiarize myself with the rest of his body and my favorite discovery is the muscles below his waist are highly defined and quite attractive. I can feel how hard they are through the towel. His body really is beautiful. I reluctantly hand him the towel that he wraps around his waist, then he gives me a kiss and pushes the door open.

He puts on shaving balm again then asks, "What next?"

"You order our dinner then select my dinner dress."

Trevor makes the call then opens the closet and comments, "These are new."

"They are part of my bridal trousseau you have seen very little of."

"Ah." He stops going through them at the cocktail dress I expect him to. "Black strapless satin, fitted and a slit up to your thigh. What goes under this?"

"Me and a black pair of panties." One eyebrow goes up and he walks over to the dresser. He gets the panties and feels the satin then gives them to me. Without hesitation I take off my towel and toss it to him. He stands there holding it, looking a bit surprised as I step into them. Then I open his drawer and select a pair of dark blue jacquard undershorts for him. I hand them to my husband and undo his towel. He locks his eyes on mine and puts them on.

"Geneviève, I have observed you trying to overcome your shyness with all your heart and now, it is as if you were never shy at all."

"That is because you look at me through adoring eyes. And I am fascinated with your body. I had no idea it would be so beautiful." I place my hands on his neck and kiss him then he steps forward and embraces me.

Minutes pass as we are lost in an expression of love. He breaks the silence by telling me, "I do not want to say this, but we need to get dressed before there is a knock on our door." I nod and begin to towel dry my hair while he gets out his black suit and tie.

We dress each other and go into the bathroom where he picks up his comb and hands it to me. I have never combed his hair and I do enjoy it, almost as much as he does. Next he pulls out the vanity bench and brushes my hair then he hands the brush to me. "This I can't do and it will probably be the one thing I will never be able to." And I begin putting my hair up in a chignon and do not use lacquer. With that done I pick up lipstick. "Why are you going to wear lipstick?"

"I'm going to blot it with your handkerchief to give you something you may carry that is a reminder of our honeymoon." He kisses me and hands it to me.

Downstairs Trevor asks, "Do you want to listen to dinner music or the rain."

"The rain. — Will you get the candlesticks and candles out of the buffet and set them up on the table?"

"Yes, ma'am. — Geneviève, these are the ones from Joanna and Mitch."

"I know."

"Baby, you don't miss a beat."

With my face beaming I pull Primrose from my bodice and hand her to him. "Will you pin her on the left side of the waist band please?"

He kneels and responds, "With pleasure. By the way, you look lovely." When he stands there is a knock on the door.

Trevor opens it and glances at me. He motions the waiter to the dining table and whispers by my ear, "I need my money clip." And off he goes.

Curiosity gets the better of me and I walk to a place I can see through the sheer in front of a window. I know I make a face, because I see a waiter standing under a beach umbrella on the veranda. That explains why he dashed upstairs. Seconds later Trevor breezes passed me and goes outside. He hands him a tip and comes back in giving me a look of, can you believe that. I slightly shake my head.

The waiter inside has everything set out, hands Trevor the check and asks, "May I get you both anything else. He tells him, "No. Thank you." Even if we did the answer would be no, so he signs the check.

We are alone at last for our romantic candle lit dinner. Trevor pulls out my chair then kisses my shoulder before he sits across from me and we proceed to eat delicacies, drink fine wine and have intimate conversation with rain softly falling as our music.

When it's time for dessert he lifts the plate covers. "You ordered petit fours."

"I couldn't help it. When I was scanning the dessert list it caught my eye. Our life together is centered on things that are sweet. It began with your scent on the day we met." Trevor picks up his plate and sets his chair next to mine then we feed each other and steal little kisses.

Next I pour us glasses of Louis XIII while Trevor selects records and we move to the sofa. Then we listen to them playing with the volume low and watch the storm that is still over the ocean just further away, savoring our nectar and each other, dancing occasionally.

After wonderful time passes a record drops and our song begins to play. He stands and offers me his hand. "My ravishing wife, dance with me." And for the second time I sing to him.

The song ends and he dips me as he kiss me passionately. While kissing my neck Trevor sweeps me off my feet and carries me to the bedroom. We kiss tenderly as I toss his jacket and tie on the bench, then he sits by them to take off his shoes and socks as I step out of my pumps. We look at each other and I see his face change. He reaches for Primrose, unpins her and places her on the dresser. Next I have the pleasure of undressing him and he stands before me only wearing the undershorts I chose.

After allowing me a moment to admire his body Trevor slides his hands along my back feeling the satin and kissing the slope of my neck. Then he feels his way to the zipper of my dress and pulls it down. It instantly falls onto the floor and without warning he pulls my body against his by my waist and kisses me passionately. Then he sweeps my legs out from under me and lies me on the bed. Kneeling beside me he puts his fingers under the top of my panties and I raise my hips. He slides them off and I suddenly sit up and push him down onto his back. This takes his breath and he doesn't take his eyes off mine. I glide my hands over his chest and down to the waistband of his undershorts and he raises his hips for me. I take them off and he lies there waiting for what I will do next.

Looking at the muscles I recently discovered I decide to begin kissing his body there and work my way up. I place my hands by his hips and hover over him. The second my lips touch his skin he sharply inhales and puts his hands on my shoulders. I move my mouth to his abdomen sliding my forearms along his sides, then a little further up and a little further up leaving a trail of small passion marks until I am at his shoulder where I leave another mark. When I finally kiss his mouth and lie across him Trevor holds me tighter than ever and his kiss is passionate like never before, because I gave him pleasure.

Our intensity reaches a new high and he rolls over to have me beneath him. When he starts kissing my neck I run my fingernails along his spine and he arches his back until my hands are in his hair. During this blur of passion he kisses my breast then before I can comprehend the pleasure, I feel his hair brush my thighs and he moves his arms under them into an embrace then his tongue slides over the place that brings me to a climax. I have been totally aroused for so long that before I expect it I climax, repeatedly. When I stop moaning he lets me go and lies over me to keep me warm. How did he know to hold me still so I could have that experience?

I hold him for a moment then lay my arms on my pillow and he entwines our fingers. I feel my body flush and tell him, "Kiss me." and he does, with passion, because he is still aroused. When he stops to draw in a deep breath I whisper, "Trevor. I want more. Make love with me." And I see his soul.

Trevor caresses my face and kisses me tenderly to calm us down. Our hearts are pounding. He stops kissing me, looks into my eyes and I ever so slightly nod. Trevor raises his hips and his hand goes across my hip bone. When he is in place he moves his hand away and puts it on the bed to hold himself steady as he slowly lowers his body into mine. The moment he is pressed against me I draw in a deep breath and so does he, because there is so much to feel. I hold him tightly and we are perfectly still, but our breathing is as if we are out of breath. When we begin to breathe normally Trevor kisses me then he begins to move at a slow rhythm and we are making love.

Soon my breathing turns to moans and he changes the rhythm then he begins to moan. His sounds make me go higher and higher, and when I reach climax I am able to feel him throbbing inside me and there is so much pleasure it is more than I thought possible. Our bodies are spent and we are lovers.

With his strength slightly regained he begins to move and literally slides down my body because of the perspiration on us until his head is lying just below my shoulder. I place my head to his chest and slide my calf's along the back of his legs. So many thoughts are going through my mind, but one keeps repeating itself and I whisper it to him. "Trevor, I love your body." He lightly laughs and tells me, "And I love yours. — Geneviève ... your body is so warm inside, it is almost hot. And you are *so* soft. It was too much to comprehend."

"If I could put it into words, how you felt, I would, but there aren't any."

"Baby — are you all right?"

"Yes. — I'm fine — just like I knew I would be. Are you?"

"I am now, because I know you are."

"The skin of your back is cool to my touch. I can reach the covers. Would you like me to pull them over us?"

"Please." The moment I do he sighs and says, "I love you."

"I love you too." And I close my eyes.

The next thing I hear is the sound of birds singing and I feel my husband's nude body against mine. Then I am overwhelmed with my thoughts and I slowly inhale. When I exhale he whispers, "Good morning, Geneviève."

"Good morning, Trevor. — I feel as if I just woke up from a dream."

"I did too, but it wasn't. We became lovers last night and then we just drifted away in each other's arms."

"Yes we did."

"All I want to do is hold you."

"Then hold me."

Eventually I feel his shoulder blade shift while we are being still. "Baby, I need to lie on my back." I let go of him and lie on my back too.

"Trevor, does your entire body ache?"

He goes, "Mmm hm. This was unexpected."

Trying to stretch we get tickled and I tell him, "So — this is how the most romantic morning of our lives is going to go." He just shakes his head. "I do not want to interrupt this, but ..."

"Say no more. I'll go downstairs. While I'm there I'll put breakfast in the oven." He lays the covers over me and slowly sits up moving to the edge of the bed. Running his fingers through his hair he scans the area then looks over his shoulder at me. "Geneviève, where did you put my skivvies?"

My eyebrows go up instantly. He turns sideways and sits there smiling, watching me think. I finally go, "Ah." and point to the foot of the bed. He scans it and the length of the bench and looks puzzled, then I see a light bulb go on in his head and he reaches under the covers. And there they are. He puts them on, gives me a wink and leaves.

Then I begin to wonder where my panties are and use my feet to feel around under the covers. When I find them I throw the covers back, put them on and step over our clothes to get to the dresser. I get a black silk camisole out and put it on walking to the bathroom.

After brushing my teeth for five seconds with just water I smooth my hair with my damp hands and when I open the door I see Trevor at the top of the stairs. When he gets closer I put my hand over my mouth and he gives me a look. "I know, I look as if I've been in a hail storm too."

I take my hand down. "We're not going to be able to go for a swim on our honeymoon are we?"

"It's looking that way. We should just cross that off our list." And he finally gives me a proper good morning kiss. "Do you want breakfast in bed?"

"I think we should eat downstairs. We've been in bed for hours."

"And I am a tad stiff from sleeping on my side since we got here. I have been sleeping in a rack on my back for the past twelve years."

"In that case you are sleeping on the right side of the bed tonight and you can be my pillow."

"I like the idea of being your pillow."

"So do I."

With robes on we go downstairs. He hands me my camera and I photograph the dining table and our glasses on the coffee table that has a little cognac left in them. By the time I'm done he has breakfast served and is standing by my chair. We have eaten only two bites of food when he tells me, "I'm going to get the serious part of our conversation started. Your body went through a lot last night and I need to know how you are."

"I am ... sensitive, but I didn't realize it until the aching of my body subsided."

"I understand what you're telling me. — This doesn't even come close to what you're going through, but a few minutes ago when I got the pan out of the oven, my back got my full attention." I whence and Trevor sighs heavily. "Geneviève, you do know I won't be able to make love with you anytime soon without being highly concerned."

"I do. How does this sound? For the next few days we will simply hone our skills of foreplay."

"It sounds good to me."

We eat our breakfast and make decisions for those days. Today we need to call room service for more salmon and a delectable dinner. We're also going to have housekeeping bring fresh linens and clean the kitchen while we sit outside on lounge chairs. Tomorrow we're going for a walk on the beach and around the gardens. On the third day he wants to go the zoo and I am looking forward to driving Blanca again.

After we eat our last bite of scone I get my camera and we go upstairs. I begin taking photographs of our clothing on the floor and he lies down on his back in the middle of the bed length wise watching me. After I finish those I begin walking around the bed taking ones of him and begin talking to him. "That day at the pool when you were about to race, I was watching all three of you standing at the deep end and I found myself thinking that is what the marble statues of the mythological Greek gods around The Parthenon would look if they came to life. I wished I could get a closer look at you and now, here you are."

"I won that race." I watch him think for a moment. "And that night I won your heart."

He gets this look on his face and I softly say, "Don't move." I step up onto the bench and onto the bed. After just looking at him I begin taking photographs again, carefully stepping around my husband then I stand over him taking more. "You can move now."

Trevor turns his head to face me as I photograph his body and he asks, "Who are you?" I lower my camera looking into his eyes and reply, "Your lover." He holds my ankle and gently tugs on it. I lower my body astride his and put my camera on a pillow. He looks at how I'm sitting and his eyebrows go up. "Trevor, I am quite comfortable. Last night I found out the muscles below your belly button are soft when you're lying down."

He nods and puts his hands on my waist under my camisole. "I remember the first time you were astride me and feeling the weight of you." I gather the hem of my camisole in my hands, take it off and lie on him. Then I get his earlobe between my lips and that is that.

Hunger brings us out of our world and he calls room service. While I rinse off he is going to gather our clothes and when I enter the bedroom he gives me a look. "You braided your hair." I respond, "And you are already dressed." He chuckles and says, "Touché. See you soon." I meet him downstairs wearing a new sundress. He showers me with compliments and kisses while we wait on lunch.

After we eat I ask him to get my camera and my cuticle scissors out of my train case. He returns with them and I photograph my tiara and veil which is where we left it on our wedding day. I pick it up and sit on the sofa. "Will you hand me the scissors please?"

"Geneviève, what are you about to do?"

"I'm going to cut my veil from the tiara. It needs to be placed back in its case before housekeeping arrives." He sits next to me visibly upset, as am I. We look at it one last time and I ask him to hold the tiara then carefully remove the veil. I go to the closet where our wedding attire is hanging and drape it across a hanger. When I close the door he dryly tells me, "That was ... traumatizing."

"Yes it was, but it had to be done. The case is upstairs in the dresser."

With it safely tucked away he holds my hands and softly tells me, "You were so beautiful that day."

"You were more handsome than I had ever seen you look, as if that were possible." I touch his bottom lip. "Donne moi ça." And he gives it to me.

Housekeeping arrives and before we go outside I stop us. "Sunglasses, we need sunglasses."

"Good call. That would've been painful." And he gives me a nice kiss then with glasses of Pellegrino and sweet tea in hand he opens the door and we timidly step out onto the veranda. "Geneviève, we've been inside too long." I laugh as he pushes two lounge chairs together. We get situated and breathe in fresh sea air.

Hearing his thoughts I tell him, "I can't stop thinking about last night either."

"It was truly a physical manifestation of how much we love each other. Baby, I honestly didn't think it was possible, because I do love you with all my heart and all my soul." He takes his sunglasses off as do I and we kiss passionately out in the open without a care in the world. I love being married to him.

Housekeeping leaves after being here longer than we thought. We have time to shower together and he orders our dinner. While his back is turned I lay what I want him to wear out on the bed. He turns around smiling and then his face goes straight as he looks at the clothing and walks to me. "I have never seen a solid black cashmere smoking jacket or black sateen undershorts. The shirt even has French cuffs. With the matching trousers and smoking slippers it almost looks like a suit. Geneviève, thank you. It's all beautiful."

"This is a gift I got for you with the intentions of giving it to you when you are my lover." That gets me a kiss. "Frankly, I thought I would be giving it to you on the weekend. I'm so pleased it isn't."

"As am I. — Baby, what day *is* it?"

"Mercredi. Now, turn around please while I get what I intended to wear on our wedding night. I'm going to get ready in that large bathroom and meet you downstairs when the servers are gone."

He chuckles and says, "See you soon."

"See you soon." A few minutes later music composed by Chopin begins to play as I put on a simple white satin nightgown with thin straps that has a white sheer chiffon robe with cap sleeves. The entire robe is trimmed with the satin and there are five satin covered buttons at my bust line. The lower part of the robe will open and look as if it has been caught by a breeze as I descend the staircase.

Trevor hears me, walks to the staircase and his jaw drops. I loosely braided my hair and strands of it are framing my face. He extends his hand and as I slip mine onto his I say, "Bonsoir." He kisses it and says, "Ravissante, tu es ravissante."

"Merci, Mon Mari."

I step down and he puts an arm around me to pull me against him and touches my hair then he caresses my face. This entire time I have my hands on his back feeling him through the cashmere. "I knew you would feel good in this. You look quite dapper."

"I actually feel dapper. — The men in my family wear smoking jackets. I forgot about them."

"Trevor, you became a man wearing uniforms surrounded by men wearing uniforms. I have always seen you as who you are, a highly refined gentlemen who chose a profession as a navigator for the United States Navy."

"My profession is not who I am. — I have been seeing the world through those beautiful brown eyes and now, I finally see me. Thank you." And I get a proper kiss.

Trevor seats me at the candlelit table where two pieces of our wedding cake are thawing and the he pulls a bottle of Cristal from the champagne bucket. "Gérard gave me two bottles of this on our wedding day for our honeymoon. I thought our first dinner together as lovers was an appropriate time to drink one of them." I pull him down to me by his lapel to kiss him then he fills our glasses.

During our dessert he asks, "What are the amenities here?"

"There are steam rooms, a masseuse and masseur ..."

He lifts his hand up. "I cannot recall the last time I had a massage. Would you mind a change in our plans tomorrow?"

"Not in the least if it means we will have a massage after our stroll around the gardens. I'll drive us back here where we will crawl onto the bed and collapse." Trevor laughs and we finish eating our wedding cake.

Our champagne glasses are empty and Trevor stands with his hand extended to me, then he waltzes us around the living room and stops by the sofa. "Tonight we are not going to be passionate; we are going to be tender with each other, like when I began courting you." Trevor takes off his jacket and cufflinks and puts his hand on my abdomen for me to roll up each sleeve with a gleam in his eyes. Next he undoes the buttons on my robe and glides his hands along my shoulders until it falls to the floor. When he sits on the sofa I lie across him then he gently pulls my lower lip into his mouth.

In the morning I wake up cuddling him like I do Christopher, because as we discussed he switched sides of the bed with me, so he could sleep on his back. And for the first time, since Trevor is comfortable, I am awake before him.

Keeping still I listen to his heart beat and from out of the blue I recall Trevor telling me he was going to take Christopher's place and get an idea of a way to wake him up, so I gently begin to squeeze my husband. The instant I am certain he is awake I softly tell him, "Good morning, Christopher." and his laugh is deep. Then suddenly Trevor rolls over, pinning me to the bed and starts playfully biting my neck. While he hovers over me I grab his wrists and look at each one. "Genevieve, what are you doing?" I dryly reply, "Looking for a bag of orange taffy." He has to turn his head so he doesn't literally laugh in my face. "I must say, I am very disappointed there isn't one." Eventually we almost get tangled in my nightgown and that is how we start our day.

When it's time to get ready for lunch Trevor chooses my undergarments and selects a light weight dress that buttons from top to bottom, because it's best not to wear something that goes over my head for my appointment. After he dresses me I look in the mirror and see passion marks on the slope of my neck. "Trevor, perhaps I will skip the massage."

"Baby, the masseuse is a professional and this *is* a honeymooner's destination. I'm sure she has seen women with passion marks several times. Let's choose a shawl to wrap around your neck and shoulders that will cover them while we are out in public and make you look even lovelier than you already do." He makes his point; I leave my camera and happily drive Blanca to the main building. We have a very nice lunch and walk the gardens until it's time for our appointments. When I am called in first he gives me a kiss.

My masseuse is a sweet young lady named Beth and while I am behind the dressing screen she asks me if I have specific areas for her to focus on. When I tell her every muscle on my body she laughs politely and I emerge nude when her back is turned and lie down on my stomach under the sheet. Beth peals the sheet down below my waist and the aches begin to go away.

Next she asks me to lie on my back, hands me a terry cloth strip to cover my breasts and turns around. I am very relaxed as I tell her, "Ready." Beth takes one look at me, gasps and then begins shaking her head. "Mrs. Lyons, I ... I beg your pardon. Please accept my apology."

"There is no need to apologize. Your reaction is completely understandable. We are going to pretend nothing happened." She nods and begins to massage my arms and shoulders.

Next she steps to the end of the massage table and starts raising the sheet. I am drawing a line at her seeing the passion marks on the inside of my thighs and tell her, "Would you please concentrate on just my feet and calf's? They still ache from all the dancing at my wedding reception."

"Yes, ma'am."

Beth does such a good job I forget about the ordeal and relax again. When she finishes I dress, thank her with a large tip and exit the room. Trevor in sitting on a chair in the corridor and he stands up reaching for my hand. "Did you enjoy your massage?"

"Aside from having the most embarrassing moment in my life, yes I did."

"What happened to *you*?"

The way he asked causes me to reply, "What happened to *you*?"

"When I rolled over my masseur asked me if I had fallen in the rock garden." Of course I get tickled and when I quiet down he says, "I'm waiting."

"My masseuse gasped when she looked at my upper body then apologized profusely. I told her there was no need and we would pretend nothing happened. When she went to raise the sheet at my feet I had her stop above my knees."

"The ones inside your thighs."

"Mmm hm."

"I talked you into this. How can I make it up to you?"

"For now you can take to me the cottage, so I can lie down."

Walking through the lobby Trevor veers us into the gift shop, goes straight to the candy counter and tells the girl behind it, "I want a pound of that orange taffy." I chuckle and kiss his cheek.

Back at the cottage we shower off and put on our fresh terry cloth bathrobes. We pile up pillows and sit on the bed then I get a piece of taffy out of the bag I put on the nightstand and pull it apart. I look at each half then give him the small one. I deserve the large piece. He smiles and takes it shaking his head. After enjoying it I say to him, "Tell me your fondest memory."

"This story begins on a Saturday afternoon when my captain and I are running errands and he looks at watch then tells me he wants to drop by a club his wife joined and meet her new friend. I suggested it might not be a good idea and thankfully he ignored me."

Trevor continues telling me the story of us including intimate details he had not shared with me before and when he ends the story he pulls me across him.

When it gets dark in the bedroom he orders dinner and once again I get dressed in the bathroom and meet him downstairs. This time I put on the Grecian peignoir set he put his foot through. Seeing me he says, "I remember that. We moved a boundary that night."

"Yes we did and now we have no boundaries to hinder us." I am dipped and kissed, then after dinner and dancing I blow out the candles and pick up our glasses of champagne. He follows me upstairs with the bottle.

We awaken in the morning to a beautiful day that is perfect for our trip to the zoo. Before we leave Trevor jokingly suggest putting the top up on Blanca, so we can we can make out on the ferry. When I hand him her keys he lights up and opens the passenger door for me.

Since tourist season is over there are not many people at the zoo, but it takes us over an hour to walk half and we get a soft pretzel and cola to share to make it through the other. He marvels at the mountain goats and we watch the elephants for a while, because there is a baby. Next we go to the predator section, which is my favorite part of the zoo. We get lucky and watch two cheetahs chasing each other at full speed. Our luck continues because the tiger has decided to go for a swim while the tigress rests under a shade tree chuffing.

At last we reach the lion's den. There is an entire pride and we stand in silence listening to them. Trevor has his arm around my waist and I place my head on his chest. A breeze blows through the leaves of the trees and the lion roars. With one swift movement Trevor pulls me around and against him. In a deep voice he tells me, "I am a lion. Hear me roar." My body flushes.

"You are not a cub anymore."

"No, I am not." And he looks deep into my eyes.

"Take me to the cottage." He sweeps my legs out from under me and starts walking to the car.

"Trevor, what will people think?"

"Do you really care at this moment?"

"Not at all." And I lay my head on his shoulder.

We are still in the parking lot leaving when I wish we were in my other car. The stick is between us and I cannot get close to him. "Trevor, it is going to take us at least an hour to get to the cottage. If you take a left two blocks down you will see The Posh." Stopped at a red light he says, "Kiss me, Geneviève." And I do.

Trevor drives up to the valet station, turns off her engine and we get out. He hands the valet a tip and tells him, "We don't have a reservation. If we aren't back in a few minutes park her under an awning please." And inside we go.

At the desk he tells the clerk, "I am Commander Lyons and this is my wife. We don't have a reservation, but would like a corner suite for the night."

"The only one available is The Honeymoon Suite on the top floor."

"Perfect. We're on our honeymoon."

Trevor signs the register; the clerk gets the key and motions to a bell hop. "We can see ourselves up and tell housekeeping we do not want to be disturbed." He gives him a tip and takes the key. When Trevor closes the door to our suite foreplay begins, because this time I pin him against a door.

Night falls and we lie on the bed exhausted. This time we devoured each other. "Baby, we should go ahead and order room service. What do you want?"

"Filet de bœuf medium well, sautéed green beans, mashed potatoes, croissant, chocolate mousse and a bottle of Roederer." He orders two of everything.

"I'm going to get us an apple out of the fruit basket I caught a glimpse of in the other room while we wait."

"I'm going to lie here under the sheet."

He comes back holding one red apple. "The others were green." He offers it to me and I tell him, "You take the first bite." After he does Trevor goes, "Oooh, you are going to love this apple." He holds it for me and I bite into the sweetest apple I have ever tasted.

When we have eaten it down to the core he goes to the bathroom and comes back carrying a wet wash cloth he wipes my sticky face with and gives me a kiss. He hangs up our clothes, lies down next to me and has to get right back up. Our dinner has arrived.

We practically inhale our food then Trevor starts a fire, we shower and settle on the bed in our bathrobes. A few minutes later he gets up, goes into the other room and returns with the thick room service menu. "I thought I would read to you in bed." I burst into laughter. "I do have a purpose. We'll know what we want for breakfast when we wake up starving." After he reads to me he turns off all the lights and we begin having pillow talk.

In the morning I wake up disoriented and so does he. "Baby, where are we?"

I see The Brava embroidered on the bathrobes draped across a chair and go, "Oh, we're at The Posh."

"It's all coming back to me now."

"Mmm hm. You seduced me at the zoo."

"Yes I did."

"What time is it?"

He gets his watch. "Time to shake a leg." I sigh and he lifts the receiver to order breakfast and then asks to be connected to the gift shop. Trevor requests a bellhop to bring up two toothbrushes, a comb and everything a man needs to shave with. We are dressed when there is soft knock on the door and he opens it to find room service and a bell hop holding a tote bag. He throws money at them and we go straight to the bathroom, brush our teeth, kiss and eat. Trevor shaves and just as we are about to leave he feels in his pockets. "Do you know what I did with the valet ticket?"

"In our haste you didn't get one. Call the valet station and ask them to bring the white convertible Jaguar up. I'm certain she is the only one."

"True."

We check out and find Blanca has been under the awning since we arrived. We get in, Trevor gives me the keys and folds down the gift bag. "Will you put this in the glove box where it should stay just in case?" I lock it away and we make it back to our cottage several hours later than we thought.

The newspaper is lying at the front door. Trevor picks it up saying, "I'll put this on top of the pile the waiters keep bring in because we don't." After glancing at the front page he drops it and then gives me a kiss. "Geneviève, today is our one week anniversary." I gasp and kiss him. "What would you like to do, Baby?"

"Take a romantic stroll on the beach, shower and put on fresh clothes. Next, make ham sandwiches for our lunch and then see if I can beat you at a game of Spades."

"You know I'm merciless."

"Mmm hm. I'll go get my sun hat."

With the bottle of Louis XIII on the table we begin to play our first real game of cards. He wins the first hand. There is no conversation between us, this is how serious we are. We are neck and neck the entire time. It's down to the wire now and I barely have the lead at 495 points to his 492. I shuffle and he cuts the cards then taps on the deck. That was aggressive.

After sorting our hand of cards Trevor says, "Write down 10 for me." That is a large bet considering there are only 13 points up for grabs.

"I'm writing 5 down for me."

"Planning on setting me back with only 8 tricks huh?"

I merely look at him and then back at my hand. I only have one diamond, the seven, and I am certain he has three of the top four and I have low spades to trump them with, therefore at least two of them will be mine without doubt. He happens to lead with the ace of diamonds and I put my down my seven. Then he lays the king down and I take it with a two of spades. His jaw drops. I just set him back one which means I will be the victor.

"Your downfall was tapping on that deck."

"I jinxed myself."

"Yes you did."

"To the victor go the spoils."

Nodding I stand up and go to his end of the table and push it away from him. He is expecting me to sit on his lap sideways, so he moves his legs together. Instead I throw my left leg over them and sit across his lap then put my hands on his shoulders. Trevor locks his eyes on mine as he puts his hands on my thighs. "This is a far more comfortable way to sit on your lap. I'm not twisting at the waist. And since you are my husband I can sit like this whenever I want."

"Once again you catch me off guard." He gives me a kiss. "What spoils do you desire?"

"For you to put on your tuxedo and I am going to wear one of the evening gowns in my bridal trousseau. Then I want you to escort me to the fine dining room where we will eat and drink the most luxurious things know to man." He lifts me by waist onto my feet and we go upstairs.

The next morning I wake up Trevor by shaking him. "What happened to good morning?"

"It's Sunday. Our wedding announcement is in the paper. I'll see you down stairs."

With my hair smoothed I slip on my Kimono and breeze passed Trevor out onto the veranda. He follows me to the dining table and we start pulling sections. "The wedding announcements are in the social section."

"Geneviève, I have it and we are on the first page," he lays it on the table, "along with the Harding's. How did they get that?"

"The lady that is the editor of this section evidently called Mother, who called Kyle. Look at us entering our reception. You were so handsome. I didn't think we would see a photograph of us until we went to see Mr. Blackwell." Trevor looks at me smiling and I have him read the article aloud that has a headline, The First Wedding Of The Season.

When he stops reading he starts turning pages looking for the announcement and eventually says, "There she is, the woman I married. — This is a beautiful photograph of you." We kiss for several minutes then he reads it to me.

After we have eaten a light breakfast from room service Trevor gets the page with our wedding announcement and sits on the sofa. "We need another copy of this. I want to carry one in my wallet."

I take the paper from him, lay it down on the coffee table and sit across his lap. "You are such a romantic man. I love you." I begin kissing his face and pull on his bathrobe to expose his neck.

We become passionate and I untie his robe. "Geneviève, I'm not wearing anything under this."

"I'm not wearing anything under mine and am about to catch you off guard. I know we can make love with me here."

"Baby, perhaps it's a little too early for us to ... advance to another place of the unknown."

"Trevor, I understand what your thinking, but I've given this some thought and it occurred to me if anything goes wrong I can merely be still. I wouldn't be pinned between you and the bed and have to use our code word."

"I do you have you pinned. — I'm glad that never entered my mind."

"So am I." I tenderly kiss him. "Trevor, listen to me. I want your arms around me when we make love and this is a way for that to be possible sooner. Do you want to make love with me here?"

"Yes."

Trevor lifts me to my feet and I open his robe then help him get his arms out of the sleeves. He sits up and as my kimono falls to the floor he kisses my lower abdomen until my legs are weak. "I can't stand up much longer and I want to feel the warmth of your body." When I am astride him I whisper, "Kiss me like you did when we were on *our* sofa like this." We get lost in our passion and begin making love. Because I know our rhythm our moans soon turn to trying to catch our breath as he holds me close.

"Geneviève."

"I'm listening."

"Do you want me to do anything?"

"Cover us with the blanket." He pulls it off the sofa and covers us up.

Eventually my legs begin to ache. "Trevor, tell me you can lie us down without letting me go."

"I can do that." And he does.

Day turns into night and night turns into day as time passes. Then one night I am nestled on the soft chair my husband becomes, listening to his voice as he reads his book to me and then he exclaims, "The End?" I sit up and look at him. "I've been reading a tragic love story to you all this time?" He closes it and lays it on the nightstand. "Geneviève, did you read this when you were in your teens?"

"I think I'll take the Fifth Amendment." Trevor tackles me down onto the bed. "In my defense you did start reading it on your own."

"Yes I did. I need cheering up." So, I start playfully biting his neck. "That feels kind of a nice."

"I know."

His eyes dance. "I'm cheered."

"Trevor, tomorrow will be our two week anniversary. What do you want to do?"

"Chose the next book I read to you." I laugh lightly as he gets still and I can see him thinking. "I know what I want to do. I want to spend the last week of our honeymoon living in our house."

"When are we checking out?"

"How does after lunch sound?"

"Splendid. Turn off the light." And he finds me in the dark.

A few hours later he wakes me up whispering, "Good morning, Mrs. Lyons."

"Good morning, Mr. Lyons."

"You've never called me that."

"I was being romantic."

"I like hearing you call me that. You've never called me by a pet name."

"Because I love to say Trevor."

"Now I know why I feel the urge to kiss you when you say it sometimes." He sighs. "Had we not made love last night this morning would go differently."

"Will you make love with me tonight, in our bed in our bedroom?"

"Yes. Yes I will."

After breakfast I take photographs of the shower and our clothing on the bench, then I reach the end of another roll of film. As I wind it up I see Trevor holding a film canister and his hand is on the closet doorknob. He opens it and tells me. "I do enjoy the little things." And we step inside.

With that done I spot the phone. "Trevor, I should call my parents and tell them we're coming home early."

"That's a good idea."

I sit on the edge of the bed while the phone rings and my mother answers, "Delcroix residence."

"Mother."

"Oh, Sweetheart, it is so good to hear your voice."

"It is good to hear yours."

"Gérard, it's our daughter." And I start to puddle.

Two seconds later he picks up the phone in the study. "Sweetheart?"

"Hello, Father."

"We have missed you and your husband."

"We missed you both too." For some reason my lips begin to quiver. Trevor motions for the receiver and I happily hand it to him.

"My wife was about to tear up; therefore I'm going to tell you the good news. We're checking out today and going to our house this afternoon." He listens then replies, "We will see you then." Trevor hangs up and puts his arms around me. "Your father suggested seeing them tomorrow for an apéritif then going to your grandparents for the Sunday dinner. Are you all right now?"

"Yes. Thank you for stepping in." He gives me a kiss and rocks me.

We pack while I photograph things and him. When we are almost finished he orders us lobster and champagne for our long overdue lunch and our conversation is about what we should do at our house today. It keeps me from being sad at the thought of leaving.

The last thing we get is our cakes and when we are about to get in Blanca I hand him her key. He looks a little surprised as he takes it. When he pulls up to the lobby I stay with her and Trevor says, "I shan't be long." and gives me a kiss.

Upon his return he looks odd as he gets in. "What do I not know?"

"It's a bit of a story." He starts her engine and begins talking.

"I walked up to the hotel clerk, told him my name and I wanted to check out. He excused himself and returned following the manager who asked me if there is a problem. I told him there wasn't and since the reason we are checking out early is personal I simply told him duty called and he was quite relieved."

"That was a good answer. Well done."

"Thank you. Here's the interesting part. The hotel picked up our bill."

"Oh my."

"Yep, it was out of gratitude for our assistance with their unruly guest."

"That was a discreet way to say that."

"I thought so too. By the way, he sent his regards."

"Trevor, thank goodness we checked out early. We spared no expense."

"That was what I thought as he tucked the bill into a folder."

After we board the ferry I get out to take one last snapshot of the hotel and Trevor stands by my side. Then we see Louise and I quietly wave. "Oh, the lift boat is gone."

"You noticed that too."

"The way you said that was very matter of fact. You're going to go on full duty after our honeymoon aren't you?"

"More than likely. It's a good thing we are going home early. We would have been exhausted every night, on the job all day and sort of moving in at night."

"Our things *are* scattered. Moving the contents of my bedroom would have been a daunting task."

"Now, we can take our time and enjoy the rest of our honeymoon. I love you, Baby."

"I love you too, Trevor."

Riding down the road looking at him I remember his words, 'I will be a good husband.' and he is. All I can think is how kind and gentle he was and how he waited patiently for me to tell him I want to become lovers. Now that we are, I realize how venerable I really was and the risk of feeling pain instead of pleasure was higher than I thought and how much it mattered that he knew everything he could about my anatomy and I knew all I could about his. It really is important to talk about these things before, not after. He would have been distraught had he caused me the slightest twinge. We learned together how to walk, then how to run and it was perfect. I would not change a thing.

While I was lost in thought Trevor pulled into a vacant parking lot. "You haven't taken your eyes off me. Is there something you want to tell me?"

"I need to hold you."

"You said need."

Trevor turns off the car, opens his door and walks around to open mine. I get out straight into his arms and hold him for the longest time letting him know how much I love him and how much I need him. When I begin to let him go he looks at me and I see his love.

When we drive through the gates I put my hand on his as he shifts down and parks Blanca in the garage. Trevor gives me a kiss. "We're home."

CHAPTER TWELVE

Going up the outside steps I think about how I have dreamed of this day when we are here as husband and wife and I cannot wait to go inside, because this is where our life together truly begins. When we enter the solarium he has a twinkle in eyes as he opens the doors to our home. Trevor dramatically sweeps me off my feet then carries me though the threshold. We kiss tenderly and he softly asks, "What next, Geneviève?"

"In movies the groom carries his bride to their bedroom, but I bet they don't have wedding and grooms' cake thawing in their garage." And his laugh is deep.

"I'm going to carry you to the sofa where we are going to make out a little while and then we'll unpack Blanca, starting with the cakes."

When we get up I notice fresh flowers are in our vases and what seems to be a painting wrapped in thick brown packaging paper on the mantle of the fireplace and motion to it. He tells me, "I'll run down and get the cakes. Wait here."

Staring at it I wonder who could have given us a painting that would cause my parents to venture into our home and set it on such a prominent place. When it occurs to me I gasp, put my hands on my face and become motionless. Trevor enters the living room. "I see you realized who that's from while I was gone."

"What has she done?"

"Let's get it down and find out."

He lays it on the dining table and I untie the twine. We carefully fold back the paper to reveal what we have. "Joanna painted us sitting on your bench at night."

"Trevor, we're wearing the clothes we had on the night you proposed."

"She worked from photographs and captured this moment for us."

"This is ... beyond words."

"Do you want to go thank her tomorrow?"

"You spoil me so."

"I'm going to put this back on the mantle then before we get serious about unpacking I'm going to pour a Pellegrino and a glass of iced tea for us, because our kitchen is stocked and there are several catering boxes from the club."

"Your mother could replace the base commander. She certainly knows how to mobilize a unit in an efficient and timely manner."

"I love it when you use Navy speak." And he gets a glint in those blue eyes.

"All right, Mrs. Lyons." He motions to the dumbwaiter. "Man your post."

"Aye, aye, sir." And the fun begins.

In time I hear him ascending the stairs and he walks in with the garment bags for my gown and his uniform. "I hope I get to see you in a blue uniform soon."

"You will. I'm Williams' best man." My face lights up. "When is that?"

"The date escapes me. You wrote in on the calendar in the mudroom."

"I also wrote it on mine. Where did I pack that?"

"You didn't tell me." He chuckles and says, "We should buy one that's ours."

"It's late September."

"The commissary always has calendars. In fact we need to get you an ID. You're my wife and you can start shopping there."

"The place where you found my Strawberry Fluff. When can we go?"

Laughing he replies, "Does after we see Joanna and Mitch sound good?"

"Yes it does. What do you think about going to Sam's for lunch before we see them? I am craving a chocolate milkshake."

"Now I am."

"That's a yes." I hug him and pick up my camera bag.

As I get out my camera and he asks, "Where do you want to put this?"

"I'll take it to my darkroom, even though it's empty."

He follows me saying, "We'll go to Blackwell's tomorrow and get the latest equipment to fill it with." Before he opens the door I kiss my husband and then enter the room. I stop so unexpectedly Trevor runs into me.

"Father. — My father."

I slowly go inside and stand in the middle of my new darkroom that has already been filled with everything I need and set up exactly like my other one. I begin touching each item and when I'm at the enlarger I hear my camera snap. Trevor has the sweetest smile when I look at him. The photo essay of our honeymoon continues. When I'm through soaking it in I go straight into his arms. With my wits gathered I get the safelight from the hotel and we go to our bedroom where he puts it in one of our bedside lamps. We stand together looking at our incredible bedroom then out of the blue Trevor tells me, "I'm famished."

"That makes two of us."

"Let's go find out what your mother had put in those catering boxes."

While dinner heats in the oven we set the table and an everyday occurrence becomes special. For the first time we are getting out our things; table linens, the china, stemware and flatware we chose along with the vase that matches the candlesticks from Joanna and Mitch for another romantic candlelit dinner. We go around the house selecting flowers from all the floral arrangements and he sets it on the table. Trevor lights the candles and opens a nice bottle of wine while I serve the food. Seated we raise our glasses for a toast and he says, "To living our lives as one." Our glasses sing when they touch and we take pleasure in each and every second of every minute.

When the candles are burned down he asks, "Are you ready to watch me shave and shower while I watch you shave those long beautiful legs?"

"Yes I am, but I do wish I my little bench was here."

"Would you like me to sneak over and get it?"

"It's sweet of you to offer. I can survive one more night without it."

"When I spotted it at the end of your bathtub I wondered why it was there. Then the first time we really showered together I understood. I thought shaving just my face every day was bothersome until I watched you. You shave two thirds of your body. And men wonder why it takes their wives so long to get ready to go somewhere. Obviously they've never bathed with them." He steps up to me and whispers, "They have no idea what they're missing."

With a fire roaring in our fireplace Trevor gets my kimono and a pair of undershorts then leads me holding my hand into the bathroom. "Geneviève, you have no idea how much I have looked forward to this. In fact while we were at the hotel I had a dream about it."

"Trevor, it's time for you to take the lead and you should begin by making your dream come true." The kiss I get takes my breath away. Then I find out while we are bathing he dreamed of bring me to a climax with his touch in the shower.

He braids my hair while pausing to kiss the slope of my neck. His mouth, his mouth, it keeps putting me in a trance. In a blur of pleasure I find myself being placed on our bed and the moment I sink into it I find the will to speak. "Trevor. — Trevor."

"I'm listening, Baby."

"I just got distracted."

"Now?"

"Mmm hm. You have to lie down on our bed to understand."

"This must be good."

"You have no idea."

Trevor rolls over and sinks into the bed just like I did. "Our bed is luxurious. Baby, the thick down comforter underneath these soft sheets feels incredible. I see our future. We're running around trying not to be late for work because we stayed in our bed far too long. I'm so glad we have a week to indulge ourselves. Foreplay is about to reach a new height." And I am beneath him.

In the morning he wakes me up rubbing my back and I go, "Mmmm. Trevor, make love with me." I roll over to look at him and see he's concerned. "We've been lovers longer than you realize. The waiting is over." He slightly nods and kisses me.

We linger in foreplay and maybe two hours later we are left with no choice, we have to get up. The need for sustenance is overtaking us. In the kitchen Trevor gets the eggs to scramble and I find out our toaster works. I pick up the coffee press then set it down. "Cola's?" He chuckles and gets them then holds his bottle up. "To cooking our first breakfast together as husband and wife." We click them together laughing and I slide an arm around his waist as he scrambles the eggs.

When Théo elongated the house he built a dressing room for Trevor between our bedroom and mine. Even though it is supposed to be my private area, I share it with Trevor. I do not like being apart from him. After we get dressed he focuses on me. "You're lovely. Only you could find a way to look feminine in gray flannel trousers." I'm wearing a petal pink turtleneck and strands of pearls.

"Thank you. I'm lucky it's September and I can wear this to cover my neck. I have no idea what I am wearing to dinner."

"We'll figure it out. I get off easy in a shirt and tie."

"You're wearing a suit?"

"It's our honeymoon."

"And you are Mr. Lyons." He kisses me and we are off to Sam's.

The diner is packed, so we sit at the counter. We even have to wait on the waitress whose name is Marge and she has been here the longest. While waiting Trevor asks me, "Do you want to share a milkshake?" Looking at him I think how romantic, but I want my own and before I could muster a yes he gets tickled. "I was joking you. I wanted to see your reaction and you did not disappoint." As he kisses my cheek Marge sets two chocolate milkshakes in front of us. "These are compliments of Sam. You order will be up shortly." I pick up mine and we wave at a very busy man. Not until the inside of my mouth is almost frozen do I sit mine down and he raises an eyebrow at me.

"You're one to talk, he who carries butterscotch discs in his pockets and rarely passes a candy shoppe."

"Touché. It all began when I noticed your candy colored toenails and it shows no sign of stopping." As we laugh Marge serves our cheeseburger and fries.

On the way to the base we decide it's good to be driving Blanca, because we can drive around without anyone realizing it's us. When Trevor parks by the curb and I see their house I tell him, "We have been so happy alone together I didn't realize I missed my family and our friends."

"Neither did I. Would you like to sit here a minute?"

"I actually would, but they might have heard us drive up. The second Joanna sees us she will be out that door."

"I have a visual. Shall we?" And we get out.

Trevor knocks and opens the door. Their backs are too us washing dishes and Joanna is handing Mitch a dish to dry as she glances over her shoulder. Apparently she was expecting to see Emily and William, because she almost drops it. "Mitch, it's our Newlyweds." I have never been greeted so enthusiastically. Even Trevor is taken by surprise by how quickly she reaches us drying her hands and throwing the towel on the dining table.

She goes for me first. "Darling, oh My Darling." And she proceeds to kiss my cheeks repeatedly then hugs me tightly. Mitch shakes Trevor's hand and gives him a real hug, not the manly one. They switch and Joanna gets Trevor while Mitch just holds me with a slight rocking motion. Oh no, emotions. Then Joanna says, "We are drinking Pellegrino's and it made us miss you two. I cannot believe you cut your honeymoon short." Trevor replies, "We didn't, we decided to spend the last week of it in our home and spotted the painting on our mantle. We couldn't wait eight days to thank you for it, so here we are." I am nodding while Mitch helps her take off her apron.

"We are so pleased you like it. Mitch and I had some fun working on it. He was my model."

"Joanna, did you just call me a model?" Trevor cannot stop a light chuckle.

"Pardon me, Mitch. He agreed to by my artists' subject. — Please take a seat. Would you both care for a Pellegrino?" We nod and sit on the love seat. Mitch is speaking to Trevor and I begin to study the features of his face. He has the clearest green eyes that compliment his dark blonde hair and his best feature is a strong squared jaw that reminds me of Trevor's.

Joanna appears with our water and sits next to Mitch. "My dear husband dressed as close to what Trevor was wearing the night he proposed and very late one night we went there so I could take photographs from the sidewalk. I wanted the proportion to be perfect. The rest is from imagination."

Trevor says, "You imagination was spot-on. It looks like you were there."

"That is by far the best compliment I have ever received." She looks at my turtleneck. "Geneviève, there is a painting technique I want to share with you. Gentleman, excuse us." She holds on to my arm and leads me into the bathroom, not her studio. "Darling, I am about to share something you will find invaluable." And she gets a bottle of leg makeup out. "The only good thing to come from war rationing is this. It is opaque and is available in any skin tone. I have been and am at present, in your shoes."

She unbuttons the top of her dress, pulls it away from her neck and puts a towel over it. Then she wets a washcloth and puts a small amount of makeup remover on it, rubs a small spot of her neck and I find myself looking at a passion mark. While she is using soap and water to clean the area she says, "Years ago I was painting with skin tones and I had an idea to cover these with liquid makeup. It took several coats." Joanna dampens a little natural sponge, puts the makeup on it and dabs it onto her neck. Next she turns it over and blends the edges. "And it is gone. Get a bottle for him too, just in case. Now neither you nor Trevor will ever have to be concerned with these again. Oh and Mitch told me this taste terrible."

I laugh and the moment she is buttoned up I give her a big hug. "You just changed our lives. Thank you ever so much."

"Consider it a wedding gift."

"I've been wearing shawls in public. Getting married in September worked out in our favor."

"I do love the pink with all those pearls. Let's join our husbands, shall we?"

Joanna and Mitch tell us how much they enjoyed getting Blanca. Trevor tells them about Gypsy and we agree to pick up our lives again on Monday next by having lunch here. We finish our Pellegrino's and they follow us outside to get another look at Blanca, then we are off to the commissary.

Inside Trevor shows our wedding certificate to this nice man and he fills out a temporary ID card for me. Trevor puts it in his wallet, picks up a shopping basket and I almost give him a kiss. "You can do that at the first red light we stop at. Where do you want to go?"

"This place is huge. I have no idea."

"We'll just walk the aisles then and you can get familiar with it."

Maybe ten minutes pass and I tell him, "This is a department store, a market, and a drug store. A person could make a home from here."

"That was how these got started. One day you're in barracks or the BOQ and the next you have a wife and housing with nothing except a foot locker to put in it. These are always open and everything here is considered supplies and sold at wholesale to us. The Navy takes care of its own."

Next we enter the drug store section. "Geneviève, is there anything in our medicine cabinet?" I begin to think. "That is a no." He gets aspirin, some first aid supplies and shakes his head. "You keep shopping. I'm trading this basket for a cart." When he returns I put the things I gathered in the cart and we move on.

"Oh good, the ladies section, I need leg makeup."

"Wait a minute. The woman I know would risk wearing trousers to work before putting that on. What do I not know?"

"I'm getting it to cover passion marks with. Joanna knew why I was wearing this turtleneck and as luck would have it she has one on her neck. She removed the makeup and showed me how it's done. Now, we don't have to worry about them ever again. Joanna said to consider it a wedding gift."

"I really appreciate this, but I am not thanking her." I burst into laughter. I love his British sense of humor.

I get the shade I need and tell him, "Undo your top button."

"I feel as if I just entered another dimension that is not of this world."

Laughing I pick up a bottle that will hopefully match his skin tone, scan the aisle and quickly hold it up. "Done. Also, Joanna mentioned this taste terrible."

Trevor sighs heavily as he buttons his polo. "I shook it off when I realized she felt as if they were on the French Riviera because she had been sunbathing topless on Willow's deck with Mitch. Obviously he told her the taste of this is terrible. — You know, he *is* my captain and she is his wife. I am *not* supposed to know this much about their private lives."

"Umm ... where's the candy section?" And I get his deep laugh as he leads the way. "Oh look, the candy is in little pre-priced bags, how convenient." I toss bags of butterscotch disc, jelly beans, cherry licorice, chocolates filled with strawberry cream and a large bag of assorted gumdrops in the cart. "What else?"

"A bag of those caramels and the toasted coconut haystacks in dark chocolate."

"Ooo ... good choices. What do you want for now?"

"An orange gumdrop."

While we eat and do a little marketing he begins talking to me. "I used to come in here sometimes and would imagine what it would be like having my wife by my side. This is not remotely close to anything I ever imagined. It's much better."

"Where is you favorite place to daydream?"

"In home furnishings."

"Our study is empty."

"There are no tufted leather pieces or a desk to match the hand crafted wood."

"There has to be things to go on a desk." He smiles and turns the cart around. After an extensive search he finds a banker's desk lamp that is perfection and while we check out I tell him, "This was fun. When are we coming back?"

"Probably soon and yes it was fun." He whispers, "I love you."

After pouncing on him when the garage door closes and we are getting out of the car he tells me, "Mrs. Lyons, go man your post." With enthusiasm I say, "Aye, aye, sir." And run like a giddy little girl into the kitchen. Each time he sends it up it feels like I'm getting presents. When I hear him ascending the stairs I almost pout.

The kitchen counters are covered and we slowly go all over the house putting everything away. We save the desk lamp for last and when it is out of the box and has a bulb in it we head to our study. He pushes the door open, I take one step, stop unexpectedly again and Trevor runs into me again. Exasperated he says, "Baby, I almost hit you with the lamp. What's in *this* room?"

"Wedding gifts." I go in so he can see why I stopped in mid-step.

"There are so many. It didn't look like this many at the reception."

"Trevor, these are going to take an entire day to open and write the list for the calligrapher to write the thank you notes by."

"We are on our honeymoon. These will still be here next week." He sets the lamp on the floor and holds my hand as he goes into the hallway and closes the door. "It's time for me to select your dinner dress and let you practice covering those passion marks."

The only clothing I have here is from my trousseau. Fortunately I didn't wear many of them, therefore he selects my dress in less than thirty seconds and we go to our bathroom. On the second try I have mastered covering the passion marks, he shaves and we begin to get dressed. Now that I get to dress him I really enjoy doing this and I am truly grateful Mother had me learn how to tie a Windsor knot in a neck tie. I love being close to his face and the look on it as he watches me.

Halfway to my parent's house I slow us down. "Geneviève?"

"It feels like I haven't been here in ages. And just hearing their voices I became emotional. I would like to walk in with a smile on my face."

"Would you like a piece of butterscotch?" He puts his hand in his pocket and I hear the wrapper.

We enter the house laughing and the welcoming of the Newlyweds begins, because Théo and Rachel are in the foyer. He exclaims, "Gené." and throws his arms around me. "I missed you too, Théo." While I get my kiss from him, Rachel kisses Trevor's cheeks then it becomes a little hectic when my parents join us.

A toast is made and instead of sitting, we all stand together in front of the crackling fire as we tell them our reactions when we received our wedding gifts from each other and Father gets praised for putting the tag for Gypsy in my new convertible. Then all too soon we hear the clock strike the half-hour.

When we are near the doors to my grandparent's house they open and we get a wonderful surprise, Claudette. "Welcome home, Commander, Mrs. Lyons." I respond, "Thank you Mrs. Côté." As she blushes I know something, her marriage has been consummated and I am happy for them.

My grandparents welcome us with open arms and thank us for seeing them during our honeymoon. When we are seated in the candle lit dining room there is another surprise, Joseph enters with a tray. He is serving us out of kindness. Then I recall he was going to receive the offer to be our next vigneron and look at Théo. He smiles and gives me a slight nod. Joseph accepted. Trevor looks at me smiling and I am so taken by him I forget we're not alone and tenderly kiss him. When it occurs to me what I did he reaches for my hand and we notice all heads are lowered and smiles are on every face.

I make a noise with my fork on a plate to let them know they may look up and my grandfather raise his glass of wine. "To the love that fills each and every one of our hearts." And we all echo him.

Sitting in pairs in the drawing room sipping Louis XIII my brother announces he and Rachel are going to finish their cognac in the solarium at the house and gaze at the stars. Trevor and I instantly look at each. We have not spent time in ours and we follow them out.

During the walk out Trevor informs them we are going to my room for him to choose a book to read to me. We say our good nights in the foyer and go up. It feels strange to be in my bedroom, because it already seems like an old familiar place to me. Once I get passed that I ask, "Trevor, you have books in our house. Why are we here?"

"I'm looking for something." Moments later he pulls a book from the shelf and shows it to me. He is holding *Alice's Adventures in Wonderland*. "When I was home for summer and in New Haven I would go to Aunt Meredith's bookstore to help stock the shelves and work the register. I was 11 years old and a girl close to my age walked in. Of course my aunt called her by name and led her to the row of children's books. I followed them at a distance and stayed hidden."

Trevor leads me over to the bench and we sit down. "She hands her a book and her voice changed. As best as I can recall she said, 'This story will fill your imagination with the most unusual things. It's about a girl named Alice and while she was outside one day she spotted a white rabbit that was walking like a person, wearing a coat and looking at a pocket watch talking to himself and then he disappears into his rabbit hole. Alice goes to it and falls in. She falls and she falls and finally lands in a place with creatures such as a talking caterpillar and a floating cat that could vanish into thin air.' I wanted to read it, but I was a boy and didn't want to be caught reading a book for girls. I'm older now and I don't care. This is what I want to read to you."

"And so you shall."

Nestled in our bed resting on my soft chair Trevor becomes, he begins to read me a bedtime story and I am hearing it being read with a British accent, just like the little girls heard as the author told them this story that he made up while they were being rowed in a boat down the River Thames.

"Geneviève."

"Mmm hm."

"You're drifting into sleep."

"The day must be catching up with me."

"And you are not getting the deep sleep you are used to by sleeping on me. Tonight you are going to sleep on the right side of the bed like you're used to."

He puts a pillow down and moves me over to it and soon the light is off and I am being snuggled under the covers by the man I love dearly.

In the middle of the night I wake up, because Trevor rolls over onto his back and his arm slides across me. Wanting to be near him I roll over, rest my head on his shoulder and place my hand on his chest. Before I am still his hand is holding mine and he softly tells me, "I was having the nicest dream. We were aboard Gypsy sailing along the coast."

"Let's make it come true."

"When?"

"There is no better time than the present. We can set sail at daybreak and spend the rest of our honeymoon at sea."

"I'm turning on the safelight. I want to see your face." He caresses it and kisses me tenderly. "I can't believe we're doing this."

"Do you not just love spur of the moment ideas?"

"Indeed I do. And I love you too."

"And I love you. Now shake a leg, Sailor." That statement gets me pinned and nibbled on.

After calling the marina, packing from three places, raiding two kitchens and leaving a note for my parents telling them our course, we leave for the marina. We gather everything we need from Willow and because we did shake a leg we are on our way out to sea just before daybreak.

Trevor has had us at full sail for about an hour when we catch a wind that makes me feel like I'm flying. He raises his voice for me to hear him over the wind. "Geneviève, my blood is coursing through my veins. It's been a long time since I've been aboard a vessel this size. I forgot how fast they can go. It's incredible. *This* is flying. And this is why I am a Sailor." She is cutting through the water and the spray is covering us. Our jackets keep us from being soaked by the sea that calls out to us, "Come to me, come to me." and we do.

When Gypsy finally slows down Trevor lowers her sails, drops anchor and we go below to make lunch. Still basking in the richness of our experience together we make love instead. Hunger eventually brings us to our senses and we feast on cold chicken and pasta, then we dress and go up for whatever will happen next.

Trevor is following me across the deck and I hear the familiar sound of a cellophane wrapper. I stop of course and turn around. He is smiling and has a piece of butterscotch between his fingers. "Even though we skipped dessert I know you want something sweet. Kiss me and I will give this to you." When I step toward him he puts it in his mouth. I kiss him and find out just how creative he is.

Before I start the engine Trevor picks up his gloves to raise the sails and asks, "That lighthouse on the cliff where you can see the rocks underwater — Point Vicente. Is that up ahead?"

"Yes. Why are you asking?"

"I'd like to climb it and see the view. We could drop anchor, put the life raft in the water and I could row us ashore. You could get a postcard worthy photograph of Gypsy from the cliff."

"You can stop talking, you had me at the thought of watching you row."

He puts down his gloves and with me standing between his arms he starts her engine. We have plenty of time to do something else on a whim, because while we packed at our house I told Trevor about the annual trip to Santa Barbara to celebrate Mother's birthday. My family takes two days to sail there. On the first one we drop anchor to watch the sunset then make dinner and settle in talking over cognac. In the morning we get up before the sun rises and sail into the harbor at sunset. We stay at the ranch for three days and then take two days to sail back. Trevor and I decide to visit the ranch just one day. After all it is our honeymoon.

When the light house is in sight he tells me, "I'll be your eyes and talk you in as close to shore as we can get." And he goes to the bow. Now I am going to find out just how good a navigator he is. When he has me drop anchor I go stand by the lifeline and get a good look at where Gypsy is and I'm impressed to say the least.

Trevor and I go below for my picnic blanket and a tote bag to put bottles of Pellegrino and fruit in, because we are about to embark on a bit of a hike and I release some of the desire for him he stirred by pinning him to our stateroom door. For a change he has to change shirts.

While he rows to shore I take several photographs. Most of them are close ups of him and his arms flexing with each stroke of the oars. Being able to admire his body without restraint is changing the way I photograph him. I cannot wait to get in my new darkroom. When he pulls the oars in I realize we are about to go ashore and I put my camera in the bag to keep it from getting wet.

Trevor holds my hand as we climb Toveemo Trail up the cliff. At the top we marvel at the view and I photograph Gypsy. "Geneviève, she is magnificent. I can't believe you gave her to me. I love our life together. I had high expectations, but they are being exceeded every hour of every day." We kiss passionately and the driver of a car on the road blows their horn at us. That ends our moment with laughter and we walk to the lighthouse.

The view from the top of it is beyond words. My arms get tired from holding the camera and I hand it to Trevor. He takes a few snapshots, puts in the bag and we soak it in. Next we go down to the lawn and spread out the blanket. Our first picnic at a lighthouse. We eat and lie down to rest a little before making our way back. While we rest Trevor rolls onto his side and takes off my sunglasses. "What are you doing?"

"Looking for the gypsy in you."

"You are a rascal."

"A rascal that wants a kiss."

"Just don't pin me to the blanket."

After a serious display of affection in public the sound of a high pitched woman's voice catches our attention. "Jim, why haven't you ever kissed me like that?" He responds, "I didn't know you wanted me to yet? Do you want to go back to my car?" They turn around and when they pass by Trevor grabs my camera and takes a snapshot of their backs. He looks at me with eyes dancing and

I tell him, "All right you rascal. I think it's time for us to be on our way." He gives me a kiss and springs to his feet.

Aboard Gypsy we decide to leave the sails down and save our strength for tomorrow. He starts her engine and takes us 5 nautical miles northwest toward Malibu far away from artificial light and another human being to drop anchor. After we watch the sunset all I want is to shower. This is when we notice sailboats have a flaw. Only one person can shower at a time. What a huge disappointment. We shower separately and move on to cooking our first meal in the galley.

During dinner Trevor slides his hand over the table. "She is unusually fast."

"That's because like all great ladies she has a secret."

"And what might that be?"

"She doesn't weight as much as she used to."

He puts down his fork and sits back. "You have my undivided attention."

"It is my guess you haven't been in a sailboat race since your days at Annapolis and I thought one day it might cross your mind to enter the club's race, which by the way is no longer a regatta. The club changed it to only one race held on Saturday. Anyway, for the purpose of racing I had her lightened by having several things done. Some are not really noticeable."

"Such as?"

"Having the cabinet maker's plane a quarter inch off the back off all the doors and instead of handles I had the small knobs put on. Ounces add up to pounds."

"Yes they do."

"Oh, this one will make your jaw drop. Switching to the refrigerator from the marble lined icebox took off almost 200 pounds. And at least 60 more came off because there is cot metal instead of wood under the mattress in our stateroom."

"That explains why it was so comfortable. Due to the circumstance we were on it this afternoon, I thought I was imaging things."

"I knew, but it was the first time I was on it too. The difference was a surprise."

"I took us off course. Where were you headed?"

"Down a list that has left my head. Umm ... what matters is this, when the job was done my father estimated she was well over a thousand pounds lighter. Théo didn't say a word, but I could tell he was chomping at the bit. He does know the race course like the back of his hand."

"In the photographs there was a four man crew."

"That hasn't changed. And yes I think Gypsy could win this year with the crew she would have. You will have six weekends together and my father will happily take the place of William and Théo while they're gone on their honeymoons."

"You're willing to give up the Saturday afternoons we have together for that many weekends."

"Of course I am, but I have an ulterior motive. I want to watch you race. And I have no doubt you will make up for us being apart at night. Also, I plan to be aboard Willow observing from a distance with my own crew."

"I no longer want to go on deck and lie underneath a canopy of stars. I want to lie underneath you."

With a lilt in my voice I respond, "What stars?"

The gentle rocking of Gypsy wakes us up. After snuggling in our comfortable bed we rise and start the day. And what a beautiful day it is. The only stop we make is for lunch. Trevor wants to see the view when we approach Santa Barbara in daylight.

The Santa Enez Mountains are in sight and I take the wheel. My husband is so awestruck by the view I take us in. When Gypsy is settled Trevor wants to walk the harbor to make sure Gypsy is the prettiest sloop here. This time we take a right and Morning Glory is up ahead. He says, "I didn't realize she was so close."

"That is why we met the Harding's. Next to her is Stargazer. She looks much nicer than the photo in the paper depicted."

"I agree. I wish we could go aboard. She's ... posh."

While Trevor laughs we hear a deep voice say, "Ahoy to the shore." We look up and see Thomas and Adeline. Trevor replies, "Ahoy to the boat." Thomas asks, "Would you like to join us for something refreshing to drink?" Adeline adds, "Feel free to decline. We are interrupting a couple on their honeymoon." Trevor's face is lit up, so I respond, "Yes we would. Thank you for asking."

They welcome us aboard and we take seats on the stern. The steward rounds the corner straightening his bow tie and stands behind the bar as Adeline asks, "What would you like to drink? Tea, still or sparkling water, or perhaps a secret indulgence Thomas has, sodas." Trevor asks, "Do you have cola?" Thomas responds, "My favorite." I add, "Make that three, please." Adeline nods at the steward and inquires, "Where is Willow?"

"She's at the marina. My wife gave me a sailboat as a wedding gift."

"The perfect gift for a Sailor."

Thomas asks, "What did you name her, Geneviève?"

"Gypsy."

"An excellent name, Gypsies are known for never staying at a place too long."

Adeline is nodding as I thank him and after we are served our host tells us they *just* returned from Catalina. Tourist season is over and Adeline adores the theatre in Avalon. As they talk I find my mind wandering, which is close to a social crime as my husband would put it, therefore when they conclude their story I decide to change the subject to what had my mind wandering and ask, "Adeline, would you mind if I discuss business for a minute with your husband?" She gives him a look and almost quips, "If it is a response to the offer my overzealous husband made at your wedding reception, of course not."

"Thomas, I've already made a decision about your offer. It is important I keep my job on the base due to world events. I would however like to work part time for Harding Publications if that is at all possible."

"I'll have you put on a retaining salary and when something catches your eye take a snapshot and then send it via one of our messengers along with a synopsis to my L.A. office. If we use it you will be compensated. You'll receive a contract, business cards with the Harding Publications logo and a press pass via messenger next week. Is that acceptable?"

"More than."

"For now we will seal the deal with a hand shake." He sits up and extends his hand. "Welcome to Harding Publications, Mrs. Lyons."

"Thank you, Mr. Harding."

"I should be the one thanking you. We have our first woman photographer." He reaches for Adeline's hand and she says, "At last. We have been placing a want ad for photographers and only men apply. May I ask why your photo credit in *The Halyard* reads G. Delcroix?" I reply, "For the sake of brevity." Thomas tells me, "We would prefer the world to know you are a woman."

I think looking at Trevor. "How does Geneviève Delcroix-Lyons sound?"

"Perfect."

Thomas and Adeline click their bottles together and she says, "Hyphenated. Brava. How delightfully European." Thomas nods then asks Trevor, "Since you are a navigator, would you be interested in seeing her bridge?"

"Yes I would."

"Excuse us, ladies."

When their backs are turned Adeline gets up, dismisses the steward and sits next to me. "I was hoping he would give me an opportunity to speak with you privately. Many moons ago I was speaking with your mother and she told me you had a job on the base in a secretarial pool that only types carbon copies. Thomas being Thomas knew what your job required and I was thrilled to find out the Navy gave women Top Secret clearances. When he showed me *The Halyard* Thomas told me he was going to hire you if was the last thing he did, so thank you for accepting his offer. You are an exceptional woman. There is more to you than meets the eye."

"Thank you, Adeline. That means a lot to me, especially since I am positive there is more to you as well."

"Since I know a secret about you I'm going to tell you one about me only Thomas and my lady's maid know, who is more of an assistant than a maid. When Thomas travels without me he tells the editors and whomever, when they need his input to call my phone line, we have five, and I will pass the information to him. I do not pass the information on."

"You run the company when he's away."

"Yes I do."

"I knew you helped him make decisions and made them as well because of the way you two interact."

"You have been observing people closely the majority of your life. The camera made it possible for you to become invisible, because for the people that do not know you, it is all they see. It is the same when I am standing by Thomas when we are among strangers and acquaintances, he is all they see and I see everything."

"Your husband is lucky to have you."

"And yours is lucky to have you. Thomas believes women are smarter than men, mainly because we do not have egos that need to be fed and he has watched egos cloud the judgment of many a man. I must admit, I am inclined to agree with him." On that we get tickled.

"Adeline, I *am* enjoying getting to know you on a personal level."

"Thank you, Dear. Likewise." She sighs. "I hear our husbands."

Trevor and Thomas walk up grinning and Thomas says, "There is no need to ask if you had a nice chat. We heard the laughter. Have we returned too soon?"

"Not at all, Thomas. Your timing is perfect, as always."

I glance at Trevor, the man I toasted for his timing with Mother, as he sits next to me. "I'm glad Geneviève turned right on our walk. It led us here. Thank you for inviting us aboard."

"Thank you for accepting given that you two were obviously taking a romantic stroll." Adeline picks up our colas. "In fact I want you both to take these and go on your way before I start feeling guilty for keeping you from it any longer." Thomas adds, "I agree with my wife." And they shoo us off the yacht.

We walk silently drinking our sodas letting what happened sink in. Then I remember I need to call my family to let them know we arrived safely. After hanging up Trevor swiftly reels me onto him with one arm and gives me a noisy kiss. "You just landed the job beyond your dreams. What do you want to do to celebrate?"

"There is a quaint little Italian restaurant on Garden Street. I want us to get a bottle of wine, an extra large pepperoni pizza, so that we have some left for later and a dozen cannoli and eat here as we watch the sky change colors. Then I want to shower and get comfortable on our bed to listen to you read until I can't keep my eyes open." I dangle the key to the Woodie in front of him and even though he knows I was kidding about getting a dozen cannoli, Trevor orders one anyway.

In the middle of the night I wake up lying across him. He is gently caressing my arm and I see his eyes are open. I whisper, "Trevor, why are you awake?"

"A wave rocked Gypsy. I'm not used to being on a vessel a wave can rock. And because you were sleeping in my arms I began thinking about when we started lying on my bed to kiss and we would have to get up when one of us got sleepy."

"Do you want to kiss me until you're sleepy and then go to sleep in my arms?"

"More than anything. I love you, Geneviève."

"I love you, Trevor."

In the morning the sun wakes me up at daybreak. I am on my side sleeping like I normally do, but with Trevor being pressed against me by the gentle rocking of the boat. His body feels so good I eventually squeeze his hand and wake him up. "Geneviève, how long have you been awake?"

"Long enough to be aroused by your body rubbing against mine by the rocking of this boat."

"I am about to give you pleasure beginning here." He touches my neck, rolls me onto my back and makes me moan immediately. So lost am I in the pleasure he is giving me I do not realize where he is until I hear him say, "Baby, I need you to raise your hips for me."

While I rest in his embrace his stomach growls and he dryly tells me, "Intimate moments being interrupted by the need for sustenance is annoying me. I'm going to put apples in here tonight, but for now I'm going to start breakfast and serve it in our bed." He kisses my cheek then begins shaking his head as he leaves. Then a spicy smell wafts into our stateroom, so I get up and go to the galley.

"Trevor, what is in that skillet?"

"Two pieces of pizza." I raise my eyebrows. "You don't know what time it is."

"Are we going to eat those while we dress?"

"Yes, ma'am. It might give us time to stop at Jed's for me a denim jacket like yours and a boot jack." I open two colas, hand him one and get plates out.

After the shortest trip to Jed's in history we are on our way to the ranch. Trevor remembers the way to the point that he pulls over in the exact same place for me to lay across him while he drives. He enjoys the view and I enjoy being in his arms.

When he drives through the gate I sit up and soon we see Helen sitting in one of the white rocking chairs on the veranda of the main house waiting for us like last time. She walks to the front to greet us and right after we all hug Cookie steps outside and rings the bell. Trevor whispers, "That was too close." Eventually Helen says, "Chow time." and we go inside.

After lunch and the men are gone Hank walks up and sets two boxes of ammo on the table. "Then men passed a hat for a wedding gift. This is what they decided on. We all know you have a .22 and one of the men knew officers carried .45's. You two know your way around, so if you will excuse me, I am needed at the stables." Helen says, "Wait on me, Hank." and gives us a wink.

Trevor stops at the back door of the kitchen and picks up the bag of tin cans for target practice. After he sets them up he picks up his .45 and tells me, "It's as if they knew I was going to bring this." And he loads his sidearm.

"Trevor, this is need to know information. We do not thank the men for gifts, it makes them uncomfortable."

"That explains why Hank didn't allow me to get a word in and left abruptly. Are you ready Little Sure Shot?"

"Actually I want to watch you and get a few photographs." He nods, fires and does not miss. I stop taking snapshots as he reloads. And once again, just like when he boxed that day, I am attracted to him, but there is nothing he can do about it. Before he takes a stance I tell him, "You are impressive." And I sigh.

Trevor looks around, puts down his sidearm and pulls me against him. "You're attracted to me right now aren't you?"

"Mmm hm."

"Hold on to that thought." And he lets me go.

When all the targets are down I say, "Trevor, I just want to ride." He gathers our things and we go to the stables where we see Helen is standing between Cody and Whiskey holding their reins with Hank hovering to the side.

"Baby, they look like they're ready to be shown. Their hooves are polished. They sure are holding their heads high."

"They know they look good."

"Yes they do."

When we are close I bolt to Cody. "There is my beautiful boy." I take his reins from Helen as I squeeze her hand and begin petting him. Trevor says, "Hello Whiskey. You look dapper today." He pets him and starts loading our saddles. Hank takes our canteens and walks off. He returns and I tell him, "First you showed up at our wedding and now you have groomed the horses. That's it, I'm going to embarrass you. Pick your poison, a kiss on the cheek or a hug?" He dryly responds, "A kiss on the cheek won't draw too much attention, but make it quick." I stand on the toes of my boots, give him a quick kiss and just smile.

Helen clears her throat before asking, "Upper trail?" I nod. "I'll be expecting you two for dinner."

Trevor tells her, "Yes, ma'am."

We walk a few feet away from the stable and I ask Trevor, "Are you ready to saddle up, Cowboy?"

"I like it when you're feisty."

I give him a kiss, go to Cody's side and we saddle up. "Since you like it when I'm feisty, you're going to love this. I came here to ride, so you better push down your hat. Whiskey will follow Cody."

When I shift my weight in the saddle Cody's ears perk and go forward. I wait until Trevor is prepared and tell him, "See you at the top. Cody. Yah." And we are off whipping around curves and kicking up dirt.

The trail begins to open up, so I pull back on his reins and slow us down. Trevor eases up beside me. "That was exhilarating."

"Yes it was. I love to go fast."

"I figured that out the first time you drove Blanca."

While we keep the horses at a trot to cool them down we drink from our canteens and savor the moment we just had.

At the rail Trevor leaps off Whiskey, secures his reins and reaches for Cody's. When his are secure Trevor pulls me off Cody and into his arms. "I know exactly how you felt watching me take down those targets as I watched you riding. You're confidence as you went around those curves working his reins. Have mercy." His kiss his so sudden and passionate it catches me by surprise. When Trevor calms down he says, "I guess I will take my own advice and hold on to that thought." I smile nodding and he exhales heavily. My slightly shaken husband keeps one arm around me and we finally look at the view.

"Geneviève, let's watch the sunset from here."

"That is really romantic, but this is the time of year I saw the mountain lion."

"He was raiding the kitchen so to speak before he turned in?"

"Yes he was. Here we watch the sunset on the veranda and then eat dinner."

"Now would be a good time for you to take that photograph you want of the horses, put on our jackets and be on our way. I really don't want to be sitting on the saddle of a spooked horse." I have to make myself stop laughing to take the photograph of the horses with the incredible view as a backdrop. Of course I take one of Trevor and he turns the camera on me.

This time we go at a normal pace and listen to the sounds of the mountains and the valley. There is a cool breeze blowing through the trees and over the creek. Trevor is riding beside me and every muscle in my body relaxes. Then everything changes when we get near the end of the trail and ride up on Helen and Hank. He informs us, "One of the men spotted a black bear in the area, so we thought we'd provide some more hoof noise to keep him away." I give them a nod and they drop back, turn around and follow us to the stables.

When we get there I hop down and go over to Trevor with Cody. He gets his feet on the ground and Hank takes Whiskey's reins. Helen takes Cody's and while they walk away Trevor says, "It has occurred to me that I have not been told the ... proper procedure when one has an encounter with a wild animal."

"That's on me. I do apologize. If it becomes aggressive just keep your horse steady and fire off a round at a tree near it and they will be on their way in another direction." He gives me a look and I bat my eyelashes at him.

Trevor hooks me around the neck. "I'm ready to go sit on the veranda in one of those rocking chairs." And we start walking to the main house.

A few minutes after we've been rocking, happily away from lions and bears, Helen steps up and slaps Trevor on the leg grinning. Then she sits next to me, holding my hand, rocking and watching the sunset. "Trevor, when Josephine called me Saturday to let me know you two would be here today I asked what your favorite foods were. I was surprised when she told me you were fond of Southern cooking. Therefore when Cookie rings the dinner bell and we go in you will find a pile of Southern Fried Chicken, a vegetable medley of peas and corn in a buttery sauce, mashed baby red potatoes, biscuits that you can butter or pour gravy on and marbled pecan pound cake."

"I have suddenly lost interest in watching the sunset." Helen and I burst into laughter and I have to give the man credit though, because when the dinner bell rings he doesn't make a dash for the door.

Cookie is at the end of the line serving the dessert as always and when Trevor holds his hand up I am a little confused until he tells him, "I'll get dessert when I come back for seconds if you don't mind."

"Commander, feel free to come back for thirds if you want. Your dessert will be here, I'll make sure of it." They shake hands on it and Trevor could not be happier and when he gets up for seconds I join him. Fried chicken takes up a lot of room on your plate, so I only got one piece and I want another one. By the time we finish eating and telling Helen about our wedding gifts to each other all the men are gone. While we talk, Cookie comes out with a white box and with just a nod he places it on the table by Trevor and walks off.

A few minutes go by and Helen blurts out, "Are you really not curious as to what's in that box?" Trevor chuckles and replies, "I can smell what's in it, more fried chicken." I tell Helen, "We should go on that note." And because it's dark outside we say our goodbyes on the veranda.

The moment we get back in the city limits I spot the market and have Trevor pull in the parking lot. I hold out my hand and he puts his money clip in it then I slide across the seat of the Woodie and get out. The fruit is out front and I walk up to it and hold up a green apple. I can see Trevor laugh as he gives me a thumbs down. When I pick up a red apple that is the same kind we had at The Posh he gives me two thumbs up and I fill a paper bag with them.

Back at Gypsy Trevor barely speaks while we take off our boots with our new boot jack, then we gather everything and go below. We take off our jackets and after he puts the chicken in the refrigerator Trevor turns around and locks his eyes on me. "Trevor, what is it?"

"I've held my thought as long as I can." My husband closes the gap between us and becomes something he has never been, aggressive. He grabs my shirt in the middle, undoes all the snaps and untucks it in one motion. Trevor puts his arms around me underneath my shirt and his kiss is intense. Then he stops abruptly. "Baby, are you with me?"

"Yes." I push him back and unbuckle my belt. We step out of our jeans and I put my arms around his neck. Trevor lifts me up with my thighs and goes toward the bow. "Where are you going?"

"To the other stateroom, we're dirty and I'm not letting you go to shower." We enter the stateroom and he puts me on my feet. In exasperation he says, "This bed is too small. We're going to wind up the floor." Keeping me pressed against him, with one arm he pulls the mattresses off the beds and onto the floor. When we are on them the last thing to go is his dog tags and I think he broke the chain. Eventually we do something we have never done, we make love twice in one night. The second time is caused by the fact we cannot stop having foreplay while we recover from the first.

In the morning Trevor wakes me up brushing my hair from my face and I notice we are on the mattress he put on the floor under a blanket with one pillow. "Good morning, Geneviève."

"Good morning, Trevor." He props up on his elbow and looks at me. "I'm fine. In fact I feel sublime. You led and I followed."

"Yes you did, to another place we have never been."

"We went there because you are no longer worried about me in the back of your mind."

"I honestly didn't think I was anymore."

"I knew in time you would stop and you did."

"My desire for you overwhelmed me. Every time I turned around yesterday I found myself wanting you."

"And you couldn't have me because yesterday was our first day out into the world. Since we've been married we went out into it for a little while then we retreated back into ours."

"In that case I motion we don't do that again until our honeymoon is over."

"I second that motion."

He lies down and breathes a sigh of relief as I look around the stateroom. It looks different lying on the floor. "Did I tell you I had a wall removed from here and turned this into one stateroom?"

"No you didn't." His eyes drift and I know what he is thinking.

"Mr. Lyons."

"I'm listening, Mrs. Lyons."

"Gypsy is for us. When I was making decisions I was taking our future into consideration. One day we will be a family and this stateroom is for our children. We are going to take them places and teach them how to sail aboard her. And speaking from experience, they will want to share a room. Théo and I did. I want our children to grow up together and be as close as he and I are."

"That is what I want too. I love you so much."

"I know you do and I love you."

"Let's go home, Baby."

We sit up and see the state of disarray around us then look at each other and get tickled. "Trevor?"

"You go shower and I'll make us a hearty breakfast then shower after we eat."

"While you're showering I'll find our watches and your ring then we can deal with the rest of this later, much later."

"We have a plan. — Please don't forget to find my dog tags."

"I won't."

"Geneviève, why did your voice just get high?"

"I'm not sure, but I think you broke the chain during our moment of unbridled passion."

"That's one way to put it." He puts his hand to his forehead and I pull it down.

"I loved every second. In fact, I intend to reciprocate."

"I hope I stay focused and don't run us aground."

"That makes two of us. I'm going to shower." Knowing the boat is going to be chilly since we did not turn on a single heater when we returned last night I keep the blanket over my breasts and gather it around me with my free hand and get up taking it with me. I open the door and walk out leaving Trevor lying nude on the mattresses laughing without looking back. Later I do find his dog tags and he did break the chain about two inches below the clasp, but he just takes the piece out and reconnects the chain. Now I realize why they're on ball chain. It's easily fixed, but those missing inches will bother him. We're going to the commissary Eh-sap.

We miss daybreak because we didn't rush around, but Gypsy more than makes it up. When it's time for lunch I talk Trevor into sailing her without me on deck and go below to make it. I take a little longer and heat the biscuits to eat with the cold fried chicken and spinach salads then I go up and take the wheel while he lowers the sails. While eating he describes what sailing alone was like.

Close to the halfway point we spot a large gray rain cloud headed our way. Trevor lowers the sails and we drop anchor close to the coast at an inlet and start securing the deck. The marine report stated it was just light precipitation with winds at 11 knots, but things change quickly out at sea and we got that report six hours ago. It is the last day of September and even though the first official day of fall was on the 23rd we think it's rolling in.

We use the unexpected spare time wisely straightening the other stateroom and gathering laundry. After rinsing off we cook a nice dinner and since we are close enough to the coast to pick up a signal from a radio station we listen to music and even get to dance to our song. Then we get in our bed early just to rest and regain our strength while we listen to the rain curled up under cozy covers. Not knowing if there is going to be daybreak due to clouds we decide to sleep until we wake up.

As expected that was fall rolling in and we dress for the temperature change then eat a big breakfast before going on deck. This is going to be a memorable last day at sea. I'm going to be at the wheel more than usual because Trevor is going to have to make sail adjustments often due to the changes of the wind we are going to run into. We touch gloves and go to our corners.

The sun comes out and peeks through the clouds after lunch and we warm up a bit. Choppy water and the sails keep us on our toes, so when we are close to San Diego Trevor lowers them and we go the rest of the way under power. When I see Willow's masts as we round the point I am so happy. I am even happier when I see the wall around Maison.

When we pull up to the garage Trevor says, "That's new." and we are looking at a mailbox.

"Stop the car. The only reason my family bought that was because the postman told them we have mail he can't deliver until we have one."

"Our first mail. I'm a little excited myself."

We get out and he lifts the lid, so I reach in and pull out a letter. "Oh my goodness, it's addressed to Mrs. Trevor Lyons. My kingdom for a letter opener." Trevor chuckles as he reaches in his pocket for his knife. He opens it and hands it to me. This gets him a big kiss on the mouth. I carefully run it under the flap and hand it back to him. "It's my permanent ID card for the commissary. I can use it tomorrow when we go to get you a new chain."

"I feel as if you read my mind constantly."

"I knew this morning they would eventually drive you crazy because they are out of place."

"You are spot-on. I've been wearing these so long I am quite used to them. It's odd that it didn't bother me not to have them on."

"It's like when I wear garters to hold up my stockings. I'm not aware of them, but if one slips out of place and I can't get to the Powder Room fast enough. Desperation has driven me into a closet every now and then."

Suddenly Trevor pulls his dog tags out from under his shirt. "Geneviève, please get these off me." I spin the chain around and find the clasp. One little click and the job is done. I drop them in his pocket and he gives me a kiss. I get in the car, he hits the button and I pull into the garage. Thanks to the dumbwaiter the car is unpacked in minutes.

Into the kitchen we go and I tell him, "I'll get two dinners from the freezer and put them in the oven."

"While you do that I'm going to turn on the heaters, the house is damp."

"Do you want to turn on the one in the solarium?"

"I see where you're going with this. After dinner I'll make my hot cocoa."

"You can tell me the secret ingredient. I am you wife now."

"You are indeed my wife. I'll show you what it is while I make it."

"Then we will settle in with my foot on your lap and you can run your hand over the skin of my leg."

"I shan't be long."

By the time Trevor returns everything is done and he traps me in the pantry. "Geneviève, we're home. We can shower together."

"Can we just stand under the water for a while?"

"Of course we can."

Trevor turns the hot water handle on and I feel better already by the mere sound of the water. Our clothes are sticky and we smell like fish and salt, so we undress ourselves and throw our clothes down the chute. My husband follows me in and adjusts the water temperature. I unbraid my hair as I rinse off then he rinses off and pushes the showerhead down. He puts his back on the stall wall, reaches his arms out and holds me as the water flows over us until even our bones are warm again.

Sitting in the solarium Trevor's hand gets still and I open my heavy eyelids in time to see him closing his. I softly say his name and tell him it's time to get in our bed. He turns off the lights on the way to our room where he kisses me goodnight and we fall asleep when our heads are on the pillow.

Something wakes me up in the morning and before I can think I go, "Ow."

Trevor chuckles. "I just made that same sound. I knew it would wake you up. Sorry, Baby." I'm lying flat on my back and so is he.

"Don't worry about it, you couldn't help it." I sigh heavily. "I'm so glad I didn't remember last night how you wake up feeling after sailing in those conditions. My arms are killing me and I wish my legs would go numb."

"I feel as if I was just in the Brigade Boxing Championships."

I turn my head to look at him. "Make a long story short."

"I'm a four-time Brigade champion."

"Not many officers can say that can they?"

"Nope."

"Modesty kept you from telling me and I'm incapacitated when I find out?"

"I regret that decision."

"I'm sure do. You can kick yourself while you help me up." He chuckles and slowly gets up.

During breakfast we discuss running errands knowing we need to work the soreness out. Trevor being thoughtful washes the dishes, I rinse and we leave them in the rack to air dry.

Backing out of the garage I tell him, "A stack of boxes has been delivered. I would say those were more wedding gifts, except some of the boxes look ... old."

When Trevor sees them he steps on the brake. "Those are the boxes I have been sending to the caretaker."

"Do you want to get out and open them?"

"Not now, but I do want to take them inside." He gives me a kiss and I watch him carefully take them in the garage.

First stop is at *The San Diego Times* to get extra copies of the paper we missed on the Monday after our wedding day and our wedding announcement. We step up to the counter and he says, "We want 7 copies from September 15th and 12 from the 21st." The clerk steps away and I raise my eyebrows at Trevor. "My entire family should get copies of each one and I got spares of our announcement in case I ever do anything stupid with my wallet." I laugh and give him a kiss.

The next errand is to get a chain from the commissary. When we go in he asks, "Do want to shop?" I reply, "Not really. I want to see what's in those boxes."

He offers me his arm and we step up to a counter that has little spindles with over a hundred chains on them. Behind the counter are two men using what looks like small printing presses. Trevor explains that they make dog tags and he lets me watch them change out the metal letters in the presses and make a few sets. "Are you ready to go, Baby?"

"Yes. This was interesting. Thank you for letting me watch."

"No need to thank me. I remember getting my first set. I was amazed and just stood there watching while waiting." He gets a chain and I get two more. His eyes are locked on mine as he takes them from me. We stand there silently until another Sailor walks up and we go to check out. I am a little flushed when I hand the clerk my ID. There is no doubt we will ever forget the first purchase we made with my card.

We are in a quiet mood, so we go to Mandarin Garden's for lunch. After he parks Blanca in the garage he tells me, "We need to empty that crate, so we can park your other car in here for me to pin you against." When I get out he does just fine without the car.

A few minutes later my husband set his boxes on the table for folding laundry. Going around it I notice he wrote fragile on all four sides of them and the city it was from. He pulls his knife out of his pocket and cuts the twine on all of them without speaking. He is remembering the past of each one and I remain quiet.

Trevor slides the one from Osaka forward that has the sake set in it. I can tell it is old and is the prettiest set I have ever seen. Opening the box from Athens he says, "I found these in a book store. They are carved from the same white Pentelic marble of the steps and columns for The Parthenon." And soon before me are two male lions sitting on pedestals. Inside the box from Barcelona is a stack of records. "These are all the music that is played for Flamenco dancing."

When he opens the one from Lisbon there are several items wrapped in layers of newspaper from there. He unrolls one on the table until an unusual piece of stemware is revealed. Setting it on the table he tells me, "This is part of a set of eight Portuguese sorbet dishes. I'd never seen clear glass dishes with black stems, therefore I had to have them. They're the first things I sent back, that was eight years ago. When we happed upon the candlesticks in our bedroom I remembered having these and was going to ring Grandmum to send these boxes, but for some reason it slipped my mind."

Trevor kisses me then slides a box marked Naples in front of him and slowly unwraps a beautiful pair of crystal candlesticks with three dolphins on each base. "Obviously I got these to remind of the fountains there." Opening another box he tells me, "My favorite thing in Amsterdam was the swans gliding in pairs along the canal and I found the contents of this box in the gift shop of an inn." Wrapped in pale blue tissue paper are two white oval bowls with graceful swans on the side.

The last box is from New Orleans and it is the largest. "You are going to love what's in here, but I want to tell you a story before I open it." And he pulls out chairs for us. "My group was wondering around the French Market and I noticed a shop across the street that had Curiosity in large golden letters on the window. I told William I was going to it and as I got closer I noticed there was a book store next door. I went there first and then The Little Curiosity Shoppe.

There was a lovely lady behind the counter with silver hair and when the bell over the door stopped ringing she said, 'Bonjour.', so I knew right away she was French. She looked up and slowly said, 'Ooh la la, an extraordinary Sailor has walked through my door." As she came out from behind the counter with her head slightly titled I wondered how many men she had enchanted over the years.

"I looked at so many unusual items as she followed me answering questions about things I had no idea what purpose they served or where it came from. Then I came upon what is in this box. — Geneviève, close your eyes." I am filled with anticipation as I listen to the sounds of crumpling paper and the hum of metal, then silence. "You may open them now."

It is as if my eyes do not believe what they see. I glance at him then find words. "Trevor — you found a Menagerie Carousel."

"I've heard about them, but had never seen one, all wild animals and not a single horse. I stood there staring at it in disbelief and she moved this little lever." He slides it backward and the carousel begins to turn and play music I recognize.

"It plays the French Carousel Theme."

Trevor nods, sits next to me with his arm around my shoulders and we watch pairs of elephants, lions, zebras, tigers, ostriches, camels, giraffes, rhinoceroses, leopards and even hippopotamuses go round and round.

Time passes and he turns it off then reaches into the box. "Last, but definitely not least." Trevor pulls out a book that reads, *The Vicomte de Bragelonne* and hands it to me. "My favorite novel of The d'Artagnan Romances was *The Three Musketeers,* but this one included the story of *The Man in the Iron Mask.* Even though I could not speak or read French, since Dumas was French I bought it.

"The one thing all these items had in common is I was drawn to them and for some time I've felt as if I was collecting them for you. It all began on the day we met when Théo mentioned the carousel you loved. Then I found you sitting on your bench reading a book in French, followed by our song that became about the gypsy I brought out in you on our first date. It reminded me of the records for Flamenco dancing made popular in Europe by Gypsies, which you know."

"Because I mentioned it on our trip."

"Yes you did. That brought it to two references for those. Then there was the sake you mentioned for our second date that few people drink, but for some unknown reason you knew I did. Next I find out you love black Art Deco and when the pod of dolphins swam by at the wharf I almost fell into the water." I burst into laughter. "The swans on our wedding invitations I thought was going to be the last of all these coincidences until you mentioned The Parthenon and that got the lions. All roads led me to you."

"And you had to keep this to yourself all this time."

"It wasn't easy, but I knew they had to be here. These things were for us, not me." And at last we kiss. "Where would you like the carousel, Mrs. Lyons?"

"On the coffee table for now."

"This is about 20 inches in circumference. I don't want to risk tripping on the staircase with it; therefore to the dumbwaiter we go."

Trevor carefully sets the carousel in it and we go upstairs. He places it on the coffee table and after we admire it he tells me, "Man your post." I say my usual response and stand by the dumbwaiter. After everything is up I put a table cloth on the dining table to move the collection onto, then I hear the dumbwaiter being sent up. I go back wondering what could possibly be in it and slide the door up to find the chains along with his dog tags. He's going to do something when he returns and I stand by the dumbwaiter in anticipation.

Trevor enters the kitchen, slowly walks to me and begins to caress my face as he softly tell me, "I am going to start a fire in our bedroom, bathe you and make your daydream come true."

After we bathe each other he leads me over to the chest filled with pillows and comforters and lifts the lid. I move the bowl of apples onto a side table and we make a cozy pallet on the rug in front of the warm fire. I stand on it and Trevor kneels in front of me. He holds me and rests his head on my abdomen. I toss my robe onto a chair and kneel. My beautiful husband lies us down and begins to make my daydream come true and then some.

The intensity when we make love has changed dramatically and it is physically exhausting. Since he regains his strength before me, Trevor gives me an apple and goes to the kitchen to put our last catered dinners in the oven taking his apple with. He returns with a wet dishtowel and when we finish them we takes turns wiping our sticky hands and faces, then we lie there to enjoy the warmth from the fire until we have to get up before our dinner burns.

During our candle lit meal we eat wearing only our robes and out of the blue I say, "Ooh la la."

"That is exactly how she said it."

"And that is the first time I have said it. I've heard in movies though."

"You've never said it. What exactly does that mean?"

"It means ... I find you desirable." His eyebrows go up. "Madame Picotte was flirting with you unabashedly."

"She was indeed." Then his face goes straight and his eyes dart around the room. "You've been going to New Orleans at Easter for years. Of course you have been in her shoppe. Why didn't you tell me earlier?"

"I didn't want to interrupt your story or change the mood."

"Ah."

"We have purchased items from her every year. One time I went in ahead of my family and asked her how she got started. Madame Picotte told me she was married to the wrong man for a month and because her family was affluent she boarded an ocean liner and thus began her traveling of the world. When an oddity caught her eye she'd send it to her parents. After traveling almost two years her parents suggested opening a shoppe to sell some of the things she had amassed."

"I understand her completely now."

"You went there a little over four years ago?"

"Geneviève, why do you know that?"

"You were in the Gulf of Mexico, so that means you were going to the Pacific."

"I feel better. Where are you going with this?"

"When you told me about your trip and what you missed I thought that if we got married we should go there and I would show the city through my eyes. Then when you told me that you standdown for 12 days when you return from a deployment I thought we should go somewhere on a passenger plane or in a car."

"And now you think we should fly to New Orleans."

"I want to share that experience I had with the bakery with you and it is very romantic at night. I would also like to take you to see Madame Picotte. I know she will remember you, because you are unforgettable. This is twice we've walked in each other's footsteps and our paths almost crossed. — Do you recall what month you were there?"

"I can tell you the exact date, because it was April Fool's Day."

"You were there just two or three days before me. Trevor, had you not been in her shoppe I would have bought that carousel."

"It was meant to be yours."

"I have chill bumps."

"So do I."

"I can hardly for us to go in there together. If we don't find anything, just seeing her reaction alone will be worth it."

"The word fate will be spoken."

"She will say la destinée."

"I love it when you speak in française."

"That reminds me, there are books from the store next door in my parents' and grandparents' studies and my room."

"Of course there is."

"Instead of an apartment we are going to stay in a place that has four stars, Hotel Monteleone, because it's on Royal Street."

"The street I missed."

"Over the years I have seen many a Sailor on Bourbon Street during the night going into one of those burlesque clubs."

"You've been on Bourbon Street at night?"

"That's where the jazz clubs are." He nods. "One night Théo and I went there ahead of the family and I had him wait outside while I went into a house of Voodoo." A piece of pork loin flies out of Trevor's mouth, lands on his plate and I get tickled.

He gives me a look then drinks a little water. "We spotted that and decided it was time turn around. Why on earth did you go in that place?"

"To photograph what was inside. The Creole woman there didn't mind and happily answered questions I did not ask."

"That's chilling. Théo was probably beside himself."

"He was. — Where did you and William go while the others were in the burlesque club?"

"The hotel across the street to have a drink in the bar."

"Did you get to eat a praline?"

He chuckles. "Only you would ask me if I had something sweet and yes I did."

"Ooo, speaking of sweets, what do you want for dessert?"

"Thanks to the power of suggestion, candy."

I jump up before Trevor can stand to pull out my chair to get the serving bowl I put all the bags of candy in and set it on the table. Strawberry creams for me and haystacks for him. "Let's have our dessert in bed and I'll read to you. Then we need to get some sleep. We have a busy day ahead of us." I forgot tomorrow is moving day, which does not surprise me in the least.

In the morning we wake up late because we haven't really rested in days. It is so late that when we go into the solarium with our second cup of coffee Théo and Rachel are washing cars.

When Trevor finishes his he tells me, "I've made plans for the last night of our honeymoon and I have to run a Top Secret errand for it today."

"I made plans for our afternoon. I thought we could spend it in my darkroom."

"Your darkroom. — Are you going to put film in your camera?"

"Mmm hm."

"I ... I need to get dressed. Baby, please wait for me here. I don't want us to be late for lunch at your parent's." I nod and he gives me a kiss.

He returns in the black polo with two buttons buttoned instead of one to cover passion marks. I pull on his collar and he smiles that smile then gives me a kiss and we go out onto the balcony. "See you soon." We kiss and I say, "See you soon." After watching my husband drive away in his car I realize this is the first time he's done that since we've been married. My heart sinks a little, so I quickly move on and dash inside to dress and make preparations for the arrival of the rest of my belongings.

A minute later I hear his car pull up and go into the living room wearing a pair of trousers. Trevor walks in and I ask, "What did you forget?"

"You." I throw my arms around his neck. "I was about to go through the gates and realized I was in a car without you for the first time since our wedding day. There is one thing though, when we're almost there you'll have to put your head on my lap."

"I have no problem with that."

He selects a blouse and a pair of shoes while I use the leg makeup. When we get in the car I roll down the passenger window and put my head on his lap. He keeps glancing down at me because I keep sighing. "Comfy?" I go, "Mmm hm. I think it's so romantic you came back to get me." And he caresses my face.

At our destination he backs into the park so I can't see where we are and he gets out. I put my feet up in the window and notice I am still wearing Gum Drop. Maybe two minutes pass and I hear his deep laugh then he rubs the top of my feet and opens the trunk.

On the way back I say, "I need a pedicure and all my things are in my vanities top left drawer."

"Then it's a good thing we're moving that into the dressing room today. And I'll finally get to start learning how to use the polish I bought."

"Something tells me I am going to enjoy that." He just smiles.

At the house he tells me to go in through the kitchen and stay then not to look in the coat closet, because my surprise is going to be in it. I hear the door close and come out. He gives me a proper kiss and we leave. Outside the place is jumping. Claudette and my grandmother are walking to my parent's house while Grand-papa and Joseph are backing up their cars. They get out and open their trunks. I notice quilts and straps in chairs on the portico and decide we are well organized.

After a wonderful lunch Théo is the first to stand and he pulls out Rachel's chair. Then we all swing into action. While the women move the contents of my closet to the cars the men start wrapping my furniture. Before they do all that we are done since there are five of us and we leave to back the cars into the garage and make good use of the dumbwaiter.

As we organize things, piece by piece my vanity, dresser, lingerie chest, armoire, jewelry armoire and book case arrive along with boxes of books. The men happily sit down and we serve them glasses of ice water then kiss their cheeks. The only thing left to do we need help with is move the few things left at what was Trevor's apartment and what is in the crate from London we went through. Rachel and Théo volunteer to help, so Trevor and I send the others on their way with our gratitude.

We go to the apartment with just one large box and I help him check every drawer and closet. He packs it and sets it on top of his foot locker. Rachel keeps her hands on Théo's shoulders to keep them balanced on the slightly steep steps. When we are finally in the garage the fellas take the lid off the crate and take up just the box. Rachel and I start getting what we can out of the crate, leaving the heavy items for our men and soon it is empty. As Théo and Rachel leave I hear her mention she would like to go into town. She wants to go shopping no doubt for something she spotted of mine. Théo glances at me over his shoulder. I just smile and wave.

Trevor and I go into our new home and I get my train case for the few items left in my bathroom. Inside my parent's house we find everyone is next door, so we go to my bedroom where I pack my train case and pick up Christopher. We stand at the door as I look around and a flood of memories wash over me. I lived in this room and this house for 25 years and I will miss it, but my last memories are with the man I married, so it eases the ache in my heart.

Trevor rubs my back and I look at him. "Baby, are you all right?"

"I'm fine. Let's go home."

Trevor carries my train case and I hold Christopher in my arms thinking as we walk across the cobblestones. "Why did you leave your footlocker in the garage?"

"The thought of lugging it up to the attic did not appeal to me in the least and I know Théo was tired too, therefore I decided to bring the contents inside later and put it in the storage room. — Do you want to see my sword." I touch my nose. "And so you shall."

We go straight to his footlocker and he lifts the lid. On top is a black leather carrying case that obviously has the sword in it, because it is long and slender at the blade and wide where the handle is, with two buckled straps to close the flap. Next to it is an elegant walnut box with a gold latch. Trevor gets them both and closes the lid.

In the living room I set Christopher and my train case in a chair and without thinking I prop Christopher's arm on the train case before I clear off the coffee table. Trevor's laugh is deep as he kisses me then sets the sword and box down.

We settle on the sofa with a bottle of wine and the show begins when he runs his hand over the top of the box. "A man in Annapolis handcrafts these for midshipmen to safely store what we wear with our swords. The brass latch and hinges are plated in 24 karat gold, like everything officers wear or carry." He opens the box and it's lined with navy blue wool felt. The first thing I notice is a black leather belt with a round buckle with a symbol of the United States Navy on it and he picks it up. "This is my sword belt. The short strap hooks on to the scabbard ring to help keep the sword close to our leg. The long one you will find interesting. It's a garter that runs under our trousers and secures to the top of our right sock. The purpose is to keep the belt from working its way off center by our constant movements. We aren't allowed to make adjustments to our uniforms publicly."

"My goodness, the Navy is strict, but they thought of everything to keep their men looking perfect."

"Yes they have. — I should tell you this now. There is something you don't know about, because I took them off before we left our wedding reception. I knew they would interrupt a moment we were going to have that night."

"You have my undivided attention."

He says with a grin, "We also wear shirt garters with our dress blue uniforms. They attach to the hem of the shirt and the top of our socks to keep our shirts tucked in tight at all times." My mouth comes open. "And that is the visual I had of you standing there catching flies the second my trousers were off."

"That explains why your shirt stayed tucked in, even after all the dancing and then carrying me trough the threshold. So — you know why I wear garters instead of a garter belt."

"It hadn't crossed my mind actually. I love the garters."

"Yes you do."

"And we are way of course. It's a good thing I'm a navigator." We get tickled and drink some wine then he continues. "The contents of the box." He picks up something golden that almost looks like a tassel, but the ends are woven together. "This is called a Sword Knot. This wraps around the guard of the sword and hangs from it. William already knew how to do the tricky part and it saved me a lot of time and trouble."

Next he slides the sword case toward us and unbuckles the straps to reveal the top of a navy blue drawstring bag made of thin brushed cotton he slowly pulls out of the case. There are two pairs of white gloves, lined and unlined in the box. He picks up the unlined pair and loosens the drawstring. At this point I hold my breath. He reaches one hand into the bag and there it is, his sword. The hilt is gold and the guard is of heavy filigree with USN on it. The scabbard is black leather and gold on the top. The tip has a gold sea serpent on it. "I never handle my sword with bare hands. The grip is wrapped in sting-ray skin between the solid gold wire."

"They chose something from the sea, how appropriate. And that's why it's such an unusual pearly white. I understand why you wear gloves."

Trevor lets go of the hilt and holds it by the scabbard for me to get a good look at it. "I only unsheathe my sword for a purpose. I haven't seen it in a while. Are you ready?" I slightly nod and he slowly unsheathes his sword and I notice over half of the blade is intricately etched. Working my way from the tip I see ornate designs that surround a shield with the stars and stripes of our nation's flag on an anchor then there is a surprise at the top, his name is engraved on the blade. I almost touch it. "Geneviève, you can touch the blade. It isn't weapons sharp, because it is ceremonial."

I slide my finger tip across his name that is engraved in Old English lettering. "Trevor, this is magnificent."

"I was awestruck when I held it the first time. It still has an effect on me."

"I understand completely. How long is it?"

"32 inches. The length is based on my height."

"That makes sense."

"It just occurred to me I never told you something. I am a swordsman in every sense of the term. Bill taught me along with William swordsmanship the way the first Admiral Snowdon learned."

"Sword fighting passed from generation to generation. That is incredible."

"It really is. I held the Admirals' curved cutlass he used in battles. Speaking of, I've held on to this long enough. Put on the other pair of gloves."

After looking at every detail I tell him, "I want to take photographs of all this."

"I knew you would."

He takes the sword and I toss the gloves. While I got my camera he put things back in the box and I went to work. Looking at the sword I ask, "Will you put this on our bench? It will show up on the black cashmere."

With sword in place I realize I can't get the shot I want. "Trevor, I need to stand in a chair. This is too long for an overhead standing here." He moves an armchair for me then suddenly says, "Wait a minute. I'm going to get one of your other cameras."

Standing in the chair photographing the sword he photographs me. "I should have started doing this a long time ago. You are always doing something that should be photographed."

I hold out my hand for him to help me down thinking that camera in his hand is going to change things. And I was right, because when we return to the living room he takes a snapshot of Christopher propped up in the chair.

After his sword is secure he tells me, "Now I want to learn how to give you a pedicure." So we go into the dressing room and he puts the sword case in the bottom of my armoire. It is the only place it will fit and I ask him to set the wooden box on my dresser. Next I hand him the polish remover and cotton balls and sit on my vanity bench then he sets the things down. "I shan't be long." Trevor walks in with the camera he has commandeered and kneels at my feet. "I want a picture of what I've been looking at since the day we married." And he takes a snapshot of my feet.

"Oh my gosh, you just turned into a shutterbug."

My husband lights up the room and we go into the bathroom where I sit on a towel on the edge of the bath tub. He removes the polish and asks, "What next?"

"Normally I would wash my feet off here, but tonight I think we should shower, then you can paint my toenails in Strawberry Fluff and we can cook dinner while the polish dries." He takes off his shirt and drops it down the chute.

Trevor puts on civvie skivvies and I slip into a camisole and panties. He picks me up and lays me on the bed and comes back with a towel to put under my feet and the bottle of polish. Caressing my feet as he paints, Trevor turns getting a pedicure into something sensual. I am spoiled. And after dinner he continues to spoil me until we drift into a deep sleep.

Trevor insisted I sleep like I normally do and when I wake up I can tell my husband is awake by the way he is holding me. It is the last day of our honeymoon and we are well aware of it. I say, "Good morning, my handsome groom." as I roll over to see his face.

"Good morning, my beautiful bride." I bury my face in his neck and he sighs heavily. "How I wish we could order room service."

"I have an idea. Trevor, will it embarrass you to get breakfast trays from my grandparents?" He picks up the receiver and dials their number.

"Good morning, Constance." Then there is a long silence, because she of course knew why he was calling, followed by him chuckling and, "She will love it. Thank you." And he sets the receiver down.

"What will I love?"

"Your grandmother and mother have wanted to do something for us since our early return. So, they are going to bring the trays here and use the dumbwaiter. I could hear the excitement in her voice."

"I bet you could. After we spruce up let's go peak through the curtains." His laugh is deep as I throw back the covers over him.

With my camera in hand Trevor stands with me between his arms, so he can separate the curtains and see over my head outside. We do not have to wait long for them to appear carrying the covered trays smiling and talking. I take a few snapshots and get a good one when they look up at the house in the exact spot we are at. Then they go under the balcony and we hear a garage door rise. I get tickled and he says, "Do tell."

"Mother just pressed the garage door button with her elbow."

"I have a visual — and our breakfast is on its way up."

We wait to watch them leave then dash to the dumbwaiter. Trevor raises the door and there is a note on top of a tray in Mother's handwriting he reads aloud. "Compliments of Maison de la Mer Bed & Breakfast. Lunch will arrive at 12 sharp. To change the time, please call the front desk." We burst into laughter as Trevor lifts the napkins off one. "This one is yours."

"How can you tell?"

"Your father put the Funny Paper on it." My face lights up the kitchen as I pick it up and take it to our bedroom with him on my heels carrying his tray.

While eating, the decision is made to wait for lunch curled up in our bed, therefore Trevor starts a fire and I put all the pillows on it so we can watch the fire dance. Settled in nicely he reads the Funny Paper to me then puts it on the nightstand and asks, "Thus far, what has been you favorite moment of our honeymoon?"

"It started when you said, 'Have mercy.' And hours later we woke up on the mattresses you pulled onto the floor."

"That night we found out there is something that goes unsaid. After learning how to run a husband and wife will eventually have wings and be able to fly."

"And we flew so high."

"So high we were among the stars."

"I love it when we talk like this." And we spend our morning in bed kissing listening to the sound of the crackling fire and talking.

The next thing I know we hear the garage door raise and I tell him, "It has been nice not having to eat an apple for sustenance today."

"Now might be a good time to tell you this. A few days ago I asked Théo if he would mind stopping at Mandarin Garden's on his way here with Rachel for the Sunday dinner. Around six o'clock a crispy duck with all the trimmings will be in the dumbwaiter." Then he looks deep into my eye as his voice drops. "I'm going to seduce you tonight." Trevor gives me an Eskimo Kiss and gets up. I linger in our bed for a minute.

After eating a wonderful bowl of Mother's vichyssoise and coconut macaroons I sit across my husband's lap. "Are you ready to go into my darkroom?"

"That is rhetorical." And he stands up with me around him then goes toward the dressing room.

"Why are you going to the dressing room?"

He kisses me and turns around. "This is going to take some getting used to."

"What is?"

"Walking around in my skivvies and seeing you in these thin white camisoles you are so fond of wearing and panties." We enter the darkroom and I turn on the safelight. He puts me down, but keeps his arms around me feeling my back. "The only reason I am going to let go of you is because I want to see what we have."

"You won't be able to see anything until tomorrow. Film takes a long time to dry. The good news is I am about to teach you how to develop film." In his enthusiasm I am dipped and playfully kissed, but it still increases my heart rate.

I get a canister off the shelf and fill a container with water. Getting a roll of new film out I tell him, "I learned how to do this with water instead of developer and film that can be exposed to light because there is nothing on it in case something went wrong." After everything is set up I say, "All right, I need you to stand behind me and look over my shoulder." Trevor has me between his arms and he places his hands on the counter as his chest goes against my back. Normally I could do this in my sleep, but my concentration is already blown, so I work slow and steady showing him each step.

When I finish the part of the lesson that is done on the counter I rest my head back on him then begin to rub his chest with my shoulder blades. He softly says, "The first time you rubbed against me like this you were aroused and you allowed me touch you."

"If you touched me now, I wouldn't mind."

Without hesitating he moves his hands from the counter onto me. Since we are standing he holds me a little tighter and his soft hair is on my neck because he lowers his head to my shoulder. Soon the ache in my body leaves and he manages to hold me steady and bring me to a climax that makes me tremble.

When my breathing becomes quasi-normal Trevor picks up the container of water. "Is this drinkable?" I get tickled and take it from him. "That's a yes." When I set it down he asks, "Baby, do you need to lie down?"

"I'm fine." I turn around and hold him. "I love you."

"I love you too."

With my wits gathered I ask, "Where were we?"

"In the middle of a lesson?"

I turn around and look at the film canister. "Actually we were at the end of the lesson. There are only two things left to do: take the canister to the sink and flush it with water for a minute and then hang the film to squeegee the water off." After he finishes I tell him, "Now you are going to go through the steps with your eyes closed until you get the hang of it."

Maybe 20 minutes later we are standing by a strip of film he developed that is hanging to dry. My husband is so happy he makes the room brighter.

We finish developing all the rolls and shut down my darkroom. Fortunately there is plenty of time to get ready for our evening before our dinner arrives courtesy of Théo and Rachel.

Showered and wrapped in towels we go to the dressing room. Trevor is elated as he opens drawers in my lingerie chest for the first time and gets out my black bustier and matching panties. He gives me a kiss and my lingerie as he goes to his chest of drawers for undershorts. Next he lays his smoking jacket out and puts on the trousers then he turns around and gets perfectly still. "Geneviève, you are more beautiful than I imagined." He caresses my shoulders and says, "Time for your surprise." I hear the coat closet door close and then his footsteps as he reaches the doorway. "Close your eyes." And he is standing in front of me when he tells me, "Open your eyes, Baby." The second I do I gasp, for he is holding a black strapless evening dress. The full circle skirting is layer upon layer of sheer chiffon and the bodice is velvet.

"I couldn't wait until New Year's Eve for you to wear velvet."

"I can't believe you had this made for me. Trevor, it's beautiful."

"There's more." And I realize his arm is behind his back. He brings it forward and I see he is holding a pair of black satin pumps with chiffon bows on top of the back of them. "I had these made for you too." At a loss for words I step between his arms and hold his face as I kiss him. When I move back his blue eyes are sparkling like pools. "Let's get you dressed."

Trevor hands me the dress and sets the shoes down then he unzips the dress and takes it. He lets it float down onto the floor and offers me his hand to step into the dress. My husband pulls it up and places one of my hands on front of the bodice to hold it up as he reaches around me to zip the dress. Trevor gives me a kiss then kneels to slip the shoes on me. He stands and admires me in his creations then offers me his hand and walks me to the mirrors.

I lift a layer of the chiffon and sway it then let it go and look at the back of my shoes. "Trevor, this is the prettiest outfit I have ever seen."

"Thank you. Mrs. Gardener told me you had black shawls in chiffon and velvet otherwise I would have had one in velvet made for you to wear to the club for dinner and stun everyone."

"Stun is the correct word."

"I also asked her not to use my idea for your shoes until you were seen wearing them in public."

"I guess we will be going to the club soon."

"I want to show off my wife."

"In this dress you will be." As we kiss we hear a car and a garage door raise. Théo is here.

Soft music plays while we eat our luxurious candle light dinner and eventually he looks a little troubled. "Geneviève, you have barely touched your sake. Do you not like it?"

"I like it, but since you are seducing me I want to keep my head clear, so I don't miss a thing."

"I see your point. Two ginger ales in glasses coming up."

The ginger ales and pineapple cakes take us back to the first time we kissed and we talk about our romance and how far it went in a short time. Then he says, "I'm going to change the subject and tell you a story about a place we went to in Havana, Cuba before going on to New Orleans." I sit back in my chair and so does he.

"Things spread by word of mouth among Sailors and the stories change along the way. We all know this, but when a lieutenant that eats with us at the captain's table mentioned a restaurant that's highly recommended because of the Argentine beef it serves we didn't give it a second thought. When Mitch, William and I accompanied by him and two others went ashore in our Tropical Whites, we decided to go there since Mitch speaks Spanish. In the taxi Mitch taught us the phrase, no hablo español and to motion to him saying nuestro capitán. Do know what I said?"

I nod and he continues. "It was a posh place with a quartet playing dinner music and the large tables were all semicircles that faced the dance floor. After we were seated we noticed several men sitting at the bar with a drink and an unusual amount of women unaccompanied by men sitting at the small tables. The women milled about asking the men if they wanted to join them for dinner. Several women approached our table asking us to dine with them, even the married ones. After our meal was served they stopped asking.

"While dessert was being served waiters went around lighting the candle lamps on the tables then the lights were turned down low and more musicians walked out onto the stage. This is when things became ... interesting. While the band warmed up couples walked onto the dance floor and stood looking at each other. When the guitarist started this elaborate intro that we recognized as tango music the men pulled the women to their chests taking a stance. It took all of about two seconds for us to find out why the Argentine tango was called the Forbidden Dance. It was sensual to the point it was more like foreplay than dancing. The men were assertive and the women responded. Their upper bodies and legs were always pressed together unless he was leading her into a turn. There was one part when the man held his partner's chest tightly to his and with her feet planted he pulled the woman across the floor lifting one of her legs up by her thigh along his."

"I ... have a visual."

"Mmm hm. At that point Mitch said, 'Gentlemen we are in uniform. When the music stops we are taking our leave.' We all said, 'Aye, aye, Captain.' and he motioned to the waiter then paid the check. I looked at my watch and the music played for six more minutes.

The music finally stopped and when we were leaving several of the couples left as well. There was an inn across the street. We got in a taxi and some of the couples went across the street."

"Trevor, those women milling about were choosing lovers."

"Yes they were."

I run my hand over the velvet and say, "You've been planning this a while."

"Yes I have. Ever since I knew you would respond."

"When was that?"

"The day you had me box for you and you asked, 'Is that all you are going to give me?' Then you dropped your voice and told me to show you what I've got. And that is when I knew."

"When you were taking me to the bed I thought that if we were already lovers we would make love."

Trevor looks deep into my eyes. "We are lovers now." He stands, takes off his jacket and blows out the candles. Then he offers me his hand. "May I have this dance?"

"You lead and I *will* follow."

Waiting on a record to drop he takes my lead hand and puts his arm around the small of my back by slowly sliding his hand over the velvet standing several inches away from me. "Separate your feet." When I do he moves his left foot between them and bends his knee lowering his body until our chests are barely touching and his face is even with mine. Then he assertively pulls me against him and presses us together. His leg is between my legs and I stand there looking at his mouth. "I bet you want to taste me. And I taste good." He just tantalized me and we are so close that when he spoke his chin touched mine and I felt his cleft. Thus the seduction begins.

Tango music starts playing and he immediately straightens my arm with his lead hand and with our sides together he does the dramatic walk across the room, stops and keeping our arms straight he puts our hands over our heads and leads me into a turn keeping his arm around me and his hand glides under my bust and over my back. Now I understand the velvet, it is what he wanted to feel me through.

He walks us to where we started and dips us with his leg against the one I extend and gets so close to my face his lips brush mine. Before I can react he abruptly stands us back up and I hook my leg around his calf to keep my balance. Suddenly he grabs my thigh and lifts it up to his and sways me to the left then to the right and then he pulls me to his chest so quickly my head almost goes back. Trevor lets go of my thigh and begins a waltz like spin around the room. I run my hand under his collar and hold on to the back of his neck. Trevor lowers his head until his mouth is close to my ear for me to feel and hear his breath just like he does during foreplay.

Trevor dips us again and this time I lock my eyes on his. I don't think I can take anymore and since my hand is still on his neck I tighten my hold and end up lightly pressing my fingernails into his skin. It causes him to clinch his jaw and we become motionless. He stands us up and while the music is still playing Trevor tells me, "I am taking you to our bed." And I am seduced.

CHAPTER THIRTEEN

The next morning we are ripped from our sleep by his alarm clock. Trevor is on his back with my head on his shoulder and since his reach is long he is able to turn it off immediately. He breathes a sigh of relief and lets his arm fall onto the bed. "That's one way to take the romance out of a morning."

"Yes it is. Do you know a way to make that thing not give us hearing damage?"

"Put it under a cheese dome?" I burst into laughter and get tackled onto my back. After he nibbles on my neck Trevor puts on his civvie skivvies and picks up his shirt. "Do you want to wear this?" I happily take it and slip it on. "That's a yes. Allow me." My husband sits next to me and proceeds to button his shirt and roll up the sleeves.

We leave our bedroom and I grab my camera to take a photograph of the dishes on the table and one of the records in the player. I walk past Trevor going to our bedroom to photograph it and give him a kiss as he starts stacking the dishes on the counter.

After eating breakfast we leave the dishes with the others and go to the dressing room. By the time I have my hair up and makeup on, including my neck, he is already in his khaki uniform and everything he selected for me to wear are on the chaise ready for me to put on. "Before you dress me I need to borrow your nail clippers." Typists have to keep their nails short and I started letting them grow out a week before our wedding, so my hands would be pretty

When he hands them to me I notice his eyes are a shade darker. "I'm going to miss those."

I look at my watch. "We have time to spare. Take off your shirt." His eyes instantly return to the beautiful shade of blue I love.

Our time together was lovely with the exception that poor Trevor found out the leg makeup does indeed taste terrible. And we move on to the garage where a vehicle decision needs to be made that is left up to me. Knowing Emily will be watching for us in the distance I choose my hardtop.

Driving to the base we have the windows rolled down to listen to the wind and when we are close he asks. "Are you ready?"

"For what? Being separated from you after being by your side for three weeks, work or Emily's exuberant greeting?"

"Ah ... all the above."

"Nope. Are you?"

"The officer in me is, but the husband I have become is not."

"I love your answer." He touches his cheek that I kiss.

The building is in sight and when we reach the entrance I see Emily hop out of the Willys. It is in this moment I realize how much I missed her rays of sunshine. When Trevor parks the car I slide across the seat, fling the door open and get out. Emily shouts, "Geneviève." and rushes toward me. When she's close Emily warns me, "I'm going to hug the stuffing out of you." I am laughing as she does. "Oh my gosh, this place is a drag without you."

"I missed you too, Emily." Glancing over her shoulder I see William and Trevor shake hands. Their smiles are so big I can see them from a distance.

She lets me go and we walk toward them. "William did everything possible to cheer me up at lunch. I received several little presents and really good food. I found out that Trevor's family spent Christmas with his, so they had not been away from each for more than a few days at a time. Then I began trying to cheer him up. We are close enough to be heard and William responds, "You succeeded." Emily blushes as she tells Trevor, "You'd get a hug too, but you're in uniform."

While William squeezes my hand Emily continues. "The day after your wedding was interesting." William shifts on his feet and his face goes straight. "During our morning break and the women began asking me questions while my back was to them as I made my coffee. 'We knew Geneviève was a socialite, but had no idea she knew Thomas Harding. Have you met him? What is he like in person? What was the private wedding like?' I turned around trying to think of a nice way to respond, because two rudes do not make a polite. Then I hear Becky dryly say, 'Ladies, I could hear your voices in the hallway. It sounded like an interrogation was underway.' You could hear a pin drop and Becky asked to speak with me in the hallway. She told me she was just rescuing me and I could join her in the reception area until the break was over. The next day the only question they asked was how I was doing and they commented on how good the coffee was."

Trevor reaches in the car and gets my handbag. "You might want to take this in case you need your dagger."

Laughter erupts and Emily exclaims, "Wanting to verbally stab those women crossed my mind when I was being interrogated. It was why I was speechless."

Taking my handbag I tell him, "Trevor, I cannot believe you brought that up."

"The door was open. I had to go in."

William adds, "I'm still waiting to use that line."

"I'm going in on that note."

Trevor kisses my hand. "I'll be waiting for you by Mitch's car. See you soon."

"See you soon."

Emily and I watch them climb into the Willys and drive off. While waiting at the stop sign they remove their covers in unison. I wonder who did the count.

It's lunch time and when Emily parks by the curb at the Mitchell's she says, "There's your husband. I'll see you inside." And we get out.

As I walk over to him he opens the door of Mitch's car. "You are a rascal."

"It's one of the reasons you love me. Please get in. You're wasting precious time." I look at my watch and get in.

A few minutes later we go inside and discover what looks like an Easter dinner. Joanna is beaming. "Welcome back." She kisses our cheeks repeatedly and Mitch patiently stands by her side waiting to greet us.

We sit down to enjoy the freshly baked glazed ham and find ourselves at an unexpected briefing. It is the 6th of October and Emily and William are getting married on the 18th, so decisions have been made and we need to know them. Emily took her father Dress Blue's to The Bridal Shoppe in order to match it with the satin the matron of honor dresses are being made from. Emily selected three patterns and Joanna made the final choice. Fortunately her taste is flawless; therefore I am not concerned in the least. We are going to be in the same shade of blue as the men and have a fitting scheduled for next Monday.

After dessert Mitch gets up and says, "Ladies, we have a surprise for you." He turns around holding three presentation boxes from Blackwell's and gives them to us. I open mine first and see a photograph of Trevor and William talking that was taken in my grandparents house on our wedding day. Mitch tells me, "Trevor asked me to bring Joanna's camera, so you could see what was going on while we waited. I'm the only one who has seen them." No one says a word and we begin looking at them until Trevor and I see one of me and his mum outside hugging by the swing set.

"When Mum quietly left the room I thought she was going to check her appearance. She slipped off to see you."

William says, "I knew that was where she was going and went to the kitchen with the camera hoping to get a good snapshot and I did." Trevor bows his head to him. We look at each other and he whispers, "I love you." I know he wants to hold me and it makes me wish we were alone.

After working what seems like the longest work day in my life yet again, the routine we have resumes and when we get in my car we are alone at last. "I have made plans I think you will like. After we pick out a new alarm clock from the commissary that will be quieter we are going to Sam's for a steak dinner. The dishes are piling up. Then I thought we could shower and get in our bed early for a little reading and some well needed rest."

"When can I kiss you and hold you?"

"The moment we get home and I take off this shirt."

After setting off almost every alarm clock in the commissary we find one and go to Sam's where I thoroughly enjoy my chocolate milkshake. Then we go home and see cars are missing and the houses and apartment are dark inside with outside lights on. We are the only ones here. Trevor pulls up to the garage door on the right. He pushes the button and gets back in the car. "I arranged for men who work for the family to remove the empty crate and put the other one in the corner today, so you could park this car in the garage too." I give him a kiss, he pulls in and gets out to close the garage door.

When he comes back to the car for me and the clock, his shirt is unbuttoned. He takes it off, slides me over and out of the car. "All I have wanted for hours is to hold you." He puts his shirt on the roof and we are finally in an embrace and kissing tenderly.

Eventually I whisper, "I want you, but I don't want to ruin this moment by showering so we can get in our bed."

"Baby, what do I not know? You seem ... I sense melancholy in your voice."

"I've been meaning to tell you about this date of the month and I kept forgetting. After tonight we won't be able to make love for a few days."

He holds me close for a minute and then tells me, "I have an idea."

"I'm listening."

"It will take me less than a minute to toss all the living room furniture cushions on the rug."

"While you do that I'll get linens and a glass of water."

"Then afterwards we can shower and have foreplay until one of us breaks and we will make love again." Trevor takes off his dog tags and lays them on his shirt.

In the morning we are awakened by our new clock that does not take the romance out of waking up together, therefore we linger in our bed. Next we make plans for lunch on our bench and start our day.

When the clock strikes noon Emily walks with me down the corridor and when we step outside she waves at Trevor and quickly goes around the corner to William. I on the other hand go slowly to Trevor. It has been a while since I have seen him propped on it with and his ankles crossed waiting on me. And since it has been a while, I become French and kiss his cheeks.

Trevor brought our usual from The Flying Dragon and we feed each other from the boxes with chopsticks and it becomes romantic. When the boxes are empty he holds the bag of fortune cookies for me to get one. I open it and read my fortune. "Everything has its beauty, but not everyone sees it."

"I quite like that. Let's find out what's in mine." He snaps it in half, pulls out the fortune and reads it to himself. "I have a quote from Confucius. 'The wise find pleasure in water.' How appropriate is that?"

"To the point it's uncanny. — Which reminds me, when are you going to tell Théo about the race?"

"At breakfast tomorrow?"

"I'll call the house when we get home."

It is a nice cool day, so we sit in silence and enjoy the fall breeze until it's time for him to walk me to the doors where he takes a risk and steals a kiss.

At home the first thing we see are the dishes and pots and pans that have accumulated. "I'm going to soak theses a few minutes." And without warning, instead of letting him get me an apron I pull my dress over my head, toss it on a chair and stand there in my slip. Trevor shakes his head then steps up to me and softly says, "You keep catching me off guard. I love living with you. I'm going to change clothes."

My husband returns and drops a strap off my shoulder and kisses it. I put my hands on his thighs and let him caress my body through the silk until his heart is content. Eventually we get everything washed and put away then I call the house to tell my parents to expect us for breakfast and Father tells me a messenger made a delivery. I grab my dress and Trevor looks bewildered. While I put it back on I tell him, "The papers from Thomas are here. I shan't be a minute." I give him a kiss and dash out the door.

Halfway there my parents step out onto the portico. They hand me the manila envelope and a business card for the messenger service and get hugs and kisses then I return to Trevor, who is sitting on the sofa with two glasses of wine and a pen on the coffee table. He gives me a kiss then I open the envelope and pull out the press pass with my new name on it. I hand it to Trevor then get out the contract. It is standard, so I just glance over the details. When I lay it on the coffee table Trevor hands me the pen. I cover my mouth and shake my head in disbelief at what I am about to do.

After the contract is signed Trevor hands me a glass of wine and picks up his. We kiss for our toast and make our glasses ring. While thinking my dream just officially came true I realize I need a photograph and get my camera bag. After I photograph the coffee table Trevor hands me the business card and my press pass. I put them in my bag along with my camera, sit back down next to my husband and we revel in the moment drinking our wine and then cook a wonderful meal.

We shower and when I enter the dressing room he is wearing his pj's and a tank then he kisses me and goes to our bedroom. When I join him in a nightgown he gets a gleam in his eyes and pats the edge of the bed. "I haven't done this in a while." Trevor kneels and gathers my gown around my legs and lifts them onto the bed. "This is the best part, getting to join you." With eyes still gleaming he walks around and gets in our bed. "Do you want to sleep or for me to read to you?"

"Read to me."

He gathers pillows and becomes my soft chair, but he reads only one sentence and stops. "You are so beautiful in that. I've missed your nightgowns and parking at our spot. Do you want to pretend we're there?"

"Yes, very much." And we do until we're sleepy.

It's a new day and we haven't had breakfast with my family in weeks and are excited when we enter the house. The smells and the sounds are so familiar, especially the scent of cinnamon. The moment we walk through the doorway I am greeted by Théo, who kisses my forehead and hands me a cup of coffee. It goes from there.

When I compliment a new dress Mother is wearing we find out my parents did go on a shopping spree in L.A. and they had a wonderful time. When they finish telling a brief story about their trip Trevor seizes the moment. "I have an announcement and question for you." He is looking at Théo, who immediately puts down his fork that had a bite of sausage on it he was about to eat. "I want to enter Gypsy in this year's race and I haven't told my shipmates yet, because I can't do this without you. Would you like to be a member of her crew?"

"My answer is yes and thank you for asking."

"I should be thanking you. My next question and is for you, Gérard." Father looks mystified. "Will you be at the helm while Théo and William are on their honeymoons?"

"This is most unexpected. It would be my pleasure." Then I look at Mother. "While they sail practice runs, I thought we, the ladies, could weigh anchor at Old Point Loma aboard Willow." Mother responds, "Oh Sweetheart, what a brilliant idea. We are going to have so much fun." I'm beaming as I nod.

Trevor adds, "We have six Saturdays to prepare, but I know we can pull it off. Théo, you know the course and Gérard, you will be sharing your knowledge with us, so we'll have an advantage we need. Then there is the fact that the rest of our crew trained at Annapolis. They don't even know about Gypsy yet." Mother asks, "When are you going to tell them?"

"This afternoon I'm going to invite them to go sailing Saturday and meet at the club for an early lunch. Of course they will be expecting to take Willow out, but when we get to the marina I'm going to surprise them with Gypsy and my plan to enter the club's race."

"That will be a lot for them to take in."

"I know. I'm really looking forward to it. By the way, you are all invited to the club and to go sailing."

Théo says, "Rachel is going to be beside herself. She's never been sailing."

I jump in, "Théo — why didn't you tell us earlier?"

"The timing was never right."

"We'll teach her the basics while you make practice runs."

"That means I need to take her shopping. Eh-sap." The Navy speak causes a burst of laughter, then we finish eating talking about the race.

Before leaving I show my family the signed contract and give it to Mother. She is going to call the messenger service for me to have it picked up. Théo gets a Stargazer for Rachel and we are ready to start the day.

During lunch Trevor carries out the first part of his plan and our friends are looking forward to sailing. After he picks me up from work we decided there is no time for cooking and washing dishes, because the film from our honeymoon has been hanging in my darkroom waiting on us to return. So, we eat at Micheletto's.

When we get into my darkroom with an extra pair of scissors we cut all the film into sections then begin to look at them on the light table. There is so much captured it takes us aback. We print contact sheets then hang those to dry. When he sits me down on the counter and stands with my bare legs around him we do not give it a second thought. Being married is changing almost everything.

Three nights fly by spent in the darkroom and we realize that 99% of the photographs are for our eyes only. Therefore we select the one I took of the dinner table the morning after we became lovers to have enlarged into a 16 x 20 and framed to place over the mantle of the fireplace in our bedroom. It seems we decided on it because it's artistic. Oh the secrets we are going to share as man and wife. I do look forward to them.

The next day is the one Trevor gets to carry out the second part of his plan. He wakes me up by pulling the covers back as he says, "Good morning, Baby." I open my eyes and look at him. "Are you ready to have some fun?" I roll over and pin him to the bed. "That would be a yes."

When we finally get out of bed to make breakfast he grabs me around my waist and we dance around the room. In the kitchen he dips and kisses me while we cook. Then as we eat my husband throws a strawberry in the air and catches it in his mouth. I laugh and tell him, "You have a hidden talent."

"I've been waiting on the right moment to put my manners aside and entertain you."

"You are in rare form today."

"Expect the unexpected." He winks and throws another strawberry.

Minutes after we get dressed I hear a freight truck drive through the gates and Trevor gathers me into his arms. "Geneviève, although making love with you on living room cushions was more than fine with me I decided to give us another option. In that truck is a bedroom suite for our guest room. I picked it out at the commissary the other day."

"You bought us another bed."

"Mmm hm and everything to go on it."

"I adore you."

"And I adore you." Trevor gives me a lingering kiss and I take it a step further by running my fingers through his hair at the back of his neck. He moans from the pleasure and then he groans.

I coyly tell him, "You opened that door." as I take my fingers out of his hair.

"And you just got even with me over the dagger comment, because now I have to go open the front one."

Trevor holds my hand and I'm laughing when we go out onto the balcony. The delivery men are sitting in the truck looking around the property, so he does that really loud whistle. "I'll move Blanca while you tell them where to park." I go back inside and he goes to the truck.

The garage door is open by the time I get there and after parking Blanca out of the way I join Trevor at the truck. The movers raise the door and I see it's full of quilt covered furniture and boxes. Trevor instructs them to leave the boxes on the table in the garage and to follow us up with the dresser.

While they get the rest of the furniture we stay and remove the quilts to reveal he has chosen a suite of warm brown walnut that has clean lines and no carving. "Trevor, had I seen this I would have chosen it. The color is rich."

"So, you like it?" He gives me a kiss and continues. "The suite had a chest instead of a bench, so I bought it to set at the foot off the bed. I found a nice quilted bedspread with an unusual pattern of white and antique white with two pillow shams that caught my eye. Everything else is solid white; the lamps, draperies and the rods, bed linens and ..." he puts his cheek against mine then whispers, "six throw pillows I bought to pile up while we eat apples." Just as Trevor was nuzzling my neck we hear a thud in the hallway. "And that's why furniture is wrapped in quilts."

From that point on we cut up and after less the 15 minutes go by we are walking down to the garage with the movers. Trevor tips them and I dash for the boxes to find the bedspread. When I do I gush, "Trevor, this is perfection."

"Oh, thank you."

"I should be thanking you." And I give him a come-hither look.

"Baby, hold that thought. We have to go to Blackwell's to drop off the negative of the photo for the mantle in our bedroom."

After pouting I say, "Let's drop the bed linens off at the laundry service on our way to the club and when they arrive Monday for pick up they can deliver them."

"You're brilliant."

"I'll pull Blanca back in while you pack the trunk."

At Blackwell's Trevor hasn't closed the door yet when Mr. Blackwell exclaims, "You two just saved me a phone call."

I gasp. "They're here."

"Yes, ma'am." He reaches under the counter and sets a presentation box down on it. The photographs from our wedding day are in front of us and I just stare at the box. "Mrs. Lyons, when you lift the lid you both are going to get a surprise."

With that said I lift the lid. Trevor and I say in unison, "They're in color." And we look at each other then back down. He chose the one of Trevor giving me a kiss to pass with the swords crossed in front of us to begin with. I tell him, "So, that's what we look like when you dip and kiss me." He replies, "That looks more like a scene in a movie of a royal wedding." Mr. Blackwell is nodding as he adds, "That's why I put it on top. The rest are in sequence."

Suddenly I look at Trevor. "We don't have time to look at them. Our friends and the family will be concerned if we're late."

Trevor sighs heavily and gives the negative to Mr. Blackwell while I put the lid back on. Mr. Blackwell tells us to take the box and go through them at our convenience. They're numbered on the back and we can return next Saturday to place our order. We thank him and leave.

When we are in the car Trevor hands me the box and I set it on the seat with my hand on it. We go a few blocks and I tell him, "I want to see these. We have waited weeks. This is pure torture."

"Yes it is. Let's talk about something else." Waiting on him to change the subject he finally says, "My mind is a blank." And he turns on the radio while we laugh.

We get to the club early and entering the lobby I see my parents looking in the trophy case. We walk over and I stand by Father. He shakes Trevor's hand then kisses my cheeks. "She looks completely different now. I doubt anyone will recognize her. Due to the changes Geneviève made and the skills of you and your crew, people are going to get a surprise since it will be your first time to race."

Trevor responds, "Thank you for the words of confidence. I've been meaning to ask, is that Reginald's son next to him in all the photographs?"

"Yes, his name is Franklin and he is the oldest. Reginald and Norah have two sons and two daughters scattered across the country. The family reunites here for their wedding anniversary on May 6th. They all stay at the ..." He asks Mother, "What does he call it?" She replies, "The Posh."

As we laugh Théo and Rachel walk up. "What did we miss?"

"We just found out you told our parents what Trevor calls The Brava and hearing Mother say, 'The Posh' was too much."

"We've been calling it that since the day I proposed."

Next we hear Emily say, "There they are." Our friends join us at the trophy case and my father tells them a short story of the races Azure won. When he winds it up Trevor jumps in, "May I suggest we go to our table? I made reservations for one poolside for our bodies to acclimate to the temperature. The high this week was 72 degrees and it will drop at least 10 more in the open sea." Mitch says, "Our jackets are in the car. We are definitely not in Hawaii anymore." Joanna adds, "I knew the water was cool here, but last week when Mitch and I went for a walk on the beach, the tide rolled up and got on our feet. I shrieked and ran from it while he stood in it hunched over trying to catch his breath." Everyone bursts into laughter and we go outside where we belong.

When lunch is over Trevor and I are followed by four cars into the marina, so when he parks at Willow, Joanna's car is even with Gypsy. When William gets out he exclaims, "Look at Willow's new neighbor. She's a beauty."

Trevor puts his arm around me and goes straight to William. "Thank you. I think so too." Jaws drop and all eyes are on him. "I would like you all to meet Gypsy. She is the wedding gift from my wife." They look at me, then back at Trevor and finally focus on Gypsy when Mitch finds words. "We should all stop staring at her and go say hello."

Trevor leads everyone to the end of her gangway. "As you may have guessed by now, we're taking her out today and the lady has secrets. In a past life she was a winner. You just saw photographs of her in the trophy case. And when Geneviève had her modified she lost a little weight. Gérard estimated she is over a thousand pounds lighter. After sailing her to Santa Barbara for the last week of our honeymoon I decided I wanted to enter her in the club's race this year." Eyebrows go up on that. "It's been change to a single race on Saturday and is no longer a regatta, making this achievable."

He looks at William and Mitch. "I would be honored if you two joined my crew. Théo has already signed up. He knows the course and the practice course Azure sailed. Also, Gérard has agreed to take the helm while Théo is gone on his honeymoon and for yours, William. After you both discuss it with your ladies, just let me know."

William looks at Emily and she gives him two thumbs up. He tells Trevor, "Count me in." Joanna tells Mitch, "I want to watch you race as much as you want to race." And he quickly says, "I'm in." Trevor shakes their hands and tells them, "Thank you, gentlemen. Now, Geneviève has something to add."

"Ladies, while the fellas are practicing we are going to be watching them aboard Willow." Emily is so excited she shakes William's entire body by his arm while Trevor announces, "Gypsy has a refrigerator, so get what's in the ice chest out and leave it." He hands out metal milk crates and instantly everyone hits high gear.

After Trevor finishes giving the tour below he starts talking, "Today we're here to have some fun with this. Fortunately for us Théo was the tactician for Azure's crew and I'm not changing that." While we nod in agreement he looks at Mitch and William, "That puts you two on the sails." They look at each other and could not be happier. Théo has to watch the wind, the current and the other sloops to advise Trevor, their captain, who is at the helm and makes the decisions. Their responsibilities are merely the sails and taking orders.

"The race is three laps on a triangular course and it begins at Old Point Loma where the pin and committee boat will be even with the lighthouse. Today we are going to make one lap around the practice course that starts and ends at the northern wall of Maison and find out how fast she can go, because Gérard is going to be timing us. Then we're going to enjoy the rest of the day."

With that said we go on deck for the tour where Mother takes Rachel under her wing and the first thing she tells her is how to keep steady by holding on to a line or the rope banisters. Théo and I immediately look at each other over our sunglasses and make eye contact smiling. When we were little Mother called the lifelines rope banisters, so it wouldn't give us a fright. After all, what child needs to hear grab a lifeline if you lose your balance?

The fellas and my father gather at the wheel for a brief discussion and I get my camera out, which alerts the ladies to get theirs out too. Trevor holds out his hand and the others stack theirs on top, then he says, "Break." and they separate to take their posts. Théo sees us and says, "It looks like the paparazzi managed to sneak onboard." Rachel dryly replies, "I'm selling mine to *The Dish.*" Laughter erupts, because that's the local tabloid. We've been in it and it irritates my grandfather.

When we round the point the crew swings into action and seem as if they have been together on this sailboat for years. The sails are up in a flash and by the time we're close to the wall Gypsy is at full speed. My father is by Trevor as he holds the stop watch up in the air and then lowers his arm which means the race against the clock has begun.

Sitting next to Mother watching Trevor, Father and Théo doing something they love together for the first time I slowly put my camera down and revel in the moment. They have her going very fast and could not be happier. Mother softly says, "Giving Trevor Gypsy is one of the best things you have ever done." And she squeezes my hand.

Sooner than I expect I see Father talking to Trevor, meaning we are already close to the second marker. I look at Mother and she tells Rachel, "We are about to make a sharp left turn, which is port side and Gypsy is going to heel, it means tilt down toward the water. We sit starboard to prevent her from heeling too much and to avoid getting soaked. Out of the corner of my eye I can see Joanna and Emily nodding who have been sitting sideways facing forward and holding on to the lifeline watching their fellas. I drop my camera in my bag, zip it up and then face forward. William and Mitch are on the lines grinning from ear to ear.

Well into the maneuver Gypsy does indeed heel and Rachel gasps loud enough for William to hear her, because he glances over his shoulder. When Gypsy rounds the marker and is no longer heeling Rachel whirls around and looks at Théo. He smiles and gives her a thumbs up. She does the same. And we have a future sailor onboard.

When we round the last marker sails are lowered immediately and we all gather at the helm when she slows down. Father holds up the stop watch facing us, "Six bodies heavy and four seconds off our best time." Arms go straight up in the air and there are shouts from the fellas. My father gives me a wink.

After dropping anchor and celebrating Trevor announces, "I'm thirsty and wet. Would anyone care to join me below?"

Like little ducks in a row we go down ladder to the galley and take off our jackets. Trevor hands me mugs as I fill them with cool water. The fellas stand around me as they drink every drop and get refills. Then we switch to sodas and Pellegrino and gather at the table for a snack and to discuss details.

During the conversation Trevor tells the crew he's going to sign Gypsy up for the race tomorrow and get copies of the regulations then bring them to lunch Monday, so William can look over them before he goes on his honeymoon. Emily's eyes start darting around. "Umm, excuse me. I am going to ask for ... a wedding gift. William shouldn't miss the first practice run and I don't want him to, so I have an idea. You all could meet early for breakfast at Sam's and make the run afterwards. That way you will be done by lunch and can eat that at the club, still leaving plenty of time to get ready for the wedding." Trevor responds, "We have a plan." William kisses Emily as if they are alone and she doesn't blush.

I see Rachel get lost in thought and she asks, "Can we go sailing some more?"

We all laugh and Trevor replies, "We'll go anywhere you want."

She thinks for a second. "South, I want to see Coronado from the Pacific."

"South it is. — I have a question for the ladies, who brought gloves?" Even Mother raises her hand. "Gentlemen, I think they should take over." The fellas all nod in agreement as Théo says, "Gené, just don't take us into Mexican waters." When I stop laughing I tell him, "Don't worry. I won't." Rachel looks at Théo, "Ooh, there's a story here and I am all ears."

"Before Gené and I were in our teens we were capable of working the sails on the main mast and from then on our parents put us on them when we went sailing. One summer day we were sailing the course we learned on, which was heading south when we left the bay and then we would come about when we could see the Tijuana lighthouse in the distance and head north to Oceanside Pier. Gené and I were sitting on the bow with our proud parents looking at us when I noticed I could see the lighthouse over Mother's shoulder, which meant we were in the territorial waters of Mexico."

Mother interjects, "Keep in mind San Diego is only 15 miles from the border."

"That's a mere 13 nautical miles and it doesn't take long to get there. So, I got her attention and pointed to it. When she saw it Mother exclaimed, 'Gérard, come about!' Father looked at her and shouted, 'Coming about.' When we were back on course, going unusually fast, Gené asked me if we were going to be pursued and I told her I had no clue. Our day of sailing met with an abrupt end as Father sailed us straight to the marina."

Father adds, "I was simply so proud of our children. It was the first and only time I ever let my focus stray."

Mother says, "That is a good note for that story to end on and for the ladies to take charge." We start shoving everything into picnic baskets and get our gloves.

I take the helm and Mother is at my side. Joanna and Emily are on the main mast and off we go. Théo has his arm around Rachel and she is smiling so much her cheeks are going to hurt. I slide my sunglasses down my nose and look at Trevor then pretend I'm holding a camera. The face he makes is hilarious as he gets out my camera.

When it's time to come about I keep tacking not to lose speed and I hear, "Gené, you are going to heel her?"

"Yes I am. Rachel enjoyed it." My father is beaming and Trevor puts my camera away just in case spray gets us.

The day of sailing is coming to a close and when we're close to the bay I motion for Trevor and ask him how he feels about my father taking her in. I get a kiss and he goes to him. My father lights up and makes his way to me. "Sweetheart, have I told you I loved you today?" He kisses my cheeks and I move over as he takes the helm. Mother is elated.

Waiting for the men to return with the cars Joanna says, "I'm starving. Since we're still in charge I motion we go to Micheletto's." Rachel seconds the motion and when the men get out she tells them, "We've decided to go to Micheletto's." Théo responds, "We had the same discussion." And they load the cars.

We have such a good time that Trevor and I forget our wedding photographs are setting on the front seat until we get in my car. Going down the driveway he suggest I go in and begin showering while he turns on all the heaters so the house will be nice and warm when we get out. The thought of a long hot shower makes me feel better already. I smell like day old fish, so when he parks in the garage I give him a kiss and hop out on the passenger side.

The tile on the bathroom floor is almost cold, so I turn on the heater first and then both showerheads to warm up the shower stall and get in immediately. While the warm water flows over me the bathroom fills with steam. Trevor finally walks in and I watch him peel off his clothes and drop them down the chute. When he gets close to the shower stall Trevor stops and looks through the glass at me. "The daydream I had the first time we were in this house of seeing you in here just came true." I push the door open, he steps in, closes the door and while he rinses off under the other shower head I go to him and put my arms around him.

"Geneviève, your body is very warm and mine isn't."

"I know, so I'm going to get yours warm. Then I am going to bathe you and intentionally arouse you then do something for you I haven't done in a while." And I reach for the hot water handle.

With our thick cozy bathrobes on we go into the living room and I find out what took him so long to join me. There are candlesticks, a bottle of Louis XIII and two glasses by the box we have been waiting to find the treasures within.

I lift the lid and we finally get to see our wedding ceremony and the reception. There are so many things we missed that are captured it's overwhelming. One of my favorites is while Trevor kissed his bride my parents touched their foreheads together as they held each other's hands. I know this happened during our kiss, because before and after the photo was the one of our first kiss as husband and wife. Mr. Blackwell must have turned around while we kissed and took it.

After we look at the last photograph he lights the candles and we curl up on the sofa sipping the cognac and reminiscing about that beautiful day. Then out of the blue he tells me, "I think it's time I taste every inch of your skin again." I blow out the candles.

In the middle of the night I am ripped from my sleep and sit straight up gasping. I am having the worst foot cramp in my life. Trevor sits up, "Baby, what is it?" The pain is so intense I can't speak. I throw the covers back and motion toward my foot. Trevor turns on the safe light and winces. When I look down my toes are drawn up to the point they appear to be broken. This causes me to collapse back onto the bed and Trevor moves to the foot of it. "I have never seen anything like this. I'm afraid to touch it." He sighs. "The first thing I do when my foot cramps is stand up and slowly put weight on it."

I nod and he leaps over me to help me up. I try to put weight on it and that doesn't go well. I cry out, "It hurts too much." Therefore he scoops me up and lies me back down.

"Baby, you are writhing in pain. Tell me what to do."

"I can't think."

A light bulb suddenly goes on in his head. "I shan't be a moment." He vanishes and I hear the front door open and then the solarium door. Seconds later he slams them both shut and I hear him in the kitchen making a lot of noise then there is silence. Trevor enters our bedroom with a large piece of aloe that he trimmed an outer layer off of. "I'm going to hurt you when I put this on. Please don't kick me in the face with your other foot." The man is quite serious and I have a bout of nervous laughter.

After he succeeds in covering my entire foot with the gel he breathes a sigh of relief as do I, because it occurred to me I might actually kick him as a reflex. Next Trevor goes to the kitchen, puts the aloe in the refrigerator and returns with a glass of cold water for us. He sits next to me and when I give it back to him he asks, "Geneviève, what did you do to your foot yesterday?" I gasp. "I was watching you and my father. When I realized you were tacking to round a marker I put my foot down too fast and it stung for a few seconds. — I did this to myself."

He runs his hand over my hair and gives me a kiss then after time passes he looks at my foot. "That was an unusual way to spend an hour. Your toes look normal, that's a good sign. I'm going to tuck you in now. I need to lie down. You're going to have to stay on your back and I'm not going to put the covers over your foot. I'll turn the heat up a tad."

When he finally lies down I notice it's still dark outside, so I make the mistake of looking at the clock. It is a little after four o'clock. "Trevor, I am exhausted, but wide awake."

"Then I will tell you your favorite bedtime story." He turns off the lamp and carefully puts his arms around me. "A long time ago there was a princess that gave her parent's, the King and Queen of the kingdom absolute fits." My heart soars as he tells the story, but Trevor is so tired from the ordeal he eventually falls asleep in mid-sentence. I put my head against his and drift to sleep listening to him breathe.

After eating a very late breakfast Trevor cooked to keep me off my foot, we decide it's take care of wedding things day and begin with selecting the wedding photographs to have printed. With that taken care of we move on to the gifts that can no longer wait. I sit down on the floor with my steno pad and he opens them seated next to me. When Trevor gets to a large one he hands me the card smiling. It's from William and Emily. I turn it over and it reads, For hot cocoa. After he opens the box I see a tray with handles wrapped in tissue paper under several items. They bought us the extravagant gift on the registry, a sterling silver tea service. This could not be more thoughtful.

Then we notice a gift that has been mailed and the return address reads, Professor and Mrs. John Wilcox. Trevor smiles and says, "It's from Sarah." He carefully cuts it open with his pocket knife and inside are five dozen formal dinner candles and a handmade candle snuffer with a sterling silver bell that has a three-masted tall ship at full sail engraved on it and a bone handle. Trevor tells me, "The ship is the USS Constitution of our Navy. She's the oldest commissioned navy vessel in the world still afloat. She was launched in 1797. William and I went to Boston and toured her during our second year Christmas leave at Annapolis." While I am at a loss for words Trevor puts it in the box and moves it to the side.

The next unexpected gift is from Helen. The box is flat and wrapped in glossy white paper with a simple silver bow. He unwraps it and reveals a cardboard box instead of a traditional white gift box. It gives him a hard time, but when he starts pulling out the contents we discover she has given us a small Chuck Wagon bell. Trevor immediately holds it by the rope and rings it. I can't write for laughing.

The list is finished and when Trevor picks up the box the bell was in an envelope falls out. "I recognize that chicken scratch. It's from Hank." He hands it to me and inside is a photograph and a note. After I look at the photograph I give it to him and say, "That's Tillie and she's in foal." Then I get out the note and read it aloud. "I thought you two might like to help raise a horse together for the commander to ride. The foal will be here mid-June. Hank".

"Do you want to take Blanca for a drive when I get back?" And I throw my arms around him. "That is a yes." I get a kiss then he sweeps me off my feet and carries me to the bed in our guest room. Trevor wants me to elevate my foot. After we're settled he says, "I can't believe my family is going to stay at The Posh."

"Your mum told us hearing the Mitchell's and the Moore's going on and on about their room service got them. You of all people should understand that."

"Our day at the zoo that ended abruptly."

"Mm hmm, because you are no longer a cub."

Trevor swallows hard. "We should change the subject." While I rearrange the pillow under my foot I remember something. "By the way, since everyone has seen Gypsy, we're finally going to take Blanca to the base."

"You kept choosing your hardtop because you were embarrassed by the extravagance of my gift." I touch his nose and there is his deep laugh, then we lie in bed talking about the foal until it's time to get ready for the dinner we are looking forward to, because my family is going to be stunned by the color proofs.

The next morning I drive Blanca to work and it takes Emily and William a second to realize it's us when I pull into the parking lot. William stands by his Willys smiling while Emily catches flies. When I park she drags William by the hand to us. We get out and I announce, "Meet Blanca, she is *my* wedding gift." William says, "Hello, Blanca. For some reason I am not surprised in the least to meet you." Emily starts shaking her head at Trevor. "You didn't have time to track her down. I'm having a visual of Mitch in his uniform with Joanna by his side intimidating men at a dealership. You are all thick as thieves." Trevor winks at her and they begin looking her over.

When Emily and I go to the Mitchell's for lunch we take my car for a change and because Blanca gives me a heavy foot we are there in no time. Once again decisions have to made, because we are going to The Bridal Shoppe for what is hopefully our last fitting. Their wedding is in four days. I personally am looking forward to seeing what I'm wearing.

After work we all meet at the Mitchell's and due to the events the last time the fellas went to The O Club alone, they decide to wait for us here. We all have a martini then the fellas put us in Joanna's car and stand in the driveway waving. On the way Emily begins turning into a bundle of nerves worrying we may need another fitting. Joanna speeds a little to get us there faster.

When we get inside the first thing Joanna does is ask Mrs. Garner to bring out a gentleman's cart, so she can make Emily another martini. While we wait, Emily goes into my dressing room and emerges with my gown. The navy blue bridal satin is pretty. I smile immediately and look at the details. It has a jewel neckline and elbow length sleeves. The skirting is pleated making it less full. "I love it. The dress has a sash like the one Trevor picked for our engagement party."

"That was the tie-breaker. Joanna liked two of the three equally and when she saw the back we were done."

Joanna gives her the martini, I take my dress then Joanna and I go into our dressing rooms. We come out in the exact same dress with satin pumps dyed to match. This is when I realize the wedding is going to be completely traditional. We match and she is getting married in a chapel, which means the train of her bridal gown and veil will be chapel length.

Since there is a dress form custom made for me, my gown fits perfectly. This is a relief and we relax and enjoy the moment. Emily has us stand side by side as she ties our sashes. With that done she steps in front of us and points to the right side of the waistbands. "The gowns need a little something extra and I was wondering if the two of you would mind wearing your fairies there?" Joanna responds while I gasp. "I have been waiting for a reason to wear her and I can't think of a better one, your wedding ceremony." The entire time she speaks I nod and Emily is overjoyed. We move on and while we are holding nosegays and letting Emily admire us my stomach makes a sound. We all get tickled and she unties our sashes. We thank Mrs. Garner and leave in such a good mood.

Joanna turns off her headlights before she turns into the driveway and tells us, "Let's see if we can sneak up on the fellas." When we stop laughing we get out and quietly close the car doors then tip toe up the steps following Joanna's lead. Suddenly she flings the door open hard enough to make it hit the wall. The fellas, who had their backs to the door, whirl around and the pot holder William was holding goes flying across the kitchen. The looks on their faces said it all. Emily holds on to me as we laugh and Joanna goes over to Mitch and gives him a kiss. "I do apologize, but I simply had to take this opportunity to get even with those two." The morning they made her shriek from the startle they gave her when we were in Santa Barbara. She settled that score.

Mitch glares at William and Trevor as he dryly tells them, "Once again I am collateral damage because of you two. Is the sake warm yet? I need to get my blood pressure down."

I stop laughing and start looking around the kitchen. He said sake. "Why are we having sake?" Trevor opens the oven door to reveal a roasted duck and all the trimmings are being warmed in it. "We decided to surprise our ladies with dinner from Mandarin Garden's." The fellas seat us and serve dinner. We laugh and talk into the night knowing in two days flights will be arriving and all meals will be a vast undertaking from then on.

The moon is almost full tonight, so when we get home Trevor and I sit in the solarium to watch the moonlight dance on the water and unwind from the day. Thank goodness tomorrow is Tuesday and Trevor will be waiting for me at what has become our bench with lunch for two.

The next day, even though we had to work, Trevor and I had a pleasant day together and when we get home I intend to make the night even better. Trevor closes the kitchen door and I push his back against it whispering, "I have wanted to tell you something since this morning. We can make love tonight and I am going to seduce you. After I have succeeded, I am going to lead you to the bathroom where we will watch each other undress and shower. Then I am going to have you lie down and we're going to find out how much pleasure I can give you."

"Geneviève, you have already succeeded."

I look deep into his eyes then go to the fruit bowl and pick up two apples. I give him one and hold his hand to lead him upstairs to our new bed.

CHAPTER FOURTEEN

The wedding festivities begin at The O Club the next day for lunch. We follow William and Emily and our plans to park Blanca under the carport are spoiled by a two black limousines. His mum told Trevor they all decided to hire them for the duration of their stay. They were picked up from the airport in them which made things easy, because the fellas are busy aboard Louise.

We go out of our way to wave at Harry and go down the corridor that leads to the private dining room. Inside it is a familiar scene. All the same people are here once again I and fully comprehend Trevor and William are more like brothers than friends and this is their very large family that continues to officially get larger. First it was my family and next they are adding the Prescott's.

On the way back to work Trevor tells me, "A situation has developed. Mum told everyone you gave me Gypsy and informed them about the race. She also mentioned you and the other ladies are going to be watching us on our practice runs from Willow."

"We don't have enough life jackets."

"Gypsy is like the Teddy Bear that sent us all to the park."

"Yes she is. — I'll have my father call Mr. Davidson."

He parks while I am counting heads in my mind. "Baby, don't forget William is moving his things into the house his parents are staying in after dinner tonight."

"I'm going to happily go sit at my desk now." Trevor laughs as he walks around Blanca to open my door.

Time flies and Emily and I are walking down the corridor in silence. We are eating at The O Club again then going to the Mitchell's. The plan is Emily and I are going to sip on martinis with Joanna and watch the fellas get William's things from their house and wait there while they pack his quarters and move him out.

The plan worked like a charm and soon Trevor and I are on our way home where we shower and lie down to pass out. He is exhausted and I am a little tipsy. Martinis are sneaky, because you sip them like cognac, but they are oh so not.

The next day is a blur of catching up over meals and staying at The Posh too late. We wake up in the morning seeking caffeine, because the wedding rehearsal and dinner that follows is upon us. We switch back to my hardtop, because time will not permit us to go home after work and I have a dinner dress hanging in the back to change into at the Mitchell's. When Trevor pulls into the parking lot it is as if we hear crickets. "Trevor, I miss them already."

"This is going to take some getting used to."

"I'm not even sure what to do with myself."

Trevor gets a glint in his eyes as he scans the area and says, "I know what to do with you." He tosses his cover on the dash and lowers me carefully out of sight.

The Prescott's and the Snowden's planned today's itinerary. Since the men in my family and Rachel work downtown near The Posh, to save some running around, my family is having lunch there with the others. Those of us on the base are having lunch at the house Bill and Judith stay in. It has two stories and looks very nice on the outside and the moment Judith opens the door I see rank does indeed have its privileges. It is beautifully furnished and has fire places in every room we go through. Upon entering the formal dining room we get two surprises, Kelly and Bobby did not go to school and the club is catering the meal. I forgot William became a member as an engagement gift for Emily.

The Snowden's entertained us and we had such a good time Trevor and I did not want to leave. Bill talked Joanna into staying, stating just because Mitch had to leave didn't mean she should miss out. So, outside I tell Trevor he should ride with Mitch back to Louise and I will meet him at the Mitchell's. Driving into the parking lot alone reminds me of my life before Joanna introduced herself. I was happy then, but compared to now that life pales in comparison. Marrying Trevor is and will be the best decision I have ever made.

When five o'clock finally rolls around I cannot leave fast enough. To my relief when I pull up to the Mitchell's, Trevor is waiting outside for me and I rush into his arms. "Geneviève, you're trembling. What did I miss?"

"Nothing. It's just that when I went back to work alone, it reminded me of my life before you and my heart ached for you. I love you so much."

"And I love you so very much." Trevor rocks me in his arms until I'm perfectly calm. "Now, let's get you inside. I'll get your dress." I wait for him where we stood and we go in together where Joanna is holding a glass of whiskey and a martini. She must have looked between the draperies to find out what was taking us so long and knew we needed a drink.

Maybe a minute passes and Joanna reaches for our drinks. "Trevor, you two can finish theses after you help her change into her dinner dress. It could take longer than you think and we cannot be late. You both know the way to the guest room." Without a word we let go of our drinks and do as we are told.

The second my dress is on Trevor goes, "Uh oh, your slip is showing at the neckline."

"This is not a problem. You just need to lengthen the straps."

"I don't how to do that yet and we're pressed for time. I'll get Joanna."

I go into the hallway and stand by the bathroom door to wait for her and hear Trevor say, "Joanna ... umm ... Geneviève needs a woman's touch." She chuckles and when she sees me she asks, "What does he not know how to do yet?" I reply, "Lower lingerie straps." She nods and we go into the bathroom. With the problem quickly solved there is time to enjoy our drinks, get my camera and pile into Joanna's car. I'm excited about seeing inside the chapel I have driven by hundreds of times and walked around occasionally for as long as I can remember.

The chapel is at the main gate. There is a single lane in front of it for vehicles to be at the entrance during an event and parking for it is at the back. As we walk around the back of the chapel Trevor and I are holding hands and he slows us to a standstill and says, "Look at those stained glass windows. They have tall ships at full sail out in the open sea. I'm so pleased the sun is still shining. We'll be able to see every detail inside."

Mitch adds, "I love being in the Navy."

Trevor and Mitch act like doormen and swing open the two doors that go into the small vestibule. Joanna and I step inside and see the rope attached to the bell in the steeple and the doors into the sanctuary have tiny windows in them. I tell Joanna, "We will be peaking through those." She smiles and nods.

Entering the chapel we were very quiet and when Emily sees us she exclaims, "They're here." to her family and William's parents. Everyone else is eating calamari at Micheletto's by now waiting for us to join them for the rehearsal dinner. I get my camera off before she reaches me and hand it to Bobby. Then she hugs the stuffing out of me and Joanna. Trevor and Mitch just get their hand squeezed and we are off to meet the Chaplin who William is talking to. Trevor and I are able to look around while the happy couple discusses details with him.

The chapel has classic interior architecture. The high V shaped ceiling is filled with an elaborate structure of wooden beams with matching wooden lighting hanging from them. There are three steps up to a stage like area where the ceremony will take place and two small rooms at the back. Candle stands are going to be on it and in order to include Bobby in the ceremony he is going to light the candles. The pews that will have floral arrangements on each end tomorrow are perfectly spaced on each side of the aisle and the best part is the stained glass windows. The sun makes them glow and it brings out the smallest detail. The largest window is between the tall ship themed ones and it has a medallion of the guardian angel watching over two children playing by a cliff which is from a well known painting by Bernhard Plockhorst that he painted in 1886.

When the rehearsal begins we realize Kelly is the only female here who is not married and she flatly refuses to be the bride, because standing with William 'would be too weird.' Emily hands her a microphone stand to walk with and pretend it's the bride. Problem solved. Bobby is going to get a few humorous photographs of that and because Emily turned into a wedding coordinator in front of our very eyes the rehearsal takes less than 15 minutes and we are on our way to join the others.

There is such a commotion when we go into the private dining room it takes Trevor and me a minute to notice Claudette and Joseph are here. Joseph is the only person here who was with them, so to speak, on their first date. After Emily and William greet their guests the dinner begins. Surprisingly there is very little conversation about the ceremony, because everyone is excited about going sailing in the morning and plans need to be made. After the dessert is served we do not stay long due to the fact we are all waking up quite early in the morning.

Trevor is finally getting his sleep routine back, because he woke up before the alarm goes off and wakes me up like we are on our honeymoon by kissing my shoulder. It pains us to get up, but the wedding day festivities are beginning in less than an hour. So we get dressed and go into the garage where he passionately kisses me before raising the door. Trevor backs my car out to where Théo is waiting in front of the house and I walk to him for my usual kiss on the forehead. I stand and wave to them as they leave for Sam's for what is being called the bachelor breakfast then go inside to have a regular breakfast with my family.

I ride with my parents and grandparents to The Posh where two limousines filled with family members pull out and follow us to the marina. When we drive through the gates we see Emily, Joanna and Rachel standing by Emily's car that has lifejackets stacked on the trunk. I get out, take a snapshot and we start handing them out. My father parks his car at the gate and my parents and grandparents get in a limousine, because the drivers are going to take us to Willow. Emily hops on the hood of the one in front. Joanna and Rachel glance at me as we climb on.

The fellas are already aboard Gypsy and someone tells the driver to blow the horn. When the fellas get to the stern their jaws drop at the scene we make arriving. They are so stunned they don't even wave, they just go to the gangway and walk over. Trevor kisses my cheek and whispers, "I can't believe you were a human hood ornament." I dryly tell him, "It was the exuberant bride's idea." He stifles his laughter and after a few minutes of the crew greeting everyone they go aboard Gypsy as several of us call out, "Fair winds and following seas."

When we are all aboard Willow, Father takes us out with Gypsy following. At the mouth of the bay they go south and we go north to drop anchor at the spot the committee boat will be on race day to wait on them while they get ready for their first true practice run.

During the wait, my family along with Rachel, Claudette and Joseph go below for binoculars. Emily's family has their own and then I watch Joanna's father hand out binoculars from a large shopping bag to Trevor's family, then to William and Mitch's parents. I stand there amazed without taking a single photograph. Joanna walks over to me and quietly says, "Thursday I was elected unanimously to go to the commissary. They all insisted on paying me for them. I had to go to the bank and make a deposit Friday morning." I get tickled as Emily and Rachel join us. Joanna tells them and we go to the stern laughing to watch for Gypsy.

Shortly I hear several footsteps and Willow feels off. I ask them, "Is it my imagination or is Willow listing?" Joanna replies, "It's not your imagination." We look over our shoulders and see everyone is standing port side looking through their binoculars. It's as if they're manning the rails.

Mother is by Father at the wheel with the stop watch waiting to time them and she doesn't have to wait long, because soon I call out, "I see Gypsy and she's closing in fast." And in a blink she is upon us. Trevor gets Gypsy so close to Willow we feel a light mist. Everyone cheers and the run begins. My heart rate escalates as I make a dash to the bow to watch her. She is magnificent and her captain is impressive. I watch through my binoculars and when he starts tacking my breath catches, because he heels her perfectly around the charted marker. This time our passengers make Willow list starboard and Father shouts, "Lifeline people." They're holding their binoculars with both hands instead of one, which could cause someone to go overboard. In the excitement they forgot the rules.

When Gypsy heads west I can barely see them go around the marker and it only takes a minute for me to see Gypsy clearly again and the boom swing. Before any of us are ready for this to end they fly passed us and the shouting begins. I go straight to Mother with Joanna on my heels and she quietly says, "28 seconds less." It takes a moment for her words to sink in then Joanna and I pretend the time was average. When Rachel and Emily get close I whisper the time to them then Rachel tentatively asks, "Why are we whispering?" Mother replies, "We do not want to take away the thrill on race day for our spectators" Right after she speaks, here they come with her sails down and their arms in the air. They slowly sail by and Father starts Willows engines.

The fellas are already on shore and we, their ladies stand eagerly by as Father, Robert and Bill lower Willows' gangway. I call out to Mother, "Get our things please." and then run to Trevor. I leap into his arms and he spins me round, "Tell me, Baby."

"28 seconds less." He puts me down, dips me and I get a proper kiss.

After we celebrate briefly, the parents of Gypsy's crew join in. Mitch's are enthusiastic about the sight of their son on her bow. Bill vigorously shakes

William's hand and he gets a hug from Judith. Father tells Théo he hasn't lost his touch then Mother kisses his cheeks and resumes taking photographs. Evelyn is speechless while she pets on Trevor and Rowland puts his arm around me as he thanks me for the unforgettable experience of watching his son.

Everyone is ashore and Emily begins looking around the crowd. "It pains me to break this up, but I have a wedding to get ready for." Faye's eyes get wide as William turns on a dime and starts running to get her car followed by the rest of the crew to get ours. Father says, "Tell them we will stay here to settle Gypsy in. Emily, we will see you at the chapel." Next we hear cars.

The entire way home we can't keep our hands off each other and the second Trevor and I are in the house he pins me against the door. After one passionate kiss he sweeps of my feet then carries me upstairs. Now we are running a little late, so after a quick shower we stand at the kitchen counter in bathrobes eating what taste good cold from the refrigerator.

Trevor puts on civvies and is ready to go before I have on my undergarments, so while sitting at my vanity dealing with my hair and makeup I tell Trevor everything I need in my train case, including Primrose. He pauses and kisses my shoulder before he gets her. Then he takes his uniform along with my shoes and gown to the car. He picks out my most comfortable day dress and happily puts it on me and we are finally off.

When I knock on the Prescott's door I announce I have a man with me and Faye is laughing as she opens it. She takes my gown and camera bag from him and he gives me a kiss then goes to the Snowden's, where the men are. When I step inside Joanna and Emily appear. Joanna is also wearing a day dress and Emily is wearing a long line bra and a crinoline slip. I gasp when I focus on her hair. "Oh good, you like it. The hairdresser left and I took off my robe. I was getting hot."

Faye tells Kelly to raise windows as I go to her. "Emily, you are beautiful."

"Thank you. I'm thinking about getting nervous." Joanna tells her, "Don't do that. Let's pop the cork and get some food in your tummy." While she pours I look around and it's obvious the house has been rearranged for the day. The living room is a dressing room now. Three different floor mirrors are placed like the ones in the salon and the only things on the coffee table are a champagne bucket, glasses and trays of hors d'oeuvre.

After a toast to the bride she motions behind me. I turn and see her bridal gown and headpiece hanging on the coat closet door. Both items are chapel length and it's made of satin and tulle. It has a bateau neckline and long sleeves with buttons at the wrist. "Emily, it is perfection."

"I think the long sleeves were a mistake."

"You won't after the sun sets."

"That's true."

I look at Joanna. "That is a lot of fabric. I motion we dress her first."

"I second that motion. Emily, are you ready to put on your gown and see what you are going to look like?" She nods and drinks all the champagne in her glass.

When the dress is successfully on her using the skills of every female in the room Faye pins her fairy to the satin bodice of her dress. Next we put her Grecian styled head piece on that has two satin covered head bands with the veil attached to the back band. She steps into her shoes then Kelly hands her a bouquet of white roses and to the mirrors we go to admire her. Emily gasps when she sees herself and needs to be fanned. She is beautiful.

Next Kelly and Faye assist Joanna and me in getting dressed then go to their rooms. While they are gone Emily helps us put on our fairies and gives us our nosegays of yellow tea roses. When Faye and Kelly come out looking very pretty Emily gets out their flowers and Faye calls Robert. Since we can't sit we stand and pose for photographs until he arrives in Emily's car. The moment he walks in wearing his very impressive Service Dress Blue's, because he is a four star admiral, emotions gets high and handkerchiefs appear. Makeup is checked and we are out the door where we discover Robert was smart and had all the car doors open. He puts Kelly in then Faye and escorts me to the back passenger side.

Next is Emily and the fun begins. Joanna and Emily hand their flowers to Robert as Emily tosses her train to me and gets in with the assistance of Joanna. After we are all in Robert hands out the flowers and closes the doors. While he walks around, Joanna and I decide to drape the train across our legs like a lap blanket to keep it from getting wrinkled. Emily gets her fan out and fans us. This causes us to laugh and her family glances over their shoulders then they laugh and we cut up the entire way to the chapel.

When Robert pulls up out front the photographer for the base walks up, the bell begins to ring to let everyone know the bride has arrived and the four swordsmen outside act like valets and start opening car doors. One escorts Kelly inside followed by Faye and her swordsman. Then the other two escort Joanna and me up the steps into the small vestibule where they go stand by the closed doors to the sanctuary. Instead of peaking through the small windows we watch Robert proudly walk with his daughter on his arm inside and then two swordsmen go outside, close the doors and stay to guard them.

Roberts asks, "Ladies, shall we begin?" Joanna steps in front of me, we all nod and then he and Emily move to the side to be out of sight. In a commanding tone he says, "Gentlemen, doors please."

They open and there Trevor is, standing tall between his shipmates looking so handsome in a uniform I have been waiting to see him in. I can hardly wait for Joanna to reach the halfway point, so I can get close to him. When she does I wink at Emily and off I go forcing myself to keep a slow pace. Finally going onto the stage I get to smile at him and there is that oh so familiar gleam in his eyes.

The pianist changes the music to the Wedding March by Felix Mendelssohn and there is the lovely bride whose face can no longer be seen even though she has the thinnest veil she could find. Only until she reaches the stairs is when I can see her face which means William finally can.

The moment Robert places her hand into William's my eyes go to Trevor's and they are already looking into mine. His eyes move down slowly as he admires me. When his eyes are once again looking into mine I slowly admire him and then the ceremony begins.

When William lifts her veil I can see the love in eyes for her and he kisses her, perhaps more than he should, but his thoughts are only of his new wife and not the fact the commander of the base is a guest.

After the Chaplin says, "Ladies and gentlemen, it is my honor to introduce you to Commander and Mrs. William Snowden." they take their first steps together as husband and wife and soon I am holding on to the arm of my husband whom I missed and cannot wait to be alone with.

The swordsmen open the doors to begin the arch of swords ceremony and in the distance Emily sees her surprise from William and slows them to a snail's pace. Since Trevor and I are on their heels we are able to hear her say, "William, you chose our wedding day to go out on the town in The Chariot. I can't wait to be in it alone with you. I love you, William."

"I love you too, Emily."

As they make it through the arch with the kiss that is required to pass, family, friends and guests see The Chariot and jaws drop. It was a secret that only William and my family knew about. Emily looks over her shoulder at me and shakes her head in disbelief of what we did for them. Her car is parked at a distance next in line and that is what we, the wedding party ride in, to the reception at the banquet hall of The O Club.

When Trevor and I are walking down the corridor in front of Mitch and Joanna he spots the coat closet, grabs the door knob and pulls me in. We hear them chuckle as he closes the door. "The things a man has to do for a bit of privacy with his wife." After he kisses me most passionately I warn him to use caution when he opens the door to avoid hitting anyone with it. Therefore he opens it slowly and peers out then opens it wide and says, "Hello, Mum." With a twinkle in his eyes he motions for me to go out. I sigh and prepare myself, then step into an empty corridor. I whip my head around and he tells me, "I do enjoy toying with you."

"Mmm hm. You're tie needs to be straightened."

Trevor immediately looks down, sees it is fine and says, "Touché." I give him a kiss and he offers me his arm grinning from ear to ear.

When we finally enter the beautifully decorated banquet hall where a quartet is quietly playing, I tell our friends, "We apologize for making you wait." William replies. "Not a problem, we're used to his antics." Emily adds, "It's nice being married isn't it?" I nod and we begin posing for photographs and adding family members as they arrive.

When dinner is served Trevor is thrilled, because they chose prime rib for the main course. All I can think is about the day steak was served at The O club and how appropriate it was for their dinner party. We did have fun that afternoon.

While eating the prime rib he informs me that after dinner and a dance the base commander and his wife will take their leave, because they are well aware how uncomfortable their presence makes all these officers. The room *is* filled with navy blue and Joanna and I blend in at the wedding party's table. Just Emily stands out as the bride and she should, this her moment to shine. And shine she does.

The cake has been cut and the traditional dances have been danced. Thus the party part begins and as Trevor said, the base commander and his wife vanish. We drink champagne and reminisce then dance late into the night. Then I notice Emily is cutting two small pieces of the wedding cake. She wraps then carefully and gives them to Joanna and me saying, "These are for sweet dreams and a token of my love for you both." Joanna and I finally pull our handkerchiefs from our nosegays.

After the bouquet is tossed we all follow them to the front tossing yellow rose petals as William helps his wife into The Chariot and we watch Elliot drive them away to a little inn on a pier they will stay at tonight then they will leave in the morning for L.A. and their bungalow at The Beverly Hills Hotel. They intend to spend their entire honeymoon there, unlike Claudette and Joseph. Instead of going back inside, several of us leave as well. It has been a long day that began at sea and Trevor and I are going to be exhausted if we stay any longer.

Mitch and Joanna follow us to the Prescott's and we go inside to get our things. We all say our goodnights on the sidewalk and go our separate ways. At the house we go straight to the dressing room. "Trevor, seeing you in this uniform was a distraction during the ceremony."

"Your beauty and seeing Primrose for the first time since our honeymoon had me distracted."

"I was distracted by my desire for you. What has happened to me?"

"The same thing that has happened to me. I love you and it fuels my desire. Now, we are going to get undressed and go into the shower to take your hair down."

"And then we are going to give in to our desires?"

"Yes. Yes we are."

A few hours later I wake up gasping for air and Trevor turns on the lamp. "Geneviève, you're frightening me. What's happening?"

"I ... I had a Telling Dream." And he looks bewildered. "Armand, I saw him standing with his back against a brick wall riddled with bullet holes. They're going to execute him. I have to tell Father." I throw the covers back and go into our dressing room. I grab a dress off a hanger, put in on over my head going down the hallway and run out the front door. When I reach my parent's house I slowly open the door and see lights are on in the study. I run to it and find my father standing by his desk then I hear Mother drop something in the kitchen.

He looks at my bare feet and asks, "What on earth has happened?"

Breathlessly I tell him, "I had a Telling Dream." and pause to think of a way to buffer what I saw. It takes me all of two seconds to realize there isn't one, so I decide to speak bluntly. As I draw in deep breath Mother enters the study and goes straight to Father's side. "It was about Armand. I saw him standing with his back against a brick wall riddled with bullet holes. I didn't see them, but I know he was facing a firing squad." Tears begin streaming down my face as Father closes his eyes. I hear the front door close as I look at mother and plea, "Tell me I saw this so we can stop it."

"You did see this so we can stop it."

Out of the corner of my eye I see Trevor is sort of dressed as he drops my slippers and then places a sweater on my shoulders. Mother is holding a kitchen towel and walks over to give it to me. While I dry my face Théo can be heard bounding down the stairs. He is barefooted and wearing his pajama's. Before he can say a word Mother fills him in on what is happening and Father sits down as he sighs heavily. "The day that letter from him arrived at the office addressed to a

François Bassot I knew he was going to begin helping La Résistance since he had no family to protect and he sent it there to protect our family in Aix. Apparently someone is going to betray him." And there is silence.

The front door opening breaks the intense silence. I whirl around, because I know it is my grandparents. Grand-mama holds her arms out to me and I throw mine around her. She begins to console me. "Je suis désolé."

"Why are you sorry?"

"It is I that has brought this upon you. This gift is a heavy burden I have had to carry and you now carry it. When you are capable, tell me what was in the dream."

I move back to see her face. "Armand was standing with his back against a brick wall of building in the town square of Aix riddled with bullet holes. He was being so brave. It was as if I was there, watching. I knew if I tuned my head left I would have seen the firing squad he was facing. Then I woke up."

While rocking me she says, "Gérard, to prevent this do you have a plan yet?"

"I am to trying to decide how to tell him when I call."

I turn around to see his hand is resting on the receiver of the phone. "Father, you cannot call him from here." Trevor interjects, "Sir, she is correct. The enemy listens to all calls and can locate the origin of them."

Mother lightly gasps and Father takes his hand off the receiver. Théo and my grandparents sit on the sofa. While their minds begin to reel, mine stops and I sit in one of the chairs in front of the desk. Trevor sits next to me and I tell Father, "It takes 45 minutes to drive to Tijuana. Check into a hotel using the name he gave you and call him collect with it. The operator will say where the call is coming from. Also, call us collect from a pay phone. Does that friend of his still live in Marseille?" My parents nod. "Tell Armand you are calling to let him know you received a letter from him and he mentioned not feeling well. You think he is worse than he is letting on and Armand should go to him as soon as possible."

Trevor says, "Genevieve, that's brilliant. They won't hesitate to give him a travel pass into a liar of the dragon." He tells my parents, "Marseille is a heavily occupied area." They nod again and my father starts taking notes.

"It is a little after 6:00 in Aix, so he will get the travel pass by 7:00 and leave immediately. He should be safely at his friends' house in Marseille in time for a late dinner. Tell him you will be waiting on him to call when he gets there to let you know how the friend is doing and say since he never can remember your phone number he should write it down and give him the one for the hotel. Armand will know to hide his car and leave on foot in the middle of the night to get papers from La Résistance to change his identity and vanish into thin air."

Théo slowly exhales and tells us, "We have a plan." Father says, "Now, we need to put it into action. Since it is Sunday all the banks are closed. I need everyone's currency from Mexico." Mother tells him, "I am going to pack an overnight bag." Théo and Mother go upstairs, my grandparents leave and my father opens the safe. Trevor tells me, "I'll get us a glass of water."

While my father gets out passports and currency from Mexico and the States he says, "When I was no longer a boy I figured out the reason we really moved here was to save my life. They did not tell me, thinking it would cause feelings of guilt. I love my life here with my wife and children and I can finally tell them how grateful I am for their sacrifice." Tears escape from my eyes again. "The only thing keeping me sane is the knowledge Trevor will take care of you while we are gone." Before I can say anything Trevor returns along with Théo who is now wearing slippers and a robe carrying a little felt drawstring bag he gives Father. We remain silent while he counts pesos.

My grandparents return still in their robes and Grand-papa hands him a pouch. "There are pesos along with gold and silver coins anyone will take. I will call Mrs. Baxter and have her reschedule all appointments for Tuesday." Mother walks in carrying their bag and her train case. Grand-mamma reaches in her pocket and pulls out a strand of pearls. "Josephine, these have no sentimental value. I bought them because the diamond and gold clasp caught my eye." She puts them on Mother leaving the clasp under her collar. "If you need assistance from a woman, not one will refuse them." They hug as my father gets his briefcase out and puts everything we gathered in it.

We all go into the foyer and Théo gets their jackets from the coat closet. Mother tells him, "In order to avoid alarming Rachel tell her we are not dressing for dinner and we would like her to stay in the guestroom tonight and to pack an overnight bag." Father tells me, "Trevor, I am certain, has many questions. Simply tell him and Théo all you know. Théo, you tell Rachel what you learn. The secrecy ends here." He begins speaking in French to his parents and I quietly translate for Trevor. "He said he loves them, and Mamma, we are going to speak openly when I return with my wife." She nods. "He is going to call here after he reaches Armand and will call again when they know he is safe."

My parents kiss each of us and we watch them go down the hallway and into the kitchen. Their race against time has begun. Grand-papa tells us, "We are going home and will be waiting by the phone." Théo says, "We will call immediately after we hear from them." And they take their leave.

"Gené, I know you need food. I'm going to start breakfast." I look at Trevor and he tells me, "Don't worry, I'm actually afraid to offer you my arm." I smile and he motions toward the kitchen. He remembers that night he won my heart and I told him if he touched me I would not be able to stop crying.

Théo is pouring orange juice when we walk in. No one needs caffeine that's for sure. Trevor pulls me out a chair and gives me a look. Théo hands me a glass of orange juice and gives me a look too. They are going to cook and I am going to watch them. The skillet Mother fried sausages in is still on the range top. Théo touches the handle with caution. "Still warm, eggs and sausages is it."

While they cook Trevor tells Théo, "I've heard of clairvoyants and chalked things up to mere coincidences around here until this morning."

"It changes your mind when find out your wife is one."

"Yes it does." And they chuckle.

After I eat my last bite of scone I notice Théo is sort of staring at me and I raise an eyebrow. "Gené, I don't mean to rush you, but I have been dangling in suspense all morning and I eventually do need to call Rachel. Are you ready to tell me what I don't know?"

"I'm guessing you don't know the real reason our grandparents moved here." He sighs heavily and shakes his head. "A long time ago it occurred to me how much our grandparents loved living in Aix and since Grand-papa was going to inherit the château and the title of nobility I decide there was more to their story and eventually I talked to Grand-mamma. When I told her my suspicion she said, 'You get more and more like me every day. I am going to tell you what your father does not even know.' She went to speak to Grand-papa and we went into the drawing room where she poured us a glass of cognac.

"When our cognac was warm she began talking. 'Early in my teen years I began having what I call Telling Dreams. They were mere seconds long. Some of them foretold good things to come and others were about danger or tragedy in the future. One morning when your father was 10 years of age I had one and saw his name carved in marble matching the marble in the Delcroix mausoleum. When I awoke I knew a war or the constant civil disputes were going to take his life. We told our families and made the decision to move to the United States without ever telling your father exactly why. We did not want him to shoulder the responsibility of being the reason we left. It was our decision and we never looked back, because we were happy here and in time we had a happily married son and two beautiful grandchildren.' Then she sipped her cognac in silence giving me time to absorb what I had learned.

"Next she told me, 'If anyone ever asks about this, give them an honest answer. We protect one other and it ends there.' No one ever asked, but when Father and I were alone briefly this morning he let me know he had figured it out when he was older and kept it to himself."

Théo looks down and softly says, "They did leave due to the civil unrest."

"It has been amusing to me all these years that I could hear thoughts and knew things inexplicably. After my talk with Grand-mamma I became concerned I too would have Telling Dreams, but time passed and I thought I was not going to have that part of the gift and one day I stopped worrying about it. — Life as I knew it just ended."

"Gené, I wish I could think of something to say to make you feel better."

"You can't, because there isn't, but I appreciate the thought. Do either of you have any questions?" They shake their heads. "Then I'm going upstairs to lie down. Trevor, will you bring a glass of cold water and my slippers up?"

"Of course." They stand as Trevor pulls out my chair and I go upstairs.

In passing I pick up the phone on the balcony and set in on my nightstand. While I rinse my feet Trevor enters the bathroom. He dries them off for me and puts on my slippers. He has already pulled the covers back on my bed, so I lie down on my side and he walks around the bed and lies down near me. "Baby, I don't know what to do."

"Hold me. I'm in a state of shock, so trust me, I won't cry." He scoots up against me and puts his arm over me. We both sigh, then we hear Théo going into his room and I find myself staring at the phone. Soon I recall why it was installed and lie on my back. "I was just thinking about the night we stayed up all night talking and kissing while we waited on your parents to call. Will you kiss me?"

"Yes, Baby."

After long tender kisses he rests his head on my pillow then I start looking around. "It's a little strange to me for us to be making out in here."

He chuckles. "Now that you mention it, I agree. And the door is wide open with your brother walking about the house. Being married is nice."

We hear a car pull up. Rachel is finally here for Théo. Not even two minutes pass when the phone rings. We flinch as we sit up and I answer it. "Hello."

"This is the international operator. I have a collect call from François Bassot in Tijuana, Mexico. Will you accept the charges?"

"Yes, ma'am."

"Go ahead please."

"Sweetheart."

"Father, it is so good to hear your voice."

"It is good to hear yours as well. Everything went as we thought. Your mother is unpacking; I am getting food and we are going to be in our room. I will venture out occasionally to check on you all. We love you."

"We love you too."

"Please tell the others. I will call back soon." Then there is that awful buzzing sound followed by the sound of Théo and Rachel quickly ascending the stairs.

Théo is dressed and has Rachel by the hand. He pulls her into my room, because she slows down when she sees us on my bed. Théo could care less. When they are standing at the foot of it I repeat the conversation word for word. Théo sits down on the bench and Rachel sits by him. Next I call our grandparents.

When I hang up Rachel says, "Théo, I would really appreciate it if we went back down stairs where you can tell me exactly what is going on." He stands and she glances at me and Trevor. "Excuse us — please." In the hallway she whispers, "For crying out loud, Théo. You had us burst into her bedroom."

"The door was open and I knew they were dressed. It will make sense to you after we talk." Trevor instantly puts his hand over my mouth and tackles me onto the bed. When I stop laughing he pulls his hand away, kisses me and we just rest and wait on Father to call.

Eventually the smells of food cooking make their way into my room and we hear Théo on the stairs. He stands in the doorway. "Rachel is cooking lunch. It will be ready in a few minutes." After he leaves we slowly get out of bed.

Before we sit at the table the phone rings and we all are on Théo's heels. He answers the phone and hangs up in under a minute. "Armand made it to his friends' house. Mother and Father will be home in the morning. They are going to call before they retire for the evening." I turn to Trevor and he literally holds me up while Théo calls our grandparents.

After we eat the last bite of the delectable lunch Rachel prepared Trevor picks up the bottle of wine. "May I suggest we finish this in the living room?" Without a word we all pick up our glasses.

Trevor sits down on the sofa and holds out his arm then I curl up next to him. Théo and Rachel settle in on the love seat and eventually I notice Rachel's wheels are turning. "If anyone has questions for me, today is the day to ask. I want to put this behind me when it's over."

Théo asks, "When did you suspect there were things you and I didn't know?"

"Remember the summer we went to the château when I was learning how to drive?" He chuckles and nods. "We were walking the vines and Grand-papa was talking about his youth and there was a touch of melancholy in his voice. Grand-mamma placed her other hand on his arm then he gave her this look and I knew."

"When did you talk to her?"

"Not long after we were home. Next question."

Rachel asks, "Since your father can't speak openly over the phone, how did Armand know what is going on?"

"Every now and then before Théo and I were going outside to play after Saturday lunches she would tell us to build a sandcastle instead of roller skating and other little things. Then one day she told us we shouldn't play on the swing set and when we were walking passed it to play on the beach Théo decided to go down the slide just one time. He went head first and when he landed in the grass he screamed and sat up holding his wrist. It began to swell immediately. He didn't cry, but I sure did. Oh, that scream.

"He had twisted his wrist and while Mother put ice on it and Father held me, Théo asked, 'How does Grand-mamma know these things?' Father replied, 'Of this I am not sure, but you should always listen to her. — I will tell you a story about how Armand and I learned to do so the hard way, as you just did.' This got me to stop crying."

Father sat back and began. 'It happened on a very hot day in August. The night before, we decided to go for a swim in a pond filled by underground spring water that is almost cold. Armand rode his bicycle to the château as always and when we were leaving with our hobo lunches she made, Mamma told us not to ride our bicycles to where were going. We always minded her, but it was too far and hot to go on foot, therefore we rode them and disobeyed her for first time. We were almost there when Armand hit a rock in the road and he went flying. His bicycle hit mine and down I went. Covered in dirt and bleeding we were. Fortunately our bicycles were not damaged; therefore we forged on to wash off in the cool water and swim. It soothed our wounds and when our clothes were dry we headed home. Mamma did not scold us as she put salve on our wounds, knowing we would never disobey her again.' Théo and I were wide eyed."

Rachel responds, "That answered my question and more."

Trevor sighs. "The answer to mine is probably going to be a Shakespearean tragedy, but I can't go through life wondering why Armand has no family."

Théo responds, "Gené, I'll take this one and yes, it is tragic. Armand's family owned a print shop in Aix and a few years after our family left they found out book printing was lucrative in Paris and moved there. Later on they heard about a new printing press that was fast and being sold somewhere in Austria. Armand was sent to investigate and make the purchase if it could improve their business. While he was there a plague stuck Paris and he wasn't allowed back into the country. When he returned he discovered his entire family had fallen to the plague. I am going to leave out the details."

I tell him, "Thank you."

Théo nods and continues. "He moved the shop back to Aix and vowed never to marry in order to avoid the heartbreak of loss again."

Trevor sighs then says, "I'm glad I asked. I was thinking he also lost a wife and children."

Rachel exclaims, "I did too. Oh thank goodness. That didn't sound right."

Théo pats her hand he is holding. "We know what you mean."

Rachel asks, "Is there anything else anyone needs to know about this family?"

I look at Théo and he replies, "I hope not, with every fiber of my being."

Trevor adds, "If Joanna was here she would say there isn't one person in this room that didn't get hit by a ton of bricks today."

I raise my glass. "I'll drink to that." The others raise their glasses and we do indeed drink.

Our glasses are empty and I tell Trevor, "I would like to go home." and tell Rachel and Théo, "We will be back in time for dinner."

At the house Trevor calls his family to explain why we will not see them today before they catch the red eye. I go straight to our bedroom, throw my dress on the chair and collapse on our bed. Trevor walks in, undresses, gets in bed and covers us up. I hold my arms out to him and he lies on my shoulder. A little bit later I ask, "Are you all right."

He chuckles. "I'm getting there. When you jumped out of bed it felt as if the alarm went off on Louise for an emergency drill and I was already lagging behind. I watched you put your dress on walking through the living room and out the door you went. That's the second time I've had to chase you. When I caught up and put the sweater on you, I just stood there feeling helpless watching you with my heart aching as you pleaded to your mother and cried in your grandmothers arms. Then you just stopped and took charge of the situation. It felt as if I was watching an officer take over in a crisis. You were remarkable."

"Thank you for telling me that. I felt as if I could have handled things better."

"If I didn't know otherwise I would've thought this was not your first time to be in that type of situation."

"It's all sinking in now. Trevor, a man's life was placed in my hands."

"There is a reason for that and it is because you were the only person equipped to handle it due to the intel you had."

"Oh my gosh, that is why. I can't thank you enough for answering the question I've been asking myself all morning."

"Why me?"

"That's the one."

"Armand is safe and everything is going to work out. You set things in motion that changed everything."

"I did." I sigh heavily in relief. "I know what Grand-mamma told me was from years of experience, but still, sleep will not come easy to me for a while."

"What did she tell you?"

"That it didn't take her long to realize she only hears what she needs to hear and she only sees what she needs to see and it gave her comfort. In ancient times we would have been called a prophetess, a seer or a soothsayer. Please don't label me."

"I would never do that and as for calling you a clairvoyant, that was to break the palpable tension in the room. Things needed to lighten up."

"That's an understatement. — Trevor, I don't want to talk anymore."

"Are you comfortable?"

"Mmm hm."

"Then close your eyes and rest. I've got you."

I do love being in his embrace, but the image of Armand keeps going through my mind. "Trevor, the dream, I keep seeing the dream. Make it to go away."

"I wish I could." And he gives me a tender kiss. Suddenly my emotions rush in and I begin kissing him passionately as I pull him on top of me.

While he kisses my neck he pauses. "Baby, when I reach a point you need me to stop tell me."

"There won't be one."

"I love you, Geneviève."

"I love you too, Trevor."

After lifting his torso up a little, I take off my camisole and he lowers his chest to my bare breasts. The only thing in my mind is how good the weight of his warm body feels and the pleasure we are going to share, because we have all the time we need, and then some.

While we get dressed for dinner he watches me put on dove gray trousers and a petal pink cashmere cardigan and shell. "Why are you watching me?"

"To know what I should wear." I nod and brush out my hair. When it's in a chignon I sit and watch him. After he's dressed he looks at me with those blue eyes and says, "You're lovely. May I select the strand of pearls?"

"I'm not wearing jewelry tonight."

"Then may I interest you in a pair of shoes and socks?"

This is when I realize I'm barefooted and reply, "Yes, please."

"There is that beautiful smile." And I get a kiss along with shoes and socks.

Sunday dinner is being served at my parent's house and when we are in the foyer we hear the usual noises coming from the kitchen and my grandparents talking. When we enter the kitchen the first thing I notice is a cake dome and under it is my carrot cake. I go straight to my grandmother and kiss her cheeks.

We have a wonderful meal and pretend nothing has happened. Then we go to the living room to have our cognac to be close to a phone. As usual, the ritual of sipping the cognac begins to relax me and then the phone rings. This time no one moves, so I stand up and go into the study. To my pleasant surprise I hear my mother's voice. "Sweetheart, I was hoping you would answer. Feeling better are you?"

"A little, Grand-mama made my cake. Is Father all right?"

"He is doing well. I cannot talk long. It will be dark soon. I need a favor."

"Anything."

"Have Trevor call Betsy in the morning and tell her you are not going to be at work. We will be home during the hours before lunch and want you there when we return. Tell everyone we send our love and will see them soon."

"I will. Bonne nuit, Ma Mère."

"Bonne nuit, Ma Fille."

I stand there listening to the buzzing sound lost in thought and then I feel Trevor's hand over mine. He slips the receiver out of my hand and hangs it up. "Is everything all right?"

"Yes, it was Mother. I wanted to talk with her longer."

He kisses my cheek and I tell him Mother's request, then we go into the living room. I tell everyone what was said and we go home.

In the morning I wake up holding Christopher and Trevor is on the other side of the bed awake. "Why am I holding him instead of you?"

My bottom lip starts to quiver as he slides over to me and caresses my face. "You were tossing and turning so much I was in the way. For some reason when I spotted Christopher I thought you might hold on to him in your sleep and get still. So I got up and gave him to you. It worked like a charm."

"I have mixed emotions about this."

"Don't give it a second thought." I put Christopher aside and hold him tight.

Rachel and Théo have breakfast cooked and ready to serve when we get there. This time we all drink coffee and a lot of it. Rachel also called in to work and poor Trevor has to report for duty.

When I walk him to the door he is so unhappy. "Geneviève, I do not want to leave you."

"I know. Kiss me." And he does ever so gently, with such longing.

"I'll call during lunch at the Mitchell's. I love you."

"I love you. Pay attention on that ship." He laughs his deep laugh and closes the door with me inside.

Still sitting at the kitchen table after over an hour goes by we switch to orange juice. "Théo, they should be here by now. If I stay in this house one more minute I am going to lose my mind."

"That makes two of us. Let's go sit on the portico, that way we can see them the moment they arrive." Rachel sighs in relief and we get up.

This is much better. The morning air is cool and the sky is blue with sun rays making their way through the white clouds. We can hear the birds singing and the breeze blowing the sea grass. Théo is sitting between us and I hold on to his arm resting my head on his shoulder. Rachel is holding his hand with their fingers entwined. This makes me smile.

We are all relaxed and settled in nicely when we see the sun reflect off the chrome bumper of a car. We expect to see my parent's car, but it's Trevor's instead. I stand immediately and he parks in front of our house. When he gets out I ask, "What on earth?"

"I was going below deck following Mitch and knocked my cover off. I forgot to remove it. Since that's never happened he put me on liberty and ordered me off his ship. On the way here I kept thinking about the last thing you said to me, 'Pay attention on that ship.' And did I? Nope."

"Trevor, you could have hit your head."

"Yep and wound up in sick bay getting stitches. So, here I am." When he is on the top step I throw my arms around him. I could not be happier he is here and he didn't get seriously injured. "Did I miss anything?"

"Not a thing. Want to have a seat and stare at the gates with us."

"Sounds good to me." After we sit down silence falls. He looks at us a few minutes later and comments, "L.A. is about 120 miles from here and the hotel in Tijuana is only 19, but because they're in another country it seems as if they're further away."

Rachel exclaims, "It does. I feel like time is standing still."

Théo adds, "We need to do something to occupy our minds."

I tell them, "I have an idea inspired by being bored with Théo while we waited out here to stay clean before we went somewhere."

"It's been years since we played that game and it sure is a good idea."

Trevor asks, "Geneviève, what are we about to play?"

"I Spy." He chuckles with eyes gleaming. "Girls against the boys and you go first. Then I get to guess first, because we go clockwise."

Rachel adds, "I just turned six years old and can't wait to say you're on fire."

Trevor replies, "I won't make you wait. I spy something black."

I shake my head. "Trevor, I saw you look at our mailbox." Rachel and Théo burst into laughter.

"Aww, I'm a little rusty. Sorry Théo, it won't happen again."

"I guessed, my turn. I spy something ... red."

Théo guesses, "The tail light on Trevor's car."

"Oooh, you are burning up."

Rachel says, "Thank you, Théo. The flag on their mailbox."

"Well done, Rachel. In less than a minute we have them two to zip. You're turn."

"I spy something gold."

Trevor guesses, "Théo's signet ring."

"You're warm."

I guess, "Trevor's wedding band."

She exuberantly says, "You're on fire."

Théo says emphatically, "Trevor's Academy ring." Théo gets a thumbs up.

Rachel and I have them four to two and it's Trevor's turn again. He looks around then flatly says, "I spy something burgundy." Heads turn to the gates and there they are, my parents.

We are on our feet as Father pulls up to the portico. Mother slides across the seat and jumps out before he puts the car in park. "What a wonderful greeting committee." Father gets out. "Gérard, all our children are here." She bounds up the steps straight to me, looks in my eyes and touches my face then hugs me. Théo and Rachel get hugs then she stands in front of Trevor. "I did not expect you. I am so pleased you are here." She carefully hugs him, because he is in his uniform.

Father steps up with his brief case and their overnight bag. He sets them down then holds his arms out to me and holds me without kissing my cheeks. He was worried about me. Next he begins to hug the rest of the greeting committee. My poor father is not being French due to the immense relief of being home.

Trevor opens the door and Théo picks up the overnight bag and Father gets his briefcase. "I am stepping into the study to call my parents." Mother asks him, "Gérard, would you like a cola?" He nods and we are off to the kitchen.

Trevor seats her as Théo open's a cola for everyone and Rachel hands them out. Mother takes a drink and begins to tell us about their trip. "There were cars lined up at every gate of the border crossing. We were there longer than it took us to drive home." She takes another drink. "In order to get home as soon as possible we entertained the thought of skipping breakfast. Fortunately Gérard noticed there was a street vendor selling those burritos they make for breakfast from the hotel window and since he keeps his thermos in his briefcase, we filled it with coffee there. Otherwise we would have starved." My tired and thirsty mother takes another drink.

"Since I have told about our departure to explain why we are late, I will tell you all about our arrival. We decided to stay at a different hotel, because we were going to use another name. After checking in we went straight to our room and Gérard called Armand before I opened the draperies. Your father told him exactly what you told him and Armand said he would call before he left for Marseille. The call barely lasted two minutes. While I unpacked your father called here and brought food back for lunch. Then the waiting began."

Father walks in shaking his head and drinks half of his cola before sitting next to her and picks up the story. "There was a Mariachi Band playing in the court yard. They were still playing after Armand called to tell us he was leaving. We collapsed immediately, being so relieved knowing he was going to make it out before ... you know. Then out of the blue my wife asked me, 'Do you think if you went down and offered each member of that band a gold coin to stop playing they would?' We laughed for the first time since Saturday. Eventually I considered it." This makes us all laugh, because we know she was being serious and so was he.

"None of you know this. I was Armand's beneficiary until the war began and he willed his business and house to Monsieur Tillett, for what I believe to be these reasons; to protect our family there by having the Delcroix name removed and if he did not make it to the end of the war Luc would keep his job and be a good provider for his wife and children. Then if he did survive he could return and easily reclaim his life.

"For Armand's safety he told Luc he was going to visit a sick friend without knowing how long he would be gone and for him to continue with business."

Theo says, "My heart goes out to Luc and his family. They will think he has been captured or killed." This leads me to ask, "Do you think they will be interrogated?"

"The Mariachi Band eventually did stop playing and your mother and I could think clearly. We came to this conclusion; the person who was going to betray Armand knew details of his actions, therefore he knew Luc was not involved. Even though the man is clearly horrid, we feel he would not want to put him and his family in harm's way. In order to do this we think he was going to the shop today to make certain Armand was there before he went to sell his soul to the enemy. After Luc tells him he is away visiting a sick friend and does not know when he will return we feel the man will wait. Hopefully the brigade will leave before he realizes Armand went underground and have to let it go, otherwise he could risk being investigated."

Trevor remarks, "Your conclusion is spot-on and the man was well aware they would put his feet to the fire wanting to know how he got information on someone in The Resistance had they not captured Armand. Their tactics are a known fact."

My parents beam as they look at each other. Mother is smiling as she says, "Moving on. I need sustenance. Sweetheart, when you and Trevor have lunch on your bench, from where do you eat most often?"

"The Flying Dragon. We are fond of eating out of the boxes."

Her eyes drift as Trevor whispers to me, "She's starving. She's going to want half the menu." The list begins with spring rolls, makes its ways to Peking Duck and ends with my cake for dessert. Théo and Rachel volunteer to get the large take out order and Father says, "I am going next door." Mother tells him, "I am going to soak." The men stand and pull out our chairs. Then Mother hands the strand of pearls to Father and he gives her a kiss that turns into a kiss that prompts us to lower our heads to look away.

While my eyes are averted it occurs to me one minute my father was getting something out of his desk and the next he needed to go save the life of his best friend. And when he gave her the kiss he realized the ordeal was over and she got him through it. This is love.

CHAPTER FIFTEEN

For the second morning in a row I wake up and Trevor is on the other side of our bed. Even though it has only been two days since I had the rug snatched out from under me I want to move passed it and wake up with him by my side. He of course is awake and sees my eyes puddle. I am in his arms before I can blink. "Baby, we fall asleep in each other's arms, it is more than enough for me. You need to give it time. It *has* only been two days."

"I need something to preoccupy mind."

"The way things move around here you won't have to wait long." This makes me smile, because I know it's true.

We cook breakfast together and when we go to get dressed I am feeling more like myself. Then a straw breaks the camel's back, there is a run in one of my stockings. I dryly say, "I'm done." Trevor turns around and asks, "With what?"

"Wearing stockings to work. I don't have enough to make it until this war ends." I toss the stocking into the air and slide a closet door open.

"Geneviève, what are you doing?"

"Probably what you think I'm doing, getting a pair of trousers." I pull out a pair of navy blue trousers.

"Good color choice." He steps up to my closet and gets a white silk blouse with a peplum. "This will cover your belt and make you look more feminine." While he buttons it up he asks, "How are you going to present your case?"

"We do not work in a public area. Not even the men who make deliveries see us. Summer is over and I have noticed a few of my co-workers are already wearing that leg make up with a line drawn up the back of their legs. More than likely they will start catching colds causing them to miss work and for what reason? We have reached desperate times that are calling for desperate measures *and* losing part of our dignity. Trousers are warm and being worn by more women each passing day. Times are changing and we need to change with them."

Trevor applauds. "Well said. I'll get those chestnut brown trouser shoes my mum sent and the matching bag for an extra touch." He does think of everything.

We go to the base in his car and standing in the parking lot he kisses my cheeks then says, "Go get her, Baby. I love you."

"I love you too."

Trevor stands by the car and waits for me to go inside. I pause at the doors, blow him a kiss, draw in a deep breath and open the door. It's probably a good thing Emily isn't here. She would be beside herself.

When I walk into the C's Room everyone gasps and I pretend not one thing is different as I get situated at my desk. The big hand of the clock reaches the 12 and Mrs. Sloan walks in. Since I sit at a desk on the front row the first thing she sees is my trousers. She doesn't miss a beat and starts handing out folders. When she makes her way back she steps up to my desk. "Mrs. Lyons, I would like to speak with you in my office." And then I hear a chair slide back.

"Mrs. Sloan, I have something I have wanted to say and the time has come." I recognize the voice. It's Mrs. Stanhope, a woman in her fifties. "Before you send her home to change clothes I want you to know I have already been reduced to wearing this ridiculous leg makeup and am trying to draw a straight line up the back of my legs. It is humiliating. I wear trousers everywhere with the exception of this place. When winter arrives I am going to freeze half to death. This fate awaits us all, including you Mrs. Sloan. Please get permission for us to wear trousers. Mrs. Lyons ..." I turn around to face her. "I want to thank you for your courage to take a stand for us all."

One by one every woman in the room stands and knocks on their desks. I place my hand over my heart and look at these women taking a stand with me. Mrs. Sloan says, "I will make some phone calls. Ladies, please begin working. We do have a quota to meet." She leaves the room and we take our seats.

At 11 o'clock the door opens. We all stop typing and look up to see Betsy standing next to Mrs. Sloan looking like she is about to burst. "Ladies, you will be pleased to know that effective immediately the women in this build may begin wearing trousers as long as you are recognizable as women." Suddenly applause begins and I watch Mrs. Sloan blush for the first time in my life.

When the clock strikes noon I take off like a shot empty handed down the corridor and out the door to Trevor who is waiting by the bench. I start running and he holds his arms out for me as I throw mine around his neck. "I knew you would win after you told me your opening statement."

"You are the only person that heard it."

"I beg your pardon."

"All I had to do was show up wearing these. I'll tell you about it on the way to Sam's. I want a milkshake." He chuckles as I grab his hand and go to the car.

On the way to the base Trevor pulls over into a parking lot, kisses me and says, "Remember, to the victor go the spoils. Be thinking of what you want."

"I already know what I want."

"And she speaks with that lilt in her voice. What do you want?"

"For you to recreate the night we returned to Gypsy after we went riding."

"You tell me this now?"

"Mmm hm. I want to find out how you will react after thinking about making love with me all afternoon and you finally get your hands on me."

"I hope I don't hit my head." My eyebrows go up instantly. "Baby, I was toying with you. It was not my intention to alarm you. Forgive me?"

"Of course I do." Then I glance at my watch and dryly tell him, "But I am not going to forgive you for making me late."

His eyes get wide and he looks at watch. Then he chuckles and says, "Touché. You got even with me in record time." Beaming he kisses my cheek and puts the car in drive.

When I walk up to him after work he says, "There she is." And my heart skips a beat. He extends his hand and I slowly slide mine onto it. The way he kisses my hand causes me to get butterflies. "I think we should dine at Mandarin Garden's. The quiet will maintain our mood." He opens the car door and I slide in.

Going down the driveway I place my hand over his heart and as I thought it is close to pounding. Trevor sighs, "Geneviève, I'm not sure if I can get us up stairs."

"Then I will." He gives me an inquisitive glance and pulls into the garage. The moment the car is still I whisper, "Catch me." and fling open the passenger door.

Going up the stairs taking my hair down I hear the garage door lowering and the chase begins. I kick off my shoes and run through the kitchen unbuttoning my blouse and drop it on the staircase that he is taking two stairs at a time on. I barely make it into the guest room when he catches me with such force we fall onto the bed. We help each other get undressed kissing passionately and when we're nude merely undressing winds up being our foreplay, because he slows our momentum enough to look into my eyes and with his he asks, now? With mine, I say yes and he takes my breath.

In the morning I wake up in our bed with my arms around him instead of Christopher. All is right with our world.

Since we missed lunch at the Mitchell's Monday I am looking forward to seeing Joanna as we go up the steps. He opens the door and when she sees me she holds out her arms to hug me and stops cold in her tracks staring at my trousers. "Darling, you got Mrs. Sloan to change the unwritten dress code. Well done. It is official, you are a force to be reckoned with." She kisses my cheeks, then Trevor's as Mitch gives me a thumbs up and we all sit down for a nice lunch.

During the conversation the wedding becomes a topic and she says, "Emily's picture in the paper was lovely. Did you get extra copies?" My face goes straight and I briefly close my eyes. Her picture was in Sunday's paper and I completely forgot. Then I clearly hear Trevor's thoughts. "They are visibly upset. Mitch sent me home Monday without knowing why. They need to be told."

I look at him and reply, "I know. I'm just trying to figure out how to begin."

He sort of smiles and tells me, "You just did." I whip my head to look at Joanna and Mitch then watch them slowly put down their forks. Trevor draws in a deep breath and releases it. "My wife has a gift and part of it is she occasionally hears the thoughts of the people she is close to."

Mitch replies, "We caught that."

Joanna smiles at me and says, "Please take your time figuring out how to tell us this story, so we can absorb what he just said." Her words trigger a bout of nervous laughter from me, so Trevor reassuringly rubs my back then I proceed to make an extremely long story short. Due to time constraints we have to leave, but I assure them we will be back when the work day is done. We see ourselves out to give them a moment alone.

Trevor parks in the back of the lot and asks, "Are you all right?"

"Yes. I'm fine."

"That makes me feel better, but it's because I knocked my cover off you had to tell them. Otherwise the family secret would have remained in the family."

"Trevor, they are family." He gives me a kiss and escorts me to the sidewalk.

As promised we return after work for drinks with the Mitchell's and when we get home a note from Théo is taped over the door knob of the service entrance inviting us to dinner at our parent's house. During the apéritif they announce Rachel turned in her two week notice today. I sense that if things go as they hope I will be Auntie Gené next year. Then while we are unwinding from the day Judith calls and invites us to dinner. We thought they were gone. What a day.

While having dinner with Joanna and Mitch at the Snowden's we find out why they stayed. Bill used his stature to benefit Emily and William by getting them a house reserved for admirals as a wedding gift. It is two stories with a study, three bedrooms and several fireplaces. The house has been unoccupied because it was one of the first ones built on the base and in need of attention the base didn't want to spend part of its limited budget on. Bill agreed to pay for the renovation with the stipulation it be given to the newlyweds. By the time they return from their honeymoon it will be ready for them to live in. Emily will be beside herself.

The next day is one we all have been looking forward to, Saturday, aka Race Practice Day. When my father is on the bow with Mitch I watch the weight he has been carrying all week due to the events surrounding Armand lift. And we, the ladies begin teaching Rachel how to sail. Sunday Trevor and I sleep late and have a lazy day spent sitting in the solarium until it is time for dinner back at my grandparent's house. Maison de la Mar is sanctuary once again.

The week flies by and I am thrilled because it's Friday and it's Halloween. Preparations have been made for it all week and Trevor has tried to get me to give him a clue as to why all the excitement and each time I tell him he has to wait and see. During lunch Monday I invited Joanna and Mitch to Maison and today I reminded them to dress in solid black and to be there before dark, so they can park inside the gates, otherwise they will have to park on the street.

When we get there Trevor sees the sign hanging from a lantern that reads, GATES CLOSE AT 8 P.M. and when he turns off the street he sees the gates are covered in Spanish moss which makes Maison look eerie. My father and Théo are wearing solid black stacking wood in the middle of the driveway at the entrance next to the fire pit that already has a fire burning in it and there are several black chairs to the side of the driveway lined with torches that go to the steps of my parent's house. Trevor drives by slowly and when we get inside our house he scoops me up and exclaims, "I can't take the suspense any longer. It looks like a play is being staged out there." I touch his nose and motion for him to follow me into the dressing room. "This must be good."

I hand him a black turtle neck sweater. "Mother got this for you and I need you to put on black everything else and go outside to help while I get ready."

As he dresses I undress and wait on him to finish and leave. "Not that I mind seeing you in only lingerie, but you're really going to be secretive to the point I will see nothing?"

"That is correct. You should give me a proper kiss before you leave, because you won't be able to for hours." He gets a glint in his eyes and runs his hands along the bare skin at my waist and starts kissing his way from my shoulder to my mouth. This makes me forget what I was going to do first.

Halloween evolved into a performance over the years. It all started when my father, in his opinion, became too old to put on a costume and walk around with his parents asking for treats. So, for the first time Grand-mamma was going to be able to hand out treats and she decided to go all out and make caramel apples. After working on them all day they were ready when night was falling and Grand-papa opened the gates. To her dismay only two children knocked on their door in half an hour.

When another child finally showed up and picked his caramel apple from the tray she held out, he told his parents he was glad they talked him into going inside the gates. The second Grand-papa closed the door Grand-mamma called Father downstairs and told him to get a tray, because they were going to greet children at the gates. Needless to say, she gave out every one to very happy children. And now I sit at my vanity patting talcum powder on my face to make my skin look pale and drawing thick lines of black liquid eyeliner to bring out my eyes then I stain my lips with the juice from raspberries and blackberries to make them a dark shade of red. All this is for me to become one of three witches conjuring a magic potion in a cauldron hanging from a roasting spit over a fire.

Next is the costume Mother, Grand-mamma and I wear. It has a simple black dress made of cotton that is hemmed to show the top of the black Victorian lace up ankle boots and when we move, the black wool stockings underneath. We wear full length gloves to cover our skin and to protect us from the heat of the flames. The best part of the costume is the dramatic hooded cape. It is made of black weighted wool which makes it stay close to our bodies and it is lined with black silk. Grand-mamma wears a large ruby brooch that is a family heirloom at the closure of hers to signify she is the most powerful witch.

Standing in front of the mirror I carefully pull the hood over my head and turn off all the lights then go stand in the solarium. The gates are closed and the torches are lit. Claudette has Joseph in black and he is helping Théo carry a bushel of red apples. Grand-papa is tending to the fire and Trevor is facing the house talking to Rachel, Joanna and Mitch. I watch him a bit and think, when you see me you will not believe your eyes. At that moment he looks up and sees me. He is close enough for our eyes to lock on each other's. I stand a minute merely looking at him and then pull the hood over to cover part of my face as I turn to leave.

Quietly I go across the cobblestones and disappear in the garden to make my way to the back of my parent's house. In the kitchen it is anything but quiet and there are two stock pots filled with caramel sauce on the range top and two antique glass apothecary bottles labeled Eye of Newt and Wolfsbane Mother and I use for the potion are on the counter.

I take off my cape and gloves to help Mother get the black cast iron kettle out of the oven where it has become nice and warm. Then Grand-mamma and Mother pour the caramel sauce and drop the long wooden spoon into it while I place the bottles on a burlap covered silver tray. As we help each other put on our capes the last glimmer of light outside disperses and it's time for the show to begin. Grand-mamma picks up the tray, Mother and I get the burlap pot holders made for this occasion and lift the cauldron. We follow our powerful witch down the hallway and she opens the doors. We step onto the portico and Grand-mamma slams the doors shut to let Grand-papa know we are outside and it's time to open the gates. Also she does it to startle the children who are standing at them peering through the bars waiting on us to appear. From this point on only my grandparents will speak and with thick accents to add to the drama.

There are three black witches' brooms propped up by the door and Grand-mamma gives one to me, then Mother and when she has hers we step into view at the top of the steps and follow her to the fire pit. When we are there we smack our broom sticks onto the cobblestones and the children's eyes get wide and some gasp, then my grandfather takes my grandmothers' broom, my father takes Mothers' and in an unexpected twist, Trevor steps up to me instead of Théo and takes mine looking into my eyes the entire time. They put them down on the cobblestones in front of the fire pit with the ends touching, five feet away from it to keep the children at a safe distance, but to make certain, my grandfather tells them, "Be warned, stay back from their brooms for we know not what they will do if you get to close to them. — The reason their brooms are black and they *wear* black is when they fly on them at night you will not be able to see them." The children who are here for the first time look up and scan the sky.

Next my father and Trevor take the cauldron from us and hang it over the fire in the roasting spit as Grand-mamma gives me the Wolfsbane and Mother the Eye of Newt. She slowly stirs the potion and says, "Eye of Newt." and Mother adds drops of the brown colored water from the bottle into the potion. "Wolfsbane." and I sprinkle cinnamon into it. Next she chants part of a spell from *Macbeth* while stirring, "Double, double, toil and trouble; fire burn cauldron bubble." Parents who are familiar with the play by Shakespeare try to keep straight faces as their children stand close to them with mouths wide open.

She waits a minute then gives an order to Trevor and Father, "Stab the apples and give them to me." Trevor raises an eyebrow and I manage to stay in character. Father takes a pointed wooden stick, stabs the apple with it and hands it to my grandfather who hands it to his glorious wife. Then Trevor stabs an apple and I find myself enjoying his reaction to all this.

Soon two of the several buttered baking sheets that have been placed on chairs are filled with caramel apples and my grandmother points at Théo. We are doing something else different. He stands and picks up one of the trays then hands it to Rachel. She immediately goes to the children to give them out. Next she points at Joseph and he looks a little uncomfortable, but he stands straight up and gets a tray for Claudette. Joanna is fidgeting in her seat, but trying to keep still as she waits for my grandmother to point at Mitch. When he hands her the tray Grand-mamma has successfully included everyone here.

When my grandfather begins to close to the gates I hear the sound of small feet running then three children dart in. I am starving. Standing over the sweet smell of the caramel for over two hours is always more than can I bare, but the last apples are handed out and when everyone is gone we make apples for ourselves and our friends. Our men hand us our brooms and we go inside, toss our capes onto the round table in the foyer and collapse at the kitchen table. A minute later my grandfather walks in with the tray of our apples followed by the others. Joanna immediately says, "Brava. Ladies, what a brilliant performance. Never have I seen anything like it. This is the best Halloween of my life." Rachel chimes in, "I could not agree more. Théo told me I would be astounded." Mitch tells us, "Thank you for inviting Joanna and me. I cannot resist saying this, it was definitely a treat." And we all have a good laugh.

All the ladies are seated and Trevor pours glasses of water that Mitch and Joseph serve while the men in my family heat the dinner from the club. When the food is warm my father goes to the wine cellar and we move to the dining room. I'm not sure if we inhaled our meal due to hunger or because we really wanted one of those caramel apples.

After the table has been cleared my grandparents are the first to leave. Then Théo announces he is taking Rachel home, because tomorrow is practice run day and Mitch along with Joseph volunteer to help clear the way out. I just want to go home, so we all say our goodnights. Trevor picks up my cape and places it over my shoulders, hooks the closure and carefully drapes the hood over my head then offers me his arm.

We go into the solarium and Trevor stops walking and steps in front of me. "I heard your voice in my mind tonight." I gasp and become motionless. "You said, 'When you see me you will not believe your eyes.' Of course I looked up and there you were, watching me. And I could not believe my eyes. Geneviève, your appearance made me feel as if I was having a vision of this beautiful creature from another world. I will never forget watching you cover your face and vanish into thin air. Then you reappeared and I watched you for two hours without saying a word. I became intoxicated. Your eyes look incredibly seductive done like this. I have to kiss this beautiful creature standing before me."

His voice and his words have me mesmerized. When his fingertips touch my face and his lips touch my lips I keep my eyes open and so does he. My head goes back and the hood falls to my shoulders while I look at his soul.

He whispers, "Geneviève, I want to build a fire in our bedroom and make the pallet on the floor then kiss you and hold you, looking at you in the glow. Then I want to make love with you until this night turns into day. Will you let me?"

"I will."

Trevor leads me to the dressing room and seats me on the chaise lounge then kneels and begins to unlace my boots. With those off he unbuttons my dress and begins to kiss my thighs, which causes me to moan. He stops and takes of his turtle neck then he takes off the wool stockings. "Baby, I know the sweet scent of you when you are aroused. Please lie back and let me taste you." Then Trevor embraces my thighs. As I catch my breath he covers me with my dress. "I would lie down with you if I could." The chaise is too small, so he kneels beside me and I feel his soft hair against my neck. When my strength returns I tell him, "Trevor, I want to bathe you." We stay in the shower until the water starts getting cool and dry each other off then finally make it to our pallet in front of the fire. This is where we wake up in the morning.

Coffee, we need coffee and go sit in the solarium to drink our second cup. With half of it still in our mugs Théo emerges from the house and starts setting up the cars to wash them. A few minutes later Rachel arrives. Trevor and I just look at each other. He needs to save his energy for the practice run, so joining in the fun is out of the question. Then the phone rings. Trevor says, "I'll get it." And I don't move a muscle, my feet still hurt.

He returns all smiles and sits back down. "That was William."

"They're back already?"

"Yep. They checked into The Posh yesterday and went to the base to find out where they're going to live and they got a trick and a treat. The treat was when they drove up to that two story house. The trick was when he carried Emily through the threshold his parents were in the living room. William told me he almost dropped her." I cover my mouth and he shakes his head. "I had to cover my mouth too. The reason he called was to find out what time to be at the marina. He said and I'm quoting, 'Emily is a little bundle of energy from her excitement over the house and wants to go sailing.' I told him to be there at 1:30."

"Trevor, I'm tired. I'm going to require more caffeine."

"You'll get the jitters. We need to start moving around."

"Thank goodness we fell asleep."

"I was going to put you in our bed, but while I was admiring you in the glow of the fire I fell asleep. We were warm and the pallet is sooo comfortable."

"Yes it is, as are you." I give him a kiss and then the phone rings again. "My turn."

Practically bouncing I stand in front of him. "What turned *you* into a little bundle of energy?"

"That was Father. Mr. Blackwell called to tell us our wedding photographs are here. When do you want to go?"

"My instinct tells me to say now."

"Good instinct. Then we can have lunch at the club." I give him a kiss and my mug then dash to the dressing room.

We are finally at Mr. Blackwell's and when we walk in he greets us then gets a faraway look in his eyes. "I must say, you look like the young lady your father used to drop off, bright and happy to be here. — These are the easels. Everything else is in the classroom."

"Thank you, Mr. Blackwell."

We clear the doorway and stop in mid-step. Mr. Blackwell has every photograph in the frame we chose for it laying on the frames' boxes and they go down the entire length of a counter. We walk slowly holding hands looking at the details of each one, because we can see them in the enlargements. In the middle are stacks of boxes with our Wedding Album in front and he chose the one for our portrait to go in the oval on the cover. Trevor asks, "Do you want to look at that here?"

"I would like to take it home and look at it there."

"That's what I wanted to do." And we walk passed it.

The last one is the black and white I took of the dining table that is going in our bedroom. "Trevor."

"I know. It's perfect." He moves to my back, puts his arms around me and rests his head against mine. "Putting aside the secret it holds, it really is a lovely photograph. You have such a good eye for angle and proportion. I'm going to enjoy having that on the mantle over our fireplace."

"Our fireplace. I love our fireplace."

He nuzzles me and when a customer leaving makes the bell ring on the door we come back to the present and I look at my watch. "We should start putting these in their boxes." I hold the box and he slides the photograph in. When I close the end I have a thought. "Trevor, we need to put initials of the recipient on these boxes now, so we don't have to open them again."

"I'll go ask Mr. Blackwell for a pen."

Trevor returns with him and a pen. He has offered to help put them away and we get a system going, Mr. Blackwell holds the box, Trevor puts in the photograph and I initial it. Trevor loads everything into the car as I work the door and Mr. Blackwell tells us he will see us Saturday when he photographs Théo's wedding ceremony. Next we have a nice lunch served by Eric, who moved up when Joseph stopped working full time and soon we are on our way to the marina.

Driving down to Gypsy I can see a line of cars and Trevor looks at his watch. I ask, "Are we late?"

"Nope, they are all early. And I see Emily's car in front."

When we pull up, only Emily and William walk our way. Everyone is going to give us a little privacy.

As soon as he opens the door she exclaims, "Trevor, Geneviève, I missed you so." Trevor gets out and after helping me out he takes a step to the side to get clear, which was a good move, because she hugs me by rocking wide to the left and the right. I laugh and tell her, "I missed you too." William shakes Trevor's hand and they have a quiet moment that said more than words could then he speaks to him. "I found one of the best things about being married is waking up to a pretty face instead of a bunch of men that need to shave." While I laugh he hugs me too and says, "It's nice to be home." And that was Emily's opening to tell us about their house and the painting Joanna gave them as we join the others.

When we are about to board Gypsy and Willow, Joanna asks me, "Where are your parents?"

"I told them Emily and William returned early. Father decided to go to the office and catch up on work. Mother decided to go to the spa at The Posh and get the works."

"A massage is what I need." as she rubs her neck. Next she asks Mitch, "Would you mind sitting in the club's lounge for an hour?" He replies, "I am not sitting on a bar stool. I am getting a massage too. I admit it, I was sore last week." Théo, William and Trevor rub a part of their bodies nodding. We give the fellas a kiss and laugh all the way to Willow. Then after another excellent run we decide to take Willow out for a short leisurely sail together and then go our separate ways.

Sitting in a booth at Micheletto's eating a pizza Trevor asks, "Would you like to go to the club for a nice massage. Mitch and Joanna will be gone and I know they'll fit us in." I respond almost whispering. "I entertained the thought and remembered I had to put makeup on our necks this morning. Even though we are married I want to keep our private lives private." With a lilt in my voice I tell him, "I'll give you a massage."

"Have you eaten enough?"

"Yes."

"I'll have the waiter box up the rest." Trevor keeps his eyes on mine as he raises his hand to signal the waiter and we have pizza and Italian cream cake for a late night snack.

In the morning we wake up in each other's arms and snuggle under the covers. It is Sunday, the only day we get to stay in bed until we're hungry. Thinking about yesterday I notice something and get tickled. "Baby, what has you tickled?"

"The house smells like pizza."

"I didn't send the box down in the dumbwaiter." When he says dumbwaiter I flinch and make him flinch. "I hope I'm not going to regret asking this, but what did you remember?"

"What is in the trunk of my car."

"I'll get the album." And he flings back the covers.

Instead of reading the Funny Paper in bed after breakfast we look through our wedding photographs. The ceremony was beautiful. I knew it was and we are finally getting a good look at it.

When the back cover is closed Trevor says, "I know what you're thinking and I don't want to wait to give the albums and those impeccably framed photographs out at Christmas either."

With the dishes done Trevor goes down to the car and I call Grand-mamma to tell her we would like to have a Christmas styled occasion. She tells me she will spread the word. When I hang up I hear the dumbwaiter being sent up then we sit at the kitchen table listening to the radio and filling the albums. Occasionally we take a break when a good song plays and dance around the house.

After a quick lunch he sends up our framed photographs and carries up an easel. We place the 20 x 24 of the family portrait on the mantle in the dining room. The 16 x 20 of our portrait is placed on the easel in the living room and last we place the one on the mantle in our bedroom. Trevor wraps his arms around me and we get lost in thought recalling the beautiful night we became lovers.

Eventually we have to press on and Trevor sends up three copies of the family portrait, our portrait and the fun one of me, Joanna, Emily and Rachel sitting on a swing with our men ready to give us a little push. When we start getting them out of the dumbwaiter it occurs to me theses were intended for Christmas and decide to get ribbon from my parent's house to tie around them. Mother always buys more than she needs. I return with two spools of red satin ribbon and when we're finished we put the family portraits and albums in the trunk of my car and I have him raise the garage door by hand to keep down the noise then drive over to my grandparents' house to deliver the gifts. Standing on the portico with our arms full I whisper, "Be as quiet as possible from now on."

"Why are we sneaking?"

"Because that is what you do when you hide Christmas presents." His eyes sparkle and I slowly open the door and listen. "They're in the kitchen cooking. Shake a leg, Sailor." Trevor shots me a look as he tries to remain quiet.

We go into the drawing room and I motion for him to follow me over to a chair in the corner and have him hide the large portraits behind it. Then we hide the albums in the credenza and sneak out. I have him leave the car door ajar as we drive back to our house. He lowers the door by hand then gets a hug and a kiss.

The first thing we do is quickly drink a glass of cold water and then go to the study for my diamond ear clips Trevor has yet to see from the safe. On the way he asks, "How do you know they're there?"

"I know my father and I'm certain he moved my jewelry and passport." We enter the room and I ask him, "Do you want to be the first to open it?"

"Yes I would." He pulls on the bookcase and there it is. He smiles and asks, "What's the combination?"

"9-14-41"

"The date of our wedding."

"It was my grandfather's idea. Years ago he chose their wedding date as the combination for the one in their house. Then it was decided my parent's safe should have theirs as the combination, because we all would remember them and be able to access the safes if need be without a problem."

Trevor opens the safe and goes, "Mmm hm. Geneviève ... I feel like I just struck gold." I begin to laugh as he moves aside. My family added a few things. There are stacks of gold ingots and a stack of emergency cash next to a felt pouch we know is filled with gold coins. I reach passed him and get the box my ear clips are in and say, "Let's go to the dressing room." He closes the safe and bookcase then leads the way holding my hand.

Trevor motions for me to sit on the chaise and I place the box beside me. "Geneviève, I don't think I'm about to commit a social crime by bring up the topic of coin, because you are my wife and I feel as if I'm keeping something from you. — When I met you I knew you were upper class, though you had a job, which is highly unusual for an upper class woman and I admired you for it. After I began courting you it slowly became evident your family is wealthy, but it is not obvious, therefore I forget about it.

"Even though I am aware you could care less because you love me, I want you to know this. The trust fund I mentioned, it had a million dollars in it. The interest from it and my pay from the Navy have my net worth at 1.2 million dollars. Therefore on my own I can provide you with the life you are accustomed to."

I give him a lingering kiss then tell him, "My first thought is I'm happy you know I could care less. My second thought is since I know how much you're worth, when are you taking me on that shopping spree in Beverly Hills?"

His head goes back as he burst into laughter. Then he asks, "What's the story that goes with that big red box?"

"When I turned 21 I received more than a partnership with Théo." I open the box to reveal the contents and he gasps. "I've worn the clips, but not the necklace. It seemed a bit much for an unmarried woman." My eyes dance and I give him a big kiss. "But I'm married now and I will be wearing this soon."

"The necklace *is* stunning. The marquise diamonds look like a garland of orchids. I can't wait to see you in it. — What are you wearing tonight?"

"I kept my dress from last year. It is the perfect shade of Christmas green."

"What am I wearing?"

"Whatever you want."

"I've only worn the tuxedo once."

"The tuxedo it is. Trevor, would you mind turning off the radio and playing one of our Chopin records while we get ready?"

"Not at all."

Trevor helps me dress and after admiring me I help him. Holding his tuxedo shirt for him to slip on and folding the French cuffs up to put his cuff links on is a simple thing, but it makes me happy just like dressing me makes him happy. I tie his bow tie then hold his jacket and slip it over his broad shoulders. I button it closed and admire this handsome man I call my husband. We pick up the small boxes then he offers me his arm. Upon entering the solarium we see the torches have been set up and lit as if it is Christmas and we light up too.

When he reaches to open the door to my grandparents' house I get a slight twinge. "I miss Claudette."

"I do too, but she and Joseph want to be alone."

"And there is nothing like being alone with your spouse."

"There really isn't." And we kiss before he opens the door.

When we enter the drawing room we exclaim, "Merry Christmas!" and they echo our words. Then I see it, the punch bowl on the liqueur cabinet is filled with eggnog. Trevor sets down the gifts and gets us a glass. He hands it to me beaming. After we finish drinking our eggnog by the fire we go to the kitchen to bring the food to the dinner table. There we discover a Christmas ham decorated with cloves and all the trimmings. I adore my grandparents.

Once we are seated in the candle lit room conversation about the wedding begins and since we are in Christmas attire Théo answers the question none of us have had the courage to ask. He and Rachel are going to be here for Christmas. We all try not to act relieved and we all fail miserably. Rachel is thrilled we are relieved and tells us that her place is here with the man she is going to marry. Plus she was tired of having to face a blizzard every year.

The reason for our concern is Rachel has a large family in New York City consisting of grandparents, aunts, uncles, nieces, nephews, cousins and several friends. They are having a wedding reception for them and the newlyweds are flying out there in the middle of their honeymoon for it. Darlene and her husband did the same thing. I felt sorry for them and since I've been on a honeymoon, my heart goes out to my brother and his future wife.

We move to the drawing room and after a few sips of warmed Louis XIII Trevor escorts me to the chair and he lifts one of the family portraits up into it. I pull the ribbon and hold on to the box as he carefully gets it out. The second he turns around for everyone to see it Rachel grabs Théo's arm and says, "Color, it's in color." Mother adds, "And it is breathtaking." Father looks confused and I tell him, "Mr. Blackwell surprised us." Rachel is so excited at the thought of their wedding photographs being in color she is squeezing Théo's arm and shaking it.

Trevor props it up on the back of the chair then reveals the two hiding behind the chair and sets one by my parents and one by Rachel and Théo. Grand-mamma tells me, "Sweetheart, once again you demonstrate how quiet you are and we find your husband is the same."

"I was trained. My wife is evidently a natural." During the laughter Grand-mamma pats his cheek and everyone stands to get a closer look.

When my family is seated I announce, "There is more." and Trevor goes to the credenza. I give each lady the one of the swings and Trevor gives the gentlemen the one of the wedding party. Last he hands the wedding albums out and silence falls. Trevor and I sip our cognac watching their faces and respond to occasional comments. The evening was perfect.

On the walk home Trevor stops me and slides off my ear clips then drops those in his inside pocket. "Mrs. Lyons, may I have the pleasure of this dance?"

"The pleasure will be mine, Mr. Lyons." We kiss and he takes a stance and looks at me with his eyes of bluest blue and waits. Then I say, "Un, deux, trois; un deux trois; un deux trois." and he twirls us around the garden among the glowing torches then makes his way to our house. At the bottom of the steps he sweeps me off my feet and carries me into the solarium where we watch the flames of the torches flicker in the breeze.

The next morning as we sit in the parking lot I tell Trevor, "I know Emily and William are on their honeymoon, but we have to extend an invitation to Mother's surprise birthday party tomorrow. Do you have their phone number?"

"Joanna probably got it from Judith. If not I'll tape a note to their door before we leave the base."

In the distance I hear several vehicles gearing up, large and small and then there they are. As they get closer I can see it is Sailors in the Navy Security Force, the military police on base. "Trevor what's going on?"

"This is a familiar site. The NSF had a drill to close the base. That means the work on the streets you listed has been completed."

"In that case I'm taking a few snapshots." Trevor hands me Blanca's keys and I hop out to open her trunk. Halfway there I remember my camera bag is in my hardtop. I just stand there and watch them go by in complete disbelief. Trevor turns around, sees me and lowers his head. I get back in and hand him her keys. "I have never missed a shot." I glance at my watch. "It's time for me to go in. Don't get out." I give him a kiss and open my door.

"Geneviève, I feel responsible for this."

"You're not. It's my responsibility and I forgot to get it. Now I'm going to go inside and kick myself." He chuckles and I bite his neck. While he catches flies I get out. "See you soon." Trevor manages to nod and I get tickled walking away.

Walking down the corridor alone to leave for lunch I see Trevor standing by Blanca with the door open. When I get close I say, "Bonjour."

"Mmm hm. I can't believe you bit me."

"I didn't, the gypsy did." He raises an eyebrow and motions to the car seat.

Trevor starts Blanca without taking his eyes off me. "Please tell her if she gets the urge to bite me again, to wait until we get home."

"Consider it done. I hope she didn't bite you too hard."

"She knew exactly what she was doing." I feel the twinkle in my eyes. "You look like the cat that ate the canary."

"Oh." I pretend to pull a feather from between my lips and toss it into the air. He gives me that deep laugh and drives.

Lunch flies by and when it's almost time to leave Trevor asks Joanna, "Do you have William and Emily's phone number?" Her face goes straight. "It's fine. I'll leave a note on their door to invite them to Josephine's surprise party."

"You write it and I will take it over there. Oh, I hope they're not home. I'll feel like a prowler lurking outside." Trevor get's up laughing and writes the note then we are off.

On the way home we listen to the radio and Trevor keeps glancing at me with this little smile and I cannot hear his thoughts. Upon entering the living room I find out why he could not stop smiling. On the coffee table are three brand new camera bags. I called Mr. Blackwell and then your mother. You will never miss another shot." All I do is look at him, because I am at a loss for words.

Trevor coaxes me to the sofa and I sit down. He pulls one forward and unzips it then lays the flap back. Next he picks up the camera. This is the newest model he has. He told me technical terms about the lens that were over my head. The best way for me to describe it is that the lens simulates binoculars and you can photograph things at a distance and the shot will look like you were close." I gasp and he hands me the camera.

"There is black and white film you can develop and color film in each bag. It turns out you can make black and white photographs from the negatives of color film after having it developed. We didn't talk long, but I learned a lot."

After absorbing this flood of information I put down the camera and in my exuberance I sit across his lap and begin kissing his face making little noises. "I do like the way you say thank you and you're welcome, Baby." This gets him a real kiss on his mouth then I undo the top buttons of his shirt and run my hands under the collar and into his hair. This causes him to softly moan and me to remember the bite I gave him. I pretend I am going to kiss his neck by touching it with my lips and then I ever so gently bite him. He sharply inhales and then I feel he is aroused.

I softly ask, "Where do you want to go?"

"No where." And the cushions are on the rug again.

When we're cooking dinner the phone rings. "That's Emily and I have to stay with this Alfredo sauce."

Trevor answers it then comes back and starts tossing the salad again. "To say she was excited would be an understatement."

"I wish I could have answered it, but I do like hearing you say, "The Lyons residence. We *are* the Lyons."

"Yes we are and this is our den."

I gasp. "Trevor."

"And the answer presents itself. The guest house is The Lyons Den."

As chance would have it we bought a bottle of Asti Spumante to go with our Italian cuisine and Trevor pops the cork to celebrate while we cook.

The next day starts with a birthday breakfast for Mother at my grandparent's. When we step out onto the balcony we see Théo going down the steps as Rachel drives up. She gets out, sets a coffee mug on her roof and we hear Théo laugh. Then the whirlwind begins.

Mother gets an early surprise, because Claudette and Joseph are there for breakfast. Next is the surprise she gets when Helen meets her for lunch at the club instead of my father. He picked her up from the train station and dropped her off. Helen decided she had not missed one of Mother's birthdays since they met and was not going to start now. Therefore she packed for the entire week to stay and help with wedding preparations and attend it.

In order to throw the surprise party Father told her he reserved a private dining room so she didn't have to stop and greet the club members they passed on her special day, which had truth in those words. Théo and I have followed them since we were hungry children that merely wanted to sit down and eat. It's why we go to The Posh for a nice dinner out, because now we have to meet and greet.

When they walk in, the look on Mother's face says it all. We did surprise her and she is thrilled. That Emily and William are here during their honeymoon means a lot to her and she makes certain they know. We said no gifts and everyone ignored us. After she got over being embarrassed with being lavished upon I know it made her feel adored by our friends and she deserves that. She put on the gift that we, her family gave her as soon as she finished looking at it. Last month Father gave us all a brochure of gold charms to pick out individually, not as couples, for a charm bracelet to adorn her wrist. I chose a pearl on top of a gold ice cream cone.

Wednesday morning was a trip to the airport for Théo and Rachel to pick up her parents, the only family members she invited. After work Trevor and I go to The Salon for the appointment to try on my matron of honor gown. Rachel couldn't make it, but Trevor is thrilled, because I let him come in. We love the gown due to the thought Rachel put into it. She had it made similar to the dress he met me in. It is made of Robin's Egg blue crepe backed satin with a squared neckline front and back, but it has long length sleeves to keep me warm and it's full length with a back kick pleat and as always it fits perfectly.

Next we go to Bertucci's for Trevor to try on his morning suit. Théo and all the men are wearing one with the exception of Mitch and William. Trevor decided to blend in with the wedding party. Also he wanted to give his Dress Blue uniform a rest. I have never seen my husband in a morning suit and he is so handsome in it. I soak up the scene of him speaking Italian while having his suit perfected and soon we are on our way home.

When my gown and his suit is hanging safely in our dressing room we go to my parent's house to have an apéritif with Helen and my grandparent's then we ride together to The Posh for dinner with Darlene and Marshall along with Rachel's parents, who are staying there as usual. When we return to Maison my father hands Trevor something after they shake hands.

Seated at my vanity getting ready to shower Trevor kneels next to me and hands me a postcard with a postal mark that reads Cannes, France from a man named Jean-Marc Clairmont in Armand's handwriting. He's safe and living on the French Riviera in Pointe Croisette, a retreat for the elite on the coast of the Mediterranean. At long last my ordeal has ended.

It is Thursday and I am drained. A quiet lunch on our bench is exactly what I need. One of the nice things about Blanca is my hair is slightly windblown from the drive to the base and I can rest my head on his shoulder. Thankfully we are not obligated to a pre-wedding function tonight; therefore I am looking forward to picking up take out from The Flying Dragon and going home. But when we arrive things are a little lively, because Théo is still here and we go to my parent's house to find out what we're missing and if we can help.

When we walk in Théo says he was about to look for us. California's Supreme Court is ruling on a case that could change a California law. Due to this, Reginald will not be able to make it for the rehearsal. He is flying in from Sacramento the morning of their wedding, staying for lunch and flying back. Théo called Rachel and her response was she had been a bride in two rehearsals recently and didn't need another one. They liked how Trevor and I did our ceremony and he asks if we mind their ceremony closely duplicates ours. Without hesitating I tell him there is no need to ask. He calls Rachel, tells her we are fine with the idea and gives me my kiss on the forehead. Théo shakes Trevor's hand and to the mud room he goes. Walking back to our den we can hear the engine of Théo's car echoing from the street.

The rehearsal day is upon us, except now there isn't going to be one, but we do need to make haste from the base for Maison to find out what the plan is. Trevor makes good time in Friday traffic and we arrive to see a familiar site, vine covered trellises. But when the garage door goes up we see Blanca is parked next to rows of golden chairs and we get tickled. The chairs and trellises must have been delivered by the men that delivered them for our wedding and assumed they went in the same places as before. Trevor backs up and parallel parks under our balcony. We go up still laughing for me to change into a dress my husband selects.

As we walk to my parent's house we hear a car engine and it's Joseph. He slows down when he sees us and waves as he drives by. Trevor tells me, "Claudette is so timid. It's hard to believe she's a sun until he is by her side and her eyes light up."

I stop us on the portico and step in front of him then place my hand on his face. "That is from a conversation we had in what seems like ages ago."

"That is because it was the first time we ate lunch together at our bench."

"I adore you for remembering."

"I remember everything about us ... especially this." Trevor places his hands on my face then takes my lower lip between his. Once again I get weak at my knees and he gathers me into his embrace. Eventually we hear the front door open and then a click as it is quietly closed.

When we enter the drawing room Théo glances at me smiling. It was he who opened the door. Mother hands us a glass of champagne I do not want to drink. I want the taste of his mouth to stay in mine. Trevor lowers his glass and we get lost into each other's eyes. Then the next thing I know Father raises the sound of his voice and says, "A toast to love ... that can deafen us all." Apparently someone spoke to us and we didn't hear them, thus my father steps in to make it all right. On that note Rachel suggests going outside even though there's not going to be a rehearsal. She wants to catch the last few minutes of the sunset.

The gardeners have the landscaping perfectly manicured and the fresh scent of the fall flowers wafts through the air. It is pleasant and I am happy to be strolling alone with Trevor.

After the sun goes into the horizon there is still plenty of light and I hear heels gaining on us then Rachel's soft hand is on my arm. "Trevor, do you mind if I have a moment with my matron of honor?"

"Of course not."

She nods and leads me away from the others down to the boardwalk. "We have not had the time alone we should have due to hectic schedules. I even missed seeing you in the gown I selected for you. It doesn't matter at this point, but do you like it?"

"Rachel, I love it. I can't believe you had it made to resemble the sundress I met Trevor in."

"I was concerned about adding sleeves to it, but I didn't want you to be chilly and then I had a thought. You can have Mrs. Parker remove them and wear it to a Summer Banquet next year since no one from the club is going to see it."

"Thank you, Rachel."

"It was nothing. By the way, your tiara is beautiful. I feel honored to wear it."

"Rachel, it is your right to have it grace your head as you become a Delcroix."

"My heart just fluttered. Gené, I am going to be a Delcroix."

"I know exactly you feel. The thought of becoming a Lyons was surreal."

"I do keep calling you Gené, because Théo says it often. I have noticed he is the only person that calls you that. Please tell me if you mind?"

"I don't mind. He is my brother and you will officially be my sister tomorrow. Forgive me for being personal, but when you have a child, calling me by two names will confuse the little one and I am going to enjoy being called Auntie Gené. After all, my full name is a mouth full and that is why Théo did start calling me that shortly after I arrived."

"In an Easter basket. He told me he was only three, but will always remember the first time he laid eyes on his baby sister." I start blinking. "Oh, I've made you emotional. Time to change the subject. It's my turn to get personal. As a recent bride, is there a tip you can give me that isn't in the books?"

I get tickled as I think of one. "Instead of wearing the nightgown that goes with your peignoir set, wear tap pants and something on your upper body that you will feel comfortable in under the robe. You can wear the set later."

A light bulb instantly goes on in her head. "When I wake up from a restless night I have found myself tangled in my nightgown. You just gave me the best tip a bride could ever receive. The mind reels at the thought." She stops walking and gives me a hug and then I see Théo and Trevor have stayed at a safe distance while they follow us and draw Rachel's attention to them. She kisses my cheeks and motions for them to join us. Théo says, "I was thinking about picking a pear. Rachel, can we pretend our rehearsal is over and go to our rehearsal dinner?" After we laugh she nods to her parent's. Her father announces, "Apparently the wedding rehearsal has ended, therefore my wife and I invite you all to Micheletto's for the rehearsal dinner."

Wine and breadsticks are on the table and the noise level is already high from excitement when Trevor and I arrive. Rachel had a longer than usual wait time to find her match and her parents are enjoying this moment. We raise our glasses several times for toasts.

Back at Maison, Trevor and I go to our den to make out while I wait on Théo to call after he parts from Rachel before midnight. When he calls he does the unexpected by inviting Trevor to raid the kitchen with us. The second I tell Trevor he has been invited his eyes light up. It will be like before we were married and all those wonderful times we spent together.

Entering the kitchen we see Théo is standing by the oven. "In here are three pieces of apple pie from Sam's and in the freezer there is a quart of ice cream I talked a waiter at The Posh into selling me." I get plates and forks while Trevor pours tall glasses of milk. Théo puts the pie on the plates and Trevor gets the ice cream and scoop. Théo puts huge scoops of the ice cream on our pie and we settle in.

Trevor picks up his glass of milk. "I know we are all toasted out, but this one has to be made." Théo and I raise our glasses. "To late night kitchen raids." We echo his words and click our glasses together. Next we all eat a big bite of the warm pie. Then Théo looks a bit melancholy. Where did he go?

"I don't know how Rachel missed one of these."

"That you will not live here shouldn't matter. In fact I have an idea. She can be at the best kitchen raid we have all year."

"The night we decorate for Christmas." I touch my nose. "Start talking, Gené."

"The two of you should pack on overnight bag before you leave and we can sleep in our bedrooms with our spouses. Then when our parents are sound asleep we can sneak down here for all the Christmas goodies."

"Mother will be overjoyed we all stay here on such a special day."

Trevor chimes in. "What am I going to be looking forward to?"

I motion to Théo. "We decorate the entire property on the first Saturday in December. Along with the customary trees and wreathes, we have fresh evergreen garlands made and limbs from Canadian spruce trees brought in. We, the men, cut and saw them into small pieces for swags and the ladies attach red bows on them. Then we hang them on every lantern on the property while they hold the ladders steady. Next we make them for the torches and proceed to put those out. We finish up by decorating the Christmas trees. This takes all day, therefore we have caterers bring the best foods associated with Christmas and we work and eat into the night, then finish off the evening with a warmed drink sitting by the fire."

Trevor looks at us. "Growing up with a sibling ... is nice."

"Rachel feels the same way. If her first pregnancy and childbirth goes well she wants to have two more." Théo's eyes get wide.

"We'll pretend you didn't say that."

"Thank you, Gené. — In that case you two can pretend I didn't say this. We hope to be a family before the end of next year."

"We guessed that already. Trevor and I are waiting until he is out of the Navy."

"I want to be here to help her if she gets sick in the morning and when her feet start to hurt from the extra weight she's carrying I'll be able to do the cooking and cleaning then dote on her with all my spare time."

Théo squeezes my hand. "Can you believe mere months ago it was just you and me?" Smiling I shake my head. "Now, you are married and I am about to be."

Trevor tells him, "The best part about being married is when you tell each other goodnight you don't leave."

"I *am* tired of leaving Rachel at the apartment door."

"That applies to any door. I thought when I started staying in the guest room I would feel better, but it was sort of worse knowing she was just a few doors down."

"I could not be happier Rachel didn't care about proper wait times. This wait was long enough. You both inspired us and we decided we could care less what people think."

"And society here has always overlooked our little infractions of the rules by saying what?"

"They are French you know."

Trevor's eyebrows go up as he looks at us and interjects, "People do say that." Now our eyebrows are up. "The first time William and I went to the club together we were wearing civvies. We realized no one recognized us when we overheard two ladies talking about how soon you and I were getting married and one of them said, 'They are French you know.'" Théo and I have a burst of laughter.

"At last, confirmation. Trevor, why did you not tell me this earlier?"

"I wasn't sure how you'd feel about it."

"Point made." And I give him a kiss.

When we finish our milk Trevor says, "I'll rinse the dishes. You two take a moment." While Trevor clears the table Théo gets up and sits next to me. He holds my hand and I put my head on his shoulder as we watch Trevor.

After rinsing the last dish Trevor walks over to the table. "Théo, don't get up." They shake hands and he says, "I hope you get some sleep and I will see you in the morning at your grandparents'. Geneviève, I will be waiting in the solarium with a glass of cognac for us." He gives me a kiss and leaves.

I put my head back where it was and ask, "Théo, why are you and Rachel keeping your honeymoon destination a secret?"

"You haven't heard. It's not a secret, we *cannot* decide."

"Oh."

"We want to go for a drive, but not a long one."

"May I make a suggestion?"

"Please."

"L.A. will be far enough and you should stay in the biggest bungalow at The Beverly Hills Hotel. It will have a kitchen that has a staff you should decline then order room service to fill the refrigerator with for three days of breakfast and lunch items, because your sleep schedule will be totally disrupted. And because of this you will not want people in a room next to yours disturbing you and Rachel."

"When I call Rachel in the morning I will tell her what you suggested. It sounds like the perfect thing to do to me." The clock strikes once, telling us it is

1:30 and we sigh heavily. "I am going to walk you to the door and pour myself a glass of cognac then sit in the solarium to clear my head."

At the door I get my customary kiss and a hug that last longer than usual. Then he opens the door and walks out onto the portico with me. When I get to the steps of the den I turn around and see he is still there. He places is hand over his heart and I do too. Then he turns and goes inside and I go up to my husband who has been patiently waiting for me.

Trevor sets down the glass he is holding when I enter the solarium and I go straight to him and lie across the man I love. The comfort of his embrace is all I want — and a shower.

CHAPTER SIXTEEN

The sound of delivery vans wake us up. This means we have over slept and we start our day laughing then tell each other good morning before we leap to our feet. Our plan is for him to cook breakfast while I start getting ready.

With the time consuming task of putting on lingerie done I move to the vanity. My hair is in a lovely chignon that has jeweled hair pins in it and I am about to start putting on makeup when I hear a sound I was not expecting, the ringing of the Chuck Wagon bell. Trevor finally has the opportunity to ring it. I begin laughing so hard I go into the kitchen with tears on my face. Trevor is still holding it and could not be happier. We get tickled out of the blue the entire time we eat thinking about that bell.

Still trying to catch up on lost time the dishes are left on the table and we go to our dressing room. After my makeup is done he buttons up my day dress then I put on his cuff links and necktie for him. I hold out his black waistcoat and cutaway coat and button both looking into is blue eyes. Then I tuck in his pocket square. Last but not least is his pocket watch which I hand him to put in his waistcoat and then he does something unexpected. He takes off his Academy ring and gets out a sterling silver box I recognize.

"Trevor, that is the box your Delcroix signet ring is in."

"Your grandmother had it sized for me at my request." He takes it out of the box and hands it to me. "You are the Marchioness of Château Delcroix and I am your Marquis. Today I should look like who I am. Would you please?" And he holds out his hand.

As I slide it onto his finger my heart is touched. This shows his commitment to me and the family. I would have never asked him to wear this instead of his ring. "Trevor, I am so in love with you."

"I'm in love with you too, Baby."

After a passionate kiss I have to straighten his shirt and necktie before we look in the mirrors. When we are standing in front of them I tell him, "I married you for the man you are. That you happen to be the most handsome man I have ever laid eyes on — is a bonus." He laughs as he gently caresses my face.

Rachel decided she would style her hair and put on makeup in the apartment while Théo got ready in the house and when he was at our grandparents' we would dress in my old bedroom. Still pressed for time I toss a few things in my train case and Trevor carries my gown. Fortunately we are in my room before Rachel. He kisses me and says, "I'm going next door and wait to drop a ton of bricks on our friends when Emily notices this ring."

"You are a rascal." He gives me a wink and leaves.

Since Théo is wearing his medal of sapphires and diamonds instead of a flower on his lapel, we had planned to tell them about our ancestry in advance, but the opportunity never presented itself. Therefore Trevor volunteered to tell them while they sip mimosas in my grandparent's drawing room before the wedding ceremony. I was not looking forward to it, but of course he is going to enjoy watching their reactions.

The bridal gown and the outfit she is going to change into for the drive was brought up yesterday and is behind the closed door of my closet. My tiara and her veil are on my bed under a silk shawl and I am tempted to peek at my tiara, but I resist and go downstairs to get the champagne an orange juice.

As I finish setting everything up on the card table Father put in my room I hear Rachel and her mother enter the house through the service entrance. When they walk in my room Rachel is carrying her train case and Elise has the tray of our flowers. To my surprise her bouquet isn't Stargazer lilies, it's white Aphrodite orchids.

I tilt my head a little and she looks at me. "You were expecting lilies. Theo will be too, but I decided to carry the first flower he ever gave me, a single white Aphrodite orchid on a wrist corsage. It was so romantic." She sighs. "I cannot wait to see the look on his face." Elise gets misty-eyed. "Mother, you promised not to get me emotional." Elise nods and I announce, "Now would be a good time to pop the cork." Rachel adds, "We should wait on Josephine and Constance." Then as if on cue we hear the front door open.

Mother enters the room and goes straight to Rachel. "My son asked me to give you this." And she gives her a small black velvet box. Rachel looks at it, slowly lifts the lid and gasps. Then she pulls out a little piece of folded paper. "This one will live forever like our love. Théo." She immediately puddles and Mother asks, "May I see?" to distract her. Rachel holds up a brooch that is a Stargazer lily and gushes, "He had my favorite flower made with diamonds and pink tourmalines." Then Rachel's eyes get wide. "He thinks I am going to be carrying my lilies. What am I going to do?"

I calmly walk over to her and say, "Pin it onto a stem inside your bouquet where it can't be seen and show it to him before the ceremony begins."

"You're brilliant, just like Théo says." She touches my cheek and tucks it away.

When the mimosas are poured we make the glasses ring without making a toast, drink and begin dressing me, which takes two minutes or less, because Mother and Grand-mamma have been doing this for decades.

Then the moment arrives to dress Rachel and she opens the closet doors, turns on the light and walks out with a gown of ivory crepe backed satin that accentuates her hair and skin tones. It has a low sweetheart neckline, elbow length sleeves and is cut on the bias. The train is court length and it buttons up in the back. Rachel is not a young woman, therefore wearing a gown that will flow over her lovely figure is befitting.

Given that the buttons go past her waist she is able to step into it with ease and is dressed in the same amount of time it took for me and the moment to place the Delcroix Tiara on her head is upon us. Rachel lifts the shawl and I see a cathedral length veil attached to it that will trail past her gown as she walks. Reaching for the tiara I realize I've never done this before. Fortunately we hear a car going fast over the cobblestones. That is Reginald, cutting it close, but buying me time to think exactly how to put the tiara on her head without wrecking her hair.

When Mother gets my footstool for her to kneel on she has a bout of nervous laughter. "Is this really happening? I feel as if I'm a character in a novel." Elise rubs her back. "Rachel, think of it like this. It is merely your something borrowed among the something old, something new and something blue." She takes a deep breath and I pick it up as Mother guides the veil. Rachel looks at me as her mother holds her hand and she kneels. Grand-mamma stands beside me with the hair pins and I manage to place it beautifully. Mother holds it still while I slide the hair pins in place and we are done.

Inspired by her words of being a character in a novel I decide to play my role to the hilt. So, I hold out my arms with palms up and as I lift them I tell her in a dramatic voice, "Miss Janssen, you may rise." Laughter erupts and we have to help her up. When she is steady Rachel looks straight into my eyes, curtsies and says, "Thank you, Marchioness."

We make ourselves stop laughing before we reach the point of tears and Grand-mamma says, "The ceremony is complete. To the mirrors we go, ladies." The bride is stunning. We shower her with compliments and she decides not to cover her face at all, wanting to see Théo's face the moment he sees her.

Rachel has a slight smile as she looks at her reflection then her eyes get wide. "I won't be able to take this tiara off to change into the outfit I'm traveling in. I'm going to need help." She looks at me and I tell her, "Your husband will help you." We watch her get lost in thought and she finally gives me this smile that says so much and I understand every word.

We finish our mimosas then put corsages on our mother's and they hand us our flowers. Elise calls her husband and we go downstairs. Soon my father opens the doors and steps aside for Hugo to come in. Then my grandfather and father walk in followed by Mitch wearing his Dress Blue's. He's escorting Elise.

When my family is gone and Hugo is with Rachel and his wife, Mitch steps up to me and says, "Geneviève, your husband sent this." And he gives me Trevor's handkerchief. He goes up to the balcony to wait and I hold it close to my face to breath in his scent. When I hear Mitch greet Elise the wedding ceremony begins.

Since Trevor and I were running behind schedule I see the grounds for the first time as I reach the trellises. Next I see Mr. Blackwell and then notice there are no torches and the swing is decorated in garlands of greenery with fall colored flowers. The same garlands must be on the arbor. Before I step into the middle, I look back at Rachel and her father. The string quartet sees me and starts playing "Fall" from Antonio Vivaldi's "Four Seasons", how appropriate. Then my eyes go straight to Trevor who is wearing a pale yellow rose which matches my nosegay on his lapel and next I look at Théo. He is beaming as he bows his head to me. I almost wave to Reginald whom I haven't seen since he officiated over our wedding ceremony, but I manage to stop myself. Then I nod at Joseph and Claudette, who are in the back row with Darlene and Marshall. After acknowledging my family I smile at William, Emily and Joanna, whom I am seeing for the first time today. The rest of the way I focus on my husband. When I am across from him the music changes to "Arioso" by Johann Sebastian Bach, this means Rachel and her father are in sight.

Trevor winks at me just before I turn my head to look at her for a moment and then I keep my eyes on Théo. When they reach us, Rachel's father places her hand in Théo's. Reginald steps back and we move away from them. They wanted to have a short conversation too and the entire time Trevor and I do not take our eyes off each other. When Reginald moves forward we do, then Théo and his bride take their vows and exchange rings.

The time flew and after Reginald tells Théo, "Vous pouvez embrasser la mariée." he puts his arms around Rachel under her veil and holds her close as we avert our eyes. Next Théo does something I was not expecting. He takes of his signet ring and hands it to Rachel who turns it around then slides it on his finger. After Reginald says, "Ladies and Gentlemen, it is my honor to introduce you to Mr. and Mrs. Théo Delcroix." we all follow them to the dining room in my parents' house where there is a roaring fire and fall floral garlands surrounding us.

While listening to a pianist play the grand piano in the drawing room we eat an elaborate luncheon of champagne, chilled pea soup and roast duck with figs followed by the cutting of the cakes. After enjoying the desserts we move to the drawing room which is missing furniture and decorated with garlands as well, then they have their first dance as husband and wife in the glow of a fire burning in the fireplace. He kisses her in a slight dip and then the traditional dances with the bride and groom begin.

Soon my brother and his bride dance once more and since everyone finally knows about our ancestry my grandfather asks our guests to accompany us to my grandparents' house for family portraits. On the way I tell him, "Trevor — I forgot to tell you something. — Since you're not in uniform it's appropriate for you to wear your sash."

"At least I have a minute to wrap my mind around that."

"Then I'll be quiet while you do." He makes a little chuckle.

Mr. Blackwell follows us inside and he knows the drill, therefore he doesn't waste time and soon we go into the study and pair off around the desk to put our things on each other.

While Trevor is putting on my sash Rachel gasps. Obviously Théo forgot to mention there is a star and signet ring for her. Trevor and I beam as he straightens my sash, but when I remove his rose and pick up his sash I turn around in time to see him swallow hard. I give my husband a kiss and he lowers his head then places his hand across his chest. I carefully go over his head, place it on his shoulder then arrange it to have the crossing of the sash toward the front of his side. Next I step back to admire him, then we all go to the drawing room.

As the family takes their places he softly says, "I'm glad there isn't a mirror in here."

Rachel whispers, "That makes two of us."

Théo asks me, "You forgot to tell Trevor about his sash huh?"

"Yes I did." And the four of us get tickled.

After we simmer down the posing for photographs begins as our friend watch in awe. Next are the wedding photos taken outside and we all return to my parents' house. With full glasses of champagne the playing on the swing set begins and the usual photographs are taken of the women taking turns on the swings.

When Théo announces they are going inside to get ready to leave we all stay outside to give them privacy. The Newlyweds eventually emerge onto the portico in travel clothing. Théo is carrying her train case and Rachel has her bouquet to toss, but the only single woman here is Helen. Being her funny self Helen steps up to Rachel and holds out her hand as she says, "Just give it to me. I'll put it in the barn with the one Geneviève threw at me." Laughter erupts because we know she is serious. My bouquet has been in her barn.

Théo puts her train case in the car and the goodbye hugs and kisses begin. I stand on the bottom step with my hand on Trevor's shoulder to get a good view and thanks to Helen's antics there are no tears, not even from her mother. Then he says something to Rachel and they begin looking at everyone. They stop when they find me.

We work our way to each other and Theo reaches his hand out to Trevor as Rachel kisses my cheeks, "Thank you for being by my side."

"It was my pleasure, Mrs. Delcroix."

Rachel gasps. "You are the first person to call me that." And my brother clears his throat with raised eyebrows. "Théo, it's different when you say it. You're my husband." And she gives him a kiss. Then she kisses Trevor's cheeks as Théo steps in front of me with a glint in his eyes and proceeds to hug me tight enough to intentionally make me exhale and kisses my forehead.

He lets me go as I draw in a breath shaking my head and say, "Bon voyage, Mon Frère."

"Merci, Ma Sœur."

He offers his arm to his new wife and they turn around to go to his car that is not decorated at his behest. Watching them I realize they did not arrange for us to have flower petals to shower them with and I look at my lovely nosegay. Then I see Trevor's hands as he slides his fingers between the roses to reveal one slightly underneath the others and I pull the petals from it, give Trevor a kiss and the nosegay then toss them into the air and they drift down on the Newlyweds. Rachel and Théo slow down and glance over their shoulder at me with the warmest smiles. I wave and watch them get into the car.

About a minute after they are out of sight Reginald announces he has a flight to catch because the fate of California is in his hands, so he dashes to the limousine and is gone. Darlene and Marshall leave next and then Claudette and Joseph go to their apartment with my grandparents not too far behind. Helen tells us it is way too early for her to be dressed formally holding a bridal bouquet and is going inside to change into day wear and listen to a radio show she likes. My parents walk to the arbor with Rachel's parents to unwind.

The only people left in front of my parent's house are the crew and after a brief conversation about the wedding Joanna and Mitch say they will see us at lunch

Monday and take their leave. When Emily tells Trevor and me she and William will see us in the parking lot that morning I remember she doesn't know we can wear trousers. The second I finish telling the story why, she hugs me and informs William she needs to go shopping Eh-sap. Nothing was said about the bricks Trevor dropped on them and in a blink of an eye they are going through the gates.

While scanning the property it occurs to me I do not have a single photograph of this day and men in trucks will arrive soon to take everything down. When I tell Trevor he dashes to get my camera bag. He returns and I ask if he minds if I work alone. Trevor informs me he is happily going to change out of his morning suit and sit in the solarium with a glass of iced tea watching me.

The first photograph I take is of Trevor at the top of the steps on the balcony. Then I take one of the rose petals on the cobblestones and begin to slowly work my way through the trellises. Even though runners are covering the cobblestone one can still hear my heels as I walk and getting close to the arbor Mother tells the Janssen's, "Our daughter prefers to be ignored while taking photographs." To give them time to adjust I go to the swing set then I walk around to the corner of the arbor to get a photograph for Rachel and Théo of her parent's sitting under the arbor with ours talking and enjoying the sights and sounds of the Pacific. I follow it up with a snapshot of their view. When I take one of the stage and four chairs on it I am done, therefore I go wish Elise and Hugo a nice flight home. They are catching a red eye tonight after dinner with my parent's at The Posh.

Carrying my nosegay and camera bag I make my way to Trevor. He opens the solarium door for me and takes my camera bag. "I am at your service, My Lady." I get tickled and tell him, "I would like you to undress me." How he does light up.

In a surprising twist he acts like a lady's maid and goes through a ritual to undress me then asks, "What would, My Lady like to wear?" I reply, "Choose for me, please." And he gets out a pair of jeans, my petal pink cashmere twin set and tan suede loafers. Denim and cashmere is an unusual choice, but I let him dress me and when he escorts me to the mirrors I discover this looks casual yet refined. The pretending ends when I guide him to my vanity bench and have him sit down in order for me to sit across his lap and kiss him until my heart is content.

When I run my fingers through his hair he asks, "What next?"

"Let's go keep Helen company."

He holds on to my thighs and stands up then proceeds to the front door. I open it and when we are in the solarium he realizes we can be seen and puts me down. Then we walk over to the house and find Helen in the living room listening to the radio sitting on the sofa relaxing.

I tell Trevor, "Perhaps we should have called first."

She immediately rises up and says, "Don't be silly. This is still your home." Then she sits up looking at me. "I like your ensemble." I motion to Trevor, so she smiles at him and says, "You are man of hidden talents." In an instant my mind goes in a completely different direction and I blush. To make my escape I turn around and tell Trevor I am going to the kitchen for a Pellegrino and ask if he would like a glass of iced tea, then excuse myself.

Walking down the hallway shaking my head I quietly ask myself, "Why did his tongue of velvet leap to mind? *Who* am I?" When I hear him reply, "My wife." I whirl around.

"What else did you hear me say?"

"I caught the word velvet and pieced the rest of it together. I must tell you I *am* looking forward to going home."

His eyes sparkle as I stand speechless and he guides me to the kitchen where he pours my water and squeezes the slice of lime in it. Then he pours two glasses of tea and my eyes get wide. "While you were lost in thought she said, 'That sounds good.' and asked for a glass too. I saw you were blushing when you turned abruptly and knew you didn't hear her. That is why I followed you and I am so glad I did."

"And I am so embarrassed."

"Baby, Helen hasn't a clue as to what happened, therefore you can breathe normally now." I get tickled when I realize I am almost holding my breath and he gives me a hug. When I have my wits about me we return to the living room and I settle in next to Helen as Trevor sits in a chair across from us. She starts the conversation by asking Trevor why his accent is so thick and he begins to tell her a condensed story of his life.

Soon my parents step in the doorway beaming, because we have been with her and tell us they are going to change clothing for dinner. Trevor continues his story as I revel in this moment while she learns how exceptional my husband is.

When my parents tell us to have a good evening Trevor has reached the part of how he met Mitch and Joanna. When he concludes this story the decision is made to investigate what is in the kitchen to cook for our dinner that is not too rich, because of what we ate for lunch. To my complete delight we discover two whole chickens in the refrigerator and I tell Helen, "Trevor has a weakness for Southern cooking."

"I picked up on that at the ranch. What do you have in mind?"

"Southern fried chicken, baby red mashed potatoes, cut green beans and biscuits for buttering."

Trevor says, "My mouth is watering. What can I do to help?"

"Do you know how to cut up a chicken?"

"As a matter of fact I do."

"All right. You get on that and we will scramble eggs then season them and some flour for the coating." As he cuts up the chicken I hear him hum for the first time. I glance over my shoulder and he is in his own little world.

After eating too much we move to the drawing room where Trevor pours us glasses of Louis XIII. A few minutes later Helen gets up and walks toward the piano. "I'm not sure if Josephine had Gérard get this piano for me or for a place to set photographs on." We laugh as she sits on the bench. "Trevor, I am certain no one told you I majored in music." She lifts the fallboard and says "For my audience that loves Chopin I will play his Harp Study." And she begins.

When she finishes playing Trevor is speechless and I request the Nocturne we floated to at the second Summer Banquet. At the end of the impromptu concert we both say, "Brava." and she stands to curtsy then joins us on the sofa.

Our glasses are empty and we thank Helen for the concert then tell her we will see her at the marina on race day, because she will miss brunch for she is catching an early train to Santa Barbara and she spends Thanksgiving with the ranch hands.

Walking to our den Trevor says, "You have been listening to her play for as long as you can remember. How fortunate you were and now I know why Chopin is your favorite composer, he wrote piano solos. — I am going to spend years getting to watch the story of your life unfold. I do love you." Inside and alone at last he sweeps me off my feet and carries me upstairs.

In the morning we race to the balcony to get the Sunday paper and Trevor lets me win. I go straight to the kitchen table and with him by my side we look for the wedding announcement putting the Funny Paper aside. We find it and see the lovely photo of the bride. I read it aloud and leave it on the table then he fills the kettle with water for our coffee and we start making omelets. We stayed up late and slept in, therefore brunch with the family is out. After we finish eating I take a good look at the date on the newspaper and ask Trevor to get the calendar. He sits down next to me with it and puts his arm around my shoulder.

Today is the 9th and there is nothing written on it until Saturday the 15th, the last day for a practice run. The 17th reads Airport, it's the morning family and relatives of our friends begin flying in for Thanksgiving on the 20th. The cocktail party for the race is on the 21st, which is also the 55th anniversary of my grandparent's. The race is on the 22nd followed by a formal banquet that night to celebrate the event and its winners. Théo and Rachel return on the 18th and are going to step into a whirlwind. November is booked up.

Trevor and I look at each and start laughing and then he slowly lifts the page to reveal December. Only four days for the entire month have something written on them, Emily's Birthday on the 5th, Christmas Decorating on the 6th and then Christmas and New Year's Eve. We get a well deserved break next month. Trevor sighs and picks up his coffee. As he drinks I start thinking and tell him. "The nights are getting cooler and more than likely the things in your footlocker and the other crate need to be brought in to protect them from the humidity."

"Yes they do and after seeing the calendar we should start on that today. If we're lucky we can be finished by Wednesday. Would you like to go sit in the solarium to finish our caffeine before we get to work?" I chuckle and nod.

A few minutes after we are settled on the sofa he asks, "Would you like to go to the commissary next?"

"Yes I would. Besides more candy what are we getting?"

He laughs and replies, "Four steamer trunks with wheels for the things we get out of the crate."

"We'll go in your car." And the whirlwind begins.

By Wednesday night, with the help of take out from various places and the dumbwaiter, we have everything from his childhood through to him becoming a young man in our den. We spend Thursday finding places for the items that didn't go into trunks taken to the attic. Among them are his Cadet uniform I ask him to keep in the closet of our guest room, so I don't have to go into the attic to admire it and a few framed family photographs we are fortunate to have, because on the evening we visited with Hilda and Tobias, he told us a decision was made by them and his parents to remove all the photographs they had from their frames and fill their suitcases with them along with one outfit of clothing. Hilda added it took all of two seconds for her and Evelyn to make the decision due to the thought of an entirely new wardrobe.

Trevor and I make a walkthrough of the house to make sure we didn't miss anything and then have a nice long shower. After eating cold vegetable lo mein we go to our bedroom and collapse.

Friday we have dinner at the club with the crew and Saturday we all gather at the marina for the last practice run, with my father taking Theo's place. I practice using one of my new cameras that allow me to take several excellent snapshots. I can tell just by looking through the lens. I cannot wait until race day. Sunday we laze in our bed drinking coffee and Trevor reads me the Funny Paper being my soft chair. Soon the plan to develop the film from the day before is put off for another day. We missed each other.

Monday the whirlwind picks up speed, because Trevor and Williams families arrive. On the way to The O Club for lunch Emily's eyes are dancing and when we walk into the private dining room I find out why when the men *and* women stand. Emily planned a little surprise for me; Evelyn, Meredith, Judith, Poppy, Hilda, Joanna, Faye, Mother and to my utter disbelief Grand-mamma are all wearing trousers in homage to me. Tobias says, "Ladies, I think you all look younger." Robert dryly tells him, "I may never see my wife in a dress again." I know every person in the club hears the laughter.

Tuesday morning Mitch and Joanna's parent's fly in and the lunch crowd at The O Club is huge once again. The best thing happens in the evening when we get home. Théo's car is parked out front. I immediately slide over to reach for the door handle and Trevor stops. As I get out he asks, "Are you going to wait on me?" I reply, "If you park out here." He laughs and puts the car in park then gets out. I grab his hand and pull him through the house to the kitchen where I hear their voices coming from.

When we clear the doorway Théo is already standing and I walk straight into his outstretched arms. Rachel is wearing my apron, because she is cooking with Mother. We settle in and Father pours Trevor and me a glass of wine, then we get filled in on highlights of their honeymoon. The red eye flights to New York City were not considered one.

After a glass of Louis XIII my parent's leave the dishes to us, and we can talk freely. Théo begins by thanking us for the tip of having the refrigerator filled and Rachel tells us the morning after dancing the night away at the hotel's formal restaurant they called to make an appointment for a massage and found out the masseur and masseuse come to the bungalow. Fortunately we were going back and forth from the dining room to the kitchen and they do not see Trevor trying not to get tickled.

They end with their return home where they discover the desk clerk had three valet carts with wedding gifts on them. They forgot Rachel's parents sent out wedding announcements since there were no wedding invitations to send and for now they are the only thing in his office. Movers will be here Monday morning to get his drafting table and the rest of his belongings.

We sit in the solarium to finish our cognac then turn off all the lights as we go out the front door. When I watch Théo's car drive away it is my first vivid reminder of the fact he no longer lives here and I do not move a muscle. Trevor to distract me asks, "Théo looked at you while Rachel was talking and it appeared he was saying something to you and then you lit up. Does that mean I could?"

"You do and it apparently hasn't occurred to you."

Trevor's eyes begin to dart from place to place and while he process my response I pull him along to our den where we go in and shower. I'm on my side of the stall and he is on his. We've only been showering for maybe two minutes when I hear him turn off the water to his shower head. I turn around and he is covered in soap lather bathing. "Trevor, are you all right?"

He gets still and replies, "I haven't done that in a while."

"Exactly what have you done?"

"It's called a Navy Shower. To conserve fresh water on vessels we're trained to turn it off while we lather up and to turn it back on to rinse off and get out."

"That makes sense." I go over to him, turn the water back on and stay.

There is a full moon tonight, so he pours us another glass of Louis XIII and we sit in our solarium to look at it and unwind from the eventful day.

CHAPTER SEVENTEEN

Wednesday Emily and I are off, because the Navy lets there female employees prepare for Thanksgiving. It was decided everyone would be on their own today and I go to the base with a picnic basket and meet Trevor for lunch at our bench. Then afterward I go to the commissary alone for the first time and it is crowded. I leave my shopping cart on an aisle after running into several women from work that have time to chat and I do not. To the market I go.

The family business is closed until Monday and when I arrive at Maison my parents are setting pumpkins on the steps of their house. It is always a nice touch for the holiday. I walk over and ask if they need me for anything and are told they will tonight. Then something happens when I go inside our den. I find myself alone in it for the first time. I am at a loss for about two minutes when I realize this is dark room time I have desperately needed.

First on my agenda is printing a 5 x 7's of the photograph Mr. Barnes took of me sitting on the blanket Trevor asked for, to surprise him with when the perfect opportunity presents itself. So, I go get the envelope, open it to get the negative and am stunned. It is a color negative. Apparently Mr. Barnes printed the black and white photo in the frame on Trevor's nightstand. This is too good to be true. Dashing down the steps to Blanca I tell my parents I am going to Blackwell's and ask if they need anything. Mother calls out, "Film." and I am in the wind.

While there I tell Mr. Blackwell this one is a surprise for Trevor and I drop of the other negatives I need prints of to give out to everyone of the past few weeks of sailing and select frames for the race day photo I know we are going to need. I get film for Mother and last I select a wooden one for the color "woman on the blanket" photo to go in his quarters on the ship and then we talk about the latest advances in photography. All too soon I have to leave, because I want to do something I have not gotten the chance for, to be cooking dinner when he gets home. On the way I stop at the bakery for petit fours.

Loading the dumbwaiter I begin to think of what he would like to see me in when he walks into the kitchen. Then it occurs to me we are going to be in the privacy of our home and recall him telling me how he loved seeing me standing in my closet barefooted wearing a slip.

After I have the chicken breast in a white wine sauce baking in the oven I jump in the shower to bathe and rinse out my hair and when it's in a loose braid I pick out a simple sheer white silk slip. I decide to wear only it and my wedding band. Looking at myself in the mirror I cannot help but smile, because I am getting ready to seduce my husband without realizing it.

Back into the kitchen I go to sauté green beans and make linguine to pour the wine sauce over. With that done I make a martini to drink as I set the table and pour him one too. The Caesar salad is tossed and I hear his car. I turn off the things that are still simmering then take a sip of my drink and a deep breath. He enters the house through the front door and goes, "Ooo, it smells good in here." I hear him walking as he talks. "What are you ..." and he stops walking.

"Welcome home, Mr. Lyons. I missed you."

"I missed you too, Mrs. Lyons. — I'm just going to stand here and look at you."

"Take all the time you want. You might want to go ahead and take off that shirt, so the ribbons don't scratch me." He tosses it on the end of the counter.

"Geneviève, you aren't wearing anything under your slip. I have never seen you look like this. You are stunning. He puts his hands on my waist and pulls my body against his. "I am going to kiss you until we smell smoke." My laughter turns to moans when he puts his mouth on my neck and drops a strap off my shoulder.

In the morning he wakes me up by running his hand down my arm to entwine our fingers. "Good morning, Baby."

"Mmm ... good morning, Trevor. Did you sleep well?

"Yes I did. You spoil me so. I will never forget the way you looked when I got home last night."

"I love you."

"I love you too." He places his head on my shoulder and I put my hand into his soft hair. In mere seconds our bliss is shattered by the sound of car doors and he inhales sharply. "It's Thanksgiving. What time is it?"

"I don't know nor do I want to." I begin to run my fingers through his hair again and then we hear more car doors.

"Geneviève, it pains me to say this, but apparently we need to get up." I look at the clock and gasp.

"Are we about to be in a rush?"

"No, but we can't take our sweet time." While I put my hair up he gets me out a casual outfit to wear. We have a long busy day ahead of us.

After brunch at my grandparent's house we are walking down the hallway and Trevor yawns, because we were awake into the wee hours. "Pardon me." My grandmother says, "I know what to do for that. Please wait in the solarium." Our eyebrows go up. We thought we were alone.

Rachel and Théo are there too and during a discussion of how this day needs to go she returns with a tray of four espressos. We all thank her and happily take them, because we are going to be part of a party of 31 people having Thanksgiving dinner here. And in order to have us all in the dining room, her table is going to be expanded to seat 24 and our dining table with chairs, that happen to match hers perfectly and seats twelve when the leaf is added, is being brought over by a team. In order to have enough china and so forth Mother and Grand—mamma decided to mix their patterns together. We are on one determined group.

Grand-mamma wants the table and chairs to be in place before friends and their families arrive. Therefore, we finish our espressos and go to the kitchen for Claudette and Joseph and we all carry quilts and rope to our den. The second we walk in Rachel comments, "My goodness, the house looks completely different with your things in it. It's lovely." I look at Trevor wide eyed and he tells her, "Thank you." Under his breath he tells me, "Your family will be the first people we invite here." We shake our heads and go into the dining room. Trevor and I always wind up in the other houses and it has not occurred to us we have not invited them to our home.

The women wrap the table and leaf while the men tie ropes around them. Trevor and Théo each take an end and Joseph holds on to the left side to push it upright and help keep it there while they maneuver it through doors, down steps, up steps and into the other dining room. Rachel and I carry the leaf and Claudette opens and closes doors. With this done successfully we stay and unwrap the quilts as the men walk back and forth to get chairs.

After the men drink a glass of water stopping only to draw in a breath, they leave to get my parent's china and goblets that were wedding gifts almost 32 years ago my mother wrapped in hand towels and packed into picnic baskets. They look frayed when Mother leads them into the dining room and Trevor dryly says, "We were gripped in fear of tripping on the cobblestones. I didn't realize how far apart the houses were until today." Théo and Joseph nod several times in complete agreement as they happily set down the baskets.

There are two 18 pound turkeys in the refrigerators of Grand-mamma and Mother that have to be put in their ovens at 12:30 sharp, because they have to bake five hours with stuffing. So we, mother's children and our spouses, follow her to the house like little ducks in a row to help make the stuffing and put the heavy thing into the oven. When our work is done we are rewarded with chicken salad sandwiches and coconut macaroons she made yesterday, served in the solarium. Then we all go our separate ways to change into dinner dresses and suits.

Our first guests to arrive are the Prescott and Snowden families whom Emily has become part of the latter. Immediately after they have all been given something to drink there is another knock on the door and standing on the other side are Joanna and Mitch with their parents. Sandra steps in first and holds up a stack of five pie boxes tied together. "We could not remember which house to bring these to and I would like to hand them over to someone." Trevor steps forward and takes them from her. Several of us get tickled. "Thank you, Trevor. I bought a ticket for these to keep them in a seat by me on the airliner to make sure they arrived from Savannah in one piece."

Trevor asks, "Are these pumpkin or pecan pies?"

"You will have to wait until dinner to find out."

Trevor gets a glint in his eyes then holds them up to his face and when he is about to inhale she takes them away from him and everyone bursts into laughter. William says, "On that note I think we should take those next door where they belong and say hello to Constance and Théodore."

As he opens the door for our exodus Emily tells me, "I think your love of sweets has rubbed off on Trevor." While those who know me well laugh, we go outside and see Trevor's family getting out of a limousine. He hugs Evelyn first and then the rest of his family. Next he steps back and says, "To my American family members, Happy Thanksgiving. As for the rest of you, thank you for being here." I hear my mother gasp and I am with her. It didn't even cross our minds the British do not celebrate our holiday ... moving on. Since the last of our guests have arrived we all go to my grandparents' house. My parents knock on the door in order not to catch them off guard with 27 people entering the house all at once.

When the rest of our guests have been served something to drink we decide to go outside and scatter among the grounds to allow the ones whom are here for their first time to leisurely look around and go where they wish. Trevor and I quietly gather his family to invite them to see our home.

After the tour I get my camera then Trevor and I step out onto the balcony and what a site we see. William is on the teeter totter with Bobby and being pushed in swings by their spouses are Sandra, Joanna, Lorraine and Faye. Emily and Kelly are watching all this from a safe distance. Théo and Rachel are sitting on the boardwalk and we go there. Eventually my grandfather shows up, so Rachel and I choose to go inside to help Mother and send Father out. Grand-mamma has Claudette and Joseph happily helping her.

Half an hour has passed when Trevor, Théo and Father walk in while the three of us are standing at the counter with bowls whisking heavy cream, milk and flour with salt and pepper together. There is a covered bowl with onions Mother sliced yesterday to avoid the ordeal of cutting today. When my father asks what they can do to help Mother tells him they can wash two bags of potatoes that need to be thinly sliced for three dishes of Potatoes Au Gratin. He announces it is time for wine and goes to the cellar then returns with two bottles of red Bordeaux.

We drink wine and cut all the potatoes then pair off with a dish each to layer the ingredients in. I look up for a moment and watch my new family preparing a meal together for the first time. Trevor sees what I am doing and gives me a kiss. After the potatoes are in the oven our husbands help us out of aprons then we take our glasses and the last bottle of wine to the kitchen table and settle in for a simple chit chat about this and that, taking turns basting the turkey.

Eventually Théo has a puzzled look and asks, "Why hasn't anyone wondered in?" Mother replies, "You two just returned from your honeymoon and we are together officially as a family today." Father adds, "Plus it is a nice fall day for our guests to stay outside and enjoy Maison." I chime in, "And our grandparents are hosting the dinner, so they should go to their house if they want or need anything."

Next Trevor gets this boyish look and asks, "Josephine, will you tell me what kind of pies is over there?" We all laugh hard as Mother shakes her head. Then he looks at me. He knows I picked up on it and I respond, "I'm not telling you either. Mitch's mother wanted it to be a surprise and I'm not going to spoil it." Mother interjects, "The turkey is ready. May I suggest you and Théo grab a handle and set it on the range top to occupy your inquisitive mind?" They reply in unison, "Yes, Mother." and go to the oven. We, the ladies, are laughing as we go to freshen up and get ready to go next door.

The turkey is on a platter my father is carrying and my parents lead us outside. We carry the potatoes and bottles of wine and as we parade passed family and friends still outside, they begin to fall in line and follow us to the solarium. We go to the kitchen and the others keep going to the drawing room. When the table is set with a turkey on each end and the candles are lit my grandmother announces, "Dinner is served."

My grandfather puts his hand on Trevor's shoulder and we stop at the end of the tables. He tells him, "This table belongs to you and your wife, therefore you should sit at the head of it." Next he escorts Théo and Rachel to the other end and seats him at the head of their table. The future of this family is in place and they are going to carve the turkeys. My grandparents and parents stand across from each other at the middle and Grand-papa tells everyone to have a seat where ever they please. Meredith starts counting chairs and when she gets to me she says, "This is the odd side." And Trevor seats her next to me." When her bell hits the edge of the chair Trevor and I smile at each other. After my grandfather says grace William immediately passes his plate to Trevor and knowing his mate, he puts a turkey leg on it. His day is made and dinner begins.

It's finally time for dessert and the Mitchell's followed by Claudette and Joseph excuse themselves. Sandra leads them back in carrying a tray. Joanna, Mitch and Albert are also carrying trays, but Joseph and Claudette are holding pitchers of milk. Sandra steps up to Trevor and lowers her tray. He smiles so big. "I knew it was going to be Southern pecan pies instead of pumpkin." He takes a piece and kisses her cheek. When Joseph and Claudette begin filling our dessert wine goblets with milk we give Sandra a round of applause.

During our coffee Théo reminds everyone the cocktail party tomorrow for the race at the club begins at five o'clock and the lottery for placement begins at six. My father advises them to take a taxi or a limousine to the marina Saturday, because only boat owner's vehicles are allowed inside the gates, otherwise they could wind up on a long walk to Willow.

Next Father goes to the buffet and takes out eight boxes, four are shirt boxes. He gives two boxes to each member of the racing crew and they open them to find white jackets and red polo shirts with Gypsy, San Diego, CA embroidered on them. I beam as I get a visual of them wearing khakis and looking like the crew they are, formidable.

Hilda asks him, "Since we're all together will you tell us details about the race?"

"It would be my pleasure. It is a harbor race and to keep it fair only 65 foot sloops may enter. This keeps it from being overcrowded and makes it very competitive. The sailboats go one nautical mile south then come about and pick up speed in order to cross the start line going as fast as possible. They make three laps on the triangular course of buoys that on the average take 16 minutes and the first one across the finish line, which is also the start line, wins." Mother proudly interjects, "Gérard's crew and Azure hold the course record for the fastest final lap of 14 minutes and 29 seconds." This triggers more questions about the race.

Soon coffee cups are empty and slowly our friends and family take their leave. Next, tackle the aftermath in the kitchens. We begin with my grandparents' and save my parents' kitchen, the easy one, for last. When the cleaning is done we all go to our homes and no doubt collapse.

Friday Trevor does not have to report for duty, so we finally wash our dishes from Wednesday we stashed in the oven to hide from his family and then we spend the day lazing about on the overlook and in the solarium. He is going to need all his strength for the race.

When evening comes we watch my parents leave early, because Mother has to work with the board members on the lottery. For the lottery they write all the names of the sailboats entered in the race on large folded tickets and put them in a footed fish bowl. Then the tickets are drawn from it to decide the placement of the sailboats when they begin sailing toward the starting line. If your ticket is drawn first you are first on the inside and so on. What happens tonight decides the tact you are going to have to take to get in the lead. Since Mother has a conflict of interest, because Théo and Trevor are in the race she is not drawing the tickets tonight, another board member is.

Trevor and I walk into The Lounge where the cocktail party is thrown that isn't crowded yet and join my parents who are with Théo and Rachel who just arrived. The rest of the crew isn't here. Théo suggests going ahead and getting something to drink and the four of us go to the bar.

When the bartender asks, "What can I get for you?" Trevor looks at me and I reply, "A Shirley Temple, please." Then I hear Joanna say, "Make that two." as she steps up to the bar beside me. Rachel adds, "I haven't had one of those in years. Make that three, please." He nods and looks at Mitch who tells him, "I'll have a gin and tonic. Hold the gin." Trevor and Théo give the bartender a nod. Not drinking anything with alcohol before a race is an unwritten rule most crews adhere to.

The lottery begins in 15 minutes and Emily and William are still not here. Trevor keeps looking at his watch and I look around the room that should be crowded and tell him, "There should more members here by now. I think they're caught in a traffic jam caused by an accident." My parents agree and I suggest going to the bar and getting their drinks for they will be thirsty when they get here.

The bartender makes the Shirley Temple first and as he sets an old fashioned glass down we hear William say, "That is for a gin and tonic minus the gin." We whirl around and I hug Emily as Trevor shakes William's hand. "It's good to see you, mate."

"It's good to see you too. I'm glad we made it before the lottery. We were caught in a traffic jam behind by an accident and were only a block and half away from it. Emily suggested I park the car and walking passed it to hail a cab, but I didn't think it would take long to clear, but we found out a car t-boned a glass company truck with several panes on it and the glass went everywhere, taking forever to sweep off the street. I'll be paying attention to my wife's intuition from now on." Emily slightly nods as she drinks the Shirley Temple I handed her while he talked.

We join the others standing around a table now and when Emily finishes telling them about their ordeal my grandparents walk in with three minutes to spare then go straight to the bar for a whiskey on the rocks and a Manhattan. They stand with us and the bell rings to signal the lottery is about to begin. You could hear a pin drop.

After a short speech by Mr. Nichols, he announces there are 11 entries in the race this year. Kyle gets in his spot then Mr. Nichols reaches into the fish bowl and draws the first ticket. "Orion." Short applause follow as the owner, Mr. Turner takes the ticket and I whisper, "She's won before." Then he says, "Vendetta" and as he gives the ticket to, Mr. Reed. Théo says, "She's the defending champion." Then Mr. Nichols draws another one. "Gypsy." And we cause a slight disturbance, because third in the lineup is considered the lucky spot. Trevor gives me a kiss then he gets her ticket and we clap louder than usual as he waves it in the air.

After the last ticket is drawn there is a round of applause for all the boat crews. The excitement in the air is wonderful. When Father holds up his glass and says, "To Gypsy and her crew." I get chill bumps. Next we walk down the corridor to a private dining room to celebrate my grandparent's anniversary. The dinner begins with salmon canapés and ends with mango sorbet. No one has coffee, because caffeine will keep us awake and we all need plenty of sleep.

CHAPTER EIGHTEEN

Race day is here. The second I wake up I am wide wake and in Trevor's arms. He is sound asleep, so I lie here and feel the rhythm of his heart and his breath in my hair for this brief moment of calm in what it is going to be a hectic day. I do not want to move until he moves and I close my eyes.

Time passes and the rhythm of his heart changes. Then he draws in a deep breath and whispers, "Geneviève."

Rolling over onto my back to see his face I say, "I'm listening."

"Thank you for today."

"Why are you thanking me now?"

"Because it's going to be incredible to experience the thrill of racing as a man for the first time and aboard a sailboat that belongs to me, because she was given to me by the woman who married me. I love you — and our life."

"I love you too and I love our life too."

Trevor kisses me on the tip of my nose. "Are you ready to get up?"

For once I shift gears on him as I fling the covers off of us. "You bet I am. I'll start breakfast while you call Mitch to get the Maritime Report."

"How did you know ... never mind."

I jump out of bed and open the draperies. "It's overcast and breezy."

"I do enjoy a challenge." He bounds out of bed, twirls me and we dance to the kitchen where we eat a hearty breakfast which includes my pancakes and for a change we wash and put away the dishes. Next we get dressed and he does looks good in red. I'm going to thank my mother at lunch for that shirt. The sailboats cross the start line at two o'clock sharp, but we have to be at the marina by 12:45. Gypsy's crew and their wives are meeting at my parent's house for an early lunch and to ride together in Trevor's car like anchovies in a can.

During the time we have before lunch we take binoculars up to the overlook and watch the wave patterns being made by the all important wind. Once he has that down we just enjoy the view and discuss our departure and arrival plans to the marina. When Théo and Rachel get here we know it's time to gather our things and pack the car. Trevor does his whistle to get their attention. At this moment I sure am glad I started walking around with my camera again. They too are in good spirits. It's been a long time since my brother participated in a race and his wife has never watched one.

Trevor's trunk is packed and I put my old top viewer camera in with the new one I keep in his back seat then check the amount of film in the camera bag and set it in the trunk. We also pack dry clothes and towels just in case we need them. He leaves the trunk up, because there is more to come from the others.

Upon entering the house the smell of cinnamon and nutmeg is in the air. We inhale deeply and then I say, "Mother made oatmeal and pecan cookies." After we go into the kitchen she gets her cheek kissed by us then Trevor tries unsuccessfully to sneak one off the cooling rack. She gets him with a dish towel and shoos us out along with Rachel and Théo to set the dining room table. Shortly there is a knock on the door and as it opens William says, "Ahoy to the house." Trevor and I step into the hallway laughing and he replies "Ahoy, Mates."

Emily and Joanna are carrying bags of potato chips, William has a large sack with some kind of bread in it and Mitch has the tray with his wife's ham on it. Trevor announces, "Lunch is here." and we start laughing. Personally I was expecting him to say the rest of the crew was here. My grandparents along with Claudette and Joseph are not far behind and we set up a buffet.

Everyone inhales their lunch and those riding with Trevor and I go out to the car. The trunk is filled and Théo and Trevor open all the car doors. The Mitchell's and the Delcroix's squeeze in to back seat and the Snowden's squeeze in next to us. The fellas manage to get the doors closed and to the marina we go.

Trevor maneuvers to the gate through the traffic and Mr. Davidson waves us through. He parks next to Gypsy and we all say hello to her and Willow then start unloading the car. The first thing I do is put on my cameras with the straps around my neck and then the fellas go aboard Gypsy and we go aboard Willow. When I see my parent's car I think I'm hallucinating, because Trevor's entire family is riding on the hood and trunk. Evelyn and Poppy are holding onto the hood ornament and their husbands. Trevor shouts, "Ahoy to the shore." as I take several snapshots. The fun has begun on a large scale now. They unload the car and Father decides to go back to gate for the rest of our group.

He returns with the Prescott's on the hood. Faye and Robert are holding onto their children and Faye is holding onto her husband trying to smile. Bobby and Kelly are beaming. The Moore's, Mitchell's and Snowden's are in the car with Father, which is where I believe Faye wishes she was. When Robert gets her off she throws her arms round his neck. And fear causes her to make her first display of affection in front of people. Emily happily photographs them.

Next we hear a car horn blow and see a taxi headed our way. Mother exclaims, "Helen." The driver opens her door and she is shaking her head. Father takes her overnight and garment bags from the driver as she joins us. "Hello all." She sighs and kisses Mothers cheeks. "One of my trains hasn't been delayed in years. I had a horrible vision of trying to hire a water taxi out to Willow, so I held a 10 up for the driver to see in his rearview mirror and told him it was his if he would speed. As you all can see, he took it and here I am." I watch father give the driver another tip and chuckle.

The fellas are ready to go out and they come ashore. They pose for a photo by Gypsy and I whisper to Joanna, "They could win best looking crew if there was a trophy for that." She stifles her laughter as our friends and family wish them luck then leave us for a moment together and we pair off.

I tell Trevor, "Lift your sunglasses please." When he does I see they are bright and blue as blue. "Happy?"

"That is an understatement. Give me a kiss for luck." I grab his collar and pull him to me and since it is for luck I give him a brief yet passionate kiss. He licks his lips and says, "Once again you catch me off guard. I love you."

"I love you too. See you soon."

With flirtation in his voice he tells me, "See you soon, Baby." While I melt he looks around and calls out, "Boat crew." Then they go aboard and wave.

We shout, "Fair winds and following seas." and run to Willow.

I photograph the fellas cast off and passing by then I help us cast off and go to the bow as Father takes her out. Suddenly Vendetta cuts between us and Joanna says. "That was rude." I respond, "It means Mr. Reed is concerned with Gypsy." Rachel is to my left and she adds, "He should be. There are three Navy trained Sailors and a man who has been sailing since he was five years old aboard her. They will handle him and his Vendetta." Emily says, "I like her." and we all get tickled.

Father drifts into the space at the bow of the committee boat and drops anchor. The best spot is saved for Willow, being the son of the clubs founder and having him aboard has its rewards. After warning everyone I am going to be all over Willow taking photographs Rachel quietly says, "Gené, Thank you for this. We are having the best honeymoon. Théo is on Cloud Nine and I am on it with him." I respond with a careful hug, because I have two cameras and a pair of binoculars hanging on me and she has one of each. Then my Father shouts, "They're hoisting sails." I whip around grabbing my binoculars then switch to my top view camera, because they will be here shortly.

Gypsy is about 300 yards away and I can see Mitch and William trimming the headsail with Théo at the cleat of the mainsail and Trevor at the helm. They are almost to the pin for the start and after they pass it, since Gypsy is black, we can easily see her bow is two feet in front of the others when they pass by us. I dart to the port side and watch Gypsy round the north marker then she gains a little more. After they round the south marker and pass the pin, the tip of Vendetta's bow is a good eight feet back from Gypsy's and our passengers cheer. I turn to Mother who has the stop watch for the first lap standing next to Father who is timing the second one. She discretely tells us, "14 minutes and 27 seconds." Two seconds less than my father's last on their first win. Usually a sailboats last lap is her fastest. I absorb this information as I go back to the port side.

A few minutes later they round the outer marker and I am starboard looking through my binoculars. Gypsy is leading on the inside with Vendetta trying to pass her on the outside and Orion is gaining on Vendetta. Seconds later something happens and I didn't see exactly what, because it happened so fast, but Vendetta is almost even with Gypsy. When they're close to the north marker I run to the bow and then watch them pass. Gypsy and Vendetta are even and Mitch is visibly upset. Mr. Reed is known for pushing the boundaries of the rules and is obviously up to his old tricks, but Trevor glances at me grinning.

The last lap begins and I watch in amazement what happens next. Gypsy moves to the outside of Vendetta after they round the north marker and head to the outer marker. Trevor drops Gypsy back a bit and then I see Vendetta's sails flutter and I shout out, "Yes." He blocked the wind from their sails and Vendetta loses her lift for a few precious seconds and drops back considerably before she can recover. When the sloops round the south marker Gypsy is in the lead. Orion gained on her, but she is several feet back and Vendetta is close to the stern of Orion as Gypsy crosses the finish line.

Trevor is standing with one hand on the wheel and his fist in the air. Théo, William and Mitch have both fists in the air and they face us, their wives, and Trevor shouts, "Yeah, Baby." I blow him a kiss then take one of the best photographs I will ever take. They sail by and when the last sloop has passed my father starts Willow's engines and we weigh anchor then drift out toward the mouth of the bay to wait on Gypsy to follow her in.

It doesn't long for her to return and she is way ahead of the other sloops letting all the spectators know she is the winner of the race. As Gypsy gets close to the bay, the fellas lower her sails and when they see us they become very animated and motion for us to follow them. After the gangways are down, four women run to their husbands who are running toward us. I leap into Trevor's outstretched arms and he spins me round and round. He puts me down and gives me a kiss. "Baby, I can't begin to describe how I feel. Racing at this level felt ... invigorating."

"Gypsy is beautiful and the way you handle her ... it was incredible to watch. I ran circles around Willow trying to keep you in my sight." Then we hear applause and I step back to see we are surround by friends and family with spectators surrounding us all. This means we're going to the podium soon for Gypsy's crew to be presented with their trophy. It's made for 12 men to stand across and has a raised center section for the four men of the winning crew.

Eventually members of the committee work their way through the crowd and lead the way to the podium as I tell Trevor, "You need to decide who you want to stand on your left, because after you are presented with the trophy you offer the other handle to that person and you both hold it up for the crowd to see."

"That does not require a decision. Théo is going to hold the other handle. We couldn't have done this without him."

"He will be honored. Also, they line the winners up to the right of the podium with second place leading, first in the middle and third place is last, which is appropriate." On that he gives me a look.

"I'll tell you later. Is that a camera crew?"

"Yes it is, the club has this filmed and show it during The Victory Banquet."

"Nice."

"A committee member is walking up. I love you."

"I love you too, Geneviève." And he squeezes my hand before he lets it go.

Mother steps up to Rachel and me to holds our hands. "Ladies, your mother's are going to take photographs of this in order for you all to enjoy the moment." We hug Mother as Joanna and Emily wave at Sandra and Faye.

They line up the men and since Mr. Reed is a bachelor, no surprise there, 11 women line up in front of the podium to wait on them. As they climb up onto the top tier with William in front of Trevor, who is followed by Théo and Mitch, I get chills. When they present Trevor with the trophy he holds it over to Théo and they lift it up, then Trevor and William raise their arms and clasp their hands. Théo and Mitch do the same as my heart soars. There they stand – the victors.

They pose for the official photograph that goes in the trophy case at the club and for *The Times* then they step down to us for a kiss and a hug as our group closes in and no one else can get to us. Father says," I motion we go aboard Willow for a private celebration and wait for this crowd to dissipate." Mother says. "I second that motion." And we are off.

On deck Father and Rowland pull up mesh bags from the water that have three chilled bottles of champagne in each. They wrap them in towels and we go below to the lounge. It only seats 16, so the men stand by their women. Trevor and I, along with his crew and their wives sit on the sofas. Champagne is poured and Father informs us they broke the course record for the fastest first lap. We raise our glasses to them and then they talk begin talking about getting ready to cross the start line.

Then Poppy interjects, "I can't wait to find this out. What happened during the second lap?" Trevor instantly looks irritated and replies, "Mr. Reed moved in close and I had to adjust our course which cost us time." Théo jumps in. "I was seething until Trevor calmly tells me, 'We'll handle him. It's time for battle tactics.' While I'm in disbelief, wondering what we are about to do Trevor shouts, 'ATTENTION ON DECK. BATTLE TACTICS. THIS IS WAR.' Jaws drop and several people gasp as I chuckle and say, "Trevor, you didn't."

"I certainly did and for two reasons. One was we didn't have a code for that and I needed William and Mitch to be on alert. The second one was I wanted to intimidate Mr. Reed and his crew." Laughter erupts and Evelyn manages to say, "I have no doubt you succeeded. I bet they almost had a stroke."

Théo says, "I could feel *my* heart pounding. They had to be on edge. And by the time we passed Willow he already had a plan. I could tell because he was grinning. Before we reached the north marker he told me to pull the mainsail boom starboard for only five seconds on his mark to slow us down." William adds, "When Trevor aligned Gypsy with Vendetta I glanced over my shoulder and saw Théo pulling on the boom. Then I watched Reed's face go white when his sails fluttered. It was sheer perfection." Mitch looks like a proud father as he nods. My grandfather crosses to Trevor and shakes his hand. "The best racing story I have ever heard. With your permission I would like to tell it at the club."

"Permission granted." And laughter erupts again.

When Rowland stops laughing he says, "Well done, Son. I am looking forward to watching the film this evening. I spotted the camera on top of the committee boat. Perhaps they will show that maneuver." Several people say, "I hope so." in unison, including me.

Our glasses are empty and Father goes on deck and returns to inform it is no longer crowded. Faye looks pale at the thought of riding on the hood again, but off she goes. Those who rode with Trevor and I stay to revel in the moment and listen to details of the race the fellas tell only us and more photographs are taken before we bid adieu to Gypsy and thank her for the wonderful time.

Upon our arrival at Maison no one lingers, because we have to get ready for The Victory Celebration. Théo and Rachel are the first to leave then Joanna and Mitch are the last. Listening to their car get further away Trevor props on the side of his car and pulls me against him as he puts his arms around me. After a few minutes of peace and quiet I say, "What a victory." Then a thought occurs to me and I turn to face him. "To the victor go the spoils. Be thinking of what you want."

"I don't need to think. All I want is for us to have a nice ... long ... hot ... shower." And I hold his hand to lead him inside.

Wrapped in towels sipping on ice water, Trevor gets out his dress blues and I get out the black evening gown I wore for our engagement dinner. When I am laying out my lingerie on the chaise I place my black long line bra on it and Trevor says, "I've been waiting to see you wear that."

"And I'm glad you're here." His eyebrows go up as I step into my panties, drop my towel and hold the bra in place. I glance over my shoulder and assure him, "All you have to do is pull on each end until they meet and put the hooks in the middle row of eyes." After he is done I turn around and he looks quite pleased with himself and I give him a proper kiss.

When I am about to put on jewelry he asks me to stand in front of the mirrors and close my eyes. "I knew you were going to were that evening gown tonight, because it's the only one you haven't worn to the club. Therefore I got you a little thank you gift to wear with it."

"What is the thank you for?"

"Gypsy." I feel a necklace being placed around my neck that is substantial in weight. What has he done? "Open your eyes, Baby." I hesitate and when I do I gasp, because there is a large cushion cut Burmese ruby surrounded by diamonds suspended from diamonds around my neck. "You are as beautiful as I imagined you would be."

"Trevor, I ... I don't know what to say."

"Then kiss me." And I do.

After a passionate moment he reaches into his pocket then holds out a matching pair of earrings. "I choose this suite because red is your favorite color."

"You spoil me so."

After I put on the earrings and red lipstick we admire each other in the mirrors. Then he drapes my wrap over my shoulders and offers me his arm.

I am eager to step out onto the portico and when we do Trevor's jaw drops as Elliot tips his hat standing by The Chariot. He closes his mouth and faces me. "I knew you were going to win. I could feel it. Plus I watched you steer us through the heavy weather when fall rolled in. You are an exceptional Sailor."

"I wish I could kiss you."

"You will on our way home. Now let's go celebrate."

Instead of champagne I had Elliot chill a decanter of water knowing we would still be thirsty. Trevor gets tickled when he spots it and asks, "Are you able to see things in that crystal ball?" And I burst into laughter.

As Elliot pulls up to the entrance of the club I give Trevor an Eskimo Kiss and we go inside to discover the Pike's are here and I exclaim, "Norah, Reginald ... I am so pleased to see you both." Reginald responds, "We decided to surprise you both and be at Willow, but the traffic was horrendous." Norah chimes in, "We watched the race from Old Point Loma and didn't even miss the start because I am convinced our limousine driver drives ambulances on the side." She pretends to smooth her hair and laughter erupts, then she focuses on me. "Geneviève, you are in full bloom tonight, no doubt due to the man standing by your side. The jewelry suite is breath taking."

"Thank you. Trevor gave it to me tonight."

She pats his cheeks and Grand-papa suggests we make our way to The Banquet Hall and motions for Trevor and me to lead the way. This time I am happy our table is front and center because it is reserved for the party of the winners. Since there are 34 members in our party the table is a long row that goes from one end of the dance floor to the other. What a difference. The last time we had this honor we had a single round table for 10.

Gypsy's crew and us, their proud wives are seated in the center quietly sipping on whiskey and Manhattan's. Joanna has Emily sit next to Trevor to get William close to him and she sits next to William. Théo is in his relatively new place to my right, because Trevor is to my left at all times now. My, how things have changed.

Finally Rachel tells us, "I feel as if I am having a déjà vous. We are all wearing the gowns from the engagement dinner." Emily responds, "Thank goodness for that weekend. I didn't have time to shop." Joanna adds, "None of us did. Our men have been taking all our spare time. Mitch interjects, "I for one am glad. I never get to see her in the same gown twice and I was fond of this one." Trevor, Théo and William say, "Hear, hear."

The main things I like about this event are although we are dressed formally the orchestra doesn't play classical music, they play current popular songs and there is a buffet instead of a seated dinner. You have a choice of prime rib, seafood or chicken and so many side dishes and desserts your decision is not easy. The best part is they serve hamburgers with macaroni and cheese for the children. Years ago Grand-mamma made a rule that if a child did not require a booster seat the child could attend this and our New Year's Eve Gala, because my parent's refused to usher in a New Year without Théo and me. Bobby is thrilled to be here and wearing his tuxedo again. I think it makes him feel as if he is all grown up. Not to mention he idolizes William. Kelly is a pretty wallflower as always and sitting by her father.

The meal is over and we are having an after diner drink when the lights on the stage go up, which means it is time for the official presentation of the trophies.

Next we get a wonderful surprise, the fellas taught Théo how to walk in unison with them and they are resplendent as they take their place center stage. When they hold the trophy up like they did at the marina they receive a standing ovation, because it was announced Gypsy broke the record for fastest first lap. This is impressive, because that is the lap when the crews get their sloops' speed up.

They return to the table and Trevor places the trophy in the center as the screen is lowered and the lights are dimmed to watch the film. He puts his arm around my shoulder and pulls me close. The club didn't show a film of the race when Azure was winning, therefore I am most excited, especially for Trevor to see what Gypsy looked like in her glory and how well they did.

The members whisper among themselves, but no one at our table says a word until Vendetta crowds Gypsy. Several members gasp and shift in their seats as Trevor tells me under his breath, "That man got closer than I thought. Things happen in split seconds. We handled that beautifully."

"I thought so."

A few minutes later we can see him maneuvering Gypsy and the mainsail being moved ever so slightly. Then there is the flutter. Almost every person in The Hall reacts and several men knock on their tables, including the men at ours. This is one of the proudest moments of my life. Father glances at me and nods toward Trevor, then I tell him, "You need to stand for at least 15 seconds in order to let them know it was you who made that decision."

"You can't be serious?"

"You're representing the Navy, not yourself." And he is on feet standing tall at attention. I silently start counting as the knocking continues and when I reach 15 he sits down. I knew he was counting. I love him.

After the film is over and the orchestra returns there is more mingling than dancing, because everyone wants to talk about the race a first time entry won. Eventually my grandfather gives us a sign that means it's time for us to stand near the table to let the crowd overtake us. And overtake us they do, because a member of Orion's crew heard what Trevor shouted just before they made their move and he told who knows who and every person in The Hall is talking about it.

While listening to the fellas answer the same question for the umpteenth time I hear a tap on the microphone and look up to see the lady that sings with the orchestra. Mother had the board do this and I am elated. Then she begins to sing "It Had To Be You" and I sigh. Trevor says, "My wife wants to dance. Excuse us please." He holds his hand out and leads me onto the dance floor. Come here, Baby." And we dance as if we are at The O Club. Eventually Mitch and Joanna are the only ones not dancing. Théo and William lost no time in making their escape and someone had to stay at the interrogation.

The song ends and Trevor tells me, "We are not leaving this dance floor. I don't care if they play a song for the Charleston." I have a small burst of laughter. Fortunately they keep it slow with "Smoke Gets In Your Eyes" and I do not have to dance the Charleston, something I did as a child for fun with Théo.

When I notice Faye and Robert pass us I see Kelly and Bobby sitting alone on one end of the table. Helen and Meredith are on the other. Next Helen motions for Eric and in record time he returns with four sundaes topped with chocolate syrup and a cherry. The lovely women leads Eric to them and Helen sits by Bobby as Meredith sits by Kelly and all their faces are beaming.

The orchestra announces they are taking a break and the pianist emerges, so Trevor leads me to the bar for fresh drinks. He orders me another Manhattan and gets his whiskey on the rocks this time. His uniform is wool. Joanna and Mitch have gone to the dance floor and we stand talking at the back of the room with Théo and Rachel to be left alone for a minute.

We are enjoying ourselves immensely until Théo says, "Gené, you will not believe who is headed our way and he is inebriated."

I gasp and Trevor asks, "Who is that?"

"The cad." He exhales heavily as the cad walks up to me.

"Mrs. Lyons."

"Mr. Franklin."

"Whenever I approached you about speaking with your father, you were either focused on studying or focused on your career. Then out of the blue you show up with the commander here and today it all made sense. You were focused on finding an officer who could win this trophy for your family again. I heard you even gave him the sloop."

"The latter does not concern you, but my rejection of your consistent advances does. Mr. Franklin, I rejected you because I knew your only interest in me was because I am a Delcroix."

"Your last name wasn't all I was interested in. I was also interested in your virtue."

While I consider throwing my drink on his face, Trevor quips, "How dare you. Don't you ever speak to my wife in that manner. In fact, don't you ever speak to my wife again. You're dismissed."

"Do you have any idea who you're talking to?"

"Yes, I do."

"I'm not going anywhere. What are you going to do about that Mr. Big Shot Navy Man?" Then he flicks the medals on Trevor's uniform.

"I have never hit a man outside the ring, but I will make an exception for you."

I take the glass of whiskey from him and Théo gets William's attention. Then suddenly Mr. Franklin swings and misses Trevor. When he is about to swing again I say, "Upper cut." and Trevor throws an upper cut that connects and the man goes flying backwards then lands on the carpet. William has to put his arm across Emily to avoid Mr. Franklin as he falls down. Trevor rubs his knuckles and I give him his glass of whiskey. He takes a drink and then the six of us remain perfectly still as we watch the chaos that ensues.

Mother has let go of Fathers' arm and has her gown with both hands as they make their way through the crowd. Mitch and Joanna pass them. Joseph, who is here as a guest, and Eric stand by Mr. Franklin who is trying to get up. They help him to his feet and keep holding on to his arms. Mother arrives and tells them, "Hold on to him until his parent's get here and I will ask them how they want to handle this. Trevor, I am assuming you do not want to press assault charges."

"You assume correctly. I do not, but I do want him away from Geneviève."

Joseph responds, "We will take him into the next room." As they take him away my parents along with Rachel and Theo follow them. His parents catch up and the doors are closed. Trevor offers me his arm and says, "Excuse us please. We are going to private dining room at the end of the hallway." We give our drinks to William and Emily.

Trevor takes us straight into the empty room and asks, "Are you all right?"

"Yes." I lift his hand and rub it. "Are you all right?"

"I'm fine. It doesn't hurt. I pulled my punch to avoid causing permanent damage to that pathetic excuse of a man."

"He would have deserved it." Trevor laughs and gives me a hug.

"Now that I've had time to think, Geneviève, where did upper cut come from?"

"I did *not* want him to hit you and I know from listening to boxing matches an upper cut knocks the opponents head back causing them to stumble backwards, thus away from you."

"Baby, you have earned the right to watch a boxing match. When we hear about the next major event I'll take you to Gioffre and have a suit made for you." I throw my arms around his neck. "Just please don't let your mother find out."

"Deal."

"Are you ready to go back?"

"Yes. I want my drink."

When Trevor opens the door to The Hall we see our table is seated, signaling they want to be left alone and the orchestra begins to play "Moonlight Serenade", therefore we go straight to the dance floor and resume our wonderful evening. The orchestra sounds like the record we have of this by Glenn Miller.

We stop dancing and see Emily holding up a Manhattan and William is holding up a glass of whiskey on the rocks. They ordered us fresh drinks and to the table we go where Joanna tells us, "This is what you missed; the Franklin's left with their son holding an ice pack on his jaw and when Mr. Reed left he gave us a nod. Last but not least, it is getting late, so Faye and Robert have been waiting on your return before taking their children home." Trevor and I glance at each other. That happened in front of Kelly and Bobby.

Seconds before I am completely undone, Kelly becomes animated and tells Trevor and me, "We had so much fun. Thank you for inviting us." Bobby is nodding the entire time and I manage to say, "We are pleased to hear that and hope to see you soon." Since she said it all, Robert has nothing to add and he is beaming as he leaves with his wife and very happy children.

Next my grandfather motions to the trophy sitting in the middle of our table. "In case anyone was wondering what happens to the trophy, it remains here and engraved replicas are given to each crew member." Rachel, Joanna and Emily beam while Trevor, William and Mitch have slight smiles at the thought. Théo of course already knew.

This prompts Rachel to ask him, "Where are your trophies?"

"I was afraid you were going to ask me that." Eyebrows go up and he continues. "My architectural models need to be where I can see them from my drafting table, so they are on a top shelf in my closet."

"Mmm hm. When we meet the movers at your parents house Monday to get your things, those will be coming with. And then we are going shopping for a trophy case to put in your office?"

"Yes we are." She gives him a kiss on his cheek.

Emily's wheels begin to turn. "William, we are going to need one of those."

"Emily, it's just one trophy. It would look nice in the middle of the mantle in our living room."

Before she can respond Trevor goes, "Oi, Mate." in an accent so thick Tobias chuckles and William's eyes get wide. "I for one intend to return next year as the defending champion." Every man at the table says, "Hear, hear." My father stands, raises his glass and then we all do. "To Gypsy and her crew." We echo his words loud and clear.

After a little time has gone by Trevor sets down his empty glass and says, "It has been an eventful day *and* night. Therefore I am going home with my beautiful wife to collapse." And we say good night to all.

Elliot is waiting out front and after he gets in I tell him, "Elliot, to The Brava please." And I begin to raise the partition. "There is an overnight bag in the trunk. We are going to need room service." I hold out my hand and he gives me his handkerchief. While I wipe of my lipstick he whispers, "I do believe we are about to make out all the way there."

"Not tonight. Earlier today I watched you use your surface warfare training and I just witnessed the true power of your boxing skills. Foreplay begins now." I hold on to his lapels and pull him to me.

This time we wake up in The Honeymoon Suite and know where we are.

CHAPTER NINETEEN

Our lives return to normal the following week and for the first time in weeks instead of sailing on Saturday we go to the commissary to shop for Christmas decorations and tree ornaments while eating peppermint candy canes and make scenes because we have so much fun.

That evening we get ready for our first dinner guests in our den, my family. They arrive and Trevor offers them a drink before beginning the brief tour of our home, because all we've decorated is the first floor. Rachel requests a martini with the brine and it sounds good to all of us. When I give Rachel hers I notice her shiny new gold bracelet. "Your bracelet is beautiful." She quietly replies, "Thank you." and takes a drink of her martini. That was an abrupt end of the topic. As I give Théo his martini he gives her an inquisitive look and she blurts out, "Théo bought it for me on my birthday. It was during our honeymoon. I asked him not to tell anyone, because I was going to turn 30, which makes me two years older than him and I was embarrassed."

I respond, "Rachel, we knew you were older and it made sense why he was attracted to you. He never did like giggly young women." My father adds, "Most men don't." The Rachel asks, "How did you know?" Théo takes this one. "I did the math. On our first date you told me the age you were when you moved here." She sighs and says "I'm changing the subject because I just noticed those unique dolphin candlesticks remind of the fountains in Italy." Trevor responds, "You have a good eye. I found those in Naples." I interject, "The majority of the unusual objects in our home were collected over several years by Trevor as he traveled around the world."

Grand-mamma adds, "The Menagerie Carousel is a stand out."

"I was on shore leave in New Orleans and wondered into a curiosity shoppe."

We all look at each other as Trevor smiles and Rachel breaks the silence that fell. "What else did you find in your travels?"

We walk around and show the other things as he tells the stories about each one. The only items left are the swan bowls in our bedroom. Since Théo was concerned about our color choices for it we tell my family they can see it if they take off their shoes. Without question they do and we hear gasps when they step in. Mother says, "I've never seen anything like this. It is ... lavish." Rachel turns to Théo, "Our bedroom is boring."

"This one is just ... going to have us redecorating ours." She kisses him and we all go to the dining room.

When we conclude our meal we move to the living room for nectar and to look at all the photographs taken before, during and after the race. Eventually Grand-papa stands and thanks us for the lovely evening then Trevor and I escort my family onto the balcony. When no one is in sight Trevor gathers me into his embrace and kisses me as if we are moments from making love. Then he softly says, "Mrs. Lyons, I want to seduce you. I will do anything you want me to."

"Kiss me like that again and consider it done." He does and it is.

The next week we begin preparing early for Emily's birthday party on Friday over several phone calls and the arrival of the Christmas trees and greenery on Saturday. Deciding what kind of tree we wanted for our home was a highlight, because we ordered two, one for the living room and one to go in the solarium for the family to see.

During lunch on Wednesday at The O Club, Emily informs us she was almost born on the fourth, but she waited three minutes to be born on fifth. With that knowledge I have an idea. The O Club won't be crowded on a Thursday night and we could meet there for dinner and dancing, then after midnight have a toast to the arrival of our Emily. I call Joanna that night and she loves my idea.

Trevor and I wake up the next morning to a very dark room and smile. We're both thinking if we're lucky it will be raining soon and we'll have lunch in my car with fogged over windows. So we pack a lunch just in case. And as we had hoped when lunch time rolls around there is a light rain falling.

After work it is still raining and we all meet at the Mitchell's for Happy Hour. Then Emily and William go home for her to change into a dress. I change into one there and we go to The O Club in separate cars. There are only two cars in the parking lot and Trevor parks at an angle under the awning. Mitch does too and this leaves room for the Birthday Girl.

Inside Harry is at the bar serving three ensign's. He greets us beginning by saying, "Captain, Mrs. Mitchell ..." Before he could finish his sentence the young men are on their feet standing at attention. Obviously they're new and don't know protocol is relaxed in here; therefore Mitch has to tell them, "As you were."

Trevor and I walk by and Harry just waves grinning from ear to ear. When Emily and William walk in the ensigns do a repeat performance and William talks to them briefly then shakes his head looking at us as they go straight to the jukebox. When they are seated Harry takes our order. He sent the waiter home.

Tonight's special is grilled chicken with a vegetable medley and rice pilaf, so we all order that along with soup to be served first followed by artichoke leaves with a cheese sauce for dipping. Emily and I switch to Pellegrino and the fellas order iced tea. Joanna orders a martini; she doesn't have to work in the morning. While Harry serves our drinks the ensigns leave. Now we have the place to ourselves.

After dessert, arms go around shoulders and we settle in talking about the future. Then I see Joanna give Mitch a nod and they tell William and Emily Mitch's retirement plan. Emily gives us temporary hearing damage and we pretend not to know, so they do not feel left out. When one of the slow songs plays Trevor asks me to dance and we all get up. Time passes with us talking and taking turns at the jukebox. During our turn, Trevor pushes the buttons for our song twice along with other good ones. When our song drops I surprise Trevor and sing to him. I get dipped and kissed.

The rain is coming down a little heavier as we keep dancing and I can hear it on the roof. Soon I rest my head on Trevor's chest, because our song is playing again. Eventually I look around to see Emily is dancing with her arms around William's neck. Mitch is standing in front of the jukebox and Joanna is sitting at our table sipping on a martini that has two of the three olives left on the pick. Harry is at his post stacking glasses and watching us.

While dancing we hear Joanna lightly tap on her empty martini glass signaling us it's midnight. We go over to the table where six bottles of cola are sitting at William's request. We pick them up and watch the clock. When the little hand clicks on the three we all start singing "Happy Birthday" and even Harry joins in. We click our bottles together and drink to Emily who is beaming.

Next I watch William reach into his pocket and he pulls out a neatly folded handkerchief saying to his wife, "I couldn't wait until the official party to give you your present." And he hands it to her. Emily places it on the table and unfolds it to reveal a pair of oval diamond earring that matches her engagement ring. She cautiously touches them as if to make sure she isn't hallucinating then she holds William's face and kisses him as if they are the only people here.

While they kiss Joanna gets out her mirrored compact and sets in on the table by the earrings. Emily does not waste time taking off her blue zircon earrings that are her birthstone and putting the diamonds on. She gasps when she sees them in the mirror. William tells her, "You look beautiful." And we all nod as she blushes.

At 12:30 Trevor and I remind them we don't live on the base and have a drive ahead of us. Cheeks are kissed, we say good night to Harry and drive home with the passenger window down to let in cool air to keep us wide awake. Plus it gives me a reason to nuzzle Trevor and keep my nose warm.

Going down the driveway I look ahead and see a package setting under the mail box. When I am able to get a good look at it there is twine around it, which means this was brought by messenger and I exclaim, "It's the trophy." We are wide awake now.

Trevor brings the box in and sets it on the trunk then he unties the twine and folds back the flaps. This reveals a grey felt bag with a silver drawstring. Trevor lifts it up and carefully sets it down then unties the half knot and loosens the bag. It falls and before us is the familiar trophy with this engraved on it:

Gypsy

The La Jolla Cup

1941

Captain:

Commander Trevor Lyons

Crew:

Mr. Théodore Delcroix

Captain Everett Mitchell

Commander William Snowden

Trevor chuckles. "I bet the engravers thought there was a mistake on the form and called the club. The captain being listed as a commander was reason enough to have them completely bewildered."

"I bet they did. Just out of curiosity I'm going to ask Mother to find out."

Trevor gives me a kiss then we shut down the garage and he carries his prize into the living room. I motion to the liqueur cabinet and he sets it in the center of the bottom shelf. We will find a better place for it another day. For now it is time to shower. When we fall asleep our hair is still damp.

The alarm goes off and Trevor glares at the clock as he turns it off. I tell him, "Me and my bright ideas." He chuckles and kisses the tip of my nose.

"You do know if we snuggle for even a minute we'll fall asleep."

"Yes, I do. Fling the covers off of me please. I haven't the strength." He laughs, leaps over me and pulls me out of our warm cozy bed to get ready for another long day.

This is what Emily knows about the little birthday party William is throwing for her at their house; it starts at 6:30, on the guest list is Trevor, me, Joanna, Mitch, Théo, Rachel and Emily's family. The club is catering a buffet and it is going to be casual. This is what she doesn't know; William and Bill put their heads together and decide to make it a covert op. When Emily and William dropped Bill and Judith off at the airport they were going to Las Vegas. She thinks they were going home from there, but they flew back here. Also Claudette and Joseph along with my entire family have been invited. While she is at work Faye, Judith and Joanna are decorating the living room and dining room with streamers, balloons and confetti. When we get off from work, William is taking her to the commissary for some last minute items in order to give the guest's time to hide their cars behind the house and be in the living room by 5:25. He feels he can delay her until 5:30 without suspicion.

After some fancy footwork we are assembled in the living room on time waiting to startle Emily because we are an hour early. I am front and center with my old top view finder camera that Trevor now calls my sneaky camera. We hear them talking and the key unlocking the door. He pushes it open, she steps in and we do indeed startle her. Shouting happy birthday makes sure of it. Emily regroups and hugs William. Next he gives her a dime which is the signal for our group to split in half, so Emily can see her gift from him, a jukebox with a big red bow on top. When she realizes it is a gift she is struck silent as she makes her way to it. Emily drops in the dime and the party begins.

It is almost midnight; there is a pile of gift wrapping paper and bows next to a table covered in gifts. Confetti is everywhere and even though music is playing Bobby is sound asleep on the sofa. When we see him Emily knows it's time for the party to end. Robert hugs his daughter and picks up his son. Faye gives Emily kisses and opens the door then the rest of us thank them for the wonderful time we had and say our goodnights.

Since the others left a park directly behind their house for us, the last people to arrive, there is a short walk we are grateful for, because this is two of three late nights in a row we are facing, because of my other bright idea, a kitchen raid for Rachel. We go home, shower and pass out knowing we can sleep late tomorrow and can make it through another late night.

Trevor and I wake up late the next morning and happily snuggle under the covers, because there is a chill in the house. December weather is finally here. The highs are in the mid-60s, perfect for working outside decorating and the lows go into the mid-50s, which is perfect for curling up in front of a crackling fire with something wonderful to drink. Tonight it will be Mother's hot buttered rum.

Being the thoughtful person he is Trevor braved the chill in his civvie skivvies to get our thick bathrobes to cook breakfast in. When the last dish is put away we hear a truck driving through the gates. I exclaim, "They're here." Then we dash to our dressing room where I toss my jeans and a white western shirt on the chaise. While I get out my denim jacket, Trevor comments, "This is one the reasons you're so happy. We're wearing our ranch duds to work in." I touch my nose then get out his denim jacket and toss it onto the chaise.

"Wear an undershirt with this to keep from getting hot." His eyes dance, because he's going to wear his hat. After 12 years of wearing a cover it is a welcome change and he looks good in it.

"By the way, Théo drives a company pickup truck for today and I want to be outside to get a snapshot of their arrival." He nods, gives me a kiss and we are ready in short order.

When we go out onto the balcony all the residents of Maison are milling about and Christmas trees are at the entrance to every home. We look at our first Christmas trees a minute and then I ask Trevor to do his whistle to get their attention. Hats are waved in the air and I get my first snapshot of the day. Trevor is wide-eyed and says, "I was expecting Joseph to look completely different, but even your grandparent's look like ranch hands." I nod beaming and we join them.

Walking up to my grandparents, Trevor does the unexpected. "Good morning, Teddy. Miss Connie." He looks at my parents and tips his hat. "Miss Josie, Jerry. It's nice to see you both." While they hold on to each other laughing Trevor keeps walking holding my hand and looks at our set up as I try to breathe.

We have two saw horses, saw's, ladders, pruning tools and a work table with 10 pairs of leather gloves in assorted sizes on it and beside it are a stack of crates filled with red metal bows and superbly scented Canadian spruce tree limbs, garlands and wreathes are here and there. The torches are lined along my parents' portico.

While I photograph him soaking all this in we hear a horn blow in the distance and soon we see Théo and Rachel in the pickup truck. He parks, gets out, tips his hat and pulls Rachel across the seat. She gets out with her face aglow because Théo asked Claudette to select her the works while she and Joseph were at Jed's doing the same for him before they went to the ranch on their honeymoon. Rachel looks around then says, "Théo told me Maison turns into a dude ranch today and he wasn't exaggerating. Thank you, Claudette, because of you I blend." Rachel looks at my family and adds, "This is a lot to take in."

Trevor interjects, "I wasn't warned and therefore I was catching flies when I walked outside."

Rachel pats his back as I tell him, "I just wanted to surprise you."

"You succeeded." I bat my eyelashes and get a kiss. Next I take off my camera, because it is time to get to work.

The first thing we do is decorate the entrance, so we put on gloves and the men start sawing the branches for the swags that hang under the lanterns and we get out the red metal bows to wire onto those, two long garlands and two large wreathes. With this task completed the men put four ladders in the bed of the truck and we all load the greenery along with a spool of wire. Mother hands the ladies wire cutters and our men pick us up and seat us on the tailgate. My grandparents get in the cab and Grand-papa drives slowly as the men follow us on foot to the gates, staying close. When he parks Trevor gets me down and I whisper, "Now you know how I feel when you are a human hood ornament." He gives me a kiss and responds, "Touché." He chuckles as he pulls off a ladder.

As we carefully unload the garlands and wreathes Trevor takes a good look at them and smiles. Grand-mamma has walnuts and cherries dipped in wax on them that make them look festive. We use wire to secure the bows on the greenery and hold ladders as our men wire the decorations onto the gates. Trevor and I hang the swag on one lantern as Rachel and Théo hang the other. With that done the entrance is decorated and we all walk across the street to admire our efforts.

While we work on the swags for the lanterns on the houses and apartments the catering truck arrives and parks in front of my parent's house. While they take in the delivery there my grandparents go home to assist them in setting up the luncheon buffet in the solarium where sawdust can fall and be swept out the door.

During the wait I discretely watch for Grand-papa as Trevor cuts a branch with the pruning loppers. He finally steps out onto the portico holding a Chuck Wagon bell. I quickly get a snapshot and look at Trevor. When Grand-papa begins ringing the bell Trevor freezes. "I know that sound." He looks up and his head goes back as he laughs. "This really is a dude ranch today." Rachel says, "As I live and breathe. Believe half of what you see definitely applies here." Trevor nods in agreement as my parents, along with Théo, Claudette and me get our bandanas out and start swatting the sawdust off our clothes. Joseph looks at Trevor and tells him, "When in Rome." And they get out theirs.

When we're done Théo holds Rachel's hand and starts leading the way to the solarium walking in the grass. With trepidation Rachel asks him, "Why are we walking in the grass?" He tells her, "To get the sawdust off our boots." Trevor chimes in, "Of course we are. This family is a well oiled machine. Have I said that before?" Everyone chuckles and we go inside.

Since we, the young couples are reasonably sawdust free the next thing on our list is to bring the Christmas trees inside. We begin with my grandparents, which is almost 11 feet in height and heavy, ladies on doors with men doing the lifting holding on to ropes and the trunk. And as always Théo inquires why can't it be dragged into the drawing room in a strained voice while Grand-mamma motions to the rugs.

With the ropes cut and their tree balanced in its stand we move on to the same ordeal with my parent's tree that is a few inches shorter. In the foyer Théo asks Trevor and Joseph, "Is it just me or is this one heavier than the other one?" They grunt at the same time then Trevor draws in a deep breath and tells him, "Stop talking and lift your share." Rachel says "Théo, for crying out loud." We all burst into laughter and they almost drop the tree.

Putting the tree in the stand we hear a van pull up. Mother announces, "The poinsettias are here." and my father goes outside. I wait patiently for the men to balance the tree then grab Trevor's hand and pull him outside to gaze upon the sea of red. Three pots of them are already placed on each side of the steps and the rest are in the bed of the pickup truck. After Trevor catches more flies he says, "I've only seen this many poinsettias outside the commissary and they're not there for decoration. Geneviève, how many pots are there?" I reply, "54. We have seven sets of steps; six go at the bottom of each and three pots set at each corner of the arbor." Rachel adds, "We are serious about Christmas here." Mother nods as she and my grandmother get in the cab of the truck then my father and grandfather sit on the tailgate. Mother looks over her shoulder at them and my father gives her a thumbs up. Trevor and I cannot help but laugh as she drives off to the apartments. I love the Navy things my family has picked up.

When the truck goes out of sight Théo tells Trevor, "Grab the other end of this step ladder." I pick up my camera and follow them with Rachel following me. As they carry it over to the garden hose on the side of my parent's house Trevor finally asks, "Are you going to fill me in on what we're doing or am I supposed to wait and find out?" Théo chuckles and replies, "Sorry, it feels as if you've been here before. We're going to rinse a year's worth of dirt and debris off. It goes inside the houses to decorate the top of the tall trees." Trevor nods as if Théo can see him.

With the ladder dripping water we join Claudette and Joseph and he asks, "What are we doing next?" Claudette motions to the torches and replies, "Make swags for those and for the French doors of each apartment." He stops smiling. "It is easier than you think. You cut the end of a branch off, we wire a bow to it and when the truck returns we load them in the bed and drive to the apartments. We will also take our tree inside." He starts smiling again and we, the ranch hands, kick into high gear and in less than an hour the last swag is being hung on a torch.

Next we all place wreathes and garlands on the doors of the main houses. Then we go to our house where we hang one large wreath on the railing of the balcony and hang two long garlands across the entire rail and take in our trees. We put away all the tools and last but not least we light the torches as the sun sets. After that is taken care of we walk the property together to enjoy the scenery.

Trevor puts his arm over my shoulder and slows us down to let everyone pass. We stroll quietly looking at the glow on my grandmother's face. She's the visionary of our Christmas Wonderland. Trevor sighs. "I wasn't ever given the opportunity to visit the residential areas in France, but I feel as if I am there now. This is the most beautiful place I have ever had the privilege to see. I live in an enchanted forest with a captivating wife." He takes off his hat and kisses me. "Trevor, let's go shower." And he turns us around. When we get out of bed to get ready for dinner it is wet from the water on our bodies, but it doesn't matter, we'll be sleeping in my room tonight.

Trevor takes our overnight bag upstairs then we drink a glass of red Bordeaux in the drawing room with our family as we wait on dinner to be served. And what a dinner it is, with a honey glazed ham covered in cherries in the center of the table. During our delectable meal Théo announces he and Rachel bought a gift for Maison and a crew of electricians will be on the property Monday setting it up. We are intrigued to say the least.

After dinner we all go our separate ways to take our time changing into PJ's and robes while the staff clears the kitchen and leaves. Then we return to the kitchen and Mother makes her hot buttered rum for us. Next we go into the drawing room and move the sofa and settees around the fireplace. My parents and grandparents sit on the settees and the newlyweds take the sofa. Then one by one the ladies take off their slippers and curl up next to their husbands. We sip our drinks, enjoying the warmth of the fire and the scent of the spruce tree listening to stories told to Trevor and Rachel about Christmas mornings when Théo and I would find cookie crumbs left by Santa and watching us play on the rug with the presents he left under the tree and eating the candy he left in our stockings.

Then Father looks wistful. "My fondest memory is the year Santa brought Théo a bicycle. I was pushing him around the room when he asked me to stop, because it was Gené's turn. Instead of me pushing her, he held on to it and had me put her on it. Then he told her to hold on tight. They laughed and laughed and by the look on his face he was happier pushing her than when he was being pushed."

Mother says, "I remember that well." She sighs then tells us, "With the tasks of tomorrow in mind that includes decorating our tree first and your grandparents before dinner I think we are going to call it a day. Sleep until you wake up. You all earned it." We all nod, repeatedly. My grandparents tell everyone goodnight and take their leave then Mother puts a blanket over mine and Rachel's legs and kisses the cheeks of all her children. When my parents go upstairs Trevor and Rachel take turns asking us questions about Christmas mornings when Théo and I were older, then we go upstairs to our rooms to lie down and wait for midnight.

Trevor and I enter my room to find the bed has been turned down and placed on my dresser is a lit pillar candle with a candle ring of the greenery on a silver tray. Trevor and I inhale the scent then he tucks me in and gets under the covers with me as we had dreamed of many, many nights before. When he begins to touch me and tenderly kiss me my heart flutters, because a dream is coming true.

Lying in each other's arms watching the candle light flicker we hear light footsteps and then Théo whisper, "Gené, it's time to raid the kitchen." I fling the covers back and we go to the door then we all hold hands as we tiptoe down the stairs into the kitchen.

Lights are on and decisions need to be made. What are we going to eat? After much deliberation while drinking colas we decide on the sugar cookies in Christmas shapes we had for lunch and the obvious scoops of vanilla ice cream. While Rachel and I put plenty of cookies on a plate she tells me, "When Darlene and I had sleep over's we would raid the kitchen, but you and Théo got to do this all the time. It is one of many reasons we want lots of children." This gets her a kiss from Théo walking by with the ice cream.

Settled at the table we each select a snowman and get tickled then Rachel rubs her hand after she sets down her cola. I ask, "Did you hurt your hand?"

"It's just soar from using those wire cutters. It pains me to admit this, but my back was so sore Théo had to give me a massage. Using the stairs more at the apartment obviously was not enough exercise after sitting at my desk all day." She looks at me. "Wait a minute, you sit at a desk."

"And I sail."

"That would do it. I enjoyed the time before the race. I do love sailing."

Trevor tells her, "Your names are on Gypsy's full access list. Whenever you two want to take her out just let us know." Théo and Rachel brighten the room.

"I'm changing the subject. How did the search for the trophy case go?"

Théo's face goes straight. "She put it in the living room instead of my office."

"And it looks nice. Although I wish we had the photographs that go with each one." I beam as Théo gives me a look and she doesn't notice. "Even though I'm going to be stiff when I wake up, it was worth it. I had the best time today. And this is a perfect way for it to end. Thank you for thinking of me, Gené."

"You're my sister."

Théo says, "Before she gets too emotional I think we should rinse off these empty dishes, not to mention I did hear the clock chime."

Eyes get wide when we realize it's 1:30 and we really should get moving. It doesn't take the four of us long to shut the kitchen down and say our goodnights then we sneak upstairs and go to our rooms.

The second he closes the door Trevor asks, "What was that look about between you and Théo?"

"He knows something the two of you do not. I can photograph photographs and it makes a negative for me to make prints from."

"I see me in your grandparents study helping you remove all those from their frames in the very near future." I give him a kiss and he tucks me in bed again. When he goes to blow out the candle I tell him, "That pillar will burn for 10 hours. I want to see you until I fall asleep. Will the light keep you awake?" He chuckles and that's a no, so he gets in bed.

Trevor runs his hand over my hair then says, "This has been one of the best days. I have never been happier. I love you so much, Baby."

"I love you, Trevor." And we kiss until we can't keep our eyes open.

CHAPTER TWENTY

Trevor wakes me up by playfully nuzzling my neck. Smiling I roll over onto my back and see his eyes are sparkling in the dim light from the sun shining around the draperies. "Good morning, Baby."

"Good morning to you too."

"So, this is what your room smelled like when you woke up in the morning. The smell from that bacon being cooked is pungent in here. I bet you never overslept."

I just smile and ask, "Hungry?"

"I'm starving. I hope you're ready to get up." Then he flings the covers off of us and gives me a nudge. I am laughing as I get up and stretch.

"Oh good, my legs aren't sore."

"I don't know why you thought they would be since I've had to chase you so many times"

"You have a point."

"Mmm hm." He gets out his shaving kit. "I'm going to shave in my old room. You need the bathroom to yourself, because your vanity is in our den." I look at where it was and he hands me my train case then gives me another nudge. He certainly is in high spirits.

Shaving takes longer than it does to re-braid my hair, so I'm tying the sash of my robe when he walks in and tosses his kit on the bench. I go over to him and slide my cheeks along his and then give him a serious good morning kiss. When I stop he says, "All right. I wish we were home." Trevor sighs and goes to the night stand and puts on his ring and watch. After he puts on his pajama top and robe he gets a glint then suddenly he grabs me and the next thing I know we're dancing the tango across the balcony. When we reach the end he dips and kisses me then spins around and we start doing the walk. At the stairs and he says, "Trust me."

Somehow he manages to get us down the stairs and we make an entrance into the kitchen dancing. Trevor twirls me passed Mother, Grand-mamma and Rachel then around the table where the rest of the family is seated. After I am dipped and properly kissed we receive applause and begin taking everything into the solarium for breakfast leaving my Funny Paper in its spot. I glance over my shoulder at it and Trevor nudges me again. This time I get tickled.

Plans for decorating the trees are the main topic. Trunks have to brought down filled with meticulously boxed and wrapped ornaments that have been collected over the years from here and Europe. A small nutcracker doll set that belongs to my grandparents of a king and his soldiers that include drummers and buglers are my favorite. Théo and I were allowed to play with them. Their arms move.

While I am eating the last bite of my potato galette Trevor picks up the bread basket to offer me my scone I have saved for last. It is made with chocolate chips instead of cinnamon as a Christmas treat we eat all month long. I pick it up and inhale the aroma, then without warning I shiver and shake to the point I drop it. Startled I sit motionless and get a strange feeling I have never had and out of the blue I say, "Something has happened." and gasp. "Grand-mamma?"

"The family is here. With whom are you close?"

"Joanna."

Trevor stands up so quickly he knocks his chair over and his napkin falls to the floor. I push my chair back and follow him into the hallway. The handset is already to his ear as he dials the last number. "Mitch, this is ... I can hear Joanna crying. What's happened?" — "As we speak?" — "Sir, yes, sir." — "Sir, yes, sir." His hand drops to his side holding the receiver.

He looks at me and his are dark blue. "The Japanese are bombing Pearl Harbor. The base will be closed. Where is your ID?"

"In my wallet."

"I need to change into my uniform. Meet me at my car. I'll bring it down."

As I stand in disbelief I watch him leave. In the blink of an eye, life as we know it ... has ended. Then I realize I need to get dressed and run up the stairs. While dressing I remember my family is downstairs without a clue as to what is going on, therefore I put on my sweater going to the solarium.

Walking through the kitchen I notice my family is not making a sound. I swallow hard and step in. "The Japanese are bombing Pearl Harbor." They look at me as if they don't hear me correctly. "Trevor is changing into his uniform. We're going to the base. Listen to the radio." I manage to take a deep breath as I place my trembling hand on my forehead. "I'm ... I'm ... going to sending my husband off to war." Mothers eyes well with tears and I tell them, "I have to go." and leave.

Walking across the portico I see he was in such a hurry he went in through the garage door instead of using the service entrance. Before I am even close to the bumper of his car I hear the kitchen door slam and there he is, wearing his service khaki uniform with the jacket for the first time and he already has his cover on. It takes him seconds to reach me. He gives me my wallet then extends his hand and helps me get in the car.

Trevor starts the car then immediately turns on the radio and the announcer says, "has just been confirmed, this is not a hoax. Pearl Harbor is being bombed by what has been positively identified as Japanese aircraft. Reports are saying it looks as if they are a swarm of locust swooping down on the ships in the harbor." Trevor sighs heavily and turns off the radio. Riding down the driveway Trevor glances down at my hands and places his hand over them. I realize I am crushing my wallet in the grip I have on it. Trevor turns onto the road speeding and we ride in silence.

My mind is a blur of thoughts. Men Trevor and his friends have known for years are under siege. They were all just there. What is happening? Since the United States went through with the oil embargo in July the Japanese ambassador and his envoy have been in D.C. in an attempt to improve the relations between our countries. When negotiations fail, they are supposed to withdraw and then declare war, not start one with a massive surprise attack on one of our military bases while they are guests in our country. This is unheard of. I feel as if I am having a bad dream and cannot wake up. My breathing is so rapid I am probably going to hyperventilate. Then I see the main gate in the distance with several cars lined up at both boom barriers.

We get in a line and get out our ID's. While I absorb the scene in front of me something occurs to me and I reach in the back seat for my camera bag. "Geneviève, what are you doing?"

"My job. This just became the most important military base in the United States. It's the closet one to Hawaii. Everything will come and go from there here. After the events of today the citizens of this country will need to know how quickly our military mobilizes and our enemies need to be aware as well." And I slide across the seat.

"You need to wait until we are at the gate and I can explain what you're going to do. Two of those sentries have a hand on their sidearm." I give him my press pass and scan the area for the photograph I want then I write Joanna's phone number on the back of my business card.

Pulling up to the gate he rolls down his window. Trevor gives our ID's to a sentry then shows him my press pass and begins talking as I get out. I walk several feet back; the boom barrier goes up, Trevor drives through and pulls over. After taking a few snapshots I approach the sentry and give him my card. "On the back of this is the number for the home of the captain for the Louisiana. A messenger from Harding Publications is going to be here shortly. When he arrives, call it please and I will meet him here." He replies, "Yes, ma'am." and escorts me to the other side of the gate.

Trevor is standing by the car and before getting in I tell him, "I need to talk to you." He nods and parks in the chapel parking lot. "Trevor, do you think they will keep moving forward and attack this base?"

"I thought about that on the way and I think they're focused on our bases in the Pacific."

"That makes sense. I'm ready to go."

Trevor parks by the curb behind William's Willys and I notice a Christmas tree is on the roof of Mitch's car. He knocks and opens the door for me then we step inside to a strangely calm scene. William and Mitch are standing by the phone in their service khaki uniforms and Emily is in the kitchen staring through them it seems. When she sees us I watch her heart sink.

Then I turn to look at Joanna and there she sits, looking exactly as I imagined. Her eyes are red and clinched in her hand is a wet handkerchief. When I hear Trevor ask Mitch, "Am I reporting for duty?" the room spins at the thought I did not have earlier. Is he? Mitch replies, "No." Out of relief I lower my head and my shoulders slump. Then I feel a hand on my back and Emily steps beside me. She guides me to the sofa and I sit next to Joanna.

Trevor asks, "What do we know?"

"Here, all the women volunteers for our Aircraft Warning Service have been called in and surveillance aircraft are flying along the coast. The men who work the airfield and aviators are preparing to fly fighter-bombers out Eh-sap to Oahu with doctors and nurses aboard along with medical supplies. The medical center was hit. The harbor is still under attack. Wheeler and Hickam Field has been hit hard to prevent our aircraft from engaging theirs in the battle to concentrate on their objective, destroying our Pacific Fleet. They're bombing Honolulu and haven't bombed the headquarters or the power station yet."

Emily gives Trevor a glass of water and he drinks half in two seconds. While I'm watching him she sets a glass of water on the coffee table for me and I realize I haven't drank anything since I began running around the house and pick it up then drink almost half as well.

Emily says, "I knew you both were thirsty. We were when got here. I was about to pour us more coffee when we heard two MA Willys driving close to the house sporadically hitting their sirens. William almost pulled down the draperies to look out the window. Then I called Dad. I got a busy signal for the longest two minutes of my life and when I got through he told me what was happening." Joanna sighs heavily. "We were on our way home from the commissary."

Mitch sighs. "Did you hear they are also attacking Midway and Wake Island?"

"No, but I knew they would."

"Here is the good news; none of our carries are at the harbor." He picks up a note pad. "The Enterprise left on November 28th for Wake Island escorted by three heavy cruisers and nine destroyers to deliver 12 Marine Wildcats. The Lexington left for Midway on the 5th escorted by three heavy cruisers and five destroyers to deliver 18 Marine Vindicators to increase Midway's air defenses. Her position of 400 miles out was scheduled to be reached mid-morning today. As soon as they heard about the attack on the harbor they launched aircraft to locate the Japanese fleet." William interjects, "The timing is ... interesting." Trevor slowly nods and Mitch continues.

"As you know the Saratoga is en route from the Puget Sound Naval Shipyard and is scheduled to be here this afternoon to embark her air group then proceed to Oahu tomorrow morning." Emily exhales heavily in relief and then the phone rings making her flinch. Mitch answers it, "Captain Mitchell speaking." in a tone of authority that gives me chills, followed by a long silence. He finally says, "Sir, yes, sir. Thank you for calling." He hangs up and looks at Emily. "That was your father. He's at his office and we will hear from him when he receives updates." Then he looks at Trevor and William. "Midway and Wake Island fought off the Japanese. The attack at the harbor is still under way." Mitch looks troubled. "I need some fresh air."

William and Mitch put on their jackets and the fellas go to the patio door. When they open it, as if on cue we hear aircraft engines start. They are ready to be on their way to Oahu with the supplies and medical personnel.

Suddenly I remember I need to call my family and Adeline. "Joanna, do you mind if I make a couple of phone calls?" She shakes her head as she comforts Emily and I get to work. Within minutes I have calmed my family and reached Adeline telling her my idea for a news story to accompany the photograph. After Joanna and Emily commend me I watch Joanna go somewhere in her mind.

"I do not understand why men of power have a problem with asking for what they need. Instead they are willing to kill for it. The Japanese were getting oil and other natural resources they need from us and other countries, but it just wasn't good enough. They have to take. The only reason they invaded French Indochina is to make their way to the Dutch East Indies because it provides a fifth of the world's supply of oil, but apparently it's not going to be enough to satisfy ... what?"

Apparently Mitch hears her and the fellas come back inside. I get up and go to Trevor as Mitch sits next to his distraught wife. Poor Emily gets up with tears welling in her eyes. William hands her his handkerchief and puts his arm around her. I place my head on Trevor's chest and hold on to him for dear life. Then Mitch tells us, "The return flights will have people aboard who sustained injuries and are able to make the flight." Just as I think he has lost his mind for saying that because Joanna is unstable, I find the man does know his wife.

Joanna looks like herself as she sits up and says, "I know where I will be, volunteering at the medical center instead of here going insane. Also we are going to need countless volunteers. Geneviève, your mother can alert the women at the club we are going to need volunteers. Medical training is not required. Anyone can feed someone who isn't able to feed themselves." I give her a nod. "Speaking of being fed, we should start cooking something for lunch." Trevor and I look at each with a slight hint of desperation. We are not hungry, at all, but it will get her mind off things. And she is on her feet.

While we cook the phone rings and I say, "That *could* be for me." Mitch responds, "You are more than welcome to answer it." So I do and it is the sentry. Before I hang up Trevor is already going to get my camera bag. He brings it in and we go into the bathroom for me to get the film out of my camera. I put it in a canister and go to the kitchen counter and write FILM on an envelope. Trevor holds my hand and says, "We shan't be long." and to the main gate we go.

I get out alone and give the envelope to the messenger, sign my name on his clipboard and he drives of in a hurry. When I get into the car Trevor comments, "You just completed your first job as a photo journalist and it was an important one. I'm so proud of you." I think about what he said while he drives back to the Mitchell's and it's hard to believe.

Trevor and I return in time to help set the table. We sit down to eat and the only sound is from flatware on the plates. Everyone is thinking or simply numb. When the phone rings nobody moves. Trevor says, "I'll get this one." He answers, "Captain Mitchell's residence, Commander Trevor Lyons speaking." Hearing him state his name firmly it occurs to me exactly where I am, in the home of a very important man with two men he relies on, heavily. Lost in thought I do not take my eyes off him. After he hangs up I come back to an even harsher reality. "The Japanese attacked our garrison in Guam and the British Dependent Territories of Singapore, Malaya and Hong Kong."

We are all stunned. When Trevor sits back down William dryly says, "So we are not the only country they attacked today. It takes months upon months to plan and carry out a strike of this magnitude. The Japanese ambassador and his envoy are pawns for them. They've been planning to go to war with us all along without declaring war." Emily adds, "The United States will do the right thing. Congress will officially declare war, probably tomorrow." Trevor pushes his plate away, moves his chair next to mine and puts his arm around me. No one says a word. The only sound is aircraft taking off headed to Oahu and I wonder where they are going to be able to land.

When the phone rings again everyone glares at it and William tells us, "My turn." He answers it and after a few seconds of listening to Robert he says,

"What?" in a slightly high pitch. We are all literally on the edge of our seats until he hangs up and tells us, "It's over. The attack on the harbor is over. Reports from the Opana radar site have been all clear." While we process what he said William sits back down. "They withdrew without bombing the dry docks, the power station or headquarters, so the base is operational." I could tell he had more to say, but he didn't and I am ever so grateful.

Trevor looks determined as he stares straight into my eyes and I hear his inner voice. "Geneviève, I want to go home." He means right now. How do I get us out of here gracefully? And it occurs to me immediately.

"We were at my parent's house with our family when we heard the news. Our departure was abrupt and I feel we should go and tell them what we know. Is any of it classified?" The fellas look at each other and Mitch replies, "I have no idea." Trevor adds, "It doesn't matter, they won't repeat a word to a sole." Everyone nods in agreement with a bit of a smile. For us to be able to leave on a good note Trevor stands and pulls back my chair. Before standing I tell them, "Please don't get up. We can see ourselves out."

Instead of holding my sweater for me, he drapes it over my shoulders, puts on his cover and picks up his jacket. He tells Mitch, "We will be going from house to house all day. If there are any changes, please call them until you find us." Then he motions toward the door.

After our rushed exit he begins talking at the bottom off the steps. "I've never been so happy you can hear what I'm thinking in my life. For some reason the sounds out here seemed to be getting louder and louder." When he opens the car door he throws his jacket to the other side of the car seat. I quickly get in and so does Trevor looking at me. "That's when I knew I needed to get off this base." He stops talking and starts the car. The sentry at the gate sees us and raises the boom barrier then waves us through. About 10 yards away Trevor begins speeding then tosses his cover on the dash and drives with both hands on the steering wheel. He is at his wits end. At a loss of what to do I pick up his jacket and lay it neatly beside me on the seat. Maybe a mile away he rolls down his window and draws in a deep breath. He finally has the silence he has been seeking.

Still not knowing what to do or say I put my left hand over my heart and look out the right side of the windshield leaving my other hand on my lap. He knows something he's not telling me and is trying to decide to tell me or not. I'm not sure I want to know. After I sigh I feel his warm hand on mine.

When we are close to the entrance of Maison I see the swag on the lantern and his words from last night echo in my mind, 'I have never been happier.' It is as if we were flying too high and one of our engines went out causing us to have a crash landing that has us trapped in the wreckage.

Trevor pulls inside the gates and stops. "My instinct tells me busy bodies from the club may become social criminals dropping by unannounced hoping to find out something because I'm in the Navy, so I'm closing the gates." With that taken care of he parks the car and tells me, "I want to walk down to the beach. Do you mind going in alone?" I shake my head. "Thank you. I will wait for you there." We get out, he squeezes my hand and we go our separate ways. I watch him until he is on the boardwalk then go inside my parent's house. It's so quiet I have to look for them and find everyone in the living room, including Claudette and Joseph. The men stand and the ladies sit up waiting on me to speak and look for my husband. "Trevor went down to the beach. What do you know?"

My grandfather replies, "More than we want."

"There is some good news. All of our carriers were elsewhere and the Naval Station is operational. They missed the power station and headquarters. My guess is our military shot down the aircraft assigned those targets. They missed the dry docks as well, which means vessels can be repaired there. Part of what I've said may be considered classified, but at the moment I have no clue."

Father responds, "None of this will be repeated elsewhere. And Trevor's mother called from her parent's house."

"I'll go tell him."

When I round the corner of the house I see Trevor standing on the boardwalk with his hands in his pockets looking southwest. He is a navigator and I have no doubt he is looking in the exact direction of Hawaii, therefore I approach him quietly and stand beside him.

"I watched thousands of officers roll through Annapolis. Each year a thousand plebes arrived and a thousand Firsties left. We all lived at Mother B. We attended classes together, ate together, rode transports to the football games and cheered the team on in the section reserved for us, The Brigade.

"After I was assigned to Louise, over the years I have had countless enlisted men under my command ..." His voice trails off and he motions for me to sit down.

Trevor sits next to me and holds my hand. "What I am about to tell you is not going to be made known to the public by the Navy, but it might get out. There were two breakdowns in communication this morning. The men at the radar station detected a large group of aircraft about an hour before the attack and reported it. An Army Bomber Group was expected to arrive and the officer they reported it to told them that was what they were seeing. The men at the station insisted what they were detecting was larger, but their concerns were dismissed."

"When Mitch said he needed some fresh air I knew it was bad news."

"This gets worse. Around the same time that inane back and forth started, a destroyer on patrol outside the harbor spotted a submarine following a ship going into the harbor and it was engaged and sunk by the crew of the destroyer. The report of the event didn't reach the commander of the fleet until minutes before the attack. This is the disturbing part." My eyes get wide and he nods. "They described it as a mini submarine."

"A mini submarine?"

"Mmm hm. Several members of the crew reported it was approximately 80 feet in length and 9 feet in height. It's not possible for a sub that size to have made the journey on its own. We think it was attached to the after deck of a full sized sub that surfaced near Hawaii for the crew to board. Another one made it into the harbor during the attack and a destroyer rammed it. The thing rolled and sank. Sightings of two more were reported outside the harbor. They are unaccounted for, but since we are aware these exist they will not make it inside the harbor."

"So these are just lurking somewhere around the island?"

"Unfortunately." Trevor exhales. "That was the last thing I had to tell you. Do you have anything to tell me?"

"Your mum called from your grandparent's house." He makes a face as if he is in pain. "Call from the study. Everyone is in the living room." Trevor stands up shaking his head.

Walking down the hallway he tells me, "I shan't be long." And he finally gives me a kiss, a sign that lets me know he is getting his equilibrium.

Trevor enters the room while I am asking, "Where are Joseph and Claudette?" Grand-mamma replies, "At their apartment decorating their tree. They needed to do something to occupy their minds." My husband asks, "When are we decorating the one here?" Mother looks at Father and he replies, "When does everyone want to?" He receives several responses all indicating as soon as possible. Therefore Trevor and I go home to change clothes.

Sitting on the chaise about to put on my trouser socks I hear Trevor slide open a drawer in his chest of drawers and look his way to discover my husband is nude selecting a pair of undershorts. I get still and admire his beautiful body as he puts on a pair. Then Trevor turns around and kneels between my feet saying, "I want your arms around me." At long last I get to hold him. He rests his head on my shoulder and we ease our minds.

While we were changing clothes our family was busy. The ladder is in the corner of the drawing room, trunks have their lids open and glasses of Malbec, a wine we drink on special occasions, has been poured to sip on while we unwrap and hang over 200 ornaments. With eight people this will move right along and with my camera close by we begin.

A little over two hours later, pieces of tissue paper are in the trunks and the ornaments are on the tree after the ladies have gone up and down the ladder many times. The men have a reach that exceeds ours, but they do enjoy holding it steady for their wives as they look at the curves of our hips unabashedly.

The only things left are the tree topper that is a golden glass star and a box with items that make our tree perfect, drop crystal prisms. Mother had the idea for them on a winter trip to Lake Tahoe before Théo was born. My parents drove up on an old estate having a sale from it. With a new home to fill they stopped and went inside. The first thing that caught Mother's eye was the chandelier hanging in the grand foyer. The sunlight on the prisms sparkled and reminded her of the icicles hanging from the eaves of the house, so they bought it, had it delivered to the lodge and removed the prisms over the duration of their trip, leaving what was left over in their cabin.

Upon returning from their trip she strung them on thin dark green grosgrain ribbons that blend in with the tree and they look like icicles hanging on the branches. My Grand-mamma loved it so much they began a search at antique shops for a chandelier with similar prisms and of course they were successful. While we hang the prisms Mother tells the story to Rachel and Trevor.

We have a custom of placing the tree toppers on last and since Théo and I were old enough to climb high on the ladder that joy has been ours. I top our grandparent's and he places the one on this tree. Mother carefully unwraps the star and hands it to Théo and then he turns to Rachel. "As the newest member of the family this privilege should go to you." She gasps and up the ladder she goes with Théo keeping it steady, smiling the entire time. He hands her the star and she places it on the tree then asks, "Is it straight? I can't tell from up here." Théo gives her a thumbs up and I get a good photograph.

With Rachel by Théo's side we gather around the tree and watch the rainbows from the icicles dancing all over the room. We hold up our wine glasses to the tree and drink to its beauty then get ready to go next door. Théo and Trevor pick up the ladder as Rachel and I go to open the front doors. When we do I see a paper tossed on the portico and announce, "There's an evening edition of *The Times* out here. Théo dryly says, "Quelle surprise." And we all breeze passed it.

Just as Rachel and I are about to pick up our pace and get ahead of them to open the doors I barely hear my father's voice until he raises it. "Sweetheart, I think you should see something on the front page." Trevor stops so fast he almost pulls Théo backwards. He puts down his end of the ladder and we go to my father who has Mother and my grandparents looking over his shoulder at the paper. We walk up and he hands the paper to me folded to where I can see the bottom half and I do not believe what is on it, the photograph I took of the main gate this morning with my name under it for the photo credit. The caption reads, US Destroyer Base, San Diego: Battle Ready. I'm looking at Trevor when Theo and Rachel step up and he asks, "Why is everyone wide eyed?"

"This is a photograph I took at the main gate to capture the fact the base was already closed to show how quickly our military mobilizes to ease the worried minds of our citizens and to let our enemies know we are prepared for them now. I sent it to L.A. via messenger to Harding Publications."

Trevor tells me, "Thomas must have sent it to them."

"I need to call Adeline."

Trevor follows me in and I have him get the phone in the hallway and stand by the door of the study. Then I lay the paper by the phone and take off my camera glancing at the paper as I dial. Adeline answers and I say, "This is Geneviève." and motion for him to pick up.

"I've been expecting your call. When I told Thomas about the photo and why you took it he said, 'This is not a scoop for Harding Publications. It should go nationwide and to Canada. Thomas sent you international first time out the gate."

"I'm speechless."

"It is a lot to take in. Oh, I'm needed on another call. We are so proud to have you on our team. Talk to you soon. Bye, Dear."

Stunned I watch Trevor hang up his phone. He walks into the study as I slowly put down the handset. "International ... Trevor, I went international."

"Yes you *did.* — That's one way to start your career, at the top. — I'm glad I was listening on the other phone." Trevor hugs me tight and softy says, "Baby, I am so happy for you."

"I have mixed emotions. The circumstances ..."

"Let's focus on the good for now."

"I love you."

"And I love you. What would you like to do next?"

"Tell our family. They are waiting outside." He holds my hand and leads me to the front doors. "Trevor, will you tell them for me?"

"I would be more than happy to."

Trevor dramatically flings a door open and we step onto the portico. "Thomas sent Geneviève international." Jaws drop then I get hugs and my cheeks are kissed as they all congratulate me. When Trevor begins to tell them the whole story I see the ladder on the cobblestones and realize I left my camera on the desk. Quietly I go back inside and have a moment to myself. While it sinks in that my 'first time out the gate' was bigger than I ever hoped for, I put my camera strap around my neck and pick up the paper. Unintentionally I see the headline. It reads, JAPANESE BOMB PEARL HARBOR: This Means War. And it does mean war. There are going to be dark days ahead, but I will think about that later. Here and now we are celebrating my accomplishment and we are about to turn a plain tree into a Christmas tree, so I focus on that and leave the paper on the desk.

Walking down the hallway I see Trevor standing in the foyer. I was so lost in thought I didn't hear him come in. "Why didn't you join me in the study?"

"You needed a minute to gather your wits and so did I." He looks at my camera. "I would hug you, but that could do me a harm."

"A harm. I love it when you talk British to me."

"In that case, fancy a proper kiss?" I get tickled as I move my camera out of the way and he does indeed give me a proper kiss.

Trevor opens the door and only Rachel and Théo are here. My brother is all smiles as he asks, "Where were we?" Laughing we go down the steps. Trevor and Théo pick up the ladder again then Rachel and I pass them to open the doors at my grandparent's house.

Entering the drawing room we see it is time for a break, because cheese boards with cheddar and apple wedges are setting next to glasses of Malbec. Trevor gets cozy next to me, picks up an apple wedge and offers to feed it to me. I feel my face blush as I carefully take a small bite off the end. He whispers, "If we were alone that would have gone differently." I hand him a piece of cheese to put an end to this. He takes it with a glint in his eyes.

Théo and I refrain from playing with the nutcrackers and the last icicle is hanging. Next my grandmother gets out the tree topper that is a tall golden glass final. She hands it to me and Trevor is smiling as he admires it until I offer it to him. After he takes it he studies it a moment. "All right, tall and slender, therefore if it's not perfectly placed it will be obvious it's crooked. Geneviève, I'm going to need you to assist me on the ground. Gérard, Théo, I need you both to hold the ladder." We all take our places, Trevor hands me the topper, I give him a kiss for luck and he slowly climbs the ladder. When he is where he can reach the top of the tree I hand it to him and he slides the final on then looks at me. I study it and say, "Back a little at your three."

"How's that?"

"A tad off. Slightly left at your nine."

"What about now?"

"Tap it on the end to your six." This time he simply looks at me and I walk a semi circle at a distance then give him two thumbs up. He gives me a thumbs up and climbs down to applause. Grand-papa tells us, "Well done. Usually that task takes longer. You two are good team." Mother adds, "Navy speak used to decorate a Christmas tree. This will be one we will not forget." Everyone agrees then we close the trunks and move them into the closet under the staircase. Next we finish our wine looking at the tree and then we scatter to dress for a casual Sunday dinner.

While we are looking at the tree and enjoying a glass of cognac after dinner by a roaring fire Mother and Father give Rachel and I each a wooden chest. She opens the lid of hers first and gasps. I immediately open ours to find Mother has robbed two more chandeliers of their crystals. Rachel and I are overwhelmed as we unwrap one, so Théo and Trevor thank them. They are beautiful.

Our glasses are almost empty when Théo flinches and tells us he just remembered they need to pack, which reminds us we need to do the same. My grandparents give us a bottle of Malbec to drink as we decorate our trees then Mother and Father decide to stay; therefore we say our good nights and walk together to the house.

On the way a sense of melancholy washes over us as we look at the decorations and think how happy we were mere hours earlier and what a drastic turn the day took. Rachel sighs and tells us, "The grounds are truly beautiful at night." Then not another word is spoken until we are packed and going outside.

Trevor tells Théo, "I closed the gates when we returned. I didn't want anyone to drop by."

"Good thinking. Thank you for the warning. I might have hit them. Oh, don't forget I have a present for Maison that I will show everyone tomorrow." I reply, "We won't." and he throws the overnight bag in the back seat and shakes Trevor's hand then gives me my kiss. Rachel is misty-eyed and simply waves then gets in the car. Since we are carrying so much, instead of watching them leave Trevor opens the garage door and puts everything in the dumbwaiter.

When our things are put away Trevor picks up the chest smiling and he is still smiling as he sets it on the coffee table. "I have to ask, what is up with you?"

"During childhood I remember being told not to play with matches or fire. Yet at Christmas the adults ignored this and put candles on the tree to light at night. I knew about forest fires, therefore I decided it was a bad idea and I would never do that. Keep in mind this was before fire extinguishers were available for homes. And now your Mother has the perfect solution. — Would you like to put these on our tree tonight?"

"Yes, I would like that."

"I'll start a nice fire and you can pour us a glass of cognac to share."

Hanging the icicles make the day go away as we watch them sparkle from the firelight sipping cognac and kissing until they are all on the tree. And without a word he goes to the sofa, removes the back cushions and arranges throw pillows at one end then he lies down with an arm out for me to lie by his side. The warmth of his body and the fire make it difficult to keep my eyes open.

The next thing I know I wake up chilly. The fire became glowing embers as we slept. Rolling onto my back wakes him up and because he was warm due to the sofa and me, he begins to cuddle and I softly say, "Trevor, we're on the sofa."

His eyes open and he looks at his watch. "It's 3:17. We should turn on all the heaters down here to warm the house and sleep upstairs. I'll get the clock."

Trevor helps me sit up and soon we are in the guest room undressing. Since he just turned the heater on he gives me his undershirt. I put it on and get under the covers. He picks up the clock and says, "I'm going to set this 20 minutes early. The gates will have lines and I have to report for duty on time." I just nod as he gets in bed and turns off the lamp. Then Trevor holds me close to get me warm and I immediately begin to drift.

In the morning we face another tough day earlier than anticipated. After going outside to get the paper before we eat breakfast he returns without it. "The headline read, Great Britain Declares War on Japan. They are eight hours ahead. We'll be next." I just look at him and serve.

Things get a little better when we are diving up to the main gate. A sentry is walking in the yellow zone between the lanes saying, "Military personnel right lane, civilians left." This is when we find out very few men live off base. Then when we arrive early in the parking lot at work things take a nasty turn, because when we get out to speak with Emily and William the first thing he does is nod and ask, "Can you believe the Japanese bombed Clark Field 10 hours after the other attacks ended yesterday and despite being warned loses were heavy?" Trevor and I look at each other. Clark Field is the United States Army air field in the Philippines. Apparently we should have read the late edition last night. Emily realizes we didn't know and after giving us a moment she changes the subject. "We couldn't help but see your photograph on the front page of *The Times*. Congratulations, but how did it get there?" When I finish answering her question it's time to go in.

At 11:00 Mrs. Sloan walks into the C's room holding a stenographers pad and Becky is following her. They stand silently in front for a minute then Mrs. Sloan begins to read aloud from the pad. "This morning President Roosevelt requested for a declaration of war on Japan to a joint session of Congress. The speech lasted only seven minutes. The vote to declare war passed by the Senate and the House of Representatives forty minutes after his speech." She sighs and they simply walk out. Our fate is sealed.

At lunch time things digress more when Emily and I are in the car with the fellas. Mitch informs us Joanna is attending orientation at the medical center and she is going to work the first shift to feed the men breakfast and read to them until it's time for lunch. This means we won't see her until after work or on weekends for who knows how long. Our lunch routine is over.

We decide to eat at The O Club and when we walk in there is a low murmur in the place and only two seats at the bar. Apparently Joanna is not the only volunteer and these men need food. Take out it is.

While Mitch orders five Today's Specials from a very busy Harry, Emily waves at someone and we see Robert sitting at a table with the base commander and two more admirals. He gets up and joins us. After greetings he asks, "Have you heard the latest?" Mitch replies, "Probably not." Robert nods and says, "I was going to request a meeting with you at 1500 hours when I returned to the office. I have an idea. Excuse me please."

Roberts speaks to the men and their waiters, picks up his briefcase and leads us to the door with a plaque that reads, SUPPLY. He gets out his keys and unlocks it. When he opens it I find myself looking at a room that resembles a corporate conference room. The base commander sits at one end of the long, wide table and Robert sits at the other. He introduces us to the admirals as the waiters file in with everything from their table and our orders, then they fill glasses with water from pitchers they leave on the table. When they're gone and the door is closed the base commander says, "Mrs. Lyons, this is fortuitous. I want to thank you for the photograph in *The Times*. It made us look good. Admiral Prescott, you have the floor. I need to eat and return to my office."

Robert opens his briefcase and pulls out a folder that looks like one I have seen a thousand times, because it has the TOP SECRET stamp on it in red ink. I wish we had gone to Sam's or anywhere besides here, but I'm stuck, so I place my napkin on my lap and pretend I've been in this room before.

Trevor winks at me and Robert starts the briefing. "This morning at 0942 hours a grounded Japanese mini-sub was found on the east side of Oahu. We seized it and a survivor that swam ashore of the two man crew it contained. During his interrogation through an interpreter we learned five of them were mounted on the after deck of a "mother" submarine. The "mother" surfaced 12 miles from the mouth of the harbor under the cover of night. The crews boarded the mini-subs and were released to advance to the harbor. The "mother" subs submerged with orders to protect the Japanese fleet located 270 miles northwest of Oahu from Navy vessels that might manage to escape during the attack. Two mini-subs are unaccounted for, but we believe they sank before reaching the harbor."

The base commander slips out the door and Robert continues. "18 ships were damaged and three were lost. Rough counts of the wounded are as follows: Navy: 678; Marine Corps: 57; Army: 352; Civilian: 31. We have reports it will take weeks to accurately list the injured, casualties and MIA's. The first flights with injured military personnel aboard and family members are arriving this afternoon. The majority will be rerouted to bases of their choosing.

"Morning briefings will be held daily with one at 0900 hours and another at 0930 beginning tomorrow in Command Headquarters for commanding officers. Captain Mitchell, as the commanding officer of a carrier strike group, you along with your key navigator and conning officer will report to the 0900."

Mitch replies, "Aye aye, sir." then glances at Trevor and William.

Robert closes the folder then adds, "Military recruiting offices across the country have men lined up along the sidewalks waiting to enlist. We are going to have immediate growing pains. To ease them we intend to have enlisted men free up space in the barracks by moving onto their ships at first light tomorrow."

"We will be ready, sir."

The rest of the admirals excuse themselves and Emily says, "Knowing those horrible little subs are not an issue anymore was good to know, the rest, not so much. But Dad, I did enjoy watching you work. Thank you for this."

"I just wanted to show you off. I am the proud father of a daughter with a Top Secret security clearance. Not many dads can say that." Emily beams as we thank our host and take our leave. On the way back to work I remember before we married, Trevor saying breakfast with my family was like morning briefings where only one or two people speak and the rest listen. Now I know from experience. I also know I do not want to attend one again ... ever.

Five o'clock finally rolls around. Emily and I are walking down the corridor when we see Trevor is propped on the bench with his arms crossed looking at the ground. Emily says, "Umm, I'm going out the side doors. I will see you in the morning." She gives me a little hug and is gone. I keep going and the sound of my heels on the sidewalk causes him to look up. As I get closer he tells me, "I thought it would be a good idea to sit on the bench before you went to the parking lot." When I reach him Trevor hugs me then we take a seat. "There was more in the late edition we needed to know. A blackout began at 11 p.m. last night and the nation's military ordered every radio station on the West Coast to cease broadcasts, stating their signals could lead the Japanese to their destinations. And this afternoon Mitch had our vehicles taken to the motor pool to have all the lights covered with translucent blackout paint. I had the ensign get me a pint for the family's cars."

"Thank you for telling me. I'm ready to go." Trevor kisses me out in the open. At this point I think it doesn't matter. He offers me his arm and we go to the car. It looks completely different.

Waiting in line to leave we watch city workers who are already expanding the street enough to add three more lanes. I'm certain men will work day and night until the job is done, therefore getting on the base in the morning will be back to normal by week's end.

Driving through the gates at Maison I sense Trevor wants to stop and close them again, but Théo's car is here, so we press on to the house in order for him to change out of his uniform. When we get on the balcony we spot another evening edition laying on it. We know what the headline is; FDR declared war on Japan. Trevor picks it up, opens the door to the solarium and tosses it on a table. No need to see it in large letters. I get us colas and he enters the kitchen wearing a camel colored crewneck sweater with loafers. I set down the sodas and run my hands along his back to feel him through the cashmere and then he holds me.

When we emerge from the solarium all the residents of Maison are standing on the portico of my parent's house waiting on us. Théo motions for us and I notice he is holding a small shopping bag. We join them and he immediately says, "Follow me." and starts walking down the driveway with Rachel. When we are close to the wall I see two gray metal boxes on each side of the entrance with thin black metal bars attached to the gates. They have us stand a few from the street facing the gates and he pulls a small metal box out of the bag and hands it to Rachel. He gives her a nod and she pushes a button on it. Next there is an odd noise and then the gates begin to close.

After we all express how amazing and wonderful his gift is my father gives him one of those looks and asks, "You went to the Home Show on your honeymoon?" Rachel instantly responds, "I talked him into it. We were driving by the L.A. Convention Center and after I read the sign I pleaded with him to take me in. Théo had forgotten about it and it was incredible. In fact we plan to go every year." Théo nods adding, "Now passersby can see how spectacular our gates look all month instead of Christmas Eve and Christmas Day."

Then he motions to the little box Rachel is holding. "That is called a remote control. It sends a frequency like a radio to the bases. The button opens and closes the gates. We have one for each person here, the postman and a backup." Rachel begins handing them out telling us, "We tested all of them, so just put them in your cars. Josephine, these are for the postman and the extra one is just in case someone winds up needing it." Théo motions to Grand-mamma and she uses hers to open them for us to go to my parent's house.

On the way my parents walk up to us and Mother holds on to Trevor's arm then quietly says, "This afternoon a couple at the club told me they were going to drop by yesterday, but our gates were closed. Thank you for closing them." He gives her a nod then she lets go of his arm and my parents get ahead of us to go inside first.

Father is pouring wine as we gather in the drawing room to unwind before dinner, but he has a look on his face as we all take seats and he gives us a glass of wine. Then he looks at Théo and Rachel. "I think you both are unaware of something I found out when I picked up the paper from last night to read the rest of it. A blackout began at 11 p.m. last night, but I think that will change very soon to sunset until sunrise. The radio stations went off air and will remain so for an undetermined time period. Mamma, Josephine, Rachel, tomorrow you all should go separately to places that sell blackout curtains and buy as many white ones as you can for the French doors of the apartments and The Lyons Den.

"Father, Théo, we need to bring home rolls of tar paper in the morning to cover what cannot have curtains and close shutters. We need doors at the entrances to our solariums and Josephine we need a drop leaf to cover the space over the sink. I will measure it tonight and have our men make and install it in the solarium and the doors up for both houses by five o'clock. Claudette, we need new flashlights and extra batteries for every car on the property. Trevor, please call your friends and tell them we have tar paper if they need it. Does anyone have a suggestion?"

I respond, "Safelight bulbs would be good for dim lighting instead of candles or oil lamps." Mother adds, "Those can be left unattended. Those can also replace the bulbs on our porticos because they do not face the beach enabling us to walk around without flashlights. I will go by Blackwell's." Théo asks her, "Will you get us five please? We only have candles." Rachel adds, "Fortunately Darlene and I purchased blackout curtains when we moved in, so I can focus on the family's needs." Mother beams as she looks at Rachel and suggests we move to the dining room. There Trevor informs everyone he has blackout paint for the car lights and since Théo's car is the only one that needs attending to tonight Trevor tells him he will change clothes and paint his lights in our garage before they go home. Joseph tells us he will take off after lunch to help, because things are slow at the club. Most people are staying home.

After everything is taken care of we go into our den and look around our living room knowing it will be different when we return tomorrow. Due to the long day we shower and rest in our bed until we fall asleep.

The next morning Trevor and I ride in silence to the base and when we're in the parking lot with Emily and William we say very little as we look at the vehicles. Too much has happened in too short a time.

An hour later Becky and Mrs. Sloan walk in with somber faces and we stop typing in an instant. Mrs. Sloan informs us the city just passed an ordinance for a blackout which begins 15 minutes before sunset until 15 minutes after sunrise. At least I was expecting that bit of news.

The day took another disappointing turn when Trevor and William arrive at lunch time and inform Emily and me Mitch will not be joining us for lunch until Joanna is no longer a volunteer. He will be eating aboard Louise while briefing his key officers. First Joanna, now Mitch.

Since it is a day Trevor and I have lunch alone we decide to eat at Sam's hoping it will lift our spirits. On the way see steps are already being taken by the city for the blackout. Stop signs are under traffic lights that will be turned off at night and bulbs for streetlamps are being removed. When we arrive, even though Sam is preparing for the blackout as well, our spirits are lifted. There's nothing like a chocolate milkshake.

At Maison I get the remote to open the gates and he slowly goes down the driveway as we absorb the drastic change in the appearance of where we live. Then as Trevor parks, my mother walks up holding an envelope and we get out of the car. "Bonsoir. This arrived by messenger late this afternoon." She hands it to me, kisses our cheeks and returns to the house. It has the Harding Publications logo and my name written by Thomas on the front. I nervously open it and pull out a note he wrote that reads, Well done. There is a check as well. I show it to Trevor and say, "50 dollars is a little more than I expected."

"Baby, look at it again."

I see another zero and exclaim, "It's for 500 dollars."

"This calls for a celebration. Dinner at The Posh?" I run into the house with him chasing me and stop in the dressing room where he kisses me immediately.

He changes into his gray suit with a burgundy tie and then dresses me in a burgundy flowing dinner dress perfect for dancing the tango. Since it is a Tuesday there is no need for a reservation and out the door we go to dine and dance in our favorite hide away.

On the way to the hotel our mood changes; the streets are dark and we drive several blocks before we met another car. All the business have their signs turned off and I think that if we did not know the way we could make a wrong turn. Trevor is concentrating and I am quietly sitting next to him with my hand on my lap. At a stop sign he lingers and says, "This is interesting."

"Interesting? It's ... it's eerie ... positively eerie."

"I was being diplomatic." I have a burst of nervous laughter and give him a kiss.

We forge on and the hotel is unrecognizable. The signs at the entrance and on the hotel are off. All the exterior lights are off with the exception of one under the awning at the valet station. He pulls up to the entrance and we see the glass of the revolving door and side doors already have blackout paint on them. We recognize the valet; his name is John and he opens the car door. "Welcome to The Brava, Commander Lyons. Mrs. Lyons. It's nice to see you both and if I may, surprising.

You two are the only locals to show up tonight." Trevor responds, "It's nice to see you too, John." As he hands Trevor a ticket he opens a side door for us saying, "The revolving door is locked. It's a bit of a hazard with that paint on it." We both nod and step inside to a dimly lit lobby that has one bellman and a desk clerk talking to each other and we can hear the orchestra playing. At the same time they stand up straight and say, "Welcome to The Brava." in a surprised tone. Trevor tells them, "Thank you." And we keep going to the dining room.

The headwaiter's eyes get wide when he sees us and he grabs two menus then escorts us to the corner table we always sit at. When he walks away we notice there are few business men eating and I am the only woman in the room. Trevor chuckles and tells me, "At least I won't have to worry about bumping into anyone on the dance floor tonight." Shaking my head I laugh. The evening proceeds as usual and we celebrate.

The next morning we wake up to the sound of thunder getting close. By the time we are leaving there is a full blown thunderstorm upon us. Trevor says, "We're catching a brake today. Aviators don't fly in lightening, not even Japanese ones." The day passes without any more upsetting announcements and we finally finish decorating our Christmas tree sipping his cocoa then we curl up on the sofa by the fire. Things are slowly feeling normal here again.

The base however is another situation all together. Aircraft begin constantly departing or arriving to make up for the day lost to the storm and transport buses filled with new recruits go to the enlisted barracks that will be full by the end of the week at the rate they are going. Trevor and I slip away with William and Emily to their house for lunch and after work we leave the base as soon as possible.

By Friday the main gates are done and we all have plans to go to the Mitchell's after work. I begin counting the minutes at two o'clock until I hear a soft sobbing from the back of the room and turn around to see Emily has her head down holding a handkerchief and her shoulders are shaking. I jump up and when I place my hand on her back she looks up and gushes, "I can't take it any longer. Listening to aircraft day and night, knowing they're transporting wounded men and casualties. William gets lost in conversations when we hear one. He tosses and turns while he sleeps. And the base being almost pitch black is ..."

"Emily, I need you to stand up. We're leaving."

Trying to stop crying she stands up, "Where are we going?"

"To Maison, but first I need to use Becky's phone."

"Why?"

"We don't have a car, so we need a ride and Joanna might be home."

Entering the office Becky stands to her feet as I help Emily sit in a chair. Mrs. Sloan hears the commotion, opens her door and asks, "What's happened?"

"I need to get her off the base and to call someone to pick us up." She nods to Becky and she sets the phone on the front of her desk. I dial the number holding my breath as it rings several times.

"Mitchell residence."

"Joanna, I'm so happy your home. We're fine, but Emily and I need a ride."

"I'll be out front in three."

After a short conversation I ask Emily what she needs from her desk and like me she only wants her handbag. Becky volunteers to get them and shut down our desk after we leave. I think she sprinted, because she returned after we had taken one drink of the water Mrs. Sloan gave us. We thank them both and when we are close to the front doors I watch Joanna park at the end of the side walk and slide over to open the passenger door. I tell Emily, "Our getaway car is here. Let's make a break for it." This causes her to laugh as we go out.

On the way to Emily's house I tell Joanna what happened and my plan. She pulls into the driveway and we help Emily pack a suitcase for her and William to make it thru to Monday. I call Mother and tell her I will explain later, but to open the gates because we are on our way. And in no time we are off the base.

When we arrive at Maison the gates are closed, but in the distance I see Mother and she holds out the remote then the gates begin to open. Emily and Joanna are stunned, but comment on how beautifully decorated they are. I blow Mother a kiss as we drive passed her slowly to the apartment, because they're looking at the Christmas decorations.

When we're parked Emily gets her suitcase and goes up the steps. I pick up a poinsettia to take inside and follow her. Inside we discover the women of Maison were busy. There is a tray of salted petit fours and a nice bottle of red Bordeaux on the coffee table and they filled the refrigerator with beverages and staples for dinner and breakfast. I give Emily the poinsettia and she sets it by the fireplace and puts the petit fours in the refrigerator. No one is hungry, but we are in need of a glass of wine, so Joanna opens it. When we're settled in I ask their plans for Christmas. Emily and William are eating lunch with her family and exchanging gifts then they are going to spend the rest of the day alone. Bill and Judith are staying home to give them privacy. Joanna and Mitch are going to spend it alone for the first time in almost a decade. Their parents are avoiding the blackout.

The time comes when Joanna must leave to meet the fellas at the pier to let them know where their wives are. Emily asks her to tell William what happened, because she doesn't want to talk about it ever again. Then she tells me she would like to sit under the arbor, so we put on our sweaters, get our glasses of wine and walk Joanna to her car.

It is in the mid-60s, the air is crisp and we sit in silence next to each other looking at the ocean sparkle in the late afternoon sun. Eventually she puts her head on my shoulder and I put my arm around her. Then she finally speaks. "I love it here. I love you too. I wish the weekend would go on for days."

"You and William are welcome to stay here for as long as you want. Pretend you're on a little get away alone in a beach cabin for at least a week. And I love you too."

"I'll talk to William when he gets here. Thank you, Geneviève."

"You are entirely welcome. We should go back to the cabin. The fellas will be here soon and we can freshen up before they get here."

"The cabin." I get her to laugh and we get up carrying empty glasses.

Emily is brushing her hair when I hear two cars going fast down the driveway. I tell her, "I'm leaving you in good hands. Call us if you need anything." and step out onto the balcony in time to see William fling open Emily's car door and bound up the steps. He slows down and looks at me. "She's fine and is waiting for you inside." William squeezes my hand and goes in to his wife. I go down the steps to my husband who is closing Emily's car door.

"Geneviève, are you all right."

"Yes, I'm fine and so is Emily. I'm going to walk to the house."

We go inside and I hand him a bottle of the wine Emily and I were drinking and take off my pants suit jacket. "Geneviève, you're not wearing anything under your blouse."

"I know and I am so comfortable. I love this time of year."

"There is my little revolutionist. And she's getting chilly. I'll get a fire going."

Trevor takes off the shirt of his uniform and starts the fire while I pour the wine and sit in the corner of the sofa sipping it as I watch his biceps flex. When he sits down I face him. "I've been thinking about something and I have an idea."

"I'm listening."

"You joined the Navy to protect this country and its citizens. You are one of the best navigators the Navy has and I know this because you are the key navigator aboard the carrier of a carrier strike group with the other vessels of the group following your orders. And when this country needs you the most you intend to resign your commission. I don't have to hear what you're thinking to know it's troubling you, because it's troubling me." Trevor shifts slightly with his eyes locked on mine.

"Here is my idea and keep in mind the decision is yours. When you return from your deployment, instead of resigning your commission I think you should take Robert up on his offer. He is well aware your surface warfare training gives you an advantage on the ground."

"How do you know so much?" Trevor moves toward me and touches my face. "You would do this for me, release me from my word?"

"Yes. I love you and I want you to be happy. But I have a request."

"Name it."

"I would like for you to get out when the war is over and resume the life we had planned."

"Your request is granted. Once again you catch me of guard. You are selfless."

"To a degree, I happen to have an ulterior motive. You are so handsome in your uniforms I wanted to see you in them a little longer." And there is that deep laugh I adore. Then he stands and offers me his hand. The moment I am up he gathers me into his arms and holds me. I can feel his heart beating slow and steady. This was troubling him more than I anticipated.

Time passes and I feel his heart starting to beat a little fast. What is he thinking? And I soon find out. "Would you like to go to Sam's and get a hamburger steak with 2 orders of scattered hash browns and a waffle then go parking in our spot?" I give him a kiss and get my jacket. "That's a yes. I'll put on a sweater." And off we go. I am looking forward to going parking after dinner and I must admit, sharing a waffle. The next morning we sleep late, very late. What a long week we had.

While I pour us a second cup of coffee Trevor goes outside to get the paper and returns without it prompting me to ask, "What do I not know?"

"I hoped it wouldn't make the news." He sighs heavily. "The Japanese took Wake Island yesterday."

"Oh no. Trevor, that gives them a place to refuel. They can reach the coast. — I am sorry I asked. In fact I think we should pretend I didn't."

"That's fine by me."

"Scoot your chair back please." He happily does and I sit across his lap then we drink our coffee planning the day.

We start off by going to my grandparent's house to photograph the trophy case photos for Rachel and Théo. While we're in my darkroom hanging the film to dry I suggest inviting our crew for dinner. They haven't seen our house since we moved in plus I miss Joanna and Mitch. Also I think Emily and William could get cabin fever. Trevor feels the same way, so I make the calls before lunch and they accept our invitation. Since we have much to do in the darkroom and the house needs straightening, along with flowers for the table, we decide Trevor will get those and pick up a three course dinner from the club and salmon canapés to serve with martinis before dinner. I will do the straightening and set the table.

Everything has been accomplished and while the food keeps warm in the oven we stand in the solarium to watch the sunset and wait on our guests. When the sun sets we feel the temperature drop significantly. Trevor smiles at me and says, "That means rain should begin during the wee hours on the three month anniversary of our wedding day. Mrs. Lyons, tell me what you see in our future."

"There is a plate on my night stand with two apple cores on it that have been there since morning and we are on the pallet in front of a roaring fire with our bodies entwined." Trevor moves in front of me and pulls my body against his and tenderly kisses making me weak at my knees.

Time passes and a car driving through the gates gets our attention. Trevor gives me another kiss and we turn to watch for headlights. Mitch parks the car where we can't see it and then we hear Joanna ask, "What are you two doing huddled under here?" Then she steps into sight and waves at us. We wave and while they climb the steps we feel bad. Emily and William saw us and stayed in the cool night air.

When they reach the balcony we see Emily is wearing the jacket of William's suit. After we welcome them to our home in the solarium we go to the living room and William leads Emily to the fireplace where she gives him his jacket and Trevor hands her a martini. And so the evening begins.

Hours later Trevor and I are awakened by thunder. It's dark; therefore it is the wee hours. I'm lying on my side with Trevor snuggled up against me and the moment I begin to roll over onto my back to hold him and go back to sleep he whispers, "Geneviève, I need you to want me." Trying to become lucid I respond, "Then taste me." Suddenly Trevor has me in a passionate embrace and begins by tasting my neck. He is ready to release all of his emotions and I want them.

The sound of heavy rain on the glass of the windows wake me up and I immediately draw in a deep breath. It makes Trevor stir and I realize our bodies are nude. His soft hair is touching my neck and when he begins to wake up it grazes my face and I cannot help but run my fingers through it. Trevor moans and says, "The sweet taste of you is still in my mouth."

"When I was waking up I thought I had a beautiful dream until I felt your skin against mine."

"I didn't give you the chance to get wide awake. I missed you. I missed us."

"I have missed you." He nuzzles my neck and rests his head on my shoulder.

Eventually the inevitable occurs, the need for sustenance. So we eat our apples and summon the will to get out of our cozy bed and go scramble some eggs. After we eat it is straight back to bed to laze the morning away. I get out our honeymoon photo album and Trevor becomes my soft chair as we look through it while listening to the fire he started and the rain falling softly on the windows.

When the need for sustenance arises again we make the pallet in front of the fire and eat shrimp with linguini and share a piece of the dark chocolate cake from dinner last night with a glass of orange cognac. When we finish the cake Trevor dips the pad of his ring finger in the cognac and runs his finger along my lower lip then gets it between his as he lies me down among the pillows. His powers of seduction overcome me once again.

Before we know it the time to dress for Sunday dinner is upon us and I call Emily and William to tell them dress will be casual tonight due to the rain. Then I join Trevor in the dressing room to discover in bright light we both are in desperate need of leg makeup, me more than he for there is a passion mark that is unusually dark on the left slope of my neck. That happened as he devoured me in the middle of the night. How I do want to stay here with him, but we have guests and I want to see Théo.

Trevor and I are the last to enter the drawing room along with Emily and William. Claudette has a soft spot for Emily and knowing about her ordeal she leaps to her feet and kisses Emily cheeks three times. Then she goes to William and does the same. Our Claudette *is* French.

My grandfather pours us all a glass of cognac and when he gives one to Trevor he quietly asks, "Théodore, I need to talk to the family about getting prepared for the growth of the city. When would be a good time?" Grand-papa replies, "There is no better time than the present." He turns and says, "Trevor would like to speak with us. You have our undivided attention."

"Married men are already bringing their families when they come to enlist. There is going to be a housing shortage by the end of next month at the rate they're arriving. I've been thinking about the not too distant future and came to this conclusion. Théodore, Gérard, you both need to start ordering building supplies in the morning and we all need to begin looking for buildings or lots for sale the company can buy to construct apartment buildings on. Théo, you should consider designing a subdivision with houses for lease enlisted men can afford."

Théo tells us, "When Rachel and I were at the home show there was a new line of appliances for apartments. The ranges are half the size of a full sized one and the cost was considerably lower. We can install those along with full sized refrigerators and cut costs." My father gives him a nod.

William adds, "I heard that over the week almost 600 young men who were still living at home boarded trains and buses with only the clothes on their backs. Issues for new recruits are being brought in from other bases."

Rachel asks him, "Why are so many coming here?"

"This is the closest base on the mainland to Oahu."

"That makes sense."

Father says, "Trevor, thank you for telling us what needs to be done. This includes our guests, if there is anything else we can do; please do not hesitate to let us know." William and Emily nod. Then Mother asks them, "Is there anything we can do for you two?" Emily replies, "Not a thing. Thank you for asking. We could not be happier. We love it here. In fact this afternoon we got an umbrella out and strolled down to the boardwalk where he proposed to me and then we stood there and listened to the waves splashing on the beach." Grand-mamma says, "How romantic." Then there is a nice silence while they admire the things that decorate the Christmas tree. Before the evening comes to a pleasant end Mother invites Trevor and I, along with Emily and William to have breakfast with them and we all happily accept then everyone goes their separate ways.

The next morning our work week begins with Father giving William and Emily a remote to the gates and it goes up hill from there. Emily and I are waiting for the fellas to pick us up for lunch when we see Mitch driving up and they are all smiling. This means Joanna is home making lunch. On the way to the house Mitch tells us things have calmed down at the medical center and they have enough volunteers for the ladies to be able to only work one shift. Joanna chose the morning one in order for us to return to our routine we all have missed.

During lunch Joanna tells us the flights have lessened considerably and there is rarely one at night, so Emily and William decide after work they are going to Maison to pack and return to their home. When five o'clock rolls around we decide to follow them and let Emily use the remote to open the gates.

After Emily happily uses the remote William puts his arm out the window and motions for us to follow them to the apartment. Trevor and I help them pack then watch our friends leave. Driving to our den we meet Théo and Rachel. When we get out of the car Théo tells us he has news, so Trevor and I walk over to them and go inside our parent's house together and straight to the kitchen where nothing is being cooked and our grandparents are here. Father has opened a bottle of Asti Spumante and fills our glasses when we are all seated.

After one sip of the sparkling wine Théo clears his throat and tells us as fate would have it the men who hired him to design the office building dropped by this afternoon to discuss details of the ground breaking ceremony. On a whim he decided to tell them about the housing shortage the city will be facing soon and due to the circumstances it could take months to lease out office spaces, but if they built an apartment building instead he guaranteed them that before the building was completed every apartment would be leased. They took his advice and he will be drafting a new design tomorrow. To celebrate we are going to Micheletto's.

Tuesday Trevor and I have lunch at Sam's and the diner is bustling as we enjoy our usual. After work Trevor announces he is in the mood to tango, so we stop at The Flying Dragon for takeout. We even change into the appropriate clothing and how we do tango.

In the morning, just before the alarm wakes us up I sit straight up breathing rapidly. Trevor sits up and rubs my back. I look at him and shake my head. "The Japanese are here."

"What did you see?"

"I was standing near the edge of the cliff at Old Point Loma looking through binoculars and in the distance there was a row of submarines rising to the surface with their periscopes up and I stood there in disbelief. They looked so menacing I dropped my binoculars and started running."

Trevor is silent and I watch him think. "Today is the 17th. The moon will be full tomorrow night. They intend to use the extra light to hunt by."

"I loathe submarines. They're predators hiding under water hunting prey."

"I feel the same way. One should be able to face one's enemy."

While I cook breakfast wishing I was drinking a Bloody Mary instead of orange juice Trevor thinks out loud. "Since Mitch knows about your abilities I'm going to speak with him first thing this morning. I want to meet with Robert Eh-sap. I'll tell him my gut instinct is the Japanese sent subs from the task force that attacked our bases in the Pacific and will make their presence known under the cover of night using the light from the moon. — Geneviève, are you ready for today?"

"I'll pretend I'm an actress trying to win an award."

He bursts into laughter. "That's one way to handle this. Another long day."

"Trevor, you do know I'm scared."

"Yes I do and you're already handing it very well, very well indeed." He gives me a kiss and sets the table.

In the parking lot at work chatting with Emily and William we both deserve awards and before we go inside Trevor and I take a moment alone. He tells me, "I'm going to go drop a ton of bricks on my superior officer. I'll see you at lunch." I needed to laugh; hopefully it will get me through until then.

Apparently it was decided to tell William what they could, because he has that too happy look on his face when they drive up. Then when we are on the sidewalk at the Mitchell's Trevor slows our pace and tells me, "We met with Robert." and nods. I instantly feel better.

Inside for some unknown reason Joanna hugs us all instead of kissing our cheeks. After she hugs me last I know she feels my heart beating, because she says, "I feel like having a glass of wine with my lunch. Ladies?" Emily replies, "I'll make a typo for sure, but thank you for offering." I dryly say, "I began drinking wine from a sippy cup." Laughter ensues and Joanna gives me a glass.

At five o'clock I want to make a run for the doors, but I walk calmly down the corridor with Emily as always. It's chilly, so we do not linger after work. About a mile from the base Trevor pulls into a parking lot and turns off the car. Oh good, I'm not going to be in suspense another minute. "I'm trying to think of where to begin, but there is one thing I can't get passed." He faces me. "Robert told us he had an uneasy feeling as well and started making phone calls while Mitch and I were there. During one phone call we could tell he was not happy and when it ended he told us the sub net isn't up. Mitch and I whipped our heads to look at each other so fast I think we pulled a muscle in our necks. A few phone calls later he found out when the net arrived there was a lack of communication with the divers. The net is up now."

"I thought that went up after our honeymoon."

"So did I. This entire time I have been thinking Louise was safe because Coronado Island blocks the view of the harbor from the Pacific and we had a net, but it turns out none of our ships were safe. We put men aboard them last week to make room for new recruits. The only thing that made me feel better about the situation was listening to him barking at the personnel involved. — One more thing, Mitch is telling Joanna about your dream. For once he knows something that isn't classified and he is tired of keeping her in the dark. It made me appreciate the fact I don't have to keep things from you."

The windows are beginning to fog over, so Trevor starts the car then he kisses me and asks, "Where would you like to go next?"

"Let's go to the market to buy the ingredients to make a pot of stew we can have for dinner and lunch tomorrow. I need to cook. I can bake us something for dessert too. What would you like?"

"Chocolate chip cookies with a glass of cold milk." And to the market we go.

Cooking takes our minds off the events of the day and we relax until we get in bed. We become wide awake the moment our heads hit the pillows and Trevor begins to get tickled. "Since we are out of chloroform would you fancy sipping a glass of cognac in front of a warm fire?" I fling the covers over him including his face and he lies under them laughing.

Trevor has just got the fire started when I return with the cognac. While he gets it going I warm it in my hands and watch him. I do like it that he sleeps in tank shirts instead of pajama tops. It seems as if every chance I get I become in awe of his body.

The fire is high and Trevor sits next to me. He takes his glass, puts his arm around me and asks, "So, when are you planning on telling me you don't want to quit your job?"

"When the time is right." And he kisses me. "How did you know that?"

"You released me from my word because the country needs me now and it needs you too, especially after today."

"Instead of turning in my notice before you standdown I'm going to request for the time off. I have seniority and should get it, but if not I will turn in my notice and work full time for Thomas."

"You'll get the time off. Her superiors will tell her to."

"What brings you to that conclusion?"

"Your personnel record that keeps getting thicker."

"The one with saliva on it?" We burst into laughter.

"Once again you catch me of guard. When we finish our cognac do you want to make out until we're sleepy?" I push the bottom of his glass up until it touches his lips.

CHAPTER TWENTY-ONE

Our worst fears are upon us. The Japanese are here and as Trevor predicted they made their presence known under the cover of night. On December 18th a merchant ship bound for our port with a load of lumber was attacked an hour before dawn 15 miles off the coast at Cape Mendoceno. The sub was surfaced hunting for a ship and found one. It began the attack by firing on it with the subs deck gun aiming for the antenna they missed. The men aboard the ship were uncovering the lifeboats when they saw the wake of a torpedo headed straight for them. Luckily it went under the ship and exploded close by. The explosion was so close fragments from the torpedo landed on the deck. The ship was listing because the members of the crew were in the process of shifting the ballast water port side and due to poor visibility in the darkness the Japanese must have thought it was sinking and disappeared into the night. Trevor tells me this after we finish washing the dinner dishes and are sitting on the sofa with a glass of wine instead of during lunch while we were eating our leftover stew and cookies. He knew it was too much to take in then go back inside and pretend all was right in the world.

After I absorb the overload of information we hold each other and I cling to him, because he is going to be deployed in a little over three weeks. We barely speak a word getting ready for bed and when we are in it I ask him to hold on to me even if I try to toss and turn in my sleep. I don't want to wake up holding Christopher again.

Friday morning I was happy to find myself in Trevor's arms when I woke up. The day was normal with the exception of concerns one of the Japanese subs lurking off the coast would attack another merchant ship. We had lunch at the Mitchell's and even returned for Happy Hour. Emily and I were thrilled, because we announced to everyone we have the time off when they standdown. Then we decide to celebrate over dinner at the club and to my surprise people just nodded as we passed, perhaps because we were not dressed for dinner. Emily and I were wearing pant suits, Joanna had on a day dress and the fellas were wearing their khaki uniforms. It was obvious we arrived straight from the base, so we dined undisturbed.

After a slow and tedious drive to our den in my car for a change we realize we have to figure out a way to park in the garage in the dark. So, Trevor raises the door, pulls the car in and leaves the dim headlights on. We get out and after he lowers the door and I turn on a light. He turns off the headlights and we sigh before ascending the stairs to go inside. Close to the top we see a note on the door in my grandfather's handwriting. Standing in front of the door I read it aloud. "We wanted you both to know the good news as soon as possible, the brigade of German soldiers is no longer in Aix and all is well." I am so relieved that when I hug Trevor he has to grab the banister to keep us from falling down the stairs.

Saturday was a busy day. It was the last chance for Christmas shopping and Trevor and I went all over town. Then we made a special stop at Blackwell's to get more film and give Mr. Blackwell a red velvet cake with holly leaves and berries on it made by the clubs Pâtissier. We ordered several to give the people in our lives that made them better which included the owners of Trevor's favorite shop, the Bertucci brothers.

We manage to get our shopping done before the blackout and as we are driving up to our den we watch Claudette and Joseph start walking toward us. They were waiting on the steps of my parent's house. I tell Trevor, "I have a bad feeling about this." He sighs heavily, parks and we get out. Joseph tells us as they approach, "Pardon the intrusion. We simply would like to speak with you both when the time is convenient about something we want to do."

Trevor looks at me and I give him a little nod, so he invites them up. When we get inside I ask them if they would like a drink and Joseph asks for a glass of whiskey, something I have never seen him drink. I glance at Trevor and pour him a glass. Claudette tells me she will have what I am having. Manhattan's it is.

The moment I sit down Joseph says, "I will go straight to the matter. Claudette and I visited a friend this afternoon who works on the docks. He told us a merchant ship loaded with lumber docked this morning and the crew was talking about being attacked by a Japanese submarine. A few crew members had shell fragments they pulled out of their pockets. They think there are submarines off the west coast from here to the Canadian border."

Claudette says, "I am here to be safe from the war and am no longer. The Germans will not return to Aix. We will be safe *there* and I want to go home. I have missed my family too long and want my husband to see his home then begin working with my father. Also, our children will be born there and know their grandparents and aunt's before they learn to walk." Her eyes well with tears.

Joseph hands her his handkerchief and looks at my uneasy husband. "We wanted to speak with you before we mention this to anyone. Trevor, is it possible for you to make arrangements to get us across the Atlantic as you did for your family?"

"I will make calls first thing Monday."

"Thank you. We hope we are not asking too much of you."

"I understand wanting to go home and will happily do this ... for you both."

Claudette's lower lip quivers then suddenly she stands and the rest of us are on our feet instantly. She goes straight to Trevor with tears streaming down her face and kisses his cheeks several times then she does the same with me. Joseph picks up his whiskey and drinks it as if it is a shot. She tells us, "Merci. Bonsoir." and turns to Joseph who nods to us and swiftly escorts her out.

Listening to them going down the steps I stand there looking at the door they left through. Trevor is motionless. Then I start thinking out loud. "Grand-mamma is going to be at a complete loss. Mother ... poor Mother, she has been caring for him almost fourteen years. I want them to go, but I will — miss them." I try to hold back tears, but fail miserably. While Trevor's comforts me I gush, "One minute I am so happy and the next I am so terribly sad. And it keeps happening. We can't even light the torches for them. I don't know how much more I can take."

My head is pressed against his chest and I notice his heart is pounding and begin to calm down. That was building up for almost two weeks. I step back and when he hands me his handkerchief he says, "That will not be sufficient. I'm going to wet a hand towel so you can wipe off your face with a cool cloth." I sniffle, nod and sit back down on the sofa.

While wiping off my face I think all I want to do is lie down next to my husband and I definitely do not feel like cooking and washing dishes. "Trevor, that's the second those two have blindsided me and it's exhausting."

"Rest in my arms for a little while and then we can figure out what to do about dinner." I curl up next to him before he finishes his sentence.

I'm getting sleepy due to exhaustion when the phone rings. Trevor answers it then tells me. "That was your grandmother. She made too much food for dinner and wanted to know if I would like to get two plates of her 'wonderful roast and vegetables' and bring them here. You two are kind of spooky." At last, a reason to laugh. He gives me a kiss and goes out the door.

A few minutes later I hear the garage door rise and close then the squeak of the dumbwaiter. I jump to my feet and raise the door to find a tray with a white tulip on it and a pastry box with one of the red velvet cakes in it. I am cheered. When Trevor walks in I'm holding the pastry box. "There she is, the woman I married. If you set down that box I'll give you a kiss." I hold on to it and pretend to give it some thought. Laughing he takes from me and after dinner he gives me more than a kiss.

That was yesterday. Today we spend most of it in bed resting our bodies and minds and he reads the Funny Paper to me. Then late in the afternoon we sit at the kitchen table drinking hot buttered rum wrapping Christmas gifts and putting them under our tree. Trevor hung mistletoe all over the house and when I say all over I mean it. He hung a piece at the kitchen sink where I stand.

Joseph and Claudette join us for Sunday dinner and they have a difficult time pretending nothing's wrong, therefore Trevor and I cover for them by creating diversions with Théo and Rachel and we all have a good time. Christmas *is* just around the corner.

Monday morning I am sound asleep until I feel Trevor trying to get out of bed without disturbing me. "I'm awake."

"Good morning, Baby. You were holding on to me in your sleep. I knew my efforts were going to be in vain. I'm going to call the embassy. I shan't be long. Keep my place warm." And he wasn't gone long at all. He gets back in our bed and tells me arrangements are being made and he is going to call for the details during lunch at the Mitchell's. It is official, Joseph is taking Claudette home. This is how the day starts.

Lunch is over and Trevor tells everyone he needs to make a long distance call. Joanna tells him he knows she and Mitch do not mind and they all go outside to give us privacy. I stand beside him watching him writing details on the notepad still in disbelief. Their flight out of Canada aboard a Liberator will be on the 15th. He gives me hug and we go outside.

On the way home we pick up dinner from The Flying Dragon and when we get there he calls Claudette and Joseph to tell them the news. While he talks I wonder when they are going to announce this and begin dreading the moment they will. Then during dinner I notice Trevor's mind is preoccupied and I summon up the courage to tell him, "I have had a sense of foreboding all day. What do I not know?"

"Robert told us this at the morning briefing. While we were busy Saturday Christmas shopping two Japanese subs were busy attacking two merchant ships. At 1:30, in broad daylight, a sub assigned to the Cape Mendoceno vicinity fired on an empty tanker with a course set for San Francisco from Seattle. The ship was about 20 miles off the coast when the surfaced sub was spotted by a crew member closing in at a high speed. An SOS was sent out immediately. In under a minute the sub closed in on the ship and opened fire with its deck gun on the ship taking out the radio antenna. The crew was given the order to abandoned ship and the captain stopped the engines then hoisted a white flag. Moments after the crew rowed away from the ship the three man crew of the subs deck gun fired a shot at the men in the lifeboats."

I gasp and ask, "Even after they surrendered the Japanese were going to shoot them?"

"We'll never know the answer to that question. They suddenly went into the sub and it quickly submerged. Our guess is they heard a radio signal that alerted them two of our bombers were en route. When they arrived on the scene one bomber dropped a depth charge near where it submerged and then they started circling the area. A few minutes later the men in the lifeboats spotted the subs periscope and it launched a torpedo that was a direct hit."

"They were so determined to sink it they risked being sunk by our bombers?"

"Yes they were, but they failed. The abandoned ship was found 85 miles from the scene. She ran aground on rocks off the coast of Crescent City. The Coast Guard rescued the crew, but they weren't sure that when the bombers returned and dropped more depth charges the thing sank."

"I hope it did."

"You're not the only one."

Trevor drinks some ginger ale and rubs my thigh then tells me, "About 330 miles south of Mendoceno another tanker headed north to Santa Cruz came under fire during the time the other one was in peril. It was 20 miles off the coast of – Monterey Bay and had a better fate, because the ship was close to a port and the sub didn't risk getting too close. Our guess is they heard the ships distress call to the Navy and when the ship was near land it submerged. Here's the interesting part, the incident made it into the local paper at Monterey. Several men playing golf on a coastal course saw the smoke pouring from the ships funnel as it headed to Santa Cruz zigzagging. They watched it a few minutes then continued to play."

"Unbelievable. Since the coast is under blackout ordinances people must think there will only be attacks at night. How ludicrous. – At least we know the location of two subs."

"And today we learned where a third one is."

"My blood just ran cold."

"Let me begin by telling you I'm making this story short and it has a happy ending." I sigh and nod. "At around 8:30 this morning a tanker was attacked 55 miles north of Santa Barbara. A crew member spotted the surfaced sub and the captain went full speed ahead. The smoke from the funnel made a smoke screen and hid the ship from the sub rendering the deck gun useless. This forced the sub to submerge and fire a torpedo that missed. Five Navy bombers responded to their SOS and were on the scene in no time. They made it rain with depth charges in the area it submerged. There were reports of loud explosions. We either sunk it or forced it flee to deep waters. Either way we have them running scared."

We sit silently looking into each other's eyes. The only thoughts I can hear are mine. I know there is a sub lurking in the deep close by. It didn't go after the ship that came into port with the lumber recently in my opinion because it's waiting on a Navy vessel to emerge from the harbor. I hope it is not going to be the one my husband is aboard.

I go to Trevor and expect him to slide his chair back, but he places his hands on the table's edge and pushes it away from him then I sit across his lap and put my arms around him. In the comfort of his embrace I want to cry, but I begin kissing him instead. Our kisses become passionate and then suddenly he releases me and glides his hands under my thighs and pulls me to him until our lower abdomens are pressed together. "Geneviève, tell me you want to make love with me. Tell me to take you upstairs."

"Trevor, I do want to make love with you. Please take me upstairs."

At the bottom of the stairs he pins me against the wall and while we kiss he takes my hair down and I undo his dog tags then drop them onto the floor where my hair pins are. With an arm around me and a hand on the banister he guides me upstairs and into the guest room where we fall onto the bed. Undressing each other in bed turns out to be wonderful foreplay, because the moment we are nude the foreplay ends.

The next afternoon we are happily eating lunch in his car when I decide to take temporary leave of my senses. "How did the morning briefing go?"

Trevor raises his eyebrows and gives me a look. "Four more merchant ships were attacked. Two of them sank and 89 of the 92 sailors involved were rescued. Three were in different locations from the others. They're using psychological warfare to instill fear."

"Well ... it's working."

"I know, Baby. We're going to pretend we didn't have this conversation. I wish I didn't have to report for duty tomorrow."

"I wish I didn't have to either." He smiles, gives me a kiss and we share the last piece of red velvet cake.

We go to the commissary after work and split up to buy stocking stuffers for each other. In a stunning turn of events I finish shopping before he does and am sitting on a bench at the checkout eating caramels waiting on him. When I see Trevor he has a candy cane hanging from his mouth like it is a cigar and I almost choke on my caramel. After he checks out he walks up with eyes gleaming and I tell him, "I see your choice of what to eat while you shopped. If I had a camera."

"I'm glad you don't. Let's get out of here. I want real food." And we make our way to the car cutting up and eating candy.

The following day not only is it Christmas Eve it is also a day for lunch at the Mitchell's and the exchanging of gifts. When Emily opens her car door we hear Glen Miller's version of "Jingle Bells" playing. The second I walk in Trevor grabs me and starts Swing Dancing with me. William and Mitch grab their wives and we dance laughing uncontrollably. And the fun begins.

The fun continues at our den. Trevor starts a roaring fire then plays Christmas records for us to listen to while we are in separate rooms filling each other's stockings. When those are hung we make eggnog and put it in our small crystal punch bowl set then we start cooking and every time I stand at the sink to do something I get kissed. Trevor stands there with his blue eyes sparkling several times and his only reason is just to be kissed.

We set the table and sit down to a romantic candle lit dinner. And when we are ready for dessert I tell Trevor, "I've been keeping a surprise about tonight for a long time and at last you are going to find out what it is."

"Do tell."

"Nope. You have to see it and it's at my parent's house." I jump up and grab his hand then pull him off his chair, get my camera and head straight to the front doors as he laughs.

"Since we haven't had dessert this has to do with something sweet for you to be this giddy." I just look at him and do not say a word with my face beaming.

Trevor opens the front door and I immediately shout, "We're here." and drag him to the kitchen where my entire family is very busy. Rachel is holding a bag of ice wrapped in a towel while Théo hits it with a meat mallet; my grandparents are arranging two chairs between the kitchen table and island. My father is opening a box of rock salt and Mother is standing at the island stirring ingredients in a large bowl and says, "Welcome to our Christmas Eve celebration, Trevor." He smiles and replies "Thank you. I think I know what's going on here." Father tells me, "Geneviève, it is in the mudroom."

Since I am still holding his hand I drag him there and when we get to the doorway he says, "I knew it, an ice cream churn." He kisses me then picks it up and I follow him back to the kitchen where Grand-mamma motions to a chair with a folded beach towel on it. He sets it down and tells me, "I'm anxious to hear this story." And I begin telling him the story as Mother pours the ice cream mixture into the metal cylinder and Théo along with Rachel and my Father pour the ice and rock salt around it. "When I was a little girl I requested homemade vanilla ice cream to be a Christmas present. Mother decided we would make it on Christmas Eve and we have been doing so ever since." Trevor tells me, "We are about to have fun huh?" And everyone smiles and nods as my grand-papa puts the crank on top and Mother places two folded beach towels over it.

The churn moves as you begin to turn the crank and to keep it still I sat on top of it as a child while it was being churned by the men. When I became older Théo and I were a team and my parents and grandparents were too. It takes about thirty minutes to freeze the liquid into ice cream, so we each had 10 minute shifts. Théo and I are married now and things are about to change.

Father says to Trevor, "Since this began with your wife, the two of you should get this thing going." Trevor lights up the room and suddenly he grabs me by the waist, moves me in front of the churn and picks me up then he sits me on top. "Are you ready, Baby?" I nod repeatedly and he gives me a kiss then sits down in the chair across from me. Rachel picks up my camera as I kick off my shoes and put my feet on his thighs and he begins turning the crank looking into my eyes. His eyes are the brightest blue. And when I begin to wiggle my toes they twinkle. Our 10 minutes fly by and after he slips my shoes on I throw my arms around his neck and he lifts my off then I give him something appropriate to the occasion, an Eskimo Kiss. This is when we discover my nose is cold and he warms it.

Next up is Rachel and Théo. While she is sitting on the churn she says, "Now I understand why my husband told me to wear trousers." Her feet are on his thighs and my brother is extremely happy.

When it is my parents turn and Father holds out his hand to help Mother up Trevor whispers, "I adore your parents." I stop taking snapshots to give him a kiss.

As Mother gets off the churn it is time for the moment we all have been waiting for, to enjoy the fruits of our labor. My grandfather takes everything off the top of the churn then Grand-mama lifts the lid. We all hold our breath until she announces, "Perfection has been reached once again." Within minutes we are all sitting around the kitchen table savoring our ice cream and the moment. We stay for a glass of mulled wine then go on our merry way home.

Curled up on the sofa listening to the crackling of the fire, breathing in the scent of evergreen and sipping nectar Trevor sighs. "So, this is what it's like to be married during Christmas. I've spent Christmas with family and friend's thinking it doesn't get any better than this. I was mistaken. It doesn't get any better than *this*. I love you, Geneviève."

"I was thinking the same thing. And I love you." I set down our glasses and lay across him. I have to kiss him.

When he gets up to move the logs in the fireplace I tell him, "On Christmas Eve the family chooses one gift from under the tree to open. Would you like to do that?"

"As a matter of fact I would. I recognize the size of one of the boxes and the suspense is getting to me." I get up and sit on the rug by the tree and he sits next to me. Then he reaches for the gift that is the photograph of me sitting on the roof of my car. Trevor has been handling frame boxes too often.

My husband smiles so as he unties the bow and tears of the wrapping paper. When he opens the box he swiftly pulls the frame out and instantly his face has a look of astonishment. "It's in color." Trevor covers his mouth and looks into my eyes.

"When I got the negative out you could have knocked me over with a feather."

"The image in my mind is in my hand. I can't believe it. It's you, the first time I laid eyes on you. Geneviève ..." Time passes as he wraps his mind around what he has and then Trevor tells me. "Your turn."

"I've been eyeing the unusually shaped box you only put a bow on and I see why. It is beautiful. The gold on the black leather tells me it is something old." I pick it up and he beams as I slide the ribbon off and raise the lid to reveal a yellow gold hair stick pin with a fairy on top with opals on her wings. "Trevor."

"Mitch sent me on an errand about a month ago and I went into that little estate shop. When I spotted her in the glass case I honestly thought for a split second I was hallucinating. I'm so glad you choose that gift. I've wanted to give her to you since I found her."

"Thank you, Trevor. She's perfect. She can go into my chignon. I'm wearing her to dinner tomorrow."

"For now what do you want to do?"

"Get ready for bed."

We go to the kitchen and put cookies on a plate then pour a glass of milk. When I get out a box of raisins he asks, "What are those for?" I respond, "These are for the reindeer." And there is his deep laugh. We set the milk and cookies on the mantle and I set the box of raisins on the hearth.

The fire in our bedroom lights the room and while we turn down the covers Trevor says, "I wish we had *A Visit From St. Nicholas*, so I could read it to you."

"We don't need it. I know the poem by heart."

"Why am I not surprised?" And he gives me a kiss.

Snuggling under the covers I recite the poem to my husband and after he lovingly kisses my face we try to stay awake as long as possible even though we know Santa is waiting for us to fall asleep.

In the morning I wake up and become a little girl. "Santa was here!" I give Trevor a kiss, bound from our bed and put on my robe. He laughs from that moment on following me to the fireplace where I see the cookies on the plate and the raisins are gone and the glass has an inch of milk in the bottom. I give him a look and he simply grins. How did he manage to get up without waking me?

Moving on. I get my stocking down and pour the contents out to find a tin of jacks among the candy. "You gave me a toy." I open the tin and the first thing I notice is something wrapped in white tissue paper. I pick it up still smiling wondering what little thing he put in with the toy. When I begin to see what it is my jaw drops, because I am holding a ring that matches my Burmese ruby suite.

Trevor slips it on my finger. "I would have given this to you when I gave you the necklace and earrings, but it didn't exist. I had this made for you." Instead of trying to find words I caress his face and kiss him. Then I point to his stocking.

I was not as imaginative as my husband. When he pours out the contents a small brown leather jewelry box is among his candy. He smiles at me and lifts the lid. "Solid gold cuff links with my monogram. These are most unexpected." He gives me a kiss.

"You wear your Navy issued cufflinks and other things with your tuxedo. I feel the two should be separate." Next I hand him several boxes. He opens them and finds he now has a black cashmere dress overcoat, a pleated tuxedo shirt with gold studs and the last silk bow tie and cummerbund in the state along with all the accessories: black socks, sock garters, braces and shoes. He is truly speechless surround by everything. "Trevor, I want you to be Mr. Lyons tonight."

"And so I shall. Thank you, Mrs. Lyons."

"You are entirely welcome, Mr. Lyons."

Next he stokes the embers in the fireplace, adds more logs and gets a fire going. Then I watch him look at a gift for me. He hands it to me and I slowly open it. When I fold back the tissue paper I reveal a satin petal pink bustier with matching tap pants and garters. I run my hand over the bustier. "Trevor, this is beautiful. You went to the lingerie shop and chose me something beautiful." His eyes are dancing and it hits me, "You went into the lingerie shop."

"Yes I did and my presence caused a small disturbance. Would you like to hear the story?" I nod. "This time I asked Mitch if I could run an errand and headed for no man's land in uniform. I parked, opened the door, raised my voice and said, 'Excuse me. I want to buy something for my wife.' The clerk was your age thank goodness and started smiling. Then she told me there was a customer in a dressing room and asked me to please wait outside. I closed the door and a few minutes later the clerk opened it to let a frayed lady out and me in."

"Who waited on you?"

"Terry and she informed me I was the first man to ever walk through the door. When I told her you were my wife she informed me since you were a customer she knew your size in everything, as I had hoped. Therefore I bought you a little of everything."

Trevor was not joking with me. Whatever a woman wears under her clothing and to bed was under the tree. By the time all the gifts were opened I was surrounded by satin and lace in lovely colors and one color I did not own, red, dark red, because it was considered inappropriate for an unmarried woman. I am married now and am as happy as could be.

We are starving by the time we finish opening gifts and the moment we are in the kitchen I see a note on the door of the dumbwaiter that reads, Open Me. I burst into laughter, because he is reading *Alice's Adventures in Wonderland* to me and walk over. When I raise the door there is a white Teddy Bear with a red ribbon around her neck and a bag of strawberry taffy on her wrist sitting there with what seems like a smile. There is a note on her lap. I pick it up and read it aloud. "Dear Geneviève, As always you are on my nice list. Her name is Celestyna and I think she will be fond of Christopher. Happy Christmas, Father Christmas." I turn to Trevor. "You are so very British sometimes. I love you."

"I thought you would enjoy that and I love you too." I hold her in my arms and kiss him.

"She's very pretty. Thank you, Trevor. Will you go get Christopher?"

He returns with him and we make the introductions. Then Trevor asks, "Will they be joining us for breakfast?" I light up the kitchen.

"I'll set the table for four." He knows me so well.

Drinking our second cup of coffee I get up and whisper close to Trevor's ear, "I think I heard Santa in the solarium last night." In the blink of an eye Trevor stands up, grabs my hand and turns into a little boy tugging me along the way. In the solarium there is a box propped up on the sofa. Trevor exclaims, "An electric train set. Geneviève, this is incredible."

"I heard that father's and son's play together with trains."

The excitement on his face changes to adoring as he looks deep into my eyes. "Baby, words fail me." So, he kisses me instead.

He takes it into the living room then announces, "This calls for hot cocoa." And while he begins making it, I get my camera. It's time to photograph Trevor.

My overjoyed husband settles down on the rug and I sit on the sofa. After reading the instructions and a good deal of time passes he puts on the caboose, turns the switch on and it works. It goes round and round and round. And to our delight the train makes a sound on the tracks.

While he is smiling at his little train I tell him, "Perhaps now is a good time to tell you this is a starter kit. There are so many thing to go with it you will not believe your eyes."

"When does the hobby shop open?" I simply laugh then Trevor glances at the clock, sighs and gets on his feet. It must be time to dress for lunch and exchange gifts at my grandparent's house.

The trunk to my car is loaded and when he pulls out of the garage we see Théo and Rachel are parked out front with their trunk open. We drive over and hug each other then fill our arms with gifts and go inside. My parents are already there and the exchanging of gifts begins. The big surprise was my parents had our wedding portrait painted. We didn't have to pose for it because there was a color photograph to give the artist. Father tells Théo and Rachel theirs will be finished soon. Next Claudette and Joseph finally join us and I take too many photographs.

Wrapping paper and ribbon is everywhere when we move to the dining room for lunch instead of the usual brunch. The three newlywed couples spending their first Christmas together was taken into consideration.

Back at our den Trevor starts putting the gifts we received in the dumbwaiter. At the same time I wonder out of the garage looking at the decorations. He steps up beside me and holds my hand. "What is it, Baby?"

"This will be the first Christmas the torches will not be lit and we won't walk through them after dinner. The Japanese chose their timing well, Hanukkah and Christmas in one fell swoop."

"I wish you weren't upset."

"I'll be fine as soon as we go inside. These rapid mood swings make me feel as if I am a living example of the drama masks that are always on display in Nouvelle Orléans for Mardi Gras. One minute I'm the tragic Melpomene and the next I'm the comedic Thalia."

"*That's* a vivid image. Let's get you inside." And he makes me laugh.

We have hours before dinner, so the moment we're in the living room Trevor adds logs to the fire then tosses every cushion and throw pillow in the room onto the floor close to our tree and the fireplace. I put a blanket over them and get one for us to snuggle under. After we undress and get under the blanket we lie there watching the rainbows dance around the room from the prisms caused by the light from the fire. The snuggling ends as he begins to caress my thighs.

We walk to my grandparent's house as Mr. and Mrs. Lyons and after one step into the drawing room Trevor makes an odd sound then says, "Geneviève, 10 o'clock." I look that way and see the portrait of my grandparent's on their wedding day is hanging in its place over the mantle. We are standing in front of it when my grandparent's join us. Trevor looks at them and dryly says, "Thank you for taking this down for me. Even though I know the whole story, it's still a lot to take in." Grand-papa pats his back. "You are most welcome. Merry Christmas, Trevor."

Théo and Rachel arrive with our parent's seconds later and we drink eggnog before the delectable Christmas dinner. Then we move back to the drawing where my grandfather pours nectar and Grand-mamma turns on the polyphone for us to dance by and it is so festive none of us are able to stop smiling as we change partners.

After we, the ladies have danced with all the handsome men in the family and our glasses are empty Théo and Rachel are the first to leave. They have to drive home and it takes longer in the darkness. Trevor and I leave shortly after and during the walk as I hold on to his arm I become amorous, because of the thought I'm wearing red lingerie my husband gave me under my evening gown. Soon, after my count, we are waltzing and I whisper, "Mercredi, vendredi ... dimanche." He draws in a deep breath as he slows us to a stop and softly tells me, "I remember when you first said those words to me. I told you they sounded like words of seduction." When we are back into the living room my gown and his tuxedo are in the solarium.

The day after Christmas I'm always off, but not this year. So, I go to the base with Trevor. When Mrs. Sloan walks in with Becky and they both are carrying folders I glance at Emily. Her mouth is open. I would like to go to the Mitchell's now instead of waiting for lunch time.

While Trevor and I ride home my fingers are tingling like they did when I was learning how to type. When he notices me rubbing my hands he asks me why and when I tell him he pulls over and kisses them then the sweet man I married rubs my hands. When I tell him the tingling has eased, he pulls back onto the road and tells me no cooking tonight; we are eating at Micheletto's.

Settled on the sofa with a glass of Italian Rosato it's obvious Trevor needs to tell me something, but he doesn't want to. To begin the conversation I say, "When we were eating lunch in the car you told me very little. Since then I have come to the conclusion not knowing is the worst. My imagination runs away with me."

By the time he finishes talking I have learned on the 22nd, the Japanese fired upon the men in the lifeboats of one of the ships that sank and there was no doubt they were trying to take their lives, which is a war crime. The attack occurred before dawn and due to poor visibility most of the shells hit the lifeboats and one almost sank before they rowed ashore six hours later. Then on Christmas Eve two more merchant ships came under fire. One escaped harm due to a Navy subchaser. The other was saved by Navy bombers making surveillance flights nearby and within minutes they were on the scene dropping depth charges. Both ships were off the coast of L.A. less than 100 miles from here. The last thing he tells me is four American men going deep sea fishing off the coast of Tijuana spotted a submarine about 12 miles from the shore and reported it to the US Coast Guard. Tijuana is only a few miles from the base. This sub is the one lurking in the shallows waiting for a Navy vessel to go out to sea.

After I absorb all the information I respond, "The Japanese are smart to hide in waters our vessels can't go into and our aircraft can't fly over. It was good of those men to report the sighting."

"Yes it was. — Geneviève, I have more to tell you. — In case the enemy knows our deployment date, it has been moved up to the 9th." I gasp and he sighs heavily. "It's on a Friday instead of the usual Sunday and we're not standing down for 12 days. They are giving us nine days beginning the day before New Year's Eve with orders to stay within 20 miles of the base." He pauses and swallows to the point I see his Adam's apple move. "Last, but not least, Sunday morning we are taking Louise out for a training exercise." I choke on my saliva.

He gets up and returns with a glass of water. I drink some and manage to say, "Details please."

"Surveillance flights equipped to see long distances report the sub is no longer where it was. All the escort ships in the strike group went out to sea yesterday patrolling for the sub hoping to draw it out and sink it, but it was nowhere to be found."

"How long will you be gone?"

"Approximately eight hours. The strike group will return before dusk and then we will have briefings late into the night. I'm reporting for duty at 0500 hours and am among the last small group of our highest ranking officers to go aboard Louise. Married enlisted men and officers have been going aboard all day at random times. This pattern will continue into the night and tomorrow until all men are aboard in case we are being observed."

"That means wives and families are staying home."

"Yes, it does."

"Trevor, I know it's early, but would you mind showering and going to bed? I want to lie down and hold you."

"I'll build us a fire."

I lie in his arms trying not to think about how worried I am. The timing couldn't be worse. There are so many Japanese submarines off the coast I've lost count and how could I forget Louise would be taken out before he's deployed after having an extensive refitting. My husband and two fine men are about to be in harm's way.

"Geneviève, your breathing is erratic. Where ever you have gone, you need to leave and come back to me."

"I'm here."

"I love you."

"I love you. Will you lie on your back and let me listen to your heart?"

Trevor rolls over and I give him a kiss. Then I place my head on his chest and listen to the sound of his heart beating steady and true.

Just as I am finally dozing off a log falls in the fireplace and I flinch. Trevor wakes up. "Baby, what happened?"

"A log fell."

"And you flinched so hard you almost jumped out of your skin. You need a glass of cognac." He starts to get up and I hold on to his arm.

"Trevor, I don't need a glass of cognac. I need you." And soon our fingers are entwined.

The next day is the last Saturday in December and we take down the Christmas decorations, beginning with the trees because we are all clean. Even under normal circumstances we are a little sad and we rarely cut up, but today it seems more like a somber occasion. When my grandfather rings the Chuck Wagon bell for lunch we quietly swat the sawdust off our clothes and go inside.

While everyone is finishing their coffee Claudette says, "Joseph and I have been waiting to ... make announcement." Trevor and I look at each other, because she is about to drop the other shoe on the family and it is going to hurt them. How I wish this was an Irish coffee. At least they waited to drop it after Christmas. Grand-mamma tells her, "Our attention you do have."

Claudette draws an uneasy breath, reaches for Joseph's hand and proceeds to tell everyone what Trevor and I already know, Joseph is taking Claudette home on the 15th. There is an uncomfortable silence and then Joseph breaks it by telling us they have decided to get a sleeper car on a train and cross the country to see more of it before their flight, therefore they are leaving on the 3rd. When he informs us tomorrow will be his last day at the club Mother speaks in a calm controlled tone.

"May I ask why you chose a Sunday?" He replies, "Of course. Sunday brunch and lunch has always been my favorite shift." My father says, "I will make us a reservation for brunch." I glance at Trevor then tell Father, "Please do not include us. I will make a reservation for lunch and invite a few of our friends." He nods and then there is yet another uncomfortable silence.

The next thing I know Théo is getting to his feet as he says, "Time for all the newlyweds to get back to the task at hand." Every man is on their feet in a split second pulling out chairs for the women and we make a hasty exit. We could all tell Mother and Grand-mamma were battling tears, because they both held their heads high to remain dignified. For once Grand-mamma didn't see something coming and how the club managed to keep Mother from knowing Joseph had turned in his notice is beyond me.

Watching Théo and Rachel leave Trevor says, "Once again, my brilliant wife, I am in awe of your ability to think fast on your feet. I wondered how you were going to get us out of brunch without letting them know I won't be around. Inviting Joanna and Emily to lunch is a good idea."

"I'm hoping the diversion will be enough for us to keep our sanity."

Instead of giving me a kiss he kisses me and there is longing in it. Then we go inside and while I call Joanna and Emily Trevor pours two glasses of whiskey. One is a double. He walks into the kitchen, hands me the double and goes to stoke the fire. I almost lose my train of thought as I make the reservation. Due to the kiss and the fact he is having a drink and I am holding a double my instincts tell me to stay in the kitchen, but I forge on and join Trevor on the sofa.

"Geneviève, I need to get something out of the way."

"The conversation that begins with I know nothing is going to happen to me, but if it does."

"That's the one."

"Trevor, do you mind if we sip on our whiskey a minute?"

"Not at all."

Looking at the man I love, I know the moment he speaks the words they will be the reality I have been avoiding since that day Emily and I went shopping, only worse, because this deployment sends him into war. In the back of mind it was my worst fear we would go to war before or while he was deployed. His life that is so cherished by me is going to be in danger and the thought is almost unbearable.

I muster the strength to give him a nod. He hands me his handkerchief, which means he expects me to cry and begins the talk. "Since you know the first part of this conversation I'm going to skip it. If something does happen to me, Geneviève I need you to promise me you will not languish in a state of grief and you will live the life you had planned before we met."

Tears stream down my face and I tell him, "I promise."

"Baby, always remember the main objective of the ships and aircraft in the strike group are to protect Louise at all cost."

"I won't forget." More tears stream down my face. "Trevor, this is worse than I thought it would be."

"I hoped with every fiber of my being I would return before we were pulled into this war. I am so sorry for putting you though this."

"There is no reason for you to be sorry for something you didn't do. I knew the risks when I said yes and I would have said yes even if we were already at war. I was in love with you. I am in love with you."

"I am in love with you and will be until the end of time. My soul is yours."

I look deep into his eyes where I see his soul then fall into his arms. And there I stay for the longest time.

The emotions we went through drained us, so when the need for sustenance forces us to get up. Trevor and I make omelets and toast, leave the dishes then go to shower and stand under the warm water in each other's arms letting it flow over us and wash our troubles away.

We go into the living room where Trevor sets a chair in front of the fire and brushes my hair to get it dry. Then he braids it for me and carries me to our bed where we curl up together. I fight sleep for as long as I can to hold him.

When the alarm goes off Trevor sits on the edge of the bed and hands me his dog tags. I put them on him as he puts on his watch and ring then he shaves and we go to our dressing room where I help him dress and caress his face every chance I get. Next he goes into his dressing room, aka the storage closet for my gowns and our luggage and returns with his seabag. Oh my gosh, he could wind up staying out longer. While the room is spinning he reaches for my hand, leads me to the door in the kitchen and sets it down. Then we kiss tenderly and hold each other for what seems like seconds.

Trevor opens the door and picks up his seabag. "I love you, Geneviève."

"I love you too, Trevor."

"See you soon."

I gasp. "See you soon."

Trevor steps out and turns on a dime as he closes the door. I stand motionless and listen to his footsteps on the stairs and then I hear the service door close. I go into the living room and listen to him start his car and let in warm up. Then I hear him put the car into drive and listen to the sound of the tires on the cobblestones. Then there is silence and suddenly I have never felt so alone in my life.

I go back into the kitchen and just stand by the table staring at the cabinets. The thoughts running through my head and cooking breakfast for only myself has me paralyzed. When the phone rings it doesn't even surprise me. I look at the clock and see I've been standing by the table over 10 minutes. Going to answer the phone I am certain it is Joanna.

"Joanna, what are you up to?"

Laughing she says, "Darling, we're going to Sam's. Put on sailing attire in order to look our usual this early in the morning. À bientôt."

When I park the car Joanna walks up and opens the door for me. "I'm so happy you're here."

"Where's Emily?"

"At home with puffy eyes."

"I cried last night too. We had the talk."

"Oh my. Let's go inside, this blackout is giving me the shivers."

We walk in and see lit candles on the tables and the only lights on are in the kitchen. I dryly say, "This is different." Joanna goes, "Mmm hm." Carla seats us and walks off to get glasses of water then Sam waves to us through the pickup window and comes out. "Glad you ladies could find the place. Did you come here for a romantic breakfast for two?"All we do is laugh. "Two Early Bird Special's?" I tell him, "Yes, but I want hot cocoa instead of coffee." Joanna says, "I'll have the same." Sam tells us, "I'll let Carla know. Enjoy." And he is off to man the grill.

After Carla serves, Joanna reaches for my hand. "I thought Trevor would have the talk with you last night. I remember having that talk with Mitch 21 years ago, but it was not under these circumstances. That is why I called this morning. I was standing at the kitchen counter dreading cooking breakfast for only me and felt the need to run for my life, so I picked up the phone."

"I'm glad you did. I was standing by the kitchen table and had been starring at the cabinets for over 10 minutes when you called." Joanna nods then shakes her head and sighs. "I didn't know you and Mitch had been married 21 years. When is your anniversary?"

"The 26th of June."

"We knew each other then. Why didn't you mention it?"

"The boys had just met the women they were going to marry and it slipped their minds, so we kept quiet knowing it would upset them."

"I won't forget. Be prepared for a party next year at Maison."

"That would be nice for a change. We've never had a party. Mitch and I only tell people the date when asked. We wanted to avoid someone throwing a party for us at The O Club and inviting people who are mere acquaintances along with the few friends we have."

"Let's plan it now. It will certainly occupy our minds."

"Indeed it will."

With the party planned and breakfast finished Joanna tells me, "The only thing truly upsetting me is this is the first time I will not be there to send him off."

"Would watching Louise go out to sea from Willow suffice?"

"You're brilliant. I'll call Emily."

"I'll pay the check." I throw money on the table and join Joanna. "What did she say?"

"Nothing. She gasped and hung up."

"Then we had better go." We wave to Sam and open the door to see it will be light soon. We speed.

Standing on Willow's deck with binoculars and a camera around my neck waiting, we look at each other and get tickled. Emily put on sailing attire without being told and it looks like we planned this in advance instead of being a spur-of-the-moment decision.

It's 6:30 and the sun is getting brighter by the second when we hear the tug boats communicating. Then Joanna asks me, "Geneviève, do you know there is a 99% chance you will see Trevor?"

"What?"

"His station is on the right side of the island."

"My entire attitude just changed. Where are Mitch and William?"

"Mitch stays in the middle and William is on his left, so we won't see them."

"I know Trevor. He will glance over here to look at Gypsy and Willow. Once he gets past the surprise of seeing us he will discreetly alert them."

Emily tells us, "I had such a good feeling about this on the drive here." Then we all wait quietly for Louise to round the curve.

A few minutes pass then her bow appears. I grab my binoculars and look through them waiting for the island to appear. Then it hits me, "Ladies, we are going to distract them." Joanna responds. "And because they are highly trained officers they will handle it. How, we will soon find out."

And there he is, my husband, alert with head held high. Then as I predicted he glances at the marina and tilts his head as he slowly moves to the glass. I lower my binoculars and wave, causing him to cover his mouth. This apparently gets Mitch's attention, because soon he is standing next to Trevor who has raised his pair of binoculars to look at me through. Next he hands them to Mitch. I take a snapshot and after maybe 30 seconds of looking at Joanna he lowers them and places his hand over his heart. I see him say something to Trevor as he turns around and walks off. Trevor stays and after I take another snapshot William appears. He stands next to Trevor and I quickly get one more shot then he looks through the binoculars at his wife. Trevor places his hand over his heart and lingers a moment then turns and goes to his station. I watch him until he goes out of sight.

Standing between Joanna and Emily with our arms around each other's waists we watch Louise disappear into the horizon. Joanna says, "This is one of those moments in life we will never forget. Geneviève, thank you for this." Emily softly adds, "It is. Thank you, Geneviève." I respond, "It was my pleasure. Let's go aboard Gypsy where it's warm below and get a glass of water to wash down the sea spray." They laugh and off we go.

Sitting in the galley after speculating about what the fellas must have said about their little surprise Joanna stops smiling and asks, "I need to get something off my chest. Do either of you mind if I get serious for a moment?" Emily and I shake our heads. "I've sent Mitch off for over two decades, but this will be the first time I send him off to war and this is your first time to send your husband's off period. I've been wondering how we're going to keep our sanity and now without a doubt I know that by being together we will get through it. I want us to make a promise to each other, no matter what the hour, if we are having a weak moment we will call on each other for strength."

"I promise you both I will, without hesitation, pick up the phone." Emily says, "I promise." After Joanna promises she reaches for our hands. "Now, let's go put on our Sunday Best and go have a delectable meal with one of the clubs finest bottles of champagne served by our dear Joseph." So we go our separate ways and meet at the club where we do have a delectable meal with excellent champagne and finish off with chocolate mousse Joseph had the Pâtissier make for me. We delay leaving at his request in order to be his last table and drink Louis XIII compliments of Joseph.

We agree to meet at the new Point Loma light house to watch for their return while waiting on the valets to bring our cars and when I get home I change into my darkroom attire. I turn on the safelight and the bulb isn't even warm yet when I turn it off and come right back out. Trevor isn't in it and I don't want to be in it without him. I pick up the phone and call Joanna. Emily is already there and they have been waiting on my call. I change back into my Sunday Best and go to the base where Joanna entertains us with the photographs of their wedding taken in a beautiful cathedral in Paris and the reception at the home her family lived in. Time flies and we go out to the cars with sodas. Emily gets in Joanna's car and we are on our way.

The new lighthouse is on the tip of the peninsula at the mouth of the bay, so we will be able to see the strike group when they crest the horizon about 12 miles away. It will take off several minutes of dangling in suspense. Also from here we are higher and almost even with the island that will be across the flight deck from us. We will be able to see the fellas standing on the bridge on her approach and they can stay at their stations to see us.

At the Point four cars are already here with women milling about. I pass them and get closer to the cliffs edge. Joanna parks next to me and I get out my picnic blanket to place on the hood to keep our cameras and binoculars from scratching the paint. As we put the blanket down I go back in time to the day Louise arrived and how Joanna was not able to recognize me. It seems as if it was a long time ago and so much has changed. The main thing is, this time I am waiting on my husband to arrive.

Unfortunately time is not flying, because we are wondering if they encountered the Japanese sub spotted off the coast of Mexico. Joanna knows about it too due to the fact the next day that bit of information was on the front page of *The Times*, because it spread like a wildfire the powers that be could not control. We barely speak and keep scanning the horizon. Eventually Joanna sighs and lowers her arms. Emily says, "There is no blood in my arms." Joanna responds, "Same here. Our Geneviève is used to holding a camera up. I'm not the only woman scanning the surface for a periscope am I?" Emily and I dry reply, "Nope." in unison.

Soon after the conversation my arms get tired and leave me no choice but to lower them. When I do I exhale in relief and we decide to take turns. It helps the time go by and we each have taken several turns when we hear the faint sound of the surveillance aircraft from the base. This means the strike group is getting close, but that is all we know. After dangling in suspense far too long I finally spot the top of the island and announce, "I see her island. Nothing has happened to them."

Tears are about to well in my eyes when it occurs to me I am going to see something I haven't seen, the strike group, and then slowly it comes into sight. Louise is surrounded. There is a destroyer at her bow, two heavy cruisers and eight destroyers by her sides then a cruiser, a destroyer and the submariner are astern. These are the ships that protect her and they appear formidable.

When the group gets within a mile or so, the ships at her port side drop back as the destroyer slows its speed and drops back to that side, then Louise slowly makes her way passed them. Of course she comes in first. I am going to have to be careful how many photographs I take. There will not be a good time to change my roll of film for I do not want to take my eyes off this extraordinary performance.

Louise draws near to the mouth of the bay and I pick up my binoculars hoping to see Trevor. And I do. He is very small at the distance he is at, but I know what my husband's body looks like. Not to mention I know approximately where he is on the bridge when Louise is underway. I think I even see William.

Trevor is looking through binoculars scanning the area and when he looks to his left he shifts his body to the left. He sees the cars and perhaps the blanket he knows so well. Then his binoculars seem to stare straight into mine and his mouth opens. He sees me. I lower my binoculars for him to be able to see my face and wave. Then Joanna says, "Umm ... I think Trevor has spotted you, Darling." And out of the corner of my eye I see her and Emily wave as I raise my binoculars then see his incredible smile. Soon we can see them all with our eyesight and when they are about to pass us the fellas touch the visors of their covers.

While the other ships enter the bay we hug each other and get in our cars. When I place my hands on the steering wheel they begin to tremble. It's over, the worrying is over and the toll it has taken on me is visible.

Pulling into the garage the thought of going into the house does not appeal to me in the least, so I go to my grandparent's house to help cook the Sunday dinner. The moment I walk into the kitchen alone Grand-mamma says, "Alas, the reason for my melancholy explained. Trevor, where is he?" I reply, "In the bay aboard Louise. He left at five o'clock this morning to take her out for a training exercise." Grand-papa asks, "In these perilous waters?" I nod and they comfort me. This is when my parents step into the doorway and Father asks, "What do we not know?" Grand-mamma answers him and I watch their hearts sink. Mother gathers herself and holds me. Next we hear Théo ask, "What did we miss? Where's Trevor?" He slightly startles us, because we didn't hear him and Rachel enter the house.

This time Father answers his questions then Rachel gasps and Théo sort of takes me away from Mother. "Gené, why didn't you tell us yesterday?"

"I didn't want the family to be worried the entire night and day."

"So, you went through this alone?"

"No, Joanna called me to meet her for breakfast right after Trevor left. Then we decided to sneak and see them off aboard Willow at the marina and Emily joined us."

"Sneak?"

"In case the enemy was watching no one was allowed on the pier to send them off. It would have alerted them Louise and her strike group were going out. The men had been boarding the ships in small groups for days."

Rachel, who had been slowly making her way over to my grandfather, begins to gush, "One day we were playing Hide and Seek and now we're really hiding." The poor thing begins to fight tears and Grandfather puts his arms around her.

Sitting in the drawing room after dinner on the settee without Trevor I get an overwhelming urge to go home. I have no idea what time he will return and I want to be there ready and waiting for him. Théo offers to escort me and at my request he settles for giving me my kiss instead. On the way it occurs to me this is the first time I have been unescorted after Sunday dinner. Either Théo or Trevor has been at my side for as long as I can remember. Why did I do this?

Aggravated I go into the dressing room and undress myself, which is depressing and try to think what Trevor would like to see me in and when I notice my reflection in the mirror I know. Wearing only a slip and being barefooted has always made him happy. So, I pour a glass of orange brandy, wrap the quilt on the sofa around me and go into the solarium to wait for my husband.

For years I have sat in my parent's solarium alone star gazing and was perfectly happy, but that isn't the case now. I miss Trevor like never before. This has been just one day and I fought the entirety of it to keep my wits about me. In two weeks he will be gone for at least six months. What am I am going to do? I was consumed with fear before he left this morning and until he returned to the bay. This was just a taste of what is to come and it is bitter indeed.

This man has become part of every aspect of my life. Before we were married he began dressing me and tucking me in. Now I go to sleep and wake up with him by my side. We cook breakfast in the morning then we shower together at night. And as he said he would, he kisses me every time he gets the opportunity even if it is for a split second, he kisses me. I am going to miss running my fingers through his soft hair and the sounds he makes. I am going to yearn for the weight of his body on mine as we make love. And I have no clue as to how I am going to make it through what will seem like an eternity without him.

Holding the quilt tightly in my hand with my thoughts running away with me I hear the door of the solarium open. The second I see Trevor I leap to my feet and the quilt falls onto the rug. "There she is." As we close the space between us he tells me, "I knew this is where you would be." Then into each other's arms we go. Just when I am on the verge of tears of relief he whispers, "I missed you. Did you miss me?" And he makes me laugh.

I look into his eyes and caress his face then notice it's freshly shaven. "You shaved?"

"After the briefings I went to my quarters to unpack a few things. When I got out my shaving kit I realized I hadn't shaved since 0400 hours and my razor stubble would take away from this moment." Next he runs his cheek along mine and kisses me with more passion than I expect. When he drops the strap of my slip off my shoulder and begins to kiss my neck he gets tickled. "You taste salty. Louise can stir up a spray. We'll talk about seeing you and the red blanket again later. For now I want to have a long, hot shower with you, take you to our bed and make you moan until you need a drink of water."

"I'll get the water while you warm the shower stall."

He gives me a kiss and softly says, "Thank you for wearing the slip. You were a vision to a man who was aching for his wife." Then we go inside and I eventually need a drink of water and so does he.

CHAPTER TWENTY-TWO

Since I am off and he is on duty, our morning begins with me taking him to Louise's pier for the first time and I drive Blanca, because we have been taking his car almost every day to the base for weeks. And when we arrive, the pier has traffic. This is when I find out how many married men are aboard Louise and her escorts. There are even two transport buses unloading.

Trevor has me pull up to where he goes onto the pier to drop him off and before he gets out we hear knocking on the trunk and William appears at my window. He tells me Emily is home at a loss for what to do, so he suggests I go keep her company. Trevor urges me to commit a social crime and gets out. I watch him go aboard with William for entertainment then leave to commit my social crime by dropping by at Emily's unannounced.

When I park Blanca in the driveway Emily is outside before I get out. No doubt she heard my girl's engine gearing down as I drove up. The moment I am standing in the driveway Emily gives me a hug and tells me, "Boy, am I happy to see you."

"William told me you would be."

"I love him. Let's go inside and I'll call Joanna to ask her to join us for a cup of coffee and to cook up a plan for something to do today."

Halfway through our cup of coffee Emily tells us she wants to go shopping, but the shops don't open until 10 o'clock. Joanna reminds us the commissary is always open and it would be a good time to buy supplies for if and when there is an emergency power outage by the city that was just announced in *The Times*. There is also the chance the blackout ordinances will be in place until the war ends and based on the amount of countries Germany occupies in Europe, military analysts predict it could last at least two more years.

Being a secretary Emily gets up and returns with a steno pad and pencil to make a list and make a list we do: six hurricane lanterns with extra wicking, six quarts of lamp oil, candles in all sizes, three propane stoves with extra propane in case they turn off the gas to our ranges and cans of meat and canned vegetables. Then we will get lunch from Micheletto's and after we eat with the fellas it is on to the shops. We have a plan.

Since I have never seen a place to buy propane stoves I decide to get three more for my family and we go into the parking lot pushing three full carts and pulling a fourth. I drove the wrong car this morning, because we have to load a third of my purchases behind Blanca's seats, on the passenger seat and strap two stoves onto the luggage rack. When our carts are finally empty it is time to go to Micheletto's. We order two large bottles of Pellegrino, six house salads, three large pepperoni pizzas and an Italian Cream Cake then sit at the bar eating calamari with a glass of Italian Rosato while we wait.

At the Mitchell's the food goes in first and while we are unloading Joanna's car the fellas arrive. Mitch looks around and says, "No need to be concerned about our wives being prepared." The fellas finish unloading her car and we go inside to set out lunch. When they are done Mitch goes to his wife. "You should be rewarded. How does dinner at the club and going to the movie theater sound."

"I'll see what's showing."

"Does it matter?" She shakes her head. I smile at Trevor while Emily blushes and then while we eat, the ladies tell the fellas our plans for the rest of the day.

Joanna and Emily follow me to the den where I simply get my other car and we shop at every place women shop and Bertucci's for the fellas. Since war rationing will begin to increase, we by everything in leather that catches our eye and all the other things women have to wear. Due to Hilda telling me what was rationed in Great Britain we know exactly what to buy. She mentioned the lingerie rationing bothered her most, so we hit that shop the hardest.

When Joanna mentions Emily and I need to think about the future and the need for maternity clothing, things take an entertaining turn. When the sales clerk in the department store inquires who is expecting Joanna quickly tells her Emily and I both are. Emily blushes almost the entire time we are there, Joanna's eyes sparkle and I barely refrain from getting tickled, several times.

Back at the pier we get out of our cars to wait on the fellas and when they appear I watch Trevor go through the process of coming ashore and am delighted I had the presence of mind to get out my camera. I of course photograph them all then we stay in the parking lot for a few minutes then get on our way.

Diving off Trevor says, "I can feel the extra weight in this vehicle. May I suggest going to Mandarin Garden's for me to get up the strength to unload?" While laughing I give him a kiss. Plus we haven't been there since we saved it.

After the attack on Pearl Harbor Trevor found out the government intended to place Japanese people living on the entire coast in internment camps. The Ehara's, owners of the restaurant, are third and fourth generation Americans. Their ancestors made their fortune during the rice growing boom of the early 1900's in Sacramento Valley and they moved here in the 20's. So, Trevor had Robert pull some strings to protect them and I called Mr. Collins to have his team of agents search their homes and the restaurant to keep other agents from tossing the places. He did tell me he was in my debt.

Since their homes are in La Jolla they are well respected and the restaurant has not been vandalized. Théo, who passes by it often and has eaten there since the attack, told us locals still go, along with the few Japanese in San Diego that have not been sent off yet.

Soon after we order Mr. Ehara walks to our table carrying an old bottle of sake followed by our server. He bows and we bow. "Please forgive the intrusion. I offer you both this sake in appreciation for what I cannot say." He bows, we bow and he is gone. Trevor places his hand on his ribbons and tells the server he is not drinking tonight, which is why he ordered us water. The server bows, tells us he will inform Mr. Ehara and the bottle will be at the hostess podium.

After dinner Mr. Ehara returns and tells us dinner is his compliments and asks if we would enjoy a stroll in the garden. As Trevor accepts the invitation I am so excited I almost lose my composure. Mr. Ehara escorts us to the entrance, unlocks the door and opens it. There is more bowing and then we enter another world.

The beauty of the garden and the sound of flowing water are still with us, therefore I place my head on his shoulder and we ride home in silence. When he parks in our garage he loosens his tie and collar then pulls me over him and we go parking in our garage.

After our new morning routine I go right back to our den for it is Tuesday and we have lunch alone, plus tomorrow is New Year's Eve and this is his last day to report for duty before being deployed. There is much to be done, because I have decided to bake a batch of cookies to go with the PBJ I think he has craving in his subconscious since the day he was reunited with his mum.

The first thing I do is change out of my clothes into a slip, because I am going to surprise him by wearing a dress. Then the baking begins. Flour is everywhere and cookies are cooling as I get out the bread, peanut butter and boysenberry jam.

With the sandwiches made I fill my thermos with cold milk and go to select a dress while the cookies cool a little longer. In our dressing room I glace at the clock and gasp. I've been using a timer and had no idea I was behind schedule. I get the dress I planned to wear and button part of it on the way to the kitchen. After I wrap everything and toss them into a paper bag, I grab the thermos and dash down to the garage. It is time to speed.

Pulling into the parking lot at the pier I can see everyone with Trevor waiting on me. I'm not late, but have only one minute to spare. He spots me and the others get in their cars and wave as I pass by. When Trevor gets in the car he inhales deeply through his nostrils. "You smell like ... warm cookies. Now I know why you were almost late, you baked cookies. You are going to get a big kiss when I park this car."

"Hello to you too." He laughs his deep laugh and drives to our parking spot on the base and the instant he parks I do indeed get a big kiss and he inhales my skin.

"Mm mm mm, you do smell good. What else is in that bag?"

"Something you want and don't know it." I hand him the sandwich and we can smell the peanut before he unwraps it and his head goes back as he laughs.

"A PBJ. You are spot-on. I have wanted one of these for months. Hand me the thermos and I'll pour the cold milk I know is in there. Are you going to whet my appetite more by telling me what kind of cookies you baked?"

"The recipe box from Mitch's parent's had recipes from their cook in it."

"You baked me pecan sandies. I love you." I burst into laughter.

When we finish eating our sandwiches he begins to look around. "Why have we been eating in the parking lot instead of here?"

"Habit. Want a cookie?" He gives me a look.

Trevor savors four cookies while I eat only two, because I ate two straight out of the oven when the pecans had cooled enough to eat. I learned a hard lesson in my youth that pecans hold heat longer than the rest of the cookie.

At the pier we get out to join the others for a brief chat about tomorrow and for him to brag I baked *the* pecan sandies for his lunch and then we watch the fellas go aboard Louise. When I inform Joanna and Emily I have to pick up my gown for the gala they gasp and send me on my way.

All my errands are checked off the list as I return to the base for Trevor. I can see Louise in the distance and I know he is there winding things up before he comes ashore. I park close as possible, get my camera and go wait with Emily and Joanna. They greet me and barely take their eyes off the gangway. And there he is, with an accelerated pace going across the flight deck. He turns to look for me and when our eyes meet he gives me that incredible smile of his.

I take snapshots of him until he is close and lower my camera. "Ladies, your husband's asked me to tell you they are being detained. We will see you at the club tomorrow. For now I am going home with my lovely wife." Trevor reaches for my hand, kisses it and leads me to the car.

He keeps looking in the rearview mirror after we drive though the gates. "I can't see the base, which means they can't see me." He pulls into a parking lot near a tree and tosses his cover in the back seat. He gives me a wink and opens the car door to get out. Soon his jacket goes by my head followed by his tie and shirt then he gets back in with a gleam in his eyes. "Geneviève, I am yours for nine whole days. What do you want to do with me?"

I look into those blue eyes and think. Then it comes to me and with the lilt in my voice he cannot resist I tell him, "Take you hostage."

"I won't resist."

"I knew you wouldn't when I spotted you. That is why I chose you."

"Lucky me."

"Drive please, while I decide what to do with you."

"Yes, ma'am." And to the den we go.

Pulling up to the garage we notice a package sitting under the mail box and Trevor says, "That's a mood changer."

"What is it?"

"My books from Aunt Meredith."

Trevor shakes his head and opens the car door. While he brings in the box I get his things from the back seat and he lowers the garage door. Up the stairs we go and into the living room where he sets the box on the coffee table. Trevor takes out his pocket knife and has a seat. I sit by his side as he opens it. "Let's see what she sent this time." He removes the newspaper packed around them and starts laughing as he looks at the spines of six books. "Apparently telling Aunt Meredith how much I enjoyed being at the ranch and showing up in our Western gear when we took the bus to the park swayed her decision making. Half of these are Westerns." I get tickled and he reads the spines to me. "*The Virginian* by Owen Wister, *Trail Smoke* by Ernest Haycox and *The Ox-Bow Incident* by Walter Van Tilburg Clark. I won't be saying that name twice."

Trevor takes all the books out one by one and reads the synopsis out loud. When he sets down the last one he looks at me with a raised eyebrow. "So, back to me being your hostage." Laughing I tell him, "I'll get you some bread and water." He grabs me by my waist and pins me on the sofa with his body. "I would rather have an apple." And our mood changes again.

The next day is his first day off and New Year's Eve, therefore we sleep until we wake up. My hostage is very playful. He nibbles on my neck before we get up, while we cook breakfast and wash the dishes that include the ones from last night. Then he wants to dance as if we are at The O Club with the addition of kissing me. When he takes a turn to passion I have to remind him my ball gown exposes my shoulders. This does not deter him in the least. He kneels, lifts my slip and kisses my abdomen. I remember the first time he did this and before I can finish my thought I find myself on our bed raising my hips for him.

The fire he started later is roaring when his stomach growls and I am still weak, so he tells me, "I'm going to heat a can of the beef and vegetable soup you bought. I shan't be long." And I lie in our bed listening to the sounds coming from the kitchen my husband is making and I feel a slight twinge in my heart. Soon I won't hear him making sounds around the house; our days together are numbered before the Navy takes him away from me.

While I stack pillows for us Trevor returns with a tray and when he sets it down I get up and hold his face in my hands then give him an Eskimo Kiss. I slowly stop and whisper, "I love you, Trevor."

"I love you too, Baby. I love you too."

After we eat I place my head on his chest to listen to his heart beat and we hold each other and talk. Keeping an eye on the time I eventually tell him, "Trevor, you have loved on me since we woke up and given me so much pleasure. Even though it isn't time to begin getting ready for the gala I would like for us to get in the shower. I want to bathe you and I want to give you pleasure." Trevor kisses me and we go shower. The room is filled with steam by the time he has to place his hand on the wall of the shower stall.

In the dressing room, still wrapped in towels we have our last passionate kiss for the year. Then he puts on his robe and I slip into my dressing gown. While he gets my jewelry out of the safe I put my hair up. When he returns Trevor kneels beside me and sets the box on my vanity and opens it. After we admire the jewelry he asks, "Is there anything else I need to do for you?"

"Not a thing, thank you."

Trevor kisses me, stands up then gets out two garment bags and sets his shoes in the hallway. "I'll be waiting in the living room." And he goes to our bedroom to put on the only uniform I haven't seen, his white tie Formal Dress.

My lips are stained and my ears are dripping in diamonds and I cannot get my ball gown on fast enough to go see Trevor. I stand in front of the mirror as I step into the black satin skirting then put on the black velvet outer layer with large satin covered buttons, glance at my appearance, grab my evening bag and gloves then slip on my black satin pumps in the hallway. I peek round the corner into the living room and he is standing in front of the fire with his hands behind his back warming them which makes him look as if he is standing at parade rest.

Trevor is more handsome than I imagined. The gold cummerbund he wore for our wedding has been replaced by a white waistcoat, the black bow tie by a white one along with Mother-of-Pearl studs and I am guessing matching cuff links instead of gold ones. I realize while soaking him in I have moved to where he can see me, because he smiles and says, "There she is, the woman I married."

As he walks toward me with his hand extended I gush, "Trevor, you look so handsome I'm not sure how to act." He chuckles.

"Take my hand and let me look at you." I slip my hand onto his. "Geneviève, you have surpassed my expectations and they were high. You are beautiful and this gown is beyond words. I do love seeing you in black and it buttons. He steps closer and places his hand on my waist and slides it around to my back. "We are going to be in public and I am not going to be able to keep my hands off of you in this velvet."

"Oh ... I won't mind. Not one bit. We are married and I am yours, tonight more than ever."

Trevor caresses my face and then he looks a little puzzled. "I just realized you're not wearing the necklace. May I ask why?"

"I decided it would be in your way."

"You spoil me so." Trevor carefully gathers me into his arms and tenderly kisses my lips, neck and shoulders. We are interrupted by the clock as it chimes once, which means it's 6:30 already. We go to the coat closet and I get out a hooded black velvet cape lined in black silk then hand it to him. As he drapes it over my shoulders he asks, "This is truly sumptuous. Why haven't I seen it?"

"I only wear it on New Year's Eve." I slide the French knot through the loop at my neck and turn around.

"Words fail me." and he slides his hands down my arms through the velvet and sighs. "We're pressed for time, so if you will excuse me." I nod and he goes into the kitchen. I hear noises as I put on my gloves and he says, "I thought you should see me in my full glory as an officer this evening." I gasp, because I know he is putting on his Bridge coat. I saw a photograph of an admiral on the front page of *The Halyard* wearing one last winter. This full length overcoat is impressive. It is navy blue with eight gold buttons on the front in four rows and shoulder boards.

Trevor steps into sight and there he is, in his full glory, which includes a white scarf and gloves. "Commander Trevor Lyons reporting for duty, ma'am."

Walking toward him I take off a glove and place my hand on his cheek. "Trevor, what is it you said that day on the mountain? — Heaven help me."

He laughs, kisses the palm of my hand and asks, "How soon do you want to leave the gala?"

"Since there is not a fireworks show tonight, after the first dance following the stroke of midnight."

"And so we shall."

I put on my glove, he cups my elbow with his hand and out onto the balcony we go. I stop cold in my tracks when I see a limousine parked behind The Chariot. "That is for us and Elliot is in the driver's seat. I intend to throw caution to the wind tonight and celebrate like never before by drinking Louis XIII and champagne until I feel the effects of it. And I am hoping you will join me."

"It is said alcohol intensifies one's emotions."

"Which is the other reason I hired Elliot, I want my hands on you and not the steering wheel." I give him a come-hither look and we descend the steps.

Trevor opens the doors to my grandparent's house and everyone, including Joseph and Claudette, are in the foyer. He immediately says, "Pardon our tardiness." Mother responds, "It is nothing. I predicted you would be wearing that coat and we all wanted to see you in your splendor. In fact I am going to ask you both to pose for a photograph." Father hands her a camera, we pose and Mother takes the photograph then kisses our cheeks. Next they all go into the drawing room. After he hangs our outerwear in the coat closet we join them and Grand-papa hands us a glass of Louis XIII. Trevor scans the room and says, "In all my years I have never seen such opulence. Everyone looks grand." My grandfather raises his glass, "To our wives." The men raise theirs and they drink to us.

Our glasses are empty and Grand-papa and Father drape fur stoles onto their wives while Théo and Joseph assist their wives into evening coats made to match their ball gowns. Joseph's eyes literally sparkle. And we are ready to go.

When Elliot turns into the parking lot we stop kissing. Trevor lowers the partition and asks him to have the car out front at 12:20. In the lobby the only lights on are the ones in the coat check area and trophy case where we all gather in front of to look at the new trophy for Gypsy and the photograph of her crew. Next I hear a familiar voice say, "There they are." It's Emily. Trevor and I turn around and there are Mitch and William, also wearing their Bridge coats with their lovely wives by their side. Where is Kyle when I need him?

Emily is wearing an ice blue satin ball gown, her diamond earrings and a necklace that matches them. William must have given it to her for Christmas. Her hair is up in order for all to see them along with her shimmering shoulders. She looks like the woman she is.

Rachel must have mentioned the color she was going to wear tonight to Théo, which explains the sapphire jewelry suite he gave her for Christmas. Joanna is wearing emerald green satin and a jewelry suite that goes with the ring she wears. When Joanna turns around for our short parade to The Hall, we all see her bare back. Now I know why Mitch has been beaming since he took off her mink stole.

The Hall is transformed into a place that immediately puts one into the mood to celebrate if you weren't already. There is a three deep layer of white, silver and gold balloons with long matching streamers on the ceiling and clusters of them tied to urns are along the walls and on the stage. Silver and gold confetti is sprinkled on the tables from the bowls around the centerpiece of a gold mercury glass vase filled with white hydrangeas. And best of all we are greeted by servers with trays of champagne, which Trevor happily hands me a glass of. When he picks up one for himself we make our glasses sing. And the celebration begins.

For our dining experience Chef has us feast on Imperial White caviar, Lobster Newburg, roasted winter vegetables and a dark chocolate tart filled with milky caramel over a dark chocolate sable, all served with champagne. At the end of the meal Eric and his staff arrive with glasses of Louis XIII and he announces they are courtesy of Captain and Mrs. Everett Mitchell. He beat Grand-papa to the punch so to speak, this delights everyone and I adore them even more.

As soon as my grandparent's stand to dance Joseph is on his feet with his hand extended to Claudette. At long last he is going to dance at our gala with the woman who had his heart the moment they met. I look at Trevor and he knows I want to watch them, so he kisses my hand and puts his arm around my shoulders. Then everyone else decides to do the same. Trevor takes the opportunity to have a bottle of Roederer brought out for us. I'm going to get tipsy with my husband.

After several dances and we are seated I begin to admire the fellas then ask my crew if they would mind posing for photographs between two urns of balloons. They too think it is a good idea and Trevor motions for Kyle. Going to a secluded spot William comments he is concerned someone is going to step on one of the trains of our ball gowns, because people are drinking more than usual. We, the ladies, quickly glance over our shoulders to see if one is in danger and the fellas get a laugh as we cling to their arms due to this fact, your head snaps back and you lose your balance if it happens.

When we return to the table Grand-mamma asks for us all to pose together on one side of it. The men seat the women and stand by us and Kyle blinds us three times. With the spots we were seeing gone we all go to the dance floor and changing of partners begins with Father asking Joseph if he may cut in, so Mother may dance with him for the first time. Before I can react Théo taps Trevor on the shoulder and suddenly I am being taken for a spin.

Back in my husband's arms we notice servers milling about filling glasses with champagne and others are with their wives and girlfriends. It must be close to midnight; therefore we make our way back to the table. Trevor pours the last of our champagne as the conductor taps his baton. Just as the countdown begins he says, "Geneviève, count for us." I nod and start the count, "Cinq, quatre, trois, deux, un." Then we kiss with passion, because no one is looking and it is our first for the new year.

"I love you, Geneviève."

"I love you, Trevor."

"Happy New Year, Baby."

"Happy New Year, Mon Amour."

We make our glasses sing once more and drink then Trevor gets a handful of confetti and tosses it high into the air above us, so high that it falls down slowly sprinkling us in gold and silver as he gives me a lingering kiss.

Next I feel a hand on the small of my back and hear Théo say, "Happy New Year, Gené." I turn around, he kisses my forehead and then I hug Rachel. That is the beginning of hugs and kisses on cheeks that last the entire time "Auld Lang Syne" is played.

Back by my husband's side he tells me, "I put in a request for the next song." and leads me to the dance floor. Trevor takes a stance, nods to the conductor and our Nocturne begins to play. As we glide around the dance floor I feel the champagne and tell him, "Trevor, avec toi je veux faire l'amour." He begins slowing us down as he translates. "With me you want — faire, to make. You want to make love with me." Trevor stops dancing, looks into my eyes and leads me to our table. Joanna gives me my evening bag and he escorts me through the doors while our song continues to play.

In the morning while sitting in my spot across his lap after a very late breakfast I ask Trevor, "What do you want to do on your days off?"

"What would you like to do, Baby?"

"Thank you for asking, but Trevor I'm not going to be out at sea six months."

"Hm ... point made. — I would like to see the rest of the zoo. I always watch a movie, no matter what's showing. — We didn't get to go parking on the cliffs. Would you like to go on a date with me tomorrow?"

"Yes I would."

"Also, I really do want to finish reading our book."

"Oh good, you can be my soft chair."

"Your soft chair? How long have you been calling me that?"

"Since the first time you read to me on our honeymoon."

"That's the night you let me touch you and give you your first climax. The next night you let me taste you. Then you followed me into the shower and asked to touch me."

"After that I had such a moment of clarity. You were being so tender I knew that when we made love you would be so careful nothing would happen to me."

"And the next night you asked me to make love with you. It was merely our fourth day as husband and wife. Fortunately I had touched you and tasted you and became very familiar with your body, so I knew if I gently pressed my body against you, there was a chance it would be everything we wanted and perhaps more."

"It was so much more."

"Yes it was. — I was so relieved I didn't harm you and I was able to give you pleasure."

"It was because we did what you said. We took our time to get to know each other physically. And you thought it through just like you did for my first kiss."

"Then soon after that night we were sitting on the sofa, like we are now, and you decided to get adventurous."

"And you tried to talk me out of it."

"And you talked me into it by telling me I would be able to hold you in my arms while we made love." Suddenly I find myself in his loving embrace.

Finally Trevor makes a noise that sounds as if he is frustrated. "Geneviève, I do not want this moment to end yet, but my legs are going numb." I get tickled and give him a kiss then get off his lap. "I've thought of something else I would like to do, buy seat cushions for these chairs." I burst into laughter. "I'm going to sit here and wait for the circulation to return to my legs. So, is there something we can do today?"

I stop laughing and respond, "We can go to the zoo."

"I didn't expect it to be open."

"They only close on Christmas. The animals have to be fed every day and since most people are recovering from last night there will be just a few visitors."

"Suddenly I'm craving a hot dog from the stand I spotted. Help me up." I am of little use. Laughter makes me weak, so I tug on him as he stands on his own.

The parking lot close to the zoo is almost empty and Trevor has a glint in his eyes. I expect him to pull me across him, but instead he begins kissing me and slowly pushes me over until I'm cornered on the passenger side. After a few minutes he stops and asks, "Are you ready?" And before I answer him he slides over to the driver's side taking me with him. He is playful again.

With my camera around my neck I lead to where we left off, the lion's den, and this time we make it to the jaguars. Two are on the highest rock lying in the sun and out of the blue he starts talking to them. "Allow me to introduce myself." And they look at us. "My name is Trevor and this lovely woman is my wife, Geneviève. She owns a car with a hood ornament of a jaguar that looks as if he is leaping from the hood. It's eye-catching, but it pales in comparison to the beauty of you and your mate." The large male looks at us and begins to make several short roars that echo through the zoo. When silence falls Trevor says, "Please tell me you captured that on film."

"I captured that on film." I get a kiss and we move on.

When we get hungry Trevor happily leads me to the hot dog stand. "What do you like on your hot dog, Baby?"

"Umm ... I've never eaten a hot dog."

Trevor has a look of disbelief. "But you went to all those high school games."

"I was working; therefore I ate dinner before going. I'll have what you have."

"Three with sauerkraut, light on one and two colas, please."

We sit on a bench and Trevor watches me as I smell the hot dog then I tell him, "Trevor anything is downhill after getting up the nerve to eat escargot as a child." He laughs, takes a big bite of his and I take a small bite of mine. "This isn't bad and it's kind of fun to eat." Trevor beams, "That's my girl." And he eats both of his while I eat mine. Then he tells me, "After a few minutes I'm ready to get the sour taste out of my mouth. Where is The Confectionery from here?" I lead the way and get a large piece of dark chocolate almond bark. He gets the same. The taste the sauerkraut left in my mouth requires a serious dessert to overcome it.

Next he takes the lead and heads toward the carousel. Business is so slow Charlie is in the booth with his wife. They light up and Charlie stands as Trevor buys 10 tickets. Walking to the carousel I ask, "You want to ride this five times."

"I want one of us to grab the brass ring and since we are alone it's going to take more than one." Charlie lets us in and when I am standing by my favorite horse Trevor puts his hands on my waist. "I know you don't need help to get on a carousel horse, but I want to." I give him a kiss and he helps me up. Trevor rides the one in front of me, because he knows I want snapshots.

Three minutes into the ride I have three iron rings on my thigh and there is one on the floor. Trevor hears it land and from that point we drop them on it. We are on our third ride and when I pull an iron ring out the brass one rolls down and I don't say a word. When we are near the arm he says, "I see the brass ring." then he grabs it. The ride ends and in his excitement Trevor dismounts and hands it to me. "Geneviève, would you like to get in the swan chariot with me for our last rides?" I give him a kiss and put my hands on his shoulders. "That's a yes."

When the rides are over and we have stolen a few kisses we go to pick up the iron rings. Charlie tells us, "I'll get those." then he breaks a roll of pennies in half and gives one to each of us and we are off to the booth where I chose a tan Teddy Bear, because he looks like Trevor in his khaki uniform, except he wears a black tie, not a bow. We thank Beatrice and walking away Trevor is beaming, because he finally won me a bear. I name him Fred and we go back to The Confectioners for our penny candy. There Trevor tells me, "I have one last thing I want to do, ride the little train." I have to lead the way.

The ride is half a mile and goes by statues of zoo animals that are close. Once again we are alone and we sit near the back. The seats are so small Trevor sits in one behind me and sits up with his arms around me. The conductor blows the horn and we are off. Up ahead we see the tunnel and Trevor says, "Ooo, a tunnel of love." And he kisses my neck until the sunlight gets bright again.

Being a bit tired we decide to eat at Mandarin Garden's and are pleased to see there are only a few empty tables and we are having an early dinner. On the way to our den Trevor tells me he wants to visit with Rachel and Théo this week. When he calls, to our delight Théo has taken tomorrow off and we are having lunch at their place. Next Trevor gets a fire going in our bedroom; we shower and get into our bed early for him to read to me. At the end of a chapter Trevor puts the book down and takes us back to the first time he became my soft chair.

The next morning we wake up starving and decide to get back in bed after we eat to rest and my husband I talk about yesterday and the highlights of it. Our decision is unanimous on the best highlight of the day, him winning Fred, who is sitting on the chair by our bed with Christopher and Celestyna.

This time we happily get up, because lunch with Rachel and Théo is next on our agenda. When we arrive Théo has the door open, the concierge announces all visitors, and he greets us with open arms. Something is up and while we are drinking an espresso following lunch we find out what. He holds Rachel's hand and says, "The building supervisor called me at work Tuesday and you two are going to be the first to know our extremely good news. The penthouse will officially be ours today. We're signing the papers to take ownership at 3:30."

Trevor and I are speechless and Rachel jumps in. "You could have knocked me over with a feather. I didn't even know he had put us on the waitlist. Not to mention the couple in it bought it less than two years ago." Trevor manages to say, "Congratulations. Did the husband get transferred?" Théo replies "Get this, he asked to be transferred to Denver. They can't deal with the blackout and will be gone by Saturday. We can go in Sunday and I can begin drafting the blueprints for the remodel Monday. — Is it too early for a champagne toast?" I reply, "It is never too early for a toast to celebrate an event such as this." Theo gets up and brings out a bottle of Cristal that was chilling in a bucket behind the drapes in the living room, which is where we move to and he fills us in on details.

Back at our den Trevor and I get ready for our date and we even dress up a bit. Upon our arrival at Micheletto's we discover it is a night that couples date on, Friday night. Thank goodness he made a reservation and now we know the movie theater is going to be packed. It's a good thing we planned on watching it and going parking instead, because we cannot be a make out couple tonight.

This evening we are not pretending to be teenagers, so Trevor orders a bottle of Asti Spumante to drink with our meal since we had champagne earlier. And he does not order a pizza, instead he orders fried baby artichokes to start and grilled quail for our main course. I find this out being served, because as usual he speaks Italian and I hang on every word. When the dish of chocolate gelato we share is empty and we are in the car I have to kiss him, because I know he tastes like chocolate and the first time he did is one of my fondest memories, the first time we went parking without intending to.

Neither of us checked to see what movie was being shown and we discover a comedy is being shown that premiered yesterday, so the lobby is overcrowded. We skip the concession stand in order to get a seat on the front row of the balcony. During the intermission he makes a dash to get us a cola, because the movie is making us laugh and oh so thirsty.

The credits roll while we wait for the crowd to clear and decide to skip getting a milkshake at Sam's and go straight to the cliffs where there is no artificial light and it makes the stars that are brightly shining sparkle on the ocean's surface even brighter. Trevor turns off the engine and cracks the window for us to hear the waves below as we sit with his arm around me and just listen to the sound of them crashing on the rocks.

In time he sighs from contentment then he whispers, "Geneviève." And I turn around in the seat. Tender kisses turn passionate in the blink of an eye and he begins to undo the buttons of my dress and discovers I am not wearing a slip or a bralette when his hand touches my bare breasts. He looks at me and starts the car then he turns the heat up. With his hand on a button he asks, "Do you mind if I undo a few more of these?" I go, "Mm mmm." And he does then he kisses the sides of my breasts. I softly moan then let out a sigh and he stops.

"Geneviève, I can hear your thoughts. And it would not be in poor taste to make love with me here. Times like these are delicate and we will lose it if we go home on the drive. It's dark and I will have to concentrate. Then this, what we are feeling now, will be lost."

"Trevor. Move us over."

My husband unbuttons the rest of my dress while kissing me and helps me up. I lift my left leg and he slides underneath me then he slides us across the seat toward the passenger side. I look into his eyes as I take his tie off and toss it on the back seat where our jackets are and pull his shirt tail out as I unbutton it. His undershirt and dog tags get tossed in the back along with everything else we do not need to be wearing.

When we are finally one my head goes back as my eyes close due to the warmth of our bodies. He puts his arms around me under my dress that is covering us and holds me still. I raise my head, fall into his eyes and kiss him with passion that is once again unbridled. When Trevor slides his hands up and around my back I know he is ready for me to move. Eventually our strength leaves our bodies and we rest in each other's arms.

On the way home Trevor spots a closed service station with a soda machine glowing by the entrance. He immediately turns in. We have empty bottles in the front seat by the time he parks in the garage.

In the morning we are awakened by the phone ringing and we are wide eyed. He answers it and says very few words before he puts down the receiver. "That was your grandmother. She asked me to bring a jar of strawberry jam."

"What she was really doing is making sure we're awake, so we aren't late for the farewell breakfast for Claudette and Joseph."

"Occasionally I think I will never get used to the two of you doing ... whatever it is you do." And we fling the covers almost onto the bench as we hastily get up. "Let the whirlwind begin. There goes our romantic morning in bed."

"We had a romantic evening in the car instead." I put my hand over my face as he pulls it away and gives me a kiss.

"I talked the gypsy into coming out."

"Yes you did ... you rascal."

"You haven't called me that in a while."

"You haven't been one a while."

"I'll have to do something about that." And there is a glint in his eyes.

Trevor gets the jam, I get a box of photographs and down the stairs we go then out the service entrance just in time to see Théo and Rachel drive up. He rolls down his window. "You two look frayed. Get in and catch your breath." Slowly driving to our grandparent's house Théo looks at Trevor in the rearview mirror and says, "Let me guess. You were asleep when Grand-mamma called and asked you to bring the jam." He nods. "We were asleep too when she called us." And he holds up a bouquet of flowers. "These are for Claudette, as if there aren't enough flowers around here for twenty bouquets." Trevor responds, "I bet there are two jars of this in her cupboard." Rachel glances over her shoulder and looks at him, "I will never get used to her ... keen intuition, but sometimes it comes in handy. I would have been so upset if we were late."

When we get out of the car all eyes go to where Joseph's car used to be parked. A few days ago he gave it to his friend from the orphanage to whom he gave the furnishings of his apartment to. Joseph has always been kind and generous in every way.

Sitting at the table looking at all of us together I hear the laughter, but I'm not sure what they are laughing about. This moment is bitter sweet. On one hand I am very happy for Claudette, the man who captured her heart years ago is now her husband and he is taking her home. As for Joseph, he is about to begin a new life with a family that is truly his. On the other hand, I will miss them so much.

Before we know it a horn blows outside. They hired two taxis to take them and their belongings to the railroad station and they're here. We all stand and file out the front door slowly. The men follow Claudette and Joseph up to their apartment and emerge with steamer trunks and luggage while we watch with hearts aching. Grand-mamma is going to be alone too much. Grand-papa should begin his semi-retirement soon. As for Mother, no one will be on the other side of the beds helping her change the linens and at the club the teenage boy who became a man under her watchful eye will no longer be there to dote on her.

The taxis are loaded, cheeks are kissed and hands are shaken. I give Claudette the box of photographs I had Mr. Blackwell print for them to look at on their trip that begin with the day she arrived and end with the one of the happy couple walking the torches the night they declared their love. When Théo hands her the bouquet of flowers she inhales their fragrance with closed eyes.

The driver of the taxi they are going to ride in is by an opened door. She stands by it and says, "We'll send post cards when we can on our trip." And she smiles at us and gets in. Joseph places his hand over his heart looking at Mother and then we watch them begin their journey home.

My grandfather cups Grand-mamma's elbow and says, "At Sunday dinner we will see you all." And he escorts her inside their house. Mother still hasn't moved and Father tells us, "It is time to escort my wife inside. We love each and every one of you." Mother nods and they are gone. Théo sighs heavily. "And that's our cue." He steps over to me and I get my kiss then Rachel kisses my cheeks while our husbands shake hands. Then Trevor I watch them drive off and find ourselves standing in the driveway alone.

"Geneviève, where do you want to go?"

"To our bench." He smiles and we walk to the garage.

We sit on our bench and since Trevor isn't wearing a uniform he puts his arm around me and we sort of cuddle. Lunch is almost two hours away and we are able to settle in. Trevor begins talking about his fondest memories here and I begin to feel better. In time a car like his pulls up to the curb and Mitch is inside. Approaching us he says, "Pardon the intrusion. Geneviève, I merely want to know how you are."

"I'm good under the circumstances and you are not intruding. In fact I'm happy to see you. How is Joanna?"

"She's fine. I think she would be delighted to see you both." And for the first time I see a true glint in his eyes and in a British accent he asks, "Fancy a visit?" I get tickled and Trevor tells him in a thick accent, "Go on ahead, mate. We shan't be long." We hear him chuckling as he returns to the car.

After waiting a few minutes to allow her to prepare for our visit we walk into the house and she exclaims, "Darling." After hugs and kisses Trevor goes to the refrigerator and get us colas then we sit at the table and find out what we missed after our abrupt departure from the gala. Eventually Mitch looks at his watch. "My wife and I were going to The O Club for lunch. Would you two like to join us?" I light up and look at Trevor who replies, "I believe that's a yes." And we are off.

When we step inside Harry is very happy to see us. "This is a pleasant surprise. I was hoping you all would drop by. Commander Snowden and his Mrs. did yesterday." Trevor responds, "We wouldn't have left without coming to see our favorite bartender."

"I'll be your waiter today. It's been slow around here during the day as you can see. Things pick up at night when the single officers trickle in."

Mitch replies, "Some things never change."

We sit in one of the booths even though there are only four of us, because it is comfortable and enjoy each other's company. While talking after dessert "Blue Skies" begins to play on the jukebox no doubt selected by one of the officers sitting at the bar. Trevor extends his hand to Joanna. "Mrs. Mitchell, let's go show off, shall we?" She puts her hand on his saying, "Yes, let's."

Mitch and I are watching them and my hands are clasped together on the table. He slowly exhales then puts his hand over them in order to stop me from rubbing them together, something I am unaware I was doing. I was smiling, but my subconscious knows Trevor is leaving.

"Geneviève." I stop watching them and look at him. "Joanna doesn't have a profession and her hobby isn't enough to fill the days; therefore I have a favor to ask. Even though I know you are going to do this, please spend as much time with her as you possibly can."

"I will." Then he gives me an adoring smile. "Mitch, do you know about the pact the three of us made?" He shakes his head. "At Joanna's behest we promised each other that no matter what time it was, day or night, if we are having a weak moment we will call on each other for strength."

"Thank you for sharing that with me. — Would you like to join them on the dance floor?"

"Please don't take this wrong, but I would rather sit here and watch them."

"Frankly, that's what I want do. I only asked to be polite." I burst into laughter and he holds his iced tea up to me.

The show offs return and Joanna, who is out of breath says, "I wish we could've called William and Emily, but I'll dance with him at the party." Her eyes get wide and Trevor's gleam. "I cannot believe I said that." I quickly tell Trevor, "Are you really going to sit there and pretend you didn't know about the surprise party for your birthday and make her feel bad for ruining it?" He finally breaks and gets tickled. Joanna swats him on his chest.

Harry brings the check; Mitch picks it up and insists we go on our way. Walking to the car Trevor tells me, "I'm glad the surprise party is out in the open, because now I can ask, is my family going to be there?"

"With bells on."

"I love you."

"I love you. Where would you like to go next?"

"For a drive until dusk. Afterwards I want to eat a pizza then I want to get in bed early to read our book. I'd like to know how it ends before I'm deployed." I nod and we get into the car and drive to places even I have never been. Then we eat a pizza and go home where he reads to me until we can't keep our eyes open.

Trevor wakes me up in the morning as he tightens his hold on me. A little time passes and I ask, "Have you decided what you would like to do today?"

"I want to go see Gypsy."

"You don't want to take her out?"

"I thought it would make you uncomfortable under the current circumstances."

"I'm not afraid of the Japanese subs. I'm a Navy wife."

"I love it when you talk to me like this."

"I know."

We get up and pack the picnic basket and Trevor leaves a note for my parent's under the Sunday paper still on their portico to let them know our course. Next we go to Sam's for breakfast and happily discover it looks normal. The blackout curtains are open and the sunlight is pouring in. Trevor and I sit in a booth next to a window and after we order Sam walks up and looks at us from head to toe. "I see you're going sailing. Not many people doing that lately. — We are alone and unafraid." Trevor nods. "Commander, Mrs. Lyons." Sam bows his head to me and walks away while I have an epiphany.

Trevor tells me, "You just earned his respect. That is a phrase Navy men say and he said it to include you."

"I've never heard that phrase. And there is truth in those words. Men in the Navy on hazardous duty are not on land where a rescue team is close by to save them. They are out in the expanse of the ocean in deep waters where danger cannot always be seen, which puts them at great risks. Yet they go willingly, knowing they will be out there alone. You are all such brave men."

Trevor silently reaches across the table for my hand and looks reassuringly into my eyes. After giving me a minute he asks, "Are you all right?" I nod slightly and repeatedly to reassure him and then I notice Annie is standing by the pickup window holding a tray trying to discreetly watch us. I tilt my head her way and Trevor lets go of my hand then we pick up our cups of coffee to let her know she may serve. I know the tray was getting heavy, because it was no longer stable.

Pouring the syrup over the stack of pancakes we are about to share I can see Trevor watching me intently. There is no need for me to be able to read his mind, because I know what he's thinking, it is going to be a while before he will watch me do this again. Similar thoughts will be in our minds over the next few passing days. I look up and smile at my husband acting as if my heart isn't aching.

Driving up to the gate at the marina Trevor's face lights up and when he parks the car he hops out and enthusiastically greets Gypsy while I get my camera bag and soon after, he casts us off. I am standing at the wheel with her engine in neutral when Trevor walks around me and puts his chest against my back as he puts his hands on my waist instead of the wheel. "Take her out, Baby." I glance over my shoulder. "I want to watch you and I don't think you've had the pleasure of taking her out." He kisses my cheek as the current moves her away from the dock.

At the mouth of the bay I cut the engine and Trevor says, "Time to put the gloves on." And he goes straight to her mainsail. When it's raised I turn the wheel a few degrees northwest and catch the wind in it. The sound the sail makes when this happens is distinct and it's exhilarating, because you know you are sailing. After he raises the headsail he returns to me, except this time he puts his hands on the wheel. I put mine on top of them and feel the subtle movements of him steering. Trevor knows the area so well he no longer needs charts to navigate and we sail and we sail and we sail.

The sun is getting low in the sky and we know it's time for this moment to end and all too soon. We speak a few words as we settle her in, but when we go ashore Trevor ... expresses what he is feeling to her. "Gypsy, thank you for today, I loved every minute of it. I have to go to work in a few days, which means I'm going away for a while, but I'll be back before the end of spring, then Geneviève and I will be here together and I promise we will make up for lost time."

I swallow so hard he hears it and gathers me into his arms. "Geneviève, I'm only going to say this once, because it will be all I can bare. I will miss you."

"And I will miss you." Then we become lost in an embrace.

Upon our return to Maison we go straight to my grandparent's house for Sunday dinner. Everyone is grateful they didn't have to dress for it, because there's a dark cloud over us. Claudette and Joseph are gone, but worst of all; soon Trevor will be gone as well. Instead of serving a formal dessert Grand-mamma serves petit fours since he is so fond of them. Only we know why and it lifts our spirits.

Walking back to our den I look up at the night sky and sigh. "I know, Baby. I've missed looking at the stars too. How does this sound? Let's turn the heaters up in the solarium, recline the settee, move the ottomans in front of it and throw a comforter over them. Then we can shower, slip on our robes and sip hot cocoa while we gaze at the stars."

"It sounds perfect."

Instead of putting on robes I get us another comforter to cover up with. Trevor and I curl up under it and I sigh again, this time out of utter contentment.

When half of my cocoa is left I decide to set it down and put my head on his shoulder with my arm around him. Trevor sets his down, pulls the comforter over me and we silently rest in each other's arms.

After a long time passes he breaks the silence. "Geneviève, no matter where I am we will still be together under the stars."

"We will be. What a lovely thought."

"It is, isn't it?"

"Mm hmm." And we are silent again.

More time passes as Trevor's breathing becomes shallow and steady then he falls asleep. I want to touch his face, but it will wake him up, so I simply watch him sleeping beside me.

The next thing I know Trevor is picking me up. "Trevor, what time is it?"

"I'm not sure, but it's still dark, so it's time for us to sleep in our bed."

Trevor puts me in our bed and covers me up. I listen to him walk through rooms turning off lights then he gets in our bed, turns of the lamp and snuggles up to me. "I love you, Geneviève."

"I love you too, Trevor." The warmth off his body makes me even sleepier.

During breakfast the next morning Trevor informs me he should return his car to the motor pool, so we take our time washing the dishes and getting dressed. Next we go to the garage and he raises the door behind Blanca then opens her trunk. Watching him empty the glove box I count the days we have together. There is only three left and I know the time is going to fly. I'm close to tears when he opens his trunk and lifts out the gym bag his boxing gear is in and I go back in time.

When Trevor says my name I come back to the present and he asks, "Where were you, Baby?"

"In your apartment the day I learned the term punch mitts." His eyes gleam.

"I didn't know what I wanted to do for the remainder of today until now." He pulls me against him with one arm. "I want to seduce my wife."

"This is a good start." And he gently bites my neck.

When he opens Blanca's door I tell him, "I need a minute to gather my wits. I'm in no condition to drive." His laugh is deep as helps me into my car.

"Leave when you're ready. I'm following you." And he gives me a kiss.

While Trevor signs paperwork I get out and look around. I see a Willys and it reminds me of William, so when Trevor walks up I ask, "Why did Joanna wish she could call William and Emily?"

"It's a tradition; newlyweds are not disturbed before the husband is deployed."

"Oh ... that's nice."

"Yes it is. — This is my first time to standdown without my mate. I kind of miss that Yank."

"You'll see him see at your surprise party Wednesday."

"I do love surprises." His eyes gleam as I walk to the passenger side and his laugh is deep as he opens Blanca's door. "I'm guessing you already planned your seduction. What can you tell me?"

"We're going to have lunch at The Flying Dragon and order several things to go that are good cold for us to eat this evening, because neither of us will have the strength to cook." He gives me a look and gets in the car.

Back at our den the refrigerator is filled with Chinese food and Trevor steps close then softly tells me, "Go to your dark room, put a new roll of film in your camera and meet me in the empty bedroom. He picks up his gym bag and I stand there for a minute wondering why I need my camera.

Bright light is shining into the hallway and when I step into the bedroom he is in dark blue trunks and lace up boots boxers wear. Trevor looks so good I almost drop my camera. "Welcome to the gym." I nod as I take everything in.

Trevor has brought in a chair that has a lamp from our guest room setting on it without the shade and a glass of water. Since I haven't moved Trevor guides me into the middle of the room. "Have you heard of shadowboxing?" My heart flutters as I gasp. "That's a yes. Do you know its purpose?"

"Not completely."

"It's mainly used as a warm up for a more physical activity such as bag work or sparring, but it is also a training tool. A boxer can watch his shadow as he envisions he is boxing an opponent to improve his technique. When I finally received private quarters I would shadowbox two or three times a week, because I was where no one was waiting to critique my performance and I was able to completely focus. It was ... liberating."

"So, if I stay out of your eye line I won't break your concentration and I can capture everything I want on film." He nods and gives me a lingering kiss.

"See you soon." He steps in front of the lamp and casts his shadow on the wall.

Slipping off my shoes while watching him loosen up I decide now would be the best time to get one of the front of his body as he watches his shadow that includes my shadow. I take it and before I get out of his eye line he looks at me with eyes sparkling and a heart stopping smile. Of course I take that one then move back several feet from the chair and he begins to shadowbox for me.

Trevor stands before me with perspiration dripping from his body as I look at him awestricken as to what he did for me. He was powerful yet graceful as he floated around the floor. He was magnificent. Thoughts are spinning in my mind while he picks up the white towel laid out and wipes the perspiration from his face. Trevor drinks the water then puts the towel around his neck and holds on to the ends. His breathing is heavy and his chest swells with each breath he takes. With eyes gleaming he asks, "Are you ready for the punch mitts?"

"Do you want me to put them on?"

"Why are you asking?"

"Because, I've seen enough."

Trevor takes the towel off and instead of unbuttoning my blouse he pulls it over my head and me into his arms. My silk camisole is soaked from his perspiration the instant our bodies collide. Soon my thighs are in his hands as he carries me to the bedroom he provided for spontaneous moments such as this.

Much later we are sitting on the kitchen table like tailors feeding each other cold lo mein by hand and I tell him, "I love it when you seduce me."

"I love seducing you." And he gives me a little kiss. "When we finish this I am going to bathe you and tuck you in, then I'm going to read you a bedtime story." I light up the room.

Trevor braids my hair and tucks me in then he briefly leaves and returns with his book of Greek Mythology. He sits on the edge of the bed and flips through the pages then becomes my soft chair and begins reading me the story of the contest between Athena and Poseidon that is about how the city of Athens was named. It does not surprise me he would choose one with Poseidon. He is a Sailor *and* unbeknownst to him it happens to be one of my favorites.

In the morning we are still in our bed after being awake several minutes when he tells me, "Geneviève, I would like for you to decide what we do today." I quickly reply, "I want to develop the film I took last night and while it dries, cook a nice lunch then print the photographs."

"Working in the darkroom. I'll get breakfast started." He kisses me and throws the covers over me for a change. I lie under them laughing and then feel a hand slide under the covers and he tugs on my ankle. I have to uncover my face in order to breathe.

The film is hanging to dry and the moment we have been looking forward to is upon us, for him to pick me up and put me on the counter. Since we are married I have on just a slip and when he picks me up it slides along my thighs as I wrap my legs around him. He is kissing me tenderly when a strap falls off my shoulder. When he discovers this, Trevor glides his mouth down to my neck. Then he gets still and holds me close with his face buried at my neck and shoulder which causes me to do the same. It eventually feels like we are holding on to each other for dear life when Trevor pulls back. "Geneviève, we're clinging to one another." My heart sinks as he heavily exhales. "We both know that after today we won't be able to make love until my return and it's already having an effect on us." I can feel my lower lip quivering and he touches it. "Baby, I have to ask you this. Is that how you want it to be, with aches in our hearts?" Words fail me. "Before we were married just being able to kiss you and have you by my side was enough for me. With the exception I *really* did not like sleeping alone." And he makes me smile.

"Get me down please. I want to go photograph the room you seduced me in."

Uh oh, there's the glint. "You're going to have to put in a new roll of a film in the camera. Will you find me in the dark again and throw yourself on me?"

I cover my eyes shaking my head. "When you put it that way, I did. I threw myself on you."

Laughing he pulls my hand away from my eyes and looks into them. "I was so glad you did. I had to wait on you to take us there and my strength was dwindling."

"I found that out the moment I said you could move."

"I am enjoying reminiscing, but I would rather be in the dark with you."

"Then get me down." And he does.

Time flies and Trevor is looking over my shoulder at the photographs hanging to dry when I ask, "Tomorrow is your birthday. What do you want to do?"

"I would like to have breakfast with your parents then I want to take you shopping and have lunch at The Posh."

"Since you know about your surprise party, would you mind going to the club to pick up your cake after lunch? It will save Mother a trip into town."

"I wouldn't mind at all. In fact I would like to go for a stroll on the beach. After that you should take charge, so you can surprise me with my party."

"You are a rascal." He goes, "Mmm hm." and kisses me.

We go around the house closing draperies and then I call Mother while he gets a fire going in the bedroom. After dinner we shower and get in our bed, because he is determined to finish reading the book.

Settled in against my husband and listening to his voice I eventually get lost in him. It is going to be a long time before he reads to me again. I return when his tone changes as he says, "The End." Trevor puts the book down and holds me. "That was a good book. The characters were quite unusual: the Queen of Hearts with soldiers that are playing cards, the white rabbit that talks as do all the creatures in the book, a cat that has the ability to disappear and last but not least, a caterpillar that smokes a hookah. If one didn't know the author was a religious man one might think he frequented Ah Sing's opium den. It operated around that time in London's Chinatown."

"How on earth do you know the name of an opium den from the 1800s?"

"I saw a photograph taken outside it at the Science Museum in London. Grandmother told me it is a well known fact the elite gentlemen of London society frequented the place. It was considered acceptable, like going to the speakeasies in this country." I merely nod, because I am at a loss for words and suddenly Trevor manages to pin me down on our bed. "Since I have rendered you speechless, let's make out while we wait for me to age another year." While I laugh uncontrollably he sets the alarm on our clock and turns off the lamp.

In the morning the alarm sounds, and after he turns it off and rolls over back to me I softly sing Happy Birthday to him. "I can already tell this is going to be my best birthday ever. I love you. Good morning, Baby."

"Good morning, Trevor. And I love you. Do we have a few minutes before we have to get up? I want to stretch and lie here with you nibbling on my neck and earlobe. Or would you prefer I nibble on you?"

"I'll do the nibbling, thank you." Then he oh so does.

During breakfast with my parent's that we have missed more than we realized, Mother announces they have received the first postcard from Claudette and Joseph. When she holds it up we all burst into laughter. It reads, Greetings from the Grand Canyon and there is a photograph of tourists on pack mules. Next Mother lights a candle in a cinnamon scone and we sing Happy Birthday to him. When we stop singing he just stares at the candle melting. So I say, "Make a wish."

"I don't know what to wish for. My usual one has been granted. I found my wife." He reaches for my hand as Mother and I sigh.

After thinking a bit he blows out the candle and cuts the scone into four pieces. As we laugh he offers the plate to each of us and we eat his birthday scone. Father stays later than usual to continue the delightful conversation with us then takes his leave. We stay a little while longer with Mother, thank her for everything and are off to the shops, including the lingerie one, where he buys whatever catches his eye then we proceed to The Posh where we have a champagne lunch. He is a man with a plan that I intend to disrupt.

When we enter the lobby of the club to pick up his cake Eric is there and walks straight to us. "Commander, Mrs. Lyons, the Pâtissier sends his apologies. The cake has met with a small accident he is repairing. We have beverages with salted and sweet petit fours set up in the private dining room adjacent to The Banquet Hall. Follow me please." I respond, "Please tell him we are in no rush and we know the way. Thank you, Eric." He bows and sprints off. Trevor looks at me and smiles. "This day keeps getting better. Petit fours that you are going to let me feed you."

"You are certainly aware it is your birthday."

"It's the one day a year everyone is eager to make me happy and I am not ashamed to admit I take full advantage of it." And he offers me his arm.

Getting close to The Hall I say, "In that case will you dance with me?"

"Under one condition, you count for us." I nod and he opens a door. "The room is lit up."

"They must have cleaned it this morning."

We step inside and when he closes the door Trevor sees all our family members and our friends with their families standing to his right in the corner. I coyly say, "Surprise." He glances at me then looks at everyone again as if to make sure he is not hallucinating. Then he looks at me and says, "I can't believe this. You surprised me." I am beaming as he gives me a kiss.

Everyone spreads out as they walk toward us with Hilda front and center. She stops and holds her arms out then they begin to sing.

"For he's a jolly good fellow, for he's a jolly good fellow

For he's a jolly good fellow, and so say all of us

And so say all of us, and so say all of us

For he's a jolly good fellow, for he's a jolly good fellow

For he's a jolly good fellow, — and so say all of us!"

While we clap for him Trevor's head goes back as he laughs wholeheartedly. "I've never heard that version."

"It's British." I begin laughing, because I have a visual of them eating lunch here and then being taught this version by Hilda and Evelyn.

The first person to greet Trevor is his mum. He throws his arms around her and gives her a squeeze that gets her tickled. Then we spend approximately 30 minutes getting hugs and kisses from 25 more friends and relatives. Mmm hm, I gathered 26 people to celebrate Trevor's birthday and to give them an opportunity to see the fellas during happy circumstances before they're deployed.

There are brightly colored balloons everywhere, a jukebox in front of the stage with a bowl of change on it courtesy of Emily and William. A table is stacked with birthday presents and another one has his birthday cake on it, which was not damaged, made of creamy dark chocolate frosting and three layers of dark chocolate cake. And a few feet away from that is a small table with an ice cream maker on a chair behind it filled with my mother's vanilla ice cream and a server standing next to it. After all this is a birthday party and you expect to eat cake and ice cream at one no matter how old the person being celebrated is.

Trevor holds my hand and we go stand at his cake. While Poppy and Hilda light the candles he whispers, "Did you hear my wish I made this morning?" I nod. "Will you make the wish with me and blow the candles out?"

"Of course I will."

"Geneviève, thank you for this." And he gives me a kiss.

After the candles are lit Evelyn leads us into singing Happy Birthday to her son and next we close our eyes to make the wish. Then he says, "On my count ... three, two, one, blow." We draw in a deep breath and blow every candle out. Everyone applauds and then Trevor cuts his cake. We each take a bite them a line forms in an orderly military fashion and we begin to serve his very rich cake. It is so rich I have to ask Eric to bring me a lemon-lime soda to cut the sweet taste lingering in my mouth in the middle of serving our guests.

Before we are all seated Mitch drops a coin in the jukebox and the party gets going. When we finish eating Trevor whisks me out onto the dance floor and soon everyone is dancing. Since we are two men short Helen and Meredith spin each around the dance floor enjoying themselves immensely. Kyle has had to change cameras twice since we got here so much has been happening.

Next Trevor opens his presents and most of them are edible items that are not going to be onboard Louise. For instance: there is a huge tin of pecan sandies from Sandra and Albert, a large bag of butterscotch disc from Poppy and Spencer and Mother boxed up the oatmeal cookies she and Father baked last night.

Next Mother and I begin handing out the party favor's to our guest and tell everyone it's just a little something to remember the day by they can open on their way home.

During a slow dance Trevor softly speaks to me, "They arrived this morning? I nod. "Are they leaving after the party?" I nod again. "Our families never liked seeing us off. What are the departure times for their trains?"

"Helen's is at 4:40, the others are taking one to Phoenix that departs at 4:55."

"Then we need to wind things down. It will take several minutes at the coat check since their bags are there too." He kisses me and twirls me around.

When the music stops Trevor thanks everyone for coming and as they file passed us he gives all the ladies a balloon in the color of their choice then we go to the lobby where it becomes ... interesting. Trevor and I are standing with Théo and Rachel when Trevor says, "Excuse me please, I'm going to help my family with their luggage. I tell him, "I'm going to stay here and cling to Théo." He chuckles, gives me a kiss and Théo offers me his arm. Next Sandra gives her son and William a tin of pecan sandies as Joanna and Emily stand close together. William hands the tin to Emily then Judith gives her son a hug. Her face looks like she is in pain one second and the next she is smiling. Rachel asks, "Did you see that, how fast she got her emotions in check?" Théo nods in disbelief and I tell her, "The thought of causing him more pain if he sees her upset gives her the strength to do that." I hear Théo swallow.

With all their things claimed and in hands I let go of Théo's arm to join Trevor and he tells Rachel, "You may need to drive, Gené cut the circulation off to my hand and it's asleep." He gives me a wink and I walk off shaking my head.

The valets already have all our cars out front courtesy of Eric alerting them we were leaving no doubt. Trunks and doors are open and they load us up. Trevor is in the lead with only his parents riding with us. We're barely out of the parking lot when he asks them, "How was the trip here?" Rowland responds. "It was not dull. Since we knew all flights to the West Coast were grounded for the duration of the war your mum had to make some calls." Evelyn chimes in. "I found out we could fly to Phoenix and catch a train here, then I called everyone and we booked the same itinerary. The airport provides buses to take passengers to the train station, which was nice." His father adds, "When we all boarded the train we took over the bar car." I can see Evelyn beaming in the rearview mirror and Trevor smiling.

All too soon we pull up to the train station and find parks together. When we get to the platforms Helen insists we all go to the Phoenix bound train since she only brought her handbag and our other guests have luggage. She says her goodbyes and my family walk with her to the platform her train is on. Then the hard part begins and it becomes a blur to me as I watch each person board the train after hugs and kisses are bestowed on the men we love so very much. When the conductor calls out, "All aboard." I focus and expect them to wave at a window, but they keep going forward to the next car and out of sight. When the whistle blows the fellas offer us their arms and we turn around. This is when I notice my family had returned.

They wave to us and go to their cars at a lively pace to give us time alone as we walk to the parking lot. I feel numb and more than likely I am not the only one. Then just as the silence is becoming uncomfortable Joanna exclaims, "I had a flash of genius the other day and have been waiting to tell you all. I was thinking about how difficult it is to get a good park at the pier and then was blinded by the flash. Tomorrow night Mitch and I are going to drive my car to the pier and park parallel across three parks. So, when you both arrive, find us and Mitch will move my car then we will be parked side by side."

William responds, "That was a flash of genius. Would you like us to pick you up?" Mitch replies, "Thank for offering, but my lovely wife and I are going to have a nice walk together."

After our friends thank me profusely for the day Trevor and I watch them drive off then I ask him, "Do you mind if I get my camera out and take a few photographs?"

"I was going to ask you if you minded staying a little while. I haven't been at a train station in a long time. This place brings back fond memories."

We wonder around as I photograph the station and when it gets too dark to use my camera we sit on a bench listening to the sounds as the station shuts down. Then Trevor sits straight up. "I've been meaning to ask, what was the party favor?"

"The photograph I insisted you and your shipmates pose for at the gala."

"That is why you and your mother gave those out at the last minute. It will stir emotions and they will treasure it. — How did you pull that off? That was taken a few days ago."

"When you weren't in the kitchen I would write Mother a note with what I needed her to do and leave it in the dumbwaiter when you stopped reporting for duty. She would sneak over and get them at random times of the day or night."

"You two planned this as if it were a Special Op."

"It was and necessary to get one over on you." And his laugh is deep.

"I have a confession to make. No one has ever been able to surprise me. One time Joanna even threw my birthday party a day early and I still picked up on it. I have to thank you for letting me know how it feels to be truly surprised."

"It was my pleasure." Then with a lilt in my voice I say, "So, Birthday Boy, where to next?"

"To the car. I've never been called Birthday Boy like that."

We lock all the doors and intentionally allow the windows to fog over just in case someone is here to keep an eye on things in the darkness.

Waiting for the windows to clear up Trevor's stomach growls and the Birthday Boy tells me, "That my cue to go eat the last pizza I will have for a while."

"Why do you stop eating pizza when you're gone?" His eyes get wide.

"I can't believe I haven't told you this. Pizzas require time the cooks aboard Louise don't have to spare."

"That explains a lot. I'm glad I like pizza."

"That makes two of us." And we get tickled.

Trevor and I go to Micheletto's where he orders a large pepperoni pizza to go and I enjoy hearing him speak in Italian more than usual. Then we go to our den where we discover a pastry box in the dumbwaiter that contains what was left of his birthday cake, courtesy of Mother no doubt. Next he gets a fire going in the living room while I select several slow songs to listen to on the record player.

After he savors every bite of the pizza, we share a small piece of the cake then we settle in on the sofa sharing a glass of Louis XIII and I listen to him talk about how much he enjoyed the day. Occasionally when something really good plays we get up and sway to the music.

Sitting on the sofa I tell him, "I've been waiting on the perfect time to give you your present." I reach for the envelope that has been on the coffee table all day and give him the envelope turning it over for him to see the front.

Trevor reads it aloud, "For my husband on his 31st birthday." and then pulls out the piece of paper inside, most likely thinking it's a love letter. He gasps when he unfolds it. "You wrote me a poem. Will you read it to me?"

"I know it by heart." Looking deep into his eyes I move closer and whisper,

"I will flow through you like a tranquil stream
I will rain on you and watch you grow
I will bathe you.

I am a sparkling pool for you to swim
I am a swift current to sweep you away
I am drink to quench a thirst

I am water
I am life."

Trevor lovingly caresses my face. "You just touched my heart." Overtaken with emotion he kisses me tenderly then glances at the poem he is still holding. "Geneviève, this is the most beautiful poem I have ever heard." He whispers, 'Tell it to me again." And I do.

When I finish he puts everything down and gathers me into his arms. "I love you so much. All I want to do is lose myself in your lovely brown eyes." So, Trevor kisses me with his eyes open and I lose myself into the blue of his.

Soon we find ourselves in bed and I have the mythology book in my hands reading to Trevor, who wants to listen to my voice as he holds me with both arms and one of his hands over my heart to feel it beating. I read and read until my eyes tire. When I close them the book falls from my hands. Trevor gets us settled and we drift into a reluctant sleep.

In the morning the need for sustenance forces us from the warmth of our bed and while we cook salmon I ask Trevor, "What do you need to do today?"

"The same thing William and I do on the day before we're deployed. Go to the commissary for things we require and things we want. We went after breakfast, because the commissary became crowded with married couples after lunch."

"I'm sure it did. Since we both dislike crowds, I think we should go after we eat. The sooner we get started, the sooner we finish."

"You have a point." And I get dipped and kissed.

While looking for a park at the commissary I tell him, "Trevor, three o'clock."

"I recognize that ponytail." And he takes the next park. "This is going to be entertaining. Something usually happens to Emily. I learned that after she got the cryptic fortune cookie. Give me a kiss and let's go before we miss it."

"You are such a rascal."

"Yes, ma'am." He opens the car door grinning. "Now shake a leg." He offers me his hand and swiftly slides me across the seat then up and out I go, laughing the entire time. Before I have my legs under me he goes, "Uh oh, they're walking at a brisk pace. We'll have to look for them when we get inside."

"Do that whistle thing and stop them." Trevor immediately puts his fingers on his mouth and my ears are ringing as they stop and turn around. The second we reach them the fun begins. William and Trevor wrestle carts free then Emily and I push them as the fellas walk in front of the carts with their hands on them guiding us along. The first aisle we hit is for grooming supplies and they count out loud in unison while putting bottles of shampoo and shaving soap in the carts. It's the same with razor blades and everything else an officer in the Navy requires.

As we round the next aisle William's arm stretches out, because Emily slows down. I look down it and see it's the one with everything they wear under their uniforms. I really don't want to watch William pick out skivvies and I'm certain Emily feels the same concerning Trevor. "Fellas, you don't need our help here, therefore Emily and I are going to be on the aisle where the nail polish is." They chuckle and Trevor replies, "We shan't be long." And we turn on a dime.

When they join us Emily and I have our hands full with the new winter color palette of eye shadows and polishes. We carefully place our finds in the cart and William asks, "Where to next?" Trevor answers, "The candy aisle." Everyone lights up.

On the way Emily begins looking around. "There sure are a lot of bachelors in here. Why are there so few married couples?" William goes, "Umm ... I'm not sure how to answer your question." Trevor glances at me and does an immediate about face while I bite my tongue. Maybe two seconds later Emily turns bright red and says, "Forget I asked." With eyes dancing William tells her, "I don't think that's going to be possible." And that is it for Trevor. He hunches over holding on to the cart trying to be quiet and failing miserably. And that is it for William and me. A hushed laughter ensues and as always laughter is contagious and she gets tickled then we keep going to the candy aisle.

While Trevor nonchalantly pulls several bags of each kind of candy my polish makes him crave and tosses them into the cart William watches him intently with a smile and then looks at me. "I see that sweet tooth of yours is contagious." Trevor responds as he makes more selections, "Yep ... and if you want some, you better get your own. I shan't be sharing." Emily gives William one of those looks and he tosses bags of caramels and jelly beans in their cart.

Waiting in line to check out after Emily and William, Trevor quietly asks me, "How does the four of us at Sam's for lunch sound?"

"Perfect."

He raises his voice. "Do you two have lunch plans?" Emily smiles at William and he replies, "We do now. Where are we going?" I blurt out, "Sam's." Emily responds, "We'll save you a seat." They pay the cashier and out the doors they go.

While we unload the cart Trevor says, "We need to have a quick conversation. The blackout paint on the cars lights render them almost nonexistent. The thought of you driving in fog after work ..."

"Say no more. You want me to stay with Emily." He touches my nose. "Bring it up during lunch." It *was* a quick conversation and we get in the car.

At Sam's somehow they managed to get the booth we sat in the first time the four of us were here and we are all delighted. Water is already on the table and when Trevor and I are seated Annie walks up and nods, "Four House Special's?" Trevor responds, "Instead of a milkshake I would like a cola. I'll be eating dessert this afternoon." I almost out shine the sun and make the same request as do William and Emily. Then Trevor wastes no time talking to Emily about our short conversation.

"Emily, before we eat I have a favor to ask."

"Ask away." This gets a chuckle.

"I don't want Geneviève driving home in fog after work and ..."

"You want to know if she can stay with me and the answer is yes. As fate would have it William and I talked about this very subject last night. Now, what are you having for dessert?"

"A scoop each of the big three with extra whipping cream."

"Oh, that's right. There's no ice cream aboard Navy vessels." My jaw drops. "The freezer space is used for more important things." I dryly ask, "What's more important than ice cream?" William and Trevor say in unison, "Hear, hear."

We spend the afternoon eating and reminiscing about the first time I brought us here pretending to be a tour guide. Emily and I only eat half our fries to save room for the same dessert the fellas order, but wind up giving them what we can't finish much to their delight.

Annie puts the check on the table and Sam walks up. After we greet each other he comments, "I see the Navy still doesn't serve ice cream to the men. Some things never change." Sliding the check off the table he says, "Ladies, don't be strangers. Gentlemen, fair winds and following seas." Then he turns around before we can respond and Emily asks, "How does he know?" William replies, "Sam is an old Sea Dog." She slyly smiles at him and asks, "Does that make you a Pup?" We burst into laughter and leave on that note.

When Trevor and I arrive at our den we put everything in the dumbwaiter then go outside. He wants to take the walk on the beach we missed yesterday. On the garden path the first thing we notice in the distance are two chairs pushed together on the boardwalk. Since the outdoor furniture was already in storage Trevor looks at me and says, "Your grandmother must enjoy doing these things." Then he gets a strange look on his face. "Can *she* hear my thoughts?" Laughing I shrug my shoulders.

While passing my grandparents solarium, to our surprise they are sitting on the sofa. I thought Grand-papa was at the office. Apparently his semi-retirement has begun. Trevor asks, "Do you think they would mind?" I reply, "I'm going to treat that as rhetorical." And he kisses me.

The moment we go toward the steps they stand looking very pleased. Trevor opens the door and they lavish us with affection that is so French. My husband does relish our customs, as do we. They offer us something to drink, but we graciously decline and he sits next to Grand-mamma. Few words are spoken while we visit with them. Looking at the view and being together are enough. They are going to miss him and he will miss them. When Trevor mentions before we go for our walk that he will call the family before we leave the house tomorrow, it takes everything I have to keep my wits about me.

My arm is around his waist and his arm is around my shoulders as we stroll along the water's edge listening to the sounds of ocean. After sitting in the chairs in silence for who knows how long, out of the blue he tells me, "I think you should take a road trip to the ranch with Emily and Joanna as soon as possible. You and Helen getting them on a horse will be a wonderful diversion. By the way, I will be expecting photographs."

"How do I send mail to you?"

"Take it to Joanna, she knows what to do. Also, I will send my letters for you to her. When things leave the base to be delivered by the postal service it takes longer." He sighs heavily. "It's getting chilly." He takes off his jacket and drapes it over me. "Just a little bit longer, then we'll go inside and I'll make my hot cocoa." I nod and he kisses me.

On the way to our den I make a mistake and glance at my watch. Time is flying as I knew it would and I am powerless to make it slow down.

After we watch the sunset in our solarium Trevor tells me, "I need to get rid of some excess energy in order to get to sleep at a descent hour. Do you mind if I go for a 3k run?"

"Not at all. In fact it will give me the chance to take care of few things."

"Please wait for me to shower."

"It wouldn't have crossed my mind not to."

We go inside and I wash our mugs from Sam's and empty the dumbwaiter as he changes clothes. I grab the towel around his neck the moment he enters the kitchen and give him a nice kiss. When he goes out the door I dash to our dressing room to stash a few things to surprise him with in his satchel. This takes all of two minutes then I turn the heat up in the bathroom. Sitting on the chaise for under a minute I am already fit to be tied. I decide to go on the overlook to watch him run and grab a blanket to wrap up in then go upstairs.

A few minutes later I see him. Trevor looks like an athlete that runs track for the long race. His pace is brisk and he is perfection. When he runs out of site I slowly begin turning in a circle to see him when he is out in the open at the sides and back of the property.

As time goes by my heart begins to sink. What am I going to without him? He's going to be gone longer than I have known him. How could things go from bad to worst so fast? I knew when he won my heart sending him off was going to be more than I could bear, but off to war is beyond comprehension. I am battling tears when he slows down near the middle of the boardwalk. Then he stops and looks out to the ocean. All I can think is how much I am going to miss him and my heart aches. "Trevor, you have to return to me for I will be lost without you. I love you so much."

Suddenly he turns around and looks up at the overlook. My thoughts were so strong. How much did he hear? He looks at me then begins running toward our den. I am paralyzed. I have done the one thing I am not supposed to do and have struggled not to day after day, let him know my emotions.

I can barely hear doors closing and getting louder as he gets closer and closer until he flings the one to the overlook open and runs to me. When I am in his arms I wrap mine around him along with the blanket and he whispers, "Geneviève, you are my wife. Let me comfort you." And he begins to rock me in his arms.

As he catches his breath from running and I catch mine from coming undone we are the closest we have ever been. I need him and he gives me the comfort I am desperate for.

Minutes later he says, "Baby, it pains me to end this moment, but we must go inside and let my body cool down, otherwise I might catch cold." Keeping the blanket around him we go down to the living room where he dries off and I sit on the sofa watching his every move. Then I tell him, "We should put a roast and vegetables in the oven. It should be done by the time we shower and dress for dinner like we did on our honeymoon." Before I have a warm spot he pulls me up from the sofa and into the kitchen.

My husband and I bathe one another and since it is going to be his last long shower for months we stand under the warm water as we express our love until the water runs cool. Then we go to our dressing room wrapped in towels and when I toss his jeans on the chaise his eyes gleam. "I like wearing those." I smile and get out one of his white shirts, because I want to roll up his sleeves and his smoking slippers, because they do not require socks.

He gives me a kiss and pulls white satin panties and a camisole from my lingerie chest to slip on while he goes through the things in my closet. Eventually Trevor takes out my white satin slippers and the lace Grecian peignoir set. He removes the robe from the hanger and puts the nightgown we got tangled in back into the closet. Trevor holds it out for me, so I turn around and slide my arms into the sleeves. Then I face him, get kissed and then he buttons the satin buttons that stop at my waist, but he keeps going down to my thighs.

Next I watch him put on his black undershorts and jeans then hold out his shirt for him to put on. I button it then he lights up as he places a hand on my abdomen for me to roll up his sleeve. When both sleeves are done he motions to the vanity and I sit on the bench to let him braid my hair then he offers me his arm and escorts me to the living room. I am going to miss all this.

Trevor turns on the record player to play all our slow songs and as we warm bread and gather things to set the table for a candlelit dinner some sort of dance begins. We waltz here and there then I am dipped and kissed as he lights the candles. Next he opens a bottle of our best red Bordeaux and dinner begins.

When Trevor fills my wine glass for the second time while he is still drinking his first, our pleasant conversation takes a turn. "Geneviève, remember when we all went to Santa Barbara and Emily asked William what his reason for joining the Navy was and his answer was he wanted to protect the country and the people that live in it. Then I basically said it was why I joined." I nod filled with trepidation. "As your husband it is my duty to protect you and it occurred to me while I was running, this deployment is the best way for me to do that."

His smile tells me the rest. Trevor has made sense out of all this and tomorrow he is going to walk up the gangway willingly, which is as it should be. The weight on our shoulders is lighter and now I have confidence I will make it through sending him off with a genuine smile for him to remember me by.

Waiting for his birthday cake to thaw we forgot to take out of the freezer for some unknown reason, I decide it's time to give him something I want him to take with and lead him into the living room. I have him sit of the sofa and close his eyes while I get it out of the coat closet and set it on the coffee table.

Seated next to him I say, "You may open your eyes." He does so looking at me and I motion to the gift. "This is the smallest camera bag in the world." He chuckles as I unzip it and get the camera out. "I am holding the camera I took the first photograph of you with." I offer it to him and he carefully takes it. "There are several rolls of color film in that and when possible I would like you take photographs and send the rolls to me. This way I will still be able to see you." He nods and gives me a kiss. "To clarify, I'm giving you the bag, but I'm loaning you my camera and expect you to return it to me in the same condition."

Trevor looks at it then up at me with a glint in his eyes. "You had to loan me this one huh?"

"Mmm hm."

"Just so you know, I am going to worry about this going overboard and I'll have to stay further in when I'm on the flight deck."

"Oh good. I saw how close you were to the edge of that deck when you were manning the rails, which by the way do not exist on the tallest ships in the Navy. Even Willow and Gypsy have lifelines." Trevor bursts into laughter as he sets the camera down then gives me a hug and a playful squeeze. "Can we eat desert now? I want to kiss you while you taste like chocolate."

"I'll pour the milk."

Trevor and I are on the sofa in a passionate embrace when our song begins to play. He stands and offers me his hand. As we sway together I make my husband very happy by singing to him. When it ends he turns off the record player and leads me to the settee in front of the blazing fire in our bedroom.

Soon he is standing before me wearing only his undershorts and I caress his face then place my fingertips on his chin. "Ancient Persians described a cleft as a deep well lovers fall into and are trapped without hope of ever getting out."

Trevor tilts his head as he places his hands on my waist. "Then I'm glad I have it." He kisses me then moves us backward holding onto my waist as he sits down. Then I fan out my robe and sit across his lap. "You are lovely in firelight. I love you, Geneviève."

"Oh Trevor, I love you too."

Looking deep into my eyes Trevor unbuttons my robe and makes it fall from my shoulders. I slide my hand down the soft hair on his lower abdomen then he gathers me into his arms and begins kissing his way down my neck. As his mouth reaches the slope he holds me tight and pulls my skin into his mouth causing me to moan. When I feel his teeth press against my skin I sharply inhale and realize he is intentionally leaving a passion mark that will be there for several days after he is gone.

Trevor slowly stops and kisses the place to make it better before he looks at me and touches the slope of his neck. Then I give him what he wants.

After making myself stop to let him catch his breath he whispers, "How do you want me to take you to our bed?"

"With my arms around your neck and your hands under my thighs."

"And I will have you beneath me, which is exactly where I want you to be."

Lying across our bed he caresses my face and we begin to kissing tenderly. Every touch, every movement is slow as our bodies entwine. This is our love and I treasure it.

The flames of the fire are low as Trevor moves down and lifts my camisole, but instead of kissing my abdomen he lays his head down holding me with his arms along my sides. His body was warm and the air feels cool on me where he was, so I lay my forearm across my breasts and my hand touches his. Trevor immediately holds it and I begin to stroke his hair. He holds my hand a little tighter then I feel a tear splash on my skin. It is so unexpected I have no idea what to do for him, so I continue to stroke his hair.

After Trevor wipes the tear away he looks up and sees my arm is over my breasts. "Oh ... Baby. You're cold." In the blink of an eye he rolls onto his side and pulls the covers over me. "I know satin is thin. I'm not sure what to say."

"There's no need to say anything. Just hold me." When I finally get warm I yawn and Trevor tells me, "It's time for us to get in bed instead of lying across it." He gets up and moves my head onto a somewhat cold pillow. "I shan't be a moment." We kiss and he turns on the heater then returns wearing an undershirt and takes it off. "I put this on to get it warm. Let's put it on you." I sit up and hold my arms out like a child and he puts it over my head then tucks me in. Trevor gets in bed, sets the alarm and lies on his back next to me. I snuggle in under his arm and lay my head on his chest to listen to his heart beat. We tell each other good night and I desperately try to stay awake, but his heartbeat is like a lullaby.

CHAPTER TWENTY-THREE

In the morning between sleeping and waking I remember after today I will be waking up alone and cling to Trevor instantly. He begins rubbing my back and whispers, "Good morning, Baby."

"Good morning, Trevor. How long have you been awake?"

"I'm not sure."

"When do we have to get up?"

"In about 25 minutes." I let out a long sigh of relief as Trevor sets the alarm then takes a drink of water and offers the glass to me. After being refreshed I lie on my back and Trevor lies his body over mine using my shoulder as his pillow. Time passes and wanting to spend our last few minutes kissing in our bed I touch his lower lip and whisper, "Donne moi çe." Trevor responds, "My first French lesson. I remember it well." He gives me his lip ... and more.

The alarm sounds and when he turns it off he kisses me once more then sits on the edge of our bed. He runs his hands through his hair and gets up then walks around to my side as I sit up. "I like it when you wear my shirts."

"I like the reasons why I wear your shirts." He pulls me up into his arms then we go into the bathroom and I watch him shave.

Trevor wants to eat in the solarium, so we turn on the heaters then go to the kitchen to make our coffee and cook the first breakfast we cooked together, Swiss cheese omelets with the addition of my pancakes that I whip up while he squeezes oranges without the juicer as always.

After we finish our omelets Trevor smiles as he gets up to serve the pancakes and syrup we put in the oven to keep warm. Then he sits down to happily watch me pour my syrup moat and I feed him for a change. Next we clear the table and make a second cup of coffee then sit together looking at the view. It is beautiful, the ocean, but it is about to take him away from me. After that thought I summon the courage to say, "Trevor, you haven't told me the date you will be back."

"I decided to wait on you to ask, because the time needed to be right."

"This can't be good."

"It pains me to tell you this, — I have no idea."

"You have no idea?"

"During times of war the superior officers for the commander of a strike group make that decision during the deployment. This is done to keep the enemy from intercepting a communication and learning its location. More than likely it will push our return beyond six months at least two or three weeks."

"Can Mitch talk them into one?" And there is his deep laugh.

When we finish our coffee we go the kitchen to wash the dishes and as always he touches my hand each time I give him a dish to dry. With the last one put away Trevor sits down at the kitchen table and I sit across his lap. "So, what do you want to do next?"

"Lie in our bed and let you have your way with my face until we have to eat lunch." His hands go under my thighs as he stands and carries me to our bedroom. Trevor sets the alarm, so we don't have to watch the clock.

The alarm goes off again and it's back to the kitchen for cold roast beef sandwiches and potatoes. He drinks iced tea and I have a Pellegrino, so of course we talk about the day we met.

When there is nothing left on our plates I tell him, "Leave the dishes, I think it's time to go to our dressing room." I hold his hand and lead him there then get out my pink bustier and a pair of scissors. When I cut off an end of the lacing he asks, "Baby, what are you doing?"

"Getting two pieces of ribbon I need." Trevor looks puzzled then his face goes straight when I place the ribbon and scissors on my vanity. "Will you get your handkerchief please?" He does and kneels beside me.

"I completely forgot about this. I knew you were letting your hair grow to cut today." Trevor runs his hand down my braid and kisses it then he kisses me.

I unfold his handkerchief and lay it on my vanity then tie the pieces of ribbon onto my braid in knots about six inches apart and look to him for approval of how much I am going to cut. He nods and hands me the scissors. I hold onto my braid, kiss it and put the blades an inch above the top piece of ribbon then cut. Trevor locks his eyes on mine as I lift his hand and place my hair in it. He lifts it up and slowly inhales the scent. After holding it in his hand my husband lays it on his handkerchief and folds it over the braid.

"The day Joanna brought this up I cringed at the thought of you cutting your braid, knowing I couldn't talk you out of it. Since then I have had a change of heart. I will have a part of you with me always and I can touch your hair every night before I tuck this under my pillow."

"You are a romantic."

"I'm simply a man who loves his wife."

Suddenly Trevor picks up the scissors and parts his hair to the other side then in an instant he cuts a lock of his hair as I gasp. He smiles as he places it on my palm and all I can think is to kiss him, so I do with his hair held tight in my hand.

We walk over to my closet and Trevor gets my pink twin set out again. "You are so lovely in this. I hope you aren't tired of wearing it." I give him a kiss and take it from him then he selects my pearl earrings while I get out dark gray trousers. Then most reluctantly I take off his undershirt and carefully fold it before laying it on my dresser. I slowly dress as he puts on his khaki uniform and lays the matching cover by his satchel. Then he does something unexpected, he gets out the garment bag his Dress White uniform is in and hands me the jacket. I have the jacket I looked at every night before I went to sleep until we married. It made me feel as if he was there in spirit. This is going in our bedroom tonight.

As my husband buttons my sweater there is sadness in this sweet gesture he has done since the day he kissed me at the concert. Yet we still smile at each other and he kisses me when he's done. Nodding he asks, "Are you ready to go?" I'm not sure and I think the only reason I nod is because he is. So, he picks up his cover, tucks it under his arm and grabs the handles of his satchel. When he slings his khaki jacket over his shoulder, which is still on the hanger, I take it from him to hold his hand as we walk out and go to the garage.

My car is loaded and we go out the service entrance to join my family for dessert. The moment he opens the door to my parent's house we hear their voices coming from the solarium then Trevor walks over to the floral arrangement and removes a white tulip. He leads me into the dining room and gets a napkin to dry off the stem. "I was counting on this being here." We kiss as he gives me the tulip.

The weekly delivery of petit fours is today and I know he has forgotten, so I look at his face when we are at the doorway. When he sees them on the platter he looks at me with eyes gleaming. I adore our little secrets.

My family acts as if they haven't seen us in ages and from that point our time together becomes a blur until we are all in the foyer and Théo kisses my forehead while Rachel hugs Trevor visibly upset. To my relief she regains her composure when the hug is ending. Fortunately my parents and grandparents handle everything beautifully, but as Trevor opens the door he tells me under his breath, "Eyes forward, Baby." Walking across the portico he adds, "I've learned not to look back the hard way." And we go to the garage.

Standing by my car I struggle to breathe normally as I hold out his jacket for him to put on. He turns around and as I zip it up he says, "Geneviève, give me one more kiss."

"But we're allowed to kiss at the pier."

"Not like this." And Trevor pins me to my car.

On the way to the base I hold his hand and his cover. We ride in silence, because he has a lot on his mind. His last day on duty was spent scheduling the departures of the other ships in the strike group that would take place over the following week and the section of coast the ship would patrol while waiting to join Louise when she is deployed, all under radio silence. Planning this for a one day training exercise is entirely different when you are making the plan to go into war.

Getting close to the gates I hand Trevor his cover and while he puts it on I notice there is only two cars ahead of us and tell him, "I was expecting more than two cars to be in line."

"Only three percent of officers in the Navy live off base. The majority of them are single."

"That's interesting. Why is the majority single?"

"Can we pretend I didn't tell you that?" I shake my head emphatically and he sighs. "Geneviève, just think about it for a minute please and give me your ID." As I give him my ID it occurs to me women are not allowed in the BOQ.

"So, until the sentry reads my ID he thinks I'm your ... girlfriend."

His laugh is deep. "There is that possibility."

"Hmm, that was not need to know information. Oh look, there's Emily and William. At least they know we're married." Trevor drives up to the gate with a straight face. I do enjoy watching him use his training.

Getting close to Emily's car, William motions for Trevor to go in front of him and she is all smiles waving as we pass them. Then things take a turn when we see our bench up ahead and Trevor tells me, "Suddenly I'm wondering why I never took a photograph of you on that bench."

"I am certain you are able to see several in your mind."

"Tis true. The one I see most often is of you sitting there the night I won your heart. I remember watching you as I walked along the sidewalk and thinking how beautiful you were in the glow of the streetlamp."

"I remember thinking how handsome you were when I looked up and you were standing there in an undershirt and the trousers of your khaki uniform. I'll be sleeping in one of your undershirts tonight."

"Will you be holding my pillow or Christopher?"

"Christopher."

"When I'm on my rack tonight staring at the overhead of my quarters I'll have a visual and the last thing I'll do is touch your hair and inhale your scent."

Driving into the parking lot at the pier Trevor slows to a roll, because children are everywhere. Happily it doesn't take him long to spot Joanna and Mitch and he blows the horn. The top is already down on Joanna's car and as Mitch maneuvers it Joanna gives him hand signals as if she is on the flight deck flagging an aircraft. Even Trevor gets tickled.

Mitch takes the middle park and we go left as William goes right. The fellas get out their satchels and set them on the hoods. And when we gather in front of Joanna's car no one speaks, because we, the ladies, are wearing matching gray trousers and twin sets in different colors. Emily says, "William pulled this out of my closet this morning." I quickly respond, "Trevor chose my outfit too." Mitch chimes in, "I had nothing to do with my wife's attire. I'm used to choosing a dress; therefore I left it up to her. I *am* a leg man." William adds, "We all are. My favorite photograph from the trip to Santa Barbara is the one Trevor took of them lying on Willow's deck that morning." The fellas nod repeatedly, smiling.

While the tug boats pull back the sub net we stand in a tight circle and reminisce about the trip until the engines go into idle. Then as if on cue the farewells begin. Mitch offers me his arm and we walk to the front of my car without speaking. Trevor stays with Joanna as William and Emily go to the front of hers. Mitch faces me with his hands clasped and breaks the silence. "Under these circumstances, Geneviève, I am probably going to say something I have before."

"Your words are always kind and I wouldn't mind hearing something you have told me a second time."

"My wife gave up everything for me and the only thing I could do was show her how much I loved her as she adapted to being the wife of an officer. The life she had was just ... gone until she met you. On the day I watched her charm the chef out of the white truffle I knew she was getting back what she had given up all those years ago. And the boys have never been happier. I owe you a debt I can never repay."

"Mitch, I grew up thinking I was happy as a person could possibly be, then your wife walked up and soon I found out I was missing so many things; the bond one has with true friends, being part of a huge family and most of all, having the love of a good man. You are not in my debt." I stop talking, because I am going to get emotional and Mitch carefully puts his arms around me to give me comfort, then he slowly moves back.

"I can feel your heart pounding. Geneviève, always remember this, I *am* his captain and will do everything within my power to make sure he returns home to you." His words are comforting, but the way he said them make me ill at ease. Not knowing what to say I smile and nod. Mitch holds my hands while he kisses my cheeks then he gives me a reassuring look and walks away.

Before I can think, William is in front of me. "This is the only day it doesn't matter if our uniforms get wrinkled. Gimme a hug." Then he throws his arms around me and lifts me off my feet. When he puts me down his face goes straight and he lowers his voice. "Have you discovered any tells Trevor has while playing cards with you?"

When I stop laughing I reply, "He cannot keep a straight face with me, so I can't help you. You're going to have to beat him on your own." William sighs heavily.

"I'm probably not supposed to tell you this, but Emily was so excited about you staying overnight when it's foggy she redecorated a guest room. So, don't forget to pack a bag and bring it to work Monday morning, just in case you need to stay."

"I'll pack tonight then put it my trunk. And I will make a fuss over the room."

"Thank you. It will make her very happy." Then the tone of his voice changes. "Geneviève, I *am* going to miss you."

"I will miss you too, William."

As he smiles looking into my eyes, without warning he kisses my forehead and turns on a dime. I gasp and feel a little light headed. Then I realize I'm holding my breath. From a few feet away I hear Trevor. "Geneviève." And he closes in fast and softly asks, "Are you all right?"

"He kissed my forehead like Théo does."

"I know. That's why I'm asking if you're all right."

Trevor caresses my face to calm me down. "This is not ..." And I stop talking.

My husband gives me a kiss and gathers me into his arms then whispers, "I'm not sure what to do, so I'm going to hold you until the bell rings." For about two seconds I wonder what bell and then I melt into his arms.

I have no idea how long he held me when I hear a bell ring twice and Mitch say, "Gentlemen, we have four minutes." And I *feel* my heart beating.

"Does that mean what I think it does?"

"Yes." He draws in a deep breath. "I remember the first time I was here and I spotted a captivating woman sitting on a blanket, then she vanished into thin air. Two weeks later I realized she was standing before me and you said something. Do you remember what it was?"

"Yes."

"Say it for me again."

"Trevor, kiss me."

As his lips touch mine everything around us fades away. His taste, his scent, his hands and our love are all there is in this world. In the middle of this moment suspended in time he pulls back enough to let me see his soul then he presses his lips to mine and inhales exactly like he did when he wanted to kiss me passionately and couldn't. Trevor ends our kiss then he holds my hands and whispers. "I love you, Geneviève."

"I love you, Trevor."

As I struggle to keep my wits about me that bell rings twice again and Mitch says, "Boys, let's get this ball rolling. We need to get our wives silk stockings."

Trevor's hands slip from mine as he smiles and stands tall, then in unison he and William respond, "Sir, yes, sir." There is a gleam in Trevor's eyes as he picks up his satchel.

Out of the corner of my eye I see Mitch give Joanna a nod and he says, "About ... FACE." Trevor looks into my eyes, turns 180 degrees and when Mitch and

William pass he follows. I stand and watch them walk away in a state of shock. That's one way to make a clean getaway. Was that it? Will I really not be able to see my husband's face for over six months?

Just when I feel as if I am hanging on by a thread I hear Joanna say, "Ladies, quickly." I look over and she is motioning for us to join her. Emily and I follow her to the trunk of her car. "I made us some things to keep our heads from spinning." Up goes the trunk and we see three large canvases. She hands one to me then one to Emily, grabs one for herself and slams the trunk closed. I look at the front of mine and see BON in large black letters. Then Emily exclaims, "Age?" Joanna says, "Oh, that one's mine." While they switch canvases I figure out the other one reads, VOY. We're going to hold up signs that read bon voyage. The fellas are going to get a kick out of this.

I ask Joanna, "What size are these?"

"24" x 36."

"The fellas should be able to see these from the bridge."

"Mitch always walks to the edge of her stern before he goes up. The boys will today." We get in the car and she says, "Ladies, take off your shoes please. We don't want to scratch the leather." Emily looks at me. "We're going to sit on top of the back of the seat." She happily begins taking off her shoes.

Sitting on our perch with our signs upside down resting on top of our feet Joanna tells us, "When the fellas are situated, on my MARK we'll hold them up."

We watch them go through the procedures at the top of the gangway and they are aboard. Two Sailors take their satchels and they begin the walk to Louise's stern. The three of them make quite a scene as they cross the flight deck. They have to salute a lot, but they don't break their pace.

At last I can see his face as they reach the edge and we simply look at each other until Joanna begins her countdown and on her MARK we hold the signs up over our heads as high as we can. Trevor's head goes back and I can see his entire body moving from laughter. William puts his hand on Trevor's shoulder to hold himself up and Mitch, being the captain, stands there slightly slumped over shaking his head. Several sailors make their way over to see what the commotion is about and we can see their various reactions. Then suddenly the fellas stand tall and we are looking at six thumbs up. Joanna says, "Mission accomplished." and we lower the signs before our arms go numb.

Very little time passes and Mitch looks at his watch. I know all this is about to end and my chest gets tight. I see Mitch say something then they place their hands over their hearts as do we. This time I can read Mitch's lips when he says, "About." Trevor and I lock eyes briefly and then he does a 180. I watch him walk across the flight deck then climb the ladders on the island and he opens the door to the bridge for his captain and his shipmate then in he goes.

My hand goes over my mouth and I stare at Louise as the sound of her engines get louder. Lines are pulled and then she slowly moves forward taking my husband to war along with two other men I adore. I am struggling to breathe instead of trying to hold back tears when Louise nears the curve where she will disappear from sight and I see the sailboats at the marina. Then I remember pleasure crafts often waited not far from shore to escort ships out to sea. I say, "Gypsy." and look at Joanna. "Do we dare?" She nods and we all drop down onto the seat as we toss the signs in the back.

Joanna slowly makes her way through the parking lot and the excitement begins when the gates are in site. She speeds up and Emily grabs my hand then stands up and holds on to the windshield as she shouts, "Look alive." to the sentry's. "Raise the gate please." One of them struggles to raise the gate we are in the lane of and the other one shouts, "Is everything all right, Mrs. Snowden?" She replies, "We're in a race against time." Then she sits down. As we go through we smile, wave and say, "Thank you."

Mere yards away Joanna steps on the accelerator and Emily has to hold on to her ponytail because we are going so fast. "I hope we don't get pulled over."

Joanna tells her, "I won't pull over. They'll have to follow us to the marina."

"We could be involved in a police chase? This is not how I saw this playing out in my mind. I had a visual of me driving to the house with tears streaming down my face, not calling my dad to get us out of jail." I chime in, "They won't take us to jail. They'll only take Joanna." And we all burst into laughter.

Fortunately we make it to the marina without encountering a policeman and Joanna starts blowing her horn when we get close to the gate. Mr. Davidson comes out as I stand up and shout, "We're escorting the carrier out to sea." He waves as we pass by.

In no time flat we are barefooted aboard Gypsy. I am at the helm as they secure the lines and we are off for the chase. Louise is in sight, but there is a gap I have to close. Luckily Gypsy is fast and I have skills and a skilled crew.

We are at full sail in record time and I decide to make my approach on her starboard side where the island is as I close the gap. While I'm calculating a safe distance, Emily goes below for binoculars and Joanna joins me. "All right, this is what is going to happen. A watchman is going to spot Gypsy and alert Mitch a sailboat has entered the area of the strike group. A destroyer is already in the lead. I have no clue when the others will arrive, but they stay a good distance from her."

"I'm going to do the same thing. She's huge and we are a speck."

Emily returns with binoculars while I was talking and begins to laugh. "She *is* huge. We have taken leave of our senses. I should have drunk a shot of whiskey when I was below." Joanna rubs her back and tells her, "We'll have one when we go back to the marina." Emily and I nod repeatedly.

Mitch has her going at about 9 knots, so they adjust the sails to slow us down as I ease closer without taking my eyes off the bridge holding firmly on to the wheel with both hands. When I'm in the perfect spot to be able to see them I breathe a little easier and keep her steady. Joanna and Emily hold on to the lifelines as they make their way port side and seconds later I see Mitch appear on the island. Joanna waves immediately as Emily moves away from her and I glance at my watch. Mitch looks at his wife then raises a pair of binoculars. When he lowers them Joanna looks briefly through hers. Next Mitch waves at me and Emily then he looks at his wife and places his hand over his heart and she does the same. And in what seems like a minute later William shows up. Mitch looks at Gypsy then at Joanna and he turns around as he hands William the binoculars.

While William and Emily have their moment Joanna makes her way to me. She steps up behind me and puts both hands on the wheel then I duck under her arm and go to the port side lifeline and wait. While watching William and Emily basically do what Joanna and Mitch did my husband suddenly appears. I move closer to Emily keeping my eyes on him and when Trevor reaches William they trade places. We have two minutes.

I outstretch my hand toward Trevor wishing with all my heart I could touch him and he holds his hand out to me. As he lifts up the binoculars I draw in a deep breath and remember to smile. The moment I do I see his smile and look straight into the lenses and let him cast his eyes upon his wife. When he lowers them I raise mine and see the blue of his eyes, and for a brief glorious moment time stands still. When I see his lips move I hear him say, "Geneviève, if you can hear me, nod." I lower my binoculars in disbelief and nod. "Once again you catch me off guard. — Destroyer's are going to be closing in shortly and you can't be here." I nod again and he lowers his binoculars. "Thank you for this. I will carry the sight of you aboard Gypsy with me always. See you soon."

"See you soon."

I look at him once more through my binoculars then look at him with my eyes and he places his hand over his heart. I place my hand over mine as I give him a shy smile to remember me by and then summon my strength to turn away. While changing Gypsy's course for the marina I was about to glance his way when I recall his words of warning for me not to look back. Even though I know Trevor is still watching me, I keep my eyes forward.

To be continued in *The Field Agent*

GLOSSARY

adieu: farewell

bien sûr: of course

bonjour: hello; good morning

bon voyage: good journey

dimanche: Sunday

exactement: exactly

hilt: the handle of a sword

la mariée: the bride

MA: Master-At-Arms, security for the US Navy equivalent to the US Army Military Police

Ma Fille: My Daughter

Ma Mère: My Mother

Ma Sœur: My Sister

Mariée: Bride

mercredi: Monday

Mon Frère: My Brother

Mon Mari: My Spouse

skivvies: Navy issued boxer shorts

toute de suite: right away

tout le mond: everybody

vendredi: Friday

vraiment magnifique: really beautiful

ABOUT THE AUTHOR

Leslie Peppers is known for being an artist. She was a child prodigy at the age of four and over time she quietly made her way through the art world into galleries and notable private collections around the world. Yet along the way she had a secret; at the age of seven she began writing short stories and in her teens she began writing poetry, also a secret. This changed in May of 2015 when she went public online at vimeo with *Coincidence or Fate?*, the true story about her involvement with the SARS epidemic of 2003. The author used her artistic skills to make the very short story into a video with pages that turn themselves as a gift to the public.

Apparently writing was in the back of her mind as she continued to create artworks, because a few months after releasing the short story she had an idea for a novel. Focused on being an artist she did not want to commit to a project that would occupy the majority of her time. Then one day the desire to tell the story overtook her. As she began to write the outline she realized it was going to take more than one book to tell. And without hesitating she dived into *The Lyons Saga* and found the water was warm.

Lightning Source UK Ltd.
Milton Keynes UK
UKHW020834151220
375245UK00004B/733